The

Solitude

of

Prime

Numbers

Paolo Giordano

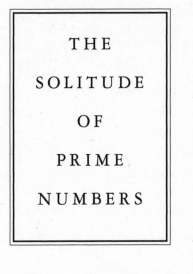

THE

SOLITUDE

OF

PRIME

NUMBERS

Pamela Dorman Books

VIKING

VIKING
Published by the Penguin Group
Penguin Group (USA) Inc., 375 Hudson Street, New York, New York 10014, U.S.A. • Penguin Group (Canada),
90 Eglinton Avenue East, Suite 700, Toronto, Ontario, Canada M4P 2Y3 (a division of Pearson Penguin Canada
Inc.) • Penguin Books Ltd, 80 Strand, London WC2R 0RL, England • Penguin Ireland, 25 St. Stephen's Green,
Dublin 2, Ireland (a division of Penguin Books Ltd) • Penguin Books Australia Ltd, 250 Camberwell Road, Cam-
berwell, Victoria 3124, Australia • (a division of Pearson Australia Group Pty Ltd) • Penguin Books India Pvt
Ltd, 11 Community Centre, Panchsheel Park, New Delhi – 110 017, India • Penguin Group (NZ), 67 Apollo Drive,
Rosedale, North Shore 0632, New Zealand (a division of Pearson New Zealand Ltd) • Penguin Books (South Africa)
(Pty) Ltd, 24 Sturdee Avenue, Rosebank, Johannesburg 2196, South Africa

Penguin Books Ltd, Registered Offices: 80 Strand, London WC2R 0RL, England

First American edition
Published in 2010 by Viking Penguin, a member of Penguin Group (USA) Inc.

10 9 8 7 6 5 4 3 2 1

Translation copyright © Shaun Whiteside, 2009
All rights reserved

A Pamela Dorman Book/Viking

Originally published in Italian as *La Solitudine dei Numeri Primi* by Arnoldo Mondadori Editore, Milan. Copyright
© 2008 Arnoldo Mondadori Editore S.p.A.

This English translation published by arrangement with Transworld Publishers, a division of The Random House
Group Limited.

"Grey Room" Testo e Musica di Damien Rice © 2006 by Warner Chappell Music Publishing Ltd.

PUBLISHER'S NOTE

LIBRARY OF CONGRESS CATALOGING-IN-PUBLICATION DATA
Giordano, Paolo, 1982–
  [Solitudine dei numeri primi. English]
  The solitude of prime numbers : a novel / Paolo Giordano.
    p. cm.
  ISBN 978-0-670-02148-2
  1. Life change events—Psychological aspects—Fiction. 2. Solitude—Fiction. 3. Psychological fiction. I. Title.
PQ4907.I57S6513 2010
  853'.92—dc22   2009041165

Printed in the United States of America
Set in Adobe Garamond Three • Designed by Carla Bolte

To Eleonora,

because in silence

I promised it to you

Acknowledgments

This book wouldn't have existed without Raffaella Lops.

I would like to thank, in no particular order, Antonio Franchini, Joy Terekiev, Mario Desiati, Giulia Ichino, Laura Cerutti, Cecilia Giordano, my parents, Giorgio Mila, Roberto Castello, Emiliano Amato, Pietro Grossi, and Nella Re Rebaudengo. Each of them knows why.

Her old aunt's elaborately trimmed dress was a perfect fit for Sylvie's slender figure, and she asked me to lace it up for her. "The sleeves are plain; how ridiculous!" she said.

—Gérard de Nerval, *Sylvie*, 1853

The

Solitude

of

Prime

Numbers

SNOW ANGEL

1983

I

Alice Della Rocca hated ski school. She hated getting up at seven-thirty, even during Christmas vacation. She hated her father staring at her over breakfast, his leg dancing nervously under the table as if to say hurry up, get a move on. She hated the woolen tights that made her thighs itch, the mittens that kept her from moving her fingers, the helmet that squashed her cheeks, and the big, too tight boots that made her walk like a gorilla.

"Are you going to drink that milk or not?" her father insisted again.

Alice gulped down three inches of boiling milk, burning her tongue, throat, and stomach.

"Good, today you can show us what you're really made of."

What's that? Alice wondered.

He shoved her out the door, mummified in a green ski suit dotted with badges and the fluorescent logos of the sponsors. It was 14 degrees and a gray fog enveloped everything. Alice felt the milk swirling around in her stomach as she sank into the snow. Her skis were over her shoulder, because you had to carry your skis yourself until you got good enough for someone to carry them for you.

"Keep the tips facing forward or you'll kill someone," her father said.

At the end of the season the Ski Club gave you a pin with little stars on it. A star a year, from when you were four years old and just tall enough to slip the little disk of the ski lift between your legs until you were nine and you managed to grab the disk all by yourself. Three silver stars and then another three in gold: a pin a year, a way of saying you'd gotten a little better, a little closer to the races

3

that terrified Alice. She was already worried about them even though she had only three stars.

They were to meet at the ski lift at eight-thirty sharp, right when it opened. The other kids were already there, standing like little soldiers in a loose circle, bundled up in their uniforms, numb with sleep and cold. They planted their ski poles in the snow and wedged the grips in their armpits. With their arms dangling, they looked like scarecrows. No one felt like talking, least of all Alice. Her father rapped twice on her helmet, too hard, as if trying to pound her into the snow.

"Pull out all the stops," he said. "And remember: keep your body weight forward, okay? Body weight forward."

"Body weight forward," echoed the voice in Alice's head.

Then he walked away, blowing into his cupped hands. He'd soon be home again, reading the paper in the warmth of their house. Two steps and the fog swallowed him up.

Alice clumsily dropped her skis on the ground and banged her boots with a ski pole to knock off the clumps of snow. If her father had seen her he would have slapped her right there, in front of everyone.

She was already desperate for a pee; it pushed against her bladder like a pin piercing her belly. She wasn't going to make it today either. Every morning it was the same. After breakfast she would lock herself in the bathroom and push and push, trying to get rid of every last drop, contracting her abdominal muscles till her head ached and her eyes felt like they were going to pop out of their sockets. She would turn the tap full blast so that her father wouldn't hear the noises as she pushed and pushed, clenching her fists, to squeeze out the very last drop. She would sit there until her father pounded on the door and yelled so, missy, are we going to be late again today?

But it never did any good. By the time they reached the top of the first ski lift she would be so desperate that she would have to crouch down in the fresh snow and pretend to tighten her boots in order to take a pee inside her ski suit while all her classmates looked on, and Eric, the ski instructor, would say we're waiting for Alice, as usual. It's such a relief, she thought each time, as the lovely warmth trickled between her shivering legs. Or it would be, if only they weren't all there watching me.

Sooner or later they're going to notice.

Sooner or later I'm going to leave a yellow stain in the snow and they'll all make fun of me.

One of the parents went up to Eric and asked if the fog wasn't too thick to go all the way to the top that morning. Alice pricked up her ears hopefully, but Eric unfurled his perfect smile.

"It's only foggy down here," he said. "At the top the sun is blinding. Come on, let's go."

On the chairlift Alice was paired with Giuliana, the daughter of one of her father's colleagues. They didn't say a word the whole way up. Not that they particularly disliked each other, it was just that, at that moment, neither of them wanted to be there.

The sound of the wind sweeping the summit of the mountain was punctuated by the metallic rush of the steel cable from which Alice and Giuliana were hanging, their chins tucked into the collars of their jackets so as to warm themselves with their breath.

It's only the cold, you don't really need to go, Alice said to herself.

But the closer she got to the top, the more the pin in her belly pierced her flesh. Maybe she was seriously close to wetting herself. Then again, it might even be something bigger. No, it's just the cold, you don't really need to go again, Alice kept telling herself.

Alice suddenly regurgitated rancid milk. She swallowed it down with disgust.

She really needed to go; she was desperate.

Two more chairlifts before the shelter. I can't possibly hold it in for that long.

Giuliana lifted the safety bar and they both shifted their bottoms forward to get off. When her skis touched the ground Alice shoved off from her seat. You couldn't see more than two yards ahead of you, so much for blinding sun. It was like being wrapped in a sheet, all white, nothing but white, above, below, all around you. It was the exact opposite of darkness, but it frightened Alice in precisely the same way.

She slipped off to the side of the trail to look for a little pile of fresh snow to relieve herself in. Her stomach gurgled like a dishwasher. When she turned around, she couldn't see Giuliana anymore, which meant that Giuliana couldn't see her either. She herringboned a few yards up the hill, just as her father had made her do when he had gotten it into his head to teach her to ski. Up and down the bunny slope, thirty, forty times a day, sidestep up and snowplow down. Buying a ski pass for just one slope was a waste of money, and this way you trained your legs as well.

Alice unfastened her skis and took a few more steps, sinking halfway up her calves in the snow. Finally she could sit. She stopped holding her breath and relaxed her muscles. A pleasant electric shock spread through her whole body, finally settling in the tips of her toes.

It must have been the milk, of course. That and the fact that her bum was freezing from sitting in the snow at six thousand feet. It had never happened before, at least not as far as she could remember. Never, not even once.

But this time it wasn't pee. Or, not only. As she leaped to her feet she felt something heavy in the seat of her pants and instinctively touched her bottom. She couldn't feel a thing through her gloves, but it didn't matter—she had already realized what had happened.

Now what, she wondered.

Eric called her but Alice didn't reply. As long as she stayed up there, the fog would hide her. She could pull down her ski pants and clean herself up as best she could, or go down and whisper in Eric's ear what had happened. She could tell him she had to go back to the lodge, that her knees hurt. Or she could just not worry about it and keep skiing, making sure to always be last in line.

Instead she simply stayed where she was, careful not to move a muscle, shielded by the fog.

Eric called her again. Louder now.

"She must have gone to the ski lift already, silly girl," a little boy said.

Alice could hear them talking. Someone said let's go and someone else said I'm cold from standing here. They could be just below her, a few yards away, or up at the ski lift. Sounds are deceptive: they rebound off the mountains and sink in the snow. "Damn . . . let's go see," Eric said. Alice slowly counted to ten, suppressing her urge to vomit as she felt something slither down her thighs. When she got to ten, she started over again, this time counting to twenty. Now all was silent.

She picked up her skis and carried them under her arm to the trail. It took her a little while to work out how to position them at right angles to the fall line. With fog that thick you can't even tell which way you're facing.

She clipped into her skis and tightened the bindings. She took off her goggles and spat inside them because they had misted up. She could ski down to the lodge all on her own. She didn't care that Eric was looking for her at the top of the mountain. With her pants caked in shit, she didn't want to stay up there a second longer than she absolutely had to. She went over the descent in her head. She had never done it alone, but, after all, they had gone only as far as the first ski lift, and she'd been down this slope dozens of times.

She began to snowplow. Just the day before, Eric had said if I see you doing one more snowplow turn, I swear I'm going to tie your ankles together.

Eric didn't like her, she was sure of it. He thought she was a scaredy-pants and, as it turned out, events had proved him right. Eric didn't like her father either, because every day, at the end of the lesson, he pestered him with endless questions. So how is our Alice coming along, are we getting better, do we have a little champion on our hands, when are we going to start racing, on and on. Eric always stared at a spot somewhere behind her father and answered yes, no, well . . .

Alice saw the whole scene superimposed on her foggy goggles as she gently edged her way down, unable to make out anything beyond the tips of her skis. Only when she ended up in the fresh snow did she understand that it was time to turn.

She started singing to herself to feel less alone. From time to time she wiped away her snot with her glove.

Keep your weight uphill, plant your pole, turn. Lean on your boots. Now shift your body weight forward, okay? Bo-dy weight for-ward. The voice was partly Eric's and partly her father's.

Her father would probably fly into a rage. She had to come up with a lie, a story that would stand up, no holes or contradictions. She didn't even dream of telling him what had really happened. The fog, that was it, blame it on the fog. She was following the others onto the big slope when her ski pass had come off her jacket. No, that's no good, no one's ski pass ever blew away. You'd have to be a real idiot to lose it. My scarf. My scarf blew away and I went back to find it, but the others didn't wait for me. I called them a hundred times but there was no sign of them; they had disappeared into the fog and so I went down to look for them.

And why didn't you go back up? her father would ask.

Of course, why hadn't she? On second thought, it was better if she lost her ski pass. She hadn't gone back up because she'd lost her ski pass and the man at the ski lift wouldn't let her.

Alice smiled, pleased with her story. It was flawless. She didn't even feel all that dirty anymore. She would spend the rest of the day in front of the TV. She would take a shower and put on clean clothes and slip her feet into her furry slippers. She would stay inside, in the warmth, all day. Or she would have, if only she'd looked up from her skis long enough to see the orange tape with the words TRAIL CLOSED. Her father was always telling her look where you're going. If only she'd remembered that in fresh snow you shouldn't put your body weight forward and if only Eric, a few days before, had adjusted her bindings better, and her father had been more insistent in saying but Alice weighs sixty pounds, won't they be too tight like that?

The drop wasn't very high. A few yards, just long enough to feel a slight void in your stomach and nothing beneath your feet. And then Alice was facedown in the snow, her skis pointing straight up in the air, and her fibula broken.

She didn't really feel that bad. To tell the truth, she didn't feel a thing. Only the snow that had slipped under her scarf and into her helmet and burned her skin.

The first thing she did was move her arms. When she was little and woke up to find it had snowed, her father would wrap her up tight and carry her downstairs. They would walk to the center of the courtyard and, hand in hand, would count to three and fall backward like a deadweight. Then her father would say make an angel, and Alice would move her arms up and down. When she got up and looked at her outline sculpted in the white, it really did look like the shadow of an angel with outspread wings.

Alice made a snow angel, just like that, for no reason, just to prove to herself that she was still alive. She managed to turn her head to one side and start breathing again, even though it felt as if the air wasn't going where it was supposed to. She had the strange sensation of not knowing which way her legs were turned. The very strange sensation of no longer having legs at all.

She tried to get up, but she couldn't.

If it weren't for the fog, someone might have seen her from above, a green stain splayed at the bottom of a gully, a few steps from the spot where a little waterfall would start flowing again in the spring, where, with the first warmth, wild strawberries would grow, and if you waited long enough they'd ripen, as sweet as candy, and you could pick a basketful in a day. Alice cried for help, but her thin voice was swallowed up by the fog. She tried to get up again, or at least to turn over, but it was no use.

Her father had told her that people who freeze to death feel very hot and, just before dying, have an urge to get undressed. Almost everyone who dies of cold is found in their underwear. And hers were dirty.

She was starting to lose feeling in her fingers as well. She took off her glove, blew into it, and then put it back on her clenched fist, to warm it up. She did the same with her other hand. She repeated this ludicrous gesture two or three times.

It's your extremities that get you, her father always said. Your toes and fingers, your nose and ears. Your heart does everything in its power to keep the blood to itself, leaving the rest to freeze.

Alice imagined her fingers turning blue and then, slowly, her arms and her legs. She thought about her heart pumping harder and harder, trying to keep in all the remaining warmth. She would go so stiff that if a wolf passed by it would snap off one of her arms just by stepping on it.

They must be looking for me.

I wonder if there really are any wolves around here.

I can't feel my fingers anymore.

If only I hadn't drunk that milk.

Bo-dy weight for-ward.

Of course not, wolves would be hibernating now.

Eric will be furious.

I don't want to race.

Don't be stupid, you know very well that wolves don't hibernate.

Her thoughts were growing more and more circular and illogical.

The sun sank slowly behind Mount Chaberton as if nothing was the matter. The shadow of the mountains spread over Alice and the fog turned completely black.

THE ARCHIMEDES PRINCIPLE

1984

When the twins were small and Michela was up to one of her tricks, like throwing herself downstairs in her baby walker or sticking a pea up one of her nostrils, so that she had to be taken to the emergency room to have it removed with special tweezers, their father would always say to Mattia, the firstborn, that his mother's womb was too small for both of them.

"God only knows what the two of you got up to in there," he said. "I reckon all those kicks you gave your sister did her some serious damage."

Then he laughed, even though it was no laughing matter. He lifted Michela in the air and buried his beard in her soft cheeks.

Mattia would watch from below. He would laugh too, letting his father's words filter through him by osmosis, without really understanding them. He let them settle at the bottom of his stomach, forming a thick, sticky layer, like the sediment of wine that has aged for a long time.

His father's laughter turned into a strained smile when, at two and a half, Michela still couldn't utter a single word. Not even *mommy* or *poo-poo* or *sleepy* or *woof*. Her inarticulate little cries rose from such a solitary, deserted place that they made their father shiver every time.

When she was five and a half a speech therapist with thick glasses sat Michela down in front of a board with four different shapes cut out—a star, a circle, a square, and a triangle—and the corresponding colored pieces to place into the holes.

Michela looked at them with wonder.

"Where does the star go, Michela?" asked the speech therapist.

Michela stared at the puzzle but didn't touch anything. The doctor put the yellow star in her hand.

"Where does this go, Michela?" she asked.

Michela looked everywhere and nowhere. She put one of the points in her mouth and began to chew on it. The speech therapist took the object out of her mouth and asked the question yet again.

"Michela, do what the doctor tells you, for God's sake," snarled her father, who couldn't quite manage to stay seated, as he'd been told.

"Signor Balossino, please," the doctor said in a conciliatory voice. "Children need time."

And Michela took her time. A whole minute. Then she let out a heartrending groan that might have been of joy or of despair, and resolutely jammed the star in the square hole.

In case Mattia had not already figured out for himself that something was not right with his sister, his classmates didn't hesitate to point it out to him. Simona Volterra, for example, during the first year of school. When the teacher said Simona, you're going to sit next to Michela this month, she refused, crossing her arms, and said I don't want to sit next to her.

Mattia let Simona and the teacher argue for a while, and then said Miss, I can sit next to Michela again. Everyone had looked relieved: Michela, Simona, the teacher. Everyone except Mattia.

The twins sat in the front row. Michela spent the whole day coloring, meticulously going outside the lines and picking colors at random. Blue children, red skies, all the trees yellow. She gripped the pencil like a meat pounder, pressing down so hard that she often tore the page.

At her side Mattia learned to read and write, to add and subtract, and was the first in the class to master long division.

His brain seemed to be a perfect machine, in the same mysterious way that his sister's was so defective.

Sometimes Michela would start squirming on her chair, waving her arms around crazily, like a trapped moth. Her eyes would grow dark and the teacher, more frightened than she was, would stand and look at her, vaguely hoping that the retard really might fly away one day. Someone in the back row would giggle, someone else would go shhh. So Mattia would get up, picking up his chair so that it wouldn't scrape on the floor, and stand behind Michela, who by now was rolling her head from side to side and flailing her arms about so fast that he was afraid they would come off.

Mattia would take her hands and delicately wrap her arms around her chest.

"There, you don't have wings anymore," he'd whisper in her ear. It took Michela a few seconds before she stopped trembling. She'd stare into the distance for a few seconds, and then go back to tormenting her drawings as if nothing had happened. Mattia would sit back down, head lowered and ears red with embarrassment, and the teacher would go on with the lesson.

In the third year of primary school the twins still hadn't been invited to any of their classmates' birthday parties. Their mother noticed and thought she could solve the issue by throwing the twins a birthday party. At dinner, Mr. Balossino had rejected the suggestion out of hand. For heaven's sake, Adele, it's already embarrassing enough as it is. Mattia sighed with relief and Michela dropped her fork for the tenth time. It was never mentioned again. Then, one morning in January, Riccardo Pelotti, a kid with red hair and baboon lips, came over to Mattia's desk.

"Hey, my mom says you can come to my birthday party," he blurted, looking at the blackboard.

"So can she," he added, pointing to Michela, who was carefully smoothing the surface of the desk as if it were a bedsheet.

Mattia's face went red with excitement. He said thank you, but Riccardo, having gotten the weight off his chest, had already left.

The twins' mother immediately became anxious and took them both to Benetton for new clothes. They went to three toy shops, but Adele couldn't make up her mind.

"What sort of things is Riccardo interested in? Would he like this?" she asked Mattia, holding up a jigsaw puzzle.

"How would I know?" her son replied.

"He's a friend of yours. You must know what games he likes."

Mattia didn't think that Riccardo was a friend of his, but he couldn't explain that to his mother. So he simply shrugged.

In the end Adele opted for the Lego spaceship, the biggest and most expensive toy in the store.

"Mom, it's too much," her son protested.

"Nonsense. And besides, there are two of you. You don't want to make a bad impression."

Mattia knew all too well that, Lego or no Lego, they would make a bad impression. With Michela, anything else was impossible. He knew that Riccardo had invited them only because he'd been told to. Michela would cling to him the whole time, spill orange juice on herself, and then start whining, as she always did when she was tired.

For the first time Mattia thought it might be better to stay at home.

Or rather, he thought it might be better if Michela stayed at home.

"Mom," he began uncertainly.

Adele was looking in her bag for her wallet.

"Yes?"

Mattia took a breath.

"Does Michela really have to come to the party?"

Adele suddenly froze and stared into her son's eyes. The cashier observed the scene indifferently, her hand open on the conveyor belt, waiting for the money. Michela was mixing up the candy on the rack.

Mattia's cheeks burned, ready to receive a slap that never came. "Of course she's coming," his mother said, and that was that.

Riccardo's house was less than a ten-minute walk away, and they were allowed to go on their own. At three o'clock on the dot Adele pushed the twins out the door.

"Go on, or you'll be late. Remember to thank his parents," she said.

Then she turned to Mattia.

"Take care of your sister. You know she shouldn't eat junk."

Mattia nodded. Adele kissed them both on the cheek, Michela for longer. She tidied Michela's hair under her hair band and said enjoy yourselves.

On the way to Riccardo's house, Mattia's thoughts kept time with the Lego pieces, which shifted back and forth inside the box like the tide. Michela, tagging a few feet behind him, stumbled as she tried to keep up, dragging her feet through the mush of dead leaves stuck to the pavement. The air was still and cold.

She's going to drop her potato chips on the rug, thought Mattia.

She'll grab the ball and she won't want to give it back.

"Will you hurry up?" he said, turning to his twin sister, who had suddenly crouched down in the middle of the pavement and was torturing a long worm with her finger. Michela looked at her brother as if seeing him for the first time in ages. She smiled and ran to him, clutching the worm between her fingers. "You're disgusting. Throw it away," Mattia ordered, recoiling.

Michela looked at the worm again for a moment and seemed to be wondering how it had ended up in her hand. Then she dropped it and launched into a lopsided run to join her brother, who had already walked on ahead.

She'll grab the ball and won't want to give it back, just like at school, he thought to himself.

Mattia looked at his twin, who had his same eyes, same nose, same color hair, and a brain that belonged in the trash, and for the first time he felt genuine hatred. He took her hand to cross the street, because the cars were going fast, and it was then that the idea came to him.

He let go of Michela's hand in its woolen glove, instantly thinking that it wasn't right.

Then, as they were walking by the park, he changed his mind again and convinced himself that no one would ever find out.

Just for a few hours, he thought. Just this once. He abruptly changed direction, dragging Michela by an arm, and entered the park. The grass was still damp from the night's frost. Michela trotted behind him, muddying her brand-new white suede boots. There was no one in the park; it was so cold that no one would have felt like going for a walk. The twins came to an area with trees, three wooden tables, and a barbecue. They had eaten lunch there once, in year one, when the teachers had taken them to collect dry leaves from which they made ugly table decorations to give to their grandparents for Christmas.

"Michela, listen to me," said Mattia. "Are you listening?"

With Michela you always had to check that her narrow channel of communication was open. Mattia waited for his sister to nod.

"Good. So, I have to go away for a little while, okay? But I won't be long, just half an hour," he explained.

There was no reason to tell the truth, since to Michela there was little difference between half an hour and a whole day. The doctor had said that her spatiotemporal perception development had been arrested at a preconscious stage, and Mattia understood perfectly well what that meant.

"You sit here and wait for me," he said to his twin. Michela stared gravely at her brother and didn't reply, because she didn't know what to say. She gave no sign of having really understood, but her eyes lit up for a moment, and for the rest of his life when Mattia thought of those eyes he thought of fear.

He took a few steps away from his sister, walking backward to make sure she didn't follow him. Only prawns walk like that, his mother had yelled at him once, and they always end up crashing into something.

He was about fifteen yards away and Michela had already stopped looking at him, engrossed in trying to pull a button off her woolen coat.

Mattia turned around and started to run, tightly clutching the bag with the present. Inside the box more than two hundred little plastic blocks crashed into one another. It was as if they were trying to tell him something.

"Hi, Mattia," Riccardo Pelotti's mother said as she opened the door. "Where's your little sister?"

"She has a temperature," Mattia lied. "A mild one."

"Oh, what a shame," the woman said, not seeming displeased in the slightest. She stepped aside to let him in.

"Ricky, your friend Mattia is here. Come and say hello," she called, turning toward the hall.

Riccardo appeared, sliding along the floor, an unpleasant expression on his face. He stopped for a second to glance at Mattia and look for traces of the retard. Relieved, he said hi.

Mattia waved the bag with the present under the woman's nose. "Where shall I put this?" he asked.

"What is it?" Riccardo asked suspiciously.

"Legos."

Riccardo grabbed the bag and disappeared down the hall.

"Go with him," Mrs. Pelotti said, pushing Mattia. "The party's down there."

The Pelottis' living room was decorated with bunches of balloons.

On a table covered by a red paper tablecloth were bowls of popcorn and chips, a tray of dry pizza cut into squares, and a row of still unopened soda bottles of various colors. Some of Mattia's classmates had already arrived and were standing in the middle of the room guarding the table.

Mattia took a few steps toward the others and then stopped a few yards away, like a satellite that doesn't want to take up too much room in the sky. No one paid him any attention.

When the room was full of children, an entertainer with a red plastic nose and a clown's bowler hat made them play blindman's buff and pin the tail on the donkey. Mattia won first prize, which consisted of an extra handful of candy, but only because he could see out from under the blindfold. Everyone shouted boo, you cheated, as he shamefacedly slipped the candy into his pocket.

Then, when it was dark outside, the clown turned out the lights, made them sit in a circle, and began to tell a horror story. He held a flashlight under his chin.

Mattia didn't think the story was all that scary, but the face, lit up like that, sure was. The light shining from below turned it all red and revealed terrifying shadows. Mattia looked out the window to keep from looking at the clown and remembered Michela. He hadn't ever really forgotten about her, but now for the first time he imagined her all alone among the trees, waiting for him, and rubbing her face with her white gloves to warm up a bit.

He got to his feet just as Riccardo's mother came into the dark room carrying a cake covered with candles, and everyone started clapping, partly for the story and partly for the cake.

"I've got to go," Mattia said to her, without even giving her time to set the cake down on the table.

"Right now? But the cake."

"Yes, now. I've got to go."

Riccardo's mother looked at him from over the candles. Lit up like that, her face was full of threatening shadows, just like the clown's. The other kids fell silent.

"Okay," the woman said uncertainly. "Ricky, walk your friend to the door."

"But I've got to blow out the candles."

"Do as I say," his mother ordered, still staring at Mattia.

"You're such a drag, Mattia."

Someone started laughing. Mattia followed Riccardo to the front door, pulled his jacket from the pile, and said thanks, bye. Riccardo didn't even reply, quickly shutting the door behind him to run back to his cake.

In the courtyard of Riccardo's building, Mattia glanced back at the lit window. His classmates' muffled cries filtered out like the reassuring hum of the television in the living room when his mother sent him and Michela to bed in the evening. The gate closed behind him with a metallic click and he began to run.

He entered the park, but after ten yards or so the light from the street lamps was no longer enough for him to make out the gravel path. The bare branches of the trees where he had left Michela were no more than slightly darker scratches against the black sky. Seeing them from a distance, Mattia was filled with the clear and inexplicable certainty that his sister was no longer there.

He stopped a few yards from the bench where Michela had been sitting a few hours before, busily ruining her coat. He stopped and listened, catching his breath, as if at any moment his sister were bound to pop out from behind a tree saying peekaboo and then run toward him, fluttering along with her crooked gait.

Mattia called Michela and was startled by his own voice. He called again, more quietly. He walked over to the wooden tables and laid a hand on the spot where Michela had been sitting. It was as cold as everything else.

She must have gotten bored and gone home, he thought.

But if she doesn't even know the way? And she can't cross the road on her own either.

Mattia looked at the park, which disappeared into the darkness. He didn't even know where it ended. He thought that he didn't want to go deeper and that he didn't have a choice.

He walked on tiptoes to keep from crunching the leaves under his feet, turning his head from side to side in the hopes of spotting Michela crouching behind a tree to ambush a beetle or who knows what.

He walked into the playground. He tried to remember the colors of the slide in the Sunday afternoon light, when his mother gave in to Michela's cries and let her have a few goes, even though she was too old for it.

He walked along the hedge as far as the public toilets, but wasn't brave enough to go inside. He found his way back to the path, which was now just a thin strip of dirt marked by the coming and going of families. He followed it for a good ten minutes until he no longer knew where he was. Then he started crying and coughing at the same time.

"You're so stupid, Michela," he said under his breath. "A stupid retard. Mom told you a thousand times to stay where you are if you get lost. . . . But you never understand anything. . . . Nothing at all."

He went up a slight slope and found himself looking at the river that cut through the park. His father had told him its name loads of times, but Mattia could never remember it. A bit of light from who knows where was reflected on the water and quivered in his teary eyes.

He went over to the riverbank and sensed that Michela must be somewhere close by. She liked the water. His mother always told how when they were little and she gave them a bath together, Michela would shriek like mad because she didn't want to get out, even once the water was cold. One Sunday his father had taken them to the riverbank, perhaps even to this very spot, and taught him to skip stones across the water. As he was showing him how to use his wrist to spin the stone, Michela leaned forward and slipped in up to her waist before their father caught her by the arm. He smacked her and she started whining, and then all three of them went home in silence, with long faces.

The image of Michela playing with a twig and breaking up her own reflection in the water before sliding into it like a sack of potatoes ran through his head with the force of an electric shock.

Exhausted, he sat down a couple of feet from the river's edge. He turned around to look behind him and saw the darkness that would last for many hours to come.

He stared at the gleaming black surface of the river. Again he tried to remember its name, but couldn't. He plunged his hands into the cold earth. On the bank the dampness made it softer. He found a broken bottle, a sharp reminder of some nighttime festivity. The first time he stuck it into his hand it didn't hurt, perhaps he didn't even notice. Then he started twisting it into his flesh, digging deeper, without ever taking his eyes off the water. He expected Michela to rise to the surface from one minute to the next, and in the meantime he wondered why some things float while others don't.

ON THE SKIN AND
JUST BEHIND IT

1991

The horrible white ceramic vase, with a complicated gold floral motif, which had always occupied a corner of the bathroom, had been in the Della Rocca family for five generations, but no one really liked it. On several occasions Alice had felt an urge to hurl it to the floor and throw the countless tiny fragments in the trash can in front of the house, along with the Tetra Pak mashed-potato containers, used sanitary napkins—although certainly not used by her—and empty packets of her father's antidepressants.

Alice ran a finger along the rim and thought how cold, smooth, and clean it was. Soledad, the Ecuadorean housekeeper, had become more meticulous over the years, because in the Della Rocca household details mattered. Alice was only six when she first arrived, and she had eyed her suspiciously from behind her mother's skirt. Soledad had crouched down and looked at her with wonder. What pretty hair you have, she had said, can I touch it? Alice had bit her tongue to keep from saying no and Soledad had lifted one of her chestnut curls as if it were a swatch of silk and then let it fall back. She couldn't believe that hair could be so fine.

Alice held her breath as she slipped off her camisole and closed her eyes tightly for a moment.

When she opened them again she saw herself reflected in the big mirror above the sink and felt a pleasurable sense of disappointment. She rolled down the elastic of her underpants a few times, so that they came just above her scar, and were stretched tightly enough to leave a little gap between the edge and her belly, forming a bridge between the bones of her pelvis. There wasn't quite room for her index finger; but being able to slip her little finger in made her crazy.

29

There, it should blossom right there, she thought.

A little blue rose, like Viola's.

Alice turned to stand in profile, her right side, the good one, as she would tell herself. She brushed all her hair forward, thinking it made her look like a child possessed by demons. She pulled it up in a ponytail and then scooped it higher up on her head, the way Viola wore hers, which everyone always liked.

That didn't work either.

She let her hair fall on her shoulders and with her usual gesture pinned it behind her ears. She rested her hands on the sink and pushed her face toward the mirror so quickly that her eyes seemed to form one single, terrifying Cyclops eye. Her hot breath formed a halo on the glass, covering part of her face.

She just couldn't figure out where Viola and her friends got those looks they went around with, breaking boys' hearts. Those merciless, captivating looks that could make or break you with a single, imperceptible flicker of the eyebrow.

Alice tried to be provocative with the mirror, but saw only an embarrassed girl clumsily shaking her shoulders and looking as if she were anesthetized. The real problem was her cheeks: too puffy and blotchy. They suffocated her eyes, when all the while she wanted her gaze to land like a dagger in the stomachs of the boys whose eyes it met. She wanted her gaze to spare no one, to leave an indelible mark.

Instead only her belly, bum, and tits got slimmer, while her cheeks were still like two round pillows, baby cheeks.

Someone knocked at the bathroom door.

"Alice, it's ready," her father's hateful voice rang out through the frosted glass.

Alice didn't reply and sucked in her cheeks to see how much better she would be like that.

"Alice, are you in there?" her father called.

Alice puckered her lips and kissed her reflection. She brushed her tongue against its image in the cold glass. Then she closed her eyes and, as in a real kiss, swayed her head back and forth, but too regularly to be believable. She still hadn't found the kiss she really wanted on anyone's mouth.

Davide Poirino had been the first to use his tongue, in the third year of secondary school. He'd lost a bet. He had rolled it mechanically around Alice's tongue three times, clockwise, and then turned to his friends and said okay? They had burst out laughing and someone had said you kissed the cripple, but Alice was happy just the same, she had given her first kiss and Davide wasn't bad at all.

There had been others after that. Her cousin Walter at their grandmother's party, and a friend of Davide's whose name she didn't even know, and who had asked her in secret if he could please have a turn too. In a hidden corner of the school playground they had pressed their lips together for a few minutes, neither of them daring to move a muscle. When they had drawn apart, he had said thank you and walked off with his head held high and the springy step of a real man.

But now she was lagging behind. Her classmates talked about positions, love bites, and how to use your fingers, and whether it was better with or without a condom, while Alice's lips still bore the insipid memory of a mechanical kiss in third year.

"Alice? Can you hear me?" her father called again, louder this time.

"Ugh. Of course I hear you," Alice replied irritably, her voice barely audible on the other side of the door.

"Dinner's ready," her father repeated.

"I heard you, damn it," Alice said. Then, under her breath, she added, "Pain in the ass."

———

Soledad knew that Alice threw away her food. At first, when Alice started leaving her dinner on her plate, she said *mi amorcito,* eat it all up, in my country children are dying of hunger.

One evening Alice, furious, looked her straight in the eyes.

"Even if I stuff myself till I burst, the children in your country aren't going to stop dying of hunger," she said.

So now Soledad said nothing, but put less and less food on her plate. But it didn't make any difference. Alice was quite capable of weighing up her food with her eyes and choosing her three hundred calories for dinner. The rest she got rid of, somehow or other.

She ate with her right hand resting on her napkin. In front of the plate she put her wineglass, which she asked to be filled but never drank, and her water glass in such a way as to form a glass barricade. Then, during dinner, she strategically positioned the saltshaker and the oil cruet too. She waited for her family to be distracted, each absorbed in the laborious task of mastication. At that point she very carefully pushed her food, cut into small pieces, off the plate and into her napkin.

Over the course of a dinner she made at least three full napkins disappear into the pockets of her sweatpants. Before brushing her teeth she emptied them into the toilet and watched the little pieces of food disappear down the drain. With satisfaction she ran a hand over her stomach and imagined it as empty and clean as a crystal vase.

"Sol, damn it, you put cream in the sauce again," her mother complained. "How many times do I have to tell you that I can't digest it?"

Alice's mother pushed her plate away in disgust.

Alice had come to the table with a towel wrapped like a turban around her head in order to justify all the time she had spent locked away in the bathroom.

She had thought for a long time whether to ask them for it. But she'd do it anyway. She wanted it too much.

"I'd like to get a tattoo on my belly," she began.

Her father pulled his glass away from his mouth.

"Excuse me?"

"You heard," said Alice, defying him with her eyes. "I want to get a tattoo."

Alice's father ran his napkin over his mouth and eyes, as if to erase an ugly image that had run through his mind. Then he carefully refolded it and put it back on his knees. He picked up his fork again, trying to put on all his irritating self-control.

"I don't even know how you get these ideas into your head," he said.

"And what kind of tattoo would you like? Let's hear," her mother broke in, the irritable expression on her face probably due more to the cream in the sauce than to her daughter's request.

"A rose. Tiny. Viola's got one."

"Forgive me, but who might Viola be?" her father asked with a bit too much irony.

Alice shook her head, stared at the middle of the table, and felt insignificant.

"Viola's a classmate of hers," Fernanda replied emphatically. "She must have mentioned her a million times. You're not really with it, are you?"

Mr. Della Rocca looked disdainfully at his wife, as if to say no one asked you.

"Well, pardon me, but I don't think I'm all that interested in what Alice's classmates get tattooed on them," he pronounced at last. "At any rate you're not getting a tattoo."

Alice pushed another forkful of spaghetti into her napkin.

"It's not like you can stop me," she ventured, still staring at the vacant center of the table. Her voice cracked with a hint of insecurity.

"Could you repeat that?" her father asked, without altering the volume and calm of his own voice.

"Could you repeat that?" he asked more slowly.

"I said you can't stop me," replied Alice, looking up, but she was unable to endure her father's deep, chilly eyes for more than half a second.

"Is that so? As far as I know, you're fifteen years old and this binds you to the decisions of your parents for—the calculation is a very simple one—another three years," the lawyer intoned. "At the end of which you will be free to, how shall I put it, adorn your skin with flowers, skulls, or whatever you so desire."

The lawyer smiled at his plate and slipped a carefully rolled forkful of spaghetti into his mouth.

There was a long silence. Alice ran her thumb and forefinger along the edge of the tablecloth. Her mother nibbled on a bread stick and allowed her eyes to wander around the dining room. Her father pretended to eat heartily. He chewed with rolling motions of his jaw, and at the first two seconds of each mouthful he kept his eyes closed, in ecstasy.

Alice chose to deliver the blow because she really detested him, and seeing him eat like that made even her good leg go stiff.

"You don't give a damn if no one likes me," she said. "If no one will ever like me."

Her father looked at her quizzically, then returned to his dinner, as if no one had spoken.

"You don't care if you've ruined me forever."

Mr. Della Rocca's fork froze in midair. He looked at his daughter for a few seconds, seemingly distressed.

"I don't know what you're talking about," he said, a slight quaver to his voice.

"You know perfectly well," Alice said. "You know it'll be all your fault if I'm like this forever."

Alice's father rested his fork on the edge of his plate. He covered his eyes with one hand, as if thinking deeply about something. Then he got up and left the room, his heavy footsteps echoing across the gleaming marble hallway.

Fernanda said, oh Alice, with neither compassion nor reproach, just a resigned shake of the head. Then she followed her husband into the next room.

Alice went on staring at her full plate for about two minutes, while Soledad cleared the table, silent as a shadow. Then she stuffed the napkin filled with food into her pocket and locked herself in the bathroom.

4

Pietro Balossino had stopped trying to penetrate his son's obscure universe long ago. When he would accidentally catch sight of Mattia's arms, devastated by scars, he would think back to those sleepless nights spent searching the house for sharp objects left lying around, those nights when Adele, bloated with sedatives, her mouth hanging open, would sleep on the sofa because she no longer wanted to share the bed with him. Those nights when the future seemed to last only till the morning and he would count off the hours, one by one, by the chimes of distant church bells.

The conviction that one morning he would find his son facedown on a blood-soaked pillow had taken root so firmly in his head that he was now used to thinking as if Mattia had already ceased to exist, even at times like this, when he was sitting next to him in the car.

He was driving him to his new school. It was raining, but the rain was so fine that it didn't make a sound.

A few weeks before, the principal of Mattia's science high school had called him and Adele to his office, *to inform them of a situation.* But when the time came for the meeting, he skirted the issue, dwelling instead on the boy's sensitive temperament, his extraordinary intelligence, his solid 90 percent average in all subjects.

Mr. Balossino had insisted on his son being present for the discussion, for reasons of correctness, which doubtless interested him alone. Mattia had sat down next to his parents and throughout the whole session he had not raised his eyes from his knees. By clenching his fists tightly he had managed to make his left hand bleed slightly. Two days before, Adele, in a moment of distraction, had checked only the nails on his other hand.

Mattia listened to the principal's words as if he were not really talking about him, and he remembered that time in the fifth year of primary school when, after not uttering a word for five days in a row, his teacher, Rita, had made him sit in the middle of the room, with all the other kids arranged around him in a horseshoe. The teacher had begun by saying that Mattia clearly had a problem that he didn't want to talk to anyone about. That Mattia was a very intelligent child, perhaps too intelligent for his age. Then she had invited his classmates to sit close to him, so that they could make him understand that they were his friends. Mattia had looked at his feet, and when the teacher asked him if he wanted to say something, he finally opened his mouth and asked if he could go back to his chair.

Once the plaudits were finished, the principal got down to business. What Mr. Balossino finally understood, although only a few hours later, was that all of Mattia's teachers had expressed a peculiar unease, an almost impalpable feeling of inadequacy, with regard to this extraordinarily gifted boy who seemed not to want to form bonds with anyone his age.

The principal paused. He leaned back in his comfortable armchair and opened a folder, which he didn't need to read. Then he closed it again, as if remembering all of a sudden that there were other people in his office. With carefully chosen words he suggested to the Balossinos that perhaps the science high school was not capable of responding fully to their son's needs.

When, at dinner, Mattia's father had asked him if he really wanted to change schools, Mattia had replied with a shrug and studied the dazzling reflection of fluorescent light on the knife with which he was supposed to be cutting his meat.

"It isn't really raining crooked," said Mattia, looking out the car window and jerking his father out of his thoughts.

"What?" said Pietro, instinctively shaking his head.

"There's no wind outside. Otherwise the leaves on the trees would be moving as well," Mattia went on.

His father tried to follow his reasoning. In fact none of it meant anything to him and he suspected that it was merely another of his son's eccentricities.

"So?" he asked.

"The raindrops are running down the window at an angle, but that's just an effect of our motion. By measuring the angle with the vertical, you could also calculate the fall velocity."

Mattia traced the trajectory of a drop with his finger. He brought his face close to the window and breathed on it. Then, with his index finger, he drew a line in the condensation.

"Don't breathe on the windows, you'll leave marks."

Mattia didn't seem to have heard him.

"If we couldn't see anything outside the car, if we didn't know we were moving, there would be no way of telling whether it was the raindrops' fault or our own," said Mattia.

"Fault for what?" his father asked, bewildered and slightly annoyed.

"For them coming down so crooked."

Pietro Balossino nodded seriously, without understanding. They had arrived. He put the car in neutral and pulled on the hand brake. Mattia opened the door and a gust of fresh air blew inside.

"I'll come and get you at one," said Pietro.

Mattia nodded. Mr. Balossino leaned slightly forward to kiss him, but the belt restrained him. He leaned back into the seat and watched his son get out and close the door behind him.

The new school was in a lovely residential area in the hills. It had been built in the Fascist era, and in spite of recent renovations, it remained a blot on the landscape amid a row of sumptuous villas; a parallelepiped of white concrete, with four horizontal rows of evenly spaced windows and two green iron fire escapes.

Mattia climbed the two flights of steps leading to the main door but kept his distance from all the little groups of kids who were waiting for the first bell, getting wet from the rain.

Once inside, he looked for the floor plan with the layout of the classrooms, so that he wouldn't have to ask the janitors for help.

F2 was at the end of the corridor on the second floor. Mattia took a deep breath and entered. He waited, leaning against the back wall, with his thumbs hooked in the straps of his backpack and the look of someone who wanted to disappear into the wall.

As the students were taking their seats, their new faces glanced at him apprehensively. No one smiled at him. Some of them whispered in each other's ears and Mattia was sure they were talking about him.

He kept an eye on the desks that were still free, and when even the one next to a girl with red nail polish was taken, he felt relieved. The teacher came into the classroom and Mattia slipped onto the last empty chair, next to the window.

"Are you the new boy?" asked his neighbor, who looked just as alone as he did.

Mattia nodded without looking at him.

"I'm Denis," he said, extending his hand.

Mattia shook it weakly and said nice to meet you.

"Welcome," said Denis.

5

Viola Bai was admired and feared with equal passion by her class-mates, because she was so beautiful she made people uneasy, and because at the age of fifteen she knew more about life than any of her contemporaries did; or at least that was the impression she gave. On Monday mornings, during break, the girls congregated around her desk and listened greedily to the account of her weekend. Most times this was a skillful reimagining of what Serena, Viola's older sister by eight years, had told her the day before. Viola transferred the stories to herself, but embellished them with sordid, and often completely invented, details, which to her friends' ears sounded mysterious and disturbing. She talked about this or that bar, without ever having set foot in them, and she was capable of giving minute descriptions of the psychedelic lighting, or of the malicious smile that the bartender had flashed at her as he served her a Cuba libre.

In most cases she ended up either in bed with the bartender or out behind the bar, among the beer kegs and the cases of vodka, where he took her from behind, covering her mouth with his hand to keep her from screaming.

Viola Bai knew how to tell a story. She knew that all the violence is contained in the precision of a detail. She knew how to work the timing so that the bell rang just as the bartender was busy with the fly of his name-brand jeans. At that moment her devoted audience slowly dispersed, their cheeks red with envy and indignation. Viola was made to promise that she would go on with her story at the next bell, but she was too intelligent to actually do it. She always ended up dismissing the whole thing with a pout of her perfect mouth, as if what had happened to her was of no importance. It was just one more detail in her extraordinary life, and she was already light-years ahead of everyone else.

She had actually tried sex, as well as some of the drugs whose names she liked to list, but she had been with only one boy, and only once. It had happened at the shore. A friend of her sister's who had smoked and drunk too much that evening to realize that a little thirteen-year-old girl was too young for certain things. He had fucked her hastily, in the street, behind a trash bin. As they walked back, heads lowered, to rejoin the others, Viola had taken his hand but he had snatched it away and asked what are you doing? Her cheeks burned and the heat still trapped between her legs had made her feel alone. In the days that followed the boy didn't say a word to her and Viola had confided in her sister, who had laughed at her naïveté and said wise up, what did you expect?

Viola's devoted audience was made up of Giada Savarino, Federica Mazzoldi, and Giulia Mirandi. Together they formed a compact and ruthless phalanx: the four bitches, as some of the boys at the school called them. Viola had chosen them one by one and had demanded a little sacrifice from each of them, because her friendship was something you had to earn. She alone decided if you were in or out, and her decisions were obscure and unequivocal.

Alice observed Viola on the sly. From her desk two rows back, she fed off the broken sentences and fragments of torrid tales; then in the evening, alone in her room, she savored every detail.

Before that Wednesday morning Viola had never spoken a word to her. It was a kind of initiation and had to be done properly. None of the girls ever knew for sure whether Viola was improvising or whether she planned the torture in advance—but they all agreed that it was brilliant.

Alice hated the locker room. Her oh-so-perfect classmates stood around for as long as possible in their bras and underwear so as to make the others envious. They assumed stiff, unnatural poses, sucking in their stomachs and thrusting out their tits. They sighed at the cracked mirror that covered one of the walls. Look, they'd say as they sized up their hips, which could not have been better proportioned or more seductive.

On Wednesdays Alice wore her shorts under her jeans so that she wouldn't have to get completely undressed. The others would look at her suspiciously, imagining the horrors that were surely hidden under her clothes. She would turn her back to take off her sweater so they wouldn't see her belly.

She would put on her sneakers and tuck her shoes, neatly parallel, against the wall, and then carefully fold her jeans. Her classmates' clothes, in contrast, tumbled chaotically from the wooden benches, their shoes scattered about and upside down because they had yanked them off with their feet.

"Alice, do you have a sweet tooth?" Viola asked.

It took Alice a few seconds to convince herself that Viola Bai was actually talking to her. She was sure she was invisible to her. She pulled the two ends of her shoelaces, but the knot came untied between her fingers.

"Me?" she asked, looking around uneasily.

"I don't see any other Alices."

The other girls giggled.

"No. Not particularly."

Viola got up from the bench and came closer to her. Alice felt those marvelous eyes on her, bisected by the shadow of her bangs.

"But you like gumdrops, don't you?" Viola continued in her honeyed voice.

"Yeah. I guess. Pretty much."

Alice bit her lip and chided herself for being so wishy-washy. She pressed her bony back against the wall. A tremor ran down her good leg. The other remained inert, as always.

"What do you mean pretty much? Everyone likes gumdrops. Isn't that right, girls?" Viola addressed her three friends without even turning around.

"Mm-hmmm. Everyone," they echoed. Alice noticed a strange trepidation in Federica Mazzoldi's eyes as she stared at her from the other end of the locker room.

"Yes, actually, I do like them," she corrected herself. She was starting to feel frightened, even though she didn't yet know why.

In the first year, the four bitches had grabbed Alessandra Mirano, the one who ended up being thrown out and going to beautician school, and dragged her into the boys' locker room. They shut her inside and two boys pulled their cocks out in front of her. From the corridor Alice had heard the four torturers egging them on and laughing hysterically.

"I thought so. Now, would you like a gumdrop?" Viola asked.

If I say yes, who knows what they're going to make me eat, Alice thought.

If I say no, Viola might get pissed off and I'll end up in the boys' locker room as well.

She sat in silence like a moron.

"Come on. It's not such a hard question," Viola said mockingly. She took a handful of fruit candies from her pocket.

"You girls back there, what flavor do you want?" she asked.

Giulia Mirandi came over to Viola and looked into her hand. Viola didn't take her eyes off Alice, who felt her body crumpling under the gaze like a sheet of newspaper burning in the fireplace.

"There's orange, raspberry, blackberry, strawberry, and peach," Giulia said. She threw a fleeting, apprehensive glance at Alice, without letting Viola see.

"I'll have raspberry," said Federica.

"Peach," said Giada.

Giulia tossed them their candies and unwrapped the orange one for herself. She slipped it into her mouth and then took a step back to return the stage to Viola.

"Blackberry and strawberry are left. So do you want one or not?"

Maybe she just wants to give me a candy, Alice thought.

Maybe they just want to see whether I eat or not.

It's just a candy.

"I prefer strawberry," she said quietly.

"Damn it, that's my favorite too," Viola said, giving a terrible performance of disappointment. "But I'll happily give it to you."

She unwrapped the strawberry candy and let the paper fall to the ground. Alice held out her hand to take it.

"Wait a minute," Viola said. "Don't be so greedy."

She bent down, holding the candy between her thumb and index finger. She rubbed it along the filthy locker room floor. Walking with her knees bent, she dragged it slowly along the whole length of the room to Alice's left, close to the wall, where the dirt had co-agulated in balls of dust and tangles of hair.

Giada and Federica were dying of laughter. Giulia nervously chewed on her lip. The other girls had figured out where things were going and left, closing the door behind them.

When she got to the corner, Viola headed for the sink, where the girls splashed their armpits and faces after gym. With the candy she wiped up the whitish slime that lined the inside of the drain.

Then she turned to Alice and held the revolting object under her nose.

"There," she said. "Strawberry, just what you wanted."

She wasn't laughing. She had the serious, determined look of one who is doing something painful but necessary.

Alice shook her head no. She pressed herself even closer to the wall.

"What? Don't you want it anymore?" Viola asked her.

"Go on," Federica cut in. "You asked for it and now you can eat it."

Alice gulped.

"What if I don't?" she summoned the courage to say.

"If you don't eat it, you'll accept the consequences," Viola replied enigmatically.

"What consequences?"

"You can't know the consequences. Ever."

They want to take me to the boys, Alice thought. Or else they'll strip me and not give me back my clothes.

Trembling, but almost imperceptibly, she held her hand out toward Viola, who dropped the filthy candy into her palm. She slowly brought it to her mouth.

The others had fallen silent, and seemed to be thinking, no, she's not really going to do it. Viola was impassive.

Alice put the gumdrop on her tongue and felt the hairs that were stuck to it dry up her saliva. She chewed only twice and something squeaked between her teeth.

Don't throw up, she thought. Do not throw up.

She choked back an acidic spurt of gastric juices and swallowed the candy. She felt it as it went down, like a stone, along her esophagus.

The fluorescent light on the ceiling gave off an electrical hum and the voices of the kids in the gym were a formless mixture of shouts and laughter. Here in the basement the air was heavy and the windows were too small to allow it to circulate.

Viola stared solemnly at Alice. Without smiling she nodded her head as if to say now we can go. Then she turned around and left the locker room, passing the other three without so much as a glance.

6

There was something important you had to know about Denis. To tell the truth, Denis thought it was the only thing about him worth knowing, so he'd never told anyone.

His secret had a terrible name, which settled like a nylon cloth over his thoughts and wouldn't let them breathe. There it was, weighing heavily inside his head like an inevitable punishment with which he'd have to come to terms sooner or later.

When, at age ten, his piano teacher had guided his fingers through the D major scale, pressing his hot palm on the back of Denis's hand, Denis had been unable to breathe. He bent his torso slightly forward to hide the erection that had exploded in his sweatpants. For his entire life he would think of that moment as true love, and would fumble around every corner of his existence in search of the clinging warmth of his teacher's touch.

Each time memories like this surfaced in his mind, making his neck and hands sweat, Denis would lock himself in the bathroom and masturbate fiercely, sitting backward on the toilet. The pleasure lasted only a moment and radiated just a few inches beyond his penis. But the guilt rained down on him from above like a shower of dirty water. It ran down his skin and nestled in his guts, making everything slowly rot, the way that damp eats away at the walls of an old house.

During biology class, in the basement lab, Denis watched Mattia dissect a piece of steak, separating the white fibers from the red. He wanted to stroke his hands. He wanted to discover whether that cumbersome lump of desire that had taken root in his head would really melt like butter simply through contact with the classmate he was in love with.

They were sitting close to each other. Both rested their forearms on the lab bench. A row of transparent flasks, beakers, and test tubes separated them from the rest of the class and deflected the rays of light, distorting everything beyond that line.

Mattia was intent on his work and hadn't looked up for at least a quarter of an hour. He didn't like biology, but he pursued the task with the same rigor he applied to all subjects. Organic matter, so violable and full of imperfections, was incomprehensible to him. The vital odor of the soft piece of meat aroused nothing in him but a faint disgust.

With a pair of tweezers he extracted a thin white filament and deposited it on the glass slide. He brought his eyes to the microscope and adjusted the focus. He recorded every detail in his squared notebook and made a sketch of the enlarged image.

Denis sighed deeply. Then, as if taking a backward dive, he found the courage to speak.

"Mattia, do you have a secret?" he asked his friend.

Mattia seemed not to have heard, but the scalpel with which he was cutting another section of muscle slipped from his hand and rang out on the metal surface. He slowly picked it up.

Denis waited a few seconds. Mattia sat perfectly still, holding the knife a few inches above the meat.

"You can tell me; you can tell me your secret," Denis went on. His veins pulsed with trepidation. Now that he had pushed himself over the edge and into his classmate's fascinating intimacy, he had no intention of letting go.

"I've got one too, you know," he said.

Mattia cleanly sliced the muscle in half, as if he wanted to kill something that was already dead.

"I don't have any secrets," he said under his breath.

"If you tell me yours, I'll tell you mine," Denis pressed. He moved his stool closer and Mattia visibly stiffened. He stared, expressionless, at the scrap of meat.

"We have to finish the experiment," he said in a monotonous voice. "Otherwise we won't be able to finish the chart."

"I don't give a damn about the chart," said Denis. "Tell me what you did to your hands."

Mattia counted three breaths. Light molecules of ethanol stirred in the air, and some of them penetrated his nostrils. He felt them rising, a pleasant burning sensation along his septum, up to a point between his eyes.

"You really want to know what I've done to my hands?" he asked, turning toward Denis but looking at the jars of formalin lined up behind him: dozens of jars containing fetuses and amputated limbs of all sorts of animals.

Denis nodded, quivering.

"Then watch this," said Mattia.

He gripped the knife in his fist. Then he plunged it into the hollow of his other hand, between his index and middle fingers, and dragged it all the way to his wrist.

7

On Thursday Viola was waiting for her outside the gate. Alice, head lowered, was walking past her when Viola grabbed her by the sleeve. Viola startled her, calling out her name. She remembered the candy and was dizzy with nausea. Once the four bitches had you in their sights, they didn't let you go.

"I've got a math test," Viola said. "I don't know anything and don't want to go."

Alice looked at her uncomprehendingly. She didn't seem hostile, but Alice didn't trust her. She tried to pull away. Let's go for a walk, Viola continued. You and me? Yes, you and me. Alice looked around in terror. Come on, get a move on, Viola urged, they can't see us out here. But . . . Alice tried to object. Viola didn't let her finish; she pulled her harder by the sleeve and Alice had no choice but to follow, hobbling, as they ran to the bus stop.

They sat down side by side, Alice pressed against the window so as not to invade Viola's space. From one moment to the next she expected something to happen, something terrible. But Viola was radiant. She took a lipstick from her bag and ran it over her lips. Want some? she then asked. Alice shook her head. The school shrank in the distance behind them. My father will kill me, Alice mumbled. Her legs were shaking. Viola sighed. Come on, show me your attendance sheet. She studied Alice's father's signature and said it's easy . . . I'll sign it. She showed Alice her own sheet. She faked a signature whenever she didn't feel like going to class. Anyway first period tomorrow is Follini, she said, and she can't see a thing.

Viola started talking about school, about how she didn't give a damn about math because she was going to do law anyway. Alice could hardly believe her ears. She thought about the day before, about the locker room, and didn't know what to call this sudden intimacy.

They got off in the square and started walking under the arcades. Viola stopped at a clothing shop with fluorescent windows where Alice had never even set foot. She was acting as if they were lifelong friends. She insisted they try on some clothes, which she picked out herself. She asked Alice her size, and Alice was ashamed to tell her. The shop assistants watched them suspiciously, but Viola paid no attention. They shared a dressing room and Alice surreptitiously compared her own body with her friend's. In the end they didn't buy anything.

They went to a café and Viola ordered two coffees, without so much as asking Alice what she wanted. Alice hadn't a clue what was going on, but a new and unexpected happiness was filling her head. Slowly she forgot all about her father and school. She was sitting in a café with Viola Bai and that time seemed theirs alone.

Viola smoked three cigarettes and insisted that Alice try one too. Viola laughed, showing her perfect teeth, every time her new friend exploded in a fit of coughing. She subjected her to a little quiz about the boys she hadn't had and the kisses she hadn't given. Alice replied with her eyes lowered. You want me to believe you've never had a boyfriend? Never ever ever? Alice shook her head. That's impossible. A tragedy, Viola exaggerated. We absolutely have to do something. You don't want to die a virgin!

So the next day, at ten o'clock break, they roamed the school in search of the boyfriend for Alice. Viola had dismissed Giada and the others, saying we've got things to do, and they watched her leave the classroom hand in hand with her new friend.

Viola had already organized everything. It would happen at her birthday party the following Saturday. They just had to find the right boy. As they walked down the corridor she pointed this and that out to Alice, saying look at the ass on that one, not bad at all, he certainly knows what to do.

Alice smiled nervously but couldn't make her mind up. In her head she imagined with unsettling clarity the moment when a boy would slip his hands under her shirt. When he would discover that, underneath the clothes that fell so well, there was nothing but chubby flesh and flabby skin.

Now they were leaning on the fire escape railing on the third floor, watching the boys play football in the courtyard with a yellow ball that seemed not to be blown up enough.

"What about Trivero?" Viola asked.

"I don't know who he is."

"What do you mean you don't know who he is? He's in the fifth year. He used to row with my sister. They say some interesting things about him."

"What sort of things?"

Viola gestured with her hands, indicating something long, and then laughed loudly, enjoying the disconcerting effect of her allusions. Alice felt her face flush with shame, but she also felt a marvelous certainty that her loneliness was truly over.

They went down to the ground floor and passed the snacks and drinks machines. Students had formed a chaotic line, chinking the coins in their jeans pockets.

"Okay, but you've got to decide," said Viola.

Alice spun on her heels. She looked around, disoriented.

"That one looks cute," she said, pointing at two boys in the distance, near the window. They were standing close together, but they weren't talking or looking at each other.

"Who?" Viola asked. "The one with the bandage or the other one?"

"The one with the bandage."

Viola stared at her. Her sparkling eyes were as wide as two oceans.

"You're crazy," she said. "You know what he did?"

Alice shook her head.

"He stuck a knife in his hand, on purpose. Right here at school."

Alice shrugged.

"He looks interesting," she said.

"Interesting? He's a psychopath. With a guy like that you'll end up chopped to pieces and stuffed in a freezer."

Alice smiled, but went on looking at the boy with the bandaged hand. There was something in the way he kept his head tilted down that made her want to go over to him, lift his chin, and say to him look at me, I'm here.

"Are you absolutely sure?" Viola asked her.

"Yes," said Alice.

Viola shrugged.

"So let's go," she said.

She took Alice by the hand and pulled her toward the two boys at the window.

8

—————

Mattia was looking out the opaque windows of the atrium. It was a bright day, an anticipation of spring at the beginning of March. The strong wind that had cleared the air during the night seemed to sweep time away too, making it run faster. Mattia tried to estimate how far away the horizon was by counting the roofs of the houses that he could see from there.

Denis was surreptitiously staring at him, trying to guess his thoughts. They hadn't talked about what had happened in the biology lab. In fact, they didn't talk much at all, but they spent time together, each in his own abyss, held safe and tight by the other's silence.

"Hi," Mattia heard someone say, too close to him.

Reflected in the glass he saw two girls standing behind him, holding hands. He turned around.

Denis looked at him quizzically. The girls seemed to be waiting for something.

"Hi," Mattia said softly. He lowered his head, to protect himself from one of the girls' piercing eyes.

"I'm Viola and this is Alice," she continued. "We're in 2B."

Mattia nodded. Denis's mouth fell open. Neither of them said anything.

"Well?" Viola said. "Aren't you going to introduce yourselves?"

Mattia spoke his name in a low voice, as if just remembering it himself. He offered Viola a limp hand, the one without the bandage, and she shook it firmly. The other girl barely touched it and smiled, looking in another direction.

Denis introduced himself next, just as clumsily.

"We wanted to invite you to my birthday party the Saturday after next," said Viola.

Again Denis sought Mattia's eyes, but Mattia responded by staring at Alice's timid half-smile. Her lips seemed so pale and thin to him, as if her mouth had been carved by a sharp scalpel.

"Why?" he asked.

Viola looked at him askance and then turned to Alice, with an expression that said I told you he was mad.

"What do you mean why? Obviously because we feel like inviting you."

"No, thanks," said Mattia. "I can't come."

Denis, relieved, quickly added that he couldn't come either.

Viola ignored him and concentrated on the boy with the bandage.

"You can't? I wonder what could be keeping you so busy on a Saturday evening," she said provocatively. "Do you have to play video games with your little friend? Or were you planning on cutting your veins again?"

Viola felt a tremor of terror and excitement as she uttered those last words. Alice gripped her hand harder to make her stop.

Mattia reflected that he had forgotten the number of roofs and wouldn't have time to count them again before the bell.

"I don't like parties," he explained.

Viola forced herself to laugh for a few seconds, a sequence of piercing, high-pitched giggles.

"You really are strange," she teased, tapping her right temple. "Everyone likes parties."

Alice had withdrawn her hand and unconsciously rested it on her belly.

"Well, I don't," Mattia snapped back.

Viola stared defiantly at him and he blankly held her gaze. Alice had taken a step back. Viola opened her mouth to give some kind of reply, but the bell rang just in time. Mattia turned around and headed resolutely toward the stairs, as if to say that as far as he was concerned the discussion was over. Denis followed, pulled along in his wake.

9

Since entering the service of the Della Rocca family, Soledad Galienas had slipped up only once. Four years ago, one rainy evening when the Della Roccas were out to dinner at a friend's.

Soledad's wardrobe contained only black clothes, underwear included. She had spoken so often of her husband's death in a work accident that she sometimes even believed it herself. She imagined him standing on a scaffolding sixty feet off the ground, cigarette between his teeth, as he leveled a layer of mortar before laying another row of bricks. She saw him trip over a tool or perhaps a coil of rope, the rope with which he was supposed to make a harness and which instead he had tossed aside because harnesses are for softies. She imagined him wobbling on the wooden planks before plummeting without a sound. The image panned out so that her husband became like a little black dot waving its arms against the white sky. Then her artificial memory ended with an overhead shot: her husband's body splattered on the dusty ground of the building site, lifeless and two-dimensional, his eyes still open and a dark pool of blood oozing out from under his back.

Thinking of him like that gave her a pleasurable tremor of anguish, and if she dwelled on it long enough, she even managed to squeeze out a few tears, which were entirely for herself.

The truth was that her husband had walked out. He had left her one morning, probably to start his life over again with a woman she didn't even know. She had never heard anything more about him. When she arrived in Italy she made up the story of her widowhood to have a past to tell people about, because there was nothing to say about her real past. Her black clothes and the thought that others

56

might see the traces of a tragedy in her eyes, a pain that had never been assuaged, gave her a sense of security. She wore her mourning with dignity, and until that evening she had never betrayed the memory of the deceased.

On Saturdays she went to six o'clock mass, in order to be back in time for dinner. Ernesto had been courting her for weeks. After the service he stood waiting for her in the courtyard and, always with the same precise degree of ceremony, offered to walk her home. Soledad shrank into her black dress, but in the end she gave in. He told her about the post office where he used to work, and how long the evenings were now, at home alone, with so many years behind him and so many ghosts to reckon with. Ernesto was older than Soledad and his wife really had died, carried off by pancreatic cancer.

They walked arm in arm, very composed. That evening Ernesto had shared his umbrella with her, allowing his head and coat to get soaked so as to shelter her better from the rain. He had complimented her on her Italian, which was getting better week by week, and Soledad had laughed, pretending to be embarrassed.

It was thanks to a certain clumsiness, a lack of coordination, that instead of saying good-bye to each other as friends, with two chaste kisses on the cheek, their mouths had met on the front step of the Della Rocca house. Ernesto apologized, but then he bent over her lips again and Soledad felt all the dust that had settled in her heart whirl up and get in her eyes.

She was the one to invite him in. Ernesto had to stay hidden in her room for a few hours, just long enough for her to give Alice something to eat and send her to bed. The Della Roccas would be going out soon and wouldn't be back till late.

Ernesto thanked someone up above for the fact that such things could still happen at his age. They entered the house furtively, Soledad leading her lover by the hand, like a teenager, and with her finger to her mouth she told him not to make a sound. Then she hastily made dinner for Alice, watched her eat it too slowly, and said you look tired, you should go to bed. Alice protested that she wanted to watch television and Soledad gave in, just to get rid of her, as long as she watched it up in the den. Alice went upstairs, taking advantage of her father's absence to drag her feet as she walked.

Soledad returned to her lover. They kissed for a long time, sitting side by side, not knowing what to do with their own hands, clumsy and out of practice. Then Ernesto plucked up the courage to pull her to him.

As he fiddled with the devilish hooks that fastened her bra, apologizing under his breath for being so clumsy, she felt young and beautiful and uninhibited. She closed her eyes, and when she opened them again she saw Alice, standing in the doorway.

"*Coño,*" she blurted out. "*¿Qué haces aquí?*"

She slipped away from Ernesto and covered her bosom with one arm. Alice tilted her head to one side and observed them without surprise, as if they were animals in a zoo.

"I can't get to sleep," she said.

By some mysterious coincidence Soledad was remembering that very moment when, turning around, she saw Alice standing in the study doorway. Soledad was dusting the library. Three at a time she pulled the lawyer's encyclopedia, the heavy volumes with dark green binding and gilded spines, off the shelf. While she held them with her left arm, which was already beginning to ache, with her right she dusted the mahogany surfaces, even in the most hidden corners, because the lawyer had once complained that she only pushed the dust around.

It was years since Alice had entered her father's study. An invisible barrier of hostility kept her frozen in the doorway. She was sure that if she placed so much as a toe on the regular, hypnotic geometry of the parquet, the wood would crack under her weight and send her plunging into a black abyss.

The whole room was saturated with her father's intense smell. It had seeped into the papers stacked neatly on the desk, and drenched the thick, cream-colored curtains. When she was little, Alice would tiptoe in and call her father for dinner. She always hesitated for a moment before speaking, enchanted by her father's posture as he loomed over his desk studying complicated documents from behind his silver-framed glasses. When the lawyer realized his daughter was there, he slowly lifted up his head and frowned, as if to ask what she was doing there. Then he nodded and gave her a hint of a smile. I'm coming, he said.

Alice was sure that she could hear those words echoing against the wallpaper in the study, trapped forever in these four walls and inside her head.

"*Hola, mi amorcito,*" said Soledad. She still called her that, even though the pencil-thin girl standing in front of her was a far cry from the sleepy child she used to dress and walk to school every morning.

"Hi," replied Alice.

Soledad looked at her for a few seconds, waiting for her to say something, but Alice glanced away nervously. Soledad returned to her shelves.

"Sol," Alice said at last.

"Yes?"

"I have to ask you something."

Soledad set the books down on the desk and walked over to Alice.

"What is it, *mi amorcito?*"

"I need a favor."

"What sort of favor? Of course, tell me."

Alice rolled the elastic of her trousers around her index finger.

"On Saturday I have to go to a party. At my friend Viola's house."

"Oh, how lovely," said Soledad, smiling.

"I'd like to bring a dessert. I'd like to make it myself. Would you help me?"

"Of course, darling. What sort of dessert?"

"I don't know. A cake. Or a tiramisù. Or that one that you make with cinnamon."

"My mother's recipe," said Soledad with a hint of pride. "I'll teach you."

Alice looked at her pleadingly.

"So we'll go shopping together on Saturday? Even though it's your day off?"

"Of course, dear," said Soledad. For a moment she felt important, and she recognized in Alice's insecurity the little girl she had raised.

"Could you take me somewhere else as well?" Alice ventured.

"Where?"

Alice hesitated for a moment.

"To get a tattoo," she said hastily.

"Oh, *mi amorcito*." Soledad sighed, vaguely disappointed. "You know your father doesn't want you to."

"We won't tell him. He'll never see it," Alice insisted with a whine.

Soledad shook her head.

"Come on, Sol, please," she begged. "I can't get it done on my own. I need my parents' permission."

"So what can I do?"

"You can pretend to be my mother. You'll only have to sign a piece of paper, you won't have to say anything."

"But I can't, my dear, I can't. Your father would fire me."

Alice suddenly grew more serious. She looked Soledad straight in the eyes.

"It'll be our secret, Sol." She paused. "After all, the two of us already have a secret, don't we?"

Soledad looked at her, puzzled. At first she didn't understand.

"I know how to keep secrets," Alice continued slowly. She felt as strong and ruthless as Viola. "Otherwise he'd have fired you ages ago."

Soledad was suddenly unable to breathe.

"But—" she said.

"So you'll do it?" Alice cut in.

Soledad looked at the floor.

"Okay," she said quietly. Then she turned her back on Alice and arranged the books on the shelf while her eyes filled with two fat tears.

Mattia deliberately made all his movements as silently as he could. He knew that the chaos of the world would only increase, that the background noise would grow until it covered every coherent signal, but he was convinced that by carefully measuring his every gesture he would be less guilty of that slow ruin.

He had learned to set down first his toe and then his heel, keeping his weight toward the outside of the sole to minimize the amount of surface area in contact with the ground. He had perfected this technique years before, when he would get up in the night and stealthily roam about the house, the skin of his hands having become so dry that the only way to know they were still his was to pass a knife over them. Over time that strange, circumspect gait had become his normal way of walking.

His parents would often find themselves suddenly face-to-face with him, like a hologram projected from the floor, a frown on his face and his mouth always tightly shut. Once his mother dropped a plate with fright. Mattia bent down to pick up the bits, but resisted the temptation of those sharp edges. His mother, embarrassed, thanked him, and when he left she sat on the floor and stayed there for a quarter of an hour, defeated.

Mattia turned the key in the front door. He had learned that by turning the handle toward himself and pressing his palm over the keyhole, he could eliminate almost entirely the metallic click of the lock. With the bandage on it was even easier.

He slipped into the hallway, put the keys back in again, and repeated the operation from inside, like a burglar in his own home.

His father was already home, earlier than usual. When he heard him raise his voice he froze, unsure whether to cross the sitting room and interrupt his parents' conversation or go out again and wait until he saw the living room light go out from the courtyard.

"I don't think it's right," his father concluded with a note of reproach in his voice.

"Right," Adele shot back. "You'd rather pretend nothing is wrong, act as if nothing strange were going on."

"And what's so strange?"

There was a pause. Mattia could picture his mother lowering her head and wrinkling up one corner of her mouth as if to say it's pointless trying to talk with you.

"What's so strange?" she repeated emphatically. "I don't . . ."

Mattia kept a step back from the ray of light that spilled from the sitting room into the hall. With his eyes he followed the line of shadow from the floor to the walls and then to the ceiling. He realized that it formed a trapezoid, only one more trick of perspective.

His mother often abandoned her sentences halfway through, as if she had forgotten what she was going to say as she was saying it. Those interruptions left bubbles of emptiness in her eyes and in the air and Mattia always imagined bursting them with a finger.

"What's strange is that he stuck a knife in his hand in front of all his classmates. What's strange is that we were convinced those days were over but we were wrong once again," his mother went on.

Mattia had no reaction when he realized that they were talking about him, just a mild sense of guilt at eavesdropping on a conversation he wasn't supposed to hear.

"That's not reason enough to go and talk to his teachers without him," his father said, but in a more moderate tone. "He's old enough to have the right to be there."

"For God's sake, Pietro," his mother exploded. She never called him by name. "That's not the point, don't you understand? Will you stop treating him as if he were—"

She froze. The silence stuck in the air like static electricity. A slight shock made Mattia's back contract.

"As if he were what?"

"Normal," his mother confessed. Her voice trembled slightly and Mattia wondered if she was crying. Then again, she cried often since that afternoon. Most of the time for no reason. Sometimes she cried because the meat she had cooked was stringy or because the plants on the balcony were full of parasites. Whatever the reason, her despair was always the same. As if, in any case, there were nothing to be done.

"His teachers say he has no friends. He only talks to the boy who sits next to him and he spends the whole day with him. Boys his age go out in the evening, try to hook up with girls—"

"You don't think he's . . ." his father interrupted. "Well, you know . . ."

Mattia tried to complete the sentence, but nothing came to mind.

"No, that's not what I think. Maybe I wish that's all it was," said his mother. "Sometimes I think that something of Michela ended up in him."

His father let out a deep, loud sigh.

"You promised not to talk about that anymore," he said, vaguely irritated.

Mattia thought of Michela, who had disappeared into thin air. But only for a fraction of a second. Then he let himself be distracted by the faint image of his parents, who, he discovered, were reflected in miniature on the smooth, curved surfaces of the umbrella stand. He started scratching his left elbow with his keys. He felt the joint twitching from one tooth to the next.

"Do you know what really makes me shiver?" said Adele. "All those high grades he gets. Always the highest. There's something frightening in those grades."

Mattia heard his mother sniff, once. She sniffed again, but now it sounded as if her nose were pressed up against something. He imagined his father taking her in his arms, in the middle of the living room.

"He's fifteen," said his father. "It's a cruel age."

His mother didn't reply and Mattia listened to those rhythmic sobs rising to a peak of intensity and then slowly ebbing, finally growing silent again.

At that point he walked into the living room. He closed his eyes slightly as he entered the beam of light. He stopped two steps away from his hugging parents, who looked at him in alarm, like two kids caught necking. Stamped on their faces was the question, how long had he been out there?

Mattia looked at a point midway between them. He said, simply, I do have friends, I'm going to a party on Saturday. Then he continued toward the hall and disappeared into his room.

The tattoo artist had eyed suspiciously first Alice and then the woman with the too dark skin and the frightened expression whom the girl had introduced as her mother. He didn't believe it for a second, but it was none of his business. He was used to tricks of that kind, and he was used to capricious teenage girls. They were getting younger and younger: this one couldn't be as much as seventeen, he thought. But he certainly wasn't in a position to refuse a job for a question of principle. He'd shown the woman to a chair, and she'd sat down and hadn't said another word. She had gripped her purse tightly in her hands, as if ready to leave at any moment, and looked everywhere except in the direction of the needle.

The girl hadn't flinched. He had asked does it hurt, because that's something you have to ask, but she had said no, no through clenched teeth.

He had recommended that she keep the gauze on for at least three days and to clean the wound morning and evening for a week. He had given her a jar of Vaseline and stuffed the money in his pocket.

Back home in the bathroom, Alice took off the white tape that held the bandage on. Her tattoo had been in existence for only a few hours and she had already peeked at it a dozen times. Each time she looked, a bit of the excitement dispersed, like a pool of shimmering water that evaporates beneath the August sun. This time she thought only of how red her skin had turned, all the way around the design. She wondered if her skin would ever regain its natural color and for a moment her throat tightened with panic. Then she banished that stupid anxiety. She hated the fact that her every action always had to seem so irremediable, so definitive. In her mind she called it *the weight of consequences,* and she was sure that it was another awkward piece of her father that had wormed its way into her brain. How she longed for the uninhibitedness of kids her age, their vacuous sense of immortality. She yearned for all the lightness of her fifteen years, but in trying to grasp it she became aware of the fury with which the time at her disposal was slipping away. The weight of consequences was becoming more and more unbearable and her thoughts began whirling faster and faster, in ever smaller circles.

She had changed her mind at the last moment. That was what she had said to the young man who had already turned on the whizzing machine and was bringing the needle to her belly: I've changed my mind. Unsurprised, he had asked her don't you want to do it anymore? Alice had said yes I want to. But I don't want a rose. I want a violet.

The tattooist had looked at her, puzzled. Then he had confessed that he didn't exactly know what a violet looked like. It's kind of like a daisy, Alice had explained, only with three petals at the top and two at the bottom. And it's violet in color. The tattooist had said okay and set to work.

Alice looked at the livid little flower that now framed her navel and wondered if Viola would understand that it was for her, for their friendship. She decided she wouldn't show it to her till Monday. She wanted to present it without any scabs, bright against her pale skin. She chided herself for not doing it earlier, so that it would have been ready for tonight. She imagined what it would be like to show it secretly to that boy she'd invited to the party. Two days before, Mattia had appeared in front of her and Viola, with that sunken air of his. Denis and I are coming to the party, he had said. Viola hadn't even had time to come up with an unpleasant remark before he was already at the far end of the hall, his back turned to them and head lowered.

She wasn't sure she wanted to kiss him, but it was all decided now and she would look like an idiot in front of Viola if she backed down.

She measured the precise point where the top of her underpants had to come to be able to see the tattoo but not the scar immediately below it. She slipped on a pair of jeans, a T-shirt, and a sweatshirt big enough to cover the lot—the tattoo, the scar, and the bumps of her hips—and then left the bathroom, to join Soledad in the kitchen and watch her make her special cinnamon dessert.

Denis took deep, long breaths, trying to fill his lungs with the smell of Pietro Balossino's car. A slightly sour smell of sweat, which seemed to emanate not so much from the people as from the fireproof seat covers, and from something damp that had been sitting there too long, perhaps hidden under the mats. Denis felt the mixture wrap around his face like a hot bandage.

He would happily have spent all night in that car, driving around the half-dark streets of the hill, watching the lights of the cars in the opposite lane strike his friend's face and then return it to the shadows, unharmed.

Mattia was sitting in the front, beside his father. To Denis, who had been secretly studying the absence of any expression on both their faces, it seemed that father and son had agreed not to utter a single word during the whole journey, and to ensure that their eyes didn't meet even by accident.

He noticed that they had the same way of holding objects, framing them with their fingers tensed, touching surfaces but not really resting on them, as if they feared deforming whatever they held in their hands. Mr. Balossino seemed to barely touch the steering wheel. Mattia's frightful hands traced the edges of the present that his mother had bought for Viola and which he now held on his knees.

"So you're in the same class as Mattia," Mr. Balossino forced himself to say, though without much conviction.

"Yeah," said Denis, in a shrill voice that seemed to have been trapped for too long in his throat. "We sit next to each other."

Mattia's father nodded seriously and then, his conscience assuaged, he returned to his thoughts. Mattia seemed not even to have noticed that scrap of conversation and didn't take his eyes off the window, through which he was trying to work out whether his perception that the dotted white line in the middle of the road was in fact a continuous line was due merely to his eye's slow response or to some more complicated mechanism.

Pietro Balossino braked a few feet away from the big gate of the Bai family's property and put on the hand brake as they were on a slight incline.

"She's pretty well off, your friend," he observed, leaning forward to see over the top of the gate.

Neither Denis nor Mattia admitted that they barely knew the girl's name.

"So I'll come back for you at midnight, okay?"

"Eleven," Mattia replied quickly. "Let's make it eleven."

"Eleven? But it's already nine o'clock. What are you going to do for only two hours?"

"Eleven," insisted Mattia.

Pietro Balossino shook his head and said okay.

Mattia got out of the car and Denis did likewise, reluctantly. He was worried that Mattia might make new friends at the party, fun, fashionable friends who, in the bat of an eye, would take him away forever. He was worried that he would never get into that car again.

He politely said good-bye to Mattia's father and, to seem like a grown-up, held out his hand. Pietro Balossino performed a clumsy acrobatic maneuver to shake it without unfastening his seat belt.

The boys stood stiffly at the gate and waited for the car to turn around before deciding to ring the bell.

Alice was crouching at one end of the white sofa. A glass of Sprite in her hand, from the corner of her eye she was peeking at Sara Turletti's voluminous thighs, crammed into a pair of dark tights.

Squashed onto the sofa they became even bigger, almost twice as broad. Alice thought about the space she occupied compared to her classmate. The idea of being able to become so thin as to be invisible gave her a pleasant pang in the stomach.

When Mattia and Denis came into the room, she suddenly stiffened her back and looked around desperately for Viola. She noticed that Mattia wasn't wearing a bandage anymore and tried to see if he had a scar on his wrist. She instinctively ran her index finger along the trace of her own scar. She knew how to find it even under her clothes; it was like an earthworm lying against her skin.

The boys looked around like hunted prey, but in truth not one of the thirty or so kids scattered around the room paid them the least attention. No one except Alice.

Denis followed Mattia's movements, going where he went and looking where he looked. Mattia walked over to Viola, who was busy telling one of her made-up stories to a group of girls. He didn't even ask himself whether he'd ever seen those girls at school. He stood behind the birthday girl, holding the present stiffly to his chest. Viola turned around when she noticed that her friends had taken their eyes off her irresistible mouth and were looking instead over her shoulder.

"Ah, you're here," she said rudely.

"Here," said Mattia, placing the present in her arms. Then he added a mumbled happy birthday.

He was about to go when Viola shouted in an overexcited voice, "Alice, Alice, come quickly. Your friend's here."

Denis swallowed the lump in his throat. One of Viola's little friends cackled into another girl's ear.

Alice got up from the sofa. In the four paces that separated her from the group she tried to mask her syncopated gait, but she was sure that that was what they were all looking at.

She greeted Denis with a quick smile and then Mattia, bowing her head and saying hi in a faint voice. Mattia said hi back and his eyebrows jerked, making him appear even more spastic in Viola's eyes.

There followed an uncomfortably long silence that only she was able to break.

"I've discovered where my sister keeps the pills," she said, beaming. "Do you want some?"

She aimed her question at Mattia, certain that he wouldn't have the slightest idea what she was talking about. She was right.

"Girls, come with me, let's go get them," she said. "You too, Alice."

She took Alice by an arm and the five girls jostled one another as they disappeared down the hall.

Denis was alone with Mattia again and his heartbeat resumed its regular frequency. They both walked over to the drinks table.

"There's whiskey," Denis observed, slightly shocked. "And vodka too."

Mattia didn't reply. He took a plastic cup from the stack and filled it to the brim with Coca-Cola, trying to get as close as possible to that limit where the surface tension of the liquid prevents it from spilling over. Then he set it down on the table. Denis poured himself some whiskey, looking cautiously around and hoping secretly to impress Mattia, who didn't even notice.

Two rooms away, the girls had sat Alice down on Viola's sister's bed to instruct her about what to do.

"No blow jobs. Not even if he asks you, understand?" advised Giada Savarino. "The first time the max you can do is a hand job."

Alice laughed nervously and couldn't work out whether Giada was being serious.

"Now, you go back in there and start talking to him," explained Viola, who had a plan in mind and a very clear one. "Then you come up with an excuse to take him to my room, okay?"

"And what excuse am I supposed to come up with?"

"How do I know? Anything. Tell him you're fed up with the music and you want some peace and quiet."

"What about his friend? He's always glued to him," Alice said.

"We'll take care of him," said Viola with her most ruthless smile.

She climbed onto her sister's bed, trampling the light green cover with her shoes. Alice thought of her father, who wouldn't even let her walk on the carpet with her shoes on. For a second she wondered what he would have said if he had seen her there, but then she swallowed back the thought.

Viola opened a drawer in the cupboard above the bed. She rummaged around, not tall enough to see inside, and took out a little box covered with red fabric, adorned with gilded Chinese characters.

"Take this," she said. She held her hand out toward Alice. In the middle of her palm was a bright blue pill, square and with rounded corners. Carved in the center was a butterfly. For a second Alice saw the filthy fruit gumdrop she had accepted from that very same hand and felt it trapped in her throat again.

"What is it?" she asked.

"Take it. You'll have more fun."

Viola winked. Alice thought for a moment. They were all looking at her. She thought this must be another test. She took the pill from Viola's hand and placed it on her tongue.

"You're ready," Viola said with satisfaction. "Let's go."

The girls left the room single file, all looking down and with wicked smiles on their faces. Federica pleaded with Viola, please, let me have one too. And Viola brusquely told her wait your turn.

Alice was the last to leave. When all their backs were turned, she brought a hand to her mouth and spat out the pill. She put it in her pocket and turned out the light.

13

Like four beasts of prey, Viola, Giada, Federica, and Giulia surrounded Denis.

"Will you come with us?" Viola asked.

"Why?"

"We'll explain why later," Viola cackled.

Denis froze. He sought Mattia's help, but Mattia was still absorbed in the quivering Coca-Cola. The loud music that filled the room made the surface jerk with each beat of the bass drum. Mattia waited with strange trepidation for the moment when it would spill over the rim.

"I'd rather stay here," said Denis.

"God, how boring you are," Viola said, losing her patience. "You're coming with us and that's that."

She pulled him by the arm. Denis resisted feebly. Then Giada started pulling as well and he gave in. As they were pushing him into the kitchen, he looked once more at his friend, who was still motionless.

Mattia became aware of Alice's presence when she rested a hand on the table: the tension broke and a thin layer of liquid spilled over the rim and settled around the base in a dark ring.

He instinctively looked up and met her gaze.

"How's it going?" she asked.

Mattia nodded. "Fine," he said.

"Do you like the party?"

"Mmm."

"Music this loud gives me a headache."

Alice waited for Mattia to say something. She looked at him and it seemed to her that he wasn't breathing. His eyes were meek and pain-stricken. Like the first time, she suddenly wanted to draw those eyes toward her, to take Mattia's head in her hands and tell him everything would be okay.

"Will you come into the other room with me?" she ventured.

Mattia looked at the floor, as if he had been waiting for those very words.

"Okay," he said.

Alice headed down the hall and he followed a short distance behind. Mattia, as always, kept his head down and looked in front of him. He noticed that Alice's right leg bent gracefully at the knee, like every other leg in the world, and her foot brushed the floor without a sound. Her left leg, on the other hand, remained stiff. To push it forward she had to make it do a little arc outward. For a fraction of a second her pelvis was unbalanced, as if she were about to topple sideways. At last her left foot touched the ground as well, heavily, like a crutch.

Mattia concentrated on that gyroscopic rhythm, and without realizing it he synchronized his steps with hers.

When they got to Viola's room, Alice sidled up next to him and, with a daring that startled even her, closed the door. They were standing, he on the rug and she just off it.

Why doesn't he say anything? Alice wondered.

For a moment she wanted to drop the whole thing, to open the door again and leave, to breathe normally.

But what would I tell Viola? she thought.

"It's better in here, isn't it?" she said.

"Yeah," Mattia agreed, nodding. His arms dangled at his sides like a ventriloquist's dummy. With his right index finger he was folding a short, hard bit of skin that stuck out from beside his thumbnail. It was almost like piercing himself with a needle and the sting distracted him for a moment from the charged air in the room.

Alice sat on Viola's bed, balancing on the edge. The mattress didn't dip beneath her weight. She looked around, searching for something.

"Why don't you sit down here?" she asked Mattia at last.

He obeyed, sitting down carefully, about a foot away from her. The music in the living room sounded like the heavy, panting breath of the walls. Alice noticed Mattia's hands, clenched into fists.

"Is your hand better?" she asked.

"Nearly," he said.

"How did you do it?"

"I cut myself. In the biology lab. By accident."

"Can I see?"

Mattia tightened his fists still further. Then he slowly opened his left hand. A furrow, light in shade and perfectly straight, cut it diagonally. Around it, Alice made out scars that were shorter and paler, almost white. They filled the whole of his palm, intersecting like the branches of a leafless tree seen against the light.

"I've got one too, you know," she said.

Mattia clenched his fist again and trapped his hand between his legs, as if to hide it. Alice stood up, lifted her sweatshirt slightly, and unbuttoned her jeans. He was seized by panic. He turned his eyes to the floor, but still managed to see Alice's hands folding back the edge of her trousers, revealing a piece of white gauze framed by Scotch tape and, just below it, the top of a pair of pale gray underpants.

Alice lowered the elastic band a couple of inches and Mattia held his breath.

"Look," she said.

A long scar ran along her protruding pelvis bone. It was thick and in relief, and wider than Mattia's. The marks from the stitches, which intersected it perpendicularly and at regular intervals, made it look like the kind of scar children draw on their faces when they dress up as pirates.

Mattia couldn't think what to say. Alice buttoned up her jeans and tucked her undershirt inside them. Then she sat down again, a little closer to him.

The silence was almost unbearable for both of them, the empty space between their faces overflowing with expectation and embarrassment.

"Do you like your new school?" Alice asked, for the sake of saying something.

"Yes."

"They say you're a genius."

Mattia sucked in his cheeks and bit into them till he felt the metallic taste of blood filling his mouth.

"Do you really like studying?"

Mattia nodded.

"Why?"

"It's the only thing I know how to do," he said shortly. He wanted to tell her that he liked studying because you can do it alone, because all the things you study are already dead, cold, and chewed over. He wanted to tell her that the pages of the schoolbooks were all the same temperature, that they left you time to choose, that they never hurt you and you couldn't hurt them either. But he said nothing.

"And do you like me?" Alice went for it. Her voice came out rather shrilly and her face exploded with heat.

"I don't know," Mattia answered hastily, looking at the floor.

"Why?"

"I don't know," he insisted. "I haven't thought about it."

"You don't need to think about it."

"If I don't think, I can't understand anything."

"I like you," said Alice. "A bit. I think."

He nodded. He played at contracting and relaxing his retina, to make the geometric design of the carpet go in and out of focus.

"Do you want to kiss me?" Alice asked. She wasn't ashamed, but as she said it her empty stomach curled with terror that he might say no.

Mattia didn't move for a few seconds. Then he shook his head, slowly, still staring at the swirls in the carpet.

With a nervous impulse, Alice brought her hands to her hips and measured the circumference of her waist.

"It doesn't matter," she said quickly, in a different voice. "Please don't tell anyone," she added.

You're an idiot, she thought. Worse than a girl in kindergarten.

She stood up. Suddenly Viola's room seemed like a strange, hostile place. She felt herself becoming intoxicated by all the colors on the walls, the desk covered with makeup, the toe shoes hanging from the closet door, like a pair of severed feet, the big photo of Viola at the beach, lying on the sand looking beautiful, the cassettes stacked haphazardly beside the stereo, and the clothes piled up on the armchair.

"Let's go back," she said.

Mattia got up from the bed. He looked at her for a moment, apologetically, it seemed to her. She opened the door, letting the music flood the room. She walked partway down the hall alone. Then she thought of Viola's face. She turned around, took Mattia's stiff hand without asking his permission, and together they walked into the noisy living room.

14

The girls had trapped Denis in the corner, near the fridge, so as to have a little fun. They had arranged themselves in front of him, forming a barrier of excited eyes and flowing hair, through which he could no longer see Mattia in the other room.

"Truth or dare?" Viola asked him.

Denis shook his head timidly, to say that he didn't feel like playing this game. Viola rolled her eyes and then opened the fridge, forcing Denis to lean to the side to make room for the door. She pulled out a bottle of peach vodka and took a gulp, without bothering to find a glass. Then she offered him some, with a complicit smile.

He already felt dizzy and a little nauseated. The whiskey had left a bitter aftertaste suspended between his nose and his mouth, but there was something in Viola's behavior that prevented him from objecting. He took the bottle and took a sip. Then he passed it to Giada Savarino, who grabbed it greedily and started to pour it down her throat as if it were orangeade.

"So. Truth or dare?" repeated Viola. "Otherwise we'll choose."

"I don't like this game," Denis objected unconvincingly.

"Mmm, you and your friend really are a drag," she said. "Then I'll choose. Truth. Let's see."

She rested her index finger on her chin and with her eyes traced an imaginary circle on the ceiling, pretending to be deep in thought.

"I know!" she exclaimed. "You have to tell us which one of us you like best."

Denis shrugged, intimidated.

"Dunno," he said.

"What do you mean, dunno? You must like at least one of us, right?"

Denis thought he didn't like any of them, that he just wanted them to get out of his way and let him get back to Mattia. That he had only one more hour to be with him and watch him exist, even at night, when usually the only thing he could do was imagine him in his bedroom, sleeping under a sheet the color of which he didn't know.

If I choose one of them, they'll leave me alone, he thought.

"Her." He pointed to Giulia Mirandi, because she seemed the most harmless.

Giulia brought a hand to her mouth as if she'd just been elected prom queen. Viola turned up one corner of her mouth. The other two exploded into coarse laughter.

"Good," said Viola. "So now the dare."

"No, that's enough," protested Denis.

"You really are a bore. Here you are, surrounded by four girls, and you don't even want to play a bit. Certainly this doesn't happen to you every day."

"But now it's someone else's turn."

"And I say it's still your turn. You have to do the dare. What do you say, girls?"

The others nodded greedily. The bottle was once more in the hands of Giada, who at regular intervals threw back her head and took a swig, as if she wanted to finish it before the others noticed.

"See?" said Viola.

Denis snorted.

"What do I have to do?" he asked with resignation.

"Well, since I'm a generous hostess, I'm going to give you a nice dare," Viola said mysteriously. The other three hung on her words, eager to discover the new torture. "You have to kiss Giulia."

Giulia blushed. Denis felt a pang in his ribs.

"Are you crazy?" Giulia asked, shocked, perhaps pretending.

Viola gave a capricious shrug. Denis shook his head no, two, three times in a row.

"You were the one who said you liked her," she said.

"What if I don't do it?"

Suddenly dead serious, Viola looked him straight in the eyes.

"If you don't do it you'll have to choose truth again," she said. "You could tell us about your little friend, for example."

In her keen, bright stare Denis recognized all the things he had always thought were invisible. His neck stiffened.

His arms at his sides, he leaned his face toward Giulia Mirandi, narrowed his eyes, and kissed her. Then he tried to draw back, but Giulia held his head, her hand on the back of his neck. She forced her tongue through his pursed lips.

In his mouth Denis tasted saliva that wasn't his own and felt sick. In the middle of this, his first kiss, he opened his eyes just in time to see Mattia coming into the kitchen, hand in hand with the crippled girl.

The others were the first to notice what Alice and Mattia would come to understand only many years later. They walked into the room holding hands. They weren't smiling and were looking in opposite directions, but it was as if their bodies flowed smoothly into each other's, through their arms and fingers.

The marked contrast between Alice's light-colored hair, which framed the excessively pale skin of her face, and Mattia's dark hair, tousled forward to hide his black eyes, was erased by the slender arc that linked them. There was a shared space between their bodies, the confines of which were not well delineated, from which nothing seemed to be missing and in which the air seemed motionless, undisturbed.

Alice walked a step ahead of him and Mattia's slight drag balanced her cadence, erasing the imperfections of her faulty leg. He let himself be carried forward, his feet making not the slightest sound on the tiles. His scars were hidden and safe in her hand.

They stopped on the threshold of the kitchen, a little away from the cluster of girls and Denis. They tried to work out what was happening. They had a dreamy air about them, as if they had come from some distant place that only they knew.

Denis pushed Giulia violently away and their mouths separated with a smack. He looked at Mattia and sought in his expression the traces of the thing that terrified him. He thought that he and Alice had said something to each other, something he would never be able to know, and his brain filled with blood.

He ran out of the room, deliberately knocking into him, to destroy that equilibrium he loathed. For an instant Mattia met Denis's red and upset eyes. For some reason they reminded him of Michela's defenseless eyes that afternoon in the park. Over the years those two gazes would gradually merge in his memory into a single, indelible fear.

Mattia let go of Alice's hand. It was as if all his nerve endings were concentrated in that single point, and when he broke away, it seemed that his arm gave off sparks, as if from a bared cable.

"Excuse me," he whispered to her and left the kitchen to catch up with Denis.

Alice walked over to Viola, who was staring at her with eyes of stone.

"We—" she began.

"I don't care," Viola cut in. Looking at Alice and Mattia, she had remembered the boy at the beach, the moment when he had refused to hold her hand, while she would have loved to go back to the others on the beach holding hands just like that. She was jealous, a painful, violent jealousy. And she was furious, because the happiness she wanted for herself she had just given to someone else. She felt robbed, as if Alice had taken her share too.

Alice leaned over to say something in her ear, but Viola turned away.

"What do you want now?" she said.

"Nothing." Alice retreated in fear.

At that moment Giada bent forward, as if an invisible man had punched her in the stomach. With one hand she held on to the kitchen counter and with the other she gripped her belly.

"What's wrong?" Viola asked.

"I'm going to throw up," she moaned.

"Gross, go to the bathroom," Viola yelled.

But it was too late. With a jerk Giada emptied the contents of her stomach onto the floor, something reddish and alcoholic, a mixture of vodka and Soledad's dessert.

The others pulled back, horrified, while Alice tried to hold her up by the hips. The air immediately turned rancid.

"Well done, you idiot," said Viola. "What a fucking awful party."

She left the room, her fists clenched furiously, as if struggling to keep from smashing something. Alice looked at her anxiously and then went back to taking care of Giada, who was sobbing gently.

———

The other guests had scattered about in small groups around the living room. Most of the boys were bobbing their heads back and forth to the music, while the girls scanned the room. Some held drinks in their hands; six or seven were dancing to "A Question of Time." Mattia wondered how they could feel so at ease, moving around like that in front of everyone. Then he realized it was the most natural thing in the world, which was precisely why he was incapable of it.

Denis had disappeared. Mattia crossed the living room and went to look for him in Viola's room. He even looked in her sister's and her parents' rooms. He looked in both bathrooms and in one he found a boy and a girl from school. She was sitting on the toilet and he was on the floor in front of her, legs crossed. They both wore sad and questioning expressions and Mattia hastily closed the door.

He went back to the living room and out onto the balcony. The hill dropped away darkly and below them lay the entire city, a series of bright white dots arranged homogeneously, as far as the eye could see. Mattia leaned over the railing and looked through the trees of the grounds of Villa Bai, but he couldn't see anyone. He went back inside; anxiety began to shorten his breath.

A spiral staircase led from the sitting room to a dark attic. He climbed the first steps, then stopped.

Where has he gotten to? he thought.

He went on, up to the top. The light that filtered from below allowed him to make out the shadow of Denis, standing in the middle of the room.

He called to him. All through their friendship he had uttered his name only two or three times at the most. He had never needed to, because Denis was always right next to him, like a natural extension of his limbs.

"Go away," Denis replied.

Mattia looked for the switch and turned on the light. The room was enormous, lined with tall bookshelves. The only other furniture was a big, empty wooden desk. Mattia had the impression that no one had come up to this floor of the house for a long time.

"It's almost eleven. We have to go," he said.

Denis didn't reply. His back was turned, and he stood in the middle of a big rug. Mattia walked over to his friend. He saw that Denis had been crying. He was blowing through his teeth as he breathed, his eyes fixed straight ahead and his half-open lips trembling slightly.

It took Mattia a few seconds to notice a desk lamp that lay shattered at his feet.

"What have you done?" he asked.

Denis's breathing turned into a wheeze.

"Denis, what have you done?"

Mattia tried to touch his friend's shoulder, but Denis gave a violent start. Mattia shook him.

"What have you done?"

"I . . ." Denis began. Then he froze.

"You what?"

Denis opened his left hand and showed Mattia a fragment of the lamp, a splinter of green glass, grown opaque from sweat, that seemed to swallow up the light.

"I wanted to feel what you feel," he whispered.

Mattia didn't understand. He stumbled back, confused. A burning sensation exploded in his gut and filled his arms and legs.

"But then I couldn't do it," said Denis.

He held the palms of his hands upward, as if waiting for something.

Mattia was about to ask him why, but didn't. The music rose up, muffled, from below. The low frequencies passed through the floor, but the higher ones seemed trapped.

Denis sniffed. "Let's get out of here," he said.

Mattia nodded, but neither of them made a move. Then Denis turned and abruptly walked toward the stairs. Mattia followed him across the living room and then outside, where the cool night air was waiting to give them back their breath.

Viola decided if you were in or out. On Sunday morning Giada Savarino's father had phoned Viola's father, waking up the entire Bai household. It was a long phone call and Viola, still in pajamas, had pressed her ear to her parents' bedroom door, but she hadn't been able to catch a single word of the conversation.

When she heard the bed creak, she had run back to her room and hid under the blankets, pretending to be asleep. Her father had woken her up saying you can tell me what happened later, but for now let me tell you that there will be no more parties in this house and, in fact, you can forget about parties of any kind for a good long while. At lunch her mother had asked her to explain the broken lamp in the attic and her sister hadn't come to her defense, because she had noticed that Viola had laid her hands on her personal stock.

She locked herself away in her room all day, disheartened and banned from using the phone. She couldn't get Alice and Mattia, and their way of holding hands, out of her head. As she scratched away the last remnants of nail polish she decided: Alice was out.

On Monday morning, locked in her bathroom at home, Alice finally removed the gauze that covered her tattoo. She balled it up and then threw it in the toilet, along with the crumbled biscuits that she hadn't eaten for breakfast.

She looked at the violet reflected in the mirror and thought that, for the second time, she had changed her body forever. She shivered with a pleasant mixture of regret and trepidation. She thought that this body was hers alone, that if she felt like it she could even destroy it, lay waste to it with indelible marks, or let it dry out like a flower picked on a whim by a child and then left to die on the ground.

That morning she would show her tattoo to Viola and the others, in the girls' bathroom. She would tell them how she and Mattia had kissed for a long time. There was no need to invent anything more than that. If they asked her for details, she would merely go along with their fantasies.

In class she left her backpack on her chair and headed over to Viola's desk to join the others. As she approached, she heard Giulia Mirandi saying here she comes. She said hi to everyone, beaming, but no one replied. She leaned over to give Viola two kisses on the cheeks, as Viola had taught her to do, but her friend didn't move an inch.

Alice stood up again and found herself looking into four hostile faces.

"We were all ill yesterday," Viola began.

"Really?" Alice asked, with genuine concern. "What was wrong with you?"

"A terrible stomachache, all of us," Giada broke in aggressively.

Alice saw Giada vomiting on the floor again and felt like saying I'm not surprised with the amount you all drank.

"There was nothing wrong with me," she said.

"Of course," sneered Viola, looking at the others. "There was no doubt about that."

Giada and Federica laughed; Giulia lowered her eyes.

"What's that supposed to mean?" Alice asked, disoriented.

"You know very well what I mean," Viola retorted, suddenly changing her tone and fixing her with her marvelous, piercing eyes.

"No, I don't know," Alice defended herself.

Giada attacked. "You poisoned us."

"What are you saying? What do you mean 'poisoned'?"

Giulia butted in, timidly. "Come on, girls, that's not true."

"Yes, it is. She poisoned us," Giada repeated. "Who knows what disgusting things she put in that dessert."

She turned back toward Alice. "You wanted to make us all sick, didn't you? Well, it worked, well done."

Alice listened to the sequence of words, but it took her a few seconds to reconstruct their meaning. She looked at Giulia, who, with her big blue eyes, was saying sorry, there's nothing I can do. Then she sought shelter in Viola's eyes, but Viola returned an empty gaze.

Giada held a hand over her belly, as if she were still having convulsions.

"But I made it with Soledad. We bought all the ingredients at the supermarket."

No one replied. They looked in different directions, as if waiting for the murderer to leave.

"It wasn't Sol's dessert. I ate it too, and I didn't get sick," Alice lied.

"You're a liar," pounced Federica Mazzoldi, who hadn't said a word till then. "You didn't even taste it. Everyone knows that—"

She suddenly froze.

"Please, stop," Giulia begged. She looked as if she were about to burst into tears.

Alice put a hand over her flat stomach. She could feel her heart beating under her skin.

"Everyone knows what?" she asked them in a calm voice.

Viola Bai slowly shook her head. Alice stared at her former friend in silence, waiting for words that didn't come but that floated in the air like tongues of transparent smoke. She didn't even move when the bell rang. Ms. Tubaldo, the science teacher, had to call her twice before she finally went to sit in her place.

18

Denis hadn't come to school. On Saturday, on the way home, he and Mattia hadn't looked at each other once. Denis had responded to Mattia's father in monosyllables, and hadn't even said good-bye when he got out of the car.

Mattia rested a hand on the empty chair beside him. Now and again Denis's words in that dark attic ran through his head. Then they slipped away, too quickly for him to get to the bottom of their meaning.

He realized it didn't really matter to him to understand them. He merely wished Denis was there, to shield him from everything beyond his desk.

The day before, his parents had made him sit down on the sofa, in the living room. They had sat in the chairs opposite him. Then his father said so tell us about the party. Mattia had clenched his hands tightly, but then stretched them out on his knees so that his parents could see them. He had shrugged and replied in a quiet voice that there was nothing to tell. His mother had gotten nervously to her feet and disappeared into the kitchen. His father, on the other hand, had come over to him and clapped him twice on the shoulder, as if consoling him for something. Mattia remembered how, when he was little, on the hottest days of summer, his father would blow on his and Michela's faces in turn, to cool them down. He remembered what the sweat felt like as it evaporated from his skin, ever so lightly, and was filled with a searing nostalgia for a part of the world that had drowned in the river along with Michela.

He wondered if his classmates knew everything. Maybe even his teachers knew. He felt their furtive glances weaving together above his head like a fishing net.

He opened his history book at random and started learning by heart the whole sequence of dates that appeared from that page onward. The list of numbers, lined up without any logical meaning, formed an ever longer trail in his head. As he followed it, Mattia slowly moved away from the thought of Denis standing in the shadow and forgot the void that now sat in his place.

During break time Alice slipped into the infirmary on the second floor, a narrow white room furnished only with a hospital bed and a mirrored cabinet with the essentials for first aid. She had ended up there only once before, when she had fainted during PE because in the previous forty hours she had eaten only two whole-grain crackers and a low-calorie snack. That day the gym teacher, in his green Diadora tracksuit, his whistle, which he never used, around his neck, had said to her think carefully about what you're doing, think very carefully. Then he had gone out, leaving her alone under the fluorescent light, without anything to do or look at for the whole next hour.

Alice found the first-aid cabinet open. She took a wad of cotton wool the size of a plum and the bottle of rubbing alcohol. She closed the door and looked around for a heavy object. There was only the wastepaper basket, made of hard plastic, a dull color halfway between red and brown. She prayed that no one would hear the noise from outside and shattered the mirror of the little cupboard with the bottom of the basket.

Then, being careful not to cut herself, she picked up a big triangular splinter of glass. She caught the reflection of her own right eye and felt proud that she hadn't cried, not even a bit. She stuffed everything into the center pocket of the baggy sweatshirt she was wearing and went back to class.

She spent the rest of the morning in a state of torpor. She never even glanced at Viola and the others and didn't listen to a single word of the lesson on the theater of Aeschylus.

As she was leaving the class, behind all her classmates, Giulia Mirandi furtively took her hand.

93

"I'm sorry," she whispered into her ear. Then she kissed her on the cheek and ran after the others, who were already in the hallway.

Alice waited for Mattia in the atrium, at the bottom of the linoleum-covered staircase down which poured a chaotic stream of pupils headed for the exit. She rested a hand on the banister. The cold metal gave her a sense of tranquillity.

Mattia came down the stairs enveloped by that foot and a half of emptiness that no one other than Denis dared occupy. His black hair fell over his forehead in tousled curls. He watched carefully where he placed his feet, leaning slightly backward as he descended. Alice called out to him, but he didn't turn around. She called again, more loudly now, and he looked up, said an embarrassed hi, and made as if to head toward the glass doors.

Alice elbowed her way through the other students and joined him. She took him by the arm and he gave a start.

"You have to come with me," she said.

"Where?"

"You have to help me do something."

Mattia looked around nervously, in search of some kind of threat.

"My father's waiting for me outside," he said.

"Your father will wait. You have to help me. Now," said Alice.

Mattia snorted. Then he said okay but he couldn't have said why.

"Come."

Alice took him by the hand, as she had at Viola's party, but this time Mattia's fingers spontaneously closed around hers.

They left the crowd of students. Alice walked quickly, as if she were escaping from someone. They slipped into the deserted corridor on the second floor. The doors leading to the empty classrooms conveyed a sense of abandonment.

They went into the girls' bathroom. Mattia hesitated. He was about to say I'm not supposed to be here, but then he let her drag him in. When Alice took him inside a cubicle and locked the door they were so close that his legs started trembling. The space not taken up by the old-style hole-in-the-ground toilet was nothing more than a thin strip of tiles and there was barely room for their four feet. There were pieces of toilet paper scattered on the ground half-stuck to the floor.

Now she's going to kiss me, he thought. And all you have to do is kiss her back. It'll be easy; everyone knows how.

Alice unzipped her shiny jacket and started to undress, just as she had at Viola's house. She untucked her T-shirt and lowered the same pair of jeans halfway down her bottom. She didn't look at Mattia; it was as if she were there on her own.

In place of Saturday evening's white gauze she had a flower tattooed on her skin. Mattia was about to say something, but then fell silent and looked away. Something stirred between his legs and he tried to distract himself. He read some of the graffiti on the wall, without grasping its meaning. He noticed how none of the writing was parallel to the line of tiles. Almost all of it was at the same angle to the edge of the floor and Mattia worked out that it was somewhere between 30 and 45 degrees.

"Take this," said Alice.

She handed him a piece of glass, reflective on one side and black on the other, and as sharp as a dagger. Mattia didn't understand. She lifted his chin, just as she had imagined doing the first time they had met.

"You've got to get rid of it. I can't do it on my own," she said to him.

Mattia looked at the glass shard and then at Alice's right hand, which pointed at the tattoo on her belly.

She anticipated his protest.

"I know you know how to do it," she said. "I never want to see it again. Please, do it for me."

Mattia rolled the shard in his hand and a shiver ran down his arm.

"But—" he said.

"Do it for me," Alice interrupted him, putting a hand to his lips to shut him up and then removing it immediately.

Do it for me, thought Mattia. Those four words stuck in his ear and made him kneel in front of Alice.

His heels touched the wall behind him. He didn't know how to position himself. Uncertain, he touched the skin next to the tattoo, to stretch it better. His face had never been so close to a girl's body. The natural thing to do seemed to be to breathe in deeply, to discover its smell.

He brought the shard close to her flesh. His hand was steady as he made a little cut the size of a fingertip. Alice trembled and let out a cry.

Mattia recoiled and hid the piece of glass behind his back, as if to deny that it had been him.

"I can't do it," he said.

He looked up. Alice wept silently. Her eyes were closed, clenched in an expression of pain.

"But I don't want to see it anymore," she sobbed.

It was clear to him that she had lost her nerve, and he felt relieved. He stood up and wondered if it would be better to leave.

Alice wiped away the drop of blood trickling down her belly. She buttoned up her jeans, while Mattia tried to think of something reassuring to say.

"You'll get used to it. In the end you won't even notice it anymore," he said.

"How is that possible? It will always be there, right before my eyes."

"Exactly," said Mattia. "Which is precisely why you won't see it anymore."

THE OTHER ROOM

1995

20

Mattia was right: the days had slipped over her skin like a solvent, one after the other, each removing a very thin layer of pigment from her tattoo, and from both their memories. The outlines, like the circumstances, were still there, black and well delineated, but the colors had merged together until they faded into a dull, uniform tonality, a neutral absence of meaning.

For Alice and Mattia, the high school years were an open wound that had seemed so deep that it could never heal. They had passed through them without breathing, he rejecting the world and she feeling rejected by it, and eventually they had noticed that it didn't make all that much difference. They had formed a defective and asymmetrical friendship, made up of long absences and much silence, a clean and empty space where both could come back to breathe when the walls of their school became too close for them to ignore the feeling of suffocation.

But over time, the wound of adolescence gradually healed. The edges of skin met in imperceptible but continuous movements. The scab peeled off with each fresh abrasion, but then stubbornly re-formed, darker and thicker. Finally a new layer of skin, smooth and elastic, had replaced the missing one. The scar slowly turned from red to white, and ended up merging with all the others.

Now they were lying on Alice's bed, their heads at opposite ends, their legs bent unnaturally to avoid any contact between their bodies. Alice thought if she turned around she could make her toes touch Mattia's back but pretend not to notice. But she was sure he would immediately pull away and decided to spare herself that little disappointment.

Neither one of them had suggested putting on some music. Their only plans were to stay there and wait for Sunday afternoon to wear itself out all by itself and it would once again be time to do something necessary, like eating, sleeping, or starting yet another week. The yellow light of September came in through the open window, dragging with it the intermittent rustle of the street.

Alice stood up on the bed, making the mattress ripple very slightly under Mattia's head. She held her clenched fists by her sides and stared at him from above. Her hair fell over her face, concealing her serious expression.

"Stay right there," she said. "Don't move."

She stepped over him and jumped down from the bed, her good leg dragging the other one behind it like something that had been attached to her by mistake. Mattia bent his chin to his chest to follow her movements around the room. He saw her opening a cube-shaped box that sat in the middle of her desk, and which he hadn't noticed until that moment.

Alice turned around with one eye closed and the other hidden behind an old camera. Mattia started to pull himself up.

"Down," she commanded. "I told you not to move."

Click. The Polaroid spat out a thin white tongue and Alice waved it in the air to bring out the color.

"Where did you get that from?" Mattia asked.

"The cellar. It was my father's. He bought it God knows when but never used it."

Mattia sat up on the bed. Alice dropped the photograph on the carpet and snapped another one.

"Come on, stop," he protested. "I look stupid in photographs."

"You always look stupid."

She snapped again.

"I think I want to be a photographer," Alice said. "I've made up my mind."

"What about university?"

Alice shrugged.

"Only my father cares about that," she said. "He can go, then."

"You're going to quit?"

"Maybe."

"You can't just wake up one day, decide you want to be a photographer, and throw away a year's work. It doesn't work like that," said Mattia sharply.

"Oh, right, I forgot you're just like him," Alice said ironically. "You always know what to do. You knew you wanted to be a mathematician when you were five. You're all so boring. Old and boring."

Then she turned toward the window and snapped a picture at random. She dropped it on the carpet as well, near the other two, and stomped on them with both feet, as if she were treading grapes.

Mattia thought about saying something to make amends, but nothing came out. He bent over and slid the first photograph out from under Alice's foot. The outline of his arms, crossed behind his head, was gradually emerging from the white. He wondered what extraordinary reaction was happening on that shiny surface and decided to look it up in the encyclopedia as soon as he got home.

"There's something else I want to show you," Alice said.

She tossed the camera onto the bed, like a little girl who's grown tired of a toy because she's spotted another, more inviting one, and left the room.

She was gone for a good ten minutes. Mattia started reading the titles of the books leaning crookedly on the shelf above the desk. Always the same ones. He combined the first letters of all the titles, but couldn't come up with a sensible word. He would have liked to identify a logical order in the sequence. He would probably have arranged them according to the color of their spines, copying the electromagnetic spectrum maybe, from red to violet, or according to height, in decreasing order.

"Ta-daaaa." Alice's voice distracted him.

Mattia turned and saw her standing in the doorway, gripping the frame as if afraid she might fall. She was wearing a wedding dress, which must have been dazzlingly white once, but which time had turned yellow at the hem, as if some disease were slowly devouring it. The years spent in a box had made it dry and stiff. The bodice fell limply over Alice's nonexistent bosom. It wasn't especially low-cut, just enough for one of the straps to slip a few inches down her arm. In that position Alice's collarbone looked more pronounced; it broke the soft line of her neck and formed a little hollow, like the basin of a dried-up lake. Mattia wondered what it might be like, eyes closed, to trace its outline with the tip of his finger. The lace at the end of the sleeves was crumpled and on the left arm it stood up slightly. The long train continued out of sight down the hall. Alice was still wearing her red slippers, which peeked out from under the full skirt, creating a curious dissonance.

"Well? Aren't you going to say something?" she said without looking at him. She smoothed the outer layer of tulle on the skirt. It felt cheap, synthetic.

"Whose is it?" asked Mattia.

"Mine, obviously."

"Come on, seriously."

"Whose do you think it is? It's my mother's."

Mattia nodded and imagined Fernanda in that dress. He pictured her wearing the only expression she ever gave him when, before going home, he would stick his head in the living room where she'd be watching television: an expression of tenderness and profound commiseration, like the one usually bestowed upon the sick when people visit them in the hospital. A ridiculous expression, as she was the sick one, sick with an illness that was slowly crumbling her whole body.

"Don't stand there gawking like that. Come on, take a picture of me."

Mattia picked the camera off the bed. He turned it around in his hands to work out which button to press. Alice rocked from side to side in the doorway, as if moved by a breeze that only she could feel. When Mattia brought the camera to his eye, she stiffened her back and assumed a serious, almost provocative expression.

"There," said Mattia.

"Now one of us together."

He shook his head.

"Come on, don't be your usual pain in the ass. And for once I want to see you dressed properly. Not in that mangy sweatshirt that you've been wearing for a month."

Mattia looked down. The wrists of his blue sweater looked as if they'd been devoured by moths. He had a habit of rubbing them with his thumbnail to keep his fingers busy and to keep from scratching the hollow between his index and middle fingers.

"And besides, you wouldn't want to ruin my wedding day, would you?" added Alice with a pout.

She knew it was only a joke, a silly game to pass the time, just a bit of nonsense like so many other things they did. And yet, when she opened the closet door and the mirror inside framed her in that white dress next to Mattia, for a moment the panic took her breath away.

"Nothing in here will work," she said hastily. "Come with me."

Resigned, Mattia followed her. When Alice got like this his legs would itch and he was seized by a desire to leave. There was something in her way of behaving, something in the violence with which his friend satisfied her childish whims, that he found unbearable. It felt as if she had tied him to a chair and then called hundreds of people, showing him off like a possession of hers, some kind of funny pet. Most of the time he said nothing and allowed his impatience to emerge through gestures, until Alice tired of his apathy and gave up, saying you always make me feel like an idiot.

Mattia followed the train of Alice's dress all the way to her parents' room. He had never been in there before. The blinds were down almost entirely and the light entered in parallel lines, so clearly that they seemed drawn on the wooden floor. The air was more dense and tired here than in the rest of the house. Against the wall was a double bed, much higher than the one that belonged to Mattia's parents, and two matching bedside tables.

Alice opened the closet and ran her finger along her father's suits, all hanging in an orderly fashion, each one protected by its cellophane covering. She took out a black one and threw it on the bed.

"Put that one on," she ordered Mattia.

"Have you gone mad? Your father will notice, you know."

"My father never notices anything."

For a moment Alice seemed absorbed in thought, as if reflecting on the words that she had just spoken, or looking at something through that wall of dark clothes.

"Now I'm going to find you a shirt and tie," she added.

Mattia stood still, uncertain what to do. She noticed.

"Will you get a move on? Don't tell me you're ashamed to get changed here!"

As she said that her empty stomach flipped over. For a second she felt dishonest. Her words had been a subtle form of blackmail.

Mattia huffed, then sat down on the bed and started untying his shoes.

Alice kept her back turned, pretending to choose a shirt that she had already chosen. When she heard the metallic jingle of his belt buckle, she counted to three and then turned around. Mattia was taking off his jeans. Underneath he had on a pair of soft gray boxers, not the close-fitting ones she had imagined.

Alice thought that she'd already seen him in shorts dozens of times, it's not like there was much of a difference with underwear, and yet she still felt herself tremble slightly under the four white layers of her wedding dress. He tugged at the bottom of his undershirt to cover himself better and quickly slipped on the elegant trousers. The fabric was soft and light. As it ran over the hairs of his legs it gave them an electric charge, making them stand up like cat's fur.

Alice came over and handed him the shirt. He took it without looking up. He was annoyed and fed up with this pointless playacting. He was ashamed of showing his thin legs and the sparse hairs on his chest and around his navel. Alice thought he was doing everything possible to make the scene embarrassing, as usual. Then she thought that, for him, she was the one to blame, and she felt her throat tighten. Even though she didn't want to, she looked away and let him take off his undershirt without her watching him.

"And now?" Mattia called to her.

She turned around. Seeing him in her father's clothes, she had trouble breathing. The jacket was a little big, his shoulders weren't quite wide enough to fill it out, but she couldn't help thinking that he was incredibly handsome.

"All you need is the tie," she said to him after a moment.

Mattia took the bordeaux-colored tie from Alice's hands and instinctively ran a thumb over the shiny fabric. A shiver ran down his arm and spine. He felt that the palm of his hand was as dry as sand. He quickly brought it to his mouth and breathed on it, to moisten it with his breath. He couldn't resist the temptation to bite one of the joints of his fingers, trying not to be seen by Alice, who noticed anyway.

"I don't know how to tie it," he said, dragging out his words.

"Mmm, you really are hopeless."

The truth was that Alice already knew that. She couldn't wait to show him that she could tie it. Her father had taught her when she was little. In the morning he would leave a tie on her bed and then, before going out, he'd stop by her room and ask is my tie ready? Alice would run to him, with the knot already made. Her father would lower his head, his hands joined together behind his back, as if he were bowing before a queen. She would put the tie around his neck, and then would tighten it and adjust it slightly. *Parfait,* he would say. One morning after the accident, Alice's father found the tie still on the bed, just as he had left it. From then on he always tied it himself and that little ritual passed away, like so many other things.

Alice prepared the knot, fluttering her skeletal fingers more than necessary. Mattia followed her gestures, which struck him as complicated. He let her adjust the tie around his neck.

"Wow, you look almost respectable. Do you want to see yourself in the mirror?"

"No," said Mattia. He just wanted to leave, wearing his own clothes.

"Photograph," said Alice, clapping once.

Mattia followed her back into her room. She picked up the camera.

"It hasn't got a self-timer," she said. "We'll just have to guess."

She pulled Mattia to her, by the waist. He stiffened and she clicked. The photograph slipped out with a hiss.

Alice fell onto the bed, just like a bride after hours of celebration, and fanned herself with the picture.

Mattia stayed right where he was, feeling those clothes that weren't his, but with the pleasant sensation of disappearing into them. The light in the room suddenly changed. It turned from yellow to a uniform blue as the last sliver of light disappeared behind the building opposite.

"Can I get changed now?"

He said it on purpose, to make her understand that he had had enough of her game. Alice seemed absorbed in thought; she arched her eyebrows slightly.

"There's one last thing," she said, getting up again. "The groom carries the bride in his arms over the threshold."

"Meaning?"

"You've got to take me in your arms. And carry me over there." Alice pointed to the hall. "Then you're free."

Mattia shook his head. She came over to him and held out her arms like a child.

"Come on, my hero," she said, teasing him.

Mattia slumped his shoulders even farther, defeated. He bent awkwardly in order to pick her up. He had never carried anyone like that. He put one arm behind her knees and the other behind her back, and when he picked her up he was startled by how light she was.

He stumbled toward the hall. He felt Alice's breath penetrate the fine weave of his shirt, definitely too close, and heard the train rustling on the floor. When they crossed the threshold, the sound of a prolonged, dry rip made him stop short.

"Damn," he said.

He hastily set Alice down. The skirt had gotten caught on the door frame. The rip was about six inches long and looked like a sneering mouth. They both stopped and stared at it, slightly dazed.

Mattia waited for Alice to say something, to give up and lose her temper with him. He felt as if he ought to apologize, but she was the one who had been so insistent on this foolishness. She'd been asking for trouble.

Alice stared expressionlessly at the rip.

"Who cares?" she said at last. "It's not like anyone's going to use it anymore."

IN AND OUT OF THE WATER

1998

Prime numbers are divisible only by 1 and by themselves. They hold their place in the infinite series of natural numbers, squashed, like all numbers, between two others, but one step further than the rest. They are suspicious, solitary numbers, which is why Mattia thought they were wonderful. Sometimes he thought that they had ended up in that sequence by mistake, that they'd been trapped, like pearls strung on a necklace. Other times he suspected that they too would have preferred to be like all the others, just ordinary numbers, but for some reason they couldn't do it. This second thought struck him mostly at night, in the chaotic interweaving of images that comes before sleep, when the mind is too weak to tell itself lies.

In his first year at university, Mattia had learned that, among prime numbers, there are some that are even more special. Mathematicians call them twin primes: pairs of prime numbers that are close to each other, almost neighbors, but between them there is always an even number that prevents them from truly touching. Numbers like 11 and 13, like 17 and 19, 41 and 43. If you have the patience to go on counting, you discover that these pairs gradually become rarer. You encounter increasingly isolated primes, lost in that silent, measured space made only of ciphers, and you develop a distressing presentiment that the pairs encountered up until that point were accidental, that solitude is the true destiny. Then, just when you're about to surrender, when you no longer have the desire to go on counting, you come across another pair of twins, clutching each other tightly. There is a common conviction among mathematicians that however far you go, there will always be another two, even if no one can say where exactly, until they are discovered.

Mattia thought that he and Alice were like that, twin primes, alone and lost, close but not close enough to really touch each other. He had never told her that. When he imagined confessing these things to her, the thin layer of sweat on his hands evaporated completely and for a good ten minutes he was no longer capable of touching anything.

He came home one winter day after having spent the afternoon at her house, where she'd done nothing the whole time but switch from one television channel to another. Mattia had paid no attention to the words or the images. Alice's right foot, resting on the living room coffee table, invaded his field of vision, penetrating it from the left like the head of a snake. Alice flexed her toes with hypnotic regularity. That repeated movement made something solid and worrying grow in his stomach and he struggled to keep his gaze fixed for as long as possible, so that nothing in the frame would change.

At home he took a pile of blank pages from his ring binder, thick enough so that the pen would run softly over them without scratching the stiff surface of the table. He leveled the edges with his hands, first above and below and then at the sides. He chose the fullest pen from the ones on the desk, removed the cap, and slipped it on the end so as not to lose it. Then he began to write in the exact center of the sheet, without needing to count the squares.

2760889966649. He put the lid back on the pen and set it down next to the paper. "Twothousandsevenhundredsixtybillioneighthundredeightyninemillionninehundredsixtysixthousandsixhundredandfortynine," he read out loud. Then he repeated it under his breath, as if to take possession of that tongue twister. He decided that this number would be his. He was sure that no one else in the world, no one else in the whole history of the world, had ever stopped to consider that number. Probably, until then, no one had ever written it down on a piece of paper, let alone spoken it out loud.

After a moment's hesitation he jumped two lines and wrote

2760889966651. This is hers, he thought. In his head the figures assumed the pale color of Alice's foot, standing out against the bluish glare of the television.

They could also be twin primes, Mattia had thought. If they are . . .

That thought suddenly seized him and he began to search for divisors for both numbers. 3 was easy: it was enough to take the sum of the numbers and see if it was a multiple of 3. 5 was ruled out from the beginning. Perhaps there was a rule for 7 as well, but Mattia couldn't remember it so he started doing the division longhand. Then 11, 13, and so on, in increasingly complicated calculations. He became drowsy for the first time trying 37, the pen slipping down the page. When he got to 47 he stopped. The vortex that had filled his stomach at Alice's house had dispersed, diluted into his muscles like smells in the air, and he was no longer able to notice it. In the room there were only himself and a lot of disordered pages, full of pointless divisions. The clock showed a quarter past three in the morning.

Mattia picked up the first page, the one with the two numbers written in the middle, and felt like an idiot. He tore it in half and then in half again, until the edges were firm enough to pass like a blade beneath the nail of the ring finger of his left hand.

During his four years of university, mathematics had led him into the most remote and fascinating corners of human thought. With meticulous ritualism Mattia copied out the proofs of all the theorems he encountered in his studies. Even on summer afternoons he kept the blinds lowered and worked in artificial light. He removed from his desk everything that might distract his gaze, so as to feel truly alone with the page. He wrote without stopping. If he found himself hesitating too long over a passage or made a mistake when aligning an expression after the equals sign, he shoved the paper to the floor and started all over. When he got to the end of those pages stuffed with symbols, letters, and numbers, he wrote "QED," and for a moment he felt he had put a small piece of the world in order. Then he leaned against the back of the chair and wove his hands together, without letting them rub.

He slowly lost contact with the page. The symbols, which only a moment before flowed from the movement of his wrist, now seemed distant to him, frozen in a place that denied him access. His head, immersed in the darkness of the room, began to fill with dark, disorderly thoughts and Mattia would usually choose a book, open it at random, and begin studying again.

Complex analysis, projective geometry, and tensor calculus had not managed to diminish his initial passion for numbers. Mattia liked to count, starting from 1 and proceeding through complicated progressions, which he often invented on the spur of the moment. He allowed himself to be led by numbers and he seemed to know each one of them. And so, when it came time to choose his thesis topic, he went with no doubts to the office of Professor Niccoli, professor of discrete calculus, with whom he had never even sat an exam and about whom he knew nothing other than his name.

Francesco Niccoli's office was on the fourth floor of the nineteenth-century building that housed the mathematics department. It was a small room, tidy and odorless, dominated by the color white—the walls, shelves, plastic desk, even the cumbersome computer on top of it, were white. Mattia drummed softly on the door and from inside Niccoli wasn't sure if the knocking was for him or for the office next door. He said come in, hoping he had not made a fool of himself.

Mattia opened the door and stepped into the office.

"Hello," he said.

"Hello," replied Niccoli.

Mattia's eye caught sight of a photograph hanging behind the professor, which showed him, much younger and beardless, holding a silver plate and shaking hands with an important-looking stranger.

Mattia narrowed his eyes, but couldn't read what was written on the plate.

"Well, then?" Niccoli urged, studying him with a frown.

"I'd like to write a dissertation on the zeros of the Riemann zeta function," said Mattia, staring at the professor's right shoulder, where a dusting of dandruff looked like a little starry sky.

Niccoli made a face, an ironic smile.

"Excuse me, but who are you?" he asked without concealing his disdain and locking his hands behind his head as if wanting to enjoy a moment of fun.

"My name is Mattia Balossino. I've finished my exams and I'd like to graduate within the year."

"Have you got your record book with you?"

Mattia nodded. He slid his backpack off, crouched on the floor, and rummaged around in it. Niccoli stretched out his hand to take the book, but Mattia preferred to set it on the edge of the desk.

For some months the professor had been obliged to hold objects at a distance to get them properly into focus. He quickly ran his eyes over the sequence of high grades. Not one flub, not one hesitation, not one try that had gone wrong, perhaps on account of a love story that had ended badly.

He closed the book and looked more carefully at Mattia. He was dressed anonymously and had the posture of someone who doesn't know how to occupy the space of his own body. The professor thought he was another of those who do well in their studies because they are unable to make much headway in life. The ones who, as soon as they find themselves outside the well-trodden paths of the university, always reveal themselves to be good for nothing.

"Don't you think I should be the one to suggest a topic for you?" he asked, speaking slowly.

Mattia shrugged. His black eyes moved right to left, following the edge of the desk.

"I'm interested in prime numbers. I want to work on the Riemann zeta function," he replied.

Niccoli sighed. Then he got up and walked over to the white bookshelf. As he ran his index finger along the spines of the books he snorted rhythmically. He pulled out some typed pages stapled in one corner.

"Fine, fine," he said, handing them to Mattia. "You can come back when you've performed the calculations in this article. All of them."

Mattia took the stack of pages and, without reading the title, slipped it into his backpack, which leaned against his leg, open and slack. He mumbled a thank-you and left the office, pulling the door shut behind him.

Niccoli went and sat back down in his chair and thought about how over dinner he would complain to his wife about this new and unexpected annoyance.

22

Alice's father had taken this photography business as the whim of a bored little girl. Nonetheless, for his daughter's twenty-third birthday, he gave her a Canon SLR, with case and tripod, and she had thanked him with a beautiful smile, as impossible to grasp as a gust of icy wind. He had also paid for her to take evening classes, which lasted six months, and Alice hadn't missed a single lesson. The agreement was clear if implicit: university came before everything else.

Then, in a precise instant, like the line separating light and shade, Fernanda's illness had gotten worse, dragging all three of them into an increasingly tight spiral of new tasks, drawing them toward an inevitable cycle of apathy and mutual indifference. Alice hadn't set foot in the university again and her father pretended not to notice. A feeling of remorse, the origins of which belonged to another time, kept him from imposing his will on his daughter and almost kept him from talking to her at all. Sometimes he thought it wouldn't take much, all he would have to do was go into her room one evening and tell her . . . Tell her what? His wife was disappearing from life like a wet mark drying on a shirt and, with her, the thread that still connected him to his daughter was slackening—it was already scraping the ground—leaving her free to decide for herself.

With photography Alice liked the actions more than the results. She liked opening the back of the camera and unrolling the new film a couple of inches, just enough to catch it in the runner, and thinking that this empty film would soon become something and not knowing what, taking the first few snaps into the void, aiming, focusing, checking her balance, deciding whether to include or exclude pieces of reality as she saw fit, enlarging, distorting.

Every time she heard the click of the shutter, followed by that faint rustle, she remembered when she used to catch grasshoppers in the garden of their house in the mountains when she was a little girl, trapping them between her cupped hands. She thought that it was the same with photographs, only now she seized time and fixed it on celluloid, capturing it halfway through its jump toward the next moment.

During the course she had been taught that the strap of the camera is to be wrapped around the wrist twice. That way, if someone tries to steal it they're forced to tear your whole arm off along with it. Alice ran no such risk in the corridor of Our Lady's Hospital, where her mother was being cared for, but she was used to carrying her Canon like that anyway.

As she walked she grazed along the two-tone wall, brushing it with her right shoulder from time to time to avoid touching anyone. Lunchtime visiting hour had just begun and people were pouring into the hospital like a liquid mass.

Aluminum-and-plywood doors opened onto the wards, each with its own particular smell. Oncology smelled of disinfectant and gauze soaked in methylated spirits.

Alice entered her mother's room, which was the second to last. She was sleeping a sleep that wasn't her own and the gadgets to which she was connected didn't make a sound. The light was faint and drowsy. On the bedside table red flowers were arranged in a vase: Soledad had brought them the day before.

Alice rested her hands and the camera on the edge of the bed, where the sheet, lifted in the middle by her mother's outline, flattened out again.

She came every day to do nothing. The nurses already took care of everything. Her role was to talk to her mother, she imagined. Lots of people do that, acting as if the patients were capable of hearing their thoughts, able to understand who was standing there beside them, and conversing with them inside their own heads, as if illness could open up a different channel of perception between people.

It was not something that Alice believed in. She felt alone in that room and that was that. Usually she would just sit there, waiting for half an hour to pass, and then leave. If she met a doctor she asked for news, which was always the same anyway. Their words and raised eyebrows meant we're only waiting for something to go wrong.

That morning, however, she had brought a hairbrush. She took it out of her bag and delicately, making sure not to scratch her face, combed her mother's hair; at least the hair that wasn't squashed against the pillow. She was as inert and as submissive as a doll.

She arranged her mother's arms on top of the sheet, extended and parallel, in a relaxed pose. Another drop of the saline solution in the drip ran down the tube and disappeared into Fernanda's veins.

Alice moved to the end of the bed, resting the Canon on the aluminum bar. She shut her left eye and pressed the other to the viewfinder. She had never photographed her mother before. She pressed the shutter and then leaned a little farther forward, without losing the frame.

A rustling sound startled her and the room suddenly filled with light.

"Better?" said a male voice behind her.

Alice turned around. Beside the window a doctor was busying himself with the cord of the venetian blinds. He was young.

"Yes, thanks," said Alice, a little intimidated.

The doctor stuck his hands in the pockets of his white coat and went on looking at her, as if waiting for her to continue. She leaned forward and snapped again, more or less randomly, as if to please him.

He must think I'm crazy, she said to herself.

Instead the doctor came casually over to her mother's bed. He took a glance at her chart, narrowing his eyes as he read, reducing them to slits. He went over to the drip and moved a wheel with his thumb. The drops started to come down more quickly and he watched them with satisfaction. Alice thought there was something reassuring about his movements.

The doctor came over to her and grasped the bed rail.

"The nurses are obsessed," he remarked to himself. "They want darkness everywhere. As if it weren't already hard enough in here to tell day from night."

He turned and smiled.

"Are you the daughter?"

"Yes."

He nodded, without condescension.

"I'm Dr. Rovelli," he said. "Fabio," he added, as if he'd been thinking about it.

Alice shook his hand and introduced herself. For a few seconds they stared at the sleeping Fernanda, without exchanging a word.

Then the doctor tapped twice on the metal bed, which sounded hollow, and walked away. As he passed by Alice he leaned slightly toward her ear.

"Don't say it was me," he whispered, winking and pointing at the light-filled windows.

When visiting hours were over Alice descended the two flights of stairs, crossed the entrance hall, and left through the automatic glass doors.

She crossed the courtyard and stopped at the kiosk for a bottle of fizzy water. She was hungry, but was used to keeping the impulse in check until she had erased it almost entirely. Fizzy drinks were one of her tricks. They were enough to fill her stomach, at least long enough to overcome the critical moment of lunch.

She looked for her wallet in her purse, hampered slightly by the camera that hung from her wrist.

"It's on me," said someone behind her.

Fabio, the doctor whom she had met just half an hour before, held out a bill to the man in the kiosk. He smiled at Alice in a way that stripped her of her wish to protest. Instead of the white coat he wore a blue short-sleeved T-shirt and a strong aftershave that she hadn't noticed before.

"And a Coke," he added, turning to the man.

"Thanks," said Alice.

She tried to open the bottle, but the top slipped through her fingers without moving.

"May I?" said Fabio.

He took the bottle from her hand and opened it using only his thumb and index finger. Alice thought there was nothing special in the gesture, that she could have done it herself, like anyone else, if only her hands hadn't been so sweaty. And yet she found it strangely fascinating, like a small heroic feat performed specially for her.

Fabio gave her back the water and they drank, each from their own bottle, glancing stealthily at each other as if contemplating what to say next. Fabio's hair was short, with chestnut curls that shaded into red where the sun struck them directly. Alice had a sense that he was aware of the way the light played on his hair; that in some way he was aware of everything he was, and all the things around him.

They moved a few feet away from the kiosk, together, as if by common agreement. Alice didn't know how to say good-bye. She felt indebted to him, partly because he had given her the water and partly because he had helped her to open it. She wasn't even sure she wanted to go so quickly.

Fabio understood.

"Can I walk you to wherever you're going?" he asked cheekily.

Alice blushed.

"I'm going to the car."

"To the car, then."

She didn't say yes or no, but smiled, looking in another direction. Fabio made an obsequious gesture with his hand that meant after you.

They crossed the main road and turned into a smaller one, where the sidewalk was no longer sheltered by trees.

It was from Alice's shadow, as they walked side by side, that the doctor noticed the asymmetry of her gait. Her right shoulder, weighed down by the camera, acted as a counterpoint to the line of her left leg, which was as hard as a stick. Alice's unsettling grace was exacerbated in her oblong shadow, making it look one-dimensional, a dark segment branching out into two proportional and equal mechanical prostheses.

"Have you hurt your leg?" he asked.

"What?" said Alice, alarmed.

"I asked if you'd hurt yourself," he repeated. "I saw you were limping."

Alice felt her good leg contracting too. She tried to correct her walk, leaning on her faulty leg as much as she could, until it really hurt. She thought of the cruelty and precision of the word *lame*.

"I had an accident," she said. Then, as if by way of apology, she added, "A long time ago."

"Car?"

"No, skiing."

"I love skiing," Fabio said enthusiastically, sure that he had found an opportunity for a conversation.

"I hate it," Alice replied crisply.

"That's too bad."

"Yes, too bad."

They walked side by side not saying anything more. The young doctor was surrounded by an aura of tranquillity, a solid and transparent sphere of security. His lips were pursed in a smile even when he wasn't smiling. He looked at ease, as if he met a girl in a hospital room every day and chatted to her as he walked her back to her car. Alice, on the other hand, felt like a piece of wood. Her tendons were on the alert, she was aware of the creaking of her joints, the stiff muscles sticking to her bones.

She pointed to a parked blue Seicento, as if to say that's it, and Fabio spread out his arms. A car passed along the road behind them. From nothing, its noise grew and then faded away again, until it finally disappeared.

"So, are you a photographer?" said the doctor, to buy some time as much as anything else.

"Yes," Alice replied instinctively. She immediately regretted it. For the moment she was a girl who had quit university and was wandering around the streets snapping photographs more or less at random. She wondered whether that was enough to make her a photographer; what was the boundary between being and not being someone?

She bit her thin lip. "More or less," she added.

"May I?" the doctor said, opening his hand for the camera.

"Of course."

Alice unwound the strap from her wrist and held it out to him. He turned it around in his hands. He took off the lens cap and aimed the lens first in front of him and then upward, toward the sky.

"Wow," he observed. "It looks professional."

She blushed and the doctor made as if to give her back the camera.

"You can take a picture if you like," said Alice.

"No, no, please. I don't know how. You do it."

"Of what?"

Fabio looked around. He turned his head from side to side, dubiously. Then he shrugged.

"Of me," he replied.

Alice looked at him suspiciously.

"Why should I?" she asked him, with a slightly malicious inflection that escaped from her involuntarily.

"Because then you'd have to see me again, at least to show it to me."

Alice hesitated for a moment. She looked into Fabio's eyes, carefully for the first time, and couldn't hold their gaze for more than a second. They were blue and shadowless, as clear as the sky behind him, and she felt lost inside them, as if she were naked in a huge empty room.

He's handsome, thought Alice. He's handsome in the way a boy should be handsome.

She aimed the viewfinder at the middle of his face. He smiled, without a hint of embarrassment. He didn't even tilt his head, as people often do in front of the lens. Alice adjusted the focus and then pressed down with her index finger. The air was shattered by a click.

23

Mattia presented himself in Niccoli's office a week after their first meeting. The professor recognized his knock, a fact that curiously disturbed him. Seeing Mattia come in, he took a deep breath, ready to fly into a fury as soon as the boy said something along the lines of there are things I don't understand or I wanted to ask you if you could explain a few passages to me. If I'm forceful enough, Niccoli thought, I might be able to get rid of him.

Mattia asked may I, and, without looking the professor in the face, set down on the edge of his desk the article that he had given him to study. Niccoli picked it up and a little stack of pages slid out, numbered and neatly written, appended to the stapled ones. He quickly gathered them up and realized they were the calculations of the article, perfectly executed and with precise reference to the text. He quickly flipped through them but didn't need to examine them thoroughly to determine that they were correct: the order of the pages was enough to reveal their exactness.

He was a little disappointed, his fit of fury stuck halfway down his throat, like a sneeze that refused to come. He kept nodding as he reviewed Mattia's work, trying in vain to suppress a jolt of envy for this boy who seemed so unfit for existence but was doubtless gifted in this subject, something he himself had never really felt.

"Very good," he said at last, more to himself than with the intention of paying a genuine compliment. Then, with apparent boredom, "A problem is raised in the final paragraphs. It concerns the moments of the zeta function to—"

"I've done it," Mattia cut in. "I think I've solved it."

Niccoli looked at him with suspicion and then with deliberate disdain.

"Oh, really?"

"In the last page of my notes."

The professor licked his index finger and flipped through to the end. Frowning, he quickly read Mattia's demonstration, not understanding much of it, but not finding anything to object to either. Then he started from the beginning, more slowly, and this time the reasoning struck him as clear, quite rigorous, in fact, although marred here and there by amateur pedantry. As he followed the steps, his forehead relaxed and he unconsciously began stroking his lower lip. He forgot about Mattia, who was still frozen in the same position since he first arrived, looking at his feet and repeating in his head let it be right, let it be right, as if the rest of his life depended on the professor's verdict. As he said that to himself he didn't imagine, however, that it really would be.

Niccoli rested the pages on the table again, carefully, and dropped back into his chair, once again crossing his hands behind his head, his favorite position.

"Well, I'd say you're all set," he said.

He was to graduate at the end of May. Mattia asked his parents not to come. What? was all his mother could say. He shook his head, looking toward the window. The glass gave onto a wall of darkness and reflected the image of the three of them sitting around a four-sided table. In the reflection Mattia saw his father taking his mother's arm and gesturing to her to let it go. Then he saw the reflection of her getting up from the table with her hand over her mouth and turning on the tap to wash the dishes, even though they hadn't finished dinner yet.

Graduation day arrived just like any other, and Mattia got up before the alarm. His phantasms, which had filled his mind with scribbled sheets of paper during the night, took a few minutes to dissolve. No one was in the living room, just an elegant blue suit, brand-new, laid out beside a perfectly ironed pale pink shirt. On the shirt was a note with the words *To our graduate* and signed *Mom and Dad,* but in Dad's handwriting alone. Mattia put the clothes on and left the house without even looking at himself in the mirror.

He defended his thesis, looking the members of the committee straight in the eyes, devoting an equal amount of time to each of them and with a steady voice. Niccoli, sitting in the first row, nodded gravely and noted the growing amazement on the faces of his colleagues.

When the moment of the announcement came, Mattia arranged himself in a line with the other candidates. They were the only ones standing in the oversized space of the great hall. Mattia felt the eyes of the audience tingle on his back. He tried to distract himself by estimating the volume of the room, taking as his scale the height of the dean, but the tingle climbed up his neck and split in two directions, wrapping around to his temples. He imagined thousands of little insects pouring into his ears; thousands of hungry moths tunneling into his brain.

The words that the dean repeated identically for each candidate seemed longer each time, and were drowned out by a growing noise in his head, so loud that he couldn't make out his own name when the moment came. Something solid, like an ice cube, obstructed his throat. He shook the dean's hand and it was so dry to the touch that he instinctively sought the metal buckle of the belt that he wasn't wearing. The whole audience rose to its feet with the sound of a rising tide. Niccoli came over and clapped him twice on the shoulder, saying congratulations. Before the applause ended Mattia was out of the hall and walking hastily down the corridor, forgetting to put his toe down first to keep his footsteps from echoing on the way out.

I've done it, I've done it, he silently repeated to himself. But the

closer he got to the door the more aware he became of an abyss opening up in his stomach. Outside, the sunlight overwhelmed him, along
with the heat and the noise of the traffic. He staggered, as if from
fear of falling from the concrete step. There was a group of people on
the pavement; Mattia counted sixteen with a single glance. Many of
them were holding flowers, almost certainly waiting for his fellow
students. For a moment Mattia wished someone was there for him.
He felt the need to abandon his own weight onto someone else's body,
as if the contents of his head had suddenly become more than his two
legs alone could bear. He looked for his parents, he looked for Alice
and Denis, but there were only strangers looking nervously at their
watches, fanning themselves with sheets of paper they'd picked up
who knows where, smoking, talking loudly, and noticing nothing.

He looked at the degree that he held rolled up in his hand, on
which was written in beautiful cursive script that Mattia Balossino
was a graduate, a professional, an adult, that it was time for Mr.
Balossino, B.Sc., to face up to life, and that this meant he had reached
the end of the track that he had blindly followed from the first year
of primary school to graduation. He was still only half breathing,
as if the air didn't have enough momentum to accomplish the complete cycle.

What now? he wondered out loud.

A short, panting woman said excuse me, please, and he stepped
aside to let her in. He followed her inside, not even she could lead
him to the right answer, and walked reluctantly down the corridor
and climbed the stairs to the second floor. He stepped into the library
and went and sat down at his usual place, beside the window. He set
his degree down on the empty seat beside him and stretched his
hands out on the table. He concentrated on his own breathing, which
was still stuck in some backwash between his throat and the bottom
of his lungs. It had happened to him before, but never for such a
long time.

You can't forget how to do it, he said to himself. It's something you simply can't forget and that's that.

He exhaled all the air and was in a state of apnea for several seconds. Then he opened his mouth wide and inhaled as hard as he could, so much that the muscles in his chest hurt. This time his breath went all the way to the bottom of his lungs and Mattia thought he could see the molecules of oxygen, round and white, scattering around his arteries and beginning to swirl toward his heart once more.

He stayed in the same position for an indefinite amount of time, without thinking, without noticing the students coming in and out, in an absentminded state of numbness and agitation.

Then something flashed in front of his eyes, a red patch, and Mattia gave a start. He focused his eyes upon a rose wrapped in cellophane, which someone had slapped rudely onto the desk. Following the stem he recognized Alice's hand with its protruding knuckles, slightly reddened compared to her white fingers, and rounded nails cut down to the edge of the fingertip.

"You're a real jerk."

Mattia looked at her as one looks at a hallucination. He felt as if he were approaching the scene from a long way away, from a blurry place that he was already unable to remember well. When he was close enough, he made out on Alice's face a deep and unfamiliar sadness.

"Why didn't you tell me?" she went on. "You should have told me. You should have."

Alice slipped into the seat opposite Mattia, exhausted. She looked outside, toward the street, shaking her head.

"How did you . . . ?" Mattia began.

"Your parents. I found out from your parents." Alice turned and stared at him, her blue eyes boiling with rage. "Do you think that's right?"

Mattia hesitated and then shook his head, a dim and distorted outline moving with him over the wrinkled surface of the cellophane.

"I'd always imagined being there. I'd imagined it so many times. While you . . ."

Alice paused, the rest of the sentence trapped between her teeth. Mattia reflected once more on how that moment had suddenly become so real. He tried to remember where he had been until a few seconds before, but couldn't.

"You never did," Alice finished. "Never."

He felt his head sinking between his shoulders, felt the moths swarming inside his skull again.

"It wasn't important," he whispered. "I didn't want—"

"Shut up," she interrupted him abruptly. Someone at another desk said shhh and the silence of the next few seconds preserved the memory of that hiss.

"You're pale," said Alice. She looked at Mattia suspiciously. "Are you okay?"

"I don't know. I feel a bit dizzy."

Alice got to her feet. She brushed her hair from her forehead, along with a tangle of unpleasant thoughts. Then she bent over Mattia and gave him a kiss on the cheek, silent and light, which in a breath swept away all the insects.

"I'm sure you did brilliantly," she whispered into his ear. "I know you did."

Mattia felt her hair tickling his neck. He felt the soft hollow of air that separated them filling with her warmth and pressing lightly on his skin, like cotton wool. He became aware of an urge to pull her to him, but his hands remained motionless, as if asleep.

Alice straightened up, then she picked up his diploma from the chair, unrolled it, and smiled, reading it under her breath.

"Wow," she said at last. Her voice assumed a radiant tone. "We've got to celebrate. Come on, Mr. B.Sc., on your feet," she commanded.

She held out her hand to Mattia. He took it, rather uncertainly at first. He allowed himself to be led out of the library, with the same disarmed trust with which years before he had been dragged into the girls' bathroom. Over time the proportions between their hands had changed. Now his fingers wrapped completely around Alice's, like the rough halves of a seashell.

"Where are we going?" he asked her.

"For a drive. The sun's out. And you need to get some sun."

They left the building and this time Mattia wasn't afraid of the light, the traffic, and the people gathered around the entrance.

In the car they kept the windows lowered. Alice drove with both hands on the wheel and sang to "Pictures of You," imitating the sound of the words that she didn't know. Mattia felt his muscles gradually relaxing, adapting to the shape of the seat. He felt as if the car were leaving a dark and sticky trail in its wake, a trail of his past and all his worries. He gradually began to feel lighter, like a jar being emptied. He closed his eyes, and for a few seconds floated on the air that fanned his face, and on Alice's voice.

When he opened them again they were on the road leading to his house. He wondered if they might have organized a surprise party for him and prayed that it wasn't so.

"Come on, where are we going?" he asked again.

"Don't you worry," murmured Alice. "If you ever take me for a drive you'll have the right to choose."

For the first time Mattia was ashamed to be twenty-two and not have gotten his driver's license. It was another of the things he had left behind, another obvious step in a boy's life that he had decided not to take, so as to stay as far as possible from the machinery of life. Like eating popcorn at the movies, like sitting on the back of a bench, like not respecting your parents' curfew, like playing football with

a ball of tinfoil, like standing naked in front of a girl. He thought
that from this precise moment things would be different. He decided
he would get his license as soon as possible. He would do it for her,
to take her for a drive. Even though he was afraid to admit it, when
he was with her it seemed it was worth doing all those normal things
that normal people do.

Now that they were close to Mattia's house, Alice turned in another direction. She pulled onto the main road and parked the car a
hundred yards down, opposite the park.

"*Voilà,*" she said. She unfastened her seat belt and got out of the
car.

Mattia stayed frozen in his seat, his eyes fixed on the park.

"Well? Are you getting out?"

"Not here," he said.

"Come on, don't be stupid."

Mattia shook his head.

"Let's go somewhere else," he said.

Alice looked around.

"What's the problem?" she insisted. "We're just going to take a
walk."

She came over to the window on Mattia's side. He was stiff, as if
someone were sticking a knife in his back. His hand gripped the
handle of the door, which was half open. He stared at the trees a
hundred yards away. The wide, green leaves covered their knotty
skeletons and the fractal structure of the branches, hiding their horrible secret.

He had never been back here. The last time was with the police,
that day that his father had told him give your mother your hand
and she had pulled hers away and stuck it in her pocket. That day
he had still had both his arms bandaged, from his fingers to his
elbow, with a thick dressing rolled in so many layers that it took
a saw blade to remove it. He had shown the policemen where

Michela had been sitting. They had wanted to know the exact spot and had taken pictures, first from far away and then from close up.

From the car, on the way back home, he had seen the dredging machines sinking their mechanical arms into the river and pulling out big piles of wet soil, then dropping them heavily on the bank. Mattia had noticed that his mother held her breath every time, until each pile disintegrated on the ground. Michela must have been in that slime, but they didn't find her. They never found her.

"Let's get out of here. Please," repeated Mattia. His tone wasn't pleading. Instead he seemed absorbed, annoyed.

Alice got back into the car.

"Sometimes I don't know whether—"

"That's where I abandoned my twin sister," he cut in with a flat, almost inhuman voice. He lifted his arm and with his right index finger pointed to the trees in the park. Then he left it hanging there in midair, as if he had forgotten about it.

"Twin sister? What are you talking about? You don't have a twin sister. . . ."

Mattia nodded slowly, still staring at the trees.

"She was my identical twin. Completely identical to me," he said.

Then, before Alice even had time to ask, he told her everything. He spilled out the whole story, like a dam collapsing. The worm, the party, the Legos, the river, the bits of glass, the hospital room, the judge, the television appeal, the shrinks, everything, in a way he had never done with anyone. He talked without looking at her, without getting excited. Then he lapsed back into silence. He felt around under the seat with his right hand, but found only blunt shapes. He calmed down, feeling remote again, alien to his own body.

Alice's hand touched his chin and delicately turned his face toward her. All Mattia saw was a shadow moving toward him. He instinctively closed his eyes and then felt Alice's hot mouth on his, her tears on his cheek, or maybe they weren't hers, and finally her hands, so light, holding his head still and catching all his thoughts and imprisoning them there, in the space that no longer existed between them.

24

They saw each other often over the next month, without ever making a real date but never really by chance. After visiting hours Alice always ended up wandering around Fabio's ward, and he always managed to run into her. They'd stroll around the courtyard, always taking the same route that they had decided by mutual agreement, without discussing it. That outer enclosure marked the confines of their story, carving out a space where there was no need to name that clear and mysterious thing flowing between them.

Fabio seemed to have a precise knowledge of the dynamics of courtship; he knew how to respect rhythms and moderate phrases as if following a set protocol. He sensed Alice's profound suffering, but remained beyond it, as if he were standing on the border. The excesses of the world, whatever form they might assume, didn't really concern him. They collided with his equilibrium and common sense and so he preferred to ignore them, simply pretending that they didn't exist. If an obstacle blocked his path, he walked around it, without altering his own pace in the slightest, and soon forgot it. He never had doubts, or hardly ever.

Nonetheless, he knew how to reach an objective, so he was attentive to Alice's moods in a way that was respectful, though slightly pedantic. If she didn't talk, he asked her if something was wrong, but never twice in a row. He showed interest in her photographs, in how her mother was, and filled the silences with stories from his own day, amusing anecdotes he picked up around the ward.

Alice allowed herself to be carried away by his self-confidence and gradually abandoned herself to it, as she had abandoned herself to the support of the water when as a little girl she played dead in the swimming pool.

They lived the slow and invisible interpenetration of their universes, like two stars gravitating around a common axis, in ever tighter orbits, whose clear destiny is to coalesce at some point in space and time.

Alice's mother's treatment had been suspended. With a nod of the head, her husband had finally given his consent to let her sink into painless sleep, under a heavy blanket of morphine. Alice merely waited for it to come to an end and couldn't bring herself to feel guilty. Her mother already lived within her as a memory, settled like a clump of pollen in a corner of her head, where she would stay for the rest of her life, frozen in the same pile of soundless images.

Fabio hadn't planned to ask her and wasn't the type for impulsive gestures, but that afternoon there was something different about Alice. A kind of nervousness emerged from the way she wove her fingers together and moved her eyes from side to side, always careful not to meet his own. For the first time since meeting her he was hasty and incautious.

"My parents are going to the beach this weekend," he said out of the blue.

Alice seemed not to have heard. At any rate, she let the sentence drop. Her head had been buzzing like a wasps' nest for days. Mattia hadn't called her since his graduation, more than a week before, and yet it clearly was his turn now.

"I thought you could come to dinner at my place," Fabio tossed out.

His confidence faltered for a moment in the middle of those words, but he immediately shook off his uncertainty. He plunged both hands into the pockets of his white coat and prepared to accept any kind of reply with the same kind of lightness. He knew how to build a shelter for himself even before he needed one.

Alice smiled faintly, slightly panic-stricken.

"I don't know," she said gently. "Perhaps it isn't—"

"You're right," Fabio interrupted her. "I shouldn't have asked you. Sorry."

They finished their walk in silence and when they reached Fabio's ward again he murmured okay, long and drawn out, as if speaking to himself.

Neither of them moved. They exchanged a quick glance and immediately lowered their eyes. Fabio started to laugh.

"We never know how to say good-bye to each other, you and me," he said.

"Yeah." Alice smiled at him. She brought a hand to her hair, hooked a lock with her index finger, and tugged on it slightly.

Fabio took a resolute step toward her and the gravel of the path crunched beneath his foot. He kissed her on her left cheek, with affectionate arrogance, and then stepped back.

"Well, at least think about it," he said.

He smiled broadly, with his whole mouth, eyes, and cheeks. Then he turned around and walked confidently toward the entrance.

Now he'll turn around, thought Alice when he went through the glass door.

But Fabio turned the corner and disappeared down the corridor.

25

The letter was addressed to Mr. Mattia Balossino, B.Sc., and to the touch it was so light and insubstantial it seemed impossible it could contain his whole future. His mother hadn't shown it to him until dinner, perhaps out of embarrassment at having opened it without permission. She hadn't done it on purpose, she hadn't even looked at the name on the envelope: Mattia never got any mail.

"This came," she said, holding the letter over the plates.

Mattia glanced quizzically at his father, who nodded at something vague. Before taking the letter he ran his napkin over his upper lip, which was already clean. Seeing the complicated circular logo, printed in blue next to the address, he had no idea what it might contain. He pressed on both sides of the envelope to take out the folded page inside it. He opened it and began to read, rather impressed by the thought that this letter was specifically for him, Mr. Mattia Balossino, B.Sc.

His parents made more noise than necessary with their silverware and his father repeatedly cleared his throat. After reading it, Mattia refolded the page with the reverse sequence of gestures with which he had opened it, so as to return it to its initial form, and slipped it back into its envelope, which he then set down on Michela's chair.

He picked up his fork again, but was momentarily bewildered at the sight of the sliced zucchini on the plate, as if someone had made them appear there by surprise.

"It sounds like a wonderful opportunity," said Adele.

"Yeah."

"Do you want to go?"

As she spoke, Mattia's mother felt heat flashing in her face. She was aware that it had nothing to do with the fear of losing him. On the contrary, she hoped with all her might that he would accept, that he would leave this house and the place that he occupied opposite her every evening at dinner, his black head dangling over his plate and that contagious air of tragedy surrounding him.

"I don't know," Mattia replied to his plate.

"It's a wonderful opportunity," his mother repeated.

"Yeah."

Mattia's father broke the silence that followed with random thoughts about the efficiency of northern Europeans, about how clean their streets were, putting it all down to the severe climate and the lack of light for much of the year, which limited distractions. He had never been anywhere of the kind, but from what he had heard that was clearly how it was.

When, at the end of dinner, Mattia began stacking up the dishes, collecting them in the same order as he did every evening, his father put a hand on his shoulder and said under his breath go on, I'll finish up. Mattia picked up the envelope from the chair and went to his room.

He sat down on the bed and began turning the letter around in his hands. He folded it backward and forward a few times, making the thin paper of the envelope crack. Then he examined the logo beside the address more carefully. A bird of prey, probably an eagle, held its wings open and its head turned to one side so as to show its pointed beak in profile. Its wing tips and claws were inscribed in a circle, which a printing error had turned slightly oval. Another circle, larger and concentric with the preceding one, contained the name of the university that was offering Mattia a place. The Gothic characters, all those *k*'s and *h*'s in the name and the *o*'s with a diagonal line running through them, which in mathematics indicated a null set, made Mattia imagine a tall, dark building, with echoing corridors and high ceilings, surrounded by lawns with grass cut to a few millimeters from the ground, as silent and deserted as a cathedral at the end of the world.

In that unknown and far-off place lay his future as a mathematician. There was a promise of salvation, an uncontaminated place where nothing was yet compromised. Here, on the other hand, there was Alice, just Alice, and all around her a swamp.

It happened as it had on the day he graduated. Once again his breath caught halfway down his throat, where it acted as a stopper. He gasped as if the air in his room had suddenly liquefied. The days had grown longer, and the dusk was blue and wearying. Mattia would wait for the last trace of light to fade, his mind wandering along corridors that he hadn't yet seen, now and then bumping into Alice, who would look at him without a word, without so much as a smile.

You've just got to decide, he thought. Go or don't go. 1 or 0, like a binary code.

But the more he tried to simplify things, the more confused he became.

Someone knocked on the door of his room. The sound reached him as if from the bottom of a well.

"Yes?" he said.

The door opened slowly and his father poked his head in.

"Can I come in?" he asked.

"Uh-huh."

"Why are you sitting in the dark?"

Without waiting for an answer, Pietro flipped the switch and 100 watts of light exploded in Mattia's dilated pupils, which contracted with a pleasant pain.

His father sat down on the bed next to him. They had the same way of crossing their legs, the left calf balanced on the right heel, but neither of them had ever noticed.

"What's the name of that thing you studied?" Pietro asked after a while.

"What thing?"

"That thing you wrote your dissertation on. I can never remember what it's called."

"The Riemann zeta function."

"Right. The Riemann zeta function."

Mattia rubbed his thumbnail under the nail of his little finger, but the skin there had become so hard and calloused that he didn't feel a thing. His nails slipped noisily over each other.

"I wish I'd had your mind," Pietro went on. "But I never understand a thing about math. It just wasn't for me. You have to have a special sort of brain for some things."

Mattia thought there was nothing good about having his mind. That he would happily have unscrewed it and replaced it with a different one, or even with a package of biscotti, provided it was empty and light. He opened his mouth to reply that feeling special is the worst kind of cage that a person can build for himself, but he didn't say anything. He thought about the time his teacher had sat him in the middle of the classroom, with everyone else staring at him like some exotic beast, and it occurred to him that it was as if he'd never moved from there in all those years.

"Did Mom tell you to come?" he asked his father.

The muscles in Pietro's neck stiffened. He sucked in his lips and then nodded.

"Your future is the most important thing," he said in a vaguely embarrassed voice. "You need to think about yourself now. If you decide to go we'll support you. We haven't got a lot of money, but enough if you need it."

There was another lengthy silence, in which Mattia thought about Alice, and about the share of money that he had stolen from Michela.

"Dad?" he said at last.

"Yes?"

"Could you leave, please? I have to make a phone call."

Pietro gave a long sigh that also contained a certain amount of relief.

"Of course," he said.

He got up, and before turning around he stretched a hand toward Mattia's face. He was about to caress his cheek, but stopped a few inches from the unruly tufts of his son's beard. He redirected his hand to his hair, which he barely touched. After all, it had been quite a while since they had done such things.

26

Denis's love for Mattia had burned itself out, like a forgotten candle in an empty room, leaving behind a ravenous discontent. When he was nineteen, Denis found an advertisement for a gay bar on the last page of a local newspaper and tore it out, keeping the scrap of paper in his wallet for two whole months. From time to time he unrolled it and reread the address, even though he already knew it by heart.

All around him, guys his age were going out with girls and by now they were used to sex, so much so that they'd stopped talking about it all the time. Denis felt that his only escape route lay in that piece of newspaper; in that address that had faded from the sweat of his fingertips.

He went one rainy evening, without really having made his mind up to go. He put on the first thing he pulled out of his closet and headed out, giving a quick shout to his parents in the other room. I'm going to the movies, he said.

He walked past the bar two or three times, circling the block every time. Finally he went in with his hands in his pockets and a confidential wink to the bouncer. He sat down at the bar, ordered a lager, and sipped it slowly, staring at the bottles lined up along the wall, waiting.

A guy came over to him a moment later and Denis decided he'd be okay, even before he looked him properly in the face. The man started talking about himself, or maybe about some film that Denis hadn't seen. He shouted in his ear but Denis didn't listen to a word. He brusquely interrupted him saying let's go to the toilet. The other guy was struck dumb and then he smiled, revealing bad teeth. Denis thought he was horrible, that his eyebrows almost joined up and he was old, too old, but it didn't matter.

In the toilet the guy pulled his T-shirt up over his belly and bent forward to kiss him, but Denis pulled away. Instead he knelt down and unbuttoned the other man's pants. Damn, he said, you're in a hurry. But then he let him get on with it. Denis shut his eyes and tried to finish as quickly as possible.

He didn't get a result with his mouth and felt completely hopeless. Then he used his hands, both of them, insistently. As the guy came he came too, in his pants. He almost ran from the toilet, without giving the stranger time to get his clothes back on. The same old sense of guilt took hold of him as soon as he was past the toilet door, and drenched him like a bucket of icy water.

Outside the bar he wandered about for half an hour in search of a fountain to wash the smell off him.

He went back to the bar on other occasions. Every time he talked to someone different and he always found an excuse not to give his real name. He never hooked up with anyone else. He collected the stories of people like himself, mostly keeping silent and listening. He slowly discovered that the stories were similar, that there was a process, and that the process involved immersion, putting your whole head under until you touched the bottom and only then coming up for air.

Every one of them had a love that had rotted alone in their heart, as his love for Mattia had done. Each of them had been afraid and many of them still were, but not when they were here, among others who could understand, protected by the "scene," as they put it. When he talked to those strangers Denis felt less alone and wondered when his moment would come, the day when he would touch bottom, resurface, and finally be able to breathe.

One evening someone told him about "the cemetery lamps." That's what they called the little path up behind the graveyard, where the only light, faint and trembling, was from the tombstone lamps filtering between the bars of the big cemetery gate. They would grope about there, it was the perfect place to empty themselves of desire without seeing or being seen, merely putting their bodies at the disposal of the dark.

It was at the lamps that Denis had touched bottom. He slammed into it with his face, chest, and knees, as though diving into shallow water. Afterward he never went back to the bar, locking himself away, more stubbornly than before, in his own denial.

Then, in his junior year at university, he went to study in Spain. There, far from the probing eyes of his family and friends, far from all the streets whose names he knew, love found him. His name was Valerio and he was Italian like him; young and scared to death like him. The months they spent together, in a little apartment a few blocks from the Ramblas, were quick and intense and they removed the useless cloak of suffering, as on the first clear evening after days of pouring rain.

Back in Italy they lost sight of each other, but Denis didn't suffer. With a completely new confidence, which he would never lose, he moved on to other affairs, which seemed to have been waiting for him for all that time, lined up in an orderly fashion just around the corner. The only old friendship he maintained was with Mattia. They spoke only rarely, mostly on the phone, and were capable of being silent for minutes at a time, each lost in his own thoughts, punctuated by the other's reassuring, rhythmical breathing at the other end of the line.

Denis was brushing his teeth when the call came. At his house they always answered after the second ring, the time it took to get to the nearest telephone from anywhere in the apartment.

His mother called Denis it's for you, and he took his time answering. He rinsed his mouth out well, passed the towel over it, and glanced once more at his two upper front incisors. Over the past few days he had had a sense that they were overlapping, because of his wisdom teeth pushing in from the sides.

"Hello?"

"Hi."

Mattia never introduced himself. He knew that his voice was unmistakable to his friend and anyway he didn't like saying his name.

"So, Mr. Graduate, how are you?" Denis said cheerfully. He wasn't upset about the graduation business. He had learned to respect the chasm that Mattia had dug around himself. Years previously he had tried to jump over that chasm, and had fallen into it. Now he contented himself with sitting on the edge, his legs dangling into the void. Mattia's voice no longer stirred anything in his stomach, but he was aware of the idea of him and always would be, as the only true benchmark for everything that had come afterward.

"Did I disturb you?" asked Mattia.

"No. Did I disturb you?" Denis teased.

"I was the one who called you."

"Of course, so tell me: I can tell from your voice that something's up."

Mattia remained silent. Something was up, it was there on the tip of his tongue.

"Well?" Denis pressed. "And this something would be?"

Mattia exhaled loudly into the receiver and Denis became aware that he was having difficulty breathing. He picked up a pen beside the telephone and started playing with it, passing it between the fingers of his right hand. Then he dropped it and he didn't bend down to pick it up. Mattia still wasn't speaking.

"Shall I start asking questions?" said Denis. "We could do it so that you—"

"I've been offered a position abroad," Mattia interrupted. "At a university. An important one."

"Wow," Denis observed, not surprised in the least. "That sounds fantastic. Are you going?"

"I don't know. Should I?"

Denis pretended to laugh.

"You're asking me that when I haven't even finished university? I'd go in a second. A change of air always does one good."

He thought of adding *and what is there to keep you here?* But he didn't say it.

"It's because something happened, the other day," Mattia ventured. "The day I graduated."

"Mmm."

"Alice was there and . . ."

"And?"

Mattia hesitated for a moment.

"Well, we kissed," he said at last.

Denis's fingers stiffened around the receiver. He was surprised by his reaction. He was no longer jealous of Alice, there was no point, but at that moment it was as if an undigested bit of the past had come back up his throat. For a moment he saw Mattia and Alice hand in hand in Viola's kitchen, and he felt Giulia Mirandi's invasive tongue forcing its way into his mouth like a rolled-up towel.

"Hallelujah," he remarked, trying to sound happy. "You two have finally done it."

"Yeah."

In the pause that followed both of them wanted to hang up.

"And now you don't know what to do," Denis struggled to say.

"Yeah."

"But you and she are now, what would you say . . . ?"

"I don't know. I haven't seen her since."

"Ah."

Denis ran the nail of his index finger along the curled wire of the telephone. At the other end Mattia did the same and as always he thought of a DNA helix, missing its twin.

"Numbers are everywhere," said Denis. "They're always the same, aren't they?"

"Yes."

"But Alice is only here."

"Yes."

"So you've already made up your mind."

Denis heard his friend's breath easing and becoming more regular.

"Thank you," said Mattia.

"For what?"

Mattia hung up. Denis spent another few seconds with the receiver pressed to his ear, listening to the silence inside it. Something within him went out, like one last ember that had stayed lit for too long under the ashes.

I said the right thing, he thought.

The busy signal sounded. Denis hung up and went back into the bathroom to check on those wretched wisdom teeth.

27

"¿Qué pasa, mi amorcito?" Soledad asked Alice, tilting her head slightly to catch her eye. Ever since Fernanda had been in the hospital she had eaten at the dinner table with them, because father and daughter facing each other, alone, was unbearable for both of them.

Alice's father had developed the habit of not changing when he came home from work. He had dinner in his jacket and tie, slightly loosened, as if he were merely passing through. He held a newspaper open on the table and looked up only to make sure that his daughter was gulping down at least the occasional mouthful.

The silence had become part of the meal and disturbed only Sol, who often thought back to the rowdy meals at her mother's house, when she was still very young and could never have imagined she would end up like this.

Alice hadn't even looked at the cutlet and salad on her plate. She took little sips of water, crossing her eyes as she drank and regarding the glass resting on her lips as seriously as if it held some kind of medicine. She shrugged and flashed a swift smile at Sol.

"Sorry," she said. "I'm not very hungry."

Her father nervously turned the page. Before setting the paper back down he gave it an impetuous shake and couldn't help glancing at his daughter's full plate. He didn't comment and started reading again, beginning a random article in the middle, without grasping its meaning.

"Sol?" asked Alice.

"Yes?"

"How did your husband win you? The first time, I mean. What did he do?"

Soledad stopped chewing. Then she started again, more slowly, to gain some time. The first image that ran through her head wasn't of the day she met her husband. Instead she thought back to that morning when she had gotten up late and wandered barefoot around the house, looking for him. Over the years all the memories of her marriage had become concentrated in those few moments, as if the time spent with her husband had been only the preparation for an ending. That morning she had looked at the previous night's dirty dishes and the cushions in the wrong place on the sofa. Everything was just as they had left it and the sounds in the air were the same as ever. And yet something, in the way things were arranged and the way the light clung to them, had left her frozen in the middle of the sitting room, dismayed. And then, with disconcerting clarity, she had thought he's gone.

Soledad sighed, feigning her usual nostalgia.

"He brought me home from work on his bicycle. Every day he came with his bicycle," she said. "And he gave me some shoes."

"What?"

"Shoes. White ones, high heels."

Soledad smiled and indicated the length of the heels with her thumb and index finger.

"They were very pretty," she said.

Alice's father snorted and shuffled in his chair, as if he found all this intolerable. Alice imagined Sol's husband coming out of the shop with the shoe box under his arm. She knew him from the photograph that Sol kept hung over the head of her bed, with a dry little olive branch slipped between the nail and the hook.

For a moment Alice felt light-headed, but her thoughts immediately turned to Mattia, and stayed there. A week had passed, and he still hadn't called.

I'll go now, she thought.

She slipped a forkful of salad into her mouth, as if to say to her father look I've eaten. The vinegar stung her lips slightly. She was still chewing as she got up from the table.

"I've got to go out," she said.

Her father arched his eyebrows.

"And might we know where you're going at this hour?" he asked.

"Out," said Alice defiantly. Then she added, "To a girlfriend's," to soften the tone.

Her father shook his head, as if to say do what you like. For a moment Alice felt sorry for him, left on his own like that behind his newspaper. She felt a desire to hug him and tell him everything and ask him what she should do, but a moment later the same thought made her shiver. She turned around and headed resolutely for the bathroom.

Her father lowered the newspaper and with two fingers he rubbed his weary eyes. Sol turned the memory of the high-heeled shoes around in her head for a few seconds, then put it back in its place and got up to clear the things away.

On her way to Mattia's house, Alice kept the music turned up, but if when she got there someone had asked her what she was listening to, she wouldn't have been able to say. All of a sudden she was furious and she was sure that she was about to ruin everything, but she no longer had any choice. That evening, getting up from the table, she had crossed the invisible boundary beyond which things start working by themselves. It was like when she was learning to ski, when she would move her center of gravity too far forward by an insignificant couple of millimeters, just enough to end up facedown in the snow.

She had been to Mattia's house only once before, and only as far as the living room. Mattia had disappeared into his room to change and she had had an embarrassing chat with his mother, Mrs. Balossino, who observed her from the sofa with a vaguely worried air, as if Alice's hair were on fire or something, without even offering her a seat.

Alice rang the doorbell and the display beside it lit up red, like a final warning. After a few crackles Mattia's mother answered in a frightened voice.

"Who is it?"

"It's Alice, Mrs. Balossino. I'm sorry about the time, but . . . is Mattia there?"

From the other end she heard a thoughtful silence. Alice pulled her hair over her right shoulder, having the disagreeable impression of being observed through the lens of the intercom. The door opened with an electrical click. Before coming in, Alice smiled at the camera to say thank you.

In the empty hallway her footsteps echoed with the rhythm of a heartbeat. Her bad leg seemed to have lost all life, as if her heart had forgotten to pump blood into it.

The door to the apartment was ajar, but there was no one to welcome her. Alice pushed it open and said, "Hello?" Mattia emerged from the sitting room and stopped at least two meters away from her.

"Hi," he said, without moving his arms.

"Hi."

They stood looking at each other for a few seconds, as if they didn't know each other at all. Mattia had crossed his big toe over his second one, inside his slipper, and by squashing one over the other and against the floor he hoped he could break them.

"Sorry if I'm—"

"Won't you come in?" Mattia broke in automatically.

Alice turned to close the door and the round brass handle slipped from her sweaty palm. The door slammed, shaking the frame, and a shiver of impatience ran through Mattia.

What's she doing here? he thought.

It was as if the Alice he had been talking to Denis about only a few minutes before wasn't the same one who had just dropped by without warning. He tried to clear his mind of that ridiculous thought, but the irritation remained in his mouth like a kind of nausea.

He thought of the word *hunted.* Then he thought about when his father used to drag him onto the carpet and imprison him between his enormous arms. He tickled him on his tummy and on his sides and he exploded with laughter; he laughed so hard that he couldn't breathe.

Alice followed him into the sitting room. Mattia's parents stood waiting, like a little welcoming committee.

"Good evening," she said, shrinking back.

"Hi, Alice," replied Adele, without moving.

Pietro, on the other hand, came over and unexpectedly stroked her hair.

"You're getting prettier and prettier," he said. "How's your mother?"

Adele, behind her husband's back, held a paralyzed smile and bit her lip for not having asked the question herself.

Alice blushed.

"Same as usual," she said, so as not to appear overdramatic. "She's getting by."

"Say hello from us," said Pietro.

All four of them stood in silence. Mattia's father seemed to stare right through Alice and she tried to distribute her weight uniformly on her legs, so as not to look crippled. She realized that her mother would never meet Mattia's parents and she was a bit sorry about that, but she was even sorrier to be the only one thinking anything of the kind.

"You two go on," Pietro said at last.

Alice passed beside him with her head lowered after smiling once more at Adele. Mattia was already waiting in his room.

"Shall I close it?" asked Alice once she was inside, pointing to the door. All her courage had deserted her.

"Uh-huh."

Mattia sat on the bed, with his hands crossed on his knees. Alice looked around the room. The things that filled it seemed not to have been touched by anyone; they looked like articles that had been carefully and calculatedly displayed in a shopwindow. There was nothing useless, not a photograph on the wall or a stuffed animal from childhood, nothing that gave off that smell of familiarity and affection that teenagers' rooms usually have. With all the chaos that filled her body and her head, Alice felt out of place.

"Nice room," she said, without really meaning it.

"Thanks," said Mattia.

There was an enormous list of things to say floating over their heads and both of them tried to ignore it by looking at the floor.

Alice slid her back along the wardrobe and sat down on the ground with her working knee against her chest. She forced a smile.

"So, how does it feel to have graduated?"

Mattia shrugged and smiled very slightly.

"Exactly the same as before."

"You really don't know how to be happy, do you?"

"Apparently not."

Alice let an affectionate mmm slip through her closed lips and thought that this embarrassment between them made no sense and yet it was there, solid and ineradicable.

"But things have been happening to you lately," she said.

"Yes."

Alice thought about whether to say it or not. Then she said it, not a drop of saliva left in her mouth.

"Something nice, no?"

Mattia drew in his legs.

Here we go, he thought.

"Yes, actually," he said.

He knew exactly what he was supposed to do. He was supposed to get up and go and sit next to her. He was supposed to smile, look into her eyes, and kiss her. It was that simple. It was mere mechanics, a banal sequence of vectors that would bring his mouth to meet hers. He could do it even if at that moment he didn't feel like it; he could trust the precision of his movements.

He made as if to get up, but somehow the mattress kept him where he was, like a sticky morass.

Once again Alice acted in his place.

"Can I sit next to you?" she asked.

He nodded and, even though there was no need to, moved slightly to one side.

Alice pulled herself to her feet, with the help of her hands.

On the bed, in the space that Mattia had left free, there was a piece of paper, typed and folded in three like an accordion. Alice picked it up to move it and noticed that it was written in English.

"What's this?" she asked.

"It came today. It's a letter from a university."

Alice read the name of the city, written in bold in the top left-hand corner, and the letters dimmed under her eyes.

"What does it say?"

"I've been offered a grant."

Alice felt dizzy and panic turned her face white.

"Wow," she lied. "For how long?"

"Four years."

She gulped. She was still standing up.

"And are you going?" she asked under her breath.

"I don't know yet," said Mattia, almost apologizing. "What do you think?"

Alice remained silent, with the sheet of paper in her hands and her gaze lost somewhere on the wall.

"What do you think?" Mattia repeated, as if she really hadn't heard him.

"What do I think about what?" Alice's voice had suddenly hardened, so much that Mattia gave a start. For some reason she thought about her mother in the hospital, dazed with drugs. She looked expressionlessly at the sheet of paper and wanted to tear it up.

Instead she put it back down on the bed, where she had been about to sit down.

"It would be important for my career," Mattia said by way of self-justification.

Alice nodded seriously, with her chin thrust out as if she had a golf ball in her mouth.

"Fine. So what are you waiting for? Off you go. Besides, it doesn't seem to me that there's anything to keep you here," she said between clenched teeth.

Mattia felt the veins in his neck swelling. Perhaps he was about to cry. Ever since that afternoon in the park the tears were always there, like a lump that was hard to swallow, as if that day his tear ducts, clogged for so long, had finally opened and all that accumulated stuff had finally begun to force its way out.

"But if I went away," he began in a slightly quivering voice, "would you . . . ?" He stopped.

"Me?" Alice stared at him from above, as though he were a stain on the bedcover. "I'd imagined the next four years differently," she said. "I'm twenty-three and my mother's about to die. I . . ." She shook her head. "But none of that matters to you. Go ahead and worry about your career."

It was the first time she had used her mother's illness to wound someone, and she didn't particularly regret it. She saw Mattia shrink in front of her eyes.

He didn't reply and in his mind ran through the instructions for breathing.

"But don't you worry," Alice went on. "I've found someone it does matter to. In fact that's what I came here to tell you." She paused, her mind blank. Once again things were taking a course of their own; once again she was tumbling down the slope and forgetting to stick in her ski poles to brake. "His name's Fabio, he's a doctor. I didn't want you to . . . you know."

She uttered the phrase like a little actress, in a voice that wasn't hers. She felt the words scratching her tongue like sand. As she uttered them, she studied Mattia's expression, to pick up a hint of disappointment that she could cling to, but his eyes were too dark for her to make out any spark in them. She was sure none of it mattered to him and her stomach crumpled like a plastic bag.

"I'll be off," she said quietly, exhausted.

Mattia nodded, looking toward the closed window to eliminate Alice completely from his field of vision. That name, Fabio, had pierced his head like a splinter and he just wanted Alice to leave.

He saw that outside the evening was clear and he sensed a warm wind was about to blow through. The opaque pollen of the poplars, swarming under the beam from the streetlights, looked like big legless insects.

Alice opened the door and he got to his feet. He walked her to the front door, following a few steps behind. She distractedly checked in her bag that she had everything, to gain another moment. Then she murmured okay and left.

Before the elevator doors closed, Alice and Mattia exchanged a good-bye that meant nothing at all.

28

Mattia's parents were watching television. His mother sat with her knees curled up under her nightdress; his father with his legs stretched out, crossed on the coffee table in front of the sofa, the remote control resting on one thigh. Alice hadn't responded to their good-bye, she didn't even seem to have noticed that they were there.

Mattia spoke from behind the back of the sofa.

"I've decided to accept," he said.

Adele brought a hand to her cheek and, bewildered, sought her husband's eyes. Mattia's father turned slightly and looked at his son as one looks at a grown-up son.

"Fine," he said.

Mattia went back to his room. He picked up the sheet of paper from the bed and sat down at the desk. He perceived the universe expanding; he could feel it accelerating under his feet and for a moment he hoped that its stretching fabric would burst and let him come crashing down.

He groped around for the light switch and turned it on. He chose the longest of the four pencils lined up side by side, dangerously close to the edge of the desk. From the second drawer he took the sharpener and bent down to sharpen it into the wastepaper basket. He blew away the thin sawdust that was left on the tip of the pencil. There was already a blank sheet in front of him.

He placed his left hand on the paper, palm down and fingers spread wide. He ran the very sharp graphite tip over his skin. He lingered for a second, ready to plunge it into the confluence of the two big veins at the base of his middle finger. Then, slowly, he removed it, and took a deep breath.

On the sheet he wrote *To the kind attention of the Dean.*

29

Fabio was waiting for her by the front door, with the lights of the landing, the door, and the sitting room all on. As he took the plastic bag with the tub of ice cream from her hands, he linked his fingers with hers and kissed her on one cheek, as if it were the most natural thing in the world. He said that dress really suits you and he meant it, and then he went back to the stove to get on with cooking dinner, but without taking his eyes off her.

From the stereo came music that Alice didn't recognize, but it wasn't there to be listened to, just to complete a perfect scenario; there was nothing casual about it. Two candles were lit, the wine was already open, and the table was tidily set for two, with the blades of the knives turned inward, which meant that the guest was welcome, as her mother had taught her when she was little. There was a white tablecloth with no wrinkles and the napkins were folded into triangles with the edges perfectly aligned.

Alice sat down at the table and counted the empty plates stacked on top of one another to work out how much there would be to eat. That evening, before leaving the house, she had spent a long time locked in the bathroom staring at the towels that Soledad changed every Friday. In the marbled-topped chest of drawers she had found her mother's makeup and used it. She had made herself up in the semidarkness, and before running the lipstick over her lips, she had sniffed the tip. The smell hadn't reminded her of anything.

She had allowed herself the ritual of trying on four different dresses, even though it was obvious from the outset, if not from the previous day, that she had already decided on the one she had worn to the Ronconi boy's confirmation, the one that her father had said

160

was the most inappropriate because it left her back uncovered to below the ribs and her arms completely bare.

Still barefoot and wearing the little blue dress whose neckline against her pale skin looked like a smile of satisfaction, Alice had gone down to Sol in the kitchen and asked her apprehensively for an opinion. You look wonderful, Sol had said. She kissed her on the forehead and Alice had been worried about smudging her makeup.

In the kitchen Fabio moved with great agility and at the same time with the excessive care of someone who knows he's being watched. Alice sipped the white wine that he had poured and the alcohol produced little explosions in her stomach, which had been empty for at least twenty hours. The heat spread along her arteries, then rose slowly to her head and swept away the thought of Mattia, like the evening tide when it reclaims the beach.

Sitting at the table, Alice carefully assessed Fabio's silhouette, the clear line that separated his chestnut hair from his neck, his pelvis, which was not especially slender, and his shoulders, somewhat inflated under his shirt. She found herself thinking of how it would feel to be safely trapped in his arms, with no more possibility to choose.

She had accepted his invitation because she had told Mattia about him and because—she was sure of it now—what she could find here was more like love than anything else she would ever have.

Fabio opened the fridge and from a stick of butter cut a slice that Alice thought was at least 80 or 90 grams. He threw it into the pan to thicken the risotto and it melted, giving up all its saturated and animal fats. He turned off the flame and stirred the risotto with a wooden spoon for another few minutes.

"Dinner's ready," he said.

He dried his hands on a dishcloth hanging over a chair and turned toward the table, holding the frying pan.

Alice darted a terrified glance at the contents.

"Just a little for me," she said, gesturing a pinch with her fingers, right before he poured a hypercaloric ladleful onto her plate.

"You don't like it?"

"It's not that," lied Alice. "It's just that I'm allergic to mushrooms. But I'll try it."

Fabio looked disappointed and stood there with the frying pan in midair. He actually lost a little color from his face.

"Damn, I'm really sorry. I had no idea."

"It doesn't matter. Really." Alice smiled at him.

"If you want I can—" he went on.

Alice hushed him by taking his hand. Fabio looked at her as a child looks at a present.

"I can try it, though," said Alice.

Fabio resolutely shook his head.

"Absolutely not. What if it makes you ill?"

He took the pan away and Alice couldn't help smiling. For a good half hour they sat talking over the empty plates and Fabio had to open another bottle of white.

Alice had the pleasant sensation of losing part of herself with each sip. She was aware of the insubstantiality of her own body and at the same time of the massive bulk of Fabio's, sitting in front of her with his elbows resting on the table and his shirtsleeves rolled halfway up his forearms. The thought of Mattia, so incessant over the past few weeks, vibrated faintly in the air like a slightly slackened violin string, a dissonant note lost in the middle of an orchestra.

"Well, we can console ourselves with the main course," said Fabio.

Alice thought she was going to faint. She had hoped it was going to end there. Instead Fabio rose from the table and took from the oven a baking dish with two tomatoes, two eggplants, and two yellow peppers, stuffed with something that looked like ground beef mixed with bread crumbs. The composition of colors was cheerful, but Alice immediately thought of the exorbitant dimensions of those vegetables and imagined them, completely whole as they were now, in the middle of her stomach, like rocks at the bottom of a pond.

"You choose," Fabio said invitingly.

Alice bit her lip. Then she timidly pointed at the tomato and he transferred it onto her plate, using a knife and fork as pincers.

"And?"

"That's enough," said Alice.

"Impossible. You haven't eaten a thing. And with all that you've drunk!"

Alice looked at him and for a moment she hated him deeply, as much as she hated her father, her mother, Sol, and anyone else who had ever counted the things on her plate.

"That one," she said, giving in, pointing at the eggplant.

Fabio served himself one of each vegetable, and before attacking them he looked at them with satisfaction. Alice tried the stuffing, barely touching it with the tip of her fork. Apart from the meat she immediately recognized eggs, ricotta, and Parmesan and hastily calculated that a whole day of fasting wouldn't be enough to compensate.

"How is it?" Fabio asked, smiling, with his mouth half full.

"Delicious," she replied.

She summoned up the courage to bite into a mouthful of eggplant. She gulped back her nausea and went on, one bite after another, without saying a word. She finished the whole eggplant, and as soon as she had set her fork down next to her plate, she was assailed by a sudden urge to vomit. Fabio was talking and pouring more wine. Alice nodded and with each movement she felt the eggplant dancing up and down in her stomach.

Fabio had already shoveled everything down, while on Alice's plate there still lay the tomato, red and filled with that nauseating mixture. If she cut it into tiny pieces and hid it in her napkin he would notice immediately because there was nothing to hide her apart from the candles, which had already burned halfway down.

Then, like a blessing, the second bottle of wine was finished and Fabio struggled from the table to get a third. He held his head in his hands and said out loud to her stop, please stop. Alice laughed. Fabio looked in the fridge and opened all the cupboards, but he couldn't find another bottle.

"I think my parents must have finished all the wine," he said. "I'll have to go to the cellar."

He exploded with laughter for no reason and Alice laughed with him, even though it hurt her stomach.

"Don't you move from there," he commanded, pointing a finger at his forehead.

"Okay," Alice replied and the idea came to her straightaway.

As soon as Fabio was gone, she picked up the greasy tomato with two fingers and carried it to the bathroom, holding it at arm's length to avoid the smell. She locked herself in, lifted the seat, and the toilet smiled at her as if saying leave it to me.

Alice studied the tomato. It was big, perhaps it needed to be cut up into little pieces, but it was also soft, and she said to herself who cares and threw it in as it was. It dropped in with a plop, and a splash of water nearly stained her blue dress. The tomato settled on the bottom and disappeared halfway down the drain.

She flushed and the water came down like healing rain, but instead of disappearing down the hole, it started filling the bowl and a less than reassuring gurgle rose from the bottom.

Alice drew back in horror and her bad leg wobbled so much that she almost ended up on the floor. She watched the water level rise and rise and then suddenly stop.

The sound of the siphon kicked in. The bowl was full to the brim. The surface of the transparent water quivered slightly and there at the bottom, motionless, was the tomato, trapped in the same spot as before.

Alice stood and looked at it for at least a minute, frozen with panic and at the same time strangely curious. She was reawakened by the sound of the key turning in the front door. She took the toilet brush and plunged it into the water, her face contorted into a grimace of disgust. The tomato just wouldn't move.

"What do I do now?" she whispered to herself.

Then, almost unconsciously, she flushed again, and this time the water began to spill out and spread over the floor in a thin layer, until it licked at Alice's elegant shoes. She tried to flush again, but the water kept flowing and pouring out, and if Alice hadn't put the rug over it, it would have reached the door and from there the other room.

After a few seconds the water stopped again. The tomato was still down there, intact. The lake on the floor had ceased spreading. Mattia had once explained to her that there's a precise point at which water stops spreading, when the surface tension has become strong enough to hold it together, like a film.

Alice looked at the mess she had made. She closed the lid of the toilet, as if surrendering to disaster, and sat down on it. She brought her hands to her closed eyes and began to cry. She cried for Mattia, for her mother, for her father, for all that water, but mostly for herself. Under her breath she called Mattia, as if seeking his help, but his name remained on her lips, sticky and insubstantial.

Fabio knocked at the bathroom door but she didn't move.

"Ali, everything okay?"

Alice could see his outline through the frosted glass of the door. She sniffed quietly and cleared her throat to disguise her tears.

"Sure," she said. "I'll be there in a minute."

She looked around, lost, as if she really didn't know how she'd ended up in that bathroom. The water from the toilet bowl dripped onto the floor in at least three different places and Alice hoped, for a moment, that she could drown in those few millimeters of water.

GETTING THINGS IN FOCUS

2003

She had turned up at Marcello Crozza's studio at ten o'clock one morning and, feigning a determination that had cost her three walks around the block, had said I want to learn the trade, could you take me on as an apprentice? Crozza, who was sitting by the automatic developer, had nodded. Then he had turned around and, looking her straight in the eyes, had said I can't pay you. He hadn't wanted to say forget it, because he'd done the same thing himself many years before and the memory of the courage it had taken him was all that was left of his passion for photography. In spite of all his disappointments, he wouldn't have denied anyone that sensation.

They were mostly vacation photos. Families of three or four people, by the sea or in tourist destinations, hugging in the middle of St. Mark's Square or under the Eiffel Tower, with their feet cut off and always in the same pose. Photographs taken with automatic cameras, overexposed or out of focus. Alice didn't even look at them anymore: she developed them and then slipped them all into the paper envelope with the yellow and red Kodak logo.

It was mostly a matter of being in the shop, receiving rolls of twenty-four or thirty-six shots, shut away in their little plastic containers, of marking the customer's name on the slip and telling them they'll be ready tomorrow, of printing out receipts and saying thank you, good-bye.

Sometimes, on Saturdays, there were weddings. Crozza picked her up from home at a quarter to nine, always in the same suit and without his tie, because in the end he was the photographer, not a guest.

169

In church they had to set up the two lights, and on one of the first occasions Alice had dropped one and it had smashed on the steps of the altar and she had looked at Crozza in terror. He had pulled a face as if one of the pieces of glass had gotten stuck in his leg, but then he had said never mind, just clean it up.

He was fond of her and didn't know why. Perhaps because he had no children, or because since Alice had been working there he was able to go to the bar at eleven o'clock and check his lottery numbers and when he came back to the shop she smiled at him and asked him so, are we rich? Perhaps because she had that bad leg and lacked a mother as he lacked a wife and all lacks are pretty much the same. Or because he was sure that she would soon get tired of him and in the evening he would pull down the security gate on his own again and set off for home where no one was waiting, with his head empty and yet so very heavy.

Instead, after a year and a half, Alice was still there. Now that she had the keys she arrived before him in the morning and Crozza found her on the sidewalk in front of the shop, chatting with the lady from the grocer's next door, with whom he had never exchanged more than a "Good morning." He paid her under the table, five hundred euros a month. If they did weddings together he would drop her outside the door of the Della Rocca house and, with the engine of his Lancia still running, take out his wallet and hand her an extra fifty, saying see you Monday.

Sometimes she brought him her own snapshots and asked his opinion, even though it was clear to both of them that he had nothing more to teach her. They sat down at the desk and Crozza looked at the photographs, holding them up to the light, and gave her some advice about exposure time, or how best to use the shutter. He let her use his Nikon whenever she wanted and had secretly decided that he would give it to her as a present the day she left.

"We're getting married on Saturday," said Crozza. It was his way of saying they had a job.

Alice was putting on her denim jacket. Fabio would be there to pick her up at any moment.

"Okay," she said. "Where?"

"At the Gran Madre. Then there's a reception in a private villa in the hills. Rich folks' stuff," commented Crozza with a touch of disdain, immediately regretting it because he knew that Alice came from that world too.

"Hmm," she murmured. "Do you know who they are?"

"They sent the invitation. I've put it over there somewhere," said Crozza, pointing to the shelf under the cash register.

Alice looked in her bag for a rubber band and pulled back her hair. Crozza watched from across the shop. Once he had masturbated thinking about her, kneeling in the gloom after they'd lowered the security gate, but then he had felt so dreadful that he hadn't eaten and the next day he had sent her home saying you've got the day off today, I don't want anyone underfoot.

Alice rummaged among the sheets of paper stacked under the counter, more to fill the time while waiting than out of genuine interest. She found the envelope with the invitation, stiff and imposingly large. She opened it and the name leaped off the page in a gilded cursive, full of flourishes.

Ferruccio Carlo Bai and Maria Luisa Bai are delighted to announce the marriage of their daughter Viola . . .

Her eyes darkened before she went any further. A metallic taste flooded her mouth. She swallowed and it was like gulping down that fruit candy from the locker room all over again. She closed the envelope and waved it in the air for a moment, thinking.

"Can I go alone?" she ventured at last, her back still turned to Crozza.

He shut the drawer of the cash register with a rattle and a ding.

"What?" he asked.

Alice turned around and her eyes were wide open and bright with something and Crozza couldn't help smiling, they were so beautiful.

"I've learned how by now, haven't I?" said Alice, walking over to him. "I can do it. Otherwise I'll never be able to manage on my own."

Crozza looked at her suspiciously. She rested her elbows on the desk, right in front of him, and leaned toward him. She was only a few inches from his nose and that gleam in her eyes begged him to say yes and not to ask for explanations.

"I don't know if—"

"Please," Alice broke in.

Crozza stroked his earlobe and was forced to look away.

"All right, then," he gave in. He didn't understand why he was whispering. "But don't screw it up."

"I promise," Alice said, making her translucent lips disappear into a smile.

Then she pushed herself forward on her elbows and gave him a kiss, which tickled Crozza's three-day beard.

"Go on, go on," he said, dismissing her with his hand.

Alice laughed and the sound of it scattered through the air as she left with that sinuous, rhythmic gait of hers.

That evening Crozza stayed a little longer than usual in the shop, doing nothing. He looked at the things around him and noticed that they had more presence, as they had many years before when they seemed to be asking him to take their picture.

He took the camera out of the bag, where Alice always put it back after giving all the lenses and mechanisms a good clean. He screwed on the lens and aimed it at the first object that came into view, the umbrella stand by the entrance. He enlarged part of the rounded edge until it looked like something else, like the crater of an extinct volcano. But then he didn't take the picture.

He put the camera away, picked up his jacket, turned out the lights, and left. He closed the security gate with the padlock and headed in the opposite direction from his usual one. He couldn't seem to wipe the stupid smile from his face and he really had no desire to go home.

The church was decorated with two enormous bouquets of lilies and daisies, arranged on either side of the altar, and with dozens of miniature copies of the same bouquet at the end of each pew. Alice set up the lights and arranged the reflector panel. Then she sat in the first row and waited. A lady was running the vacuum cleaner over the red carpet that Viola would walk down in an hour. Alice thought about when she and Viola used to sit on the railings and talk. She couldn't remember what they had talked about, only that she had looked at her rapt from a place just behind her eyes, a place full of jumbled thoughts that she had kept to herself even then.

Over the next half hour all the pews filled up and people accumulated at the back, where they stood fanning themselves with the order of service.

Alice went outside and waited on the cobblestones for the bride's car to arrive. High in the sky the sun warmed her hands and its rays seemed to pass right through them. As a little girl she had liked looking at her palms against the light, the red peeking through her closed fingers. Once she had shown it to her father and he had kissed her fingertips, pretending to eat them.

Viola arrived in a gleaming gray Porsche, and the driver had to help her out and pick up her cumbersome train. Alice madly snapped away, more to hide her face behind the camera than anything else. Then, when the bride passed by, she lowered it deliberately and smiled at her.

They looked at each other for only a moment and Viola caught her breath. Alice couldn't study her expression, because the bride had already passed her and was entering the church on her father's arm. For some reason Alice had always imagined him taller.

She was careful not to lose so much as a moment. She took various close-ups of the happy couple and their families. She immortalized the exchange of rings, the reading of the promises, the communion, the kiss, and the signing of the register. She was the only one moving in the whole church. It seemed to Alice that Viola's shoulders stiffened slightly when she was near her. She increased the exposure time still further, to obtain the blurry quality that, according to Crozza, suggested eternity.

As the couple left the church, Alice walked ahead of them, limping backward, bending slightly so as not to alter her height with a low perspective. Through the lens she became aware that Viola was looking at her with a frightened half-smile, as if she were the only one who could see a ghost. Alice exploded the flash in her face at regular intervals, about fifteen times, until the bride was forced to narrow her eyes.

She watched them get into the car and Viola darted her a glance from behind the window. She was sure she would immediately start talking to her husband about her, about how strange it was to have come across her there. She would describe her as the class anorexic, the cripple, someone she had never hung out with. She wouldn't mention the candy or the party or all the rest. Alice smiled at the thought that it might be their first half-truth as a married couple, the first of the tiny cracks that would eventually converge into a gaping hole.

"Miss, the bride and groom are waiting on the riverbank for you to photograph them," said a voice behind her.

Alice turned around and recognized one of the witnesses.

"Certainly. I'll be right there," she replied.

She quickly went into the church to dismantle her equipment. She was still putting the various pieces of the camera in the rectangular case when she heard someone calling to her.

"Alice?"

She turned around, already sure who had been speaking.

"Yes?"

Standing in front of her were Giada Savarino and Giulia Mirandi.

"Hi," said Giada ostentatiously, approaching Alice to kiss her on both cheeks.

Giulia stayed where she was, staring at her feet as she had done at school.

Alice barely brushed Giada's cheek with her own pursed lips.

"What on earth are you doing here?" shrieked Giada.

Alice thought it was a stupid question and couldn't help smiling.

"I'm taking photographs," she replied.

Giada responded with a smile, showing the same dimples she had had at seventeen.

It was strange to find them here, still alive, with their shared bits of past that suddenly counted for nothing.

"Hi, Giulia," Alice forced herself to say.

Giulia smiled at her and struggled to speak.

"We heard about your mother," she said. "We're really sorry."

Giada nodded repeatedly, to show her agreement.

"Yeah," replied Alice. "Thanks."

She started hastily putting things away. Giada and Giulia looked at each other.

"We'll let you get on with your work," Giada said, touching her shoulder. "You're very busy."

"Okay."

They turned around and walked toward the exit, the crisp click of their heels echoing off the walls of the now empty church.

The couple was waiting in the shade of a big tree standing some feet apart. Alice parked next to their Porsche and got out with the shoulder bag. It was hot and she felt her hair sticking to the back of her neck.

"Hi," she said, walking over.

"Alice," said Viola. "I didn't think—"

"Neither did I," Alice cut in.

They pretended to hug, as if not wanting to rumple their clothes. Viola was even more beautiful than she had been at school. Over the years her features had grown milder, the outlines were softer, and her eyes had lost that imperceptible vibration that made them so terrible. She still had that perfect body.

"This is Carlo," said Viola.

Alice shook his hand and felt how smooth it was.

"Shall we start?" she asked, cutting her short.

Viola nodded and sought her husband's eyes, but he didn't notice.

"Where shall we stand?" she asked.

Alice looked around. The sun was at its zenith and she would have to use the flash to eliminate all the shadows from their faces. She pointed to a bench in full sunlight on the riverbank.

"Sit down there," she said.

She took longer than was necessary to set up the camera. She pretended to busy herself with the flash, mounted one lens and then swapped it for another one. Viola's husband fanned himself with his tie, while she used her finger to try to stop the little drops of sweat trickling down her forehead.

Alice left them to stew for a bit longer as she pretended to find
the right distance to take the picture.

Then she started issuing brusque orders. Put your arms around
each other, smile, now serious, take her by the hand, rest your head
on his shoulder, whisper in her ear, look at each other, closer, toward
the river, take your jacket off. Crozza had taught her that you mustn't
let your subjects breathe, you mustn't give them time to think, because it takes only a minute for the spontaneity to evaporate.

Viola obeyed, two or three times asking apprehensively is that all
right?

"Okay, now let's go into the field," said Alice.

"More?" asked Viola, startled. The red of her flushed cheeks was
starting to show through her foundation. Her eyeliner was already
slightly smudged, the edges were getting jagged, making her look
tired and slightly shabby.

"You pretend to run away and let him chase you across the field,"
Alice explained.

"What? You want me to run?"

"Yes, run."

"But . . ." Viola began to protest. She looked at her husband and
he shrugged.

She snorted, then lifted up her skirt and began running. Her heels
sank a few millimeters into the ground, and kicked up little clumps
that dirtied the inside of her white dress. Her husband ran after her.

"You're going too slowly," he said.

Viola turned around all of a sudden with a look that reduced
him to ashes, a look that Alice remembered all too well. She let
them run after each other for two or three minutes, until Viola
freed herself clumsily from her husband's clutches, saying that's
enough.

Her hair had come undone on one side and a lock fell down her
cheek.

"Yes," said Alice. "Just a few more shots."

She took them to the ice-cream stand and bought two lemon ice pops, which she paid for herself.

"Hold these," she said, extending them to the couple.

They seemed not to understand, and unwrapped them suspiciously. Viola was careful not to get the sticky syrup all over her hands.

They had to pretend to eat them, arms crossed, and then offer the other a lick. Viola's smile was becoming increasingly tense.

When Alice told her to hold on to the street lamp and use it as a pivot to spin around, Viola exploded.

"This is ridiculous," she said.

Her husband looked at her, slightly intimidated, and then looked at Alice, as if to apologize.

Alice smiled. "It's part of the classic album," she explained. "That's what you asked for. But we can skip that sequence."

She forced herself to sound sincere. She felt her tattoo pulsating, as if it wanted to jump out of her skin. Viola stared at her furiously and Alice held her gaze until her eyes burned.

"Have we finished?" said Viola.

Alice nodded.

"Let's go, then," the bride said to her husband.

Before letting himself be dragged away, he came over to Alice and shook her hand politely once more.

"Thanks," he said.

"My pleasure."

Alice watched them climb back up the slight slope to the parking lot. Around her were the usual sounds of Saturday, the laughter of children on the swings and the voices of the mothers looking after them. There was music in the distance and the rush of cars on the road, like a carpet of sound.

She wanted to tell Mattia, because he would have understood. But he was far away now. She thought that Crozza would be furious, but he would forgive her in the end. She was sure of it.

She smiled. She opened the back of the camera, took out the film, and unrolled it completely under the white light of the sun.

WHAT REMAINS

2007

His father phoned on Wednesday evenings, between eight and a quarter past. They had seen each other rarely over the last nine years and it had been a long time since the last visit, but the phone call in Mattia's two-room apartment had become a ritual. In the long pauses between words the same old silence arose between the two of them: there were no televisions or radios on, never any guests rattling their cutlery.

Mattia could imagine his mother listening to the phone call from her armchair without changing her expression, with both arms on the armrests, as when he and Michela were in primary school and she sat there listening to them recite poetry by heart and Mattia always knew it while Michela said nothing, incapable of doing anything.

Every Wednesday, after hanging up, Mattia found himself wondering whether the orange floral pattern of that armchair was still the same or whether they'd replaced it, since it had been threadbare even back then. He wondered whether his parents had grown old. Of course they had, he heard it in his father's voice, which was slower and wearier, more like an attack of breathlessness.

His mother came to the phone infrequently and her questions were a matter of form, always the same. Is it cold? Have you had your dinner yet? How are your classes going? We eat dinner at seven over here, Mattia had explained the first few times. Now he merely said yes.

"Hello?" he said, speaking in Italian.

There was no reason to answer the phone in English. Only about ten people had his home number and none of them would have dreamed of calling him at that time of day.

"It's Dad."

The delay in his reply was only just perceptible. Mattia meant to get a stopwatch to measure it, to calculate how much the signal deviated from the straight line of more than 1,000 kilometers that connected him and his father, but he forgot every time.

"Hi. Are you well?" said Mattia.

"Yes. And you?"

"Fine. . . . And Mom?"

"She's right here."

The first silence always fell at that point, like a mouthful of air after swimming a lap underwater.

Mattia ran his index finger along the scratch in the pale wood of the round table, a few inches from the middle. He couldn't even remember whether he had scratched it or whether it had been the old tenants. Just under the enameled surface it was compressed chipboard, which got under his fingernail without hurting him. Each Wednesday he dug that furrow a few fractions of a millimeter deeper, but a lifetime wouldn't be enough for him to break through to the other side.

"So you saw the sunrise?" his father asked.

Mattia smiled. It was a joke they had between them, perhaps the only one. About a year before, somewhere in a newspaper Pietro had read that watching the dawn over the North Sea is an unforgettable experience, and in the evening he had read his son the clipping over the phone. You absolutely have to go, he had advised. Since that day he asked from time to time so have you seen it? Mattia always answered no. His alarm was set to seventeen minutes past eight and the shortest way to the university was not along the seafront.

"No, no dawn yet," he replied.

"Well, it's not going anywhere," said Pietro.

They had already run out of things to say, but they lingered for a few seconds, the receivers pressed to their ears. They both breathed in a little of the affection that still survived between them, diluted along hundreds of miles of coaxial cables and nourished by something whose name they didn't know and which perhaps, if they thought too carefully about it, no longer existed.

"I'll say good-bye, then," Pietro said at last.

"Sure."

"And try to keep well."

"Okay. Say hi to Mum."

They hung up.

For Mattia it was the end of the day. He walked around the table. He looked distractedly at the papers stacked up on one side, the work he'd brought back from the office. He was still stuck on the same step. No matter where they began the proof, he and Alberto always ended up banging their heads against it sooner or later. He was sure that the solution lay just beyond that final obstacle, and that once past it getting to the end would be easy, like rolling down a grassy slope with his eyes closed.

But he was too tired to go back to work. He went into the kitchen and filled a pan with water from the tap. He put it on the stove and lit the gas. He spent so much time on his own that a normal person would have gone crazy in a month.

He sat down on the folding plastic chair, without completely relaxing. He looked up toward the unlit bulb dangling in the middle of the ceiling. It had blown just a month after he'd arrived, and he'd never bothered to replace it. He ate with the light turned on in the other room.

If he had simply upped and left the apartment that very evening and not come back, no one would have found any sign of his presence, apart from those incomprehensible pages stacked on the table. Mattia had put nothing of himself into the place. He had kept the anonymous pale oak furniture and the yellowed wallpaper that had been stuck to the walls since the building was constructed.

He got to his feet. He poured boiling water into a cup and immersed a tea bag in it. He watched the water turn dark. The methane flame was still lit and in the gloom it was violently blue. He lowered the flame until it was almost out and the hiss faded. He held his hand over the burner. The heat exerted a faint pressure on his devastated palm. Mattia brought it down slowly, and closed it around the flame.

He had spent hundreds and thousands of identical days at the university, and consumed innumerable cafeteria lunches in the little low building on the edge of the campus, but even now he remembered the very first day when he had walked in and copied the sequence of gestures of the other people. He had joined the line and, taking small steps, had reached the pile of plastic imitation-wood trays. He had picked one up, set the paper napkin on it, and helped himself to cutlery and a glass. Then, once he was in front of the uniformed woman who served up the portions, he had pointed to one of the three aluminum tubs, at random, without knowing what was in them. The cook had asked him something, in her own language or perhaps in English, and he hadn't understood. He had pointed to the tub again and she had repeated the question, exactly the same as before. Mattia shook his head. I don't understand, he had said in English in a loud and nervy voice. She had raised her eyes to the sky and waved the empty plate in the air. She's asking you if you want sauce on that muck, said the young man next to him in Italian. Mattia had spun around, disoriented, and shook his head. The young man had turned toward the dinner lady and simply said no. She had smiled at him and finally filled Mattia's dish and handed it to him. The young man had chosen the same and had brought it up to his nose and sniffed it with disgust. This stuff is revolting, he had observed.

You've just got here, then? he had asked him after a while, still staring at the thick puree on the plate. Mattia had said yes and the young man had nodded with a frown, as if it were a serious matter. After paying, Mattia had frozen in front of the cash register, his hands gripping the tray. He had looked around for an empty table, somewhere he could avoid feeling people's eyes on him and eat alone. He had just taken a step toward the back of the room when the young man from before had overtaken him and said come on, over here.

Alberto Torcia had already been there for four years, with a permanent research post funded by the European Union for the quality of his most recent publications. He too had escaped from something, but Mattia had never asked him what. Neither of them, after so many years, could have said whether the other was a friend or just a colleague, in spite of the fact that they shared an office and had lunch together every day.

It was Tuesday. Alberto sat down opposite Mattia and, through the glass of water that he brought to his lips, glimpsed the new mark, pale and perfectly circular, on his palm. Alberto didn't ask any questions, but merely gave him a crooked glance to let him know that he understood. Gilardi and Montanari, sitting at the same table, were sniggering over something they had found on the Internet.

Mattia drained his glass in one gulp, then cleared his throat.

"Yesterday evening an idea came to me about the discontinuity that—"

"Please, Mattia," Alberto interrupted him, dropping his fork and flopping back in his seat. His gestures were always very exaggerated. "At least have pity on me when I'm eating."

Mattia looked at the table. The slice of meat on his plate was cut into identical little squares and he separated them with his fork, leaving between them a regular grill of white lines.

"Why don't you do something else with your evenings?" Alberto went on more quietly, as if he didn't want the other two to hear him. As he spoke he drew little circles in the air with his knife.

Mattia said nothing and didn't look at him. He brought a little square of meat to his mouth, chosen from the ones on the edge whose fringed borders disturbed the geometry of the composition.

"If only you'd come and have a drink with us every now and again," Alberto continued.

"No," Mattia said brusquely.

"But—" Alberto protested.

"Anyway, you know."

Alberto shook his head and frowned, defeated. After all this time he still insisted, even though in all the years they had known each other he had managed to drag him out of the house only a dozen or so times.

He turned to the other two, breaking into their conversation.

"Have you seen her over there?" he asked, pointing to a young woman sitting two tables away with an elderly gentleman. As far as Mattia knew, the man was a geology professor. "If only I wasn't married, Christ, what I could do to a woman like that."

The others hesitated for a moment, because it had nothing to do with what they were talking about, but then they shifted gears and joined in, speculating about what such a babe was doing with an old windbag like that.

Mattia cut all the little squares of meat along the diagonal. Then he reassembled the triangles so as to form a larger one. The meat was already cold and tough. He took a piece of it and swallowed it almost whole. The rest he left where they were.

Outside the dining hall Alberto lit a cigarette, to give Gilardi and Montanari time to move away. He waited for Mattia, who was following a rectilinear crack along the ground and thinking about something that had nothing to do with being there.

"What were you saying about discontinuity?" he said.

"It doesn't matter."

"Come on, don't be a dick."

Mattia looked at his colleague. The tip of the cigarette between his lips was the only color that brightened that entirely gray day, the same as the one before and doubtless the same as the one that would follow.

"We can't escape it," said Mattia. "We've convinced ourselves that it exists. But I may have found a way to get something interesting out of it."

Alberto came closer. He didn't interrupt Mattia until he had finished his explanation, because he knew that Mattia didn't talk much, but when he did it was worth shutting up and listening.

32

The weight of consequences had collapsed on her all at once one evening a few years before, when Fabio, as he pushed inside her, had whispered I want to have a baby. His face was so close to Alice's that she had felt his breath sliding along her cheeks and dispersing among the sheets.

She had pulled him to her, guiding his head into the hollow between her neck and shoulder. Once, before they were married, he had told her it was the perfect fit, that his head was made to slip into that space.

So what do you think? Fabio had asked her, his voice muffled by the pillow. Alice hadn't replied, but had held him a bit tighter. She hadn't had the breath to speak.

She'd heard him closing the drawer with the condoms in it and had bent her right knee a little more to make room for him. Rhythmically she stroked his hair, her eyes wide open.

That secret had crept after her since her school days, but it had never taken hold of her mind for more than a few seconds. Alice had set it aside, like something she would think about later on. Now, all of a sudden, there it was, like an abyss cut into the black ceiling of the room, monstrous and irrepressible. Alice wanted to say to Fabio stop for a moment, wait, there's something I haven't told you, but he moved with disarming trust and he certainly wouldn't have understood.

She felt him come inside her, for the first time, and imagined that sticky liquid full of promise that he deposited in her dry body, where it too would dry.

She didn't want a baby, or maybe she did. She hadn't ever really thought about it. The question didn't arise and that was that. Her menstrual cycle had stopped around the last time she had eaten a whole chocolate pudding. The truth was that Fabio wanted a baby and she had to give him one. She had to, because when they made love he didn't ask her to turn the light on, not since the first time at his house. Because when it was over he lay on top of her and the weight of his body canceled out all her fears and he didn't speak, just breathed, and anyway he was there. She had to, because she didn't love him, but his love was enough for both of them, enough to keep them safe.

From then on sex had assumed a new guise. It bore within itself a precise purpose, which had soon led them to abandon everything that wasn't strictly necessary.

For weeks and then months nothing had happened. Fabio had himself examined and his sperm count was good. That evening he told Alice, being very careful to hold her tightly in his arms as he spoke. He immediately added you don't have to worry, it's not your fault. She pulled away and went into the other room before bursting into tears, and Fabio hated himself because he thought—in fact he knew—that it was his wife's fault.

Alice started feeling spied on. She kept a fictitious count of days, drawing little lines on the calendar beside the phone. She bought tampons and then threw them away unused. On the right days she pushed Fabio away in the dark, telling him we can't today.

He kept the same count, without telling her. Alice's secret, slimy and transparent, wormed its way between them, forcing them further and further apart. Every time he hinted at doctors, treatments, or the cause of the problem, Alice's face darkened and he was sure that it wouldn't be long before she found a pretext for an argument, any random nonsense.

Exhaustion slowly defeated them. They stopped talking about it and, along with the conversations, sex too had grown less frequent, until it was reduced to a laborious Friday night ritual. They took turns washing, before and after doing it. Fabio would come back from the bathroom, the skin of his face still gleaming with soap, wearing fresh underwear. In the meantime Alice would already have slipped on her T-shirt and would ask can I go now? When she came back into the room she would find him already asleep, or at least with his eyes closed, facing the wall and with his whole body on his side of the bed.

There was nothing very different about that Friday, at least at first. Alice joined him in bed just after one, having spent the whole evening shut up in the darkroom that Fabio had given her as a third anniversary present. He lowered the magazine he was reading and watched his wife's bare feet walk toward him, sticking to the wooden floor.

Alice slipped between the sheets and pressed herself against his side. Fabio let the magazine fall to the floor and turned out the bedside light. He did everything he could to not make it look like a habit, a duty, but the truth was clear to both of them.

They followed a series of movements that had become consolidated into a routine over time, and which made everything simpler, then Fabio entered her, with the help of his fingers.

Alice wasn't sure that he was really crying, because he held his head tilted to one side to avoid contact with her skin, but she noticed that there was something different in his way of moving. He was thrusting more violently and more urgently than usual, then he would stop suddenly, his breath heavy, and start again, as though torn between the desire to penetrate more deeply and the desire to slip away from her and from the room. She heard him sniffing as he panted.

When he finished he quickly withdrew, got out of bed, and went and shut himself in the bathroom, without even turning on the light.

He stayed there for longer than usual. Alice moved toward the middle of the bed, where the sheets were still cool. She put a hand on her stomach, in which nothing was happening, and, for the first time, thought she no longer had anyone to blame, that all these mistakes were hers alone.

Fabio crossed the room in the semidarkness, climbed into bed, and turned his back to her. It was Alice's turn, but she didn't move. She felt that something was about to happen, the air was full of it.

It took him another minute, or perhaps two, before he spoke.

"Ali," he said.

"Yes?"

He hesitated again.

"I can't do this anymore," he said softly.

Alice felt his words gripping her belly, like climbing plants sprouting suddenly from the bed. She didn't reply. She let him go on.

"I know what it is," Fabio went on. His voice grew clearer. As it struck the walls it assumed a slight metallic echo. "You don't want to let me in, you don't even want me to talk about it. But this . . ."

He stopped. Alice's eyes were open. They were accustomed to the dark. She followed the outlines of the furniture: the armchair, the wardrobe, the chest of drawers and on top of it the mirror that didn't reflect anything. All those objects sitting there, motionless and terribly insistent.

Alice thought of her parents' room. She thought how similar they were, that all bedrooms in the world were similar. She wondered what she was afraid of, losing him or losing those things: the curtains, the paintings, the carpet, all that security folded carefully away in the drawers.

"You barely ate two zucchinis this evening," Fabio went on.

"I wasn't hungry," she replied automatically.

Here we go, she thought.

"The same yesterday. You didn't even touch the meat. You cut it up into little pieces and then hid it in your napkin. Do you really think I'm that stupid?"

Alice clenched the sheets. How could she have thought he would never notice? She saw again the hundreds, thousands of times in which the same scene had repeated itself before her husband's eyes. She was furious about all the things he must have thought in silence.

"I expect you also know what I ate the evening before and the evening before that," she said.

"Tell me what it is," he said, loudly this time. "Tell me what it is that you find so repellent about food."

She thought of her father bringing his face down to the plate when he ate soup, the sound he made, how he sucked the spoon rather than simply putting it in his mouth. She thought with disgust of the chewed-up pulp between her husband's teeth every time he sat in front of her for dinner. She thought of Viola's gumdrop, with all those hairs stuck to it and its synthetic strawberry flavor. Then she thought about herself, without her T-shirt, reflected in the big mirror in her old house, and the scar that made her leg something slightly apart, something detached from her torso and useless. She thought of the balance, so fragile, of her own silhouette, the thin strip of shadow that her ribs cast over her belly and which she was prepared to defend at all costs.

"What is it you want? Do you want me to start stuffing myself? To deform myself to have your baby?" She spoke as if the baby were already there, somewhere in the universe. She called it your baby on purpose. "I can do some sort of treatment if you're so keen on the idea. I can take hormones, medicine, all the junk necessary to let you have this child of yours. Maybe then you'll stop spying on me."

"That isn't the point," Fabio shot back. He had suddenly regained all his irritating self-confidence.

Alice moved toward the edge of the bed to get away from his

threatening body. He rolled onto his back. His eyes were open and his face was tense, as if he were trying to see something beyond the darkness.

"Isn't it?"

"You should think about all the risks, particularly in your condition."

In your condition, Alice silently repeated to herself. She instinctively tried to bend her weak knee, to demonstrate to herself that she was in full control, but it barely moved.

"Poor Fabio," she said. "With that wife of his, crippled and . . ."

She couldn't finish her sentence. That last word, already trembling in the air, caught in her throat.

"There's a part of the brain," he began, ignoring her, as though an explanation might make everything simpler, "probably the hypothalamus, which controls the body mass index. If that index falls too low, gonadotropin production is inhibited. The mechanism is blocked, and menstruation stops. But that's just the first of the symptoms. Other things happen, more serious. The density of minerals in the bones diminishes and osteoporosis ensues. The bones crumble like wafers."

He talked like a doctor, listing causes and effects in a monotonous voice, as if knowing the name of an illness were the same as curing it. Alice reflected that her bones had already crumbled once, and that these things didn't interest her.

"Raising that index is enough for everything to return to normal," Fabio added. "It's a slow process, but we still have time."

Alice lifted herself up on her elbows. She wanted to leave the room.

"Fantastic. I suppose you've had all this ready for a while," she remarked. "That's all there is to it. Easy as that."

Fabio sat up as well. He took her arm, but she pulled away. He stared into her eyes through the gloom.

"It's not only about you anymore," he said.

Alice shook her head.

"Yes, it is," she said. "Maybe it's what I really want, haven't you thought of that? I want to feel my bones crumbling, I want to block the mechanism. As you said yourself."

Fabio thumped the mattress, making her start.

"So now what do you want to do?" she said provocatively.

Fabio sucked in air through his teeth. The compressed violence in his lungs made his arms stiffen.

"You're just selfish. You're spoiled and selfish."

He threw himself on the bed and turned his back to her again. All of a sudden things seemed to return to their place in the shadows. There was silence again, but it was an imprecise silence. Alice noticed a faint whirring sound, like the rustle of old films in the cinema. She listened, trying to work out where it was coming from.

Then she saw the outline of her husband bobbing slightly up and down. She became aware of his suppressed sobs, like a rhythmical vibration of the mattress. His body asked her to stretch out a hand and touch him, to stroke his neck and his hair, but she didn't lift it. She got up from the bed and walked toward the bathroom, slamming the door behind her.

33

After lunch Alberto and Mattia headed down to the basement, where nothing ever changed and you measured the passing of time only by the heaviness of your eyes as they filled with the white light of the fluorescent bulbs on the ceiling. They went into an empty classroom and Alberto sat down on the teacher's desk. His body was massive, not exactly fat, but to Mattia it seemed as if it were constantly expanding.

"Fire away," said Alberto. "Tell me everything from the start."

Mattia picked up a piece of chalk and broke it in half. A fine white dust settled on the tips of his leather shoes, the same ones he had worn on the day of his graduation.

"Let's consider things in two dimensions," he said.

He started to write in his neat hand. He began at the top left corner and filled the first two blackboards. On the third he copied out the results that he would need later. It was as if he had performed this calculation hundreds of times, when in fact it was the first time he had pulled it out of his head. He turned toward Alberto every now and again, who nodded at him seriously, while his mind scampered to keep up with the chalk.

When he got to the end, after a good half hour, Mattia wrote "QED" next to the framed result, just as he had done when he was a boy. The chalk had dried the skin of his hand, but he didn't even notice. His legs were trembling slightly.

For about ten seconds they stayed there in quiet contemplation. 197 Then Alberto clapped his hands and the noise echoed through the silence like a whiplash. He got down off the desk and almost fell on the floor, because his legs had gone to sleep from dangling like that.

He put a hand on Mattia's shoulder and Mattia found it both heavy and reassuring.

"No bullshit this time," he said. "You're having dinner with me tonight; we've got something to celebrate."

Mattia smiled faintly.

"Okay," he said.

They cleaned the blackboard together. They took care that nothing legible was left, that no one would be able to make out so much as a shadow of what had been written on it. No one would really have understood it, but they were already jealous of the result, as one is of a beautiful secret.

They left the classroom and Mattia turned out the lights. Then they went upstairs, one behind the other, each savoring the little glory of that moment.

Alberto's house was in a residential area exactly like the one where Mattia lived, but on the other side of the city. Mattia took the bus, which was half empty, his forehead resting against the window. The contact between that cold surface and his skin soothed him, and made him think of the compress that his mother used to put on Michela's head, nothing but a damp cloth handkerchief, but enough to calm her in the evening when she had those attacks that made her tremble all over and grind her teeth. Michela wanted her brother to wear a compress too, she said so to her mother with her eyes, and so he would lie down on the bed and stay there, waiting for his sister to finish writhing.

He had showered and shaved, and had put on his shirt and black jacket. In a liquor store he had never entered before he had bought a bottle of red wine, choosing the one with the most elegant label. The lady had wrapped it up in a sheet of tissue paper and then put it in a silver-colored bag. Mattia rocked it back and forth like a pendulum as he waited for someone to open the door. With his foot he arranged the doormat in front of the door so that the perimeter aligned precisely with the lines of the paving.

Alberto's wife came to the door. She ignored both Mattia's outstretched hand and the bag with the bottle. Instead she drew him to her and kissed him on the cheek.

"I don't know what you two have been up to, but I've never seen Alberto as happy as he is tonight," she whispered. "Come in."

Mattia resisted the temptation to rub his ear against his shoulder to get rid of an itch.

"Albi, Mattia's here," she called.

Instead of Alberto, his son Philip appeared from the hall. Mattia knew him from the photograph that his father kept on his desk, in which Philip was still only a few months old, and round and impersonal like all newborn babies. It had never occurred to him that he might have grown. Some of his parents' features were forcibly making their way beneath his skin: Alberto's long chin, his mother's not-quite-open eyelids. Mattia thought about the cruel mechanism of growth, the soft cartilages subject to imperceptible but inexorable changes, and, just for a moment, about Michela and her features, frozen forever since that day in the park.

Philip came over, pedaling his tricycle like a boy possessed. When he noticed Mattia, he braked suddenly and stared at him in astonishment, as if he had been caught doing something forbidden. Alberto's wife gathered him in her arms, lifting him from the tricycle.

"Here's the horrid little monster," she said, burying her nose in his cheek.

Mattia gave him a forced smile. Children made him uneasy.

"Let's go in. Nadia's here already," Alberto's wife went on.

"Nadia?" said Mattia.

Alberto's wife looked at him, confused.

"Yes, Nadia," she said. "Didn't Albi tell you?"

"No."

There was a moment of embarrassment. Mattia didn't know a Nadia. He wondered what was going on and feared he already knew.

"Anyway she's in there. Come on."

As they walked toward the kitchen, Philip studied Mattia suspiciously, hiding behind his mother's back, his index and middle fingers in his mouth and his knuckles gleaming with saliva. Mattia was forced to look elsewhere. He remembered the time he had followed Alice down a longer hall than this one. He looked at Philip's scribbles hanging on the walls instead of paintings and was careful not to trample his toys scattered on the floor. The whole house, its very walls, was impregnated with a smell of vitality that he was unused to. He thought about his own apartment, where it was so easy to decide simply not to exist. He already regretted accepting the invitation to dinner.

In the kitchen Alberto greeted him, shaking his hand affectionately, and he responded automatically. The woman sitting at the table stood up and held out her hand.

"This is Nadia," Alberto said. "And this is our next Fields Medal winner."

"Nice to meet you," said Mattia, embarrassed.

Nadia smiled at him. She made as if to lean forward, perhaps to kiss him on the cheeks, but Mattia's motionlessness held her back.

"A pleasure," she said, and nothing more.

For a few seconds he remained absorbed by one of the big earrings that dangled from her ears: a gold circle at least five centimeters in diameter, which when she moved began swinging in a complicated motion that Mattia tried to decompose into the three Cartesian axes. The size of the earring and its contrast with Nadia's jet-black hair made him think of something shameless, almost obscene, that frightened and aroused him at the same time.

They sat down at the table and Alberto poured red wine for everyone. He grandly toasted the article they would soon write and obliged Mattia to explain to Nadia, in simple terms, what it was about. She joined in with an uncertain smile, which betrayed thoughts of a different kind and made him lose the thread of the conversation more than once.

"It sounds interesting," she observed finally, and Mattia looked down.

"It's much more than interesting," said Alberto, waving his hands around as if imitating the shape of an ellipsoid, which Mattia pictured in his mind.

Alberto's wife came in holding a soup tureen, from which emanated a strong smell of cumin. The conversation turned to food, a more neutral territory. A tension that they hadn't previously been aware of dissipated. Everyone, apart from Mattia, expressed nostalgia for some kind of delicacy that they couldn't get here in northern Europe. Alberto talked about the ravioli his mother used to make. His wife remembered the seafood salad they used to eat together in their university days, in that restaurant facing the beach. Nadia described the cannoli filled with fresh ricotta and dotted with tiny chips of dark black chocolate that the only pastry shop in her little village made. As she described them she kept her eyes closed and sucked in her lips as if she could still taste a little of that flavor. She caught her lower lip with her teeth for a moment and then let it go. Mattia fixed on that detail without realizing it. He thought there was something exaggerated about Nadia's femininity, in the fluidity with which she rolled her hands around, and the southern inflection with which she pronounced her labial consonants, almost doubling them when there was no need. It was as if she possessed a dark power, which depressed him and at the same time made his cheeks burn.

"You just need the courage to go back," Nadia concluded.

All four of them remained in silence for a few seconds, as if each were thinking about what it was that kept them so far from home. Philip banged his toys against one another a few feet away from the table.

Alberto was able to keep a tottering conversation alive all through dinner, often embarking on long monologues, his hands waving above an increasingly untidy table.

After dessert, his wife got up to collect the plates. Nadia made as if to help her, but she told her to stay where she was and disappeared into the kitchen.

They sat in silence. Lost in thought, Mattia ran an index finger along the serrated edge of his knife.

"I'll just go and see what she's up to in there," said Alberto, getting up as well. From behind Nadia's back he darted a glance at Mattia, which meant do your best.

He and Nadia were left on their own with Philip. They looked up at the same time, because there was nothing else to look at, and they both laughed with embarrassment.

"What about you?" Nadia said to him after a while. "Why did you choose to stay here?"

She studied him with her eyes half closed, as if trying to guess his secret. She had long, thick eyelashes and Mattia thought they were too still to be real.

He finished lining up the crumbs with his index finger. He shrugged.

"I don't know," he said. "It's as if there's more oxygen here."

She nodded reflectively, as if she had understood. From the kitchen came the voices of Alberto and his wife talking about ordinary things, about the tap that was leaking again and who would put Philip to bed, things that at that moment seemed tremendously important to Mattia.

Silence fell again and he forced himself to think of something to say, something that seemed normal. Nadia entered his field of vision wherever he looked, an awkward presence. The dark color of her low-cut top distracted him, even as he was staring at his empty glass. Under the table, hidden by the tablecloth, were their legs and he imagined them down there, in the dark, forced into a strained intimacy.

Philip came over and put a toy car in front of him, right on his napkin. Mattia looked at the miniature Maserati, then looked at Philip, who observed him in turn, waiting for him to decide to do something.

Rather hesitantly he picked up the toy car and made it go back and forth on the tablecloth. He felt Nadia's dense gaze upon him, assessing his embarrassment. With his mouth he imitated a shy vroom. Then he stopped. Philip stared at him in silence, slightly annoyed. He stretched out his arm, took the car back, and returned to his toys.

Mattia poured himself some more wine and drained it in one gulp. Then he realized that he should have offered some to Nadia first and asked her would you like some? She said no, no, drawing in her hands and hunching her shoulders, as people usually do when they're cold.

Alberto came back into the room and made a kind of grunt. He rubbed his face hard with his hands.

"Sleepy time," he said to the child. He lifted him up by the collar of his polo shirt as if he were a doll.

Philip followed him without protest. As he left he glanced back at his toys piled up on the floor as if he had hidden something in the middle of them.

"Maybe it's time for me to go too," said Nadia, not quite turning toward Mattia.

"Yeah, perhaps it's time," he said.

They both contracted their leg muscles as if to get up, but it was a false start. They stayed where they were and looked at each other again. Nadia smiled and Mattia felt pierced by her gaze, stripped to the bone as if he could no longer hide anything.

They got up, almost at the same time. They put their chairs next to the table and Mattia noticed that she too had the foresight to lift hers off the ground.

Alberto found them standing there, not knowing how to move.

"What's happening?" he said. "Are you off already?"

"It's late, you must be tired," Nadia replied for both of them.

Alberto looked at Mattia with a smile of complicity.

"I'll call you a taxi," he said.

"I'll take the bus," Mattia said quickly.

Alberto gave him a sidelong look.

"At this time of night? Come on," he said. "And besides, Nadia's place is on the way."

34

The taxi slipped along the deserted avenues on the edge of town, between identical buildings without balconies. Few windows were still lit. March days end early and people adapt their body clocks to the night.

"The cities are darker here," said Nadia, as if thinking out loud.

They sat at opposite ends of the backseat. Mattia stared at the changing numbers on the taxi's meter, and watched the red segments going off and on to compose the various figures.

Nadia thought about the ridiculous space of solitude that separated them and tried to find the courage to occupy it with her body. Her apartment was only a few blocks away and time, like the road, was being consumed in a great hurry. It wasn't just the time of that particular evening, it was the time of possibilities, of her nearly thirty-five years. Over the past year, since breaking up with Martin, she had begun to notice the foreignness of the place, to suffer from the chill that dried her skin and never really left her, even in the summer. And yet she couldn't make up her mind to leave. She depended on the place now; she had grown attached to it with the obstinacy with which people become attached only to things that hurt them.

She reflected that if anything was going to be resolved, it would be resolved in that car. Afterward she would no longer have the strength. She would finally abandon herself, without remorse, to her translations, to the books whose pages she dissected by day and night, to earn her living and fill the holes dug by time.

She found him fascinating. He was strange, even stranger than the other colleagues that Alberto had introduced her to, to no avail.

205

The subject they studied seemed only to attract sinister characters, or to make them so over the years. She could have asked Mattia whether Mattia had been attracted by math because he was weird or if math had made him weird, to ask something funny, but she didn't feel like it. And yet, "strange" conveyed the idea. And disturbing. But there was something in his eyes, a kind of shining molecule drowning in those dark pupils, which, Nadia was sure, no woman had ever been able to capture.

She could have turned him on, she was dying to. She had pulled her hair to one side so as to reveal her bare neck and she ran her fingers back and forth along the seams of the bag that she held on her lap. But she didn't dare to go any further and she didn't want to turn around. If he was looking elsewhere, she didn't want to find out.

Mattia coughed quietly into his clenched fist, to warm it up. He noticed Nadia's urgency, but couldn't make up his mind. And even if he did decide, he thought, he wouldn't know what to do. Once Denis, talking about himself, had told him that all opening moves were the same, like in chess. You don't have to come up with anything new, there's no point, because you're both after the same thing anyway. The game soon finds its own way and it's only at that point that you need a strategy.

But I don't even know the opening moves, he thought.

What he did was to rest his left hand in the middle of the seat, like the end of a rope thrown into the sea. He kept it there, even though the synthetic fabric made him shiver.

Nadia understood and in silence, without any abrupt movements, she slid toward the middle. She lifted his arm, taking it by the wrist as if she knew what he were thinking, and put it around her neck. She rested her head against his chest and closed her eyes.

She was wearing strong perfume and it nestled in her hair; it stuck to Mattia's clothes and forced its way into his nostrils.

The taxi pulled up on the left, in front of Nadia's house, with its engine running.

"Seventeen-thirty," said the taxi driver.

She sat up and they both thought how much trouble it would be to find themselves like this again, to break an old equilibrium and build a different one. They wondered if they'd still be able to do it.

Mattia rummaged in his pockets and found his wallet. He held out a twenty and said no change, thanks. She opened the door.

Now follow her, Mattia thought, although he didn't move.

Nadia was already on the sidewalk. The taxi driver watched Mattia in the rearview mirror, waiting for instructions. The squares on the taximeter were all illuminated and flashing 00.00.

"Come on," said Nadia and he obeyed.

The taxi set off again and they climbed to the top of a steep flight of stairs, with the steps covered in blue carpet and so narrow that Mattia had to walk with his feet at an angle.

Nadia's apartment was clean and very well kept, as only the home of a woman living on her own can be. In the middle of a circular table there was a wicker basket full of dry petals, which had stopped giving off any perfume a long time ago. The walls were painted in strong colors, orange, blue, and egg-yolk yellow, so unusual here in the north that there was something disrespectful about them.

Mattia asked may I come in? and watched Nadia take off her coat and lay it on a chair with the confidence of someone moving in her own space.

"I'm going to get something to drink," she said.

He waited in the middle of the sitting room, his ravaged hands hidden in his pockets. Nadia came back a few moments later with two glasses half full of red wine. She was laughing at a thought of her own.

"I'm not used to all this anymore. It hasn't happened to me for a long time," she confessed.

"That's fine," replied Mattia, rather than say that it had never happened to him.

They sipped the wine in silence, looking cautiously around. Each time their eyes met they smiled faintly, like two children.

Nadia kept her legs folded on the sofa, so that she could get closer to him. The scene was set. All that was required was an action, a cold start, instant and brutal as beginnings always are.

She thought about it for another moment. Then she set her glass down on the floor, behind the sofa, so as not to risk knocking it with her foot, and stretched out resolutely toward Mattia. She kissed him. With her feet she slipped off her high heels, which fell resoundingly to the floor. She climbed astride him, not leaving him the breath to say no.

She took his glass from him and guided his hands to her hips. Mattia's tongue was rigid. She began rolling hers around his, insistently, to force it to move, until he began to do the same, in the opposite direction.

With a certain awkwardness they rolled onto one side and Mattia ended up underneath. One of his legs was dangled off the sofa and the other was extended straight, blocked by her weight. He thought of the circular movement of his own tongue, its periodic motion, but soon he lost concentration, as if Nadia's face squashed against his own had managed to obstruct the complicated mechanism of his thought, like that time with Alice.

He slid his hands under Nadia's top and contact with her skin didn't repel him. They got undressed slowly, without pulling apart or opening their eyes. There was too much light in the room and any interruption would have made them stop.

As he busied himself with the unfastening of her bra Mattia thought it happens. In the end it happens, in some way you couldn't imagine before.

35

Fabio had gotten up early. He had switched off the alarm clock so that Alice wouldn't hear it and had left the room, forcing himself not to look at his wife, lying on her side of the bed, with one arm out of the sheet and her hand stretched out as if she were dreaming about clutching on to something.

He had fallen asleep out of exhaustion and passed through a sequence of nightmares that gradually became more and more gloomy. Now he felt the need to do something with his hands, to get himself dirty, to sweat and wear out his muscles. He considered going to the hospital to do an extra shift, but his parents were coming for lunch, as they did every second Saturday of the month. Twice he picked up the phone with the intention of calling them and telling them not to come, that Alice wasn't feeling well, but then they would have phoned to find out how she was doing, and he would have had to talk to his wife again, and things would have gotten even worse.

In the kitchen he took off his T-shirt. He drank some milk from the fridge. He could pretend nothing was wrong, behave as if nothing had happened the night before and carry on like that, as he had always done, but deep in his throat he felt a completely new sense of nausea. The skin of his face was taut with the tears that had dried on his cheeks. He splashed his face with water at the sink and dried himself with the dish towel hanging next to it.

He looked out the window. The sky was overcast, but the sun would come out shortly. It was always like that at this time of year. On such a day he could have taken his son out for a bike ride, followed the track that ran along the canal all the way to the park.

There they would have drunk from the fountain and sat on the grass for about half an hour. Then they would have come back, on the road this time. They would have stopped at the bakery and bought some pastries for lunch.

He wasn't asking for much. Only for a normal life; the one that he had always deserved.

He went down to the garage, still in his underwear. From the top shelf he took down the box of tools and its heaviness brought him a moment of relief. He took out a screwdriver, a size 9 and a size 12 wrench, and started dismantling his bike, piece by piece, methodically.

First he smeared grease over the gears, then he polished the frame with a rag drenched in alcohol. With his fingernail he scraped away the spots of mud that were stuck to it and also cleaned thoroughly between the pedals, in the cracks that his fingers couldn't enter. He put the various pieces back together again and checked the brake cables, adjusting them so that they were perfectly balanced. He pumped up both tires, testing their pressure with the palm of his hand.

He took a step backward, wiped his hands on his thighs, and observed his work with a weary sense of detachment. He knocked the bike to the ground with a kick. It folded in on itself, like an animal. One pedal started spinning in midair and Fabio listened to its hypnotic swish, until silence fell once more.

He was about to leave the garage, but then he turned back. He lifted the bike and put it back in its place. He couldn't help checking to see if it was damaged. He wondered why he was incapable of leaving everything in a mess, of giving vent to the rage that flooded his brain, cursing and smashing things. Why he preferred everything to seem as if it were in its proper place even when it wasn't.

He turned out the light and climbed the stairs.

Alice was sitting at the kitchen table. She was sipping tea thoughtfully. There was nothing in front of her but the sweetener container. She raised her eyes and looked him up and down.

"Why didn't you wake me up?"

Fabio shrugged. He went over to the tap and turned on the water full blast.

"You were fast asleep," he replied.

He poured dishwashing soap onto his hands and rubbed them hard under the water to remove the black streaks of grease.

"I'll be late with lunch," she said.

Fabio shrugged again.

"We could just forget about lunch," he said.

"What's this, a new development?"

He rubbed his hands together even harder.

"I don't know. It's just an idea."

"It's a new idea."

"Yeah, you're right. It's an idiotic idea," Fabio shot back through clenched teeth.

He turned off the tap and left the kitchen, as if in a hurry. Shortly afterward Alice heard the thunder of water in the shower. She put the cup in the sink and went back to the bedroom to get dressed.

On Fabio's side the sheets were crumpled, full of wrinkles flattened by the weight of his body. The pillow was folded in half, as if he had kept his head underneath it, and the blankets were piled up at the end of the bed, kicked away by his feet. There was a faint smell of sweat, as there was every morning, and Alice threw the window open to let in some fresh air.

The pieces of furniture that the night before had seemed to her to have a soul, a breath of their own, were nothing but the same old pieces of bedroom furniture, as scentless as her tepid resignation.

She made the bed, stretching the sheets out properly and tucking the corners under the mattress. She turned down the top sheet so that it was halfway down the pillows as Sol had taught her and got dressed.

From the bathroom came the buzz of Fabio's electric razor, which for some time she had associated with drowsy weekend mornings.

She wondered whether the previous night's conversation had been different from the others or whether it would be resolved as always. Would Fabio, just out of the shower and still not wearing his T-shirt, hug her from behind and keep his head pressed against her hair, for a long time, long enough to allow the rancor to evaporate? There was no other possible solution, for the time being.

Alice tried to imagine what would happen otherwise. She was transfixed by the sight of the curtains swelling slightly in the draft. She became aware of a sharp sense of abandonment, like a presentiment, not unlike what she had felt in that snow-filled ditch, and then in Mattia's room, and which she felt every time, even now, as she looked at her mother's neatly made bed. She brought her index finger to the pointed bone of her pelvis, running it along the sharp outline that she was not prepared to give up, and when the buzz of the razor stopped she shook her head and went back into the kitchen, with the more solid and imminent worry of lunch.

She chopped up an onion and cut off a little chunk of butter, which she set aside in a small dish. All those things that Fabio had taught her. She was accustomed to dealing with food with ascetic detachment, following simple sequences of actions, the end result of which would not concern her.

She liberated the asparagus stalks from the red elastic band that kept them together, held them under the cold water, and laid them out on a chopping board. She set a panful of water on the burner.

She was alerted to the presence of Fabio in the room by a series of small approaching noises. She froze, waiting for contact with his body.

Instead he sat down on the banquette and started distractedly flipping through a magazine.

"Fabio," she called to him, not really knowing what to say.

He didn't reply. He turned a page, making more noise than necessary. He gripped one corner between his fingers, uncertain whether to tear it or not.

"Fabio," she repeated at the same volume, but turning around.

"What is it?"

"Can you get me the rice, please? It's in the top cupboard. I can't reach."

It was just an excuse, they both knew that. It was just a way of saying come here.

Fabio threw the magazine on the table and it struck an ashtray carved from half a coconut, which began to spin. He sat there for a few seconds with his hands resting on his knees, as if he were thinking about it. Then he suddenly rose to his feet and walked over to the sink.

"Where?" he asked angrily, taking care not to look at Alice.

"There." She pointed.

Fabio pulled a chair over to the fridge, making it squeak on the ceramic tiles. He climbed up on it with bare feet. Alice looked at them as if she hadn't seen them before, and found them attractive, but in a vaguely frightening way.

He picked up the box of rice. It was already open. He shook it. Then he smiled in a way that Alice found sinister. He tilted the box and rice started spilling onto the floor, like thin white rain.

"What are you doing?" said Alice.

Fabio smiled.

"Here's your rice," he replied.

He shook the box harder and the grains scattered all around the kitchen. Alice came over.

"Stop it," she said, but he ignored her. Alice repeated it more loudly.

"Like at our wedding, remember? Our damn wedding," shouted Fabio.

She gripped him by a calf to make him stop and he poured the rice over her head. A few grains stuck in her smooth hair. She looked up at him and said again stop it.

A grain hit her in the eye, hurting her, and with her eyes closed Alice slapped Fabio's shin. He reacted by shaking his leg hard, kicking her just below her left shoulder. His wife's bad knee did what it could to keep her upright, bending first forward and then backward, like a crooked hinge, but then it let her drop to the ground.

The box was empty. Fabio stayed standing on the chair, bewildered, with the box upside down in his hand, looking at his wife on the floor, curled up like a cat. A violent shock of lucidity flashed through his brain.

He got down.

"Ali, did you hurt yourself?" he said. "Let me see."

He slid a hand under her head to look at her face, but she squirmed away.

"Leave me alone!" she yelled.

"Darling, I'm sorry," he pleaded. "You are—"

"Go away!" shouted Alice, with a vocal power that neither of them could have suspected she owned.

Fabio pulled away. His hands trembled. He took two steps back, then stammered an okay. He ran toward the bedroom and came out wearing a T-shirt and a pair of shoes. He left the house without turning to look at his wife, who still hadn't moved.

36

Alice pushed her hair behind her ears. The cupboard door was still open above her head, the lifeless chair in front of her. She hadn't hurt herself. She didn't feel like crying. She couldn't manage to think about what had just happened.

She started picking up the grains of rice scattered over the floor. The first few she picked up one by one. Then she started sweeping them together with the palm of her hand.

She got up and threw a handful into the pan, in which the water was already boiling. She stood and looked at them, carried chaotically up and down by convective motions. Mattia had called them that once. She turned off the flame and went and sat on the sofa.

She wouldn't put anything away. She would wait for her in-laws to arrive and find her like that. She would tell them how Fabio had behaved.

But no one arrived. He must have warned them already. Or he had gone to their house and was telling them his version, saying that Alice's belly was as dry as a dried-up lake and that he was fed up with living like this.

The house was plunged into silence and the light seemed unable to find a place for itself. Alice picked up the telephone and dialed her father's number.

"Hello?" answered Soledad.

"Hi, Sol."

"Hi, *mi amorcito*. How's my baby?" said the housekeeper with her usual concern.

"So-so," said Alice.

"Why? *¿Qué pasa?*"

Alice remained silent for a few seconds.

"Is Dad there?" she asked.

"He's asleep. Shall I go and wake him up?"

Alice thought of her father, in the big bedroom that he now shared with only his thoughts, with the lowered blinds drawing lines of light on his sleeping body. The rancor that had always divided them had been absorbed by time; Alice could hardly remember it. What oppressed her most about that house, her father's serious, penetrating glance, was what she missed most now. He wouldn't say anything, he hardly ever spoke. Stroking her cheek, he would ask Sol to change the sheets in her room and that would be that. After her mother's death something had altered in him: it was as if he had slowed down. Paradoxically, since Fabio had entered Alice's life, her father had become more protective. He no longer talked about himself, he let her do the talking, losing himself in his daughter's voice, carried along by the timbre rather than the words, and responded with thoughtful murmurs.

His moments of absence had begun about a year before, when one evening he had confused Soledad with Fernanda. He had pulled her to him to kiss her, as if she really were his wife, and Sol had been forced to give him a gentle slap on the cheek, to which he had reacted with the whining resentment of a child. The next day he hadn't remembered a thing, but the vague sense of there being something wrong, an interruption in the cadenced rhythm of time, had led him to ask Sol what had happened. She had tried not to reply, to change the subject, but he hadn't let it go. When the housekeeper had told the truth he had grown gloomy, had nodded and, turning around, had said I'm sorry, in a low voice. Then he had holed himself up in his study and stayed there until dinnertime, without sleeping or doing anything. He had sat down at his desk, with his hands resting on the walnut surface, and had tried in vain to reconstruct that missing segment in the ribbon of his memory.

Episodes such as this were repeated with ever greater frequency and all three of them, Alice, her father, and Sol, tried to pretend nothing was wrong, waiting for the moment when that would no longer be possible.

"Ali?" Sol urged. "So shall I go and wake him up?"

"No, no," Alice said quickly. "Don't wake him. It's nothing."

"Really?"

"Yes. Let him rest."

She hung up and lay down on the sofa. She tried to keep her eyes open, directing them at the plastered ceiling. She wanted to be present at this very moment, in which she noticed a new, uncontrollable change. She wanted to be witness to the umpteenth little disaster, memorize its trajectory, but after a few minutes her breathing became more regular and Alice fell asleep.

37

Mattia was startled to find that he still had instincts, buried beneath the dense network of thoughts and abstractions that had woven itself around him. He was startled by the violence with which these instincts emerged and confidently guided his gestures.

The return to reality was painful. Nadia's foreign body had settled on his own. Contact with her sweat on one side and the crumpled fabric of the sofa and their squashed clothes on the other was suffocating. She was breathing slowly. Mattia thought that if the ratio between the intervals of their breath was an irrational number, there was no way of combining them to find a regularity.

He tried to take in some air by stretching over Nadia's head, but it was saturated with heavy condensation. He suddenly wanted to cover himself up. He twisted one leg because he felt his member, flaccid and cold, against her leg. He clumsily hurt her with his knee. Nadia gave a start and raised her head. She had already fallen asleep.

"Sorry," said Mattia.

"Doesn't matter."

She kissed him and her breath was too hot. He remained motionless, waiting for her to stop.

"Shall we go to the bedroom?" she said.

Mattia nodded. He would have liked to go back to his apartment, his comfortable void, but he knew it wasn't the right thing to do.

They both became aware of how embarrassing and unnatural the moment was, as they slipped beneath the sheets from opposite sides of the bed. Nadia smiled as if to say everything's fine. In the darkness she huddled up against his shoulder. She gave him another kiss and quickly fell asleep.

Mattia too closed his eyes, but was forced to open them again immediately, because a jumble of terrible memories lay in wait for him, piled up beneath his eyelids. Once again he had difficulty breathing. He reached his left hand under the bed and began rubbing his thumb against the iron netting, at the pointed juncture where two meshes met. In the darkness he brought his finger to his mouth and sucked it. The taste of blood calmed him for a few seconds.

He gradually became aware of the unfamiliar sounds of Nadia's apartment: the faint hum of the fridge, the heat that rustled for a few seconds and then stopped with a click of the boiler, and a clock, in the other room, that sounded to him as if it were going too slowly. He wanted to move his legs, to get up and out of there. Nadia was still in the middle of the bed, depriving him of the space he needed to turn around. Her hair stung his neck and her breathing dried the skin of his chest. Mattia thought that he would never manage to close his eyes. It was late already, perhaps after two. He had to teach the next day and was bound to make mistakes at the blackboard; he would look like a complete idiot in front of all his students. At his own place, on the other hand, he would have been able to sleep, at least for the few remaining hours.

If I'm quiet about it she won't notice, he thought.

He remained motionless for more than a minute, thinking. The sounds were becoming more and more apparent. Another sharp rattle from the boiler made him stiffen and he decided to leave.

With little movements he managed to free the arm that was underneath Nadia's head. In her sleep she felt the lack and moved to try to find him. Mattia drew himself upright. He rested first one foot on the floor and then the other. When he got up the bed squeaked slightly as it settled.

He turned to look at her in the semidarkness and vaguely remembered the moment when he had turned his back on Michela in the park.

He walked barefoot to the sitting room. He picked up his clothes from the sofa and his shoes from the floor. He opened the door, as always, without a sound, and when he was in the corridor, still clutching his trousers, he finally managed to breathe deeply.

38

On the Saturday evening of the rice incident, Fabio had called her on her cell phone. Alice had wondered why he hadn't tried on the home phone first and then thought that perhaps it was because the home phone was an object that belonged to both of them and he didn't like the fact that there was something they shared at that moment any more than she did. It had been a short call, in spite of the drawn-out silences. He had said for tonight I'm staying here, like a decision that had already been made, and she had replied as far as I'm concerned you can stay there tomorrow as well and as long as you like. Then, once these tiresome details had been worked out, Fabio had added Alice, I'm sorry, and she had hung up without saying me too.

She hadn't answered the telephone again. Fabio's insistent calls soon abated, and she, in an attack of self-commiseration, had said to herself you see? Walking barefoot through the flat she had picked up at random a few things of her husband's, documents and a few items of clothing, and put them in a box, which she had then dumped in the hall.

One evening she had come back from work and found it wasn't there. Fabio hadn't taken away much else. The furniture was all in place and the closet still full of his clothes, but on the living room shelves there were now gaps among the books, black spaces that bore witness to the start of the breakup. Alice had stopped to look at them and for the first time the separation had assumed the concrete outlines of a hard fact, the massive consistence of a solid form.

With a certain relief she let herself go. She felt as if she had always done everything for someone else, but now there was just her and she could simply stop, surrender, and that was that. She had more time for the same things, but she was aware of an inertia in her actions, a weariness, as if she were moving through a viscous liquid. She finally gave up performing even the easiest tasks. Her dirty clothes piled up in the bathroom and, lying on the sofa for hours, she knew that they were there, that it wouldn't take much effort to pick them up, but none of her muscles considered this a sufficient motive.

She invented a case of the flu so as not to go to work. She slept much more than necessary, even in broad daylight. She didn't even lower the blinds; she had only to close her eyes to be unaware of the light, to cancel out the objects that surrounded her and forget her hateful body, which was growing weaker and weaker but still clung tenaciously to her thoughts. The weight of consequences was always there, like a stranger sleeping on top of her. It watched over her even when Alice plunged into sleep, a heavy sleep saturated with dreams, which was coming more and more to resemble an addiction. If her throat was dry, Alice imagined she was suffocating. If one of her arms tingled from being under the pillow too long, it was because a German shepherd was eating it. If her feet were cold because the blankets had fallen off them in her sleep, Alice found herself once more at the bottom of the crevasse, buried in snow up to her neck. But she wasn't afraid, or hardly ever. Paralysis allowed her to move only her tongue and she stretched it out to taste the snow. It was sweet and Alice would have liked to eat it all, but she couldn't turn her head. So she stayed there, waiting for the cold to rise up her legs, to fill her belly and spread from there to her veins, freezing her blood.

Her waking life was infested with half-constructed thoughts. Alice got up only when she had to, and her drowsy confusion faded slowly, leaving milky residues in her head, like interrupted memories, which mixed with the others and seemed no less true. She wandered through the silent apartment like the ghost of herself, unhurriedly following her own lucidity. I'm going mad, she thought sometimes. But she didn't mind. In fact, it made her smile, because at last she was the one making the choices.

In the evening she ate lettuce leaves, fishing them straight from the plastic bag. They were crunchy and made of nothing. They tasted only of water. She didn't eat them to fill up her stomach, but just to stand in for the ritual of dinner and somehow occupy that time, which she didn't know what else to do with. She ate lettuce until the flimsy stuff made her feel ill.

She emptied herself of Fabio and of herself, of all the useless efforts she had made to get where she was and find nothing there. With detached curiosity she observed the rebirth of her weaknesses, her obsessions. This time she would let them decide, since she hadn't been able to do anything anyway. Against certain parts of yourself you remain powerless, she said to herself, as she regressed pleasurably to the time when she was a girl. To the moment when Mattia had left and, shortly afterward, her mother too, on two journeys that were different but equally remote from her. Mattia. That was it. She thought of him often. Again. He was like another of her illnesses, from which she didn't really want to recover. You can fall ill with just a memory and she had fallen ill that afternoon in the car, by the park, when she had covered his face with her own to prevent him from looking on the site where that horror had taken place.

No matter how hard she tried, from all those years spent with Fabio she couldn't extract so much as one image that crushed her heart so powerfully, that had the same impetuous violence in its colors and which she could still feel on her skin and in the roots of her hair and between her legs. True, there had been that one time at dinner with Riccardo and his wife, when they'd laughed and drunk a lot. She'd been helping Alessandra wash the dishes and had cut the tip of her thumb on a glass that had shattered in her hands. And as she dropped it she had said ouch, not loudly—she had barely whispered it—but Fabio had heard and come running. He had examined her thumb under the light; leaning forward he had brought it to his lips and sucked a little of the blood, to make it stop, as if it had been his. With her thumb in his mouth he had looked up at her, with those disarming eyes that Alice couldn't resist. Then he had closed the wound in his hand and kissed Alice on the mouth. She had tasted her own blood in his saliva and imagined that it had circulated throughout her husband's body and come back to her cleaned, as though through dialysis.

There had been that time and there had been an infinite number of others, which Alice no longer remembered, because the love of those we don't love in return settles on the surface and from there quickly evaporates. What was left now was a faint red patch, almost invisible on her drawn skin, the spot where Fabio had kicked her.

Sometimes, particularly in the evening, she remembered what he had said. *I can't do this anymore.* She stroked her belly and tried to imagine what it would have been like to have someone in there, swimming in her cold liquid. *Tell me what it is.* But there was nothing to explain. There was no reason, or not only one. There was no beginning. There was her and that was that and she didn't want anyone in her belly.

Perhaps I should tell him that, she thought.

Then she picked up her cell phone and ran through her contact list till she got to *F.* She rubbed the keyboard with her thumb, as if hoping to activate the call by mistake. Then she pressed the red button. To see Fabio, talk to him, rebuild: it all seemed like an inhuman effort and she preferred to stay there, watching the furniture in the sitting room being covered with a layer of dust that was getting thicker by the day.

39

He hardly ever looked at the students. When he met their clear eyes directed at the blackboard and at him, he felt naked. Mattia wrote out his calculations and made precise comments, as if he were explaining them to himself as well as to everyone else. The classroom was too big for the dozen fourth-year students who were taking his course in algebraic topology. They arranged themselves in the first three rows, more or less always in the same places and leaving an empty seat between one and the next, as he himself had done in his university days, but in none of the students could he spot anything that reminded him of himself.

In the silence he heard the door at the back of the classroom close but he didn't turn around until the end of the proof. He turned a page in his notes, which he didn't really need, realigned the pages, and only then noticed a new figure in the topmost margin of his field of vision. He looked up and saw it was Nadia. She had taken a seat in the back row; dressed in white, she sat with her legs crossed and didn't greet him.

Mattia tried to conceal his panic, and moved on to the next theorem. He almost lost his thread, said I'm sorry, and tried to find the step in his notes, but was unable to concentrate. A barely perceptible murmur ran through the students; the teacher had never once hesitated since the beginning of the course.

He started over and made it to the end, writing quickly, his writing sloping more and more toward the bottom as it shrank toward the right-hand edge of the blackboard. He crammed the last two steps into a top corner because he had run out of space. Some of the students leaned forward to make out the exponents and subscripts that had gotten jumbled up with the formulas around them. There was still a quarter of an hour to go before the end of the lesson when Mattia said okay, I'll see you tomorrow.

He set down the chalk and watched the students get up, slightly puzzled, and give him a little wave before leaving the classroom. Nadia was still sitting there, in the same position, and no one seemed to notice her.

They were alone. They seemed very far apart. Nadia got up in the same instant as he stepped toward her. They met more or less halfway across the lecture hall and stayed a good meter apart.

"Hi," said Mattia. "I didn't think—"

"Listen," she broke in, looking resolutely into his eyes. "We don't even know each other. I'm sorry I just turned up like this."

"No, don't—" he tried to say, but Nadia didn't let him speak.

"I woke up and didn't find you, you could at least have . . ."

She stopped for a second. Mattia was forced to lower his gaze because his eyes stung, as if he hadn't blinked for more than a minute.

"But it doesn't matter," Nadia went on. "I don't chase after anybody. I don't feel like it anymore."

She held out a piece of paper and he took it.

"That's my number. But if you decide to use it don't wait too long."

They both looked at the floor. Nadia was about to lean forward, and wobbled slightly on her heels, but then suddenly turned around.

"Bye," she said.

Mattia cleared his throat instead of responding. He thought that it would take a finite amount of time for her to reach the door. Not enough time to make a decision, to articulate a thought.

Nadia stopped in the doorway.

"I don't know what's wrong with you," she said. "But whatever it is, I think I like it."

Then she left. Mattia looked at the piece of paper, on which there was merely a name and a sequence of numbers, mostly odd numbers. He picked up his papers from the desk, but waited for the hour to finish before leaving.

In the office Alberto was on the phone, the receiver pinched between his chin and his cheek, so he could gesticulate with both arms. He raised an eyebrow to Mattia in greeting.

When he hung up he leaned back into his chair and stretched his legs. He gave him a complicit smile.

"So?" he asked. "Were we up late last night?"

Mattia deliberately avoided his gaze. He shrugged. Alberto got up and went and stood behind Mattia's chair, massaging his shoulders like a trainer with his boxer. Mattia didn't like to be touched.

"I understand, you don't feel like talking about it. All right, then, let's change the subject. I've jotted down a draft for the article. Feel like casting your eye over it?"

Mattia nodded. He drummed gently with his index finger on the o of the computer, waiting for Alberto to take his hands off his shoulders. Some images from the previous night, always the same ones, ran through his head like faint flashes of light.

Alberto went back to his desk and slumped heavily into his chair. He started looking for the article amid a shapeless pile of papers.

"Ah," he said. "This came for you."

He tossed an envelope on Mattia's desk. Mattia looked at it without touching it. His name and the address of the university were written in thick blue ink, which must have soaked through to the other side of the paper. The *M* of Mattia started with a straight line, then, slightly detached from it, a soft, concave curve set off, continuing into the right-hand vertical. The two *t*'s were held together by a single horizontal line and all the letters were slightly sloped, piled up as if they had fallen on top of one another. There was a mistake in the address, a *c* too many. He would have needed only one letter, or nothing but the asymmetry between the two potbellied loops of the *B* in Balossino, to recognize Alice's handwriting straightaway.

He gulped and reached around for the letter opener, which was in its place in the second drawer down. He turned it nervously around in his fingers and slipped it into the flap of the envelope. His hands were trembling and he gripped harder on the handle to control himself.

Alberto watched him from the other side of the desk, pretending to be unable to find the papers that were already sitting in front of him. The trembling of Mattia's fingers was apparent even from that distance, but the piece of paper was hidden in the palm of his hand.

He watched his colleague close his eyes and stay like that for a good few seconds, before opening them again and looking around, as if lost and suddenly far away.

"Who's it from?" Alberto ventured.

Mattia looked at him with a kind of resentment, as if he didn't even recognize him. Then he got up, ignoring the question.

"I've got to go," he said.

"What?"

"I've got to go. I think . . . to Italy."

Alberto got up as well, as if to stop him.

"What are you talking about? What's happened?"

He instinctively walked over to him and tried once more to peer at the piece of paper, but Mattia kept it hidden between his hand and the rough fabric of his sweater, pressed against his stomach, like something secret. Three of the four white corners stuck out beyond his fingers, giving a clue to its rectangular shape and nothing more.

"Nothing. I don't know," Mattia shot back, with one arm already in the sleeve of his Windbreaker. "But I've got to go."

"And what about the article?"

"I'll look at it when I get back. You just go ahead."

Then he left, without giving Alberto time to protest.

40

The day Alice went back to work she turned up almost an hour late. She had switched off the alarm without even waking up and as she got ready to go out she had had to stop often, because every movement put an unbearable strain on her body.

Crozza didn't tell her off. He needed only to look at her face to understand. Alice's cheeks were hollow and her eyes, even though they seemed to pop too far out of her head, looked absent, veiled by an ominous sense of indifference.

"Sorry I'm late," she said as she walked in, without really meaning it.

Crozza turned the page of his newspaper and couldn't help glancing at the clock.

"There are some pictures to be printed by eleven," he said. "The usual crap."

He cleared his throat and lifted the newspaper higher. He followed Alice's movements from the corner of his eye. He watched her putting her bag in the usual place, taking off her jacket, and sitting down at the machine. She moved slowly and with excessive precision, which betrayed her efforts to make everything seem all right. Crozza watched her sitting lost in thought for a few seconds, with her chin resting on her hand, and at last, after brushing her hair back behind her ears, deciding to begin.

He calmly assessed her excessive thinness, hidden beneath her high-collared cotton sweater and in her far-from-skintight trousers, but apparent in her hands and even more in the outline of her face. He felt a furious sense of powerlessness, because he played no part in Alice's life, but by God she did in his, like a daughter whose name he hadn't been able to choose.

They worked until lunchtime without speaking. They exchanged only indispensable nods of the head. After all the years they had spent in there, every gesture seemed automatic and they moved with agility, sharing the space fairly. The old Nikon was in its place under the counter, in its black case, and they both sometimes wondered if it still worked.

"Lunch. Let's go—" the photographer said hesitantly.

"I've got something to do at lunchtime," Alice interrupted. "Sorry."

He nodded thoughtfully.

"If you don't feel well, you can go home for the afternoon," he said. "There isn't much to do, as you can see."

Alice looked at him in alarm. She pretended to rearrange the things on the counter: a pair of scissors, an envelope for photographs, a pen, and a roll of film cut into four equal segments. All she was doing was swapping them around.

"No, why? I—"

"How long is it since you've seen each other?" the photographer interrupted.

Alice gave a slight jump. She stuck one hand into her bag, as if to protect it.

"Three weeks. More or less."

Crozza nodded, then shrugged.

"Let's go," he said.

"But . . ."

"Come on, let's go," he repeated, more firmly.

Alice thought for a moment. Then she decided to follow him. They locked up the shop. The bell hanging from the door jangled in the shadow and then stopped. Alice and Crozza set off toward the photographer's car. He walked slowly, without showing it, out of respect for her laborious gait.

The old Lancia started only at the second attempt and Crozza muttered a curse between his teeth.

They drove down the avenue almost as far as the bridge, and then the photographer took a right and followed the road that ran along the river. When he changed lanes and switched on the right blinker to turn again, this time in the direction of the hospital, Alice suddenly froze.

"But where . . . ?" she tried to say.

He pulled up outside a shop with its security gate half closed, across from the entrance to the emergency room.

"It's none of my business," he said, without looking at Alice, "but you've got to go in there. To Fabio, or some other doctor."

Alice stared at him. Her initial puzzlement gave way to fury. The road was silent. Everyone was tucked away at home or in a restaurant for lunch. The leaves of the plane trees fluttered soundlessly.

"I haven't seen you like this since . . ." The photographer hesitated. "Since I've known you."

Alice considered that *like this* in her head. It sounded ominous and she glanced at herself in the mirror, but it showed only the side of the car. She shook her head, then unlocked the door and got out of the car. She slammed the door and without turning around she resolutely walked in the opposite direction of the hospital.

She walked quickly, more quickly than she really could, to get away from that place and Crozza's damned insolence, but after about a hundred meters she had to stop. She was out of breath and with each step she took her leg hurt more and more, pulsating as if asking her for mercy. The bone seemed to penetrate the living flesh, as if it had come out of joint again. Alice moved all her weight to the right and just managed to keep her balance, leaning one hand against the rough wall beside her.

She waited for the pain to pass, for her leg once more to become inert as usual and her breathing to become an unconscious action again. Her heart pumped blood slowly, without conviction, but she could hear it even in her ears.

You've got to go in there. To Fabio, or some other doctor, Crozza's voice echoed in her head.

And then? she thought.

She turned back, toward the hospital, walking with difficulty and without any precise intention. Her body chose the way as if by instinct and the passersby she met on the sidewalk stepped aside, because Alice was staggering a little, although she wasn't aware of it. Some of them stopped, unsure whether to offer to help, but then walked on.

Alice stepped into the courtyard of Our Lady's Hospital and didn't think back to the time when she had walked along the same little avenue with Fabio. She felt as if she didn't have a past, as if she had found herself in that place without knowing where she had come from. She was tired, with that tiredness that only emptiness brings.

She climbed the steps holding on to the handrail and stopped in front of the doorway. She wanted only to get there, to activate the sliding doors and wait for a few minutes, just long enough to collect her strength and leave. It was a way of giving chance a little push, nothing more, to find herself where Fabio was and see what happened. She wouldn't do what Crozza said, she wouldn't listen to anyone, and she wouldn't admit even to herself that she really hoped to find him.

Nothing happened. The automatic doors opened and when Alice took a step back they closed again.

What did you expect? she wondered.

She thought about sitting down for a few seconds, hoping it would pass. Her body was asking her something, every nerve was screaming it, but she didn't want to listen.

She was about to turn around, when she heard the electric swish of the doors again. She looked up at the sound, convinced that this time she would really find her husband standing in front of her.

The door was wide open, but Fabio wasn't there. Instead, on the other side of the doorway, a girl was standing. It was she who had activated the sensor, but she didn't come out. She stood right where she was, smoothing her skirt with her hands. At last she imitated Alice: she took a step back and the door closed again.

Alice studied her, curious about that gesture. She noticed that she wasn't all that young. She might have been the same age as Alice, more or less. She kept her torso bent slightly forward and her shoulders tightly curved, as if there wasn't enough room for them.

Alice thought there was something familiar about her, perhaps in her facial expression, but she couldn't place her. Her thoughts closed in on themselves; they spun in the void.

Then the girl did it again. She stepped forward, put her feet together, and a few seconds later stepped back.

It was then that she looked up and smiled at Alice from the other side of the glass.

A shiver ran down Alice's spine, vertebra by vertebra, before losing itself in her blind leg. She held her breath.

She knew someone else who smiled like that, merely arching her upper lip, barely revealing the two incisors, and leaving the rest of the mouth motionless.

It can't be, she thought.

She stepped forward to see better and the doors remained wide open. The girl looked disappointed and stared quizzically at her. Alice understood and stepped back to let her go on with her game. The other girl continued as if nothing was wrong.

She had the same dark hair, thick and wavy at the bottom, that Alice had managed to touch only a very few times. Her cheekbones protruded slightly and hid her black eyes, but as she looked at her

Alice recognized the same expression that had kept her up till late so many nights: the same opaque gleam as she had seen in Mattia's eyes.

It's her, she thought, and a feeling very like terror gripped her throat.

She instinctively fumbled for the camera in her bag, but she hadn't brought so much as a stupid Instamatic.

She went on looking at the girl, not knowing what else to do. She turned her head toward her and her vision dimmed from time to time, as if her crystalline lens couldn't find the right curvature. With her dry lips she pronounced the word *Michela,* but not enough air came from her mouth.

The girl didn't seem to tire of this. She played with the automatic door like a child. Now she was taking small jumps, back and forth, as if to catch the doors out.

An old lady walked over from inside the building. A big rectangular yellow envelope protruded from her bag, X-rays perhaps. Without saying a word, she took the girl by the arm and led her outside.

The girl didn't resist. When she passed by Alice, she turned for a moment to look at the sliding doors, as if to thank them for amusing her. She was so close that Alice was aware of the displacement of air produced by her body. By holding out a hand she could have touched her, but it was as though she were paralyzed.

She watched the two women as they walked slowly away.

Now people were coming in and out. The doors were constantly opening and closing, in a hypnotic rhythm that filled Alice's head.

As if suddenly coming to, she called Michela, this time out loud.

The girl didn't turn around and neither did the old lady who was with her. They didn't alter their pace by one iota, as if the name meant nothing to them.

Alice thought she should follow them, look at the girl from closer up, talk to her, understand. She put her right foot on the first step and drew her other leg forward, but it remained frozen where it was, fast asleep. She found herself toppling backward. With her hand she sought the handrail, but didn't find it.

She collapsed like a broken branch and slid down the two remaining steps.

From the ground she just had time to see the women disappearing around the corner. Then she felt the air becoming saturated with moisture and the sounds growing rounder and farther away.

41

Mattia had taken the three flights of stairs at a run. Between the second and the first he had bumped into one of his students, who had tried to stop him to ask something. He had brushed past him saying sorry, I've got to go, and in trying to avoid him he had almost stumbled. When he reached the entrance hall he had suddenly slowed down, to compose himself, but still walked quickly. The dark marble of the floor gleamed, reflecting things and people like a stretch of water. Mattia had given a nod of greeting to the doorman and gone outside.

The cold air had taken him by surprise and he had wondered what are you doing?

Now he was sitting on the low wall in front of the entrance and wondering why on earth he had reacted like that, as if all he had been doing all those years was waiting for a signal to go back.

He looked again at the photograph that Alice had sent him. It was of the two of them, by her parents' bed, dressed up as a bride and groom with those clothes that smelled of mothballs. Mattia looked resigned, while she was smiling. One of her arms was around his waist. The other held the camera and was partially out of the frame, as if she were now holding it toward him, as an adult, to caress him.

On the back Alice had written only one line and below it her signature:

> *You've got to come here.*
> *Alice*

Mattia tried to find an explanation for the message and, even more, for his own peculiar reaction. He imagined coming out of the arrivals zone of the airport and finding Alice and Fabio waiting for him on the other side of the barrier. He imagined greeting her, kissing her on the cheeks, and then shaking her husband's hand by way of introduction. They would pretend to argue about who should carry the suitcase to the car and on the way they would try in vain to tell each other how life had been, as if it could really be summed up. Mattia in the backseat, them in the front: three strangers pretending to have something in common and scratching the surface of things, just to avoid silence.

It's pointless, he said to himself.

That lucid thought brought him some relief, as if he were taking control of himself again after a moment of bewilderment. He tapped the photograph with his finger, already intending to put it away and go back to Alberto, to get on with their work.

While he was still lost in his thoughts, Kirsten Gorbahn, a postdoc from Dresden with whom he had recently written some articles, came over to peer at the photograph.

"Your wife?" she asked him cheerfully, pointing at Alice.

Mattia twisted his neck to look up at Kirsten. He was about to hide the photograph, but then he thought it would be rude. Kirsten had an oblong face, as if someone had pulled it hard by the chin. In two years spent studying in Rome she had learned a little Italian, which she pronounced with all the *o*'s closed.

"Hi," Mattia said uncertainly. "No, she isn't my wife. She's just . . . a friend."

Kirsten chuckled, amused by who knows what, and took a sip of coffee from the polystyrene cup that she was holding in her hands.

"She's cute," she remarked.

Mattia looked her up and down, slightly uneasily, and then looked back at the photograph. Yes, she really was.

42

When Alice came to, a nurse was taking her pulse. She still had her shoes on, and was lying at a slight angle on top of a white sheet on a hospital bed by the entrance. She immediately thought of Fabio, who might have seen her in that terrible state, and suddenly sat up.

"I'm fine," she said.

"Lie down," the nurse ordered her. "We're going to do a checkup."

"There's no need. Really, I'm fine," Alice insisted, overcoming the resistance of the nurse, who tried to keep her where she was. Fabio wasn't there.

"You fainted, young lady. You have to see a doctor."

But Alice was already on her feet. She checked that she still had her bag.

"It's nothing. Believe me."

The nurse raised her eyes to the sky but didn't stand in her way. Alice glanced around, lost, as if looking for someone. Then she said thank you and left in a hurry.

She hadn't hurt herself when she fell. She seemed merely to have banged her right knee. She felt the rhythmical pulsation of the bruise under her jeans. Her hands were a little scratched and dusty, as if she had dragged them along the gravel in the courtyard. She blew on them to clean them.

She walked over to the reception desk and bent down to the round hole in the glass. The lady on the other side looked up at her.

"Hello," said Alice. She had no idea how to explain herself. She didn't even know how long she had been unconscious.

"A little while ago . . ." she said, "I was standing there . . ."

239

She pointed to the spot where she had been, but the lady didn't move her head.

"There was a woman, by the entrance. I didn't feel well. I fainted. Then . . . You see, I need to find out the name of that person."

The receptionist looked at her, bewildered, from behind the counter.

"I'm sorry?" she asked with a grimace.

"It sounds strange, I know," Alice insisted. "But you've got to help me. Perhaps you could give me the names of the patients who had appointments in this department today. Or examinations. Just the women, I only need those."

The woman looked at her. Then she smiled coldly.

"We aren't authorized to give out that kind of information," she replied.

"It's very important. Please. It's really very important."

The receptionist tapped with a pen on the register in front of her.

"I'm sorry. It really isn't possible," she replied irritably.

Alice snorted. She was about to pull away from the counter, but then she approached again.

"I'm Dr. Rovelli's wife," she said.

The receptionist sat up straighter in her chair. She arched her eyebrows and tapped the register with her pen again.

"I understand," she said. "If you like I'll let your husband know you're here."

She picked up the receiver but Alice stopped her with a gesture of her hand.

"No," she said, without controlling the tone of her voice. "There's no need."

"Are you sure?"

"Yes, thanks. Never mind."

———

She set off toward home. All the way there she couldn't think about anything else. Her mind was becoming clear again, but all the images that passed through it were obliterated by that girl's face. The details were already blurring, plunging fast into the midst of an ocean of other memories of no importance, but that inexplicable sense of familiarity remained. And that smile, the same as Mattia's, mixed with her own intermittent reflection on the glass.

Perhaps Michela was alive and she had seen her. It was madness, and yet Alice couldn't help believing it. It was as if her brain desperately needed that one thought. Clinging to it to stay alive.

She began to think, to formulate hypotheses. She tried to reconstruct how things might have gone. Perhaps the old lady had kidnapped Michela, had found her in the park and taken her away, because she had a violent desire for a little girl but couldn't have children. Her womb was defective or else she was unwilling to make a bit of room in it.

Just like me, thought Alice.

She had kidnapped her and then brought her up in a house a long way from there, with a different name, as if she were her own.

But in that case, why come back? Why risk being discovered after all those years? Perhaps she was being devoured by guilt. Or else she just wanted to tempt fate, as she herself had done outside the door of the oncology department.

On the other hand, perhaps the old woman had nothing to do with it. Maybe she had met Michela a long time afterward and knew nothing about her origins, her real family, just as Michela remembered nothing about herself.

Alice thought of Mattia, pointing from inside her car at the trees in front of him, his ashen, absent face that spoke of death. She was completely identical to me, he had said.

Suddenly it seemed to her that everything made sense, that the girl really was Michela, the vanished twin, and that every detail now fell into place: the blank expanse of her forehead, the length of her fingers, her circumspect way of moving them. And more than anything that childish game of hers, that more than anything.

But just a second later, she realized she was confused. All those details collapsed into a vague sense of weariness, orchestrated by the hunger that had clenched at her temples for days, and Alice feared losing her senses all over again.

At home, she left the door half open with the keys still in it. She went into the kitchen and opened the cupboard without even taking off her jacket. She found some tuna and ate it straight from the can without draining off the oil. The smell made her feel sick. She threw the empty can into the sink and picked up a can of peas. With her fork she fished them from the cloudy water and ate half of them, without breathing. They tasted of sand and the shiny skin stuck to her teeth. Then she pulled out the box of cookies that had sat open in the cupboard since the day Fabio had left. She ate five, one after the other, barely chewing them. They scratched her throat as she swallowed, like bits of glass. She stopped only when the cramps in her stomach were so strong that she had to sit down on the floor to withstand the pain.

When it had passed, she stood up and walked to the darkroom, limping openly, as she did when she was alone. She took one of the boxes from the second shelf. The word *Snapshots* was written on the side in indelible red pen. She spilled the contents onto the table and spread out the photographs with her fingers. Some were stuck together. Alice quickly inspected them and at last found the one she was looking for.

She studied it for a long time. Mattia was young, and so was she. His head was bent and it was hard to study his expression to determine the resemblance. A lot of time had passed. Perhaps too much.

That fixed image brought others to the surface and Alice's mind stitched them together to re-create movement, fragments of sounds, scraps of sensations. She was filled with searing but pleasurable nostalgia.

If she had been able to choose one point from which to start over, she would have chosen that one: she and Mattia in a silent room with their private intimacies, hesitant about touching each other but their outlines fitting precisely together.

She had to let him know. Only by seeing him could she be sure. If his sister was alive, Mattia had the right to know.

For the first time, she perceived all the space that separated them as a ludicrous distance. She was sure that he was still there, where she had written to him several times, many years before. If he had moved, she would have been aware of it somehow. Because she and Mattia were united by an invisible, elastic thread, buried under a pile of meaningless things, a thread that could exist only between two people like themselves: two people who had acknowledged their own solitude within the other.

She felt around under the pile of photographs and found a pen. She sat down to write, careful not to smudge the ink with her hand. At last she blew on it to dry it. She looked for an envelope, slipped the photograph inside, and sealed it.

Maybe he'll come, she thought.

A pleasant apprehension gripped her bones and made her smile, as if at that very moment time had begun again.

43

Before seeking the runway, the plane on which Mattia was traveling crossed the green patch of the hill, passed the basilica, and flew twice over the center of the city in a circular trajectory. Mattia took the bridge, the older one, as his point of reference and from there followed the road to his parents' house. It was still the same color as when he had left it.

He recognized the park nearby, bounded by the two main roads that flowed together into a broad curve bisected by the river. On so clear an afternoon you could see everything from up there: no one could have disappeared into nothingness.

He leaned farther forward, to look at what the plane was leaving behind it. He followed the winding road that climbed part of the way up the hill and found the Della Roccas' building, with its white façade and its windows all attached to one another, like an imposing block of ice. A little farther on there was his old school, with the green fire escapes, their surfaces, he remembered, cold and rough to the touch.

The place where he had spent the first half of his life, the half that was now over, was like an enormous sculpture made of colored cubes and inanimate shapes.

He took a taxi from the airport. His father had insisted on coming to collect him, but he had said no, I'll come on my own, in that tone that his parents knew well and that was pointless to resist.

244　　After the taxi had driven off, he stood on the sidewalk on the other side of the street, looking at his old house. The bag that he carried over his shoulder wasn't very heavy. It contained clean clothes for two or three days at the most.

He found the entrance to the apartment block open and climbed to his floor. He rang the bell and heard no sound from inside. Then his father opened the door and, before they were able to say anything, they smiled at each other, each contemplating the passing of time in the changes that had occurred in the other.

Pietro Balossino was old. It wasn't just the white hair and the thick veins that stood out too much on the backs of his hands. He was old in the way he stood in front of his son, his whole body trembling almost imperceptibly, and leaned on the door handle, as if his legs were no longer enough on their own.

They hugged, rather awkwardly. Mattia's bag rolled off his shoulder and slipped between them. He let it fall to the floor. Their bodies were still the same temperature. Pietro Balossino touched his son's hair and remembered too many things. Feeling them all at the same time gave him a pain in his chest.

Mattia looked at his father to ask where's Mum? and he understood.

"Your mother's resting," he said. "She didn't feel very well. It must be the heat these past few days."

Mattia nodded.

"Are you hungry?"

"No. I'd just like a little water."

"I'll go and get you some."

His father quickly disappeared into the kitchen, as if looking for an excuse to get away. Mattia thought that that was all that was left, that parental affection resolves itself into small solicitudes, the concerns his parents listed on the telephone every Wednesday: food, heat and cold, tiredness, sometimes money. Everything else lay as if submerged at unreachable depths, in a mass of subjects never addressed, excuses to be made and received and memories to be corrected, which would remain unchanged.

He walked down the corridor to his bedroom. He was sure he

would find everything as he had left it, as if that space was immune to the erosion of time, as if all the years of his absence constituted only a parenthesis in that place. He felt an alienating sense of disappointment when he saw that everything was different, like the horrible feeling of ceasing to exist. The walls that had once been pale blue had been covered with cream-colored wallpaper, which made the room look brighter. Where his bed had been was the sofa that had been in the sitting room for years. His desk was still at the window, but on it there was no longer anything of his, just a pile of newspapers and a sewing machine. There were no photographs, of him or of Michela.

He stood in the doorway as if he needed permission to enter. His father came over with the glass of water and seemed to read his thoughts.

"Your mother wanted to learn to sew," he said, as if by way of justification. "But she soon got fed up with it."

Mattia drank the water down in one gulp. He rested his bag against the wall, where it wasn't in the way.

"I have to go now," he said.

"Already? But you've only just got here."

"There's someone I have to see."

He walked past his father, avoiding his eyes and sliding his back against the wall. Their bodies were too similar and bulky and adult to be so close to each other. He took the glass through to the kitchen, rinsed it, and set it upside down on the draining board.

"I'll be back this evening," he said.

He nodded good-bye to his father, who was standing in the middle of the living room, at the same spot where in another life he was hugging his mother, talking about him. It wasn't true that Alice was waiting for him, he didn't even know where to find her, but he had to get out of there as quickly as possible.

44

They wrote to each other during the first year. As with everything else that concerned them, it was Alice who had started it. She had sent him a photograph of a cake with a rather clumsy *Happy Birthday* written with strawberries cut in half. She had signed the back only with an *A*—and nothing more. She had made the cake for Mattia's birthday, and then had thrown the whole thing into the trash. Mattia had replied in a letter of four closely written pages, in which he told her how hard it was to start over in a new place without knowing the language, and in which he apologized for leaving. Or at least that was how it seemed to Alice. He hadn't asked her anything about Fabio, either in that letter or in the ones that followed, and she hadn't talked about him. Both of them were aware, however, of his strange and menacing presence, just beyond the edge of the page. Partly for that reason they soon began to reply to each other's letters coldly and at increasingly longer intervals, until their correspondence faded away entirely.

A few years later Mattia had received another card. It was an invitation to Alice and Fabio's wedding. He had stuck it on the fridge with a piece of tape, as if, hanging there, it would inevitably remind him of something. Each morning and each evening he found himself standing in front of it and each time it seemed to hurt him a little less. A week before the ceremony he had managed to send a telegram that said *Thank you for invitation must decline due to professional obligations. Congratulations, Mattia Balossino.* In a shop in the city center he had spent a whole morning choosing a crystal vase that he had sent to the couple at their new address.

It was not to this address that he went when he left his parents' house. Instead he headed for the hill, to the Della Roccas', where he and Alice had spent their afternoons together. He was sure he wouldn't find her there, but he wanted to pretend that nothing had changed.

He hesitated for a long time before pressing the buzzer. A woman replied, probably Soledad.

"Who is it?"

"I'm looking for Alice," he said.

"Alice doesn't live here anymore."

Yes, it was Soledad. He recognized her Spanish accent, still quite noticeable.

"Who is looking for her?" asked the housekeeper.

"It's Mattia."

There was an extended silence. Sol tried to remember.

"I can give you her new address."

"That's okay. I've got it, thanks," he said.

"Good-bye, then," said Sol, after another, shorter silence.

Mattia walked off without turning to look up. He was sure that Sol would be standing at one of the windows watching him, recognizing him only now and wondering what had become of him in all those years and what it was he had come back in search of. The truth was that even he didn't know.

45

Alice hadn't expected him so soon. She had sent the card only five days before and it was possible that Mattia hadn't even read it yet. At any rate she was sure that he would call first, that they would arrange to meet, perhaps in a bar, where she would prepare him calmly for the news.

Her days were filled with waiting for some kind of signal. At work she was distracted but cheerful and Crozza hadn't dared to ask her why, but in his heart he felt he deserved some credit for it. The void left by Fabio's departure had made way for an almost adolescent frenzy. Alice assembled and dismantled the image of the moment when she and Mattia would meet; she studied the scene from different angles and adjusted every detail. She wore away at the thought until it seemed not so much a projection as a memory.

She had also been to the local library. She had had to get a card, because she had never set foot in it before that day. She had looked for the newspapers that reported on Michela's disappearance. They were upsetting to read, as if all that horror were happening again, not far from where she was. Her confidence had wavered at the sight of a photograph of Michela on the front page, in which she was looking lost and staring at a point above the lens, perhaps the forehead of whoever was taking the picture. That image had instantly undermined the memory of the girl at the hospital, superimposing itself over her too precisely to seem believable. For the first time Alice had wondered if it might not all be a mistake, a hallucination that had lasted too long. Then she had covered the photograph with one hand and gone on reading, resolutely dispelling that doubt.

Michela's body had never been found. Not so much as an item of clothing, not a trace. The child had simply vanished. For months the line of a kidnapping had been pursued, but to no avail. No suspects were ever named. The news had gradually moved to the margins of the inside pages before finally disappearing altogether.

When the bell rang, Alice was drying her hair. She opened the door distractedly, without even asking who's there, as she arranged the towel on her head. She was barefoot and the first thing Mattia saw of her was her bare feet, the second toe slightly longer than the big one, as if pushing its way forward, and the fourth bent underneath, hidden away. They were details he knew well, which had survived in his mind longer than words and situations.

"Hi," he said, looking up.

Alice took a step back and instinctively closed both sides of her bathrobe, as if her heart might burst out of her chest. Then she focused on Mattia, took in his presence. She hugged him, pressing her inadequate weight against him. He circled her waist with his right arm, but kept his fingers raised, as if out of prudence.

"I'll be right there. I'll just be a moment," she said, rushing her words. She went back inside and closed the door, leaving him standing outside. She needed a few minutes on her own to get dressed and put on her makeup and dry her eyes before he noticed.

Mattia sat down on the front step, his back to the door. He studied the little garden, the almost perfect symmetry of the low hedge that ran along both sides of the path and the undulating shape that broke off halfway through a sine curve. When he heard the click of the lock he turned around and for a moment everything seemed as it had been: he waiting outside for Alice and she coming out, well dressed and smiling, then walking down the street together without having decided where they were going.

Alice bent forward and kissed him on the cheek. To sit down next to him she had to hold on to his shoulder, because of her stiff leg.

He moved over. They had nothing to rest their backs against, so they both sat leaning slightly forward.

"You were quick," said Alice.

"Your card arrived yesterday morning."

"So that place isn't so far away after all."

Mattia looked at the ground. Alice took his right hand and opened it palm side up. He didn't resist, because with her he had no need to be ashamed of the marks.

There were new ones, recognizable as darker lines in the middle of that tangle of white scars. None of them seemed all that recent, apart from one circular halo, like a burn. Alice followed its outline with the tip of her index finger and he was barely aware of her touch through all the layers of hardened skin. He calmly let her look, because his hand told much more than he could in words.

"It seemed important," said Mattia.

"It is."

He turned to look at her, to ask her to go on.

"Not yet," said Alice. "First let's get away from here."

Mattia got up first, then held out his hand to help her, just as they had always done. They walked toward the street. It was difficult to talk and think at the same time, as if the two actions canceled each other out.

"Here," said Alice.

She turned off the alarm of a dark green station wagon and Mattia thought it was too big for her alone.

"Do you want to drive?" Alice asked him with a smile.

"I don't know how."

"Are you joking?"

He shrugged. They looked at each other over the roof of the car. The sun sparkled on the bodywork between them.

"I don't need to drive there," he said by way of justification.

Alice tapped her chin with the key, thoughtfully.

"I know where we have to go, then," she said, with the same playfulness with which she announced her ideas as a girl.

They got into the car. There was nothing on the dashboard in front of Mattia, apart from two compact discs, one on top of the other with their spines facing him: Mussorgsky's *Pictures at an Exhibition* and a collection of Schubert sonatas.

"So you've become a fan of classical music?"

Alice darted a quick glance at the CDs. She wrinkled up her nose.

"No way. They're his. All they do is put me to sleep."

Mattia writhed against the seat belt. It scratched his shoulder because it was set for someone shorter, Alice probably, who sat there while her husband drove. They listened to classical music together. He tried to imagine it, then he allowed himself to be distracted by the words printed on the side-view mirror: *Objects in mirror are closer than they appear.*

"Fabio, right?" he asked. He already knew the answer, but he wanted to untie that knot, dissolve that awkward, silent presence that seemed to be studying them from the backseat. He knew that otherwise the conversation between them would stall right there, like a boat run aground on the rocks.

Alice nodded, as if making an effort. If she explained everything all at once, about the baby, the quarrel, and the rice that was still stuck in the corners of the kitchen, he would think that was the reason she had called him. He wouldn't believe the story about Michela, he would think of her as a woman having a crisis with her husband, trying to reestablish old relationships to keep from feeling so alone. For a moment she wondered whether that was actually the case.

"Do you have children?"

"No, none."

"But why—"

"Drop it," Alice cut in.

Mattia fell silent, but didn't apologize.

"What about you?" she asked after a while. She had hesitated to ask, for fear of his answer. Then her voice had come out all by itself, almost startling her.

"No," Mattia replied.

"No children?"

"I don't have . . ." He wanted to say *anyone*. "I'm not married."

Alice nodded.

"Still playing hard to get, then?" she said, turning to smile at him.

Mattia shook his head with embarrassment, and understood what she meant.

They had reached a large, deserted parking lot near the truck terminal, surrounded by huge prefabricated buildings, one after another. No one lived there. Three stacks of wooden pallets wrapped in plastic leaned against a gray wall, next to a lowered security gate. Higher up, on the roof, was a neon sign that must have shone bright orange at night.

Alice stopped the car in the middle of the parking lot and turned off the engine.

"Your turn," she said, opening the door.

"What?"

"Now you drive."

"No, no," said Mattia. "Forget it."

She stared at him carefully, with her eyes half closed and her lips pursed as if she were only now rediscovering a kind of affection that she had forgotten about.

"So you haven't changed that much," she said. It wasn't a reproach; in fact she seemed relieved.

"Neither have you," he said.

She shrugged.

"Okay, then," he said. "Let's give it a go."

Alice laughed. They got out of the car to switch seats and Mattia walked with his arms dangling exaggeratedly to demonstrate his total resignation. For the first time they each found themselves in the role of the other, each showing the other what they thought was their true profile.

"I don't know where to start," said Mattia, with his arms high on the steering wheel, as if he really didn't know where to put them.

"Nothing at all? You've never driven, not even once?"

"Practically never."

"So we're in a bit of a fix."

Alice leaned over him. For a moment Mattia stared at her hair falling vertically toward the center of the earth. Under the T-shirt that lifted slightly over her belly he recognized the upper edge of the tattoo, which he had observed close-up a long time ago.

"You're so thin," he blurted out, as if he were thinking out loud.

Alice jerked her head around to look at him, but then pretended nothing was wrong.

"No," she said, shrugging. "No different from usual."

She pulled back a little and pointed to the three pedals.

"Right, then. Clutch, brake, and accelerator. Left foot only for the clutch and right foot for the other two."

Mattia nodded, still somewhat distracted by the proximity of her body and the invisible smell of shower gel that lingered.

"You know the gears, right? And anyway they're written down here. First, second, third. And I have a feeling that'll do for now," Alice went on. "When you change gears, hold down the clutch and then slowly release it. And to start too: hold down the clutch and then release it while giving a bit of gas. Ready?"

"And if I'm not?" he replied.

He tried to concentrate. He felt as nervous as if he were about to take an exam. Over time he had become convinced that he no longer knew how to do anything outside of his element, the ordered and transfinite sets of mathematics. Normal people acquired self-confidence as they aged, while he was losing it, as if he had a limited reserve.

He assessed the space that separated them from the pallets stacked at the end of the parking lot. A good fifty meters, at least. Even if he set off at top speed he would have time to brake. He held the key turned too long, making the motor screech. He delicately released the clutch, but didn't press hard enough on the accelerator and the engine stalled with a gulp. Alice laughed.

"Almost. A bit more decisive this time though."

Mattia took a deep breath. Then he tried again. The car set off with a jerk and Alice told him to hit the clutch and put it in second. Mattia changed gears and accelerated again. They drove straight until they were almost ten meters from the factory wall, when he decided to turn the steering wheel. They did a 180-degree turn that threw them both to one side and returned them to the point they had started from.

Alice clapped her hands.

"You see?" she said.

He turned the car again and performed the same move. It was as if he knew how to follow only that narrow, oval trajectory, even though he had a huge lot all to himself.

"Keep going straight," said Alice. "Turn onto the road."

"Are you mad?"

"Come on, there's no one there. And besides, you've already figured it out."

Mattia adjusted the steering wheel. He felt his hands sweating from the plastic and the adrenaline stirring his muscles as it hadn't done for ages. For a moment he thought he was driving a car, the whole thing, with its pistons and greased mechanisms, and that he had Alice, so close, to tell him what to do. Just as he had imagined so often. Well, not exactly, but for once he resolved to ignore the imperfections.

"Okay," he said.

He steered the car toward the exit. Once there he leaned toward the windshield and looked in both directions. He delicately turned the steering wheel and couldn't help following its movements with his whole torso, as children do when they pretend to drive.

He was on the road. The sun, already low in the sky, was behind him and shone in his eyes from the rearview mirror. The arrow of the speedometer pointed to 30 kilometers an hour and the whole car vibrated with the hot breath of a domesticated animal.

"Am I doing okay?" he asked.

"Brilliantly. Now you can change into third."

The road went on for several hundred meters and Mattia looked straight ahead. Alice took advantage of the situation to observe him calmly from close-up. He was no longer the Mattia from the photograph. The skin of his face was no longer an even texture, smooth and elastic: now the first wrinkles, still very shallow, furrowed his brow. He had shaved, but new stubble was already emerging from his cheeks, dotting them with black. His physical presence was overwhelming; he no longer seemed to have any cracks through which one could invade his space, as she had often liked to do when she was a girl. Or else it was that she no longer felt she had the right to. That she was no longer capable of it.

She tried to find a resemblance to the girl from the hospital, but now that Mattia was here, her memory grew even more confused. All those details that seemed to coincide were no longer as clear as they had been. The color of the girl's hair was lighter, perhaps. And she didn't remember the dimples at the sides of her mouth, or those eyebrows, so thick at the outer ends. For the first time she was really worried that she had made a mistake.

How will I explain it to him? she wondered.

Mattia cleared his throat, as if the silence had gone on for too long or as if he had noticed that Alice was staring at him. She looked elsewhere, toward the hill.

"You remember the first time I came to pick you up in the car?" she said. "I'd had my license for less than an hour."

"Yeah. Of all the possible guinea pigs you chose me."

Alice thought that it wasn't true. She hadn't chosen him over all the others. The truth was that she hadn't even thought about anyone else.

"You spent the whole time clutching the door handle. You kept saying slow down, slow down."

She cried out with the shrill voice of a little girl. Mattia remembered that he had gone against his will. That afternoon he was supposed to be studying for his mathematical analysis exam, but in the end he had given in, because it seemed so damned important to Alice. All he did all afternoon was calculate again and again how many hours of study time he was losing. Thinking about it now, he felt stupid, as we all do when we remember all the time we waste wishing we were somewhere else.

"We drove around for half an hour in search of two free parking spaces because you couldn't get into a single one," he said, to banish those thoughts.

"It was just an excuse to keep you with me," Alice replied. "But you never understood anything."

They both laughed, to stifle the ghosts let loose by her words.

"Where do I go?" asked Mattia, becoming serious.

"Turn here."

"Okay. But then that's enough. I'll let you have your seat back."

He changed from third to second without Alice having to tell him, and took the curve well. He turned into a shady street, narrower than the other one and without the dividing line down the middle, squashed between two rows of identical, windowless buildings.

"I'll stop down there," he said.

They were almost there when a tractor trailer truck appeared from around the corner, heading straight toward them and taking up most of the road.

Mattia gripped the wheel tightly. His right foot didn't have the instinct to hit the brake, so he accelerated instead. With her good leg Alice searched for a pedal that wasn't there. The truck didn't slow down, but merely moved slightly to its side of the road.

"I can't get by," said Mattia. "I can't get by."

"Brake," said Alice, trying to seem calm.

Mattia couldn't think. The truck was a few meters away and only now did it show any sign of slowing down. He felt his foot contracting on the accelerator and thought about how he could pass it. He remembered how he used to ride his bike down the ramp of the bike path and how at the end he'd have to brake abruptly in order to get between the posts that blocked the cars entering. But Michela never slowed down, she'd go right between them on her bike with training wheels, but never once did she so much as brush them with the handlebars.

He turned the steering wheel to the right and seemed to be heading straight for the wall.

"Brake," Alice repeated. "The middle pedal."

He pressed it down hard, with both feet. The car jerked violently forward and came to a standstill just a few feet from the wall.

The recoil made Mattia bang his head against the left-hand window, but the seat belt held him in place. Alice rocked forward like a bending twig, but held on tightly to the door handle. The truck, two long, red segments, sped past them, indifferently.

———

They sat in silence for a few seconds, as though contemplating something extraordinary. Then Alice started laughing. Mattia's eyes stung and the nerves in his neck pulsed as if they had all been suddenly inflated and were about to explode.

"Did you hurt yourself?" Alice asked. It was as if she couldn't stop laughing.

Mattia was terrified. He didn't reply. She tried to become serious again.

"Let me see," she said.

She freed herself from her seat belt and stretched over him as he stared at the wall directly in front of them. He was thinking about the word *anelastic*. About how the kinetic energy now making his legs tremble would have been unleashed all at once on impact.

At last he took his feet off the brake and the car, its engine off, slipped backward slightly, down the almost imperceptible slope of the road. Alice pulled on the hand brake.

"You're fine," she said, brushing Mattia's forehead.

He closed his eyes and nodded. He concentrated to keep from crying.

"Let's go home and you can lie down for a bit," she said, as if home were their home.

"I have to go back to my parents' house," protested Mattia, but without much conviction.

"I'll take you back later. Now you need to rest."

"I have to—"

"Shut up."

They got out of the car to swap seats. The darkness had taken over the whole of the sky, apart from a thin, useless strip running along the horizon.

They didn't say another word the whole rest of the way. Mattia trapped his head in his right hand. He covered his eyes and pressed his temples with his thumb and middle finger. He read and reread the words on the side mirror: *Objects in mirror are closer than they appear.* He thought about the article he had left Alberto to write. He was bound to make a mess of it; Mattia had to get back as soon as possible. And then there were lessons to prepare, his silent apartment.

Alice turned to look at him, worried, taking her eyes off the road from time to time. She was doing all she could to drive gently. She wondered if it would be better to put on some music, but she didn't know what he would like. In truth she didn't know anything about him anymore.

In front of the house she went to help him out of the car, but Mattia got out by himself. He swayed on his feet as she opened the door. Alice moved quickly, but carefully. She felt responsible, as if it were all the unexpected consequence of a bad joke.

She threw the cushions on the floor to make room on the sofa. She said to Mattia lie down here and he obeyed. Then she went into the kitchen to make him some tea or chamomile or anything that she could hold in her hands when she came back into the sitting room.

As she waited for the water to boil she started tidying up, frantically. Every now and again she turned to glance at the sitting room, but all she could see was the back of the sofa, its bright, uniform blue.

Soon Mattia would ask her why she had summoned him there and she would have no escape. But now she was no longer sure of anything. She had seen a girl who looked like him. So? The world is full of people who look alike. Full of stupid and meaningless co-incidences. She hadn't even spoken to her. And she wouldn't have known how to find her again anyway. Thinking about it now, with Mattia in the other room, the whole thing seemed ridiculous and cruel.

The only certainty was that he had come back and that she didn't want him to go away again.

She washed the already clean dishes that were in the sink and emptied the potful of water sitting on the stove. A handful of rice had been lying on the bottom of it for weeks. Seen through the water, the grains looked bigger.

Alice poured the boiling water into a cup and dipped a tea bag in it. It gushed dark. She added two heaping spoonfuls of sugar and went back into the living room.

Mattia's hand had slipped from his closed eyes to his throat. The skin of his face had relaxed and his expression was neutral. His chest moved regularly up and down and he was breathing only through his nose.

Alice set the cup down on the glass table and, without taking her eyes off him, sat down in the armchair next to him. Mattia's breathing restored her calm. It was the only sound.

She slowly began to feel that her thoughts were regaining coherence. At last they slowed down, after dashing madly toward some vague destination. She found herself back in her own sitting room as if she had been dropped in it from another dimension.

Before her was a man whom she had once known and who was now someone else. Perhaps he really did look like the girl in the hospital. But they weren't identical, certainly not. And the Mattia who was sleeping on her sofa was no longer the boy she had seen disappearing through the elevator doors that evening when a hot, unquiet wind came down from the mountains. He was not the Mattia who had taken root in her head and blocked her path to everything else.

No, what she had in front of her was a grown-up person who had built a life around a terrifying abyss, on terrain that had already collapsed, and yet who had succeeded, far away from here, among people Alice didn't know. She had been prepared to destroy all that, to disinter a buried horror, for a simple suspicion, as slender as the memory of a memory.

But now that Mattia was there in front of her, with his eyes closed over thoughts to which she had no access, everything suddenly seemed clearer: she had looked for him because she needed to, because since the night she had left him on that landing, her life had rolled into a hole and hadn't moved from there. Mattia was the end of that tangle that she carried within herself, twisted by the years. If there was still some chance of untying it, some way of loosening it, it was by pulling that end that she now gripped between her fingers.

She felt that something was being resolved, like a long wait coming to an end. She sensed it in her limbs, even in her bad leg, which usually never noticed anything.

Getting up was a natural gesture. She didn't even wonder if it was appropriate or not, if it was really her right to do so. It was only time, sliding and dragging itself after more time. Only obvious gestures that knew nothing of the future and the past.

She bent over Mattia and kissed him on the lips. She wasn't afraid of waking him, she kissed him as you kiss someone who is awake, lingering over his closed lips, compressing them as if to leave a mark. He gave a start, but didn't open his eyes. He parted his lips and went along with her. He was awake.

It was different from the first time. Their facial muscles were stronger now, more conscious, and they sought an aggression having to do with the precise roles of a man and a woman. Alice stayed bent over him, without getting onto the sofa, as if she had forgotten the rest of her own body.

The kiss lasted a long time, whole minutes, long enough for reality to find a fissure between their clamped mouths and slip inside, forcing them both to analyze what was happening.

They pulled apart. Mattia gave a quick smile, automatically, and

Alice brought a finger to her damp lips, as if to make sure it had really happened. There was a decision to be made and it had to be made without speaking. They looked at each other, but they had already lost their synchronicity and their eyes didn't meet.

Mattia stood up, uncertainly.

"I'll just go . . ." he said, pointing to the corridor.

"Sure. At the end of the hall."

He left the room. He still had his shoes on and the sound of his footsteps seemed to be slipping away underground.

He locked himself in the bathroom and rested his hands on the sink. He felt stunned, groggy. He noticed a little swelling that was spreading slowly where he had hit his head.

He turned on the tap and put his wrists under the cold water, as his father had done when he wanted to stanch the blood gushing from Mattia's hands. He looked at the water and thought about Michela, as he did every time. It was a painless thought, like thinking about going to sleep or breathing. His sister had slipped into the current, dissolved slowly in the river, and through the river she had come back inside him. Her molecules were scattered all through his body.

He felt his circulation returning. Now he had to think, about that kiss and about what it was that he had come in search of after all that time. About why he had been prepared to receive Alice's lips and about why he had then felt the need to pull away and hide in here.

She was in the other room waiting for him. Separating them were two layers of brick, a few inches of plaster, and nine years of silence.

The truth was that once again she had acted in his place, had forced him to come back when he himself had always yearned to do it. She had written him a note and had said come here and he had jumped up like a spring. One letter had brought them together just as another had separated them.

Mattia knew what needed to be done. He had to get out of there and sit back down on that sofa, he had to take her hand and tell her I shouldn't have left. He had to kiss her once more and then again, until they were so used to that gesture that they couldn't do without it. It happened in films and it happened in reality, every day. People took what they wanted, they clutched at coincidences, the few there were, and made a life from them. He had either to tell Alice I'm here, or leave, take the first plane and disappear again, go back to the place where he had been hanging for all those years.

By now he had learned. Choices are made in brief seconds and paid for in the time that remains. It had happened with Michela and then with Alice and again now. He recognized them this time: those seconds were there, and he would never make a mistake again.

He closed his fingers around the jet of water. He caught some of it in his hands and bathed his face. Without looking, still bent over the basin, he stretched out an arm to take a towel. He rubbed it over his face and then pulled away. In the mirror he saw a darker patch on the other side. He turned it around. It was the embroidered initials *FR,* placed a few centimeters away from the corner, in a symmetrical position in respect to the bisecting line.

Mattia turned around and found another, identical towel. At the same point the letters *ADR* were sewn.

He looked around more carefully. In the water-stained glass there was a single toothbrush and next to it a basket of things all jumbled together: creams, a red rubber band, a hairbrush with hairs attached to it, and a pair of nail scissors. On the shelf under the mirror lay a razor, with tiny fragments of dark hair still trapped beneath the blade.

There had been a time when, sitting on the bed with Alice, he could scan her room with his eyes, identify something on a shelf and say to himself I bought that for her. Those gifts were there to bear witness to a journey, like little flags attached to stages of a voyage. They marked out the rhythm of Christmases and birthdays. Some he could still remember: the first Counting Crows record; a Galilean thermometer, with its different-colored bulbs floating in a transparent liquid; and a book on the history of mathematics that Alice had received with a snort but had actually read in the end. She preserved them carefully, finding an obvious position for them, so that it would be clear to him that she always had them before her eyes. Mattia knew it. He knew all that, but he couldn't move from where he was. As if, in yielding to Alice's call, he might find himself in a trap, drown in it, and be lost forever. He stayed there, impassive and silent, waiting until it was too late.

Around him now there was not a single object that he recognized. He looked at his own reflection in the mirror, his tousled hair, his shirt collar slightly askew, and it was then that he understood. In that bathroom, in that house as in his parents' house, in all those places, there was no longer anything of him.

He remained motionless, getting used to the decision he had made, until he felt that the seconds were over. He carefully folded the towel and with the back of his hand he wiped away the little drops that he had left on the edge of the sink.

He left the bathroom and walked down the hall. He stopped in the doorway of the living room.

"I have to go now," he said.

"Yes," replied Alice, as if she had prepared herself to say it.

The cushions were back in their place on the sofa and a big lamp lit everything from the middle of the ceiling. No trace of conspiracy remained. The tea had grown cold on the coffee table and a dark and sugary sediment had settled at the bottom of the cup. Mattia thought that it was merely someone else's house.

They walked to the door together. He touched Alice's hand with his as he passed close to her.

"The card you sent me," he said. "There was something you wanted to tell me."

Alice smiled.

"It was nothing."

"Before you said it was important."

"No. It wasn't."

"Was it something to do with me?"

She hesitated for a moment.

"No," she said. "Just with me."

Mattia nodded. He thought of a potential that had been exhausted, the invisible vector lines that had previously united them through the air and had now ceased to exist.

"Bye, then," said Alice.

The light was all inside and the darkness all outside. Mattia replied with a wave of his hand. Before going back in, she saw once again the dark circle drawn on his palm, like a mysterious and indelible symbol, irreparably closed.

46

The plane traveled in the dead of night and the few insomniacs who noticed it from the ground saw nothing but a little collection of intermittent lights, like a wandering constellation against the fixed black sky. Not one of them lifted a hand to wave to him, because that's something only children do.

Mattia got into the first of the taxis lined up in front of the terminal and gave the driver his address. As they passed along the seashore a faint glow was already rising from the horizon.

"Stop here, please," he said to the taxi driver.

"Here?"

"Yes."

He paid the fare and got out of the car, which immediately drove away. He walked across about ten meters of grass and approached a bench, which seemed to have been put there especially to look at the void. He dropped his bag on it but didn't sit down himself.

A strip of sun was already appearing on the horizon. Mattia tried to remember the geometrical name for that plane figure, bounded by an arc and a segment, but it wouldn't come to him. The sun seemed to be moving faster than it did in the daytime; it was possible to perceive its velocity, as if it were in a hurry to come up. The rays grazing the surface of the water were red, orange, and yellow and Mattia knew why, but knowing added nothing and didn't distract him.

The curve of the coast was flat and windswept and he was the only one looking at it.

At last the gigantic red orb detached itself from the sea, like an incandescent ball. For a moment Mattia thought of the rotational motion of the stars and the planets, the sun that fell behind him in the evening and rose there in front of him in the morning. Every day, in and out of the water, whether he was there to look at it or not. It was nothing but mechanics, conservation of energy and angular momentum, forces that balanced one another, centripetal and centrifugal thrusts, nothing but a trajectory, which could not be anything other than what it was.

Slowly the tonalities faded away and the pale blue of morning began to emerge from the background of the other colors and took over first the sea and then the sky.

Mattia blew on his hands, which the brackish wind had made unusable. Then he drew them back into his jacket. He felt something in his right pocket. He pulled out a note folded in four. It was Nadia's number. He read the sequence of numbers to himself and smiled.

He waited for the last purple flame to go out on the horizon and, amid the dispersing mist, set off for home on foot.

His parents would have liked the dawn. Perhaps, one day, he would take them to see it and then they would stroll together to the port, to breakfast on smoked salmon sandwiches. He would explain to them how it happens, how the infinite wavelengths merge to form white light. He would talk to them about absorption and emission spectra and they would nod without understanding.

Mattia let the cold air of morning slip under his jacket. It smelled clean. Not far away there was a shower waiting for him, and a cup of hot tea and a day like many others, and he didn't need anything else.

47

That same morning, a few hours later, Alice raised the blinds. The dry rattle of the plastic slats rolling around the pulley was comforting. Outside the sun was already high in the sky.

She chose a CD from the stack next to the stereo, without thinking too much about it. She just wanted a little noise to clean the air. She turned the volume knob to the first red notch. Fabio would be furious. She couldn't help smiling as she thought about how he would say her name, shouting to make himself heard over the music and lingering too long over the *i,* jutting his chin.

She pulled off the bedsheets and piled them in a corner. She took clean ones from the closet. She watched them filling with air and then falling back down, undulating slightly. Damien Rice's voice broke slightly just before he managed to sing, *"Oh cuz nothing is lost, it's just frozen in frost."*

Alice washed calmly. She stayed in the shower for a long time, her face turned toward the jet of water. Then she got dressed and put a little makeup, almost invisible, on her cheeks and eyelids.

By the time she was ready the CD had been over for some time, but she didn't notice. She left the house and got into the car.

A block from the shop she changed direction. She would be a bit late, but it didn't matter.

She drove to the park where Mattia had told her everything. She felt as if nothing had changed. She remembered it all, apart from the pale wooden fence that now surrounded the grass.

She got out of the car and walked toward the trees. The grass crunched, still cold from the night, and the branches were full of new leaves. Some kids were sitting on the benches where Michela

had sat so long before. In the middle of the table, cans were arranged
on top of one another to form a tower. The kids were talking loudly
and one of them was moving wildly around, imitating someone.

Alice walked over, trying to catch scraps of what they were saying, but before they could notice her she had walked on and headed
for the river. Since the city council had decided to keep the dam
open all year, hardly any water ran at that point. The river looked
motionless in the elongated puddles, as if forgotten, exhausted. On
Sundays, when it was hot, people brought their deck chairs from
home and came down here to sunbathe. The bottom was made of
white stones and a fine, yellowish sand. The grass on the bank was
tall; it came up above Alice's knees.

She walked down the slope, checking with each step to make
sure that the ground didn't yield. She continued on to the riverbed,
to the edge of the water. In front of her was the bridge and farther
away the Alps, which on clear days like this seemed incredibly close.
Only the highest peaks were still covered with snow.

Alice lay down on the dry pebbles. Her bad leg thanked her by
relaxing. The larger stones pricked her back, but she didn't move.

She closed her eyes and tried to imagine the water, all around and
above her. She thought of Michela leaning over from the shore. Of
her round face that she had seen in the papers reflected in the silver
water. Of the splash that no one had been there to hear and the wet
icy clothes dragging her down. Of her hair floating like dark seaweed.
She saw her groping with her arms, waving them awkwardly and
swallowing painful mouthfuls of that cold liquid, which dragged
her farther down until she almost touched the bottom.

Then she imagined her movement becoming more sinuous, her
arms finding the right gestures and describing circles that gradually
became wider, her feet stretching out like two flippers and moving
together, her head turning upward, where some light still filtered
in. She saw Michela rising back up to the surface and breathing,

finally. She followed her, as she swam on the surface of the water, in the direction of the current, toward somewhere new. All night long, all the way to the sea.

When she opened her eyes the sky was still there, with its monotonous and brilliant blue. Not a cloud passed across it.

Mattia was far away. Fabio was far away. The current of the river made a faint, somnolent swish.

She remembered lying in the crevasse, buried by snow. She thought of that perfect silence. Also now, like then, no one knew where she was. This time too, no one would come. But she no longer expected them to.

She smiled at the clear sky. With a little effort, she could get up by herself.

✧ A Celtic Childhood ✦

A
Celtic
Childhood

➤ ❖ ❮

Bill Watkins

Hungry Mind Press
ST. PAUL • MINNESOTA

Published by Hungry Mind Press
1648 Grand Avenue
Saint Paul, MN 55105

ISBN: 1-886913-31-5
LCCN: 99-73220

10 9 8 7 6 5 4 3 2

Dust jacket design by Randall Heath
Book design by Wendy Holdman
Typesetting by Stanton Publication Services

Printed in the United States of America

Dedicated to my father, who never lived to see the Celtic Revival,
and to my mother, who did

Special dedication to my Native American friend,
Ingrid Washinawatok,
who gave her life in the pursuit of peace and justice,
Colombia, March 4, 1999

Preface

In a Scottish library, on a wet afternoon in 1972, I finally finished reading Frank O'Connor's autobiography, *An Only Child*. The postscript puzzled me: "Written in New York 1958–60." Why would an Irish writer go to America to write a book? My answer came in a crowded Wisconsin kitchen on Thanksgiving Day in 1995.

"Bill, why don't you go upstairs and write something? What is it your mother says? 'You're neither use nor ornament here!'"

In the stillness of the airy bedroom, an exercise book lay virgin and mocking under my quivering pencil. Without warning, a torrent of images cascaded through my mind, finding release in a swift scrawl of spiderous graphite. Seven chapters later, the Thanksgiving holiday was over, and the first book in my trilogy, "The Once and Future Celt," was under way. Like O'Connor before me, I had forged the understanding that being too close to your subject can be distorting and that distance, indeed, brings forth focus.

Acknowledgments

My thanks go to the following: In Minneapolis, Patrick O'Donnell, Kieran Folliard, Tim Fitzgerald, Kevin Finger, and all the crew at Kieran's Irish Pub; the staff, musicians, and regulars at Molly Quinn's; and Liam Óg Watkins, Matthew Lamphear, Kristi Johnson, Ethna McKiernan, and Mary Byers; in St. Paul, Jim Brooks, Mary Sue McFarland, and Seán T. Kelly at the *Irish Gazette;* Dermot and Molly O'Meara at Irish on Grand; Nick Potter, Jerry Brennan, and Jim Rogers; Pearl Kilbride, Amy Bell, and Dallas Crow at Hungry Mind Press; and Chad McNally; Chris Dale in Los Angeles; Johnny Carr and Seán Hannon in Berlin; Andy M. Stewart, Dick Gaughan, and Robbie Coltrane in Scotland; John Dingley in Wales; Danny Watkins, Jer and Eithne O'Leary, and Sean O'Driscoll in Ireland; and Cara and Amber Watkins in England.

Special thanks to my Wisconsin girls: Ma Muehlbauer for giving me the embryo of an idea and Katie Muehlbauer for being the midwife of the ensuing four-year pregnancy.

Glossary

of Words and Phrases and Their Derivation

Acting the gussie: fooling, being silly (probably from *acting the goat*)

Adam and Eve it: believe it (*rhyming slang*)

Amadawn(s): idiot(s) (Gaelic: *amadan,* fool)

An Buachaill Caol Dubh (un buckle kyl doo): the dark slender boy (Gaelic)

Avast!: Stop! (Dutch: *houd vast,* hold fast)

Banjaxed: surprise attack (Gaelic: *banaghaisge,* the surprising feats or exploits of a woman)

Barney: an argument or fight (British slang)

Blackshirts: British Union of Fascists, founded by Sir Oswald Mosley in 1932

Blaggarding: being disruptive or undisciplined (from *blackguard,* the soot-faced pot stirrers and fire tenders of a medieval army)

Blenching: flinching, drawing together, especially of eyebrows (Old English: *blencan,* to deceive)

Bloke: a man (Gaelic: *buachaill óg,* young man)

Bobbyhowler: a moth that batters itself to death on a light fixture

Bollocks, bollix: hot ashes, used as a curse (Gaelic: *beolach,* live ashes)

Boreen: a lane usually overhung with trees (Gaelic: *botharín,* little road)

Bosch: World War I slang for the German army (French)

Box: smack or hit (Old Gaelic: *bosc,* to hurt; origin of the term *boxing*)

Brummy: a native of Birmingham (Brummyjum), England

Buachaill on Eirne: the lad from Loch Erne (Gaelic)

Bum gaff: derelict house unfit for shelter (Gypsy slang)

Bumsteer: a noisy chap (Gaelic: *buamasdairish,* a turbulent fellow)

Butty: sandwich, from bread and butter (British slang)

Cabbage crates: green-brown camouflaged aircraft (World War I RAF slang)

Cantle: the rim or edge of something (Scots)

Ceol an Gael Abú! (key-owl un gale aboo): Forward the music of the Gael!

Chélidh (kay-lee): impromptu musical gathering (Gaelic)

Coddin': chiding or chaffing (Irish slang: Codology, joking, putting someone on)

Comhaltas Ceoltóiri Éireann (kowltass key-owltory airann): the Irish traditional folk music and dance society

Craic (krak): fun, also witty conversation (Gaelic)

Crikey: a contraction of "Christ help me"

Croesus: Celtic king of the Lydians, noted for his wealth (sixth century B.C.)

Croix de Guerre: French military decoration for gallantry

Cuirassiers: French light cavalry (from *Cuirass,* armored breastplate)

Culshie: a country person, a peasant (Gaelic: *culcheumnaich,* backward)

Dagda: father of the Celtic gods

Designtly: by design, on purpose (Irish)

Doolally: to go mad at someone (Hindi: *Deolali,* a military lunatic asylum in Bombay)

Duffer: an unlearned person, a dunce

Earwig: to overhear or eavesdrop (British slang)

Eejit: idiot (Irish)

Empire Loyalists: right-wing 1950s movement against colonial freedom

Flash Harry: a famous wartime spiv, or black marketeer (World War II slang)

Fleádh (flaa): festival (Gaelic)

Fleádh Cheoil (flaa key-owl): music festival (Gaelic)

Fong: a kick (Limerick slang)

Gaatch: someone's way of walking, gait (Irish)

Gallowglasses: warriors in the service of an Irish chieftain (Gaelic: *galloglach*, stranger soldier)

Git: a fool (from *get*, an archaic form of *bastard*)

Glic: wise (Gaelic)

Gombeen: a sort of village idiot (Irish)

Gorsedd: Druid enthronement (Welsh: *gorseddu*, to enthrone)

Gossoon: a young lad (Gaelic, *garsun*)

Hessians: mercenary soldiers recruited by the British from Hesse in Germany, renowned for their brutality

Hold your whist! Shut up! Shush! (Gaelic: *éist*, listen)

Hookers: prostitutes (Dutch: *hoeker*, an old sailing vessel)

Huckstered: cheated by a greedy salesman (Dutch: *hoekster*, retailer)

Iechyd da! (yacky-da): Good health! (Welsh)

Keelhaul: maritime punishment involving dragging a sailor under the ship's hull by a rope passed under the keel. Few survived this ordeal. (Dutch origin)

Keening: the wailing for the dead (Gaelic: *caoin*, lament, cry, weep)

Kibosh: the end, from the judge's black cap signifying the death sentence (Gaelic: *caip bas*, death cap)

Kidney: temperament or humor

Knackered: tired out (British slang)

Langer: penis (Irish)

Langers: very obviously drunk (Irish)

Memsahib: the wife of an English officer (Hindi)

Milesian: Irishman (ancient descendant of Mil, king of Celtic Spain and Scota, daughter of the Egyptian pharaoh Nectanebus)

Moggy: a scruffy-looking stray, usually a tabby or feral cat (perhaps from Welsh: *mwg*, smoky, a common name for a cat)

Muileann d' Or (moolin door): mill of gold (Gaelic)

Natter: idle talk often during knitting (British slang, probably from knit + chatter)

Nawney: Irish slang, the meaning of which my mother *still* won't tell me!

Nicked: stolen (British slang.)

Nuxed: dead (British slang.)

Oggin: the sea (from *floggin the oggin*, sailing the hogwash)

Orangeman: Protestant bigot, follower of King William of Orange

Paggering: a severe beating (Gypsy, probably from Spanish: *pagar,* to pay out)

Palaver: idle or lengthy talk (Portuguese: *palavra,* speech.)

Pen and ink: stink (rhyming slang)

Plantangenet: name of the royal house ruling England from 1154 to 1485 and descended from Geoffrey, Count of Anjou, who liked to wear a sprig of broom in his hat (Latin: *Planta Genista*)

Pong: a terrible stink (perhaps from Chinese *pong chi,* a loom for weaving cloth with fiber from the malodorous silkworm)

Pooky my breeks: shit my pants (Gaelic: *pocaich mo briogais*)

Prat(s): foolish person(s)

Quotha!: Forsooth! (archaic, more contemptuous form of Indeed!)

Rakes: lots of, an abundance (Irish)

Ransacked: to search thoroughly (Gaelic: *rannsaich,* search)

RUC: Royal Ulster Constabulary, British armed police force in Northern Ireland

Scallywags: petty criminals, jokers (Old Norse: *skjalla-weg,* a swaggering loudmouth)

Scarper: run away (Gaelic: *sgapadh,* to scatter)

Scouse: a native of Liverpool (from *lobscouse,* a seafarer's meat stew)

Scran: scavenged food (probably from Old Norse: *skrann,* lean, slim pickings)

Second sight: the Celtic gift of seeing into the future

Shanks's pony: using your legs; walking (British slang)

Sinne Fianna Fáil, Atá fá gheall ag Éirinn: Soldiers are we, Whose lives are pledged to Ireland (Irish national anthem)

Skivvy: a kitchen maid or pot washer (British slang)

Slán leat (slaawn lat): good-bye (Gaelic: *Slán,* go safe. Origin of U.S. term *so long*)

Spivs: ne'er-do-wells, idlers, black marketeers (from *spiffy,* well dressed)

Splice the Mainbrace: to give the crew extra rum ration for good work

Spree: to have fun (Gaelic: *spraoi,* to make sport)

Taking the mickey: to mock, literally, taking the piss (Latin: *micturire,* to urinate)

Tanner: an old silver sixpence (Gypsy: *tanno,* coin)

Tat: scrap metal (Gypsy: *tot*)

Teddy-boys: violent youth gangs, wearers of Edwardian (Teddy) frock coats

Ticketty-boo: That's fine (Hindi: *tikai babu,* it's all right, sir)

Tinker's cuss: an inferior type of malediction

Tipplers: people enjoying small amounts of drink (Old Norse: *tipla,* a wee drop)

Tír na nÓg: land of eternal youth—heaven (Gaelic)

Tosser: a small coin (British slang)

Tosspot: derogatory term for a drunkard (probably from *despot*)

Tubal-cain: the first blacksmith (Genesis 4.22)

Wabe: the grass area around a sundial (perhaps from Scots: *wab,* a web)

Wanker(s): equivalent U.S. term *jerk off*

Wizard prang: spectacular raid (World War I RAF slang)

✦ A Celtic Childhood ✦

✦ Chapter 1 ✦

"DOUSE THE LIGHT THERE, LIAM."

"What's that, Nana?"

"The light, yer mother left the light burning. Would youse ever quench it for me? I don't like touching them yokes, the bloody squitch stung me once when the old crock cover fell off it. Put the heart crossways in me, tobeJasus!"

"I'm comin', Nana," says I, scraping the old green spindled-backed chair across the flagstone floor and over to the light switch. With the fearless dexterity of a five-year-old, I climb up. *Click!* The kitchen's solitary, fly-encrusted lightbulb goes off.

"You're a good boy, Willie, so ya are." Nana sits down at the scrubbed pine table and begins humming to herself. Her eyes, just as soft as the golden era of gas mantles, are intently fixed on the job in hand. She lovingly fills the oil lamps with tangy-smelling paraffin and then adds a pinch of table salt, "so's the glass won't blacken."

"Yes, yer a good wee lad for your nana, Liam."

"He's a good boy—where the good boys don't answer," cries my mam, sweeping in from the garden with a wicker basket full of dry washing.

"Come here," she says, plucking me up like a rag doll and standing me back on the chair.

"You look like no one's child."

I squirm. She tucks in my shirt and pulls my shorts straight.

"And look at yer socks—mother of God! Yer like a ragamuffin."

"They won't stay up, Mammy."

"No," she says. "The elastic's perished. Go'way and play outside, 'tis a lovely day—go on! Yer like a hothouse plant stuck inside of the room on a grand day like this. Gowanoutnow, while the going is good." She claps her hands as if shooing chickens out of the kitchen.

"And don't be playing by the drain—ye'll get the scarlet fever!" says Nana.

I drag the green kitchen chair outside and lay it on its back on the grass—there now! Next I take the short window-cleaning ladder and place it on the front legs crosswise. This becomes the wings of my biplane, just like Captain Biggles in the comics. Suitably attired in what I think pilots wear, I sit cross-legged on the chair back and thus am able, by leaning left or right, to bank and turn my plane. This is great craic altogether, and the top legs projecting forward from under the ladder are my machine guns, which despite the occasional jam, strike terror into the cold heart of German air ace Baron von Richthofen and his flying circus.

The back garden disappears in the clouds of my imagination as my trusty Sopwith Camel tears across the turf and, with a gentle pull on the stick, speeds like an arrow into the rare blue skies over Ireland. Soon I am in enemy airspace over Belgium.

> *I know that I shall meet my fate*
> *Somewhere among the clouds above;*
> *Those that I fight I do not hate,*
> *Those that I guard I do not love . . .*

W. B. Yeats is reading his First World War poem to me over the radio as I glide like a war hawk above the green fields of France.

"Did you get that, Willie?"

"I did, Mr. Yeats. What's it called?"

"'An Irish Airman Foresees His Death.'"

"Roger Wilco, Mr. Yeats—a nice poem!"

"Willie! Willie, do you heed me?"

Through the static-filled ether another voice is calling on my frequency, a faint familiar voice from far, far away.

"Willie! Are ye deaf, ya wee bugger?"

"Is that for you or me, Mr. Yeats?"

"I think it's for you, Liam!"

"Roger, over and out!"

A quick glance about the sky, no sign of the Hun, make a turn for home, once more descending into the green patchwork quilt of Mother Ireland to land next to the threaded silver embroidery that marks the course of the ancient river Shannon.

Engine spluttering, I straighten the rudder and ease the nose up. The voice in my earphones is still calling, shrill above the din. A sudden crosswind tears at the airframe and flips my crate over like a flapjack. As the starboard wingtip jars in the soft earth, the aircraft tears itself asunder. Pulling myself from the mangled wreckage I saunter toward Fighter Command HQ. At the kitchen door I glance back at the carnage. What is it they say? "Any landing you can walk away from is a good landing." 'Tis true for you!

"Willie! I've been calling you for ages! Go ye up to Paddy King's for the evening newspaper and fetch back half a stone of spuds from Fred Rice's. You can get yourself a patsy-pop for going."

"I will, Mam, and I'll take the handcart."

Mam wraps a silver shilling in the note, which reads: "7 lbs. potatoes please Fred, Put them in Liam's cart—Thanks."

I meander up the road, hard by the Shannon wall, where rows of hungry seagulls wait for our dinner scraps. Behind me I pull my two-wheeled cart by one handle.

In my other hand is a large copper penny with a Celtic harp on one side and a chicken on the other. This coin is an inch across and four of them weigh an ounce, but more important, this is the price of a patsy-pop, which is a kind of frozen orange juice on a stick—perfect rations for a fighter pilot on such a hot day.

I balance the cart handle on the worn boot scraper outside of the shop and, with trepidation enhanced by squeaking rusty hinges, push open the huge red door with its moldy brass handles.

A shaft of daylight and myself creeps into the earthy gloom of the greengrocer's emporium. It is dank and smells like a cemetery. Standing on tiptoes, I place the note and its shilling on the black oak counter. My penny escapes and for a while rolls in diminishing circles before shuddering to a stop. I snatch it back to the safety of my pocket as, in the eerie darkness above me, an enormous face and two gigantic hands appear floating, seemingly detached in the dingy light. With a puzzled look at me and then the note, the face says, "What are ye dressed like that for, ya eejit? Do you have the earache or something?"

Looking around cagily, I catch sight of myself in a Jacob's Biscuit mirror. Sure I am a quare enough sight for such a fine warm day: silk scarf tied around my neck, a rubber swimming cap on back to front, and Mam's furry earmuffs over the top of it.

"So I'm still wearing my flying gear, mister! What of it? You should be grateful that fighter aces like me are here to stop the Bosch from making off with your spuds!"

"A foighter pilot, are ye? Glory be! We can all sleep safe in our beds tonight, knowing that Holy Ireland is being protected by Fly-by-night Foster, or is it All-Day Murphy?"

The room shakes as great cannon shots of laughter echo around the earthen vault. Even in the cool dark an angry red flush stings my face and neck. Mute rows of cabbages transform into wrinkled green choir-boys silently mocking my embarrassment. Pallid cauliflowers like freshly trepanned skulls jeer and jostle with needled-nosed carrots to get a better view, whilst sly parsnips thrust forward raggedy roots to eavesdrop on the fullness of my discomfort. I am anxious to quit this turnip-filled tomb with its guffawing owner tumbling several pounds of prize King Edwards into my cart.

"There are old pilots and bold pilots, but there are no old, bold pilots." My inner voice comforts me as I make the safety of the sunlit portal and bang the door out on my tormentor.

Across the road Paddy King's is a haven of sanity. The shop is bright and airy and romantically infused with the rich aroma of printer's ink, aniseed balls, and black Balkan pipe tobacco. I take my place in the queue behind the ample backside of old Mrs. Morrisey, who although she smells of fish paste and old cabbage water, gives excellent cover as I surreptitiously pore over a *Captain Biggles* comic. There was the chiseled-jawed fighter ace striding from his battered biplane, chummed as always by the ever-cheerful Ginger and his Scottish side-kick, Jock.

"That was a wizard prang, sir! I saw the Jerry spin out of control just as you let fly with the Hotchkiss guns."

"Yes, Ginger, but that Hun in the sun nearly took your tail off, old boy!"

"Aye, Captain, but you were there to save the day as usual," Jock chimes in.

"What is it you want, Liam?"

"Word has come of Jerry massing for an attack on the line of the Somme River."

"Liam!"

"We must move quickly and get as many cabbage crates ready to fly as possible."

"LIAAM!" The magazine, like its hero, shoots skyward and I discover myself standing alone in the middle of the newspaper shop. Mrs. Morrisey is gone.

"Ooh, sorry! The *Limerick Leader,* please, Paddy, and a patsy-pop for going."

"Here," says Paddy. "You can have this old copy of *Biggles Flies at Dawn.* I can't sell it with a torn cover. Wasn't your uncle Bill MacDonagh in the Royal Air Force?"

"He was, sir, yes, a tail gunner in Lancaster bombers."

"Fair play to him—he did well to survive. He lives in London now, so he does?"

"He does, sir, in Hammersmith, sir."

"Your dad's away in the army, isn't he?"

"He is, to be sure—somewhere in England, so."

"But you want to join the air force and become a pilot when you grow up?"

"No, sir, I want to go to sea and be a sailor, that's all."

"You could be a navy pilot, so you could. No? Don't fancy that? Well, regards to your mam and your nana anyway, off you go home now. Jasus, will ye just look at the cut of you. You look the part—*Biggles Flies Undone.*"

Ah yes! That's more like it, a bit of respect from the civilian populace, a patsy-pop for going, and a free comic to boot.

God is in his heaven and all is right with the world as I lie next to my crashed plane reading my comic book. Biggles is not so lucky. He has been shot down and is recovering in hospital. As he lies there, surrounded by pretty French nurses, he dreams of his boyhood days in England and tries to remember back to his earliest recollections. He can only see back as far as his third birthday party. Jasus! I can do much better than that. I can remember it all, from day one! Let me see, what did happen?

I came into this world on a snowy April morning in 1950, an event I recall very well. I am told that many people can remember their birth but, it being a disagreeably messy experience at best, choose to forget.

Life is a sea of blobs and wiggly dark shapes moving in a blue light. Of sounds, too, and voices. I feel unbearably cold and I hear a voice saying, "Move Mrs. Watkins to isolation." All is blue and cold.

My mam is very ill and I have been a difficult birth. Luckily for my mother, she is able to have her confinement in Britain as my father is in the British army. She also can take full advantage of the free medical treatment that was not available in Ireland in those austere postwar days. I am christened William after my Irish grandfather and James after my Welsh one. These forenames translate into Liam and Seamus in the Irish tongue.

Whilst Mam is recovering in the hospital they give her two bottles of Guinness a day "to thicken the blood." Since I am breast-fed and prone to hiccups, my mother blames the stout. Either way, I thrive and my mam is soon up and about and on the mend.

The day comes when we are to return to Limerick. I am three weeks old and a testimony to the newly formed National Health Service. Mam is fit and feisty, which is unfortunate for the hospital discharge clerk.

"Ma'am, where it says nationality of infant, you've put Irish. If the child is born here it should say British." Mam is well able for him.

"If a cat has kittens in a baker's shop, does it make them currant buns?"

Later that day we take the boat train to Holyhead in Anglesey, Wales. Waiting at the quay is the ferry boat to Ireland.

After we set sail, my mam takes me out on deck, wrapped up in a plaid shawl for my first sense of the sea. From my woolen cocoon, I remember the salty tang of it well. It is the start of a love affair.

We arrive in Limerick in a big cloud of steam and wonderful smells.

It's smell that best weaves the tapestry of time into the endless knot we call memories. The use of this sense is still the best transportation across the decades and grand for pinpointing events, places, or even people—though there's some smells you would probably like to forget!

We take a horse-drawn sidecar taxi here to my grandmother's house in Thomondgate. This is to be our home, on and off, for the next five and a half years.

Any excuse for a party. Our homecoming is a big event! I am passed around a circle of smiling blobby faces that I later know as my aunts, uncles, and grandparents.

Over the next few weeks, although I sleep most of the time, I try to make sense of my surroundings and am conscious of my need to communicate with my family. It seems that with a little effort on both sides, a fine chat might be had.

The river Shannon lies thirty feet from our front door behind a low wall. At this point, just in front of the salmon weir, she must be a quarter mile wide—or so it seems. One stormy night, my mother takes me to an upstairs window and stands with me in her arms. The river is wild in flood; crashing and boiling on the rocks below, and a dull clanging pervades the house. Its cause is the tidal flap on the sewer main, which empties straight into the Shannon. I try to say "vibrations," but my infant tongue can only manage "bulberations."

My startled mother takes me downstairs to the kitchen, where she tells the assembled tribe, "The child just said 'bulberations' as plain as day!"

Soon a sea of blurry faces are asking me:

"What are bulberations, Willie?"

"Say 'bulberations,' Liam!"

I give up trying to converse sensibly with my folks and resort to the *goo-goo, bow-wow, choo-choo* noises they seem more comfortable with.

There is a strange gray box in the corner of the kitchen that has pipes going in and out of it. I am now old enough to crawl, but have trouble holding my head up for long periods. I notice that when my aunt Frances puts the kettle on the stove, the magic box started up clicking and whirring. I make a beeline for it and for the first time get to it before being grabbed from above by an overprotective minder. I rear up my head to take a bloody good look at my prize, and my rubber neck gives out. *Thunk!* I split my head open on the corner of the gas meter.

The shock jolts me back on my haunches. I sway to and fro, blood streaming into my eye, but I feel no pain. What is far more interesting is that half of my visual field has taken on a lush red color. All at once, pandemonium breaks out and I am snatched up by screaming adults with terrifying looks on their faces.

"The child! Oh, Holy Mother—the poor child!"

This puts the fear of Jasus into me and I start to cry. Though many long years have passed and gone, lying here on the battlefields of France, I still bear the battle scar of my encounter with the ferocious killer gas meter! It was great to be able to remember such a lot of the past. Poor old Captain Biggles could only remember his third birthday party; I was ahead of him in that respect and had war wounds to prove it. I lie on my back and stare up the arse of a skylark, frolicking in the azure firmament above. In my head my own comic strip is forming. What happened after the gas meter? Ah, yes! I turned one year old.

There I am sitting in a high chair at my first birthday party. Now the faces of my family have much more form and features, and I am able to tell one from another.

My grandda, Willie MacDonagh, is a lovely, quiet gentleman, who has a fine head of soft white hair and a merry twinkle. He makes me the present of an aerodrome made of brightly painted tinplate, and when the handle is turned, little airplanes with tiny propellers fly around in a circle about a central pivot. All of the adults have great sport with it, but I want to play with the solitary flickering candle on my birthday cake. From my position of honor at the head of the table, enthroned in my food-splattered high chair, the candle entices me. It is so bright, playfully dancing, and by hook or by crook, I am going to eat it. It is in reach and everyone's attention is taken up by the airplanes. I grab it, it is mine. *OWEEE!* The bloody thing bites me!

"Willie! Willie, are you daydreaming again? Get up off that wet grass, ye'll get piles. And don't forget to put away that ladder an' bring in the chair an' wash yer kisser. It's time to go to mass."

"What, again?"

"Yes again, and enough of yer moaning—yer worse than yer father!"

"Why do we have to go to mass all the time?"

"Because we're Catolicks. You should be thankful that we're not like the godless pagan English, hammering on the pearly gates while Saint Peter cocks a deaf ear to them! Come on now and be a good boy, and we'll maybe go on a mystery tour at the weekend!"

I shuffle to and fro with the bits of my plane in some contentment. Things are indeed looking up. Partaking of railway mystery tours beats the socks off of going to mass any day. The mystery tours are a great laugh altogether, and on the following Saturday the whole family troops down to Limerick station and boards the waiting train. Most of the men drink stout and play cards, whilst the older womenfolk chatter, natter, and knit away in shawly groups and the younger ones sit studying the railway maps, speculating on the possible destination of the trip. As we clatter along the iron road the railway carriage is filled with singing and folks clapping their hands in time. Us kids run wild from one end of the train to the other, not knowing or caring where we are bound.

After about an hour, we steam to a screeching halt in the small Tipperary town of Cahir during a thunderstorm of biblical proportions. Two hundred or so passengers scurry into the town to find the funfair and amusement park waterlogged, the shops and cafés shut, and the pubs closed for the holy hour. The only thing open to visitors is a ruined castle, which, being open to the sky, affords no shelter. There is almost a riot. The men, some of whom were now the worse for drink, are wanting to lynch the train driver and his fireman for what they think is a practical joke. It takes three local policemen and the parish priest to calm things down. Eventually we reboard the Mystery Express and the train crew comes out of their hiding place to take us back to Limerick.

On the way back home, Mickey Galvin tells a story about his poor old mother in Galway, who at the age of eighty-two, comes down on the train to visit him one summer in Limerick. Well, Mickey, a bachelor, was a great outdoors man, and he couldn't imagine his elderly mam wanting to go hiking or bicycling. So the second day, at a loss to know what to offer her in the way of entertainment, he takes her on a mystery tour. Only this time, the mystery train was going back to Galway! As she recognizes her home town, she looks at him, with tears welling up in her eyes, and says, "Could you not have let me stay on for just a couple more days, son? I won't be any trouble, son."

Disaster or not, you couldn't beat the old mystery tours!

The weather had broken, as they say in these parts, and it was soft over Clare. Great white cumulous billows of wind-lashed clouds sail up the Shannon like a fleet of Spanish galleons. I stare at the wan puddles they leave in their wake, whilst rivulets of silver-gray rainwater saturate my runway. No chance of flying a sortie in this deluge, so I play cards with my teddy bear. He wins by cheating.

A sudden rake of excitement in the house. My father is coming to see us. He is on leave from the army, and he hopes to slip into Ireland quietly for a few days and see his son for the first time. Mam is excited.

"Now you'll see something!" she says, reading his letter in the far corner of the kitchen. "I hope he gets into the country all right."

"What do you mean, Mam?"

"Well, Willie, Ireland stayed neutral in Hitler's war and soldiers from either side weren't welcome here. So with the whole shebang just after finishing, the government do be frightened by rumors of spies and secret agents and God knows what and especially suspicious of British soldiers. Godhelpus, hasn't Ireland suffered enough from the British soldiers? Your father will have to keep a low profile."

"Jasus! Reg keep a low profile? Go'way! Ye might as well be asking a leopard to change his spots!" As it turns out, Nana's words weren't far off the mark.

It being near Bonfire Night, the November fifth celebration of the failure of Guy Fawkes's attempt to blow up the English Parliament in 1605, as tradition would enlist, Dad brings me over some fireworks. How is he to know that such harmless amusements are highly illegal in Ireland?

In trying to gain entry at the Irish port of Dun Laoghaire, either his military bearing and service haircut, or his hastily assembled civilian attire, catches the attention of the ever-watchful security police.

"Excuse me, sir! What have you there in that army rucksack?"

"Er . . . it's nothing, just some presents for my son."

"It's explosives, Sergeant!" says the other one, peering in.

"Jasus!" says the sergeant as they hustled him away. "Who's your son? Dangerous Dan the dynamite man, is it?"

My poor father is deported back to Britain. So as luck would have it, I never get to meet him until the following year.

"Well, now!" says me mam. "If Mohammed won't go to the mountain, then the mountain must go to Mohammed, and there, Willie boy, we can kill two birds with one stone, can't we?" I sit on the green wooden chair, nodding assent and dangling my legs in puzzlement. Grown-ups were an odd bunch with their moving mountains and dead birds—it was a trial to keep up. My mother was best left to her own devices and in time all would be revealed. As indeed it was, later that night around the kitchen table.

"He needs to get that eye fixed or he'll be looking round corners all his life."

"We can't let him off to school with the other kids shouting, 'Hey, Willie! Is that yer eye—the white thing?'"

So I was born with a lazy eye, or a cod eye as they say in Ireland. It caused me no grief, for you never miss what you've never had, but my family didn't want me growing up and people taking the mickey out of me. It is decided that I be taken back to Britain for free medical treatment on the National Health Service. As I have no say in the matter, I am stoic.

On the downside, it means leaving all I'd ever known for a while. On the other hand, it meant a great trip on the train and a ride on a ship. Also, the chance to live with my other grandparents for a wee bit and maybe see my dad if he can get leave from his unit.

As the day of departure approaches, all pervading waves of doom threaten to scuttle the frail craft of my optimism. My older cousin Joe explains it best: "Don't be worried, they just cut out yer bad eye and put a pickled onion in!"

We take the steam train from Limerick to Dun Laoghaire, where we board the ancient steamship *Princess Maud,* a floating relic of the 1920s. Mam sings an old ditty as we tramp up the gangplank, arms linked:

Bobby Shaftoe's gone to sea
Silver buckles on his knee
He'll come back and marry me
Bonny Bobby Shaftoe.

Having only the cheapest third-class tickets, we are confined to green cast-iron park benches bolted to the stern deck. There is only a tiny indoor lounge, and it is already packed full, twice over.

At last the great steam hooter blows. The blue peter is struck from the foremast head and we are off, straight into the teeth of a howling gale. To the exposed cheeks the raw wind is like emery paper, but I discover that by changing the shape of my mouth, the wind could be made to play little tunes that only I could hear.

"What are ye pulling faces like that for? Stop it now, ye'll have people think yer fooly, making faces like a fish, ya eejit. Oh, my God, *fish!*" Mam lurches to the rail and shares her breakfast with squabbling seagulls, bobbing on the boiling foam, thirty feet below. At that moment as we cross the breakwater, the wind freshens and the stern fantail is lashed by a following sea. Mad green crests spill over the aft deck rail and threaten to soak us all. Great eddies of freezing Irish seawater swirl toward our ankles, forcing us to sit like gargoyles, knees under chin. As the pilot boat leaves for shore, a bevy of kind sailors appears and within minutes jury-rig a big green tarpaulin over us to keep off the worst of the salt spray and rain. My poor mam continues to be terribly seasick, but I love every aspect of this seagoing enterprise; it awakens some long-slumbering leviathan within me! Fascinated, I watch the sailors brace against the wind, coiling hawsers, stowing docking gear, and checking davits. The old tub pitches and rolls, whilst I, with arms outstretched as a crucifix, ricochet around the aft capstans like a well-upholstered orb in a giant pinball machine. I have marvelous fun trying to keep my balance and come to no harm at all.

"Mam!" says I, "this is great!"

My mam peers out from under her blanket.

"You're in league with the devil," comes her baleful reply.

A big bearded sailor snatches me up in his arms.

"Steady as she goes! Here's a wee fellow who has his first sea legs! One of these days you'll might make a grand sailor, my young bucko!"

He doesn't have to tell me. I am already of that conviction!

We dock in Holyhead the following morning. Mam is still green in the face but after a cup of tea at the station café feels more the ticket. I am still exhilarated, but my joy is short lived.

Mam fishes in her handbag, producing a lipstick-stained white linen handkerchief. Then she dribbles a long plume of spittle onto it and scrubs my face with the resultant infusion. It is a horrible indignation for a sailor to suffer!

"There you are, a cat's lick and a promise to see you through the day."

So, if *that's* what makes me a Catolick, then I could well do without it!

On dry land now, but my little legs could still feel the pull of the ship.

I weave from side to side in my effort to maintain equilibrium.

"Look, Mam, I'm drunk!"

"That's all I need, a drunken sailor to look after, what shall we do with you?"

> *What shall we do with a drunken sailor?*
> *What shall we do with a drunken sailor?*
> *What shall we do with a drunken sailor?*
> *Early in the morning.*
> *Ohray up she rises, ohray up she rises,*
> *Ohray up she rises, early in the morning.*

Arms linked again in song, we skip past the huge, hissing monster of a Pacific class passenger locomotive and find good seats in a carriage just a few compartments down from the coal tender stacked high with its polished jet-black nuggets.

With two sharp blasts of the whistle, the great iron beast heaves his steel connecting rods and, squealing into movement, belches a hoarse roar of steam. Having thus asserted itself, the tamed tyrant gets down to the business of the day and clanks off into the hinterland of Wales. Mam starts to sing a nonsense song to entertain me:

Paddy was a Welshman, Paddy was a thief
Paddy came to our house, and stole a leg of beef.
We went to Paddy's house, Paddy wasn't there.
So I catched him by the two legs, and threw him down the stairs.

"Mam, who was Paddy?"

"I dunno."

"Why was he Welsh if he was a Paddy?"

"I dunno!"

"How can you throw him downstairs if he isn't there?"

Mam begins to snore and I am left to figure out the mysterious Paddy for myself.

Wales speeds by.

"Will you look at that now," says my mam, waking up from her snooze. We are pulling into a station, the name of which is displayed on a sign that runs the entire one-hundred-foot length of the platform. It reads:

LLANFAIRPWLLGWYNGYLLGOGERYCHWYRNDROBWLLLLANTYSILIOGOGGOG

"What does it mean, Mammy?"

"Jasus, don't be asking me. It could be the Welsh word for teacup for all I know. Ask your dad when you see him. He speaks Welsh, so he'll know how to say it."

So there it was, my father, of whom I had heard so many heroic tales, could also pronounce the Welsh word for teacup. My, my.

"Tickets, please, ladies and gentlemen. Tickets, please!" The blue uniformed conductor enters the carriage. He has a thing like a pair of pliers in his hand and a black peaked cap with a badge of a silver lion holding a wheel on the front. The man looks at the small oblong green tickets and punches a hole in each.

"Thank you, ma'am!"

"The young fella wants to know what the sign reads, yonder?"

"Oh, yes, indeed. I wish I had a shilling for every time someone has asked me that. It means 'Saint Mary's Church of the pool of the white hazel, near the rushing whirlpool, Saint Tysilio's Church, near the red cave.' Lovely, isn't it?"

"What about the teacups?"

"Teacups, is it? Teacups, there's plenty of teacups under the other sign over there. Café, see?"

They're at it again, grown-ups! Ask a civil question and they give you nonsense about saints and hazel trees and red caves. The man looks puzzled, Mam shrugs her shoulders, and I stare out of the window as the train moves off.

The boat train continues over the Telford bridge across the Menai Strait and on into mainland Wales. As we round the sea cliffs the enormous battlements of Conway heave into view. The almost perfectly preserved city walls built by the English king Edward the First are dominated by one of the largest and most formidable castles in Europe. I notice with glee that the railway tunnel entrances are all turreted and castellated in the same style as the Norman fortress above.

My mam is less impressed by this masterpiece of Plantangenet military technocratics.

"All that to keep the poor Welsh down in their own country. BloodyEnglish!" She dozes off again.

I am nearly twenty years old before I realize that *Bloody English* are two different words!

The fatigue of my seaborn adventure sweeps over me and I join Mam in restful sleep. I wake up in New Street Station in the heart of the second biggest city in Britain.

Here in Birmingham, I get my first ride on the top of a double-decker bus and sit right at the front so that I can pretend to steer. The view is terrific and the bustling streets teem with lorries, cars, and tramcars whose sleek steel rails channel through the shiny black cobbled streets like veins of silver. I am even too curious to mind the inevitable spit-soaked hankie catlicking away at my cheeks. This is the biggest city I have ever seen, bigger than anything in Ireland. World War Two was only over eight years since and vast tracts of the urban area are still fireweed-covered wastelands—bomb sites, courtesy of Herr Hitler's Luftwaffe.

"Do they not have horses here, Mam?"

"No, not many. They have a few, but not like over home."

"I don't see any donkeys either, nor dogs wandering the streets."

"No, you won't. The English keep their dogs inside of the house."

"Oh, yes, dogs inside of the house, that will be right! Ha-ha, dogs inside of the house, indeed. I suppose they keep chickens in the parlor, too!"

"Of course they do, and cheeky little sods like you are locked up in the coal hole! Now hold your whist a minute or we'll be missing our stop to get off."

Mam knows her way about the town, and she tells me her story. As a young girl, she had been here during the war, working in a munitions plant making machine guns. As the blitz continued, every night the German bombers were overhead showering death and destruction on the city. One night my mam was too ill with the flu to do her shift. Her roommate, another Irish girl, said she would put her name on the sick list at work and tell the foreman. That night the Nazi bombs found their elusive target and the factory was blown to pieces. Most of the workers were in the basement canteen on their tea break when the bombs hit. The four floors above came crashing down upon them, burying them alive under hundreds of tons of heavy machinery and bricks. The ones who were trapped had not the slightest chance of escape, there being no equipment available on the home front to lift such massive debris. As the weeks went by, the cries of the entombed faded and were still. My mother's friend, whom she had traveled with from Ireland, never returned. Mam gave out a long low sigh, and I tried to quickly change the subject.

"Brick, brick, and more brick! Sure everything here is made of bricks."

"That's true, the English like their bricks, so they do."

"I bet you don't know a song about bricks, Mam?"

"Oh, don't I?"

> *The county jail is made of bricks*
> *And the gates are made of I-ron*
> *With a big tall window and a big strong door*
> *To keep out Boody Byron*
> *When Boody Byron made a fart*

I thought the stink would blind me
Then he made another and I thought I'd smother
For the girl I left behind me.

Never can I beat Mam with this challenge—she has a poem or a song or a bit of old nonsense for everything. I resolve to take in the sights as Mam does the commentary.

"Things are on the move here, by God. After the destruction of six years of war, the entire place has to be rebuilt. Ye could make your golden fortunes here, you couldn't lose! Sure with full employment, being out of work is almost impossible. But some lazy buggers still manage it, just to stay on the dole." Mam goes on to tell me that at this time, there are tens of thousands of Irish workers in England, and the chiefs amongst these fellas are the far-famed Irish navvies, who are mostly unskilled, but fiercely hard-working, short-contract laborers. They are so clever that they can build houses, roads, railways, docks— in fact, anything. They take their name from the navigations or canals that were dug throughout Britain in the last century. Many who start with nothing but a pick and shovel go on to make a good living, and some end up owning their own construction firms or fleets of trucks and then go back and buy big houses in Ireland.

Schools, houses, pubs, factories speed past—even some of the streets are made of brick. It's marvelous. Ireland has little in the way of brick buildings, so all the more noticeable here are the curves and bastions of yellow, red, brown, and the beautiful gunmetal-colored Staffordshire blue bricks. However, if it all looks different, when we get off the bus it smells even stranger. Whereas in Limerick the pervading odors are of leather tanning, horseshit, peat smoke, and the ever-present tang of the river Shannon, Birmingham's atmosphere bears the piquancy of coal dust, gasworks, and asphalt. Sure enough, there are tar boilers every-where, sending their glorious reek skyward, and around these, little knots of men lean furiously on rakes and shovels, waiting "for the tae to boil." Whether or not they mean the tar in the boiler or the tea kettle sit-ting on its brazier, you can only guess. Occasionally my mam will spot a familiar face amongst the tarmac gangs and stop to exchange the news about what is happening over home. She smiles at everyone.

"Odd folk, the English. Most like to get on well with the Irish immigrants, but as anywhere, some folk can be awful spiteful and then they call you a Mick or a Paddy or a bog trotter or even a duck egg!"

"Why a duck egg?"

"Well, they reckon that like duck's eggs, one out of every three Irish people is a bad egg. It's all water off a duck's arse to me," says Mam. "Sticks and stones may break my bones, but names will never hurt me!"

Our journey ends at a little group of apartments, squat and square oblongs of urban utility, coy and effete, each rectangular window opaque with lace-curtain privacy, standing sternly above a prim pinafore of red sand bricks.

→ Chapter 2 ←

UNIFORMED AND MUSTACHIOED, GRANDDAD JIM WATKINS glares down from his First World War portrait above the fireplace. He has those eyes that follow you around the room, and I am very put off by the stern look of him. He looks like a baddie out of the films.

My granny, Mary-Anne, seems very nice. She is a skinny little woman and has long auburn hair tied up in a bun. Her maiden name was Bentley, and she is of Irish and Breton descent. She tells me that "Gentleman Jim Bentley," the bare-fist boxer, was her father and therefore my great-grandfather and I should be proud of him. She says he was very tough and, when training for a prizefight, would sit at the kitchen table with his fists pickling in hot salty water called brine to harden them up.

An actress and dancer in her youth, she had met my grandfather, Sergeant Major James T. Watkins, whilst he was serving with the Allied army in France in 1915. She offers us tea and while she's out of the room Mam whispers a song in my ear that gives me a fit of the giggles:

> *Mary-Anne the dancer,*
> *Wouldn't say her prayers,*
> *Catch her by the two legs,*
> *And throw her down the stairs*
> *The stairs went crack!*
> *Mary broke her back!*
> *And all the little ducks went,*
> *Quack! Quack! Quack!*

Mam points to a photograph on the mantelpiece. It shows a woman in a long skirt and buttoned boots, pushing a huge-wheeled baby carriage from which two moonfaced boys grin toothless smiles. In the background, two older boys in knee breeches hold ancient bicycles almost as tall as themselves.

"That's your granny there, and the baby with the squashed nose is your dad. The younger one is your uncle Ronny and the two other boys are your uncle Harold and your uncle Jimmy. When was this taken, Mary-Anne—about 1920?"

"It would be around 1922. Ronny was just a year old, Monica."

Mary-Anne arranges the tea set, which has hexagonal china cups and saucers, very posh indeed. I'd never seen the like. With a gurgle, the hot brown infusion swirls in the silver tealeaf strainer and a tippet of milk is added from a fine floral jug. Mam picks up a pair of silver tongs and drops a small white cube into her cup.

"It's sugar," she whispers, answering my questioning look. The tea has a taste all its own and is very nice. Perhaps it was Chinese tea—we had nothing like it in Ireland. Granny and Mam both sup at the tea with their little fingers pointing stiffly out from the cups. It looks very odd and is called manners. Gran gives us biscuits along with the tea, the sort the Americans call cookies, but I'm warned against dipping them into my cup, as that's called *bad* manners.

After tea, Gran sits chatting with my mother and I take this as my cue to explore the room, which is warm and cozy with heavy braided velvet curtains and a coal fire. I've never seen upholstered chairs before, or the big fat seat called a settee. In Ireland, chairs are made of wood and don't have matching flowery cushions all over them. Here, each armchair has a white linen handkerchief draped over the top. Mam says these are called antimacassars and are used to keep men's hair oil from staining the fabric. One corner of the room contains a harmonium, which I'm not allowed to play with, and a long bookcase with the titles showing through the leaded-glass doors. Opposite, two electric reading lamps in the shape of bronze soldiers hold green glass lampshades above an old Singer sewing machine, and in the farthest corner, the wireless talks quietly to itself and an attendant audience of beautifully ornate antique glass paperweights. For all the novelties, it is the coal fire that intrigues me the most. Being only used to the slow smoldering glow of a peat fire, this is altogether quite different. Queerly shaped twisted tongues of flame flicker in a dainty dance from the black nuggets. Hissing jets of coal gas squirt out from their cracks, gray and vaporous, then catching light, jig and gyrate in ragged crescents of orange, red, and yellow. Veins of intrusive copper ignite, sending arcs of iridescent blue shooting up the chimney, and the sulfurous tang of soot provides the atmosphere with a new and subtle aroma. I am mesmerized.

There is a noise in the hall.

"Here's Jim now," says my gran, tucking a loose piece of hair behind her ear.

I hide behind the settee to avoid being seen by those cold staring eyes. The door opens, and, instead of the Joseph Stalin character from the photograph, there enters a smiling, round-faced, bald old chap, with wire-rimmed glasses and a walrus mustache.

"Hello, Monica," says he, looking around. "Where's the young fellow? I've got something here for him."

I wiggle out of my hiding place and am presented with a small toy army tank. It is made of tin and is driven by clockwork. When allowed to run, it trundles along and suddenly flips over in a mechanical somersault. It is brilliant, and so is my granddad Jim for finding it for me. He says it was made by German prisoners of war, who were very clever at such things, and to beat it all, they made everything out of old sardine tins turned inside out. The tank is vividly painted with bright colors and held together by a system of slots and lugs. I later learn to undo these tags with a teaspoon, and it is true—they were old sardine tins and you could see the labels with fishermen painted on them!

The ice is broken and Granddad Jim is my best pal. I spend many hours sitting on his knee while he reads to me. He sees little merit in kiddies' books and only reads to me from the likes of George Eliot, Sir Arthur Conan Doyle, and Francis Brett Young.

"You're putting an old head on young shoulders, Jim."

"Nonsense, Mary-Anne, he's better reading this than that drivel in the comics."

Granddad is also very keen on Sir Walter Scott and, particularly, the *Waverley* novels. He has a great love of anything Scottish, and my grandparents spend most of their holidays up there.

When Granddad Jim isn't in the mood for reading, he tells me stories of his childhood and the rich history he grew up with, long ago.

"Did you know I was born in Bleddfa in the heart of Welsh Wales, where our people had held land since before the Roman invasion? Oh, yes, indeed! The battle of Pylleth was fought on our ancestral land centuries ago, and the great Welsh patriot and freedom fighter, Owain Glyn Dŵr, used our hidden valleys as a base to attack and harry the English in 1400. A very great man, was Owain. A Celtic hero to be proud of!

"Well, in the late eighteen hundreds, you see, the Great Western Railway Company began to forge its iron sinews into the heart of wild Wales, and legions of Irish navvies flooded into the construction camps and shantytowns that sprang up along the railhead. They needed the work, see? I was only twelve and had just left school. Ever the enterprising, I made lemonade and sold it by the pint to the thirsty workers. Loved it, they did! So anyway, one hot summer's day when I was plying my trade amongst the rail crew, a near parboiled Irishman stopped his toil and leaning on his pick wiped the sweat from his brow. He began to sing 'There's Trouble in My Native Land,' a song now sadly lost, I believe. Soon there wasn't a man jack working on the entire cutting. He finished his song to tearful applause and cheers. As an encore and to lift the heart, he launched into this old Napoleonic war song.

'Bad luck to this marching
Pipe claying and starching
How neat we must be to be killed by the French . . .

Now I love "Garryowen"
When I hear it at home
'Tis a marvelous tune, with an elegant lilt,
But the strength of the beat
Doesn't sound half as sweet
When you're facing the French and about to be kilt.'

"After some remonstration, the foremen and gangers got the men grudgingly to resume work, and the young James Watkins—that was me, you see—was left with an experience that I never forgot and an unquenchable thirst for Celtic music that stayed with me ever since. You know, I love to hear your mother sing those antediluvian Irish songs."

"That's typical of Jim . . . use ten words where one would suffice."

"I'll give you one word in a minute, Mary-Anne, that you won't hear in church!"

This new life in postwar Birmingham is full of oddities and exotica. There is marmalade, which I didn't care for; and bread and goody, which I did. The latter is made of broken-up crusts of bread soused with hot milk and finished with a wee dusting of brown sugar. It is a great favorite of my granddad Jim, who eats it twice a day, and later on I am to find out why.

Soon I am settled in and begin exploring. The back garden teems with blackberries, red currants, black currants, and gooseberries, or goosegogs, as they are commonly called. My gran makes a lot of jams and jellies, and I like to help her in the kitchen, which she always refers to as the scullery. One chilly morning, Mam puts together the sticks and paper makings of a fire and stares into an empty matchbox.

"Were out of lucifers, Mary-Anne."

"You can get a light off of the geyser in the kitchen, Monica." Mam goes out of the room only to return puzzle-faced a minute later.

"There's no one in the kitchen, he must have left!"

"No, she means the water heater, Mam, the thing on the wall by the sink. It's called a geyser."

Luckily, I had previously been introduced to this bizarre apparatus by my granddad Jim. It has a little blue flame that just peeps out of its burner, but when the hot tap is turned on—*whoosh!* The entire thing lights up with hundreds of gas jets. Very spectacular! But how on earth does it know when to flare up? I give it a wide berth anyway, in case it is some way in league with its Irish cousin, the dreaded gas meter, and it takes a notion to attack me.

I settle into life in 1002 Warwick Road, Acock's Green, Birmingham, like a cat with a new cardboard box. There is still no sign of my dad and thankfully no mention of the eye hospital or pickled onions.

The whole town is abuzz with talk of the forthcoming coronation of

Queen Elizabeth II, or the "Old Baked Bean," as my granddad Jim calls her in rhyming slang.

"It's a shame you Irish don't have a royal family," says the woman at the grocery shop.

"We've more sense," says my mam. "And anyway, if we wanted one, there's more royal blood in my little finger than in the whole lot of them jumped-up buggers!"

The shop girl is scandalized, and my mother sweeps out of the grocer's like an empress—royal finger and all.

"They make me sick, with their sucking up to the royalty, bloody bunch of inbreeds who wouldn't piss on you if you were on fire! They should have more sense. BloodyEnglish!" Mam is in an acidulous mood, and she pokes her tongue out at the Union Jack banner proclaiming the message "God Bless the Queen."

"God bless my old aunt Fanny! And that bloody awful dirge they call a national anthem—Jeesus! It gives me a pain in the nawney!"

"What's the nawney?"

"Never you mind."

Through the red, white, and blue bunting–filled streets we march to the sweetie shop. I'm in good spirits because this is to be my once-a-week treat. Mam swings her arms like a trooper and sings the stirring Irish national anthem, "The Soldier's Song":

Sinne Fianna Fáil
Atá fá gheall ag Éirinn . . .

Wartime rationing is still in force, and I have my own identity card and ration book. There are coupons for clothes, meat, fish, and eggs, but at my age, it is just the sweet coupons that interested me. I only get two a week, though, and even then they don't buy very much, Godhelpus!

May is the white-haired old lady in the little Victorian confectionery shop at the end of the street. She always seems to enjoy my weekly visit to her sweet-smelling emporium, which looks like a scene from a Charles Dickens novel, all dark oak, polished brass handles, and bull's-eye glass windows.

"Is it your usual then, Willie?"

She knows it is.

"Yes, please, May, two marshmallows, one in a bag and one in my hand."

I think she gets a kick out of my childish ways and funny Irish accent.

Confectionery remains rationed until I am seven, which does me no harm and indeed did well to keep me out of the dentist's chair. Of all the things I miss about the old country, it was the patsy-pop that I could really go for, but there was none to be had hereabouts, more's the pity. On my return home, I will be straight up the road to Paddy King's, to purchase for a penny what could not be got for love nor money in pagan England.

The road back from May's sweet shop is festooned with large colorful enamel advertisement signs screwed to the dark red brick on every street corner. Mam reads every one of them out loud, so I can learn the big words.

"Tizer the Energiser!" the one showing a big bottle of pop reads. Next to it a cheeky-looking monkey stares at his reflection in a newly scrubbed frying pan: "USE MONKEY BRAND SOAP!"

Across the street, a large orange-and-black sign entreats us to "Drink Brooke Bond Tips . . . the Tea you can really TASTE!"

"Drink VIMTO," demands a purple-tinted bottle of pop.

One large and colorful sign depicts the Holy Father sitting in the Vatican supping beef tea. Mam reads the slogan: "Two things Infallible—The POPE and BOVRIL!"

And like a call from back home in Ireland: "GUINNESS IS GOOD FOR YOU!"

The rag and bone men come around in their horse and carts, blowing old brass bugles and calling out, "Rags, bottles, and bones." If you give them something useful they would often swap you a balloon or a goldfish. In these years after the war, little goes to waste. All metal is recycled, and each family has a pig bin to put waste food—potato peelings, rotten apples, or what have you—for the wee porkers. I like the horse and carts clip-clopping along the cobbled streets and the way my granddad Jim scurries after them with a bucket and shovel to collect shite for his roses.

Entering the hallway of the house I realize something is different.

The air smells of cigarettes and there is a large army kit bag in the hall. I run into the living room to investigate and fall straight over the sausage-shaped draft excluder. As I lie sprawled facedown into the red-and-brown Chinese carpet, a voice in the air above me says, "OOPS-a-daisy!"

I arise tearlessly and towering above me is a huge soldier in full dress uniform. He is like the ones I've seen in the toy shop, but to me, he seems sixty feet high! His trousers have a red stripe running down each leg, and he has a brown mustache.

I do not know what to make of him or the long steel and wood thing he has with him. It looks like a toy gun but is of a weight that surely none could lift. He tells me it's a Lee-Enfield Mk. IV 303 rifle. He picks me up and gives me a kiss—he needs a shave.

This, then, is my dad, Bombardier Reginald Watkins, a noncommissioned officer of the Royal Artillery, home on leave before parading as part of the guard of honor at the queen's coronation in London. It's odd to see him with my mam. I feel a bit jealous.

Some days later Mam and Dad take me shopping. It is our first family outing.

Dad carries me up on his shoulders and I get a first-rate view of the world from above the top of my dad's head, plastered with this shiny Brylcreem stuff. Dad has his attention fixed upward at me and fails to notice the ice cream sign straddling the pavement. He promptly falls over it. This projects me in an arc, cometlike, from his grasp. But being well upholstered against the chilly spring air, I bounce along the sidewalk like a rubber beach ball, all with little ill effect.

The next minute I am snatched up. My father is furious. He dives into the nearest shop door, towing me in the air behind him.

"Are you the manager?" he demands.

"Yes, sir. I am indeed," says the man in the white coat, venturing a discreet smile.

BANG! My father hits him square on the nose. As the ill-starred shopkeeper slips gently to the floor, my father is roaring at him.

"You stupid bastard! The child could have been killed!"

"Reg! Reg!" My mother is pulling at his arm.

"Bloody stupid place to leave a sign!"

"Reg! For Christ's sake!" Father, in his "battle fury," takes no notice.

"REEEGGG!" Mother is desperate. "YOU'RE IN THE WRONG SHOP!"

Dad produces a wiggly face like one of the cartoon characters from the news theater and looms over the counter.

"Sorry, pal, my mistake!" He comforts his cowering victim, then he is gone like a shot from a gun, us following.

A few days later we go downtown on the bus and into an imposing-looking building that smells of iodine and disinfectant. I don't like it one little bit.

The doctor at the eye clinic gives me a ragged, old one-eyed teddy bear to hold, which does nothing at all for my confidence. Then, sitting me in a giant, cold, leather chair, he wheels over a thing that shines a bright light into my eyes. After some poking about in a drawer, he leans into me, peering into his space gun. I can see right up his nose!

"I'm afraid the right eye will always be weak, Mrs. Watkins, but he'll most likely grow out of his squint."

"Very good," says Mam. "Will he have to have glasses?"

"Indeed, yes, and he'll have to wear a patch over his good eye to force the other to improve."

Well, this was great news! No pickled onions, and I always fancied glasses because clever people wear them. Apart from this, I have the bonus of a pirate's eye patch that makes you grow "out of your squint," whatever that was. It all seems very grand and it looks like the visit is worthwhile after all. He even lets me look into his space gun, but all I see is a round blob of light.

On the way home we venture into the fish market. The building is just walls now, open to the heavens, the roof having been destroyed by German bombs in November 1940. I eat three plates of cockles drowned in malt vinegar, which I then drink. It is lovely!

By the time the spectacles arrive, I have quite forgotten about them. Granddad Jim comes in with a big pile of mail.

"Your gig lamps are here, Willie."

Mam slowly opens the parcel, putting aside the brown paper and string, and there they are, little round specs with . . . Agh! Horrors! PINK RIMS!

"I can't wear these, they're for girls!"

"You bloody well shall and you bloody well will, by crikey! No son of mine will ever look a gift horse in the mouth!"

I have no idea what she is talking about, but I know better than to argue. To add insult to injury, a special plaster sticks them to my face, so there is no escape from the poxy things. I look in the mirror, wishing to see a scientist-type chap reflected, but instead, staring back dolefully at me is the village idiot.

Mam must be feeling sorry for me. She takes me to see *Bambi*.

"We better test your new glasses," she says.

I wanted to test them with a hammer.

At any rate I knew it was Mam's custom, after the movies, to go next door to the Oxford Restaurant. There they serve the finest sausage and stuffing in the world, and it is my favorite. The forest fire rages, Bambi's mother dies, Mam sobs into her handkerchief, and I sit in the darkness, my stomach rumbling like a volcano, dreaming of sausages and stuffing.

"Have you no heart at all, child?" Mam says, appalled at my indifference.

"Sure 'tis only an old filum," I say, the steam from the sausages condensing on my glasses and gravy running down my chin.

"What did you feel when his poor mother died?" she entreats.

"Hungry," says I.

Mam shakes her head in resignation, and the dreaded lipstick-and-mascara stained handkerchief makes its appearance.

"You're a muck savage," is her final word on the matter, as she spits on the hankie.

Dad, resplendent in his best uniform, says he's going off to London, "to look at the Queen," like the old nursery rhyme would have it. Mam and I go with him to the railway station, where he mingles with a great squad of other soldiers all dressed the same. The military police won't allow civilians onto the platform, and Mam and I have to wave from behind the iron railings. There is a huge press of people, cheering and waving flags at the troop train. But I'm crying. With all the soldiers looking so much alike, I can't see which one is my dad anymore. My mother doesn't notice me until I get my head stuck in the bars of the gate and howl even louder. In the ensuing panic I miss the final departure of the London Coronation Special altogether, as I'm busy being scolded for sticking my head through the bars and getting my ears rubbed with stinky soap by the stationmaster.

I'm still crying when we get on the bus to go back to Granny's. Mam says Dad is only going away for a few days and I'll see him soon enough. I'm not convinced.

We go to the Freemans' house to see the coronation on a new televisor. I am very excited, as I have never seen a TV in action. Granddad Jim tells me that television had begun transmitting from Alexandra Palace, London, in the late 1930s, but the broadcasts were suspended at the outbreak of the war. The coronation of 1953 is the BBC's attempt to reestablish the service, and thousands, like the Freemans, have bought new television sets for the special occasion.

The house is as crowded as a wasp's nest, as this is the only TV in the entire street. Everyone has been invited, and the Brits are in a festive mood. There are sandwiches and pop for the kids, and beer and spirits for the older folk.

A great silence falls upon the eager crowd. Mr. Freeman checks his pocket watch and, with somber ceremony, switches on the television. The set begins to warm up and after what seems like an age, the sound comes on first with a loud drum roll and everyone stands up as a fuzzy picture appears. A mournful, lethargic tune fills the room like a funeral march. The TV image sharpens. It shows a man in military uniform, standing on a stone column.

"There's my dad!" I shout, pointing with certainty at the granite statue of Admiral Lord Nelson standing atop his pillar in London's Trafalgar Square.

"Quiet, child! Have you no respect for the national anthem?"

"No, it gives me a pain in the nawney!"

⇥ Chapter 3 ⇤

THE SEASONS TURN AND DAD GOES BACK TO HIS UNIT. THERE
is much weeping, and I want to go with him. He tells me I must stay
behind to look after my mam on the trip back to Ireland, as she is such
a poor sailor. Once again, Dad disappears from my life, and two days
later we take off for my other home over the water. This time sailing
from Liverpool on the B+I steamer *M. V. Munster.* The crossing is pleasant, and Mam is able to sit inside, as third-class accommodation is far
superior to the old S.S. *Princess Maud.* The voyage is much longer, however, and it is nighttime when we sail up the treacle-black river Liffey
and dock amid the golden glow of Dublin's North Wall pier.

The city is afire with neon signs, the first I have ever seen. One in an
alley off Dame Street shows a before-and-after baldy man, frowning
under his naked neon dome, then seconds later—Exulted!—colorfully
crowned with his flashing electric wig!

"I bet you don't have a song about a baldy man, Mam?"

> *Hey there baldy over there*
> *What's it like to have no hair?*
> *Is it hot or is it cold?*
> *What is it like to be bald?*

"Got me again, Mam."

Another spectacular display is at the end of Grafton Street. It takes
up the full parapet of an entire block and depicts a cheery neon pig frying two sausages in a pan. The piggy, having decided the bangers are
ready, gives them a flick and *Wheeee!* The pair of links loop the loop
across the building and land square on the plate of a smiling diner.

"Give me a song about sausages, Mam. I bet you can't."

Oh, the next time you visit your grocer
Tell him no other sausage will do sir.
The next time you visit your grocer
It's Donnelley's Sausage for you.

"Oh, Mam, you're a terror!"

The train ride down from Dublin is a cozy affair. We have the compartment to ourselves and lollop across the brown-braided seats, as snug as seals on a sandbar.

In the dim carriage light, Mam fishes out a copy of the *News of the World*.

"'Twill be nice to be home again, eh, Willie?" She flicks through the newspaper.

"'Twill so, Mam, but why is it home when we have a home in England as well?"

"Ah, well, that's the Irish for you—always on the move, taking their homes with them on their backs like a snail." She nods agreement with herself and ruffling the folds of her gossip sheet, reads aloud the curious headline: "'HOW THE WELFARE WORKER'S MODEL WIFE FELL FOR THE CHINESE HYPNOTIST FROM THE CO-OP BACON FACTORY.' Jasus, who'd of thought it . . . shocking . . . *tut-tut!*"

Mam turns over the pages to be shocked and reshocked again and again. Although I doubted the wisdom of distracting my mother from her weekly dose of scandal, I'm left in some puzzlement by her previous explanation and venture another query.

"Mam?"

"What now?" says the distracted voice coming from behind the newspaper.

"Mam, I don't get it. What's the thing about the snail? What does it have to do with us having two homes—and what on earth is that story you're reading?" Mam's paper crumples into her lap. She stares at me like a cat about to pounce on a field mouse and chastises my interruption with a bit of poetry:

"You are a funny fellow," says a puppy to a snail.
"As far as anyone can see, you haven't got a tail."

"My tail is not a waggy-one. It's in my house upstairs,
And I don't poke my nose like pups, in other folks' affairs!"

Jeez, that's rich coming from Mam, who not only minds her own business but kindly accepts the burden of everyone else's besides.

"The priest says it's a sin to read that newspaper!"

"Does he so? Maybe he's feared there'd be a story about him in it."

I wake up in a brightly lit Limerick station. A taxi ride through the streets proves the worth of the taxi driver, who is telling us of the great electrification scheme going on all over Ireland since the building of the hydroelectric plant on the Shannon at Ardnacrusha.

"Sure the 'lectric light is a marvel, missus. It don't be flickering like the ould gas lanterns, and you can see for miles with it."

It's true. Lights twinkle out in the darkness, way off on the hills of Clare, and it's hard to tell where the streetlights stop and the stars begin.

The car arrives at Nana's house. Electric light spills from every window.

On entering the old homestead, I notice a change of smell. The aroma of peat smoke is still present, but the sweet tang of warm paraffin oil no longer wafts from the now redundant kerosene lamps.

My relatives greet me with a flurry of head pats and "My, hasn't he grown, Monica." Behind their heads, a big new painting of Jesus gazes down from the top of the stairwell, illuminated by a red neon crucifix glowing beneath. After the teapot has made its second circuit around the kitchen table, I excuse myself and sneak upstairs for a surreptitious peek at the mysterious holy picture.

Jesus' long brown hair curls down to his shoulders and his bearded mouth is fixed in a benign hint of a sad smile. His blue eyes are whirlpools of sorrow as he points to the raw red thing sticking out of his bared chest. Stuck through with jaggy, spiked thorns and surmounted by hot flicks of flame, the heart-shaped object on Our Savior's breast is a fearsome sight. What could it all mean? I wasn't going to ask my folks and get called an ignorant pagan again. I'll have to work this one out for myself. What did it mean? Then it dawns on me. Of course! This must be what the grown-ups call heartburn! Flushed with the pride of discovery, I look for confirmation on the little brass name plaque fixed to the gilt frame beneath. In the dim bleed of light from the neon cross, I trace out the letters with my finger, making the sounds like Granddad Jim had taught me: T . . . H . . . E . . . S . . . A . . . C . . . R . . . E . . . D . . . H . . . E . . . A . . . R . . . T.

"The Scared Heart!" I find myself whispering in the blood-colored gloom.

Poor Jesus, with heartburn to contend with, it's little wonder he looks so melancholy. 'Tis true what Mam says: "He suffered for the sins of the world."

Later, as I climb the stairs to my bed, I glance once more at the sore-looking sacred heart and pray that Jesus might be allowed a glass of Andrew's Liver Salts to ease his pain.

The next morning, in the full brightsome of day, Christ appears much more at ease with his complaint and seems to have a merry twinkle in his eye. Ah, there's great power in prayer, I'm thinking, as I dive downstairs to a fried Irish breakfast that would give a goat indigestion.

The kitchen door opens and in comes a bicycle. Behind the bicycle is a smile and behind that, in his postman's uniform, is my uncle Seán. He is always laughing and joking and acting the gussie with us kids. He's like a big kid himself, and he speaks lovely Irish.

Breakfast done with, I am sitting in the peat house, just off the kitchen, trying to build an igloo with rectangular blocks of turf. It is grand to be home and busy constructing something. It's no easy matter getting the cuts of dried peat to stack in concentric circles and my previous attempts lie like the ruins of the ancient monks' cells on Skellig Island.

"You'll get fleas, playing in that turf," says Seán.

I grin like a gombeen.

"Here's a tosser for you," he says, flicking me a silver sixpenny piece.

I miss the catch—and it is consumed by the piles of peat.

"You'll have your work cut out for ye, finding that!"

And I do, but it was worth six patsy-pops!

"The boys will be over later and we'll all go to the pictures," says my uncle.

"Terrific!" says I, and spend the rest of the morning scratching around in the peat for the elusive sixpence. At last I see the glint of it just as the back door almost leaves its hinges, and the querulous circus of humanity known as my cousins fall, flop, and flounder on the kitchen floor.

These are Joe, Mikesy, and Willum, my aunt Frances's boys, all screeching and squabbling, like cats in a passion.

"What's all this, lads? I never heard such a din!" Seán picks up his dinner plate left warming above a hissing pot on top of the ancient gas stove.

"Mammy said I was to hold the sweetie money," says one.

"No, she didn't! She said I could!" says another.

"Well, I'm the eldest, so it should be me!" joins the third.

"Enough! Enough!" says Seán, still smiling. "It goes to the quietest!"

This psychological ruse has instant efficacy and the Buckleys sit at the table like the three wise monkeys, Hear No Evil, See No Evil, and Speak No Evil.

I emerge from the store triumphant, holding my tanner coin aloft.

"There now," says Seán, "who says there's no money in farming?" He removes the saucepan lid covering his meal and stares at the food with a convulsive shudder.

"Did yer mam cook this for me, Willie?"

"She did, Seán. It's Tuesday, so it's chops, peas, and potatoes. Is it all right, so?" He shudders again.

"Would you ever get a fork and mash up them peas for me? I can't be atein' them like that, they give me the heebie-jeebies, they do."

So it was true after all, what Mam had told me, a long time ago, that Uncle Seán wouldn't eat anything round! I suppose that on this occasion Mam had forgotten about the peas, but sure enough, word had it that he couldn't face a baby spud, or a wee tomato, nor button mushrooms, nor any of their ilk. Cherries, peas, pickled onions, and gobstoppers all fell foul of his spheraphobia and were immediately mashed into a mushy pap or dismissed to the bin of seagulls' scraps. He would have hated brussels sprouts, but there were none of them to be had in Ireland. Still, it takes all sorts to make a world, and Seán finishes his pulverized repast with relish and we strike out bold for the Treaty Stone.

Outside St. Munchin's Church we meet up with Nana, my mam, Seánin and Martin Franklin, my aunt Maura's lads. We are soon joined by cousin Breda, who, like me, lived at Nana's house. We all troop up to the Thomond cinema or the "Flea Pit," as it was known. It was the sort of place you might want to sit on a newspaper and wipe your feet when you come back out. On Saturdays you could get in to the pictures for a jam jar, and it was fun to see the lines of rowdy kids trying to smash each other's jelly jars for devilment. Anyway, we see Errol Flynn in *Robin of Sherwood,* and it is mighty!

For the next few weeks wee wild lads in Lincoln Green terrorize the locality with homemade bows and arrows and try to rob the rich and the poor, too, for that matter! Cinema is all the rage and acting out the stories is the most thrilling thing in the world to small lads with more imagination than common sense.

Evenings around the kitchen table are great craic all together. We play cards and have beetle drives and there are stories, always stories. My favorite are the Fleádh nights. These get-togethers, impromptu as they are, happen as often as not at the end of the month, when money is running short. A crate or two of stout arriving at the house will sooner or later give rise to a mighty night of story and song. My folks all do their party pieces, as like as not in the old Irish language. Mam sings "Ar M'Eiri Dhom Ar Mhadin," which means "I Arise at Morning," then maybe recites "The Siege of Athlone," both from the Williamite wars. Maura offers "Bridgín Bhán Mo Stór" (Bright Bridget My Treasure) or "Maidrín Rua" (The Little Red Dog—The Fox, in other words).

Grandda plays jigs and reels on the wooden flute and beautiful slow haunting airs such as "Rosín Dubh" (My Small Dark Rose—a secret freedom song, in which Ireland is portrayed as a tiny rose), or the "Coolin," a lament for the ponytail that the ancient Celts wore until its banning by the BloodyEnglish!

I like to sit quietly under the table and bother no one, as my more vociferous cousins get sent home for blaggarding or off to bed for falling asleep. Sitting in my tent of legs and ankles like a hermit in his cloister, I hear Grandda recite *The Sixpence,* an uproarious tale of a day in the life of a coin and all the people whose hands it passed through. My lovely grandda, Willie MacDonagh, has a great voice for lilting and a generous supply of Celtic songs and tall stories for all social occasions.

One I particularly liked and made well to memorize was "Dinny Burns the Piper." So here follows a wee snatch of it:

In the year '98 when our trouble was great,
It was treason to be a Milesian
And the blackwhiskers said that we'd never forget,
And our history tells us there were Hessians,
In these troublesome times; everything was a crime
And murder it never was riper
In the town of Glensheed, not an acre from Meath
Lived one Dinny Burns the piper.

Neither wedding nor wake would be worth a shake
If Dinny was first not invited
For at squeezing the bags, or emptying the kegs,
He astonished as well as delighted.
In these times poor Dinny, he could not earn a penny
Martial law had him stung like a viper,
And it kept him within, till the bones of his skin,
Were grinning through the rags of the piper.

Nana's favorite song is "Long Shadows on the Grass" and it is woefully sad. She also sings "Ching Chang Chinaman, Chop—Chop—Chop," which is a funny Victorian music hall song. Sometimes, when in a more mellow mood, Nana croons a slow haunting air called "The Spinning Wheel," which tells the tale of a secret courtship in sumptuous imagery. It so easy to picture it all in the mind's eye and it moves me to have memories way beyond my own childish experiences.

After hearing these songs so many times over in childhood, I find that they have slowly sunk into my head through some wonderful Celtic osmosis.

I especially like the strong, stirring lyrics of Canon Sheehan's fine old song "Seán Ui Dhuir a Ghleanna," or John O'Dwyer of the glen, as it is in English. This song has a special meaning for us, for our little house stands on the very spot where, legend has it, he forded the Shannon in 1690, and, in consequence, our old Shannonside house was called O'Dwyer's Villa:

> *After Aughrim's great disaster*
> *When our foe in sooth was master*
> *It was you who first plunged in and swam*
> *The Shannon's boiling flood.*
> *And through Slieve Bloom's dark passes*
> *You led your gallowglasses*
> *Although the hungry Saxon wolves*
> *Were howling for your blood.*

This is all wonderful stuff. I love history, and my little world was saturated with it.

King John's castle, dating from the 1200s, glowers at us from across the river. This was the same Bad King John that the English barons forced into signing the Magna Carta in 1215. Grandda Willie has a book about it and one evening proceeds to give us a lecture and all.

"Hm . . . hm . . . the Magna Carta. This charter of English liberties has over the years been much vaunted, by some politicians, as a bill of rights. Even a cursory reading of the text shows that it is no such thing; sure it guarantees rights mostly for the nobility and the bigwigs, not the ordinary folk who were mostly slaves, serfs, and villeins!"

He reads: "'For the holding of general council of the kingdom . . . we shall cause to be summoned the archbishops, bishops, earls and the great barons of the realm. Furthermore we shall summon our sheriffs, bailiffs and all others who hold us in chief.' In other words, let's keep it in the family!

"They're still the same and the legacy lives on in the nonelected, hereditary House of Lords. The Americans had the good sense to rebel against this lot and elect their upper house. Anyway, after King John had grudgingly signed the Magna Carta, the barons of Merrie England decided they now had the power to get rid of the bugger once and for all. So with their wonderful sense of English fair play, they dumped the mad monarch on the necks of the poor Irish in that castle yonder. And do you know what happened then?"

"No, Grandda."

"He died of a surfeit of lampreys."

"What's lampreys?"

"They are boiled eels! And he ate so many of them that he burst! Too good for him! The greedy old sod! As if the English royals weren't revolting enough, the antics of some of the commoners were just as bad!" He went on to tell me of the time in Irish history called the Curse of Cromwell, no book this time, he spoke only from memory.

"Opposite the castle stands the house where Oliver Cromwell's equally nasty successor and son-in-law, General Henry Ireton, set up his headquarters in 1651. He and his army besieged the walled township of Limerick in an attempt to starve out the native Irish defenders. The English Roundheads and self-styled Sons of God were spoiling for more blood after taking part in the infamous massacres of men, women, and children in Drogheda and Wexford in 1650. With God Is Love painted around the mouths of their cannon, they began their bombardment.

"After six months, the remnants of the plague-ridden garrison surrendered. Five thousand had died of the epidemic and thousands more in the defense of the walls. After reassurances to the contrary, Ireton had most of them put to death. And, as if the murderous excesses of these Puritan English bigots was not enough, the few survivors were shipped as slaves to the Americas—the first of those unfortunates to be sent there!

"However, fate had a trick up her sleeve and within the year the foul Ireton died of the same plague, screaming for a priest, as the story goes and too good for the rat. Even the English eventually had their revenge upon him; Ireton's body was exhumed from its place of honor in Westminster Abbey and, to add insult to injury, burned at the gibbet on Tyburn Hill, shortly after the fall of Cromwell and the restoration of King Charles the Second."

Grandda takes a long pull on his pint of stout and starts afresh.

"Up at the end of the street there stands the Treaty Stone of 1691, commemorating yet another bloody siege and the subsequent treaty with the English under William of Orange, in which terms the Irish people would enjoy civil and religious freedom if the city's garrison of some fifteen thousand agreed to surrender and take ship for exile in

France. With their commander, Patrick Sarsfield, the survivors of the siege boarded a fleet of French ships and sadly departed for the Continent. As soon as the sails were out of sight, the English broke every article and covenant of the agreement, and so Limerick became known as *the city of the violated treaty.*"

He thumps the table and sits down. We all clap and cheer, and he takes a bow.

Mam, as ever, knows a song about those events so long ago and strikes up:

> *When William stormed with shot and shell*
> *At the walls of Garryowen,*
> *In the breach of death my Donal fell*
> *And he sleeps near the Treaty Stone.*
> *That breach the foeman never crossed*
> *While he swung his broadsword keen.*
> *But I do not weep for my darling lost,*
> *For he fell 'neath the flag of green.*

Mam says, "You can't spit without hitting a piece of history around here."

"And neither is it the dry old stuff of books either!" says Seán. "The castle is always there as a reminder of a ruthless enemy, and d'ya see the bullet-riddled houses along the Shannon wall? It was the Black and Tans did that, in 1920."

Nana sups her tea and tells of the day when a woman walking with her was shot dead by the Black and Tans at the end of our street.

"Those whore's melts were recruited from every jail an' mental asylum in England, supposedly to fight the IRA. Bunch of bloody cowards they were. They kept well away from our boys, an' spent most of their time getting langers in the pubs an' refusing to pay for it, too! This day they get ordered out of a bar by their senior officer an' they're like a pack of wild animals, cursing an' firing at anything that moves an' threatening to shoot their own commander. They grabbed poor Joseph O'Donoghue an' dragged him off. Next day he was found with eighteen bullet holes in him. The Tans see me an' another woman running up Farron Seon. The bastards start shooting at us an' me with baby

Frances in me arms. I hear the woman next to me cry out. I look around an' she's lying there dead in the gutter with the drunken bastards laughing at her—may they roast in hell!" She stares out of the window, teacup in hand.

"Jasus sure they shot the mayor of Limerick, poor Michael O'Callaghan, in front of his whole family! Nothing but a bunch of blaggards and murderers, Godhelpus! What sort of mothers brought them into the world at all?" Nana sighs, the memory of those awful days of British occupation still vivid in her mind; she smiles over at Frances.

It was Sunday, and Sundays had a rare, brisk quality about them. Necks were scrubbed and inspected for tide marks, then without further ado, off to morning mass at St. Munchin's.

"Mam, why is the church called Saint Munchings? Was he a priest that was always eating?"

"No, his name was Munc-een, which is Irish for a little monk."

"It's a quare name anyway. Why was he so famous?"

"Sure, didn't he build the church yonder and put a curse on the Limerick people that wouldn't help him erect the steeple? It was left to some strangers who were passing by to help the poor old monk, and he said that from that day forward, strangers would always prosper in Limerick at the expense of the local population, who were a lazy bunch of goodfornothings. There they are—look, idle buggers, still as he left them!"

She points to the huddle of men sitting around the steps of the Treaty Stone and on the parapet of the Thomond bridge, waiting for the Treaty bar to open. The granite blocks of these archaic landmarks are polished to a fine luster over the years by the languid attentions of a million recumbent backsides squirming the minutes away till opening time. She sings:

> Saint Munchin was pleased with the job
> And laughed with devout satisfaction
> He gave every stranger a bob
> Along with his best benediction
> "May the strangers henceforward!" he cried

"In Limerick fast prosper and flourish
While like a bad foam on the tide
The natives will dwindle and perish
With plenty of nothing to do!"

"Does that mean we're cursed, too, Mammy?"

"No, no atall! Sure the curse was on Limerick and we live in Thomondgate, which is in County Clare. UP CLARE! AND DOWN THE RABBLE!" Mam punches the air with her fist, then crosses herself demurely when she sees the parish priest staring at her.

We go back home to a great feast of a meal, which was either breakfast or dinner, I don't know. Afterward, I take the scraps out to the squabbling seabirds that line the Shannon wall. You're not allowed to eat or drink before taking Holy Communion. I'm too young for the sacraments, but I starve along with the others. "'Tis good for your immortal soul," says Mam. I am usually as hungry as the seagulls.

The night service, or benediction, is a much more enjoyable undertaking. You are fed for a start, and kneeling before the looming alabaster statues is less unpleasant on a full stomach. The challenge is to stay awake! I like going to church better when I don't have to leave a nice warm bed. I love the singing in Latin and having the smell of incense around, but the second part of the service is a bit mystical and scares me.

God lives in a big, gold, spiky thing inside a round-topped house called a tabernacle. The priest goes up to the altar, opens the door of the tabernacle, draws back the curtain, and takes out the spiky thing. Then, holding it above his head, he recites some old incantation or other and turns to face the pews. He thrusts the spiky thing straight toward us. Mam and Nana make the sign of the cross, and I, peeping through my fingers, see the "eye of God" staring right into my sin-ridden soul.

I knew I had sins, but I didn't know how or why I got them. My nana, who I considered to be a living saint, was forever going to confession, but why was that? What could a God-fearing, righteous woman possibly do each week that required such frequent penitence? I decided to ask her straight out.

"Nana, what have you been doing so bad, that you must be telling the holy father?" Nana is momentarily stunned by my directness and looks uneasy.

Mam and Aunt Frances take up the job.

"Yer, come on now, Mam, what have you been up to?"

"Well . . . ," says Nana, with a sheepish grin. "I called Paddy the butcher, a . . . a . . . robbing bugger, Godforgivemeforswearing! An' he is so, so he is! Trying to sell me scrag end of mutton an' charge me for lamb!" She is fuming with indignation at the thought of being huckstered by a mere meat merchant.

"Anyway, the sin's on his own head," she said, tying on her plastic rain hat.

"The good Lord will forgive me—an' kick his arse into the bargain! So he will, Godforgivemeforswearing. Robbin' bugger, that he is, so he is!"

Behind my agitated grandmother, I can see Mam and my aunt making for the front door with their shoulders heaving with silent mirth.

Nana, Nelly Kelly, as she was born, is a great feast of a woman and a joy to be with. Although she never drinks liquor, she enjoys the company of those that do and loves a party. She can dance a jig and play the mouth organ at the same time. I never recall her having anything but white hair and a merry twinkle in her eye. Her laugh is ludicrously infectious, and almost anything will set her off into fits of giggles.

Mass being over, Mam and Nana sit in the kitchen, eating periwinkles, both of them helpless with laughter, recounting tales of Limerick's many odd characters and likewise their antics.

The cast of quare ones, as these worthies were known, was as never ending as the stories. Nana kicks off.

"Do you remember 'Old Wirey,' the quare fella who rode the bicycle all festooned with wires and sundry contrivances?"

"Oh, Jasus, how could ye forget him? He had dynamos, lights, horns, and all connected by curly wires, sticking into his pockets and coming out of his sleeves and up his arse and God knows where else. Sure he looked like Frankenstein's monster!"

"What do think he gained from that paraphernalia?"

"I dunno, but he was always as nice as ninepence to talk to."

"He was. He's dead now, TheLightOfHeavenToHim, so he is, and he had no one belonging to him. Do you remember the other old man? The fella who the same time every day walked up Lovers Lane outside of the house. I would see him from the kitchen window. He had a curly walking stick, the poor old chap, padding along in slow motion like a snail going to Jerusalem. 'Here's Mickey-walk-aisy,' you kids would all shout—Godhelpus, the poor crater!"

"Oh, God, yes! And do you mind the other unfortunate soul who had the spinal condition that had him bent nearly S-shaped?"

"Here's-me-head-me-arse-is-coming."

"That's him, and when the pair of them met in the lane from the opposite ends—oh, Jasus! It was like the clash of the Titans."

"Ah, now, the gaatch of the pair of them. They would meet in the middle of the lane and say hello. Then they'd be into odd maneuverings, trying to get a-past one another. 'Twas like a couple of old swans doing a courtship dance. They'd be shuffling this way and that to get the advantage, then all of a sudden break off the engagement and slip past each other like as if nothing had happened."

"Oh, good gentle shepherd, we won't see their like again."

"Unya-Conya was another quare hawk. Mind him sitting in his pew at the mass, rocking himself backwards and forwards, eyes shut tight, crooning away—*Unya-conya . . . unya-conya . . . unya-conya . . .* no matter what the hymn, his response was always the same—*Unya-conya!*"

"Maybe it was Latin, Mam?" I offer hopefully.

"Aye," says Nana. "Bloody bog Latin."

"It was always a blessing when he rocked himself to sleep."

"And the other bloke, what was his name? Steve-Mack. Remember how he was forever late and he always managed to come in the church just as the choir were singing the hymn to the Virgin Mary. 'Immaculate . . . Immaculate,' they'd be singing. 'Steve-Mack, you're late,' we'd be giving him, but he never took no notice."

"Danny-the-bags, coming home from his job at Rank's flour mills. He would be covered in fine white dust, and when you asked what he had been doing, he'd say, 'Bagging fog!' or 'Bagging daylight into a dark cellar!' He was a good sport, and he would beat his coat with his flat cap, sending up clouds of flour. Right enough, he was a good old stick."

At Hassett's Cross lived the legendary Jim Hassett. I never met him, but he was constantly referred to in our house. Whether some article of clothing was too big or too little, it would fit Jim Hassett. Whoever he was, he must have had the Druids' power of metamorphistic shape-changing to fill such a position in local folklore.

The majority of these souls were harmless, but as in all societies there were some bad-uns and some were positively malefic.

One such was Clack-a-Bone. He was a cantankerous old body who hated children and, even in passing, often dealt the unsuspecting a violent blow with his stick. He had an orchard dripping with apples, which was a terrible temptation to the young kids every autumn. A scrumping raid on his domain was always a risky business. If you were spotted, he would erupt with surprising agility from his back door, screeching: "I'll clack yer bones! I'll clack yer bones!" and demonically waving his cudgel. If caught, you could expect an unmerciful thrashing. All this, however, added to the dare factor and thus the thrill of it.

Another great dare is to climb over the Shannon wall and shin down the telegraph pole stay-wire. At low tide the river bank gives up its treasures. I find six of the Dutch General Ginkle's cannon balls that had bombarded the walls of Garryowen in the 1690–91 siege of Limerick that my grandda had told me about. I give them into the museum in town. Also one day, I see something round sticking in the crack of a rock. It is a bronze badge depicting a phoenix rising above a fire, surrounded with Celtic knotwork. A scroll underneath bore the Gaelic motto, "Forfaire agus Tairiseact," which I take to mean, "Watchful and Loyal."

From the same wall I fish, using just a reel of line and a big wormy hook with a lead weight. I catch an eel, which wraps around my wrist as I try to unhook it. I think it's cute and take it home as a pet.

"Get that slimy thing out of my house an' don't you bring serpents in here again!" Nana chases me out with the yard broom. I can outrun her, but others I can't.

Sabu Binn is a nasty piece of work, and teasing him is very dangerous and thus highly daring. I am far too small for this enterprise, but go along and watch from a safe distance as the older boys get near enough to the house to shout obscenities.

The upstairs window flies up and a head appears, cursing and blinding like a soul in the throws of demonic possession. What makes this apparition more bizarre is that the head wears a First World War German spiked helmet. He looks like a demented Kaiser Wilhelm! If he was good and drunk, it was certain he would remain in the house, but if not, he will give chase and an awful hiding to anyone he catches. This at least gives some respite to his own wife and kids, whom he abuses violently, in public as well as in private.

Like many of his ilk, he does no work himself, but his frail wife works as a skivvy to keep him in beer money. For her pains, she is forever sporting black eyes and bruises.

One day she brings home some Jeyes fluid, a powerful drain cleaner, in an old Guinness bottle and leaves it on the table. Sabu staggers in and downs it in a one 'er. He dies an agonizing tortuous death as befits such a tyrant and is no bloody loss to anyone, according to my nana.

"TheLightOfHeavenToHim," she adds in divine supplication.

Directly over the river stands the Island Field, or St. Mary's Park, as the city fathers had renamed it. We, on the Clare side of the Shannon, call it Hollywood due to the pageant of odd and exotic people who make up its populace, the likes of which you might only see on the silver screen. Ironically they have the last laugh—sure didn't they give us the great Irish actor Richard Harris.

It is pleasant to lie at night with the windows open, looking at the dancing lights of the Island Field across the roaring Shannon and smelling the tang of the distant sea.

Mam tells me stories like "The Colleen Bán," about an unfortunate girl seduced into robbing her father of his life's savings in 1820, then horribly murdered—drowned by her callous suitor. "Murder will out," as the old ones say, and sure enough her body was discovered floating in the Shannon. The rope knot tying the poor girl's neck to a large stone came undone—as indeed did the wicked plans of the young squireen, who danced the Devil's Jig on the gallows. This time there was no mistake about the knot, a looped noose of thirteen turns. The hangman knew his trade well.

In the warm darkness, my mother tells me tales of Drunken Thady and the Bishop's Lady and of the pig who went out to dig one fine day in Roscommon and the Kilkenny cats, who were so ferocious that they would fight each other until only their tails were left. Before I go to sleep each night, she teaches me how to count in Irish and say my prayers, like a good little boy. This simple life seems as endless as the hot summer, but with the first cries of autumn a cold wind blows in from the east and with it comes unexpected news.

"There's a letter here for you, Monica. It's from over in England." Uncle Seán shows me the new threepence stamps with the queen's face on them. Mam reads the letter and sits down with it open in her hand; she is trembling.

"Is it from me dad, Mam—is it?"

"Go outside and play, Willie."

"But Mam, I want to see the letter."

"Go on now and don't be annoying me, you bold boy, or I'll break you in half and fight the pair of you! Go out now, before I scatter your ashes to the four winds!"

I go out into the yard and sit under the kitchen window. I can hear the news.

"It's Reg. He's out of the army and has borrowed enough money to set up house in a . . . in a caravan!"

"JESUSMARYANDHOLYSAINTJOSEPH!" interjects Nana. "You'll be living in a trailer, like a tribe of gypsies, Jasus! A gypsy caravan, is it? Whatever next?!"

My heart sinks. I sit on the kitchen wastepipe with the familiar smell of the stinky drain wafting around me. Like any Catholic in trouble, I take to praying.

"Please, God, don't let them take me away from here! I'll be good and I won't moan when I go to mass, I promise!" With my eyes tight shut and my fist white-knuckled with clenching, I am oblivious to all but my little world of misery.

"Jasus, child, what ails ye?" says a voice. It's my uncle Paddy, looking in from his job on the Salmon Weir. "What are ya doing down there? Ye look like yer taking a shite!"

In a desperate attempt at staying behind with my family in Ireland, I take to my bed and feign illness. My folks are not to be kidded so easily and give me a dose of cod liver oil that gets me well acquainted with the bathroom. Even the prospect of the long sea voyage fails to rouse my spirits, proving that blood is thicker than water. When the morning of departure finally comes, I howl unmercifully, like a banshee with a bellyache. Through the blurry torrents of tears I see someone take a photograph of me and that sets me off.

"Don't ye be taking pictures of me when I'm crying—I'll kick the shins off ya!" All the effect this threat has is to raise a roar of laughter at my expense. Raging at this further indignity and very distraught, I rail on at them. Why could they not understand? I didn't want to be amongst strangers in a strange land, where I only knew my grandparents and Miss May at the sweetie shop. It was all so unfair!

Mam tries to drag me out of the door, but I hold on to the kitchen chair. How can I leave my old green plane? That faithful friend that has flown countless dangerous missions and carried me through the maelstrom of dogfights with the fearful Red Baron.

"The taxi's here, Monica."

"Come on now, Willie. You can see your dad tomorrow."

"NO! I don't care, I'm not going!"

"The taxi's waiting—come on!"

"No, I'm not going!"

"We can stop at Paddy King's for a patsy-pop!"

"OK, then!"

What can't be cured must be endured, especially when Mam puts things into proper context with the bribery of a patsy-pop.

The train heaves forward with a gaseous grunt, as over the orange glow of my ice lollipop, I watch distant Limerick City dissolve into a languid lake of gray mist, dreamily supporting the pugnacious turrets of King John's dark castle.

Mam looks very glamorous and has no shortage of admirers on the passage over the water. Some of the more optimistic men buy me sweets and sodas, in order to get acquainted with Mam, and I'm not about to complain to anyone.

Mam is less impressed by the amorous attentions of these hopefuls.

"They can try as they may and a fat lot of good it will do them. Men—bunch of goodfornothings, they're only after one thing! *Tut, tut, tut,*" she says, raising her eyes briefly to heaven. Mam wraps her coat around her knees and reads her *Ireland's Own* magazine. She seems sad.

I'd quite forgotten my woeful departure and thrill as the great steamship plunges into a rhythmic roll.

"Oh, my Gawd!" says Mam, looking green around the gills and clutching her stomach. I take great solace in sailing again on the high seas. For some unknown reason it gives me a tremendous feeling of adventure tinged with a distant memory of sadness.

It is a night crossing, and my poor mother, prostrate with mal de mer, lets me go out on deck in the company of one of her once hopeful Don Juans.

"Yer mother's not much of a sailor, Liam. Sure the sea's calm enough this night!"

" 'Tis true for you. Me grandda says she get can seasick standing on a wet carpet."

For what seems like an age, I stand in silence with the kindly stranger at the stern rail, somehow knowing that my great adventure was about to begin.

A gigantic seagull flutters almost motionless against an ink-black sky. I could taste the salt spray, see the green and red navigation lights of the passing ships, hear the *whoosh!* of the bow wave, and gazing back to Ireland, see the solitary finger of Howth Head lighthouse, sweep the sea and flicker out, like a lone birthday candle.

✦ Chapter 4 ✦

EIGHT MILES FROM STRATFORD-ON-AVON AND THREE FROM Henley-in-Arden, at a bend in the A34 trunk road in the green rural heart of England, nestles the ancient and picturesque village of Wootton Wawen. A Celtic cross stands before the square tower of the eleventh-century Saxon church, recording the fallen of two world wars. Opposite, a row of black-and-white Tudor period houses winds down the hill and halts at the Bull's Head tavern built in 1320. The church and its environs straddle the top of a low hill, where once the Druids practiced their rites. Behind the hill and almost hidden from view by a blaze of exotic imported trees, somber and time-worn, towers the gray solid mass known as Wootton Hall.

This Georgian pile was indeed built by one of the King Georges to keep his mistress Lady Fitzherbert well away from the wagging tongues of the London court. Now in more austere times, it had been converted into apartments and is surrounded on three sides by a caravan site. In the old kitchen garden, which once supplied fare for milady's table, amid a crisscross of cinder track roads, stands a sixteen-foot green caravan.

"This is it, our first family home!" Dad is fired full of boyish enthusiasm. He opens the door and we go in. It smells of wood and varnish and seems larger inside than out. It has two folding beds, a stove, a bottled gas cooker, and a tiny sink. Mam turns on the water tap and nothing happens.

"Where's the water?"

"I'll get it connected tomorrow," says me dad. He never does.

"There's no toilet either!"

"Jasus, woman, would you ever be aisy. I'll dig a bloody soak-away as soon as I buy meself a spade." And dig one he does—five years later.

Despite her reservations, Mam soon gets used to our new home.

"There's not room to swing a cat! At least there's no place to lose anything, and I suppose we won't be throwing any parties."

"Why would anyone want to swing a cat?" Mam was fussing about storing my meager belongings, so I thought it best not to ask.

"Your job will be to get buckets of water for washing and cooking, Willie. We'll need one in the morning and one at night. The tap is just over the road. OK?"

I wander over to the freestanding water tap and try to turn the big brass handle.

It won't budge. I climb up the wooden support and try again, to no avail. Then I slip, and a jagged razor-sharp piece of metal gashes my left leg, almost slicing off my calf muscle. Dad sews the flapping skin back into position, and I nearly bite the arm off my teddy bear with the pain. He does a grand job, albeit without the proper tools, disinfectant, or anesthetics. So once again, without provocation, an inanimate object has made a direct attack on my person for no apparent reason. Gas meters and water taps and anything with pipes are in conspiracy against my well-being and should be judged accordingly. I have a new battle scar but have become very wary of such apparatus.

I am laid up for a while until my leg mends and I can resume my aquarian duties. As the hot summer days suppurate, the drain below the water tap effuses a deathly stench as people empty their shite buckets and piss pots down the grating. In winter the plastic bucket chafes the calves of my legs raw and tips icy splashes of freezing water into my Wellington boots. Often the tap freezes up, and I have to melt snow and ice to fill the tea kettle. The joys of living in rural England!

As I grow older and stronger my water-gathering task is made easier by my ever resourceful father: he kindly buys me another plastic bucket to hump about.

Most of the young people I have met so far have been very nice, but some tend to take the rise out of my singsong Irish accent. I try to talk like an Englishman, but that makes matters even worse and Mam steps in.

"Ner'mind dem bunch of eejits," Mam says. "They don't know 'A' from a bull's arse about nuthin', all talking like they've a mouthful of plums—bollocks to 'em!"

It's only when my ear gets attuned to the angular speech of the British that I realize Mam uses words and idioms that no longer exist in modern English. Mam's everyday speech is full of quaint colloquialisms.

"I was after seeing Mrs. Arrowsmith down the market. She was coming-a-past me. When I saluted her, she didn't recognize me atall. I don't think she did it designtly, so she didn't. Mind you, that daughter of hers, the tatty-headed one with the pencily eyebrows, she wouldn't give you the steam of her piss since she got herself a bloke. You should see the gaatch of her, all airs and graces, fur coat and no knickers, the durty hewer!"

Mam's language is rich and sometimes puzzling; the more I get used to hearing the local people talk, the more I notice her peculiar way of putting things.

"The weather is a wee bit adjacent today, Willie, mind and take yer raincoat. I'd run you to school on the back of me bike, but I'm after feeling a little previous myself."

I become a bit self-conscious about my own accent, especially after being sent down to the pub to call my dad home for his dinner. I am about five years old.

I open the barroom door and there, surrounded in a haze of blue cigarette smoke, are Dad and his "boozing pals," as my mother calls them.

"Come away out of dat, and don't be drinking all dat porter!" I shout with all the authority I could muster.

"Out of the mouths of babes and sucklings!" quotes one of Dad's mates above the din, and my enjoinder is greeted with hoots of laughter and derision. At a total loss, red-faced and shamed, I run away home crying.

Mam uses a lot of words and phrases that I mistakenly take to be commonplace.

"Don't ye be deifying me with that brazen face, you bold boy, or I'll give you a lifter under the chin and a fong up the arse!"

It is oftentimes a struggle to crack the nut of my mother's meaning, and many is the kernel of connotation that escapes me entirely. Maybe she did it to tease me.

"Mam, what have we got for dinner today?"

"Currant cake and great sport!"

"Mam, what can I get to eat?"

"Shit tied up in a whisp to frighten you naked!"

"Mam, what's for dinner?"

"The full of yer hole of roasted snow!"

Sure Maxim's of Paris could not boast a more exotic menu!

"Mam, I don't like carrots."

"If you hadn't it, you'd ate it."

Well, as the old saying goes: "If the English love to hoard words like misers, the Irish love to spend them like sailors!" And likewise in Mam's peculiar patois: "If we all had the makings of ourselves, we'd be beautiful!"

"You'll be starting school next week, so we better get you some decent clothes," says Mam.

We have taken the bus into Stratford and it is market day. I dread the thought of school. There would be dozens of kids taking the mick out of my accent. We turn into a shop that proclaims "Back to School Sale." A very tall man who looks like an undertaker comes forward, rubbing hands that are long-fingered, parchment white, and bony. He has a cadaverous visage that gives him the appearance of a skeleton with skin stretched tightly over it, and a plummy English accent that you could butter a muffin with.

"Kin eye help you, Modom?"

"Yes, please, the child needs a school uniform."

"Which educational establishment will he be attending, Modom?"

"Wootton Wawen Roman Catholic," says Mam.

I am kitted out with short gray trousers, a white shirt, navy blue sweater, socks, and a black blazer jacket. These are the first new clothes I've ever had, and they even smell new. I look in the mirror, very smart, like a sailor.

"We have a large selection of school caps, ties, and pocket crests. Would Modom care to see?"

"Modom would!"

The man rummages in the big wooden drawers; for some reason he has a cloth inch tape around his neck, no doubt for measuring corpses. He hums away to himself and after some ferreting, produces a blue-and-yellow striped tie and a blue badge with a gold Celtic cross, embroidered with the letters A.M.D.G.

"Ave Maria Deo Gratias! That's Latin," the gaunt gargoyle of a shopman informs us.

"Oh," says I, my nightmare closing in. It was bad enough being stuck with a load of English kids, but now there was Catholics and Romans as well—all speaking Latin!

"What are you looking so worried about? Ye'll all be dressed the same at school, so no one will take the mickey out of your clothes. Isn't that right, sir?"

"Indeed, it is, Modom. Clothes maketh the man, Modom!"

We walk through the town. I'm glad to be out of the shop with its spindly proprietor. The air is warm and moist on the banks of the Avon. American tourists watch the rowing club scull their way through sedately swimming swans. Mam sings us through the Tudor shops of Market Street, past the Shakespeare Memorial Theatre, and up to the bus station:

> Bobby Shaftoe's gone to sea
> Silver buckles on his knee
> He'll come home and marry me
> Bonny Bobby Shaftoe.

The feared day arrives, and Mam dresses me for school. I feel awkward in my new getup, and my stomach is churning. Mam takes me down on the back of her bicycle, and I am presented to the head mistress; the dark, tall, obsidian-eyed Mrs. MacArthur.

"Nora, come ye hereabouts and look after this wee laddie," she burrs, in what I later find out is a Scottish accent. I try hard to choke back the tears as I see my mother wave good-bye and disappear up the road on her great clanking bicycle.

"Don't you be giving me any trouble now. I'm two years older than you and I'm a school monitor," says Nora. She is very bossy and bears an uncanny resemblance to Lassie the Wonder Dog. She gives me a board with little wooden pegs in it and a small wooden mallet.

"You tap the pegs through the board."

"Then what do I do?"

"You turn the board over and tap them back of course, ya idiot!"

"I'm not doing a stupid thing like that! Do ya take me for an eejit or something? I can read, you know, real words and everything!"

"If you don't do it, I'm telling miss and you'll get the cane across yer arse."

She grabs me by the collar of my new shirt and I give her a slap of the wooden hammer. She is shrieking and caterwauling and everyone is looking over. Then the head teacher pulls me out to the front of the class by my earhole. She shouts and bawls at me, but I could make out little of what she is saying on account of her accent. I do catch the word *hooligan,* however, as I know people of that name back over home. For punishment I have to stand in the corner until break time. This is very tedious, and my legs hurt. I try to stand on one leg like a stork, but I fall on my arse and get another row in Scottish for gooning around. When playtime comes I discover my new status as a holy terror has done me no harm at all. The other boys gather around eager to meet the new-comer. I am relieved and even a bit grateful to Nora.

"Where are ya from?" they ask.

"Ireland."

"Sure most of us at this school are from Ireland, ya eejit! What part?"

"Limerick City."

"Me too!" says a lanky lad with black hair. "County Limerick, that is."

"Me and my sister are from Kerry." I grin and nod.

"We're from Dublin," says one of a bunch of obviously related freckle-faces.

So fate has cast the dice and here I am, in the land of the stranger, surrounded by my own people, the far-flung children of the Gael. Despite my foreboding, my first day at school ends happily with me sitting four to a table with my newfound friends, Jeremiah Daly, Liam Cosgrave, and Steven O'Donnell.

"All the kids at school are Irish, Dad! Except a little French kid called Jean-Paul something or other. How is that?"

Dad looks up from his newspaper and regards me with curiosity.

"Their parents come over to lift the corn harvest and the potatoes and such like. Then when the season's over, they just stay on. They're what's called migrant laborers except most of them have stopped migrating. Of course they'll all be Catholics, being Irish, and the French are left-footers, too!"

"Why do people call Catholics left-footers?"

"Because they dig their spades with their left foot, of course!"

The school is unique and picturesque. Started by the monks in the Middle Ages, it is housed in an old flour mill and sits in the fork of two rivers. Behind the main buildings is a mill pool where great thrashing fish consume our leftover dinner scraps. The playground is full of mature trees—oak, ash, and beech—and is great fun to cavort around in, when the leaves lie thick in the autumn. There are two green corrugated iron bicycle sheds and two rows of outside toilets marked *Boys* and *Girls*. The main schoolroom is a single long hall with windows to the south that had been a flour store in its time. It is divided into three areas by two thick black velvet curtains.

At the end of this is the infants' room, where I found myself. My teacher is a tall, gaunt, kindly lady called Miss Hathaway. She is a descendant of Anne Hathaway, the wife of William Shakespeare, and had lived in the same house that they had once occupied. Enthusiastic and rightly proud of her heritage, she tells us much of the history and folklore of the local area and it is fascinating.

"Wootton Wawen is an old Saxon name meaning the 'Woodland of Woden.' He, you will remember, was a pagan god," she goes on. "The Saxons settled here and eventually became Christians. Some of your Irish monks were responsible for that!"

"Did they build the flour mill, miss?"

"I don't think so—or maybe they did. Anyway, they built the church that still stands on the hill yonder."

"Were they Protestants, miss?"

"No, no, they were Catholics."

"But the church is a Prody church!"

"It wasn't then. That was hundreds of years ago, before the Reformation."

"What's a reformation, miss?"

"Miss . . . ?" "Why . . . ?" "What . . . ?" "When . . . ?" A dozen hands shoot up with a dozen questions. *Clang-ker-clang!* goes the school bell, and as lively as eels, we spill out past our weary teacher into the sunlight.

The other components of the teaching staff are the accident-prone Mr. Bury and the dinner lady, Mrs. Dunscombe, whose son, Tommy, becomes one of my best friends and as a result I get bigger helpings at lunch. The operation is masterminded and directed under the eagle eye of the formidable Mrs. MacArthur, who in her own words, "Will brook no nonsense from you unruly lot!"

The parish priest comes around twice or more a week and the nit nurse once a month. She checks our hair for *visitors* and he checks our *souls* for sins. The *souls* in question were pieces of white paper pinned to the wall with our names printed underneath. If you misbehave or are found guilty of some heinous crime, such as talking in class, a small black blob is added to your record. If your sin is more serious, like cursing or giving cheek to the staff, the blot is larger. I was always a bit of a tearaway, and as a result my *soul* usually looks like the backside of a Holstein cow.

The priest teaches us two subjects: religious instruction, where we have little idea of what he is talking about, and moral instruction, where *he* has little idea of what he is talking about.

Dad objects to me being schooled by the priest and tries to argue with Mam.

"Bloody rubbish! What do they know? A Catholic priest advising you about sex is like a vegetarian telling you how you want your steak cooked."

Not that sex is ever mentioned by our priest, but he is very heavy on "the sins of the flesh" in his Sunday sermons. He seems to take a great delight in recounting the interminable horrors that await the sinful in the next life. We are told, for instance, that as Catholics, we would of course make it through to salvation, but our sins require a time in purgatory. In this place of lost souls, flames come out of the taps when you try to wash your hands.

There were venial sins—swearing, white lies, and the like—which could be forgiven with ease, and mortal sins, which killed your soul stone-dead. The latter included murder, rapine, blasphemy, and worst of all, becoming a Protestant, whatever the hell that was.

Every Wednesday we go through our own purgatory. This takes the form of morning mass at the little chapel in the graveyard behind the school. The building is unheated, and in winter we suffer greatly, kneeling without hassocks on the cold terra-cotta tiles.

Each week we pray for the conversion of Russia, not that one of us knew where Russia was or why it required converting. This is the secret of the smug priest. Eventually curiosity gets the better of me and I resolved to ask Mam.

"Mam, who are the Russians?"

"The Russians is it? Sure they're worst than the Germans! They murder priests and everything!"

Suddenly I look upon these Russians in a new, benign light.

"Ah yes!" I think, remembering a recent beating I'd received from the cleric.

"They sound like the boys for me, all right!"

Only Miss Hathaway refrains from dealing out corporal punishment. Even the dinner lady is capable of giving you a crack with a soup ladle if you are naughty.

The final authority is the florid-faced priest, who when telephoned in the most serious cases, screams down the hill to the school on his bike and like an avenging angel, delights in dealing out wicked bone-splitting raps from his long bamboo cane.

This day the cantankerous cleric is doing his rounds of the school, when he begins to inquire what various children want to be when they grow up.

"I want to be a holy father like you," offers Joseph "the saint" Ryan, sitting coyly under his spotless *soul*.

The priest's blue-jowled grin beams down apostolically upon him.

"Little creep!" I whisper to Jerry Daly, who lets out a stifled giggle.

Father spins around. "Well, Daly, what do you want to be?"

"A fireman, Father."

"H'em. And you, Watkins?"

"A sailor, Father," I say, with what I thought was a nautical grin.

He shakes his head and mutters, "Godless lot." For balance, he turns to one of the girls. "Elspeth O'Neill, what about you?"

I suppose he is hoping for the answer, "A nun, Father." If so, he doesn't know wee Elspeth O'Neill.

"I want to be a striptease dancer!" she blurts, her eyes like big blue saucers.

The priest looks like he'd been stung by a wasp.

"Now, child, I'm sure you don't even know what that is."

"Oh, I do, Father! It's a woman who takes her clothes off in front of men!"

The priest's visit was cut mercifully short by a hastily remembered appointment—elsewhere!

Mr. Bury takes us for science, in which I have a great interest. He is tall and gangly with a pointy nose and a mop of sandy brown hair, both of which accentuate a pair of peering brown eyes that give him the aspect of a perplexed rat looking out of a hayloft.

He does have an odd way with the world, and it sometimes seems that inanimate objects conspire to frustrate his efforts and thwart his every turn.

In common with the other teachers, Mr. Bury seldom partakes of the free school meals delivered each day, but prefers to make his own food in a small kitchen attached to our cloakroom. I witness him put a tin of baked beans on the hot plate of the cooker and then go searching for the can opener. Perhaps he had forgotten about Boyle's law and the expansion of hot gases. There is an enormous bang and the air is full of flying beans. The hapless young teacher spends the rest of dinner hour scraping them off the ceiling.

A week later, he plugs in the electric tea kettle and leaves it to boil on the wooden cloakroom floor. The first frost of winter has frozen some of the water pipes, and myself, coming in from the outside toilets, goes to the sink to wash my hands. I turn on the tap and expectantly hold the soap under it. Instead of water, a nasty hissing sound issues forth. *"Aargghh!"* What the priest said was true: the flames of purgatory are coming out of the pipe! I instinctively leap back, and my heel catches the spout of the boiling-kettle, which obligingly empties its bubbling contents into my shoe. Severely scalded, I am off school for a good few weeks. Maybe it was a punishment from God, but it sure was nice to be lying snuggly-buggly-boo in my bunk, far from the chilly chapel with its bare stone floor, icy arctic drafts, and frozen specters of unconverted Russians.

Whilst I am settling down to my new school, my father tries his hand at being a traveling salesman for a leading fire extinguisher company. He is sent to Morcombe Bay in Lancashire for training in shock sales technique, a startling new 1950s concept that works something like this.

After gaining entrance to someone's abode, the trick is to immediately grab a coat or scarf, spray lighter fuel on it, and set it aflame. As the horrified owner stands agape, the salesman, with a flourish, whips out the extinguisher and—*fooosh!*—the fire is out! The carbon tetrachloride base of the appliance leaves not the slightest trace of damage on the material.

All is going well and the tactic is proving effective. Dad has won some small orders from housewives and shopkeepers, but he decides that a big order might ensue from one of the many-roomed, stately Victorian mansions that dot the local vicinity.

Briefcase in hand, he walks the long, tree-lined drive to Manstell Manor. The only resident is His Lordship, an old retired Indian army officer. Dad is met courteously enough by the lord, who takes him into the gun room.

"What have you to show me, young man?" he says, in an affable enough fashion.

With a lightning sweep of the wrist, Dad snatches off the old chap's hat, douses it in petrol, and sets it alight.

"What the—?!" The general is caught completely off guard by this assault.

"Now the GREAT MOMENT!" shouts Dad, grabbing the fire extinguisher from his bag. He points it at the blazing hat and depresses the handle. *Phut! Phsssh!* A tiny whiff of gas escapes from the empty cylinder. "Bugger!" says Dad, all fingers and thumbs, trying desperately to screw on a fresh refill. The bug-eyed general stares at the funeral pyre fast diminishing on the marble floor.

"My hat! My favorite hat!!"

Dad looks up to apologize, but too late.

His Lordship, beetroot purple in the face and eyes like hot rivets, is reaching for a fine double-barreled shotgun. "GET OUT OF MY HOUSE! GET OUT!!!"

Dad needs no further encouragement—the sound of the gun being loaded is enough. He grabs his stuff and flees for his life through the front door. As my father sprints in Olympic fashion down the tree-lined drive, buckshot whizzes about his ears and clips leaves from the poplar branches. Behind him, like a charging rhino, the old boy is still running down the path, roaring. "GET BACK TO RUSSIA, YOU BLOODY BOLSHEVIK!"

→ Chapter 5 ←

SLOW—SCHOOLS, DEMANDS THE BLACK-AND-WHITE ROAD sign, depicting the torch of learning surmounted by a large red warning triangle. I stop dead in my tracks and stare at it as if I had never seen it before. Suddenly the revelation comes to me that I pass this sign at more or less the same times every day. I had not thought about it before, but the days were cyclic and so too were the weeks. From the peculiar feeling this dawn of realization gives me, I make a small mental jump into intellectual no-man's-land.

I perceive that somehow it's all connected. The days, weeks, months, and years, too—all planned out by some unseen hand, some mastermind. It must be God! Every morning I pass the school sign and each afternoon I go past the other way. In between times, I labor under the jurisdiction of Mrs. MacArthur and the school rules, but when I pass the sign on my way home, I am *free!* This sense of freedom is uplifting but hard to understand. Time becomes a fuzzy observance that I try to come to grips with. It is best measured by food. I know what day of the week it is by what is on the dinner table. It is said that a man's stomach is the best clock you can have, but we had a calendar too, which, when times were good, seldom varied:

SUNDAY: Roast beef, pork, lamb, or chicken, served with boiled and roasted potatoes, greens and gravy. Dad traditionally cooks this repast.

MONDAY: Cold meat from the Sunday joint, homemade pickled onions, steamed spuds, and English mustard.

TUESDAY: Chops, peas, and potatoes, with Sunday's gravy.

WEDNESDAY: Gammon, broad beans, potatoes, and lashings of bacon fat poured over it all as a gravy. (My favorite!)

THURSDAY: Belly pork grilled, baked beans, and mashed spuds.

FRIDAY: Fried fish and chips, served in newspaper with pickled onions, malt vinegar, and salt.

SATURDAY: (Winter) Irish stew, hotpot, or beef stew. (Summer) Fresh salads from our own garden.

We have the typical Irish appetite for potatoes and eat pounds of them every week. I would sometimes even eat them raw like apples. There were, of course, changes to the routine, as in the traditional boiled bacon and cabbage for Saint Patrick's Day and other Irish occasions. None of us has ever even seen a turkey, so it is roasted chicken for Christmas with sage-and-onion stuffing. Our meager rations are sometimes supplemented by nocturnal hunters called poachers. These gentlemen provide us with various game dishes like pheasant, venison, and salmon. These are bartered for with Dad's home-brewed beer.

The biggest changes in the family diet are brought about by our occasional dips below the poverty line. Dad is fired from his job due to setting alight the old general's hat and because his temper gets the better of him and he tells his boss that he doesn't suffer fools gladly and to stick the nozzle of his fire extinguisher up his arse.

He has always tried to grow enough potatoes, cauliflowers, cabbages, and kale on his allotment to see us through to better times, but supplies are low and he's drunk all the home brew. He sits moodily, the stub of a cigarette fuming in his nicotine-stained fingers.

Mam, with a wizardry to shame Merlin, conjures up a Sunday dinner for three out of two ounces of corned beef and some spuds.

This severe trough in our fortunes is marked by the daily ingestion of bread and dripping. Great pallid gobs of white pork fat spread cold on crusts and sprinkled with salt are better to eat than look at. For a change I try a "dip in the fat," which is the same idea, only hot. Condensed milk, dribbling like candle wax from the tin, alternates with brown sauce to make a sandwich filling.

Lean times have come upon us. Dad goes off cursing to the labor exchange to look for a job. Ominous black clouds leaden the sky, and I watch the blue flame on our tiny gas cooker fade into a wee peep as Mam tries to boil the kettle for the tea. A heavy rain is thundering on our thin aluminum roof, making lighting a campfire out of the question. Mam dons her raincoat and ventures outside. She stands at the back of the caravan, furiously shaking the gas bottle; the flame rallies for a moment, then splutters into oblivion.

"What's happening, Willie?"

"It got bigger, then it went out, Mam."

"The curse of Saint Malachy and the seven fiery devils to it. I don't think I've enough money for a refill!" She sits back at the fold-down kitchen table and pours the contents of her little leather purse onto the linen tablecloth. There are no banknotes and more miraculous medals of the Virgin Mary than coins. A gray slanting light from the side window picks out the normally invisible logos on the white linen cloth. "Ranks Flour Mills—LIMERICK" spells the ghost of the bleached-out imprint.

"We're one and ninepence short. Come on, Willie, and we'll see if Aladdin will give us a recharge on tick." I find the bottle-changing wrench, and Mam screws the brass regulator away from the cylinder. The rain subsides as we load the gas bottle onto my soapbox cart and trundle our way through the dripping trees, down to the storeroom where a little wizened woman who reeks of heating oil sells bottled gas and kerosene to the site dwellers. In the stinky darkness the wee witch-like wife sits wrapped up like a tattered mummy, wearing an odd assortment of men's clothes. She is completely permeated with paraffin. She huddles dangerously near a single hurricane lamp to read a faded newspaper. She is a walking Molotov cocktail, but this was her normal way. "Like Aladdin in the magic cave," Mam once said, and so the nickname stuck.

"Hello, Aladdin, would ye ever give us a refill for the gas? I'm needing to cook my husband's tea and I'm just one and nine short, but I can pay you on Thursday."

"Then you can get your bloody gas on Thursday."

"I thought we were friends?"

"We are, but there's no sentiment in business, Mrs. Watkins." The old vendor pushes the door closed against the wind. Mam stands dejected, on the verge of tears; the thin drizzle has started up again. I am embarrassed for my mother and annoyed that she has been rebuffed in such an offhand manner by a human lampwick. Betwixt anger and frustration I kick into the gravel surface of the old stable yard with the toe of my boot. Something odd is glinting pallidly up at me from the stones. It looks like a small set of chain links about three inches long. I bend down and pick it up. The crusty verdigris that holds the coins together crumbles and seven threepenny pieces separate in my hand. I stare in disbelief at the brass bits, exactly one shilling and nine pence.

"Mam! Look what I've found—one and ninepence. It's just exactly what we need!"

Mam takes the money from my trembling hand. Her eyes are large and round.

"Oh, thank you, thank you, Saint Jude, thank you!" she cries skyward.

"Saint Jude, me arse! It was me that found them, right over there, in the ground!"

I knew little of the patron saint of lost causes, but over the years I have heard my mother invoke his help on my behalf so many times, that along with Saint Anthony, the saint who helped you find lost items, they become invisible members of the family.

Back at school I tell my story to the priest during my communion class. I get the feeling that he doesn't believe me.

"What is Saint Jude the patron saint of?" he asks.

"Is it the obscure?" I offer, remembering something my granddad Jim had read me.

I pass the sign on my way home from school. I'm free again, free to explore my environs. I stroll toward the ivy-grown limestone mansion.

An ancient bronze sundial stands on a hexagonal stone pillar in a grassy wabe at the front of the great hall. I climb up to watch the shadow creep imperceptibly across the roman numerals incised on the plate. It has almost reached IV when the great bell of the old Saxon church chimes four o'clock. Looking up, I lose my footing, and the world spins through sky and garden as I spiral down like an autumn leaf to destruction on the ground. The interruption of the force of gravity knocks the wind from my lungs, and I lie stunned and sickened by the sudden stop. Unable to cry for the numb pain that has become my universe, I lie on my back, staring up through the branches of a giant redwood tree that towers one hundred and fifty feet above the park. No one has seen me fall except a long, lean marmalade tomcat, who now scampers toward me and begins licking away the salty tears running down my cheeks.

"*Purrow*," says the cat, as it rubs along my grazed legs. I stretch out a hand to stroke it and it bites me, dancing off sideways.

"*Perrow, perrow.*" He comes back, nuzzling my face and causing me to pull myself up to get a better look at it. What a quare orange moggy this was. One eye missing, the opposite ear missing, one incisor broken off, and only half a tail. He tumbles about in my lap, teasing and playing like a kitten. If I move my hand too quickly, he bites me, then licks the same spot whilst purring like a well-oiled sewing machine. Having distracted me from my painful plummet, I recover enough to stand up. This he doesn't like and repairs posthaste to the thick rhododendron bushes from whence he had come.

From his green hidey-hole he meows at me balefully until I sit down again, and, purring away, he rejoins me. We become firm friends and after some cajoling he follows me all the way home, where I secrete him in the cupboard underneath my bed.

"There's an awful pen and ink in here! It smells like cat's piss!" My dad's face is all screwed up like a sucked orange. Oh, my God! I'd forgotten about the cat.

"I'm off to get the water, it's bath night," says I, anxious to get out of the van.

"Yea, if that's you that's making that pong, you need a bloody bath! Leave me some water for a good wash tonight. I'm going to put in a few hours on the allotment, bastard-trenching my potato patch, then I'll be fit for a couple of pints at the Bull's Head. I think I'll grow some sprouts this year. D'you know your mother's never eaten one?"

"Neither have I. In fact, I've never so much as seen a sprout. Cheerio now, so!" I take off toward the tap with my two plastic buckets. As I splash my way back, I see Dad, two empty beer bottles in hand, swinging his way up the cinder track road, with a garden spade on his shoulder.

"It's OK, puss, he's gone!" I open the cupboard and with a flash of furry orange, the imprisoned cat shoots out of the caravan door, leaving an airborne slipstream of watery yellow shite in its wake. The small red fireside carpet, the front step, and myself are liberally coated in a malodorous defecation that only a frightened feline or a dyspeptic demon could be called on to produce. *Now* what can I do? Mam is due home soon, and it is Thursday—belly pork, beans, and spuds—but apart from that, it's bath night, which means boiling rakes of water, standing naked on a towel, and washing yourself down from head to toe. All this and the house swimming in shite! I throw the red mat into the garden and wriggle out of my black jeans and tartan shirt carefully, so as not to spread the poom all over me. There is shite on the wee pearly buttons, so I can't undo them. In pulling the shirt over my head, the stench just an inch from my nose makes me gag. No time to get dressed! I put a kettle full of water on to boil and hide my clothes in the old traveling trunk, rusting in the garden outside. In a fluttering panic, I begin to scrub away at the pungent excrement on the step. Luckily, a dousing from a full water bucket does the trick and flushes the offending feces from the linoleum. The red mat is a bigger problem. I try to wash a bit of it, but it makes the cat shit spread. Standing in my ragged underwear in the junk-filled garden I must have looked a pretty sight.

A girlish giggle erupts behind me. I spin around to see the nice little Burmese lady from the corner caravan.

"What are you doing all naughty like this? Hee-hee-hee!"

"I'm trying to get the stain out of this rug and it won't shift."

"Let me see. Oh, stinky stink! It is shit! It is shit!" She lets the mat drop and leaps backward. "SHIT! IT IS SHIT!"

"I know what it is! How do you get rid of it?"

"Oh, so sorry! Dry by the fire and brush it off with firm brush. But brush hard, very hard. It is SHIT!"

When Mam comes in the mat is clean and dry, the deposit having left the carpet in little clouds of khaki dust with each fervent stroke of a wire suede brush. The little square enameled stove is lit, and I am drying myself in front of it after my strip-wash. Mam is somewhat taken aback.

"It's not like you to have a bath without being yelled at. You must be courting. That's it—you've got a wee girlfriend somewhere!" I go red and Mam sniffs the air.

"There's a queer stink in here. I know we're hard up, but has your father been smoking those horseshit cigarettes again?" I stay red, as red as the mat I'm standing on.

I didn't see the motley old mouse hound for a while. No doubt it was off on its rounds of erstwhile benefactors, burgling, begging, and biting the hand that feeds it.

My rotund friend, Fatty Roger, and myself stroll in chitchat cheeriness up to our caravan to find the war-torn ginger tomcat sitting on the front doorstep, back leg erect, studiously licking its hole. Roger recognizes him.

"That's Candy, that is. He's a wild cat, fights with foxes and badgers and everything! You can't stroke him, you know. He'd have yer hand off!"

"Get on out of it! *I* can pet him. He's my pal, so he is!" I put my hand out and the moggy turns into a hissing ball of ear-back malevolence, rolling onto his side and lashing the air with sickle-sharp claws. I leap back in dismay.

"Some pal you've got there." Fatty Roger chucks his school cap at the cat, who shoots into the dark shadows beneath the van from whence his one eye gleams like a coal and a low growl curses our impudence. We go into the caravan and raid the food cupboard. Under a plate I find two cold pork chops, which we wolf down with dry bread and mustard, totally oblivious to the fact that they are all my mother can afford for the dinner. Mam is furious when she comes home. Roger runs, leaving me to my fate.

"For Jasus' sake, Willie, you can't keep bringing home other people's kids and feeding them! We've hardly enough food for ourselves, and Roger's people are well off compared to us. And anyway, it's not as if he's wasting away, is it?" She is right enough. Like most kids I never think of where food comes from or how much it costs.

"I'm sorry, Mam. I didn't know it was Dad's dinner. It's just that Roger said he was awful hungry."

"He's always hungry. He's like a bloody termite! Jasus, he eats his poor mother out of house and home. BeGod she can't keep up with him for sure. He's a big lad so, and it's plain that he makes great use of his food, but he gets plenty to eat at home."

"Well, I'll not do it again, Mam, so I won't."

"Good lad, you're too bloody generous to others altogether. One of these days you'll give yer arse away and ye'll have to shit through yer ribs!"

Mam is always very forthright in her use of language. When first I heard my teacher talk about something called cursive, I thought of my mother.

I go into the sitting room, where curled up on my dad's black coat is the purring form of a sleeping marmalade tomcat.

"Arggh! Get that mangy bugger out of here!" Mam begins doing the Highland fling and throwing everything at hand at the swiftly departing pussycat. Like an amber arrow, he shoots out of the open window and away toward the shrubs lining the main road.

"Durty bugger, he is! Look where he was lying on your father's coat. Look—bloody HOPPERS!" There in the warm dent left behind by the rudely awakened Candy, a small colony of cat fleas, having lost their host, is wandering about aimlessly.

"Did you bring that scruffy specimen into the house?"

"No, Mam. He must have jumped in through the window."

"Well, I believe you, thousands wouldn't! But if I see that flea-ridden bleeder again he's going to get a fong up the arse that will knock him into the middle of next week! Right, watch this carefully. Ye might have call to do this yourself one day, the way you carry on!" She goes over to the sink and picks up the soap. Slowly she walks to the spot where the old moggy had been lying, and, *dab-dab-dab* with the bar of soap, the fleas were gone! Mam turns the underside of the bar toward me and there are the tiny parasites imbedded in the bottom, firm prisoners of the carbolic soap.

"That's them wee buggers nuxed!" She smiles with all the primeval satisfaction of the ancient huntress and, stepping outside, scrapes them off onto a fence post, singing:

> *There was an old man at the fair*
> *He didn't know what he was at*
> *He was taking them out of his hair*
> *And cracking them on his old hat!*

She takes up a washboard and places it in a zinc bucket full of suds on the kitchen table. Mechanically she rubs away at the grime in my school shirt collar.

"You know there's people in America have machines that can do this."

"Goway! Machines that can do the washing, whatever next?"

"'Tis true, and they have refrigerators and vacuum cleaners, too. Even the poor people have them, so they do!"

"Why would you want to clean a vacuum? Sure Mr. Bury says, there's nothing at all in a vacuum."

Mam picks up the basket of wet clothes and pulls a puzzled face. She shrugs her shoulders and steps down into the garden.

"Oh, Jasus! It's me that's over!"

Mam slips on her duff whilst hanging out the washing and, in trying to stay herself, plucks the washline like an archer with a giant bow. This has the effect of launching all of the unused clothes-pegs skyward from the rope like a salvo of Minuteman missiles. She is not best pleased! Two straight lines like a number eleven appear on her forehead as she struggles up. The warning sign of the number eleven bus!

"What are you laughing at?"

"Nothing, Mother."

"Well, if you laugh for nothing, you'll laugh a bloody lot for a halfpenny, you cheeky young pup, you! And don't be giving me any of your old guff or I'll box yer ears for you. Now get this garden tidied up and dump some of this bloody junk. It's like Duffy's Circus here with all this crap lying about. Get rid of it!"

Loaded down with a heavy heart, old wind-up gramophone parts, and empty paint tins, my wooden box cart squeaks a weary mile to the trailer park rubbish dump nestled in the heart of the wilderness. I chuck the garbage onto the pile and go for a look-see about.

The dump lies in a wide clearing surrounded with trees and shouldered by nearby Top River, a straight stretch of water that had been, long ago, channeled in artificial banks as a tributary of the river Alne. This supplied the giant heron lake at the head of the wilderness, which feeds in turn, by means of a waterfall, Bottom River. Brown and turgid, this watercourse sluggishly bisects the wild woods, making the dump an island accessible only by one of three ancient stone bridges. The whole area is about a mile square.

I root around in the detritus of the dump for treasures. Nothing big, mind—I don't want Mam putting on her number eleven scowl and giving out to me again about the amount of old tat in the garden, half of which was my dad's junk anyway.

Overhead the round leaves of the poplar trees whisper and rustle in the light breeze, and from afar a strange whooping, yelping noise carries on the west wind mixed with a sound like a castrated car horn. Intrigued, I scamper up to the riverbank, where my view westward is not encumbered by the trees. There is a queer-looking beast swimming at full tilt down the dappled waters of Top River straight toward me. Ten yards away the beaverlike creature abruptly turns to its right and hops onto the grassy bank, shaking fine mists of water droplets from its pelt. It pees briefly in my direction and, seeing no threat, dives into a culvert and swims through the watercress patch to where the stream enters a nearby tarpaper hut. "Water Works—Keep Out!" reads the sign above the half door.

I glance back upriver, where a blur of red dots is moving about and the unmistakable baying of hounds mingles with the cries of huntsmen and the sharp bugling of the hunting horn.

What could all this carry-on be in aid of? Then it dawns on me. Oh, my God! This must be an otter hunt and they're chasing that wee beastie. It also occurs to me that the dogs are way ahead of the huntsmen and would get here first, probably tearing me to shreds in the process! You couldn't fool me! I'd seen the like in the film *The Hound of the Baskervilles. Arggh!*

Adopting the instinct of the beast pursued, I crash through the undergrowth to the refuge of the mysterious hut. The otter has wisely wriggled under the half door and is hiding behind a thing that looks like a big porcelain lavatory bowl, except this gives out a regular banging noise as it gushes water from out of its top. I bolt the top half of the door shut and climb on top of the shack. In no time at all my sanctuary is surrounded by a garish tangle of snarling dogs, and I am in fear of my mortal life.

"Come on now, Saint Jude, get me out of this one. I'm sorry I claimed the finding of the one and nine, so I am!" I lie face down on the asphalt roof. The tarry smell reminds me of those first visits to Birmingham, oh so long ago, and now I am to be ripped asunder by these devil's hounds. "Oh, Saint John Bosco, pray for us!"

"BECK! Beck, I say! Orf hownds, beck off!" In the pandemonium of trumpeting horns and hysterical dogs, two black-gloved hands appear over the cantle of the roof, soon to be followed by a red-jacketed man with a face like boiled shite.

"OH, DEM IT ALL! It's not the scent—it's jest some bloody kid!" bellows Shiteface. "CALL ORF THE HOWNDS!" he shrieks to the harbinger, who dutifully lays about the squabbling pack with a nasty-looking long whip.

The querulous gaggle of inbreeding moves off, man and dog alike. Only when they are far removed from the cover of the wilderness, way out in the lush open meadows beyond, do I wiggle myself down and open the door of the shed. To my great relief, the little brown otter is still there, his wee eyes glinting like chocolate buttons. We regard each other with benign interest. I feel we are brother survivors with something deeply elemental in common. As to who has saved whom? It doesn't matter a tinker's cuss. The point was, we are both free.

Later I ask my dad about the queer tarpaper hut and its weird machine.

"Oh, that's a Montgolfier water ram, the nearest thing ever invented to a perpetual motion machine."

"But what does it do?"

"The water runs down a slope, where it picks up energy from gravity. This hits the low-pressure diaphragm of the hydraulic ram, which pushes up, forcing some of the water at high pressure through a valve and into the pipeline. It's where our tap water comes from and all the taps on the site. Ingenious, eh? It was invented by the fellows who made the first manned balloon flight at Paris in 1783. The other nice thing is you can grow watercress in the gravity run because cress only likes to grow in shallow, fast-running water."

"OK, know-it-all, stop filling the child's mind with pumps and balloons and watercress and lay the bloody table. The dinner's ready." Mam's chide is leavened by the fact that Dad has found a job and the number eleven has disappeared from her forehead. Practical as ever, she is cooking: chops, peas, and potatoes. Hurrah! It must be Tuesday!

"Dad, why do them people hunt the otters?"

"Those upper-class twits will hunt anything! If you ask me, they're still lusting after the days when their aristocratic Norman forefathers hunted down people like us and hung them. They'd rather shoot peasants than pheasants. Bunch of bloody oxygen thieves!"

"They didn't have any horses with them though."

"No, they only use the horses for the fox hunt. Oscar Wilde rightly called them, 'The unspeakable in full pursuit of the inedible!' He wasn't too far off the mark, as usual. D'ya know, Willie, the misfortunate wee fox was introduced to Ireland by the English just so they could hunt the poor bugger. That's how it became a symbol of resistance to the downtrodden native Irish!"

After the unexpected events of the day, I knew fine how it felt to be hunted and I didn't care for it.

The evening meal arrives at the table in its welcome cloud of savory steam. Gratefully we tuck in to the best feast we have had in a while, accompanied by the sound of my mother singing an old Irish song: "An Maidrín Rua"—The Little Red Fox.

There he was in my mind's eye, having outwitted hounds and hunter alike, boldly lying in the bulrushes with his two little ears sticking up:

> Maidrín rua, rua, rua, rua,
> An Maidrín rua atá dána,
> An Maidrín rua 'na luí sa luachair
> Agus bárra a dhá chluais in áirde.

✦ Chapter 6 ✦

THE AUTUMN IS GIVING WAY TO WINTER. MR. BURY LIGHTS the potbellied stove that heats the whole school, and soon the entire place is engulfed in acrid smoke. As luck would have it, crows have made their nest in the chimney during the summer, and the smoke is going everywhere rather than up the stack. It is imperative to put out the fire. The unfortunate teacher lifts the fire extinguisher and stares at it: *non comprende.*

This was my moment to leap up from my seat and take charge of the situation.

"This is how you do it, sir!" I strike the knob as I had seen my father do.

I manage to put out the fire and soak the teacher in one fell swoop. I sit down a hero!

My heroics do not last for long—pride comes before a fall.

Mam wants me to wear a particularly ghastly cream-colored Aran sweater that has been sent to me from Ireland. I hate it and when she won't take no for an answer, I tell her that it will get me picked on in school. This is an out-and-out lie, but she demands the name of the bully. In my panic, I name the last person I'd talked to in class, thinking it would go no further. My mam, outraged, marches me to school and demands satisfaction. The child quite rightly denies it, but I am too craven to recant. As the poor innocent lad is flogged across the backside, he stares at me with such a lost, pleading look in his eyes. I look away in shame and guilt; his hurt will heal, mine won't. I do my all to make amends after this awful experience, and myself and the victim of my dishonor become firm friends. He is a gypsy lad named Paul, and his people have left the highways and byways to settle down for a while in the heart of England. Their eldest girl is at university, a thing totally unknown to us. They live in two caravans connected together in an H shape by a central veranda. There are lots of kids in the family, and it becomes my second home. For the first time I hear a recording of Tchaikovsky's *1812 Overture*. I am spellbound. "Good Golly Miss Molly," by Little Richard, has me jitterbugging around the room. Dinnertime is a feast of the bizarre. I eat hitherto unheard of things like spaghetti bolognese, sago pudding, and hedgehogs roasted in balls of clay, which helps pull off the prickly spines when you break them open. Under the supervision of the eldest lad, Nicky, I learn how to take car engines to bits and motorcycles to pieces and reassemble them with not too many pieces left over. Happily I dwell with these gypsies in their wonderful, surreal pied-à-terre and as a result spend less time at home.

Mam has an important announcement for me.

"I'm going to have a wee baby!" She grins.

This is great news. I have always wanted a brother or sister. Mam gets bigger day by day and knits lots of little woolen things from the old socks and jumpers that I unravel for her. She packs a suitcase and tells me it's time to go and get the baby. I want to go with her, but I have to stay and run the household. Dad is away at work. A car comes, and my mother waves at me as it drives her to the hospital. In an old drawer I make up a crib and put my teddy bear in it to keep warm for the baby.

Dad comes in late and won't eat his dinner. He is very drunk and holds me so tight that I can't breath. He rocks me back and forth, all the time crying and muttering in Welsh. The smell of stale beer and cigarettes is horrible, and the rocking motion makes me gag. I am terrified, and glad when he finally goes to sleep. Women call at the caravan and ask me what I need. Days pass and Dad still comes home stinking of drink; he lies awake half the night. I hate the acrid sting of sulfur from struck matches as he lights the roof of the caravan with the orange glow of another cigarette. Please, Mam, come back soon!

Mother comes home alone, there is no baby with her. My little brother, Keith, had lived only four days. He only comes home to be buried, and even then I never see his face. Mam says he looked like an angel. His coffin lies in the corner of the caravan until Davy Windle has finished digging the tiny grave at the back of our school chapel. After he was gone into the earth, Mam sits for hours cradling my teddy in her arms and singing, "Shule, shule, shule, aroon." A lament for a lost loved one, as heavy as the cloud of misery that hangs above the corner where we live. The keening notes drift upward to heaven and into a lifeless sky, as gray as my mother's face.

Something has to be done to turn the luck: Dad sobers up.

"I've got a better site," he says, turning up one day on a old Ferguson tractor. After much palaver and arsing about, he pulls the caravan some fifty feet to the shelter of a tall ivy-grown red brick wall. Mam, still mourning her loss, is singularly unimpressed. I also notice with gloom that this move puts me even farther away from the water tap.

"This thing here," says me old fella, pointing to an old army ammunition box bolted to the wall, "is an electricity hook-up and we shall have electric light!" Mam is almost impressed and raises an inquiring eyebrow.

"What about the toilet then?" She likes asking awkward questions and is enjoying twisting my dad's tail. It is good to see her smile again.

"All in good time, woman! Didn't it take God seven days to make the world?" This divine allusion from my atheistic father is calculated to rile my devout mother, and it works.

"Seven days, me arse! What would a pagan like you know about it? He worked six days and on the seventh he rested, ya bloody heathen! You do it all arse backwards, one day's work and six days' bloody rest—mostly in the public house!"

Dad puts his thumb up to his nose, waggles his fingers and speeds off on the little gray tractor. I try the same gesture at Mam and get a slap round the earhole for my pains.

Months later, Dad, true to his word, installs a single forty-watt bulb in the caravan. Mam says, "Whoopee!! We're back in the twentieth century!" But I miss the yellow gas light burning hoarsely in its fragile lime mantle. On the other hand, we now have a socket to run the ancient Sobell valve wireless that has sat in its box for over a year. With this aid, we can tune in Radio Eireann from its transmitter in Athlone and get the Irish news from home. The BBC has a lot of plays and on Sunday mornings runs *As I Roved Out,* a program of traditional folk songs from all parts of the British Isles and Ireland. This is presented by A. L. Lloyd, the famous folk music collector, and features many old songs that we know. Sadly, the tuning cord eventually breaks and the radio remains stuck on the frequency of some European station that plays the "Harry Lime Theme" from the film *The Third Man,* over and over again. We soon have enough of that. The wireless goes into Dad's "must fix it pile," where it stays until I fix it myself, many years later.

Winter is now upon us, but we are cozy in our little environment. Mam asks me to help tidy up the rest of the garden before the snow comes.

"Now let's get you wrapped up," she says, tying a scarf around my neck. "We don't want the damp to get you!" I glance nervously over my shoulder as the wind shakes the bushes behind me.

My large tin trunk has been left outside in the elements and is disintegrating with rust. Mam forces it open and inspects the contents. Shaking her head in disbelief, she picks up my cowboy suit, a present from my great-uncle who's a cop in New York. It is green with mold and in tatters.

"Oh, dear, look at all this stuff. It's ruined." She holds up one of my picture books. The cover slides off and the pages are all in decay.

"What causes all this, Mammy?"

"It was the damp, son."

A cold shiver runs through me. So the damp has been in our garden, causing havoc while we lay asleep in our beds!

"It's a good thing we lock our door at night, Mammy. Only the other day I heard the neighbors talking of a murder! Did you hear old Mrs. Mackay was found dead in her caravan? Oh, yes, they say it was the damp that killed her. Yes, it was the damp all right. Why don't they get a posse together and hunt it down, Mammy, before it gets us all?" Mam shoots me a queer look.

"You'd better go inside, I think you're coming down with something," she says.

"Hellooow!" The queer figure I had been idly watching as it trudged through the snow turns out to be my dad. The tracks behind him have a definite wavy quality, and his nose is red. He has a bow saw in one hand and a hip flask of brandy in the other.

"Come on, get your coat! We're going to cut timber for a rustic garden fence."

Off we march into the wilderness, that magical enclave of wild nature, now a stretch of ice-covered scrub bushes, frosty silver tree trunks, and frozen lakes. We cut several lengths of sapling about ten feet long, then with much grunting and swearing on my dad's part, we drag them home. On the way back, we see two big brown hares sitting in the rays of the setting winter sun.

"We'll come back for those buggers tomorrow—with a gun!" whispers my dad with an expeditious wink. Blue shadows fill our footprints as we march home through the snow in the indigo twilight.

"Here's the shotgun, Reg, and six cartridges. They're all I have just now."

"Ticketty-boo, sahib," Dad answers. I notice he often speaks to his old army chums in strange words and phrases; sometimes Arabic or in this case, Hindi, meaning: "That's fine, sir."

We crunch our way back to the wilderness, while Dad gives me a lesson on the etiquette of firearms.

"You *never* point a gun at anyone, always assume a gun is loaded, never carry a loaded gun with the safety off, and when hunting, always break a shotgun at the breach."

"There's one!" says Dad. The .410 discharges its shot, and the big brown hare falls still in the snow. I get such a fright from the bang, and because my ears are still ringing, I don't hear my dad say, "Hold this!" He thrusts the single-barreled shotgun into my hands, and I, totally unprepared for its weight, watch helplessly as the barrel spins round and sticks in the snow.

Dad is running over to his kill as I retrieve the gun and brush the snow off of the long blue barrel. He has not seen me drop it, and I say nothing.

"Now," says Dad, "this is what you do." He takes the one back leg of the hare and pushes it through the sinew of the other, forming a carrying handle.

"You hold it," he says, and reluctantly I do—at arm's length.

A little farther off, Dad motions me to be still—he has spied another. As he raises the newly loaded gun and takes aim, a miracle happens! The hare I'm holding suddenly jerks and kicks so violently that I let go of it and it takes off, zigzagging across the snow. The damn thing had only been stunned! I am even more stunned and take off running in the opposite direction. At the same instant, Dad fires and the end of the gun, packed with snow, mushrooms out in splinters.

It was a long walk home, with Dad muttering darkly to himself. As we reach our caravan he suddenly brightens up.

"Get my tools, Will, I have a plan."

For the next few hours my father saws, files, and smooths until the gun looks as good as new. Then with a blowtorch, he tempers the barrel until the metal is the same beautiful, uniform, blue color all around.

"There, he'll never know the difference," he says with some pride, scrutinizing the gun, now three inches shorter.

The next day we take it back to his mate. There is a unsuspected fly in the ointment, however. The owner takes the gun and is set to notice nothing until, to my Dad's wiggly-mouthed chagrin, he produces a case for it. Dad shuffles nervously as the man puts the gun in its walnut box. The man blinks, stares again, and utters, "The f—ing thing's shrunk!"

"Oh," says Dad, used to thinking on his feet, "it must be this cold weather!"

"What!" says his pal. "I've never heard of such a thing." Dad warms to his ruse.

"Do you know aught about the coefficiency of gun metal alloys?"

"No," says his mystified friend.

"Well, there you are. It's ten below out there!" Dad's superior knowledge wins the day and we leave his pal scratching his head.

The next summer, his mate duly reports that the barrel has never recovered from its mysterious shrinkage.

"Aye," says Dad. "That was a bloody cold winter!"

It is fast approaching Christmas. Dad has found a decent job as a signalman for British Railways. All is very pleasant at school, and we spend a lot of time making Christmas decorations and rehearsing for the school nativity play.

I had long wanted to have a go at acting and hoped for a star part. It was not to be. Like so much in life, I am passed over for someone whose only talent is not getting into trouble. The best parts go to those with the most spotless *souls*.

Amongst these chosen few, Mary O'Malley is given the part of Jesus' mother because she is the only Mary in the school. The fact that she is extremely timid and can't remember her lines is glossed over by the first-time director, Mr. Bury. The saintly Joseph Ryan is a triumph of miscasting for the same reason, and although he is playing Mary's consort he is too shy even to hold her hand.

I wanted to play King Herod, but Mr. Bury cut that role and I am given the only remaining speaking part—the innkeeper! Well, at least I have an apron, so my costume won't be expensive.

We rehearse in the school, but the play is to be held at the Firemen's Memorial Hall in nearby Henley-in-Arden. As the opening night approaches, I notice that the leading players are almost fainting with fear at the prospect. They should be more like the shepherds, who are scallywags and, with no lines to say, are having a ball. Even the angels, whose elaborate wings never seem to want to stay on, are having fun. I am in my element and delight at Mr. Bury as he strides around, wringing his hands and intoning, "This is going to be a disaster!" For once he was right, dead right!

During rehearsals the shepherds watched their flocks by night around a pile of rulers, which was their makeshift campfire. Now on opening night, Mr. Bury, our resident Jonah, builds a pile of twigs center stage to add a little realism. For color, he wraps a hundred-watt lightbulb in red cellophane and plugs it in. He flashes it up and it does look very pleasant, bathing the shepherd's faces with a warm glow. We are all set.

The choir are sweetly singing "O Little Town of Bethlehem," and from the scraping of the chairs and excited chatter, we know we have a full house.

At last the houselights dim, the curtain opens, and Mr. Bury's "fire" looks very realistic.

"Go—lighting cue one," comes a whisper. Nothing happens. Dark shapes move around the stage and collide with each other. The audience, sensing that something is amiss, begins to titter.

"Lighting cue one—GO!" bellows the director and the stage lights shoot up to discover an angel, with wings like Pegasus, wedged firmly in the doorway. The shepherds, far from being sympathetic, begin laughing. The determined seraphim, mustering all the strength of an indignant ten-year-old, bursts free of his encumbrance and marches on stage.

"I have come to tell you the Good News!"

"You've given up flying!" shouts an irreverent voice offstage, and the audience is in transports of delight.

"This is not supposed to be funny!" Mr. Bury is nearing the edge of his patience, and his stage whispers are in danger of drowning out the actors' dialogue.

Funny or not, it was getting realistic—he trapped lightbulb had reached the flash point of the cellophane, which had burst into flames.

"Holy Christ!!" shouts a new figure in the play, leaping into the midst of the confused gaggle of shepherds.

"FIRE! FIRE!" The tall man in the shiny brown suit is doing a jerky jig on top of the campfire in front of puzzled actors and audience alike. Mr. Bury has made his stage debut, as a fire dancer!

With great presence of mind, a young actor whose father once worked for a fire extinguisher firm douses them all down with a fire hose and never even asks for thanks.

The curtain closes prematurely on the first act, and Mr. Bury sits dripping and disconsolate in the wings.

I thought it had gone quite well, and the audience seems to be enjoying it. In fact, news of the fun had reached the fire station next door, and the backstage area is now full of men in firemen's gear. They tell us that we can proceed with the show once they have turned off the fire alarm, which is threatening to deafen us all.

Eventually the time comes to do my bit. There isn't much to it, so I make the most of it. "Saint" Joseph knocks timidly at the inn door, his pregnant wife beside him. This was it! I throw open the door and roar, "NO ROOM! NO ROOM AT THE INN!" But before I can finish, Joseph has fled off stage and Mary gets such a fright, she drops the infant Jesus, which had been secreted in her garments, and stares in horror as the Messiah's head flies off, rolls down the raked stage, and lands in the orchestra pit. The final curtain comes down on our pantomime production and likewise on Mr. Bury's career in show business. The befuddled audience is wild with appreciation, and even the firemen are cheering.

Later, as we make our way back in the winter chill, knowing that on the morrow our luckless teacher must explain the night's bizarre events to the stern Mrs. MacArthur, my gift for parody comes to the fore. Borrowing the melody of "Ding Dong Merrily on High," I offer "Ding Dong Bury's Gonna Die." Our little group takes up the chant as we walk the two and a half miles home through the snow.

Our wee school is blessed with two bequests from long-dead estates: the first amounts to sixpence for each child and the second to half a crown. Both are payable at Christmas. This makes a total of three shillings in sterling money and is a princely sum.

An ice cream costs a penny and there are thirty-six pennies in three shillings. The lowest-value coin is the farthing. Even this will buy you a boiled sweet, and there are four farthings to a penny, so the mathematics are simple: 36 ice creams = 144 boiled sweets.

The farthing is a neat little coin about the size of an American penny. On its face side, it has the monarch of the day, whilst the obverse bears the likeness of a wren.

Whether the Royal Mint in London realized it or not, this tiny creature was the smallest bird known to the ancients and is the Celtic king of the birds.

Mam had told me the story of the wren-king back home in Ireland

when I was wee, and so I present it to the class as my Christmas mono-
logue:

> The birds were deciding who should be their leader. "I
> am known to be the wisest," said the owl. "The swiftest
> should rule," squeaked the swallow. "How about the
> most graceful?" asked the swan. In a terrible uproar, each
> pressed his case, except the humble wren, who consid-
> ered himself unelectable on account of his diminutive
> size. He instead went to sleep in the warm feathers of the
> eagle's back.
>
> Knowing his ground well, it was the eagle now who
> spoke. "The title shall go to he who can fly the highest!"
> None dared argue and the contest began. One by one, as
> they climbed and wheeled, the various species reached
> their limit. Soon only the swifts, martins, and hawks
> were left. Still above them, climbing even higher, was the
> mighty eagle. Finally, in a last show of prowess, he flew
> higher than any eagle had flown before. At the very edge
> of his strength, he hovered and the rest of the birds whis-
> tled and squawked in approval.
>
> This awoke the sleeping wren, who flew straight up to
> see what all the commotion was about. The eagle, crest-
> fallen, admitted defeat, and the wren became the king of
> the birds.

In Ireland, the pagan ceremony of wrening still persists. On the day
after Christmas, boys dress up and go hunting for a wren. The object is
to capture one and parade it around the village in a cage. People give you
money for good luck and then the bird is released. It is considered very
unlucky to kill a wren, and if you do, you will be struck by lightning
within the year. I finish the story with a song I also learned from Mam:

> *The wren, the wren, the king of all birds,*
> *St. Steven's Day, was caught in the furze.*
> *Though he is little, his family is great,*
> *I pray you, good Landlady, give us a treat.*

The school term is over for Christmas and we have ten glorious days off! We are all very excited and even the prospect of midnight mass seems thrilling. Indeed, it was easy for the meanest of spirit to feel a little more *bon vivant!* at this time of year.

The big church at the top of the hill, next to the railway station, is very different from the freezing old barn of a school chapel. The statues are all nicely painted and look like real people. The altar boys have incense, and best of all—it is heated!

Christmas Eve comes with a light fall of fine snow that crisps under foot. The bells of the old Saxon church cascade in syncopated peals. This is great! It is nearly midnight, and I am so wrapped up against the cold, I am impervious to the many slips and falls we all have on the way up the hill. Many of the once a year devout traveling with us have just come out of the Bull's Head tavern, and giggling is the common currency of their conversation.

The priest is less pleased at seeing these annual revelers and warns them about swigging from secreted bottles during the mass. The great organ swells into a mighty crescendo, and we launch into "Adeste Fidelis."

The service seems very holy until about the halfway point, when the great nail-studded doors at the back of the church are flung wide open, letting in an icy shaft of air. Everyone turns to see the cause of the draft. I shiver and so does Mam. She recognizes the stumbling figure weaving his way toward the altar.

"Mother of Good Counsel—it's your father!"

Dad has inbibed a little too much of the Christmas spirit and is as drunk as a bobbyhowler. He is wearing both his work overcoat and his khaki army greatcoat, the pockets of which clink with beer bottles. He kneels down in the nave and begins to wail: "Oh, Jesus, forgive a poor sinner . . . oh, Jesus!"

He falls forward, giving his head a mighty clout on the altar steps. Two bottles of stout escape from the prison of his pockets and shoot across the marble floor. Dad goes after them sideways like a crab, all the time grabbing at the air, as they roll out of reach beneath a pew.

"Cummeeer, ye wee bashtards!" Dad slurs. "Whoops! Shorry, missus, was that yer leg?"

The priest, having recovered a little from this unwarranted intrusion, explodes!

"HOW DARE YOU BRING ALCOHOL INTO THE HOUSE OF GOD!!!" he thunders.

Dad wheels around on one foot, blinking in disbelief at the raging cleric.

"Shorry, mister, shorry, God!" Dad shuffles out toward the porch, tucking his prodigal Guinnesses back in his greatcoat pockets. Mam has her head buried in between the leaves of her gilt-edged prayer book.

"Has he gone?" she whispers. He has, for the time it takes him to line up his six bottles of stout in the vestry and return, waving his arms about and smiling like a prat.

"Happy Chrishmash!" he wishes one and all. "Peassh to all men."

"I'll give him peace when I get him home!!" Mam hisses, gritting her teeth into her missal. "I'll give him such peace it'll kill 'im."

The verger, a nervous man, decides to position himself near the telephone in case the assistance of the village policeman is required. In his haste, he neglects to see Dad's choir of beer bottles standing to attention across the vestry floor. He scatters them like ninepins. The unmistakable sounds of disaster send my father scurrying and cursing back up the aisle, where he confronts the terrified verger.

"YOU STUPID FU—!"

To the relief of all, especially the priest and my mother, Dad's voice is drowned out as the organ strikes up with, of all things, "Silent Night."

A Christmas Day truce is observed by Mam and Dad, "for the sake of the poor child." I appreciate it no end and stare at the solitary Christmas present under the tree. After breakfast I'm allowed to open it; it's a small red Dinkytoy fire engine.

Soon my mother, enlivened by a glass of sherry, is in better kidney and laughing about the previous night's doings.

"My God, Reg, you put the fear of the devil into that verger. When me and Willie last saw him, on our way home, he was hiding in the graveyard as white as a ghost!"

"If I'd have caught the bugger, he would *be* a bloody ghost by now! By the way, how do you like your Christmas present, Will?"

I was sitting on the floor, playing with my fire truck.

"It's terrific, Dad. Thanks!"

"We could have used that the night of the play," Mam says and proceeds to fill Dad in on all the disastrous details.

"There's a party at the big hall on New Year's Eve," informs my mother, who has started working as a part-time barmaid there. "It's a western-style barn dance cum fancy dress party. The theme is cowboys and Indians!"

"There's no shortage of either around here," says Dad.

"This will be old Mr. Mayer's last New Year's bash, as he's selling the estate in the spring," she says, pouring another sherry for herself and one for Dad.

The news of the sale saddens me, as I liked the old chap. Even though Mr. Mayer was seldom seen around and was a bit of a recluse, when he did venture out, he was pleasant to chat with and sometimes handed out silver sixpences. Each year, in the country gentleman's tradition of noblesse oblige, he threw a party in the grand ballroom for the estate workers and caravan site dwellers. He did not attend the revelry himself, but would stand at the door shaking hands with everyone before retreating to his lonely rooms above. Mr. Mayer's apartments in the Georgian mansion were spacious and crammed full of bric-a-brac from all over the globe. Mam said he had been well traveled as a youth and had made a lot of money in the United States before coming back to buy the hall. He also told my mother that what he missed the most about America was the pancakes.

In the British Isles, we only eat pancakes once a year, on Pancake Day, or Shrove Tuesday, as it's properly called. Being the start of Lent, this is the time to be shriven of sins and to use up all your flour and eggs before the fasting of the Lenten weeks begins. Last Pancake Day, we remembered old Mr. Mayer and brought some hot pancakes up to him. He was delighted, and although he was Jewish and didn't celebrate the feast day, he said he was very touched by Mam's simple act of kindness. He gave me a wooden camel from Egypt, which I treasure, as a memento of a kindly old man, who, though as rich as Croesus, lived a solitary life and hardly seemed to have a friend in the world.

Mam pours a small glass of sherry for me and gives us the toast: "We have come through some hard times—a happy Christmas and peace on earth!"

"And sod the begrudgers!"

"REG! That's enough of that sort of language in front of the child!"

Christmas dinner over, we all fall asleep where we sit, like giants surrounded by the bones of their slain.

The New Year's Eve party is a great success. A western barn dance scene is created, using bales of hay and old wagon wheels for effect.

Mam and Dad look very fine dressed as cowboys and have their photograph taken by the local paper. Dad has drawn a funny mustache and beard on his face with an indelible marker and finds that it won't wash off. People put a lot of care into their get-ups and everyone sports cowboy hats; Mam wears my hat and belt when she gets up to sing with the band:

> *I'm a rambler, I'm a gambler*
> *I'm a long way from home*
> *So if you don't like me*
> *Then leave me alone!*
> *I eat when I'm hungry*
> *I drink when I'm dry*
> *And if the moonshine don't kill me*
> *I'll live till I die!*

So the year was almost over. I get to go to the kids' party that precedes the grown-ups' fancy dress on Old Year's Night. To my amazement, there in the ballroom of the great hall, I meet with a quare-looking character, the likes of which I've never seen before. My friends say he is called Old Father Time. He has a well-worn, tattered robe of sable, a long white beard, a scythe over his shoulder, and a thing called an hourglass in his hand. I asked him what he is and why he was dressed like that?

"I am death!" comes the voice from within.

✦ Chapter 7 ✦

IN PREPARATION FOR THE SALE OF WOOTTON HALL AND ITS lands, hordes of workmen are recruited to do a spruce-up job on the three-hundred-year-old building.

The hall had been commandeered by the army during the war, and somehow, in the defense of king and country, the soldiers had managed to set fire to the roof. As a result, it was far from weathertight and needed major repairs.

In due course, huge flatbed trucks arrive carrying trusses, A-frames, stringers, and beams. All this makes a grand playground for us kids, both while stored under tarpaulins on the ground or rigged in place on the roof. The laborers, all of whom we know, are for the most part oblivious to our presence and pay us no heed.

One evening, I overhear some of the workmen chatting at the end of their shift.

"So they've finally managed to eradicate the damp, I hear," says a big, red-faced geezer.

"Yes, Mr. Bullivant, and none too soon either. It had eaten halfway through some of the timbers supporting the west wing. We caught it just in the nick of time!"

I am glad of our deliverance, but still curious. I'd never been face-to-face with a real monster.

"Can I see it?" I says to the construction fella.

"See what?"

"The damp, of course!"

"Well no, it's gone, dead! Not a trace left. Kaput!"

"Damn!" says I. "What did it look like?"

"Er . . . it was green and yellow spots mostly, and it really did stink!"

So there I had it, firsthand, from a man who had seen the ghastly murderous beast with his own eyes. The dreaded damp that had terrorized our neighborhood for ages was *dead*. We had been saved from the big stinky thing!

I lie in my bunk at night and watch the myriads of stars in their punctual progression around Polaris. I feel very small, very safe, and very happy.

The day dawns to a new brighter age and with it I arise confident to explore my terra incognita. The first thing is to acquire a trusty steed. This comes in the form of a tall, black, 1910 BSA bicycle. It is given to me by an old lady who'd had it from new. She called it a sit-up-and-beg, but my mam tells me it is a Thin Lizzy. It's a single-geared machine and has mechanical brakes. Although it is old fashioned, I love it.

Dad checks it over and after some tightening and adjusting, he pronounces it safe and roadworthy.

"See this thing, here?" he says, tapping the chain guard with a wrench. "This gadget was invented by your great-granddad to keep ladies' crinolines out of the works." I nod approval. "Now, let's oil her up and when the weather's better, I'll teach you to ride the beast."

Learn to ride, I did, sitting way up in the air on that ancient and venerable old bike. I got a great view of the entire world from up there!

Bright Phoebus vied for control of the northern skies and General Winter, sensing defeat, retreated his storm troopers, southward to the Antipodes. Spring was born.

"Rabbits!" shouts my Dad from his bed.

"What was that?"

"Rabbits! It's traditional to shout 'Rabbits!' on the first of March, for good luck."

"Ah, now, Reg, don't be filling the child's head with superstitious old nonsense. You're as mad as a March hare and you'll have the child as daft as yourself," Mam contends.

After my hunting experience, I'd had quite enough of hares, March or otherwise, but when I look outside, the snow, like the accursed damp, is gone.

"In like a lion and out like a lamb," Mrs. MacArthur says, turning over the calendar page and placing the red marker on March 1st. 1957.

"You're supposed to say 'Rabbits!' miss," I blurt out, as blithe as a butterfly. She turns and fixes me with a viperous eye. My heart stops.

"Beware the hides of March!" she warns me, or it could have been the eyes of March—I couldn't tell with that quare Scottish "Och eye the noo" accent of hers.

"What was that again, miss?" I entreat, trying to get into her good books.

She turns a serpentine stare back toward me.

"I don't boil my cabbages twice," she hisses mysteriously and fills my conviction that grown-ups like to answer proper questions with odd allusions to vegetables! Luckily for me, the old school wireless set crackles to life with an important announcement.

"This is the BBC Schools Service. We begin today's Broadcast of Scottish Country Dancing in five minutes. *PEEP! PEEP! PEEP!*"

"CLEAR THE DECKS FOR ACTION!" Mrs. MacArthur has become transformed. "You there, Patrick Whateveryournameis, stack those chairs!" She has become Captain Bligh! "Clear the tables away! Move it! MOVE IT! Mister Bury! Where are you? MISTER BURY, GET IN HERE!!!"

Mr. Bury, still on his morning break, appears in the doorway. Teacup in one hand and half-dipped digestive biscuit held high in the other.

"Er, what is it, Head? Er . . . um," he bumbles, staring around in disbelief as the normally well-ordered schoolroom is stripped as clean as the gun deck on a frigate.

"I'm still on my . . . er . . . tea break!"

"GET STUCK IN!!" she barks. "The DANCING will start in two minutes!!"

"I . . . um . . . yes . . . em!" All this is as new to Mr. Bury as it is to me and whilst his mind vacillates between incomprehension and hope, the soggy end of his biscuit breaks off and disappears down his shirt sleeve.

"MISTER BURY—DO SOMETHING!!!" she orders, clearing away the blackboard. He does and in his eagerness to please, he tries to do two different tasks simultaneously. Unfortunately, they are at opposite sides of the classroom and his confused corporance, in defiance of the laws of anatomy, attempts to move his bottom half to the right and his top half to the left. Still with teacup and half biscuit in hand, it gives him the appearance of a bemused hula-girl on coffee break.

"Mr. Bury, stop those gyrations and come here!" she says, pointing to a spot on the floor. "That's it—guid!" Clapping her hands three times, she calls, "RIGHT NOW! Let's get fell in. Guid! Guid! Two lines, girls to the left, boys to the right, facing each othe—? Michael Dwyer!!! Do you not know what gender you are???"

"No, miss," he says in all honesty, as we hadn't done gender yet.

"Well, that butters no parsnips with me! Get in line!"

"Mrs. Mack's gone veggie again!" I confide to Steve O'Donnell, who gets the giggles. The teacher spins around, but we are saved as the wireless strikes up with a skirling Scottish march and Mrs. MacArthur, her eyes blazing like Queen Boadicea mowing down the Roman legions, stomps up and down the assembled rows of children, swinging her arms and blowing odd bagpipe-type noises out of the corner of her mouth.

"The Campbells are coming . . . *Puh—Paw—Puh—Paw!* The Campbells are coming . . . *Puh—Paw—Puh—Paw!!*" It is all very unnerving.

The brisk signature tune fades and the lesson proper begins.

"Now each of you take a partner." She grabs Mr. Bury, who pales visibly. To my horror, though I try to maneuver myself down the line, I get stuck with Nora.

The music begins with an eightsome reel, and whether Nora had forgotten the incident with the hammer two years ago, I don't know, but being taller and older than me, she throws me around the room like a terrier does a rat. I am glad when the final *Deh!—Dah!* comes and we all can rest.

Mr. Bury looks like he's been filleted. His body has gone to jelly and he is having trouble keeping it on his chair. One of his legs has taken to doing a solo twitching dance, and with his face the color of an overripe tomato, he is sweating profusely.

The headmistress, however, is bristling like a sergeant major's waxed mustache. Her eyes gleaming like the hot coals of hell, and with a determined stride, she swans up and down the ranks, rubbing her hands with glee.

"Well done! Well done, children, a very guid show!"

This unexpected praise spurs us on to new efforts, and we all get thoroughly into the swing of things; all except the recumbent Mr. Bury, who sits like a broken toy in the corner, nursing a supposed dislocated shoulder and complaining of nausea.

"You should eat more *porridge,* sonny!" Mrs. Mack teases as she circles past the fallen teacher clutching her new dancing partner, the terrified Michael Waterson. In her exuberance she fails to realize that Mike, being half her size, has become airborne; his little legs describe spindly arcs in her turbulent wake.

After half an hour of Scottish country chaos, we file past a proudly smiling Mrs. MacArthur and into the sunlit playground where we sit in little groups, supporting each other like earthquake victims. The aftershocks of the jigs and reels still shudder in our small bodies like tremors, and despite the warm day, Mike's teeth are chattering.

Break over, we troop back into the classroom to find the genie out of the bottle. The florid-faced parish priest is there with an unwelcome announcement.

"Tomorrow there will be a special mass to celebrate Pope Pius the Twelfth's eightieth birthday. Also, his seventeenth year as the Holy Father. You will all attend. There will be NO EXCEPTIONS!" He says the last bit loud enough to drown out our groans.

As if this isn't bad enough, the next subject is the dreaded arithmetic or sums, as we called it, and that is the one subject I have the most trouble with.

Now, it isn't that the idea of adding and subtracting, multiplying and dividing is all that strange. The problem lies in the teaching methods and the British school's standard math textbook. The course work relies heavily on allegory, which is fine for teaching fables or parables, but to me mathematics is abstract and is best dealt with in abstraction.

I could readily understand that $1 + 5 = 6$, but to the Celtic mind, one carrot + five carrots = a bunch of carrots and nothing else. Similarly, $3 - 1 = 2$, fair enough, but the book would ask: "You have three apples in one hand and you take away one, what have you got?" To the Anglo-Saxon, the simple answer is two. To the visually minded Celt, however, you have two apples in one hand and one in the other. Apples and carrots, me arse; I'd rather be fishing.

The lesson begins with a cane being rapped on the face of the blackboard to draw our attention, and Mr. Bury, now on firmer ground, feels like he's back in control.

"John Costello, if it takes one man one hour to dig a hole, how long does it take two men?"

"Two hours, sir!"

"No, no, no! How could it be two hours? Come on, John, think about it!"

"Well," says John, "the second fella would be getting in the first fella's way for a start and then they'd be talking and wisecracking an' carrying on. Then they might stop for a smoke and then—"

"Stop, stop, stop! The answer is simple: half an hour! OK?"

"Noshataall!" continues John. "There'd be no hole dug in half an hour that could accommodate two men with picks and shovels and them both working!"

We all support his irrefutable logic and we know full well that John's dad is a ganger for Ryan Construction and so he knows what he is talking about.

Mr. Bury is stunned to silence, probably lamenting the fact that he had spent all those years at college just to be worsted by a young gosoon from the wilds of Connemara. Mind you, no teacher back home in Ireland would ever be so errant as to argue digging holes with a Culshie.

"They just don't seem to grasp it, Miss Hathaway," our young teacher confided over a cup of tea.

"You should try taking the little tykes for history! I only had to mention Oliver Cromwell and they nearly took the hide off me! They take it all so personally!"

This is true. History to us is a living, breathing beast. A composite of people and events that directly effects and involves our lives. Wasn't Thomas MacDonagh, the poet and patriot, who signed the Declaration of Irish Independence in 1916, a living kinsman, before he was executed by a British firing squad!? He was! Didn't General Sir John Cope, another distant relative, have the good sense to take one look at the Highland Scots' army and run away from the battle of Prestonpans in 1745? He did! Who was it that got hung for organizing the Spithead naval mutiny in the 1700s? Thomas Watkins, that's who! Mind you, Uncle Walter reckons our family are direct descendants of Old King Cole, but that's Uncle Walter for you! Anyway, the English history that we are now obliged to learn is merely a long list of kings, queens, and battles that would put a glass eye to sleep! To us, history is still in the making. On New Year's day this very year, a small force of volunteers of the Irish Republican Army has attacked Brookeborough RUC barracks in Northern Ireland. The gunfight that ensued left two IRA men dead and three wounded. The fallen were Fergal O'Hanlon, aged nineteen, from Monaghan, and the raid's legendary twenty-seven-year-old leader, Seán South, the family of whom we knew well.

> *At early dawn, the Colleen bawn,*
> *Put on her long black veil.*
> *She told me then, of two young men*
> *Who fell on freedom's trail.*
> *The seagulls cried, for those who died*
> *All along the Shannon's shore.*
> *God rest you brave, Seán Sabhat.*
> *We will ne're see you more.*

The funerals for the two young men were the largest in living memory. In Limerick, 36,000 people followed the coffin, including the U.S. ambassador. Seán was buried with full military honors in the same graveyard as countless past generations of my own family. That's the sort of history we are used to—not the despotic antics of some obese, syphilitic, ax-wielding old tosspot like Henry VIII.

The long plod home from school is rewarded by a grand yeasty aroma emanating from the vicinity of our caravan.

Mam is in good fettle, making bread and singing a wee song away to herself:

> *Ireland was Ireland,*
> *When England was a pup.*

And Ireland will be Ireland,
When England's "buggered up"!

"Mam, do you hate the English?"

"Good God, no, Willie. There's enough hate it this world without me stirring up some more. You shouldn't hate anything in this life, except hatred itself. The poor old English, they're more to be pitied than scorned, with their cricket and tiddlywinks and their passion for keeping up with the Joneses. As Brendan Behan says, 'Take them away from their kings and queens and rifles, and they're decent enough people!'"

There is a blue van sounding its horn at the end of the road. The back doors are opened, and old Mr. Westmacote, the greengrocer, stands waiting by his weighing machine, wearing a grubby white apron.

"Willie, go up to the van and buy me five pounds of spuds and a cabbage. I've a lovely piece of boiling bacon and tomorrow is Saint Patrick's Day."

"On my way, Mam. Where's the money?"

"Take a pound out of my purse and make sure you get a nice firm little cabbage."

Shopping bag in hand I saunter up to the mobile shop.

"Five pounds of potatoes, please, and I'll take one of these." I set the small green orb on the weighing scale. The needle hardly moves.

"Do you only want one of them?"

"Yeah, there's only the three of us."

"OK, you're the boss!"

I stroll back to the caravan. Mam stares at my purchase in disbelief.

"Is that the cabbage he gave you?"

"It is."

"Jasus! What sort of daylight bloody robbery is going on here atall? That skinny little thing wouldn't feed a flea, ifeverawomansuffered!" She grabs the goods and storms off to the vendor.

"What sort of a cabbage do you call that?"

"I call it a brussels sprout, madame!"

"WILLIE! Willie! You bleeder, I'll kill you for making me look an eejit!" She chases me back to the caravan to the great delight of the departing grocer.

What is with vegetables? Why are they always trying to get me into trouble?

It's a great day for the Irish! March seventeenth. Saint Patrick's Day is here again and all of the kids in the school have green, white, and orange tricolor ribbons with wee gold harps on them. Everywhere little tufts of wild green shamrock sprout from coat collars. The atmosphere is unusually festive, and even Mrs. Mack, Miss Hathaway, Mr. Bury, and wee Jean-Paul are all decked out with the three-leafed wonder. We sing:

> *Hail glorious Saint Patrick, dear Saint of our Isle*
> *On us, thy dear children, bestow your sweet smile*
> *And as you look down from your mansion above*
> *On Erin's green valleys, look down in thy love.*

The priest arrives and beams at us during our hymn singing. Father rambles on about St. Patrick being a slave and how he lit a fire to annoy the Druids, then showed the king of Ireland that a shamrock had three leaves, and that's what saved us all. He sets us an essay to write on the subject of "The Real Catholic Meaning of St. Patrick's Day."

I had heard my father say, "It's a good thing to have *real Catholic tastes.*" Hence, ignoring the patron saint of Ireland and his driving out the snakes an' all, I begin:

> Bacon and cabbage is made like this. First you must boil
> a lump of shoulder bacon or corned beef, in a big pan of
> water for two hours, add no salt as it comes out from the
> meat. Then add a chopped up cabbage straight into the
> same pot and leave it alone. Then boil up loads of spuds
> and eat it all together with Colman's mustard on it. Then
> you will have a happy Saint Patrick's Day.

March goes out like a lamb and then 'tis April, just before my seventh birthday.

A bright yellow General Post Office Telephones van pulls into the main drive of the hall and its crew begins rigging poles and wires to a new phone box at the end of the road. It is always a curiosity when a government agency makes a rare visit to our secluded environment.

Mostly we only see the village postman on his red bicycle or the occasional policeman on motorcycle patrol, so the arrival of a GPO van is noteworthy. The post office has a unique place in public life. Not only does it run the postal service, but also the national savings bank and the telephone and telegraph networks.

The linesmen are busy in the field with their cables and poles, and I wander over to take a closer look at the operation. Behind the open back of the telephone truck, much to my surprise, I stumble headlong into my father doing something furtive.

"What are you doing, Dad?"

"Shooosh! Shsh!" He winks and flashes a roll of copper wire that he has concealed under his coat. With a sideways glance at the oblivious workmen, he sidles away whistling the old military march "Colonel Bogey."

The next day the wire is hanging high above our caravan, suspended on a pair of porcelain insulators, between two poles. What could it be? I soon find out.

"Happy Birthday!!!" Mam and Dad usher me into the caravan and there on my bed is a small white box with dials and switches and a pair of earphones. It's a crystal set.

I put on the headphones and tune the dial around. There it is: the BBC "Light Programme" on 1,500 meters long wave! A flick of the switch to medium wave and there is the BBC "Home Service" and, further down the frequency, the "Third Programme." This is truly a mystical experience, the sorcery of which intrigues me.

"Does it have batteries, Dad?"

"No, no, it works only on the signal voltage coming down the aerial wire."

"Is that the stuff you nicked from the GPO van?" Mam's smile fades.

"You said you found that wire! You thievin' bugger!" She gives him a dig.

"I did find it—just before it was lost!"

At night in the darkness, I tune in the world. I can hear stations from all over Europe and beyond. It is totally different from the big wireless set that hums. This is quiet, and the reception is crystal clear. My excitement gets the better of me.

"Dad! Dad! Radio Moscow has just announced that they've launched a spaceship called a sputnik!"

"Go to bloody sleep, Marconi. I've got to get up for work in four hours."

As a result of my ear on the world, I become a walking encyclopedia of news, comment, terrestrial trivia, and litanies of unrelated facts.

"Oliver Hardy died last night," I tell the postman.

"Oh," he says. "What a shame, I liked him."

The school crossing lady is edified by the splendid news that there is now a brand-new tunnel under the Hudson River in New York.

"That's nice, dear. Watch out for the traffic now!"

"Mam, thousands of Hungarians are arriving in Britain. They're called refugees, and they had to get out of Hungary because of the fighting!"

"Yes, the poor hungry Hungarians," she says, looking troubled. She tucks me in and takes off my earphones. I sense something is badly wrong.

"Mam, tell me a poem about Hungary?"

"OK," she says, still distractedly poking the old stove:

> *Long legged Italy,*
> *Kicked little Sicily*
> *Into the Mediterranean sea.*
> *Germany got angry,*
> *Austria got Hungary*
> *And ate a bit of Turkey,*
> *Fried in Greece."*

"Now give me a real poem—the 'Siege of Athlone' or suchlike."

"No, not tonight. I've too much on my mind, son," she says, turning off the electric light to sit quietly in the amber glow from the little stove.

Dad comes home and I wake up a little. They sit sharing a bottle of Ansell's Nut Brown Ale. As I drift in and out of sleep, I try to follow their conversation.

"The priest has given him the last rites," Mam says.

"God, it couldn't have come at a worse time, Monica. With this non-sense going on in Cyprus, I might have to go. The army may call up all the reservists."

"There's never a good time to get cancer, Reg."

"I know," says Dad, putting his arm around her. "I think the world of your da. We've had many's the spree together. You had better get the boat train tomorrow."

The next morning Mam is up early, packing her old brown suitcase. In my sleepy state I don't notice at first, but as she fusses and folds, she is crying.

"So it wasn't all a bad dream then?"

"No, Willie."

"Then Grandda is going to . . . ?" I can't say the word.

"Yes," she says. "Now be a good boy and pack your things."

"Am I going back over home with you, Mammy?"

"No, you're going to your granddad Jim's house in Birmingham for a few weeks." I am strangely relieved. I don't want to see my lovely Irish grandda on his deathbed.

Mam and me take the Midland Red bus to New Street railway station in Birmingham. My granny Mary-Anne is waiting on the platform to see Mam off and take me back to granddad's house. Granny looks as care-worn as Mam.

"Be a good little soldier now for your mammy and don't be bold to your grandma!" I nod up and down, biting my lower lip hard so I won't cry.

From along the platform, the guard waves a green flag and blows a shrill shriek on his whistle. Like the keening of a banshee, the engine's siren wails a mournful farewell and the train slowly squeals away, leaving grandma and me wrapped in shrouds of white steam. When it clears, all I can see is the red oil lamp of the departing carriages glowing like a cinder in the funereal darkness of the long black tunnel.

"Bye, Mam," I whisper to the retreating taillight.

Granddad Jim's house seems huge and scary after the confines of a sixteen-foot trailer home, and to make it worse, I am given a double bed in the spare room. I've never slept in a room on my own before and

I'm very nervous. The lofty oak furniture, dark and terrifying, towers around me, creaking for no apparent reason. I feel alone and frightened. From one wall of the bedroom stares the ghostly face of an old oil painting. It's the portrait of a man in early Victorian garb. He has a lace ruff around his neck and his eyes are dark like damsons. His forehead is adorned with a row of little kiss-curls, his lips are cherry red and in the shape of a cupid's bow; like Mary Pickford or the famous "It Girl," Clara Bow. This, my granny tells me, was my great-uncle Leman, who had been a dandy and who eventually died in a duel, his gambling debts paid on the point of his creditor's rapier. This is not the bedtime story I was hoping for, and I long to be back in my tiny caravan, where, sitting on my pillow with the black Bakelite headphones on, my teddy bear was keeping abreast of the world's events on the crystal wireless set.

Life at the grandparents' place is a lot different than I remember from the last time I stayed there. Grandma seems more remote and can't be bothered with me. She says odd things and wanders about a lot. Granddad Jim is tired most of the time and sometimes very grumpy. I like to look inside the fragrant-smelling walnut writing bureau, where is kept ink, drawing pens, and colored pencils.

"Stop that meddling!" comes the call from Granddad Jim.

"But, what is this thing?" I'm holding a glass paperweight with beautiful nodules of colored coral entrapped in the lead glass.

"It's a lay hole for a meddler. Now put it down before you drop it and it's smashed!" He holds his stomach and moans.

"Willie, make me up some bread and goody, there's a good boy."

"He who asks, don't get. He who don't ask, don't want!" I says in jest, repeating one of his own maxims.

He manages a smile and indicates the scullery. "Go on now, Willie, and be a good lad. I must go and lie down."

When Granny comes home I ask her what is wrong with him.

"His stomach . . . in tatters. What do you expect? Years at the whiskey bottle. Should have spent more time at home with me. Always off swilling down Scotch with your uncles and their cronies at the Masonic Lodge. One foot in the grave . . . bread and milk and Andrew's Liver Salts." She walks nimbly over to the curtains and yanks them open as if expecting to find someone hiding behind them. The doorbell rings and I get a fright!

It's Dad with the grim news that Grandda in Ireland has died and Mam is coming home in a few weeks' time. Then he leaves and I'm sitting at the fireside with Mary-Anne.

"He was here again, you know? That little boy. I saw him looking through the window, upstairs."

"Gran, what little boy? Gran, we don't have a window upstairs. This is a ground floor flat."

"There he is again, looking at me!" She stabs the air with a crooked forefinger and the heart is put crossways in me. I spin on my chair; there is nothing at the window except a pale twilight moon peeping above the lime trees. I am scared. She puts on an old fur coat and goes out.

"Where are you going, Gran?" The bang of the front door is my only answer.

What my granny does in the daytime I don't know. She seems to like going shopping, but all she keeps bringing back is dried yeast and marmalade. We have cupboards bursting with it. I spend many hours each day with Granddad Jim, who now seldom gets out of bed. He says he is very poorly. I make bread and goody for us both; luckily bread and milk are delivered to the house. I sit day by day, reading to him. It makes him laugh when I mispronounce words or read things without knowing their meaning.

Granny is gone more often; time passes; Granddad grows worse. He calls for an enamel bowl and then sends me out of the room. Standing in the hallway, I can hear him being sick. The bowl is full of brown liquid that stinks like cat shit. I pour it down the toilet and pull the chain.

I doze off by the fire. Again Granddad Jim is shouting. He calls for the bowl, but he's too weak to hold it. I put pillows behind his back and hold it as he vomits a bowl full of thick black blood. I flush it down the toilet and ask if he wants some liver salts made up. He nods no. He closes his eyes, but in a weak voice asks for the shoe box from on top of the wardrobe. I get it down for him. It contains a silver-mounted Colt .45 pearl-handled revolver and a small brass padlock key.

"This is for you!" he whispers, giving me the pistol. He asks for a drink of water and I fetch it for him. Taking the small key he puts it into his mouth and swallows it. Then finally, lying back with the palms of his hands flat on the green eiderdown, he says, "You're a good boy, Willie," and then he dies.

Previously in the long talks we had as he lay in his sickbed, he told me not to mourn death, but celebrate life. Alone in the apartment with his body, I didn't know what to do. I wander from room to room like my granny does, just wishing my dad would come. I want to cry, but I can't. As if in answer to my plight, the door bell rings. I nearly jump out of my skin with fright. "Please, God, let it be Dad!"

It isn't Dad. It's two strange men in suits and bowler hats. They push past me. One goes straight into granddad's room and nods to the other one when he comes back out.

"We've come for your granddad's things," says the taller of the two.

The other geezer, a squinty little bloke with glasses like the bottom of milk bottles, tries to engage me in childish conversation. I'm not having any of this old soft soap. I might be just a kid, but I know he is trying to distract me while the lanky one is snooping around the house. I ask the tall bloke what in the name of Jasus he thinks he's doing. He puts a hand on my shoulder and leers at me with a smile like a boiled herring.

"Oh, a little Irish boy!" he smoothes, with what I take to be total contempt. I make a mental note where the revolver is.

"Maybe a clever little boy like you knows where your granddad's secret key is?" he probes in the clipped tones of the BloodyEnglish upper class. I make my way nearer the shoe box.

"Well, tell us, Sonny Jim," says the kipper-lipped one.

"He swallowed it, with a glass of water, just before he died."

"Ah good." They nod knowingly at each other.

"Well, we won't detain you any longer." They pick up granddad's large trunk that contains his sword and weird clothes and walk outside with it.

"His things are in here, we'll look after them," says Squinty, patting the lid.

"Bye-bye, Sonny Jim," adds the fish-faced one, as he pulls the door shut on a seven-year-old boy and a sixty-seven-year-old corpse.

There is a policeman at the door with my granny. She is babbling about the little boy who sets fire to things, looking in the window. He says that my gran is not well and is having delusions. He wants to see Granddad Jim. I show him in. He talks to Granddad Jim for a bit and then just stands there in silence. Then he grabs Granddad's wrist.

"He dead!" he says to me, going all white and big eyed.

"I know!"

"Suffering Jasus!" My father is incandescent with rage. "Those fucking cockroaches come in here without so much as a by-your-leave, take away Dad's Masonic regalia, and leave a little boy alone with his dead grandfather and a grandmother with senile dementia! It's outrageous, totally beyond belief. What the hell do they think they're playing at!"

My two uncles nod and shuffle their feet. Granny doesn't seem to know what's going on and keeps saying that it's getting late and she must make Granddad's dinner.

"It's all a terrible mistake, Reg. I'll see that questions are asked at the next lodge meeting."

"Fuck the lodge—and fuck you both as well!" roars my father, bundling me into the front seat of a waiting car.

On the long journey back to the caravan site, Dad thumps the dashboard of the borrowed car with his fist. I have never seen him so angry. He seems to have forgotten all about me. He just shouts that fuck thing, that Mam said was a soldier's word, and hits the car. For the first time in all this, I begin to cry. Dad's anger is gone. He realizes he is not alone and puts his arm on my shoulder.

"You poor wee bastard. You've lost both your granddads in seven weeks!" he sighs.

So that was just seven weeks. It had seemed like an eternity. I had never fully understood time before. It just sort of happened, like passing the school signpost every day. Now it is all too real, painfully real. I remember the Old Father Time character I met last New Year's Eve.

"I am Death!" he had said—and now death had a face.

Chapter 8

MAM HAS BEEN BACK FOR A FEW WEEKS. IN HER FRAILTY, SHE seems wizened with worry and is full of distractions. It's been desperate hard on her, with three deaths in the family and poor old Mary-Anne now locked up in a mental home, but as Mam is wont to say, "There's always someone worse off than yourself." To take her mind off things, my mother busies herself with something called relief work. She sorts out seldom-worn clothes and puts them in a pile.

"This is going to be a cold winter like the year before last. The rowan berries are heavy on the trees and that's always a sure sign of a rough winter." I look up from playing with my little red fire engine by the glowing cast-iron stove.

"Aye, but we'll be warm enough, eh?" I am thinking of the big pile of hard, shiny anthracite coal we have just been delivered by Mr. Snell the coalman.

"Yes, we're all right, but what about the poor refugees up at Snitterfield? They need everything and the poor misfortunes have nothing. Do you have any toys you don't play with anymore, or things you've grown out of? There's little kiddies up there with bugger all and sure Christmas is only a couple of weeks away."

"Yeah, I've a rake of old toys and things. I'll round them up so."

We pack a big bag of stuff and hitch a ride on the Red Cross collection truck that is doing the rounds. In twenty minutes we are at the old RAF base that serves as temporary shelter and housing for the survivors of the Hungarian uprising.

They are indeed the sorriest-looking bunch of folk I have ever seen and no wonder: most are penniless, some are recovering from wounds, all are stateless and homeless, and as in any war, there are many widows and orphans. Their gratitude for our meager donations sees no bounds. My arm aches from having my hand shaken, and Mam has been kissed more times than General de Gaulle liberating Paris.

In the midst of this cold war flotsam of humanity, I see a young girl like no other I'd ever seen. She has high cheekbones, dark eyes, black hair, and flawless white skin. I am reminded of the faces on the angels in St. Munchin's Church in Limerick, and let's face it, you never see an angel with red hair and freckles. She is holding a toy monkey that I have donated. I wave at her, but she looks away. I think she is shy.

As I'm boarding the truck to get a ride home, I look back to the rows of corrugated iron Nissen huts, and there she is, still hugging her monkey.

She smiles and shouts, "Dank yew!"

I feel like the risen Christ!

We later hear that despite everything, the Hungarians had a good Christmas after all and we are pleased. Ours was a little subdued, as you would expect, but Dad has a stroke of luck. He has been hired by the site manager to clean out some old storerooms that are full of junk.

"Just get rid of it all and sweep the place out. I don't care what you do with the crap." And crap there is, but buried under piles of old Leyden jar batteries, moldy books, and pigeon droppings is an army officer's personal traveling trunk..

This cornucopia of yesteryear is full to the brim with old photographs, personal letters, Victorian postage stamps, a silver-mounted hipflask (still containing red rum), a silver "Albert" for decorating a pocketwatch chain, and a Sam Browne belt complete with holster containing a .38 Webley revolver. Further investigation in the floor cavity produced twenty-four eight-ounce tins of army issue metal polish, three boxes of .303 rifle ammunition, and an ammo box full of hand grenades, all very saleable on the black market. Never ones to look a gift horse in the mouth, it seems that the year 1958 might be treating us more kindly than the previous one.

We have a handcart full of treasures to trundle along the cobbled pathway home. Turning up the cinder track to our part of the site, we bump into Mrs. Ayers. She is an old Shakespearean theater actress who long ago had hit the gin bottle and now thinks she is the reincarnation of Lady Fitzherbert.

"Isn't it a cold day, Mr. Wilkins?" says the old starlet.

"Watkins!" corrects my dad.

"What is? The day of course—damn cold, I said!"

"Have a drink!" says Dad, offering the ancient hip flask. She doesn't need a hearing aid this time!

"Thank you, Mr. Wilson, that is a lovely drop of stuff!" She smiles as she returns the rum and waddles away like an inebriate Queen of Sheba.

The new owners of the hall and its lands are the Allen family. The day they arrive I am sent down to open the big wrought-iron gates to let them in. To my astonishment, on a chill spring day, they drive up in an enormous white American Oldsmobile with the top down. I am black-affronted by this unexpected show of wealth and prestige. Damn it all, just who do these millionaires think they are?

"What's your name, kid?" says Mr. Allen, giving me a sixpenny tip.

"I'm Willy Watkins, and we're having SALMON sandwiches for tea!" That's shown them that they're not the only ones who live high on the hog.

The car speeds off in a cloud of dust toward the hall. I follow, pedaling furiously on my ancient bicycle. All the way down the long drive I thought I could hear the people in the Yankee car laughing. What's the big joke?

The Allens soon settle in and we become firm friends. They have three kids: Mark is a bit younger than me, Neil is a bit older, and John is very, very old, fourteen or something!

Mr. Allen is a big, leonine chap with a sense of humor. He isn't one of the landed gentry and that wrinkles a few noses amongst the country set. Wisely, he had sold his successful garage business in Birmingham and used the proceeds to buy the hall. This story isn't good enough for some of the busybodies on the caravan site who challenge its veracity. Rumors fly about that he is some sort of underworld gang boss who has retired from crime. Some say that he is a government agent sent to spy on them, and others have an even more outlandish theory. Before the outbreak of World War II, they allege that he took a risky gamble. When it was obvious that war was inevitable, he took the six new cars that he had in his showroom, greased them thoroughly, and wrapped them up in wax-soaked cotton sheets. He then secreted them in a barn in the Welsh mountains, far from the eyes of the military, who would surely commandeer all civilian vehicles. The begrudgers said that he would always get more than double his money back, in sterling or Reichsgeld, depending on the war's outcome. Mam's take on this was typical.

"If that's true, then good luck to him for having some foresight, and if it isn't, then some of those gossips down at Obnoxious Corner have more petty imagination than is good for them."

Mrs. Allen is a tall, thin lady called Edna. She is very nice to us raga-muffins and even sets up a television in the hall so that we can watch *Children's Hour.* The TV is the size of a chest of drawers and has but one black-and-white channel. It is an adventure just to watch the test-card transmission. We sit in the darkness waiting for the test-card to fade and the plummy Queen's English voice to announce:

"Theese is the BHEE BHEE SEE CHILDRAWNS HAAR! And NHAA we have the LEARN RAINJHA and TONTO!"

"HI! HO! SILVER . . . AWAAAY!!!" We all shout and make gal-loping movements sitting back to front on our chairs.

Mrs. Allen tells me that there is an odd coterie of people called high brows who can listen to the "William Tell Overture" and never once think of *The Lone Ranger.*"

On the way back up the hill I meet Dad; he has a bucket of paint and is furious.

"What's wrong, Dad? Where are you going with that paintbrush?"

"Come and see what some sick bastard has done to old Mr. Feidel-man's caravan."

At the point where the cinder track turns sharply into the kitchen gardens, a little moss green wooden caravan stands covered with garish white Nazi swastikas. Across the side is scrawled "JUDEN RAUS!" Dad helps the owner to paint over the mess, but the color is a poor match.

"After six years of war, I thought we'd put an end to this load of bol-locks once and for all! If I catch the bastard who did this—"

"What does that mean?" I point at the words now disappearing under the pea-green paint.

Old Mr. Feidelman looks at me sadly. "It means, Jews get out!"

The weather takes to the warm side, and I am able to venture farther afield in search of diversion. I take a notion to go fishing, and being surrounded by two rivers, a canal, and dozens of little lakes, there is no shortage of good spots. My first rod is a piece of willow branch broken straight off the tree. The tackle comes from the same source and consists of about fifteen feet of line, a float, three lead sinkers, and a hook—all salvaged from the branches, where some unlucky bugger had snagged it on a back cast.

"You'll never catch now't with that!" one of the weekend fishermen down from the big city says, laughing.

"Ah, you never know. What are you fishing for?"

"Perch," says his mate. "But I don't reckon there's any in here. We've been here all morning and caught just two roach and a skinny little gudgeon!"

"You never know your luck in a big town!" I sit about twenty feet away from them, catching four nice perch in the space of ten minutes. To make matters worse, I put them back upstream of the fishermen and all their fancy gear.

"There you are, boys, that will give you a chance at them!"

"He's taking the piss! Go on, get out of it, you scruffy little sod."

I laugh all the way home.

My horizons are to expand in more ways than one. I was always a bit of a daredevil and suffer from enough insatiable curiosity to fill the nine lives of a dozen cats.

Michael Waterson lives just around the corner from me and up a small hill. His caravan sits in a fork in the road and is hidden by trees. I never meet his dad; he is always away on business, which usually means in jail. His mum is very glamorous and a walking monument to Max Factor. I think her name is Trixie or something like that.

I like going up to Mike's place because there's never any parents around to chastise you for blaggarding or acting the goat.

He has a mandolin and is delighted when I get a tune out of it. I manage a ragged version of "Brian Boru's March," but I can't make much of a fist of it because the strings are so rusty. Mike, though, is thrilled. To him the tune is as magical and inaccessible as Elgar's *Enigma Variations*.

"Could you show me how to play that?" I try, but he has no ear.

"That's great!" He lays the instrument down. "Let's have a drink!"

A bottle of port and two glasses appear. "It's my dad's, he doesn't bother with it!"

Well, we bother with it all right—all afternoon, until it's empty!

The world has seemingly taken on an Alice in Wonderland quality and as I speed downhill home on my bike, I fancy that I'm riding through a mental kaleidoscope. The time comes to make the turn. I feel neither the power nor the will to do so. My trusty velocipede flattens the white picket fence and strikes a concrete lawn ornament. It stops dead. I don't, however, and fly like Flash Gordon toward a pea-green hardboard-built caravan. Mr. and Mrs. Feidelman had just finished their dinner when a large child going "Wheeee!" crashes head-long through the wall and lands squarely on the dinner table.

It is as well for me that the impact knocks me out for a while. My incoherent ramblings, on regaining consciousness, are put down to concussion. The truth is that I'm steaming drunk and can feel nothing.

The next day, lying in my bed, I can't find a part of me that doesn't hurt! Mam quizzes me suspiciously:

"When I picked you up, there was the smell of drink on you?"

"Yes, Mrs. Feidelman gave me a glass of brandy, or the like—to revive me!"

"I believe you, thousands wouldn't!"

"Is Mr. Feidelman really mad at me? Will we have to pay for his caravan?"

"No, he was pleased in the end. The old van was a mess after that graffiti business, and now he can get a new one with the insurance money."

"Oh, that's a bit of luck then!"

Later that day, when I try to stand, my luck runs out. I have managed to rupture myself during the crash and Mam has to take me to the doctor's. As I lie on the surgery table, I experience the worst pain

I have ever known, as the poor doctor, apologizing profusely, tries to push and probe my missing gonad back into its ancestral home.

For many weeks afterward, I have to wear a sort of cottonwool diaper with a little hole cut in it, for my toodle to hang out!

All this pain from one afternoon's drinking. What had I learned? Well, drinking and driving is not on, and drinking and flying is lethal—unless you want to sing soprano with the Treorchy Male Voice Choir.

School holidays provide the best opportunity for getting into trouble. I am in the shit whether I'm the perpetrator or not. The fact is, I suffer from a severe case of alliteration!

A broken window, a scratched car, a stolen bicycle, or a sudden outbreak of foot-and-mouth disease will all be, sooner or later, laid at my door by the simple tripping-off-the-tongue phrase "Willy Watkins did it!"

I'm no saint of course, but for me to accomplish half of what I'm blamed for, I'd have to work a 120-hour week.

My little bunch of ruffians spend most of our free time playing with all the army surplus uniforms and military equipment left lying around after the end of World War Two. Tin helmets, bayonets, webbing belts, even binoculars, and leather map cases are there for the taking, moldering in long-abandoned dumps. It is fun to dress up and play soldiers, but it can make for dangerous games.

Without thought of the consequences, we wilderness warriors throw handfuls of .22 bullets into the refuse dump bonfire to make our war games more realistic! The rubbish dump becomes the bullet-riddled Berlin bunker of a doomed Third Reich, its blazing ruins still crawling with S.S. storm troopers and Death's Head fanatics. In a brave attack on the burning tip, we engage our imaginary enemy with .22 rifles and BB guns, whilst the answering fire from the exploding bullets whizzes and whistles over our heads.

"Rocket Attack!" screams Michael Waterson, tossing a clip of moldy .303 rifle ammunition into the flames. This time the resultant explosions are a lot more spectacular. The bullets go off with a very loud series of reports, and it's quickly realized that our barricade of old cars and rusty kitchen appliances doesn't stop them. We run for our lives! Twenty yards away and in full retreat, I'm brought down by a .22 bullet that lodges in the back of my knee. I'm carried home on an ex-army stretcher. Fatty Roger drapes the Stars and Stripes over me, covering my face. My mother faints amongst the junk in the front garden. Dad takes great pleasure in removing the slug with a razor blade, without of course, any anesthetic.

"That will bloody teach you to play about with live ammunition, you stupid young prat! I hope you've learned your lesson?" He thrusts tweezers holding the small lead .22 almost up my nose.

"That bullet could have lodged in your fucking thick head!"

We later find out that another bullet had passed through the caravan belonging to old Mrs. Cheshire. It shattered a mirror and that, to us superstitious Celts, was an omen of bad luck. My pals and I resolve to play less dangerous games. There will be no more live rounds used in our war games. Had we fully learned our lesson? Hell, no!

It is the end of term when traditionally school's rigid regime relaxes a little. The headmistress feels confident enough to attend a teachers' conference in Blackpool. This leaves us in the affable hands of the calamitous Mr. Bury, who has come up with an idea. I think he must have read about "Show and Tell" in some American journal, for it is totally unheard of in our part of the world.

"Now, class, you must all bring something of interest into school tomorrow and tell us a little about it."

"What sort of thing, sir?"

"Anything at all! Pets, hobbies, weird objects, anything that you find interesting or unusual."

The next day, the classroom is alive with bizarre goings-on. Jean-Paul's French-speaking budgerigar has escaped and is being chased around the room by three kids and Katie Coughlin's cross-eyed cat. The poor bird screams Gallic blue murder in its panic, and the hubbub is increased by the antics of Paul Mead, who's shouting German-sounding gobbledygook and goose-steps up and down, wearing a Nazi tin helmet on his head and doing "Heil, Hitler" salutes each time he passes the wall mirror.

In the corner, someone's windup gramophone gives out a hiss-and-crackle rendition of Count John McCormack singing "Macusla,"—in concert with the screams of Mary O'Malley, whom Gypsy Paul is having great sport terrorizing with a shoe box containing a long, green grass snake! Nora Hedderman sits oblivious to all this, playing "Frère Jacques" on her recorder, whilst, in her element, naughty Elspeth O'Neill, wearing a tutu, is attempting to show the contents of her knickers to anyone who's interested. Saintly Joseph Ryan has been trying in vain to get someone into the stock cupboard to see his luminous Infant of Prague. Elspeth jumps at the chance and seconds later, young Joseph, with a face as red as a beetroot, erupts from the stockroom, shoots out of the door, and locks himself in the boys' toilet.

"What's wrong with ya, Joe?"

"Elspeth showed me her willy!"

"Girls don't have willies, Joe."

"I know that now!"

In the midst of the carry-on, Mr. Bury, telephone in hand, is trying to assure the absent Mrs. MacArthur that everything is under control.

"Yes, Head, yes, fine . . . that noise? Er . . . it's the wireless! Yes! OK, I'll see you after the holidays. Bye-bye!"

I sit at my table in the eye of the storm, between a stuffed owl and a model of Thor Heyerdahl's raft *Kon-Tiki* made completely out of lollipop sticks.

This is great! This is what school should be like all the time. I fondle my show-and-tell item, my pièce de résistance: a live hand grenade!

Mr. Bury has to resort to smacking the blackboard with a cane to restore order. Finally satisfied, he moves like a judge in a flower show amongst the tables, nodding approval, congratulating, and praising. He is enjoying himself—until he gets to me.

"What? What is that? What is that thing?" he says, pointing and backing off at the same time.

"It's a Mills bomb, sir, commonly called a hand grenade."

"It's disarmed though, isn't it, Watkins? Made safe, eh?"

"No, sir, it's still primed and armed. This is where the fuse screws in and here is where they pack the cordite. You hold this bit and pull out this pin and that plunger drops and BOOM!"

He goes white and begins muttering.

"Oh, my God! What to do? Call the police? Oh, my God! Oh, no, better not." He picks up the telephone, stares out of the window, and puts it down again.

"The gardener!" he shouts, finger raised in the air in triumph. He creeps over to my table and gingerly picks up the grenade as if it is going to bite him. Holding it at arm's length, he walks in slow motion to the book cupboard and places it softly on top. It is now way out of our reach.

"Don't you dare touch that!" Like a thing possessed, he tears out of the door in search of Mr. Giles, the school gardener and ex-soldier, who lives in a cottage at the back of the mill. I could have told him he wasn't there. I'd seen him this morning, all dressed up, waiting for the Stratford bus, off to the horse racing no doubt.

With Mr. Bury tear-arsing around the grounds, it is time for action.

"Come on, lads, give me a hand!"

Steven and Jerry rock the cupboard until the grenade does a little dance, then drops down. I catch it. To avoid any more trouble, I scarper off home, leaving the offending Mills bomb in a hollow tree by the river.

Later that evening, a small posse of us retrieves the grenade, and I resolve to destroy the evidence in the most spectacular way I can imagine.

Our little commando group sneaks through the undergrowth to where the languid river Alne runs through a small tree-lined gorge. Here, in a great show of bravado, I pull out the pin. With my thumb keeping the handle depressed, I show it around the semicircle of my friends. They are awestruck! I let go of the handle, which flies off into the gorge and with an overarm motion, I throw the grenade in a wide arc after it, John Wayne style. Nothing happens.

"It's a dud!" says Paul Mead, ever the pessimist.

Mike is pointing to something that is out of my view and is about to speak, when there is a tremendous explosion and a column of water shoots skyward. The echoes die away and the water crashes back down. Mike is spluttering!

"There was two fishermen down there!!!"

"Where? You're kidding me."

"Sitting on the pipe over the river. Look—there they are!!"

I move to where I can see farther upstream and sure enough, two bedraggled anglers are wading out of the water. Unseen, we melt back into the bushes and without further ado, disperse homeward.

My father tells me later of the two damp fishermen he met in the tap-room of the Bull's Head Tavern. They were still puzzling over the queer sight that they had witnessed.

An enormous pike, some hideous freak of nature that, through some odd biochemical chain reaction, had detonated itself with such force that the blast had killed a whole lot of lesser fish, decimated the pike, and blown them off the pipe and into the water. All that remained of the unstable leviathan was the head and tail, floating some eight feet apart, and by this they judged its size.

"Spontaneous combustion!?" offers my Dad.

No better explanation for the exploding fish is ever found, and thus it passes into local legend. I have no intention of setting the record straight.

There is, however, a bigger problem. Even though the summer holidays are eight weeks long, I fancy Mr. Bury's memory will match them. A word to Mrs. MacArthur about me and the disappearing grenade episode and I am doomed!

Deliverance comes in an unsuspecting way. The balmy breezes of June rustle the long vertical stalks of the osier beds as we three friends make our way through this ancient plantation of the old Celtic Britons.

Osier is a type of bog willow and grows dead-straight. Our ancestors used it for basket making, hurdle fencing, and ribs for coracles, the small Celtic one-man boats. We use it to fashion spears, which when tipped with lead make a handy javelin.

This day it is the river far beyond the osiery that is our destination. Gypsy Paul has it on good authority that fine bream have been caught there, and we are up to the chance.

We dawdle along on our bikes, going nowhere fast, and eventually we find the shade of the tree-lined river.

The gray-green water moves slowly, noiselessly spinning into eddy currents. Sweet the air is, suffused with the scent of wild garlic, and where the trees open to the sky, the river reflects every passing cloud above. Stretched out on the lush green sward, surrounded by trees and bushes, we are hidden from the world and especially the old water bailiff, who will fine us for fishing without a permit.

The afternoon sun drenches our golden glade, a delicious torpor envelopes us, and slowly, one by one, we fall asleep.

In my dream, I can see my fishing float jerk, dip twice, and then shoot away under the undulating stream. The end of my rod is whipping with tension. My arms strain to pull ashore the huge, flapping bream. *Splish! Splash!* It mocks, flailing the water and defying my efforts. *Splash! Splish splash!* I wake with a start to find Gypsy Paul pissing in the river about three feet away from my head.

"Get out of it, ya durty bugger!"

He raises a finger to his lips: "Shush!"

"What is it?"

"Listen!" He cocks his ever alert ear to the prevailing wind.

Mike sits up on his elbow. "What?" he mouths silently. I say nothing, but I can pick out a voice or a giggle or something.

Paul slips stealthily into the bushes, the blood of generations of clandestine poachers pulsating in his veins. In a twinkling he is back.

"What's your report number one?" I say, like Jack Hawkins in *The Cruel Sea*.

"It's crumpet, sir!" he smiles, picking up the theme.

"Bearing?"

"Green thirty, range two hundred yards."

"Rig for silent running," I whisper, and we all crouch low in our green oasis.

"Oooh!" says Mike dreamily. "Crumpet!"

Lying doggo, we choke in silent mirth, listening to the *cooeees!* and answering giggles as they move closer to us. Suddenly the shrubbery parts, and with a girlish laugh, a young woman springs into our midst.

"Oh, my goodness!" she says, trying to do up her blouse buttons. "I'm so sorry!" And with that she dives into the other side of the overgrowth and is gone.

We are just enjoying this spectacle when the bushes to our left begin thrashing about and a voice inquires, "Fufkin! Fufkin! Where are you?" Mike gets the giggles, causing the voice to report.

"I can hear you, Fufkin!"

"I've got you!" says the head as it thrusts out of the foliage.

"Good afternoon, Mr. Bury!!!" we cry out in almost perfect three-part harmony. The face first goes quite pale, then, as quickly as a chameleon, a fine ruby wine color.

"Er . . . em . . . I . . . I . . . am looking for my friend . . . er?"

"Fufkin!" I remind him with relish. "She went thataway," I say, pointing. He nods his head in thanks and disappears. We are helpless with merciless merriment.

"I know her," says Mike finally. "She teaches at the Church of England school in Henley. That's Miss Foster."

"Fufkin Foster," says Gypsy Paul in realization. "What a moniker!" We fall about laughing again.

"I can't wait to tell everyone at school."

"No, Mike, we must tell no one! It will be our little secret. This way he'll never mention the grenade business for fear we'll tell Mrs. Mack about him consorting with the enemy!" And so it turns out, a classic Mexican standoff.

Being eight is just the right age. You are glic enough to know most of what is going on roundabouts, but too young to have much responsibility foisted upon you.

An bliadhna d'ór—the golden years, as our old language has it.

Mam is getting fat and has started knitting again. I help her with hanking the yarn and she tries to teach me some simple stitches. I can't make a fist of it at all, but I'm good at unraveling the wool from old knitwear. I take great delight in tearing asunder my god-awful cream Aran sweater. The same one that made me tell lies and got Gypsy Paul the unwarranted beating at school, the time long ago.

"You never got much wear out of that! Sure it's shrunk now. 'Twould only fit Jim Hasset. Why did you take such a spite to that jumper anyway? It was lovely!"

"It stunk of old sheep and made my skin itchy, an' I didn't like the color, or them daft wiggly patterns in the stitch."

"Well, those sweaters are made for the fishermen of the Aran Islands and the sheep oil keeps out the sea spray and rain. The patterns have a special purpose, too, as every family on the Western Islands have their own distinctive weave. If someone is drowned, you can tell who they are by the cut of their jumper."

"Why not just look at their faces?"

"Because their faces get all eaten away by the fishes."

I was going to say, "Do you have a song about fishes eating your face off?" But Mam has already started:

> *With swelling sail, away! away!*
> *Our boat goes bounding o'er the bay*
> *Farewell, farewell, old Aranmore*
> *She curtseys, curtseys, to the shore.*
> *Farewell, fond wives and children dear*
> *From every danger, keep you clear*
> *Till through the surge, we stagger back*
> *As full of fish as we can pack.*

Mam places a pair of lemon-colored baby's booties in the seldom-opened drawer where she keeps little Keith's never-worn baby garments. She carefully places a layer of white tissue paper over the tiny clothes and sprinkles several miraculous medals on top of it. She whispers an ancient Irish prayer into the drawer before gently closing it:

> *If harm comes near thee, may the three greats in heaven,*
> *Who cast all evils into the sea, protect thee,*
> *And the seven angels of God, watch over thee. Amen.*

The big boys down at the Post Office corner are taunting me.

"Your mammy's a pregnant prostitute!" Derrick Davies shouts across.

"No, she's not—she's a Roman Catholic!" I shout back.

"Come over the road and I'll give you a bloody good hiding, you little bog trotter."

I go home and tell Mam what the older boys had said.

"That fat eejit Davies is right about one thing, I am having a baby in a few weeks. Now you keep away from that bunch of bullies. They're a bad lot, and you'll be led astray."

I need little encouragement to stay away from this gang. They go to the Church of England school, so I seldom see them and they don't hang around with us much, anyway.

The time comes and Mam departs in the taxi again. She takes her old battered brown suitcase, which somehow looks much smaller now. Through a cloud of cinder dust she waves at me and Dad.

Mam gives birth to a little girl who only lives for a few short minutes. The doctors know the baby has no chance, and Mam is seriously ill.

"What do you want to call the baby, Mrs. Watkins?"

"Mary," Mam breathes in a thin voice, her mind fixed on the Blessed Virgin.

"Any middle names?"

"No, just Mary."

Mam's life is draining away, and despite all efforts the doctors cannot stanch her hemorrhage. The priest is called with his oils and unctions to perform the last rites. Before I am taken to the hospital to say my last good-bye, I go alone into the woods to pray. Through my tears I see a small bunch of white snowdrops growing in a clearing. Plucking them up, I take them with me and the nurse puts them in a vase of water by Mam's bed. Mam manages a weak smile and closes her eyes.

"Mr. Watkins, the surgeon wants a word with you." A kindly nurse takes my hand.

"Come along now and let your mother sleep." Dad and I are taken to an office downstairs. The surgeon looks up from his notes; he is grave.

"Mr. Watkins, there's a new procedure I have been reading about in the British medical journal, *The Lancet*. It might work. Your wife will require a hysterectomy and if we can get it, a course of snake-venom coagulant they've just devised in West Africa."

Dad looks doubtful.

"What have we got to lose? But if it's only available in Africa, how do we get hold of it in time?"

The surgeon picks up the telephone.

"Let's try the Royal Air Force!" he says, fingering his RAF ex-officer's necktie.

Later that day, an RAF Vulcan jet leaves Lagos, Nigeria, with the life-giving serum on board.

In the days that followed, Mam shows signs of improvement, her bleeding stops, but we are not out of the woods yet. She needs the hysterectomy.

"I can't have the operation without the permission of the Catholic Church, Reg. Don't you understand? I asked Father, but he won't sign the release form!" Mam starts to cry.

"H'm, I'll talk to him," says Dad.

On the way back, we stop in at the vestry and Dad argues with the priest. I am scared stiff that with Mam dying, God will strike my dad down for shouting in the church, and I'll be left on my own, with no one belonging to me.

"No! No, I won't sign! It's contraception, and that's no better than murder, so it is!" The priest is sweating and his eyes are darting around the room for some form of divine assistance.

"If you don't sign, she will die and what will that be?" asks my father.

"The will of God, that's what!"

My father stares long and hard at the perspiring cleric. He doesn't much care for "God botherers" as he calls them. He told me once of a fascist priest holed up with a rifle in the bell tower of his church during the Spanish Civil War.

"The bastard opened fire on the people sitting around the village fountain—his own parishioners!"

Dad went on to say that this so-called man of God had killed three women, an old man, and a child before he was flushed out by a group of volunteer Welsh miners from the Fifteenth International Brigade. His excuse was that he "thought his victims were communists!"

Dad said they tied the bell rope around his neck and threw him out of the tower. With grim satisfaction, they saw his head fly off!

My father is in no less a belligerent mood this day, and I fear the priest might meet a similar end if he doesn't put pen to paper. Heart thumping like an echo sounder, I stand in the corner, hiding my face in my hands and peeping through my fingers.

"You *will* sign!!!" Dad grasps the priest by the dog collar and draws his hamlike fist back slowly.

"I will not!"

Like the twang of a bow-string, my father lets fly a withering punch. The priest's knees sag, but to his credit, he recovers.

"I won't! I won't!"

Dad hits him again. This time, the priest's resolve caves in as fast as his nose, and in a very shaky hand, he signs the release form.

Later that day, we make the long journey back to the main hospital. Mam is seemingly much improved from the magic potion. Dad and I go in and gave her the crumpled paperwork. My mother looks at the brown spots surrounding the scrawled signature on the form.

"This looks like blood? Was this won under duress? You didn't hit the priest, did you? Jesus! Reg, you'll go to hell!"

"No, no, not at all," says Dad, looking as innocent as a lamb. "After I made my position clear to him, the priest couldn't wait to sign it!!!" Mam looks at me and I close my eyes in panic. In my mind's eye I can see my father surrounded by fire and brimstone, holding the devil by the throat and drawing back his fist with relish.

My mother takes a long time to recover after her operation, and it is grand to have her home again. Mam tells me what it was like when she was dying. She said she flew back over home to Ireland and even had a chat with Grandda, who was long since dead. Sometimes she flew feet first toward a giant mouth that gaped open on her approach. She knew this was the point of no return and would scrunch up her toes and try to think of something else, something nice.

"What did you think of, Mammy?"

Mam smiles. "I thought of the snowdrops that you brought me and how I was too weak to say thank you."

My sister, Mary, is laid to rest in the same plot as my wee brother, Keith, together forever in the tiny nettle-filled graveyard behind our school chapel. The priest is very short with his service and stares at me over the sticking plaster across his nose. "Suffer little children to come unto me," he quotes, and gives me a menacing glance. He will make me suffer all right, if he gets the chance. It's just as well he's afraid of Dad.

It feel odd when I pass the little green bump that marks the grave of two of my lost siblings. Now when I kneel in the cold chapel my thoughts dwell on what might have been. Looking up I can see the faces of the angels staring down from the stained glass windows. There is Keith and over there is Mary, and here on my knees is me. The priest has the whole school praying, that some guy called John Fitzgerald Kennedy might become the next president of the United States of America.

Filing out of the mass, past their graves, I make the sign of the cross and think of Granddad Jim quoting a Rupert Brooke poem:

In that rich earth, a richer dust concealed.

✦ Chapter 9 ✦

MAM IS STILL RECUPERATING AT HOME AND I GET USED TO doing most of the household chores. I like having a go at cooking, and if I make a bollix of it, no one complains. Washing clothes is the hardest job, as I can't boil enough water on the stove to wet the really big things and I'm no good at rubbing them up and down the zinc washboard.

Mam takes short walks into the countryside. She never mentions her loss, but when I go to tidy out the baby clothes drawer, she tells me to leave it alone and not go near it. I ask my dad what I should do.

"Give her time, Willie, to mourn for the wee ones and she'll be fine."

Mam adopts a little abandoned tortoiseshell kitten that she calls Fluff. The purring ball of fur soon grows into a big strong cat and Mam's attentions to its welfare have been rewarded.

One day, out of the blue, she jumps up and takes to rubbing her nylon pinafore together with her hands. The friction produces a warble of tortuous, squeaking noises.

"Listen to the birds in Mummy's apron, puss! Listen to the birds!"

Both myself and the cat are caught unawares and regard my mother with mystified silence. She dances a jig around us, squeaking her pinny whilst entreating, "Listen to the birds in Mummy's apron!"

The cat's face becomes a row of blurry eyes as it shakes its head to dislodge the squealing noises from its ears. In a trice, Mam scoops the cat up in her arms and swirls around the kitchen, singing:

> *Pussycat, pussycat where have you been?*
> *I've been to London to look at the Queen.*
> *Pussycat, pussycat, what did you there?*
> *I frightened a little mouse under the chair.*

The dismayed cat scrambles free of Mam's clutches and darts under the bed. She grabs me instead and the waltz becomes a gavotte.

> The thunder rolled, the lightning cracked
> And all the earth was shaken
> The little pig cocked up his tail
> And ran to save his bacon.

The gavotte becomes a polka:

> There was a little man and he had a little gun
> Up the mountain he did run
> With a belly full of fat and a big tall hat
> And a pancake stuck to his bum, bum, bum!

Exhausted, we succumb to gravity in the middle of the red mat.

Mam's imagination, aided by a flowery nylon apron and some invisible birds, has made the long journey back from grief accompanied by a royalist pussycat, a paranoid pig, and a rotund, diminutive, armed mountaineer with no dress sense! This is much more like it! Mam's back to normal! She has walked out of the mist and is her old self again. This is a great boon to us all. In no time at all, she resumes her position as the head of the household and it feels good knowing Mam's hand is on the tiller, even though this ends my brief reign of freedom and I'm now accountable again.

"Willie, come here to me now and tell me this? What were you doing hanging around with those corner boys down at the post office again?"

"I wasn't doing anything, Mammy, just chatting."

"Well, I don't want you chattin' with them durty sods, always spitting on the floor and trying to look up under your clothes, filthy buggers. Anyway, what were you chattin' about?" Mam is eating tinned spaghetti in tomato sauce.

"Segs. We were talking about segs, that's all."

"What the bloody hell you mean, 'Sex, that's all?' What in the name of Christ the Almighty do you know about sex?" She stops eating, obviously intrigued by my tale.

"More than they do and that's a fact. Those older boys are always talking about segs, but not one of them has a clue. They're way off the mark. It's all to do with the way you walk. Now, I tend to walk hard down on my right heel and that wears the back of my shoe away at an angle, giving rise to the problem. So you must get a packet of segs. They work great in leather, but when I tried one in rubber, it kept falling out, until I hit it hard with the coal hammer and it went in fine. See . . . it's still there!"

I lift up the sole of my boot to show the crescent-shaped metal seg neatly hammered into my worn heel. "See? Dad had shown me how to use that wee three-legged anvil, called a cobbler's last. He says the last is the first thing a cobbler uses!"

Like a baby bird waiting to be fed, Mam sits open-mouthed. I never thought that an explanation of a wee bit of do-it-yourself shoe repair could be so spellbinding, but as I have previously observed, Mam is a woman of mysteries and best left to her own devices. She sits in a trance whilst white worms of spaghetti continue to uncoil from her motion-less fork. Happy to be relieved of my duties as chief cook, bottle washer and handyman cobbler, I return to playing with my Dinkytoy fire engine on the little red hearthrug in front of the fire. Mam is back in command and makes me feel as secure as the segs in the soles of my hob-nailed boots.

Motorcars are still quite a rarity in these parts, and a posh one arriving is always a cause for a crowd to gather. I liked cars, but preferred rural Ireland, where the horse and jaunting car still held sway.

"Come and get a load of this!" says Dad one Saturday afternoon. We walk into the courtyard and there stands a cream-colored Austin-Healy sports car.

"It belongs to Sabrina the film star!"

"Wow! Will you look at all that leather and chrome—what a monster!"

"I'll give you half a crown to wash and polish it," offers Dad. "All the stuff you need is over there in that bucket."

I don't need asking twice and am soon working up a good lather on myself as well as the car. Two shillings and sixpence is a half crown and could buy goodies beyond the dreams of avarice!

Dad disappears toward the bar, chuckling to himself. I later find out why. He had been given five shillings to clean the car and had subcontracted the donkeywork to me, thus earning the price of a good few pints of best bitter for very little effort on his part.

Sabrina becomes a regular weekend visitor to the hall, and the weekly ritual of Dad's so-called cleaning of the car is established. The young starlet, a busty peroxide blond, is a Marilyn Monroe look-alike who had a few small parts in some of the racy comedy films that were in vogue at that time. She certainly does turn men's heads, and her erstwhile mentor, the manager of the country club, takes a special interest in her development. She's very nice to me and one day gives me a wee trip up to the petrol station in her sports car. Unfortunately, none of my pals are there to see us, and next day they all call me a bloody liar.

Dogs, too, were a rarity on the caravan site. Most folk had cats as they were good for keeping down the rats and mice, and large dogs were discouraged by the site managers.

Mr. Allen, of course, owned the place and so had a huge black-and-white harlequin Great Dane. The monster dog was all bollix and no brains.

This day he's outside our caravan slobbering around Mrs. Ayers's Pekinese. I'm having great sport watching him trying to cock a leg over a tiny dog some three feet below him. The bitch wanders off uninterested, leaving the giant spotty hound in oblivious ecstasy, probing the gravel path with his raw-looking toodle. Mam appears.

"Jasus! What's wrong with that dog at all? Gowan, bugger off with ya! Get out of it, ya durty big eejit!"

She chucks a bowl of washing-up water over him and he stands there dripping, looking mystified, then with a heartfelt sigh he waddles off home.

"Durty bugger, that fella! Forever sniffing everyone's arse and making a spectacle of itself, with his old langer sticking out! Durty sod he is and thick as a brick too."

"Why is it the dogs are always sniffing at each other, Mam?"

"Ah well you see, some of the greatest minds in the world have tried to fathom out the riddle of that. Here's what I think:

'The dogs once held a meeting, they came from near and far
Some came by helicopter and others came by car
And so inside the city hall, no one dared to look
As each dog took its arsehole off and hung it on a hook.
There they were, sitting there father, son, and sire
Sitting round looking round, when someone shouted FIRE!
Up they got and out they ran, without no time to look
They snatched the nearest arsehole, from off the nearest hook
And so my friend sometimes you see your doggy leave his bone
To sniff another's arsehole, he's just trying to find his own.'"

It must be common enough that you think your parents are above criticism and can do little wrong. I take everything my mother says as verbatim. How is it that a simple poem I learn from my mam gets the arse leathered off me when I quote it during my weekly poetry class? Adults live in a strange world!

It's early morning and Mam is up with the lark and doing something very odd in the kitchen. Twisting herself into a queer contorted version of Aphrodite rising from the waves, she stands in an immodest state of undress in front of a large mirror. To the accompaniment of much wheezing and grunting, she draws long black lines up the back of her legs with an eyebrow pencil.

Now I'm not as naive as some of my pals. I knew that women did secret things, like the times when I would be sent to the shop with a note that I wasn't allowed to read. The shopman would read the note and wrap up something in a brown paper bag. "Take this home to your mam," he'd say, "and don't be peeking inside!" Well, bollocks to him and his rules! I had a good gander into the bag, but all it contained were long cottonwool pads with loops on the ends. Later, I asked my pals. Gypsy Paul, ever the worldly wise, responded first.

"My mam gets them, too, and so does my older sister. I think all the women have them." Mike Waterson nodded his head in mute assent, but I needed more information.

"But what are they?" Mike added what little he knew to the mystery.

"I don't know what they are, but I think they're called No-Nos.

Whenever I ask my mom to tell me what's in the bag, she says, 'No-No.'"

My father once told me to ask if I didn't know and he'd always try to give me an answer. I caught up with him on his way to work.

"Dad, what's them cloth things with the hoops that Mam sends me to the shop for every month?"

"Oh, that's one of women's secrets!"

"Well, if you tell me what they are, I'll keep it a secret from Mam!"

He was as good as his word and I was able to tell my astounded pals that they were hammocks for pet mice.

"But where do our moms keep the pet mice?"

"I don't know. Dad said that's a secret he hadn't discovered yet."

So I was aware that women were full of mysteries, but now my mother, seemingly content with the straightness of her pencil lines, is rubbing Bisto Gravy Browning powder all over her legs. I'm getting alarmed, thinking that she might be slipping away with the fairies.

"Mam! What are you doing?"

"Jasus, Willie! You gave me a fear! I thought you were still asleep!"

"But what are you doing with that food stuff?"

"Oh, I'm going for a job and I've no nylon stockings, so this is a trick we used to do in the war—see!" She pulls on her dress and sure enough it does look like she's wearing dark brown, seamed stockings. She wriggles into her high heels and admires her handiwork.

"American Tan, wouldn't you say? Very stylish!" Mam trips out the door.

"I'll see you later!" She waves. I go back to the land of nod.

I'm awoken by rain pounding on the aluminium roof of the tiny caravan. A short time later, I'm sitting drinking tea when the door opens and the bedraggled remains of my mother staggers into the kitchen.

"It's me that's wet!" she splutters, casting the remnants of an inside-out umbrella back out the door. Her best frock is ruined, and her white shoes stained brown from the gravy running down her legs. She rubs her face vigorously with a towel, smearing cherry-red lipstick and blue eye shadow in vivid arcs all over her face.

"Oooh, that's better," she says, oblivious to the effect. "Your dad should be home soon from the night shift."

"He *is* home!" I advise as my father enters the caravan.

Dad takes his cap off and stares at my dripping, multicolored mother with all the bemused expression of a man stepping into an empty elevator shaft.

"Dear God, Monica! You didn't have to dress up special for me!"

Mam gets the job, working back at the country club. I am lying in my bunk at home with the cat asleep on the quilt and my Eagle comic book recounting the tale of Captain Nemo and the Space Eels.

Mam enters, followed by my dad, who is dead drunk and falls asleep on the floor.

"Oh, Willie, you should have seen yer father tonight. He was marvelous!"

"What did he do?" I stare at the pile of father snoring by the stove. Normally Mam would be hopping cups off his head for coming in langers.

"What didn't he do? He came to walk me home from work an' when he comes into the club there's this gang of teddy boys all setting about the village policeman."

"Who? That big bloke, Copper Smith?"

"Yeah, well, yer dad pulls the one fella off the copper and puts his head through the wall. He gives the next one a fong in the bollocks that has the eyes pop out of his head and down he goes! Then the leader comes at your father with a cutthroat razor. Yer dad stands there, motionless like a statue. 'I hope you know how to use that, sonny?' he says, like Gary Cooper in *High Noon,* he was. The fella makes a swipe at your dad and Reg grabs the boy's arm and cracks it over his knee, then he gives him a dig with the flat of his hand into the throat, and the punk turns blue and falls down. The rest run like the beJasus, and your dad is dusting down Copper Smith, who was all cuts and bruises. If yer father hadn't have turned up when he did the policeman would be dead now, the kicking he got!"

"Me dad did all that fighting, in that state?"

"Notatall, he got free drinks till midnight off the manager, and I had a few myself—*hic!*"

Mam likes working as a barmaid at the club and sometimes sings there with a little five-piece band and the local skiffle group. I'm not so keen on it because it means I'm left alone often after dark when my dad's on night shift. But it's not too bad, I have my books and my crystal set, and if I do get scared, there's always the .22 rifle with two hundred rounds of long ammunition that Dad swapped for the .38 Webley revolver we found in the old trunk.

The next week when the postman comes around on his red bicycle, Dad receives a letter from the Warwickshire chief of police.

He opens it warily, as if it contains a bomb, but to his relief it is a commendation for bravery.

"Good!" says Dad. "I always sleep better when the coppers owe me a favor."

Dad's job on the railways has the yearly advantage that it provides two free return tickets to anywhere in Britain and Ireland. Mam and I decide to go over home for the summer holidays, and I am excited to see my family again. A few days before our departure, Dad comes home as drunk as a fiddler's bitch. He has been in the pub all day with his pal MacBride, who has won a "fistful on the gee-gees," as he would say. Celebrating the good luck, they have both got completely langers. Dad stotters up to the caravan and, looking quizzically at me, says, "I know what it is you need? A haircut. You look like a fuzzy-wuzzy!"

I didn't know my father could cut hair, but he rummages around in the kitchen drawer and comes out with a pair of hand-operated hair clippers that he'd sent away for from some mail-order catalogue or other.

With supreme confidence that my father can do anything, I sit as he hacks and chops at my flowing locks. Then he stops and blinks, swaying unsteadily.

"Oh, dear!" he says. "I've made a bit of an arse of it. Sorry, old chap!"

I look in the mirror and see that my once thick mop is reduced to a bald stubble with ragged tufts sprouting out at random, like a confused pineapple. Mam appears.

"Sweet Mother of Jesus! What have you done to the poor child?"
She is not impressed by father's tonsorial expertise and quickly reaches

melting point. "What do you think yer on, coming home and doing that to Willie just before his holidays! You're worse than a bloody kid, ya drunken sod!"

Mam marches me off to a real barber, who just shakes his head. He has no choice other than to cut off all my hair to make it even. I stare morosely at the baldy figure in the mirror. I look like a young, sad Humpty-Dumpty.

When we get home Dad has succumbed to an alcoholic haze and is in bed. Mam busies herself getting dinner ready, rattling pots and smashing pans on the cooker top as noisily as she can to spite him. It has no effect.

"Will ya look at him, drunken Thady, lying there farting and snoring like a warthog! I must of had shit in me eyes when I married that fella, Godforgiveme!"

I hate it when Dad comes home with a rake of drink taken and fills the tiny caravan with acrid blue smoke and stale beer fumes. Mam adds to the bad atmosphere by cursing Dad lying there, his bare chest covered in curly gray caterpillars of cigarette ash.

"Why *did* you marry him, Mam?"

"Ah now! Sure he was a handsome bloke in his day. I always thought he looked a bit like Robert Mitchum and sure wasn't he in uniform when I first saw him—very dashing he looked!" She stares dreamily out of the window.

Dad moans and rolls over in his stupor, noisily scratching his arse.

"Jeez, who'd of thought it, but all the girls were mad for him during the war, you wouldn't get a look in. They should see him now, beJasus, lying stinking in his pit!"

"How did you end up with him then?" Mam glances at me, sitting sorrowfully at the kitchen table, and laughs.

"I went out with some of the girls from the factory one night. All of a sudden, the air-raid sirens went off and Jerry started dropping bombs all over the place. Well, we couldn't find the shelter, so we ran into this little pub under a railway bridge. The place was packed and no one gave a bugger about the blitz outside. 'Live for today and sod tomorrow!' was the cry. I was making for the ladies loo, when I overheard this fella, common as shite he was, passing a durty remark behind my back."

"What did he say? Was it Dad?"

"No, no, he is standing next to your dad, he was another soldier. Anyroadup, he says, 'I bet she's had more pricks than a secondhand dartboard!' I turned to give him a look as good as a summons, just in time to see your father fetch him a belt in the gob for being disrespectful to a lady. Oh, very chivalrous, your dad, very gallant! Well, it was love at first smite—and Jasus, look at me now, living in the lap of luxury with Happy Harry there pissing his week's wages up the public house wall. Jasus Christus! Look at the gaatch of him? Robert Mitchum, me arse. You'd get more life out of Robert Emmet and he's long since dead! Ifeverawomansuffered!"

Dad didn't know that Mam called him "Happy Harry." It was our secret. Mam didn't know that Dad called her "The Dragon." That was Dad's and my secret. Being an only child could be a pain. Often, being piggy-in-the-middle during family disputes and rows, I learned that a good bit of tolerance and a huge amount of diplomacy could go a long way. My parents were like big kids themselves, either loving or hating each other and most often managing to do both at the same time. Both were consummate actors. Mam leans toward the melodramatic, whilst dad had a flair for comedy.

Father smiles in his torpor, blissfully unaware that Mam is pulling ghastly, gargoyle faces at him. She might be mad at him, but at least she sees the funny side of my predicament.

"Hey, Yul Brynner, I've got a riddle for you!"

> *A little white and round house,*
> *and it is full of meat.*
> *It has no doors and windows,*
> *to let me in to eat!*

"What is it then, Willie?"

"Is it an igloo?"

"No, no, to be sure, igloos have doors."

"Och, I don't know, I give up!"

"It's an egg!" she says, laughing, and taps me on the bald head with a spoon.

✦ Chapter 10 ✦

THE DAYLIGHT SEA CROSSING FROM THE PORT OF HOLYHEAD is warm and calm. I discover to my great delight that the vessel's aft deck contains a ship's wheel, a compass inside a brass binnacle, and a ship's telegraph to relay commands down to the engine room: "Full Ahead! All Stop! Astern!" There is no one around, so I play sea captain. "Ahoy there! Splice the main brace! Avast behind!" I know these terms are nautical, but I don't know what a hoy is, or what a spliced main brace looks like, and I was vexed to see the significance of somebody's vast behind. Ah, but the sea is full of glorious mysteries!

There is a long cable going from a neat-looking, brass-dialed instrument affixed to the ship's stern rail. It trails off to sea in the wake of the vessel. My curiosity gets the better of me and I reel in the yards of cable, to find it is a brass, torpedo-shaped thing with little wiggly fins down the sides. I let it fall to the deck for a closer inspection. As I kneel down I am enveloped in the umbra of a large shadow.

"What the bloody hell do you think yer doing? Throw that thing back overboard!" Terrified, I look up into the black shape of an angry sailor, the flames of the afternoon sun flashing a coarse halo around his hat.

"I'm sorry, mister, I didn't mean no harm. I just wanted to know what it was. What is it?" The seaman laughs and, realizing I'm just a curious kid, crouches down by my side and pokes the dripping instrument.

"This is the ship's tracking log. It records our speed in knots and how far we have traveled in nautical miles, so you should have let it be."

"Yes, I'm sorry. What's a knot?"

"A knot is the way of reckoning speed at sea. One knot is the speed of one nautical mile per hour."

"How long is a nautical mile?"

"Six thousand and eighty feet, just a wee bit longer than a land mile, to compensate for the curvature of the earth." He picks up the log spinner and hurls it off into the ship's wake.

"There now, matey, no harm done and that's the log back into the oggin. Now don't be messing with the ship's equipment again, or we'll to have ye keel-hauled—*har-har!*"

By the time I get to Limerick a short velvet of hair has grown back across my bald pate, but hairstyles like that you only saw in American films or in magazines. My cousin Mikesy is the first to see me and the first to take the piss.

"Gee tonight! Look at the Yank!!" And so that becomes my nickname and it sticks for the rest of the summer.

And what a grand summer it is. We spend a lot of time in County Clare, mostly in Kilkee on the wild Atlantic coast.

"The next parish over is Boston," people would joke, pointing westward across the emerald green waves.

"And many's the thousands that joined that parish from hereabouts," someone would add.

"Where are you down from?" they ask.

"We're from up in Limerick."

"Sure the Limerick people are no good for Clare. They bring their own sandwiches with them!" The locals contend, trying to get the rise out of us.

I love eating dilsg, which is a form of red seaweed. "Full of iodine," Mam would say. Also winkles—I can't get enough of them. Just eating them is fun. They are small sea snails boiled in saltwater, and you have to pull them out of their shell with a pin. Hence the term "to winkle him out." Another delicacy is crubeens, which are boiled pig's trotters, These are Mam's favorite, whilst mine is pork pie, or pig's willy pie as they are known. Dad says that every part of the pig gets eaten except the squeak.

In summer you can buy all these tasty things from vendors' barrows as you walk along the circular harbor wall. Every second house in Kilkee is a pub, and they don't mind having kids in — if they behave themselves. I like the smell in these places. They have the aroma of times long past. You would know the smell of the right old pubs if ever you sniffed the inside of an old fiddle or an ancient piano.

We go up to the cliffs of Moher and peer cautiously over their brink to the thrashing ocean 668 feet below. We saunter along the strand to Spanish Point, where ships of the Spanish Armada were wrecked in 1588.

From the long white beach at Lahinch, I wade with my cousins into the Atlantic foam and try my hand at swimming. Unfortunately, like St. Columba before me, I step on a flounder buried in the sand and it shoots out from under my foot, turning me topsy-turvy in the surf. Spluttering under the waves, I guzzle more than my fair share of seawater and now understand why the good saint cursed the flounder to have both its eyes on the same side of its head, always looking up.

Back on shore, spitting sand and seaweed, I resolve never again to try to learn to swim. I realize that I'm never going to be amphibious, and like a cat, I don't like being wet anyway. There's something most unnatural being in the sea without the hull of a good boat around you.

I'll not be venturing into the water again without at least an aqualung to help me breathe. The same thought probably occurred to John P. Holland of the little village of Liscannor, about three miles away: in 1880 he astonished the world with his new invention — the first practical submarine!

There is a horse fair in Kilrush and we go along for the craic. The streets are teeming with horses and crammed with folk of every social stratum and walk of life.

> *The young the old,*
> *The meek the bold,*
> *The poet and musician —*
> *The relics of humanity*
> *In every known condition.*

I hear a queer noise and, turning a corner, I come face-to-face with a man playing an odd instrument. He has a box around his neck which is crisscrossed with fine wire strings. These he hits with two little leather thongs. It makes a lovely, tremulous, tinkling sound and I'd never seen or heard anything like it before. It is a hammer dulcimer.

In the alley by Crotty's pub, two ragged-arsed tinkers are rubbing brown shoe polish on the hind quarters of a venerable old horse. This serves to mask the gray and white hairs of the elderly beast. A young traveler lad is holding a bucket of oats and Guinness slops that the nag is slurping down with gusto.

Within the space of ten minutes a transformation takes place in the animal. Its belly starts to swell and the bony protruding ribs begin to disappear. Suddenly the old die-er is a young prancing pony again. The magic elixir of oatmeal and stout has transfused life into the creature's sagging frame, which now, as tight as a bow string, looks surprisingly youthful. Obviously enjoying the elation, the tipsy horse snorts and stamps its hooves, sending showers of tiny sparks up from the black cobbled road.

This display catches the attention of an English chap who is looking for a pony to give his daughter for her twenty-first birthday. After a lot of spitting on hands, bidding and bartering, the final hand shake is made and the deal is done.

The duped Englishman guides the frisking cuddy into a horse box, towed by a Land Rover. He gives it a playful slap on the rump and then stares incredulously at his sticky, brown stained hand. Lifting its tail, the horse lets off a string of beery farts and its ribs reappear! The mystified buyer looks around questioningly, but the tinkers are nowhere to be seen.

"Jayzus!" says a bystander. "That horse will be a sorry sight in the morning."

"A sorry sight with a hangover," adds another.

Buses are the great mode of transport. Everyone starts singing as soon as the bus is in motion. Not just on outings or mystery tours, but on regular commuter buses. It is a gas, right enough!

A common entertainment for us kids is to try and count the number of castles or ruined fortresses between Limerick and Kilkee. It comes to about thirty, I think.

Most of these represent the seat of some ancient clan chief, or king as they preferred to be known. At one time there were over two hundred and fifty small kings in Ireland, several queens, five regional big kings and an *Ard Rí,* or high king, presiding over the lot of them. It is no idle boast to say that even the humblest Irish person has royal blood—for all that's worth.

"Mam, did we have any royalty in our family years ago?"

"Oh, yes," she says. "Somewhere down the line, we're descendants of Aoibheal the fairy queen of Thomond!"

Good grief! A fairy queen on one side and Old King Cole on the other. It all seemed a bit nursery rhymish! After that revelation I give up on the royalty bit.

> *Imperial Caesar,*
> *Dead and turned to clay,*
> *Will plug a hole,*
> *To keep the wind away!*

"That's a good one, Mam!"

On the way back home on the bus, my die-hard Fianna Fáil nana is celebrating the results of the recent Irish election by singing:

> *Vote vote vote for De Valera,*
> *Vote vote vote for Fianna Fáil*
> *and we'll break the Union Jack*
> *Over Cosgrave's humpy back,*
> *and we'll crown De Valera*
> *King of Irrrrrrrrrrrrreland!*

"A Spaniard will free Ireland," the old prophecy stated, and as far as Nana is concerned that can only mean Eamon De Valera. However, half the family think he's the biggest crook unhung, and there's always a good slagging match to be indulged in whenever his name comes up.

A spectacular event is taking place in Limerick. Uncle Seán hurries in with the news.

"Jeez! Sure the whole town is up in flames! Todd's store is burning out of control and the wind is spreading the fire all over the place—the city center's aflame!"

Sure enough! From the front garden of our house we can see the huge pall of black smoke climbing into the skies above King John's castle.

Excitedly we cross over the river bridge for a closer look. It seems like every fire engine in Munster is in attendance. The roads are a tangle of large canvas fire hoses, many of which are leaking at the big brass knuckle joints.

The corner of Todd's is gutted and the four-story blackened shell, windowless and roofless, is still steaming from the drenching it received from the hose.

The fire is raging farther up the block and has gotten as far as Lipton's tea shop. Behind the large street windows of the store, a curious gray fog has appeared that swirls about obscuring the goods inside. Two firemen in the street outside begin to run, leaving their hoses to snake about wildly, spraying everything but the conflagration. It isn't before time! A tiny point of yellow light glows for a split second in the center of the smoke, then mushrooms into a billowing red fireball that shatters the plate glass windows to smithereens. The crowd of gawkers, ourselves included, scream and flee to a safer vantage point. Some are wounded by flying glass splinters and are taken away to waiting ambulances.

Within minutes the roof caves in and a shower of sparks shoots skyward. These are joined by exploding bags of sugar, streaking and coursing through the smoky air, like distress-signal rockets.

Suddenly an eddy of wind sucks out the blazing contents of the shop and belches it into the molten sky. The whirlwind picks up pace and spreads the fire to the next block. The squads of firefighters run after the new threat and begin evacuating buildings in its path. The door of Teasey-Weasey's bursts open and a bevy of women with their hair in curlers, or crowned with cones of shampoo, flees the doomed salon, which is soon consumed by the holocaust. The brave teams of firemen play their battery of hoses on the buildings directly in line of travel to the fire. This tactic is proving successful until the note from the pump engines rises abruptly in scale and the water from the firehose nozzles is reduced to a piddling dribble.

The bewildered fire crews soon find out why. The water is being pumped directly out of the Shannon and the tide has gone out, leaving the syphon hoses high and dry, sucking air!

It takes several days for the fire to be completely terminated, by which time much of the area is in ruins. To us kids picking through the debris of the burned-out shops for treasures, it was a great hoot altogether, but the old ones said this was the greatest disaster to befall the city since the destruction brought by the civil war of 1922.

Fortunately, Limerick survives and is soon rebuilt. Living up to its tough motto carved into the rock of the Treaty Stone. "Urbs antiqua fuit studasque asperima belli"—An ancient city, well studied in the arts of war.

We are on the move again. Returning to Britain and this time no tears! It has been a great holiday and despite fire, brimstone, and near drowning, we've all had loads of fun, but I'm looking forward to going back to my little enclave of the Gael. People forget that Britain was once a Celtic country and still is—"In quiet places where the moss grows green," to quote a Scots poet.

The journey back is at night under a full moon. A harvest moon hangs like a ripe peach: *An Gealach*—the bright one, mirror of the Celtic soul, the Triple Goddess. She illuminates our voyage across the Irish Sea with warm honey-colored light. There is little wind, and the sea is a slab of black marble; the moonlight ripples through the surface like streaks of rose quartz. In the cabin, Mam sleeps like a baby.

I stay on deck absorbing every sight, sound, and smell that I can savor. The old sea shanty "Santa Anna" goes round and round in my head and I feel at home.

> *We'll sail across the river to Liverpool,*
> *Heave away, Santa Anna.*
> *Heave her up and away we'll go*
> *All around the bay of Mexico.*

I wonder if I have been a sailor in a previous existence.

No one in my family has gone to sea in nearly two hundred years, to my knowledge. The last one was the unfortunate Thomas Watkins, who had the temerity to speak out against the depravations and hardships of the Royal Navy and ended up swinging from the yardarm with a hemp necktie. Dad said he should have known that the King's Navy was built on three English principles: rum, sodomy, and the lash. He would have been better off in the Merchant Navy, which was more rum, bum, and concertina.

Wild and mysterious, the train journey from Holyhead to Birmingham is mighty and my mind is ablaze with its captured images. Everywhere red and green signal lanterns glow in the night, mixed with the white and amber lights of the point switches. We thunder through Angelsey, the Welsh teacup station my mother had shown me years ago; LLAN—BLUR—GOGGOG hurtles past the window.

Digedydee digedydaa digedydee digedydaa. The sound of the wheels become a hypnotic heartbeat broken only by *Digedydig dig Da dig dig dig,* as we clatter through sets of points before settling back into the incessant rhythm. Phantoms of flickering flashes spring from other passenger trains plunging past us in the opposite direction, probing our carriage with stark stroboscopes of filmlike montage. Somewhiles the shrill shriek of the steam whistle heralds the ear-popping vacuousness of an unexpected tunnel, from which we emerge moments later to see the soft moonlight spangle the midnight-dark Menai Strait in bands of quicksilver, and the jagged peaks of Snowdonia's mountains thrusting their quiet majesty into a silent star-washed sky.

The head of the train makes a long curve and looms into view. The glow from the footplate fire box is clearly visible, and the great steam-belching engine sends showers of hot cinders to join the plume of smoke in its wake.

Our friendly moon continues to keep us company, and while Mam sleeps in the darkened carriage, I rest my head against the window, watching the lunar visage play hide-and-seek with scurrying clouds, or dance along the transient telegraph wires until, swirling in steam, she is lost in the Conway tunnel.

Autumn is closing in and school is looming on the horizon. I make one of the last trips of the year to my favorite place—the rubbish dump. Quite often I find useful things, but this time I hit the jackpot and come home loaded down with books.

I was never conscious of learning to read; it just happened. Once I get started there is no stopping me. I will read anything, even the back of a sauce bottle. And trying to keep me supplied with good reading material keeps Mam busy. There is a small library at school, but they won't let you take books home. The county library in Stratford doesn't want our custom because we live on a caravan site, and so we are not only book thieves but probably murderers as well. Maybe the hours I spent with my granddad Jim triggered some osmosis. Anyway, my reading age is quite advanced and eclectic; even the school grudgingly acknowledges this when I win the prize for General Knowledge.

The books I have found are a godsend. Whereas the average school curriculum revolves around the well-known three R's: reading, 'riting, and 'rithmetic—we are encumbered by three more: religion, righteousness, and rubbish. With the aid of my booty of books, I can strive to transcend the guilt-ridden fetters of Rome.

These fabulous old tomes, all beautifully bound, deal with chemistry, physics, general science, botany, biology, geology, geography, anthropology, astronomy, French and Russian literature, English language, radio and TV engineering, and the Second World War!

How they came to be in a refuse tip is beyond me! Who would throw away a book? Well, people are odd, and odd people are even odder. These volumes become my constant companions. I do my best to suck the last kernel out of each one. Through their pages I journey to Peru in the time of the Incas, revolutionary Paris with its blood-spattered guillotine, the galvanic effect of electricity on a frog's legs and a universe burgeoning with facts, words, fantasies, ideas, and most of all stories of other folks' lives. "Give kids the love of books and they'll educate themselves," so said my granddad Jim, who ministered to me in that respect and grateful I am too. He would quote Kipling:

Let us now praise famous men,
Men of little showing . . .
For their work continueth,
And their work continueth,
Broad and deep continueth,
Greater than their knowing.

School starts up again, and to our relief Mr. Bury says nothing about the hand grenade business last term. He has probably forgotten all about it, as he told us he'd been on holiday in Greece most of the summer.

"What's it like in Greece, sir?" asks Nora.

"Well, after dinner we shall see. I've brought in some slides that I took!"

True to his word, after we eat, the curtains are drawn and Mr. Bury fumbles with the archaic brass slide projector.

There is a lot of giggling as we sit in the dark, waiting for something to happen. Then a shaft of stark white light, the shape of a playing card, hits the far wall, followed in glorious color by the appearance of a car on its roof with its wheels in the air next to an odd-looking policeman standing on his head!

"Damn thing's upside down!" the teacher murmurs to himself. After some pushing and pulling at the ancient mechanism, he manages to show us a picture of a Greek policeman standing next to his patrol car.

"Now," he asks, "has anyone heard of the Acropolis?" Two hands go up in the dingy light. "Well, Daly?"

Jerry looks hopeful. "Is it that new coffee bar in Stratford, sir?"

"Don't be daft, Daly. Cosgrave, tell him," our leader suggests with confidence.

"It's the horse fellas, sir, the four riders, *you* know! The four horsemen of the Acropolis, that's it!"

Mr. Bury chooses to ignore this dazzling display of ignorance and goes back to his slides.

"This is the Acropolis, the very citadel of the Greek capital. And this is the Parthenon, the temple of Athena, who gives her name to Athens. This is another shot of the temple showing the fine Doric columns . . . and here we have the view from the steps of the Parthenon showing the full extent of the Acropolis . . . !"

"The bloody place is in ruins!" whispers Gypsy Paul, unaware of its antiquity.

"I wouldn't go there if you paid me!"

"Shoosh!" I breathe, trying to stifle the giggles, but he won't shut up.

"Fancy going all that way to a dump like that—it's falling to bits!"

"It might have been in one piece when he got there and he wrecked it himself," says Steve O'Donnell. At this point I lose the ability to stifle my laughter and a stream of frothy orange juice comes out my nose and all down the front of my shirt.

"Pay attention there, whoever that is! Now this is the Aegean Sea named after Aegeus, the king of Athens and father of Theseus, and this is—"

"Mr. Bury's crumpet!" erupts Mike, as pandemonium breaks out at the sight of the young and lovely Fufkin Foster, stretched out on the beach in a two-piece swimsuit!

Mrs. MacArthur appears in a flash and calls out the names of those she thinks responsible for the cacophony.

"Daly, O'Donnell, Cosgrave, Dutton—report to me after school is over!"

I can't believe it! For once I'm not on the list!

"It wasn't them, miss."

"Who was it, Nora?"

"Willie Watkins, miss."

I don't even bother protesting my innocence. I know it is a waste of time. Nora has got her revenge from all those years ago when I hit her with the mallet.

From Mrs. Mack I receive the penance to write up a project of my choice as extra homework. Bugger! I'd rather have the cane and get it over with.

⇥ Chapter 11 ⇤

STRATFORD-UPON-AVON, JUST EIGHT MILES AWAY, IS A VERY ancient town. I decide to do my school project on it because of Shakespeare and everyone has heard of him. Also, it has two annual fun fairs, and this gives me the excuse to go. I start my research, first, on the name elements, and here Dad helps me. After that I'm on my own.

Stratford-upon-Avon.

Strat is from the Latin: Strata meaning a paved Roman road. Ford is from the Welsh: Fford corresponding to the English: way, or crossing place and Avon from the Gaelic Abhain, pronounced Avon, the word for river.

The town still has a medieval charm and a lot of black and white striped houses. Most of them would be familiar to Willie Wagglestaff, which was Shakespeare's real name before he joined the theatre. It is a market town and has a large cobble-stoned square and lots of pubs where Willie wrote plays in the afternoon.

Here you get the Stratford Mop every year. This is a traveling fair and was used to supply the wealthy folk with slaves. These were black women called Mrs. Mops because they were cleaners and skivvies. Some of the slaves escaped only to be recaptured and resold three weeks later when the fair returned. This is why the second fair is called the Runaway Mop.

Mrs. Mack said my history was very good and funny. She stuck a silver star onto my paper soul on the wall. It was the first one I'd ever had. It was the last one I ever got!

Mam is proud of the star and takes me to the Mop.

The fairs are now just carnivals, dodgem rides, big wheels, ox roasting, sideshows, cotton candy, toffee apples, and the smelly throb of diesel generators.

A thousand children lost in a maze of a million lightbulbs and me at the rifle-shooting gallery, winning a goldfish for Mam—four targets, three bull's-eyes, and an off center. After the first shot, I notice the rifle is sighted to fire high and left and compensate accordingly. The man gives me a quare look and a goldfish in a plastic bag.

The journey home on the Stratford Blue bus is fun. Mam and myself start to sing as if we are back home in Ireland. The locals frown at us and we don't care a bit:

> *Westering home with a song in the air,*
> *light in the eye and it's good-bye to care.*
> *Laughter of love, and a welcoming air,*
> *heart of my heart—my home land.*

"We need something to put the fish in. He can't live in there." Mam is staring into the caravan sink.

"How about this?" Dad has come up with a large pickled onion jar. "This should do!" He rinses out the jar with clean water and sniffs it. "Pooh! It still has a bit of a pen and ink about it. I hope he doesn't mind."

Mam is busy trying to catch the goldfish in her hands, accompanied by whoops of laughter.

"It tiddles when I try to grab him!" Mam giggles. Dad, ever the practical, scoops the wee fish up in a pint beer mug and pours it into the pickle jar.

"There you are, home sweet home, whatever your name is."

"Ooh! That's right. We haven't given him a name."

"How about Tiddles, Mam? You said he tiddles your hand."

"Yeah, that will do fine. Hello, Tiddles!"

"Now, Willie, people think goldfish lead a boring life, but someone once told me that they only have a tiny brain and can remember things for less than a second. If that's true, then each revolution would present them with an entirely new vista, as they can't remember the old view."

"Go'way, Reg, and leave the poor child alone. Ye'll have him puggled!"

"That's science, my dear wife. This is science I profess."

"Go'way with yer old guff. What are ye? Professor of Fermented Beverages?"

With the first frosts of winter, the air smells clean and crisp. The night sky hangs heavy with stars and bright planets traverse the heavens in elliptic excursions.

"That's the Milky Way, that long pale streak, and the W-shaped thing is the constellation of Cassiopeia. If you look down from the W, you see three stars equally spaced. Right at the end of the top one is a vague hazy blob. That's the spiraling Andromeda nebulae!"

Dad is giving us a lesson in astronomy and apart from the crick in my neck, I love it. Mam says she thinks she needs glasses.

"You see the three stars over there, about the same brightness? Well, that's the 'Belt of Orion.' Hanging down from the middle one are the three stars that make up his sword, and there's Rigel and Betelgeuse, and the two other stars, Ballatrix and Saiph, make up the famous Orion the Hunter.

"Who is this Orion, Dad, and what did he do to become so famous?"

"Ah!" says Dad. "I'm afraid you've got me there. I think he was a Greek."

"He was in his arse—he was Irish!"

"Glory be, woman! How in the name of the wee man do you make that out?"

She sings:

> O'Ryan is a mighty man
> Within the Irish nation,
> And hunting is his heart's delight
> And constant occupation.

She goes on to sing us an unlikely tale of O'Ryan the Hunter's encounter with a starving traveler who turned out to be St. Patrick. The hunter takes him in and feeds him on roast hare and Irish whiskey, which is called poteen. To repay this kindness, the saint promises O'Ryan a plethora of good hunting and sport in the afterlife:

Saint Pat—he supped the whiskey sweet
And says "Good luck attend ye,
And when you're in your winding-sheet
To the heavens I will send ye."

And so old Mick O'Ryan's might
Is famed throughout the nations,
You'll see him on a winter's night
Amongst the constellations.

"I tell you, Willie, that mother of yours is a walking encyclopedia of
Irish bullshit!"

We are now in *An lathan dubh*—the dark days, as wintertime is known
to the Gael. I arrive home from school and am walking down the path
to our caravan, when something catches my eye. Mam often puts
Tiddles outside for an airing and a change of scenery, but this time she
has forgotten to bring him in and his water has frozen solid.

I pick up the pickle jar and gaze at my friend suspended in his frozen
world. There is a loud *bang!* and I watch helplessly as the fish, still in
its icy cocoon, smashes to the ground in a shower of glass. I go to
pick up the spinning ice block containing its captive aquatic, but to my
horror a large wedge-shaped piece of glass is sticking out of my wrist.
My screams alert Mam, who wraps a tea towel around the wound, glass
and all!

Mrs. Allen, who was an ambulance driver in the London blitz, drives
at breakneck speed to get me to the casualty department at Stratford
Hospital. There they remove the glass carefully, the sliver being just a
fraction of an inch away from my main artery. The doctor says that it
was the heat from my hands that caused the frozen glass to explode.
He goes on to say that any attempt to yank out the glass would most
likely have severed the artery and I would have bled to death. The re-
moval of the glass and the subsequent stitches are administered without anesthetic, but I'm getting used to that. Still, it is bloody sore!

We get home, Tiddles is still lying where he has fallen, motionless
in his glacial stasis. Mam picks up the block of ice and puts it in a sink

full of cold water. Within the hour Tiddles is swimming and frolicking in the sink, none the worse for his experience.

And so my little pal—won at a slave auction, incarcerated in a vinegar-smelling jar, frozen by mistake, dropped by accident, spun by gravity, and defrosted by Mam—continues to live a full life with his circular window on the world, now illuminated by the first shafts of warm spring sunshine.

My parents buy a new caravan. This time it is a twenty-six-footer and affords me a room of my own. It seems enormous. There is a bathroom complete with a long plastic bath. My father, for reasons as mysterious as Stonehenge, rips out the bathtub and throws it into the garden. There it lies undisturbed for the next three years, in the midst of all the other junk, full of leaves and rainwater. The new trailer is very nice, but we still have no hookup to running water, no toilet, and now no bathtub either, not that it mattered a great deal to me!

Bathing takes place at a communal bathhouse in a section of the big hall that is reserved for washing clothes. There are coin slots on the doors of the three bathrooms, and it costs sixpence. I think it is a complete waste of money. Over home you could get six patsy pops for a tanner! I'm forced to have a bath once a month, whether I need it or not. I hate Mam scrubbing me with the hard black soap called Durback, which not only kills fleas and lice, but stings the eyes out of your skull. Still, it's better than breaking the ice on the water bucket, so's to rinse your bollocks down on a cold and frosty morning.

There are spiders up in the washhouse roof the size of dinner plates, and I would be feared one would fall off the ceiling and land on top of me. The two biggest black spiders, known as George and Georgina, have been there for centuries, producing millions of spidereens that migrate to every part of the known world.

Many spiders make the trek across to the whitewash and lead-piped realm of the public toilets, where they weave gossamer grids of fly-trapping thread over the dingy fanlights of grime-ridden windows. The lavatories are a long way from where we live, the nearest being at least a quarter of a mile away. Whereas you can pee around the back of the caravan, anything more exotic requires a long walk and sometimes a long wait at the other end if the khazzi is occupied. These facilities are not heated and going to the loo in the depths of winter puts enough iron in the soul to build a battleship. The lavatory walls are festooned with crude drawings of various male and female genitalia and lewd poems of the type described as limericks:

> *There was a young man from Clyde*
> *Who fell down the toilet and died*
> *Along came his brother who fell down another*
> *And now they lie in-turd inside.*

You're better off going for a shite in the woods. At least it don't stink, and Kilroy hasn't been scribbling his name all over the place.

Summer arrives with its attendant hordes of buzzing black flies and whirring swarms of iridescent bluebottles. These filth hounds of Hades congregate like a biblical pestilence, plaguing any visitor so brave as venture into ablutions. Even from a safe distance, the toilet buildings hum like electricity transformers, and the mixed smell of excrement and its Elsan Disinfectant antidote would be enough to make a tapeworm gag.

"Phew What A Scorcher!" says the headline in the local paper and then goes on to tell that factories and workplaces all over the country are closing down because of the heat wave. Anyone with any money heads to the seaside, where the fresh breezes and cool water calm the savage brow. We are of course stuck here in a caravan trailer as hot as a bread oven, with neither refrigerator nor ice box to keep milk from becoming a solid and butter from becoming a liquid. The only thing hotter than the weather is my mother's temper.

"Bad scran to you!" she says, throwing the last of the meat supplies out into dustbin.

"What's wrong with it, Mam?"

"It has the flyblow on it. The feckin' bluebottles are after laying their eggs all over your dad's pork chops, Godforgivemeforswearing. Curse this feckin' heat. We've nothing but tatties and vegetables for dinner. Your father will be raging. Ah, well, if the ouldfella doesn't like it, he can lump it! Being a vegetarian was good enough for great men like George Bernard Shaw and Mahatma Gandhi, so it better suit old baldy, too, or he'll get my boot up his hole!"

I leave my mam to her cursing and wander off around the corner to where the little Burmese woman, who'd told me how to get the shit out of the carpet, lives. She is out in the garden and her wee baby boy crawls around in the shrubbery, getting covered in shite and putting everything he finds into his mouth. She pays him no heed and bustles around the vegetable patch, clipping little green sprigs of herbs and uprooting quare-looking plants for their evening curry. Dad says the best way to preserve meat is to curry it; this makes Mam pull faces and say that curry gives you the skitters and that's why Indians and Pakistanis don't wear trousers. I decide to ask the Asian lady if what Dad says is true.

"Oh yes, yes, yes, spicy very good—make meat not go bad, not stinky stink. You watch, I show," she says, spreading spices and garlic over a large flat-topped boulder that grows out of the earth in front of her old hardboard caravan. The "Memsahib," as my dad calls her, then lays a piece of meat over the stone and pulverizes the living Jasus out of it with a big wooden club. Bits of flesh and peppercorns fly in all directions as she attempts to pound the raw steak into the cold cranium of the living rock beneath. It's a spectacular sight—like yer man wielding the jawbone of an ass in the Old Testament. Aromatic herbs and exotic flavors hang on the breeze, and soon the meat is diced and put into a large pot shaped rather like a cauldron.

"Must wait now for all to cook nice," she says, snatching up her little lad and making for the cool of the veranda.

"You come back later, I give you chipatti," she says, smiling, and closes the fly screen. Later, when I do return, she hands me a rolled pancake containing tangy, golden curry. I'm amazed at the taste and texture of it and, despite my mother's caution, discover that spicy food is wonderful and doesn't give me the runs either. I am glad to be friends with the Asian lady, with her great cooking and never to be forgotten advice: "Brush very hard, it is SHIT!"

The days continue sultry, sweltering affairs, made all the more irritating because bathing in the river has been declared out of bounds by the health ministry because of the great polio scare sweeping the nation. We are all vaccinated by the mobile hospital units that visit every town and village in Britain, but for some, it's already too late. The epidemic grows into a scourge which takes the lives of many and cripples even more. I'm glad when the summer finally fades and the sweaty sleepless nights give way to more tolerable circumstances.

It is a lovely autumnal day. With the onset of winter just around the corner, I think it is a good idea to get out and about while I still can. I am helping Dad down at the old piggeries where we are off-loading a pile of wooden lattice fence sections from the site manager's Jowett truck. The weight of these units is too much for me and, bandy-legged, I begin dropping my end.

"Jasus, Will, have ye no strength atall? Yer like a man made of smoke! I don't know why we bother feeding you. Put your back into it! I've seen more life in a tramp's underpants!"

"I'm doing my best, for the love of Mike! I'm nearly deaf with effort!" Wobbling most precariously, the entire load succumbs to gravity and slides majestically to the road.

"OK, let's take one at a time and stack them against the wall yonder."

"What are they for, Dad?"

"Well, the powers that be think that by fixing these trellises to the piggery walls and growing some Tudor roses up them, they can convert the pigsties into luxury weekend apartments for the city toffs and no one will ever know the difference."

"It seems a shame to turf the poor ould piggies out, just so some city slicker can play country squire for the weekend. I like feeding the wee pigs and scratching their backs for them—they're cute."

"Yes, I like pigs, too. D'you know they say that pigs can see the wind?"

"That's handy."

"No, really, they're amazing animals, almost human. It's reckoned that dogs look up to you, cats look down on you, but pigs treat you as equals! I think I might buy one of them when the auction comes."

"Where will we keep it, Dad?"

"With us in the caravan, of course!"

"What about the smell?"

"The pig will get used to it." Dad chuckles away to himself.

"Will they change the name? I mean, 'The Piggeries' doesn't sound much like a posh address, does it?"

"Yeah, Will, I believe they're going to rename it 'The Mews,' or some such nonsense, but it will still be the piggery to me." Dad stacks the last lattice against the pigsty wall as the incumbents within squeal with the expectancy of a good scratch.

"You know what Shakespeare said, Dad: 'A rose by any other name would smell the same.'"

"So would pig shit, my son."

We tarry with the porkers for a while, feeding them windfall autumn apples and rubbing their coarse hairy shoulders with sticks. The pigs whine and fret when we leave them to return the truck. Two weeks later they whine all the more as they're bundled off to Stratford market. The piggeries fall silent, until one day when a pig of a different kind appears, roaring at me and my friends.

"If I catch one of you scruffy gypsy bastards around here again, I'll have the hide off your backs! Especially you—I'll skin you alive, you little shit! Go on, Raus! Raus! Get out of here!" The old curmudgeon swings his knurled walking stick at my head. This is my first meeting with Grumpy, a nasty-tempered retired British army general who has become the self-appointed *Obergruppenführer* of the pastoral part of the trailer park. He acts like the emperor of this part of the site, which my mother has dubbed Obnoxious Corner.

This lace-curtain and rose water enclave of the bourgeoisie is infested with old military men, failed Conservative MPs, blue-rinse harridans of the "whip'em and hang'em brigade," empire loyalists, ex-Blackshirt fascists, and oddbods who think that "Herr Hitler wasn't such a bad chap, he was just a little misunderstood." To them we are anathema and represent the thing they fear most: tomorrow!

The big problem is that their citadel of refined reaction is directly adjacent to the two places we visit the most: the rubbish dump and the old livery stables. We constantly raid the refuse tip for raw materials, and the stables at the rear of the pigsties have been converted into garages and workshops where we can repair soapbox carts, bicycles, and help people mend their motorbikes. With the pigs gone, Grumpy has expanded his borders until these facilities lie within his self-proclaimed territory.

In the square courtyard of the piggeries there stands an old cast-iron hand pump that presumably drew water for the horses that were once stabled there before the pigs moved in. We resolve in the interests of physics to get it working—and we do! By priming it with tap water through a hole in the top, we are able for the first time in maybe a hundred years to pull up the water from the ancient well below. The handle, worked loose of its rust, swings free. With all the vigor of expectant youth, we pump like the mad apprentices of the biblical blacksmith Tubal-cain. There is a gurgling, sloshing, whooshing sound—with an eminence like a sperm whale blowing off. The entire apparatus erupts in a fountain of the foulest-smelling, rancidly stagnant water any of us has experienced since bath day. To us young scientists, it is a triumph; to Grumpy and his henchmen, it's another sign that educating the underclasses is fraught with danger and should therefore be a treasonable offense!

Before we are aware of it, a posse of the great like-minded descend upon us like the Spanish Inquisition and begin dealing out summary punishment. Some of my mates get an awful thrashing, but I am nimble and jump up onto the garage roof to run for my life. At a safe distance, I turn just in time to see Grumpy pick up my bicycle and throw it at the wall. It bounces back and lies, wheels spinning, on the cobblestones. With great glee, he leaps up and brings his considerable bulk down on the front wheel, which buckles beyond repair.

"Raus, you stinking Gypos! Raus!"

This *Raus* business is familiar. I remember Mr. Feidelman's caravan and begin to put two and two together. I don't get four carrots, I get a declaration of war!

"Right, lads! As my dad says, 'If you cross an Irishman with a pig, you'll get a pig that can hold a grudge for a thousand years!' We don't need that amount of time, we just need a good working plan!"

For the next few weeks, myself and my battered lieutenants conceive a dastardly counterattack that, in the fullness of time, is to prove devastating.

"What happened to your bike?" Dad asks, as I seek to replace the front wheel with another, two sizes too small.

"Er . . . nothing, just a stupid accident."

"That old Hooray-Henry of a general was down at the club last night, boasting that he'd worsted a gang of local hooligans? Dy'know anything about it, youngfella?"

"No," I says. I meant it, too. We had only received a cuffing, not a worsting, and we hadn't yet even replied to the challenge.

"Operation Moonstrike" goes into effect at the next full moon. We have three commando teams of two; each has a separate job. Every job is synchronized to the bells of the old Saxon church, which toll the hour, quarter, half, and three-quarters. This gives parameters of fifteen minutes for each phase.

We are well versed in this clandestine military stuff—we've just sat through two showings of *The Guns of Navarone* at Stratford Cinema.

It is 8 o'clock: Zero hour. The advance party moves forward to the corner of the piggeries and props a ladder against the garage roof nearest Grumpy's caravan.

8.15: The assault party climb the ladder with a large piece of turf, which they place over the caravan's chimney pipe.

8.30: The observation party monitors the buildup of smoke and the opening of doors and windows to let out same. An intelligence report confirms: *Grumpy cursing and waving smoke out of door with his hat.* Excellent!

8.45: The coup de grâce, the assault party removes turf and replaces it with a garden hose.

9.00: All rendezvous. Remove ladder, turn on water hose, and withdraw. The mission is complete!

This puts the kibosh on old Grumpy as far as we're concerned. He is left knee deep in soot and water, with "Nazis Raus!" painted on the roof of his caravan!

The next day our action is followed by a serendipitous event that places us kids beyond any repercussions that may occur.

A mysterious bearded bloke called Pikey, who for the last year has wandered around the caravan site wearing sandals and talking poetry to himself, pays Grumpy a visit, carrying a large metal container. Grumpy is on a ladder trying to scrub the graffiti from his roof.

"We have all, like, heard about what happened to you, general man, and have, like, taken up a collection, dig?" Grumpy smiles and the lanky beatnik throws the contents of an Elsan shit bucket all over him.

"Revenge is a dish best eaten cold," say the Sicilians, and as luck would have it, I have learned a lot about exotic dishes this year!

News of our part in the daring raid spreads around the web of intrigue that makes up the multistranded universe of the prepubescent. By some lapse of security or most likely a comrade's boast, made no doubt in the strictest confidence, the Bulldog Gang hears of it.

This unsavory outfit is the remote, but nevertheless, feared group of older boys who hang around the post office. They are mostly the sons of servicemen and live in a distant enclave of the caravan site. Their leader is the fat git called Derrick Davies who once called my mam a pregnant prostitute. He bears a remarkable resemblance to his pet: a squat, snarling, slobber of a bulldog from which they take their gang name.

Like most of my pals, I give these guys a wide berth when I can. They go to the Protestant school in Henley, and so are doomed anyway. If that isn't bad enough, they are all over twelve, and indeed some are fourteen! The main currency of their everyday conversation seems to be the esoteric world of masturbation, a presumed rite of passage at this time still alien to us in thought, word, and deed. The old air raid shelter at the back of the railway station is their headquarters, and to this den of dexterous depravity I am duly summoned by a pair of Derrick's hard-faced shock troops.

I enter the dingy shelter, festooned with pinup girls from *Parade* magazine and smelling heavily of stale spunk and mildew. In the half-light, surrounded by his faithful, *Obergrossenführer* Davies sprawls across a canvas-backed chair like a half-inflated zeppelin.

"So you want to join our gang, do you? We heard of the raid on Grumpy—good work!" Beside his master's chair, the drooling dog shakes its head, sending whiplashes of snot in a silvern arc about it.

"Who the hell has told him that?" I wonder, shuddering at the thought of joining this lot.

"Well, don't be a scaredy-cat! Do you want to join a real gang or keep hanging out with those little prats from the kitchen gardens? Can you fetch?"

"Fetch what?"

"Fetch your cock off? Have a wank? Shake the vinegar bottle? Come yer custard? For fuck's sake, give him the book, somebody!" At the flabby Führer's request, I am handed a stained, dog-eared copy of *Health and Efficiency* magazine, a monochrome tabloid of naked, beach-ball-throwing females, curiously devoid of any traces of pubic hair. My initial feeling of fear and trepidation is now approaching panic! What do they want me to do? If it's *that*, forget it! *That* is a mortal sin and I don't know how to do it anyway! The elbow-nudging storm troopers piss themselves laughing at my bewilderment amid cries of, "He's never done it!" "He hasn't got one!" "He needs two hands, one for the magnifying glass and one for the tweezers!"

The dirty book is slapped across my face and returned to the shelf. In the stinging silence that follows, I have a chance to reassess. What am I doing here? I don't want to be in this stupid gang of wankers!

Derrick is still pushing for my loyalty.

"If you want to join us, you must go though the initiation ceremony. First you must swear the oath of secrecy. Then you must cut your thumb with a razor blade and give it to the dog to lick. Then you must kiss the dog's dick!"

I stare around the ring of stern, cheerless faces, now all nodding approval to these arcane rituals. Tough, intimidating faces, eyes defiant and mouths set hard, mouths that, *mouths that*—oh! my Christ!—had kissed a dog's cock!

The tiny gene of the absurd that I have inherited from my mother causes me a convulsion of irrepressible mirth that not only drives away fear and foreboding, but makes me impervious to the blows of fists that rain down upon me. I am forcibly ejected into the clean crisp air of the countryside where, still being kicked and beaten, I jackknife my way home more aware of my ribs aching from hysterics than violence.

"Holy Jasus, child, what ails ye?" Mam is hanging up the washing as I reel into the yard, blood, snot, and merriment shining on my face. Still holding my splitting ribs, I recount to her the story of the dreaded dog's cock kissers.

"Durty fuckers!" says Mam. "Taking advantage of a poor dumb animal like that! It's little wonder they're always spitting on the pavement!" I commence back to roaring and howling with agonizing glee.

The Bulldog Gang never recover from their betrayed secret and subsequent crippling loss of face. No longer does this pack hang out at the post office corner, shouting obscenities at girls, smoking cigarettes, and gobbing on the street. They are only seen in shamefaced ones and twos, except when they march on Sundays with the Protestant Boy's Brigade troop. Then we cheer them on with *"Woof! Woof!"* noises combined with lip-licking kissy sounds.

Now with the opposition defeated and in disarray, we have the place to ourselves!

It is a great revelation when I find out that I won't be struck by a celestial lightning bolt when I dare go into a non-Catholic church. The truth is that most of the interesting ancient churches are Church of England or the like, and the Catholic ones are nearly all modern, some as recent as the 1890s.

There are many Saxon, Norman, Tudor, and Gothic buildings in everyday use all over the county, most within a good bike ride. I visit many such places and marvel at the tombs of crusaders, barons who knew Simon de Montfort, men-at-arms in stone chain mail, knights in armor with their feet resting on a lion to show they'd died in war or on a dog to signify that they met their demise at home, in time of peace.

Dad shows me how to take brass rubbings from the ancient tabloid effigies of long-dead knights of the realm, in the old churches. This process involves placing paper over the inscribed knightly representations and rubbing with a wax crayon or preferably a cobbler's heel-ball. The resulting image is very pleasing and educational. The unfortunate thing is that all of these old churches are now post Reformation and as a result Protestant!

Dad doesn't give a fling about this and neither do I—until I write a story about us going to an old Norman church in Alcester and rubbing the brasses.

My teachers are not amused.

"So you go into Protestant churches, do you? Do you know that's a mortal sin? What do you have to say for yourself?" I am not to be intimidated. My father has briefed me well.

"The brasses I rubbed were of good Catholics who had never heard of a Protestant. They were well dead long before Henry the Eighth, Cromwell, or any of them was pupped." I am very indignant! "And if they didn't think they were still Catholics, why did Cromwell's Iron-sides deface so many of the statues and old knights in these churches?"

Mrs. MacArthur looks at Mr. Bury, who in turn looks at Miss Hathaway. Miss Hathaway looks out of the window, and I look at her reflection and see her trying not to laugh.

They had been totally unprepared for such a vigorous defense. Mrs. Mack takes up the inquisition.

"Your father encouraged you to do this, isn't that right?"

"Yes, miss."

"He's not of the faith, is he?"

"No, miss."

"I've heard he's an atheist. Is that true?

"I don't know, miss!"

"Well, does he go to church?

"Only at Christmas, miss."

"Oh yes, I heard all about that. He doesn't have much love for our parish priest, does he?"

"I don't know, miss."

"Of course you know. He tells you everything. What's his opinion of our own holy father?"

"No different to how he sees the rest of the priesthood, miss."

"And what does he say about them, pray tell?

"He says if priests wore their trousers around the same way as their collars, there would be fewer bastard children in the world."

There is a long silence. They are dumbfounded. It is decided more appropriate that the priest should confront my father with a list of my ill doings, and thus I would get my comeuppance at home. I am dismissed.

Weeks go by and nothing happens. I thought I'd gotten away with my outburst, and though I had seen the priest at church and at school, he had never made any attempt to converse with me, let alone give me a punishment. One day, however, the past catches up with me whilst I am playing with my toy soldiers on the kitchen table.

Dad has finished his rotating early shift and is having a kip on the settee, when there is a knock at the caravan door.

"See who that is, Will?" I open the door and there is a chap I vaguely knew, but who is he? A little ferret-face bloke with a familiar hunted look.

"Er, I'm Mr. Timmins. I work with Father. Can I have a word with your parents? If it's not too much trouble."

"Daaad?" I begin, but he is already up, pulling on his braces and looking suspiciously at the interloper.

"Who's this arsehole?" he says to me, ignoring the outstretched hand of the verger. "What does he want, waking me up in the middle of the bloody daytime?"

"Eh-hrm! I'm here on behalf of the priest to have a little chat with you about the behavior of your son."

"You're what?" says Dad, taking stock of the nervous stranger for the first time.

"Your son, he's bee . . . n . . ."

He trails off, aware that Dad is regarding him with jaundiced eye.

Dad cracks his knuckles with a sickening snap, before saying ,"*Listen you,* whoever you are! If that devil dodger wants to talk to me, he can come here his bleeding self! I don't parley with any bugger's fart catcher. I prefer to talk to the shovel, not the shit! Do you understand, lickspittal?"

"Yessyessyes!" agrees the poor verger, making his way back to his bicycle like a surreptitious sideywise crab.

"I will be going now—good-bye!" says the layman, throwing his leg over the crossbar and pedaling off, head tucked in, legs a-blur, down the cinder track road.

Dad is just about to close the door when a spark of recognition flashes in his eyes. He throws the door open wide.

"I remember you from last Christmas, ya shifty wee bastard!"

His words are lost on the fast-diminishing figure of the verger, who has sped away as swiftly as his 1930 three-geared Hercules Roadster can convey him.

"So what have you been up to that's pissed off the old sin bosun?"

"I told my teacher that you are an atheist and they called the priest about it."

"Well, it's no bloody business of theirs what I am—and anyway, I'm an agnostic!"

"What's that, Dad?"

"Well, when I joined the army, we had our first Sunday church parade and the regimental sergeant major has us all lined up in rank and file. *Right, you 'orrible lot!'* he shouts. *'Catholics move to the left! Protestants move to the right! On my command, FALL OUT!'* This left myself and a long drink of water called Private Abel Goodman standing in the middle of the parade ground. The RSM goes to gangly Goodman and says, *'So what the bleedin' 'ell are you?'*

'I'm Jewish,' says Goodman.

'Hmm,' says the RSM, making his way over to me.

'So what are you, Private Watkins? Are you Jewish as well?'

'Erm, no, I'm an agnostic, Sergeant.'

'What in the name of buggery is an agnostic, Watkins?'

'Well, Sarge, I believe in a God of sorts, but I haven't made my mind up about what exactly it is yet!'

'WELL, NOW'S YOUR BLEEDING CHANCE! IT'S THAT LOT, THE OTHER LOT, OR THAT LANKY BASTARD OVER THERE! NOW GET FELL IN, YOU GODLESS LITTLE MAN!'"

✣ Chapter 12 ✢

DAD WALKS SLOWLY DOWN FROM HIS SIGNAL BOX AT HENLEY Station. It is two in the afternoon, and he has just been relieved by the second shift. Crossing the road by the Three Tuns public house, he roots in his greatcoat pocket and produces the grand sum of his wealth: a single copper penny bearing the head of Queen Victoria and on the reverse, Britannia sitting gazing at the ocean, shield and spear in hand.

"Not much good to man nor beast—well man anyway," he muses, popping the penny into a horse-shaped charity box labeled "The People's Dispensary for Sick Animals."

"Cast ye, your bread upon the waters and what shall ye receive in return? Soggy bread!" Dad begins the long walk home, but something catches his eye, fluttering like a small green woodpecker in a pile of brown autumn leaves. It is a one-pound note!

"Let joy be unconfined!" shouts Dad to the gray skies above. The smell of beer is enticing from the taproom of the Golden Cross Tavern.

"In for a penny, in for a pound!" Dad makes to venture over to the pub.

He pauses at the curbside. A lorry load of cattle breezes past and trundles down the High Street.

On the fulsome wind that follows its wake, a staccato voice drifts up from the offtrack betting shop. "Three minutes to go here at Newmarket before the Cesarewitch October Stakes is run. Here at this historic race, named after the czar of all the Russias, the field is as follows: Superfine, seven to four favorite; Hal's Lad, two to one; Continuous Wave, eleven to two; Lucky Note, ten to one; Bar, twelve to one. Two minutes to the off!"

"Lucky Note?" Dad stares at the pound in his hand and then back across to the alehouse. He tries to walk to the pub, but his legs take him into the bookie's.

"They're at the starters line here at Newmarket."

"Och! To hell with it. One pound, Lucky Note—to win!"

"And they're off!"

A big black car noses its way up the cinder track and stops outside our caravan.

"Willie, tell that fella to park somewhere else. If your dad comes home he'll have his guts for garters."

"Mam! Maaam! It *is* my dad!"

"Isn't she a beauty? I got her for ten quid."

"Ten pounds? Glory be, that's a week's wages! Where in the name of Christ did you get ten pounds?"

"It's a long story and you wouldn't believe me."

"Try me."

I inspect the sleek monster. It is black with big chrome headlights and looks like Al Capone had given it away to charity, a grand old rust bucket held together with holes.

Dad opens the bonnet and stares into the Medusa's head of coils, wires, and hoses.

"She's an Austin Ten, stoutly built. She's survived many's the long winter, and there's life in the old dog yet!" He slams the hood shut and the horn blares. He pulls at some wires and the horn never works again.

At the weekend we go on expeditions into the country. Off to the glorious west, Shropshire, Herefordshire, and over the border into the heartland of Wales.

Dad takes me to Bleddfa, the tiny hamlet where my grandfather was born and generations of Watkinses had farmed the lush pastures. The valleys of Powys are tree lined, verdant fingers, stretching in a fecund flourish from the Brecon Beacons over Offa's Dyke into the flatlands of Mercia. The air is rich and suffused with pine scent.

We still have kin living in mid-Wales and it always is a pleasure to visit and listen to them talking. Whether they speak English or Welsh, their voices have a musical quality that is sweet on the ear. They can make "Bugger off or I'll shoot your dog!" sound as pleasant as Dylan Thomas reading "A Child's Christmas in Wales."

My great-uncle, George Lloyd, is a bard of the old school, foremost in the art of Celtic storytelling and likewise the symbiotic Druidic craft of brewing. He talks in Welsh a lot with my father and calls him Rhienallt, the Welsh for Reginald. Me he refers to as Gwylym bach, little William.

Here in a little tumbledown house, behind Auntie Sis's post office in the village of Presteigne, he holds his impromptu Gorsedd court.

Shadowy figures, some of which are kin and some strangers, flit between fireside and ale barrel, like silent specters thirsting for the spoken word. In the focus of a concave arc of expectant faces, Old George is enthroned on a carved oak settle. In his left hand he nurses a glass of thick, home-brewed, Red-Rag cider, in the other a black briar pipe.

Master of intrigue, he knocks the dottle out of his pipe and lights the replenished bowl. The story does not begin until the pipe draws well and the room is silent except for the crackling of a log fire and the pendulous ticking of the longcase clock standing sentinel by the doorway. Pull your chair into the fire and listen to him now:

> Great-uncle Jack knew about horses, you see. He and generations before him had bred native Welsh ponies on the green hills of wild Wales. These stocky, sturdy little ponies are known to be good all-rounders; fine for working or carrying supplies in side panniers or maybe, when required, just right for riding. They can pull a medium-size barrel-top living wagon or a ladened flat cart and stay out on the mountain in all weathers. Strong and willful, they are the embodiment of the divine horse goddess, Epona, from which they take the name pony.
>
> The men and women that farmed these upland pastures are no less rugged and have clung on tenuously to the land of Cymru. They have defied famine, invasions, civil unrest, wars of all kinds, and even the pestilence of Palug's cat, who ate one hundred and eighty warriors before Cei ap Cynyr killed it on Ynys Môn, which is also called the Isle of Anglesey.
>
> It is the newly married Jack whom we see setting up

home with his wife just as the black ravens of war are gathering over Europe.

The king of England, the kaiser of Germany, and the czar of all the Russias are busy thumbing their royal noses at each other and spoiling for a fight. These three first cousins are in turn being watched by a score of second and third cousins, who make up the other crowned heads of Europe. Who will jump here? Who will jump there? Who will not jump at all when the battle royal commences?

It takes them four long years to finish their family feud. Eight million soldiers lie dead, and one of the fallen, whose name liveth forever on a Welsh village's war memorial, is the legendary great-uncle Jack.

It is 1916. The British army has lost so many men in the Battle of the Somme, nineteen thousand killed in one day alone, they feel they must introduce conscription.

Jack receives his call-up papers in the autumn of that year and grudgingly reports for duty in Cardiff. He doesn't approve of this imperialist war. If the English are seriously concerned about the freedom of small nations, why don't they pull out of Wales and leave it for the Welsh? Well, now, look you! If Jack must go, he wants to join a Welsh-speaking regiment. The British find out that he is a horse breeder and he is sent instead to the Royal Horse Artillery.

After his training as a horse gunner, he find himself in war-stricken France. He and his battery are sent to a small evacuated hamlet on the frontline. Their mission is to support a tiny detachment of dismounted French cavalry who are attempting to hold this part of the salient.

Horse units are still being sent forward by the generals at GHQ in Paris. Surely they must know they are useless against mud, barbed wire, and machine guns? Cavalry men are ill-equipped to fight on foot with their bright sabers, riding breeches, slim leather boots, and short-range saddle carbines. It is hoped that the presence of a few twenty-five-pounder field guns might discourage an attack at this weak point. It is not to be.

The first salvo of shells to leave the Allied battery gives away their position to the enemy spotters, and a withering fire is returned by the massed German heavy guns.

The German gunners are no beginners. They know well their trade. Their fire is meticulously accurate and sustained. In the first volley, Uncle Jack's field gun flies into the air like a toy and lands a hundred yards away, a crumpled wreck. A second shell rips into the ammunition carts parked next to their makeshift stables. In that one enormous explosion, all of the batteries' horses are blown to pieces, along with the British battery commander, the French colonel, and their entire staff.

Within minutes of the opening shots, every Allied field piece has been silenced. The gun crews lie around their posts where they have fallen. Jack has been blown clear off of his own gun and into a haystack, which catches fire. He dives for shelter into a ruined wine cellar until the first barrage ceases, then scurries to where the field headquarters had been established. There is nothing left but a smoking crater in the soft muddy earth. Not a single soul has survived the attack.

In the unearthly quiet following the deafening engagement, Jack hears the fall of hooves and cries of "Aller! Aller!" He jumps up and through the swirling dust he sees the remnants of the detachment of cuirassiers beating a hasty retreat on their mounts. He calls out to them, but they are out of earshot and riding hard.

There are but six of them left, and the last, in trying to clear a ruined wall, falls heavily from the saddle and lies still on the scattered stones.

Jack climbs over the piles of rubble to where the rider lies staring at the gray sky. He was a young captain who had previously won the Croix de Guerre. Now he is beyond all earthly help. Jack takes the man's papers from his top pocket. His name was Capitaine Jean-Baptiste Laurence. Jack will give these to the first casualty officer he meets. Then on a sudden impulse, he removes the medal, wraps it in its silken ribbon, and puts it in his own pocket. There is a *crump!* from the German lines and a single shell whistles over and falls in the pile of debris that once had been a farmhouse.

Jack makes his way back to his shelter, darting from cover to cover. Another solitary shell homes in and bursts behind him. "At least I'm going in the right direction!" he thinks, "away from the gunfire!" Diving like a rabbit into his sanctuary, he makes a bed out of a bale of straw and tries to sleep. All night long the desultory shelling continues and Jack has the wildest dreams.

Standing before him is the young cavalry officer, pale and deathly.

"Seek you the white Arab, lead him to safety, seek you the white Arab and save him. He is the last of his line. Restore the honor of my family and then I can rest."

In the dream Jack takes out the Croix de Guerre from his pocket and offers it to the pallid specter.

"No you must keep that. You will need it. Save the white Arab!"

Jack wakes, shivering as if ice water is running in his veins. The first fingers of the sun are probing the shadows and with the dawn he expects the counterattack that will have him killed or taken prisoner. It doesn't come! Maybe the Germans are still asleep or perhaps they fear a trap!

Emerging from his hidey-hole, he looks around. The visitation from the night before is now a distant memory in the melting warmth of morning. Way out in no-man's-land, he sees a stallion! A white stallion! A white Arab stallion! The poor horse is lost and confused, wandering amongst the barbed wire and shell holes, bloody and covered in mud.

Jack whistles and does his best to coax the charger over, but the horse is shy of him. Searching about in the remains of the orchard, he finds some apples and leaves them where the steed will smell them. This tactic works fine and soon he and the horse are pals. He is very relieved to discover that the bloodstains on the stallion are not the horse's but its unfortunate rider.

Staying holed up all day, Jack expects relief from the Allies or a German attack, but nothing occurs. Except for the horse, he is alone in a cellar, encompassed by the wastelands of futile Armageddon.

In fitful sleep, once again he is taunted by the ghost of the young officer. No words are spoken, but the officer takes the Arab's bridle and hands it to Jack. A ghostly finger points to the west. Go, the eyes of the Frenchman beckon. Go!

Jack wakes and lies in thought. The phantom is right! Enough of this war business. There's no glory here, just death—not only of iniquitous mankind but of beautiful innocent horses. What couldn't he do with an Arabian stud sire like this back home in Wales?

"Needs must when the devil rides!" Jack tells himself.

Jack ties a red neckerchief around his throat and looks at himself in the shattered mirror of a long abandoned bedroom dresser. "I could pass for a civilian!" he thinks, fingering the stubble on his unwashed chin. In the ruins of the farmhouse, he finds old clothes scattered where they had fallen during the hasty evacuation. Divesting himself of all traces of military garb, he dresses in a hotchpotch of civilian attire. A lone shell hums over his head and explodes beyond the poplar trees. Jack throws his army identification discs into the mangled morass where the first shell had fallen. The loose leaves of his army paybook flutter like butterflies over the stinking corpses.

"Now to disguise the horse!" An old blacksmith forge yields a large rasp file. This he uses to take off the French army brand, from the charger's right hoof. It works well and a good feed of apples will make up the difference in hoof horn.

The stallion is also branded on the lip. This seems a problem until Jack finds a tin of army metal polish. This he rubs into the brand, causing it to swell and blister until formation of a scab completely obscures the mark!

He fashions a bridle out of rope and replaces the French cavalry saddle with an old red velvet curtain, He mounts his mud-covered prize and slowly rides away from the insanity they call the First World War!

It takes Jack many weeks to thread his careful way across the French countryside. In the confusion of the front, he isn't even challenged. He's just another lost peasant refugee on the road to nowhere, mingling with the other dispossessed and evacuated. Horse and rider are of no interest to the army except as a bloody nuisance to be cleared rapidly out of the way.

His initial navigation relies on having the sound of the guns to his rear and joining the flow of other civilians fleeing the war zone. After which, he travels only at night and uses the stars for pointers. Early one morning, when he is many miles from the battle line, he runs into his first real trouble.

A platoon of recently arrived British soldiers is bivouacked across the road, and Jack, riding almost fast asleep, clatters straight into them.

"*Halt! Who goes there?*" challenges a London Cockney private, his rifle raised. "*Friend or foe?*"

"Bore da!" says Jack, in Welsh, just wishing the soldier a fine good morning. The sentry looks unsure and calls out, "*Sergeant! I think I've caught a German spy!*"

The sergeant runs up with two more armed soldiers. Pistol in hand, he orders, *"Hände hoch!"* Jack looks blankly from one to another. The sergeant tries again. *"Spreckenzee Deutsch, Fritz?"*

"Bore da!" says Jack, smiling and beginning to enjoy their discomfort.

"That's what he says to me, Sergeant!"

"Right, you, what's your game? Where do you come from? Who's your king?" The sergeant was trying a bit of psychology.

Jack, still staring down the muzzles of four guns, replies, "Beird byt barnant wyr o gallon, Diebyrth e gerth e gynghyr!" The poets of the world judge those to be men of valor, whose counsels are not revealed to slaves!

"There you are!" says the sergeant, *"I knew it! He ain't no bloody German! He's a bloody Gypsy! Now get that Gypo bastard out of here before he steals something!"*

To Jack's delight, he is given a British military escort through the camp and out into the open country beyond.

He passes unseen through the thickly hedged lanes of Normandy and into the Argoat, which is Breton for the Country of the Trees. Here in Brittany, he is amongst fellow Celts who speak his language and also have little love for the war. Many resented being conscripted into the army of France, who they considered to be an occupying force in their beloved Armorica. Uncle Jack can well understand that!

He and his horse are fed and watered by sympathetic families and guided from village to village. Within two days, they reach the coast at the tiny fishing port of Tréguier. Now only the sea stands between him and Wales.

Jack's helpers have informed him that fishing boats from Wales often call in to pick up sardines from the smaller Breton fishing smacks and that this is his best chance at getting across the Channel. His luck is holding.

In the small stone harbor is a French coaster about to set sail for Pembroke to pick up a flock of Cheviot sheep. Jack tries to secure passage by offering to work for his trip. The captain shakes his head. *"Have you no money?"* The captain pats Jack's coat pockets to emphasize the point.

"No, I have nothing." The skipper delves into the jacket pocket and draws forth a long blue, white, and red ribbon with its silver fourchée.

"My God! You have the Croix de Guerre! For that I will give you free passage and two bottles of apricot brandy!"

Jack and his Breton helpers drink a toast. Then he and his mount set sail for Wales.

No one takes the slightest notice of the scruffy, bearded figure leading his horse away from the bustling Welsh port. With an army to be fed in France, every coastal town is choked with livestock being loaded or penned up, waiting for ships. The streets are thronged with drovers, agents, farmers, and the other attendants that keep an army marching on its stomach.

All this Jack leaves behind and, mounting his steed, he turns for Powys and home.

Now Jack has to be careful, see? Because he is a deserter, which would get you shot, and also a horse thief, which would get you shot again! He makes his way to the cottage of a kinsman called Blind Old Harry, where he lies up for a while in secret.

Jack's poor wife has been notified by the war office that he has been killed in action. Old Harry gets word to Jack's grieving widow that there's an impediment in law about her ownership of the farm and will she come to Llandrindod Wells for a meeting. This she duly does, and waiting there for her is her bearded husband, Jack.

They say that she fainted clean away and thought he was an angel. Well, Jack might have been a lot of things you know, but he was no angel! They maintain a secret liaison until a respectable time is past. Then Uncle Jack marries the love of his life for the second time. They move to another part of Wales, and there, with the aid of the Arab stallion, who they named Captain Laurence of Arabia, they raise fine horses and four children. Black, white, gray, and piebald they were—the horses that is, not the children! And do you know? Until the day she died, Jack's wife received a war widow's pension from the English government. She donated it all to the People's Dispensary for Sick Animals.

He finishes his tale with a section from *The Gododdin,* the epic sixth-century war saga by the great Brythonic poet, Aneirin:

> *"Gredyf gwr oed gis*
> *Gwrhyt am dias*
> *Meirch mwth myngvras*
> *A dan vordwyt megyris.*
>
> *He is a man in mind, in years a youth*
> *And gallant in the din of war:*
> *fleet, thick-maned chargers*
> *Are ridden by this illustrious hero."*

The room fills with cheers and clapping. Old Uncle George motions me to join him outside.

"There be only one thing more thirsty work than telling a story and that be a-listening to it!" Uncle George contends and shuffles off into the outhouse, where he keeps his cider vats.

"Come and give me a hand, Gwylym bach, and we'll get these good folks a drink!"

The bottom of the oaken vats are covered with the bare bones of small animals which, bleached white, gleam through the murky cider.

"Was that story true, Uncle George?"

"Well, it all depends on what you want to believe!"

"Why do you put beasts into the cider, uncle?"

"It be to improve the flavor and give it body. Do ye want a flagon, young master?"

"I'm not old enough, uncle."

"Rubbish!" He scoops me up a pewter mug of the festering infusion. "I've been drinking this since I was a sprog, an' it ain't done me no harm either!"

There is no way out and I sup at the wizard's brew. The sensation of swallowing this stuff beggars belief, but once down, it gives a pleasing glow followed seconds later by a rush of blood to the brain that sends me reeling into the fresh air.

"Har, har, har! That's what happened to me when I was a sprog! It fetched me such a tightener. Har, har, har! It be like a red rag to a bull, that old zyder! I tell ye, Gwylym bach, our family be blessed by longevity here in the clean air of Wales. Aunt Sis is over a hundred herself and her father died, only after falling down an apple tree when he was one hundred and three years old. I'm telling you, it's that red rag cider that kept us young. Har, har, har!"

With trays filled with flowing pints of scrumpy, we rejoin the convocation. Uncle George taps out his pipe once more and that's the signal for quiet. When all is still, he recites:

Silver John is dead and gone,
and buried in Cole Harbor.

When I was a little boy, I remember the old men in
the village talking about the events that were current
when they were children the same age as me. People lived
to be over a hundred, so could go back two hundred
years of history in just two generations. Bonnie Prince
Charlie and George Washington and Napoleon it was
that were giving the English a run for their money
around the world. Heroes they were to the old ones,
who didn't care for the Saesneg.

One of my forebears, who didn't make it to quite such
a ripe old age, was foully murdered whilst still a youth
of seventy-four. His name was Dr. John Lloyd or Silver
John, as he is better known. He was a traveling boneset-
ter and plied his trade through the highways and byways
of mid-Wales and the border country beyond in the

1700s. His nickname came from the silver buttons on the great flared overcoat he liked to wear and the solid-silver buckles on his shoes. The unfortunate doctor is returning home one night from New Radnor, when he is attacked by a party of brigands. Although he tries to fight them off, they get the better of him and beat him senseless. His attackers strip the silver adornments from his clothes and then with great callousness push his unconscious body beneath the ice of the frozen Llyn Hielyn. "Murder will out," the old saying goes and sure enough it do! Under the ice his body lies until the spring thaw, when the lake boils and bubbles to the amazement of all and with a terrible eruption casts his body forth! They say the doctor's vengeful spirit still haunts the banks of the lake, seeking revenge on his murderers!

His assailants are never brought to justice, but it is said that to this day the grass never grows on the grave of Silver John.

One night, it was, when I was a sprog, I had been staying out too late and the sun had gone down quicker than I expected. Making my way back home, along the twilight filled lane that passes close by the shore of Llyn Hielyn, I begin to tremble.

A rustling noise dogs my footsteps from the other side of the hedgerow. It could only be *Silver John's Ghost!* I hasten my pace without trying to appear frightened. The accompanying footfalls take on speed, too. I stop, they stop. I creep forward, they creep forward! Finally I take off as fast as my legs can carry me, still paced by my invisible nemesis. At the end of the lane the hedgerow abruptly finishes and I clatter headlong into my phantom! A large saddle-backed pig it was, lying there with me in the mud. I'm up and running in my bare feet and the pig is calling after me, "Siors Lloyd, run hard, for a great storm approaches," and I run as fast as I can, for I know that pigs can see the wind. Lightning strikes the trees around me and great peels of thunder rend the air. The stones in the road sting my feet and hail the size of hen's eggs strikes the road behind me. "Take my shoes, Siors bach, and be fleet of foot!" I look down and a pair of black shoes with silver buckles appear on my feet, giving me new strength to outrun the storm. I gain the safety of my gate and run into the kitchen.

"Mam! Mam! Look at my feet!"

"I see them—they are a disgrace! You will go to bed without any supper!"

I look down and my feet are muddy and bare.

"But Mam—"

"There will be no buts. Wash those feet and off to bed, and it's sorry you'll be for missing supper! Your uncle killed his old saddle-backed pig this morning and brought us over a roast!"

There is a sigh from the assembly, the briar pipe is knocked out on the hearth of the old fireplace, and Uncle George drains the last of his pint.

"Tangnefedd fo gyda chwi, nos dawch a ffarwel!"

Peace go with you, good night and farewell!

We course through the night, our one headlight picking out the cat's eyes marking the median of the road.

"Are they real cat's eyes, Dad?"

"No, they were invented by a man who was out one night, when he saw a cat walking towards him, with its eyes reflecting his car lights. He made up similar reflectors out of glass and rubber."

"To help make the roads safer?"

"That's right! If the cat had been walking away from him, he would've probably invented the pencil sharpener!"

"Reg! That's enough of that filth in front of the child!"

"Do you believe in ghosts, Dad?'

"No."

"No, of course he doesn't, Willie. Yer father is what they call a daylight atheist. He doesn't believe in God unless he's at death's door, and then you should hear him. Oh, Jesus help me! Oh, my God! What is it they say?

> '*The devil was ill—the devil a monk would be.*
> *The monk got well—the monk a devil was he.*'"

"Well, at least I don't pray to some bug-whiskered old bollix up in the sky."

"No, you'd rather put your faith in trees an' stones an' cats an' dogs and them bunch of beauties you go boozing with down at the Bull's Head tavern!"

"You see, Will, though your mother doesn't credit it, most religions are like used car lots for the soul. Here the dealers—priests, vicars, rabbis, what have you—offer their best price on what you've got, provided you trade in your good sense, your free will, your obedience, and often all your money. Then you can drive away in their new model, which ultimately you hand in at the company headquarters. They check it over and if it's well kept, you're kitted out with something more luxurious that will last you for eternity! If you've thrashed it, then it's the scrap heap for you!"

"Listen to him and his lies! Your father is like the fella in the story, walking past the graveyard at night and shiting himself with fear. 'God is good!' he says out loud and feels better. A wee bit further on, an owl hoots and he is shiting it again, so he cries out, 'God is good!' Again he feels easier. Then he thinks to himself, what if the Devil is lurking around and hears me saying this? He might not be too pleased and he'll jump out and get me. So next time, he shouts, 'God is good, God is good—and the Devil ain't such a bad fella when you get to know him!'"

"I'm telling you this, wife. For all these buggers extolling the virtues of the next life, I've never found one in too much of a hurry to get there!"

"Goway, with you! What does it say in the Bible? 'Man who is born of woman has but a short time to live and is full of woe!'"

"Which I take to mean, Monica, Man has but a short time to live and is a miserable bastard!" Dad crosses himself in mock parody of the Catholic blessing. "Spectacles, testicles, wallet, and watch!"

"Reg, I'm warning you!"

He takes no heed other than to bless my mother with the sign of the cross.

"Ashes to ashes, lust to dust. If God don't take ye, the Devil must!"

"Reg, you're going too far!"

Between the solid rock of my mother's devout Catholic beliefs and the whirlpool of my father's paganism, I steer an erratic course. I'm put in mind of the child Taliesin tossed in his fragile Celtic coracle betwixt Scylla and Charybdis.

It is only then I realize that the Druidical circle of eternity encompassing the Christian crucifix gives us the Celtic cross. This fusion is something that both my parents can live with.

Despite my father's dislike of the church corporate, he does give the Welsh Protestant chapels the credit for preserving the ancient Cymric language. Without their insistence on using the Welsh Bible and singing hymns in the old tongue, it can be argued that English alone would be the dominant language nowadays. It would indeed be a tragic day when the Welsh phrase "Dim Saesneg" (I have no English) is heard for the last time in the hills of wild Wales, the land of my fathers.

> *Their Lord they shall praise,*
> *Their language they shall keep,*
> *Their land they shall lose*
> *Except wild Wales.*
> Taliesin, *Destiny of the Britons* (sixth-century)

Great-uncle George lives several years past his hundredth birthday. He dies peacefully and now sleeps in the ancient graveyard at Presteigne beneath a tall yew tree that will draw plenty of nourishment from his bones. Uncle George would like that.

→ Chapter 13 ←

A NARROW, DARK, TREE-SHROUDED LANE LEADS FROM THE main road half a mile to the rear environs of Wootton Hall. Known as Spook's Path, this eerie service way is surrounded entirely by evergreen laurels, firs, and holly bushes. Its purpose was to obscure the everyday traffic of servants, laborers, and lowly-born from the delicate sensibilities of the Georgian upper crust. Summer or winter, the peasants were well hidden from the nobility promenading the broad main drive just a mere hundred feet away. The lane terminates at the graveyard of the old Saxon church in a thicket of ancient yew trees. Dad is looking for a likely tree branch to cut and form into a longbow. He tells me the tale.

"These trees are only found in medieval graveyards on account of their poisonous qualities when eaten by livestock. In the Middle Ages there were few walled enclosures. Beasts grazed where they liked, with the exception of walled burial grounds, where the intrusion of animals would be considered profane. Here the yews could grow in safety. The yew was one of the most important commodities in the economy of the warring Normans because it yielded the springy wood for the English longbow."

He goes on to tell me that this artifice of war was the most feared instrument of battle known in its day. A master archer could fire off three cloth-yard shafts before the first one hit its target, and this rapid-fire technique proved devastating to the French armies on more than one occasion during the Hundred Years War in the fourteenth century.

Dad continues: "These soldiers were so feared by the French that when they captured an archer they would cut off the plucking fingers of his bow-drawing hand. Without the means to fire an arrow, he was then sent home as a pensionable drain on the English crown's war chest. By medieval law the practice of archery each Sunday in Britain was compulsory. This formed a huge pool of likely recruits to fill the ranks, where they would wave their two intact fingers in the air in defiance of the enemy. This gave rise to the popular 'Up yours!' gesture, the one-fingered version of which our American cousins refer to as 'flipping the bird.' The old law is still on the statute books, but the practice of Sunday archery eventually evolved into the game of darts, which you play inside the tavern, not out in the pissing rain."

It takes Dad many weeks to manufacture the six-foot yew longbow, fashioned as per the descriptions in the old tales. Furthermore, he creates three cloth-yard arrows tipped with .303 rifle bullet ends. On a crisp Sunday morning, we test the bow and arrows in the safety of the wilderness.

Dad stands, legs spread apart for balance, one behind the other, with his shirt sleeves rolled up the elbows. He draws the bowstring back to the side of his mouth. There is a strange creaking sound akin to fingernails on a blackboard. Writhing muscles in my fathers forearm rise and twitch like electric sausages. His face contorts in a vile grin of effort, falling flaccid the instant the bow discharges and the arrow, with a screech of freedom, streaks away, thwacking straight through the walls of the old tar-paper pumping shed a hundred yards away.

"By Jove, that felt good! Do you want a shot, Will?"

He hands me the curve of tensioned yew and the keenly fletched arrow. I place the nock into the bowstring and draw back with all of my strength. To my chagrin, the bow hardly bends and I realize that the force required to pull the bow is far in excess of that keeping my sphincter in closed condition. On the verge of digestive disaster, I hand the weapon back to Dad with a half-apologetic smile.

"Och, no dishonor there, lad. It was all I could do to pull it myself. She's a tough one and no mistake!"

He shoots a second arrow up into the sky to test distance. It becomes a black dot that falls way out over the heron lake, where it disappears and is never found. I have visions of someone wearing it through their skull.

On the third firing the bowstring breaks.

"Oh, bugger! That was the strongest string the man in the shop had.

I think I'll have to trim some face wood off of the curve to ease the tension and make it more pliable."

That put an end to our archery caper, but it was fun while it lasted—even if I did nearly pooky my breeks. Dad is pleased with the experiment and sings an old ditty as we make our way home through the woods:

> *Here's to the bow,*
> *The bow was made in England,*
> *Of yew wood, of true wood,*
> *The wood of English bows.*

Directly over the road from the churchyard and down a little lane lies Finch's Fields. This is an undulating area of mysterious mounds, hillocks, and tumps. It has a quaint archaic feeling about it. A small tributary of the river Alne snakes through the rough green rises and its sandy banks are home to iridescent blue kingfishers, who build their tunneled nests in the soft earthen cliffs.

Fatty Roger and myself are convinced that one of these mounds contains a Viking longboat burial like the one discovered at Sutton Hoo, Suffolk, in 1939. This was thought to be the grave of King Raedwald of the East Angles, who died around A.D. 625.

We try unsuccessfully to excavate our mound; first into the top of it, then into the side, all to no avail. Alas, we know little about the sheer mass of impacted soil that required moving even to go down through one century in archaeological time line.

Though thwarted in our attempt, we still cling to the belief that there's something down there. And albeit this area is as far from the sea as you can get in Britain, we are sure it is a ship.

Summer comes and with it a posse of people in anoraks who divide up the field with wooden posts and lines of string. My father shows me a piece in the local paper. It reads: "Saxon burial ground discovered at Wootton Wawen!" There is no ship find, of course, but we have been vindicated in our conviction that this is indeed a tumulus. Roger and I go down to the dig and tell the attendant archaeologist that we have always known it was a burial site.

"Oh, yeah. Even the fool is wise after the event. What are you, psychics?"

"No, it's true! You can see where we tried to dig down over there!"

"Well, you could get into a lot of trouble, digging up archaeological sites without a permit. Now, bugger off! I've got work to do!"

"How did we know then, mister? A sixth sense maybe?"

"Listen, kids, that's a load of bollocks!"

"I don't care what you use to keep your ears apart, bollock brain!"

We run away giggling, but we were right! Perhaps we had absorbed some kind of feeling from the place. Maybe the knowledge was still in folk memory and we'd unwittingly picked up word of it from some idle overheard conversation or perhaps it was a lucky guess. I don't know. I ask my dad.

"You have a good point there, Will. I once heard author Laurie Lee talk about a tumulus near the village of Leonard Stanley in Gloucestershire. I think it was called Hetty Pegler's Tump. Lee asked his mother what it was and she told him, 'Oh, that's where the young prince is buried'. And sure enough, eventual archaeological investigation revealed the Bronze Age burial of a young warrior, who by his dress and grave goods must have been a nobleman or princeling some two thousand years before Christ. Yet that folk knowledge was handed down through some hundred and thirty-three generations, unmarred by time. A remarkable feat, indeed!"

"You're not kidding! But that university bloke down at the dig said we were talking bollocks, so he did!"

"Pay no heed to them geezers. You can have more degrees than a thermometer and still be as thick as shit! Mark my words."

Sitting at the kitchen table in the twilight of an amber setting sun, I study a Ordnance Survey map of the local area. Suddenly I realize that four of the ancient forts marked are in a dead straight line with each other.

"Hey, Dad, look at this! These old earthwork sites all line up! It's amazing!"

"Ah, ha! You've found a ley line! Just like Alfred Watkins, who wrote 'The Old Straight Track.' That's all about ley lines. You should read it!"

"Do we have that book, Dad?"

"No, we don't, but your granddad Jim had a copy. Maybe the library in Stratford might let you have one, if you lie about where you live."

"What are they, these ley lines?"

"Well, they seem to be ancient ways connecting significant points of the landscape—like standing stones, forts, tumuli, crossroads, and often churches that are built on old pagan sites like the one in Bleddfa."

"Oh, so people walked along from one landmark to another. But what are they looking for?"

"The folk years ago, for instance, had to travel to get salt, you know? It is a number one necessity and many people were paid in salt because it was so valuable. Hence the old terms 'To be worth your salt' or to 'Draw your salary.' Many of these ley lines terminate at a place called White Hill or Salt Hill because that's where the salt fairs are held at certain times of the Celtic year. Town names that end in *wich* are old salt sites, like Nantwich, Ipswich, Sandwich, and the like."

"Droitwich?"

"Yeah, that's the idea."

"So who was this Alfred Watkins? Was he a relative of some sorts? I've never heard tell of him before."

"Aye, he was a distant relation on your aunt Winnie's side, down in Hereford. A lovely part of the world. Great cider, the best! *Hhmm!*" Dad savors the thought before continuing. "They were the brewing side of the family and d'you know, the soldiers, on the eve of the Battle of Crécy in 1346, sang a fine old bawdy song called 'Watkins Ale'? Oh, yes! Watkins were the boys for making beer, all right. They had a brewery in Dublin, too, making stout! They sold it to Guinness in 1913, but it was destroyed by British shelling in the Easter Rising three years later."

"Aunt Winnie was in the last war, wasn't she?

"Yes, she was a wireless operator with the Special Operations Executive, very hush-hush. Both she and her partner trained together so that they would always recognize the unique style of each other's Morse code."

"Why did they do that, then?" I try to get the creases of my map to fold in the right order.

"Well, this was very important, as one would be in Britain and the other parachuted behind enemy lines into occupied France working with the French resistance. If the operator and her code book were captured, the Germans might begin sending false information. The London-based operator could tell by the sound, or fist, as they call it, that the transmission was fraudulent. Every transmission had to contain a deliberate mistake, a Morse letter sent wrong, or the like. The Germans always tried to send perfectly. So if the fault wasn't there, the operators knew it was a fake transmission and sent back false information."

"I'd love to be a wireless operator and send Morse code like Auntie Winnie. She must have been very brave, don't you think?"

"She was and received a medal for it. What she was most proud of was being on Hitler's death list—here, give me that!" Dad takes my unruly map and folds it up like an expert.

"If you want to learn Morse code I can teach you myself. I did it in the army."

Fatty Roger and myself bike over to as many old forts and earth-works as we can find in the vicinity. Most are Celtic Iron Age hilltop forts from the period just before the Roman invasion. And sure enough, you can see the other forts way off in the distance in line of sight, some clear into Wales. At night, signal fires on these hilltops would be visible for miles, and, as a result, many such sites bear the name Beacon Hill.

I do my school project on local history.

> The castle mound at Beaudesert, in Henley-in-Arden, was hand built by the slave-labour of the Saxons, who had lost at the battle of Hastings in 1066. They were forced to erect a mote and bailey fortress for the famous Norman knight, Sir Simon de Montfort. He was very powerful and became the Earl of Leicester and leader of the Baron's parliament in London. All was well until he fell out with King Henry III whose ambitious son, Edward the first, killed him at the battle of Evesham in 1265. The Saxon word for slave-labour is graft and this word is still in common use today meaning, hard work.
>
> After the Norman invasion and the subjugation of

the Anglo-Saxons, two classes of English people emerge: the upper class; Barons, Earls, Knights, Lords and other gentry, and the peasant class; the once mighty Saxons now reduced to feudal bondage. The beasts of the field have Saxon names like; cows, sheep and pigs, but when killed and cooked for the table, become the Norman-French; beef, mutton and pork. The lesson is simple; the peasant class raise the animals, for the ruling class to eat.

Miss Hathaway loves my history project, but Mrs. Mack says that it sounds like *The Communist Manifesto*. I tell Dad this and he laughs his head off and says, "Good lad yourself!"

People were forever telling us to "Know your place!" and not to "Get above your station!" If you attempt to improve yourself in any way, you're told, "Don't ape your betters!" No doubt, this is a legacy of the bloody Magna Carta.

I hate to see old men doffing their caps when spoken to by one of the bigwigs.

My father treats the nobility with the same contempt as he does the royals and the clergy. "Nothing but a bunch of oxygen thieves and space wasters!"

One exception to Dad's "aristocrats to the guillotine" philosophy is old Lady Lucy. We first meet her when Dad gets a part-time job delivering soda pop to the outlying areas around Stratford-upon-Avon. I go along for the ride and it is a great way to see the lush green countryside. Miss Lucy lives in a massive ancient hall at Hampton Lucy and is a direct descendant of the Baron de Lucy, who came over from Normandy with William the Conqueror in 1066.

She has a beer ready for my dad and likes to chat with him. I think she admires his bluntness and total disregard for formality. I like to go to the hall with its wondrous expanse of gardens and wood-paneled rooms full of suits of armor. The kindly old lady tells me that she is the last of her line and when she dies the Lucy family name will die with her. She offers to adopt me and put the fear of beJasus into me.

Driving back home again in the old pickup truck, we pass through miles of orchards, their trees weighed down with apples. Dad begins reflecting on the many hundreds of apple varieties that have been lost since the Second World War with the shift to corporate farming policy.

"Potatoes, too. There were over four thousand species of the humble spud worldwide. Now some countries have whittled it down to a mere four or five kinds. I can remember one type of Scottish tattie called a Forfar, which was bright blue on the outside and a creamy yellow on the interior."

"It sounds a bit yucky to me! Blue and yellow mashed tatties? Ugh!"

"Naw lad, they were delicious! The same genetic destruction has happened to hops. Each town and village had its own brewery, you know? Likewise, its unique supply of hops. So as a result, each area of the country had a local type of beer, most likely differing from its near neighbors in texture, color, and taste. Marvelous it was! Both the local water supply and the indigenous ingredients would produce a singular brew that would be common to that region alone. And as the French wisely say, 'Vive la Différence!' " This last retort he shouts out of the window at a puzzled farmer as the ancient Bedford lorry hurtles through the Warwickshire countryside and disappears up a leafy lane.

The trip home is interrupted by a stop at the Dun Cow Inn just off the Stratford road near Wilmcote, a village of black-and-white half-timbered Tudor houses with elegant thatched roofs and tiny diamond-shaped, lead glass windows. This once was the home of the redoubtable Shakespeare, hence the name William's cote or William's hamlet.

The pub itself is contemporary with the Bard and was much frequented by him from all accounts. Near to the fireplace, a shallow depression has been worn in the ancient flagstone floor by the iron rings used in the game of quoits, a game rather like horseshoes. It's easy to imagine young Willie having a throw of quoits with his pals after a hard day of knocking out *Henry V,* part I, or *A Midsummer Night's Dream* and then wandering off to court my teacher's ancestor with his quill pen stuck nonchalantly behind his ear.

"No maiden has stole my heart, yet Anne Hath-a-way!" Dad mocks as he climbs into the cab and begins singing in a rich baritone:

> *Shakespeare was a very merry wit*
> *And on his shirt tail was some sh* . . . tea leaves

One day whilst walking by St. Paul's
A young girl grabbed him by his ba . . . shirt
Says he, "Young maid, you have a lot of pluck
Let's go round the back and have a fu . . . cup of tea."
This he did, then does a bunk
And leaves the young girl all covered in sp . . . tea leaves.

The green sunken lanes meander between soaring hedgerows studded with the lofty elm trees that almost obscure the sky. It's like driving through a leafy green tunnel.

"The old boreen. That's what your mam always says whenever we drive down one of these lanes."

"Talking of Mam, when are we going home?"

"Hang on, I think we're lost. Where in the name of the wee man are we?" Dad peers out of the cab of the battered lorry. The radiator hisses and sweats at the anonymous crossroads.

"I saw a sign back there, Dad, but it was overgrown with ivy and I couldn't read it."

"Yeah, I saw that too. We must be near Wellesbourn or somewhere round there—I have an idea!" He jumps down from the cab and puts his coat on inside out. He proceeds to walk three times clockwise around the truck, then jumps back in and speeds off down the left turn of the crossroads. Hardly two minutes pass when we break free from our prison of foliage onto the main road hard by Stratford horseracing track.

"What was all that about?" I ask as we pulled into the depot.

"The bloody fairies were leading us astray, Will! So I put my coat on inside out and by running sunwise around the truck, confused them so that they would leave us alone—and it worked!"

"What took you so long today, Reg?" the foreman asks, anxious to lock up the pop warehouse.

"We were away with the fairies, weren't we, Will?"

From the old Victorian railway station we take the train for our eight-mile trip to Wootton Wawen. I can see the horses limbering up for a run of some sorts. I ask Dad what they might be doing.

"Maybe there's a steeplechase on this weekend and they're training for it."

"Oh! Aren't they the old races they used to have between one town and another, over all the hedgerows, walls, and all that?"

"Yes, that's right. They raced between one town's church steeple and another, but now it's run over the hedge jumps and water jumps on the local racecourse. Your nana in Ireland is the one to talk horse racing with. I only bet on the Grand National apart from that day when I found the pound and bet on Lucky Note. Your nana likes to have a flutter every week!" Dad disappears behind his *Stratford Herald* newspaper.

This much I know. I remember asking Nana once how her horse had done in the big race at Leopardstown one Christmas.

"Jasus, that cripple—Godforgivemeforswearing! He was so far down the field he never saw so many arseholes in his life! Godhelpus! Sure he stopped to shit and he's shitting still!" She has a neat way with words, just like Mam.

"Ha ha ha!" I chuckle out loud at the thought of Nana's luck at the gee-gees. This involuntary machination coincides with the acidic pronouncement of one of two gossiping ladies who share our carriage.

"Men! They know nothing about pain, they don't, no! They have it easy, men do, yes! Yes! *Yes!* You may laugh, sir!" she intrudes, mistakenly aiming her remark at my innocent father. "You may laugh! But you have never endured the pain of childbirth, have you? Go on, admit it!"

"Very true," says Dad, folding his paper as the train pulls into Wootton station. "I have never experienced the pain of childbirth. However, you've never had to contend with a kick in the bollocks, have you, madam? Good day to you now!"

When we get back to the caravan Mam asks about our trip and I tell her about how we got lost and Dad doing the thing with his coat.

"Ah ha! An Seachdran na Si, the Fairy Straying. You were being fooled by the little people into getting yourselves lost. Jasus, it's a wonder they let you back! They could have kept hold of your father and turned him into an ogre. With an ugly puss like his, he'd be great for frightening the children at Halloween! Away with the fairies, eh? It used to happen a lot to my father when he drove the milk lorry for Cleaves's Creamery in Limerick—usually after a couple of glasses of the whiskey, so I hear!"

"Hey, Mam, while we were gone, Dad taught me a song"
"Oh, that's nice! Sing us a stave or two of it?"

> *Shakespeare was a very merry wit*
> *And on his shirt tail he had some sh—*

"Reg!"
Mam has her hand clamped tightly over my mouth.

❖ Chapter 14 ❖

A POLICEMAN IS STANDING AT THE CARAVAN DOOR.

"Can I speak to your dad?"

"Daaad?"

"Reg, your relief signal man has been killed in a line accident. Can you go in quick? There's no one on duty in the signal box."

"Oh, my God! The poor wee bugger. Yes, of course. I'll grab my coat." Dad looks at his pocketwatch. "Jasus! We'd better hurry. The Cornishman Express is due through in fifteen minutes and if the loop points aren't changed, she'll wreck!"

"Right, Reg, let's go. I can run you there in the squad car."

Bell trilling and blue lights flashing, the Wolsley six-eighty police car disappears up the track in a pall of cinder dust. Heart in my mouth, I count the minutes until, from a distance of two miles, I hear the Cornishman's steam whistle scream through Wootton Wawen station unscathed. Dad had saved the day and unbeknownst to driver and passengers alike, the West Country Express darts safely across the Midland plains to the high moors of Devon.

Dad has to work double shifts until a replacement can be found for the young chap who had been killed by the train.

"I'm on all over Christmas and New Year, too. You and Willie might as well go to Ireland, as I won't be seeing much of you."

"OK, we will, if you can get free passes in time."

"That won't be a problem with me getting the company out of a hole."

Later that week, I wave to my dad as the train passes the signal box. Dad waves back and pulls a daft face.

At Liverpool docks the wind is blowing sleet sideways into our faces. The sailing timetable carries the message "Morning sailing canceled due to bad weather." We have eight hours to kill before the night boat sails.

The wind is at our backs as we walk up Water Street, trying to find a decent restaurant to get breakfast. We stop at a neat little corner café called the Khardoma.

Mam watches the office girls shuffling through the rainy streets on their way to work. They are all dressed in the same drab way.

"Just look at us! We need a bloody good shake-up! The war has been over for fifteen years and you'd hardly know it. The fashions are almost unchanged since the nineteen thirties. This country needs a good fong up the arse to get it going, a bit of vigor, a bit of zest!"

We spend a few hours in the news theater watching *Casper the Friendly Ghost* and *Bugs Bunny*. Pathé News is showing the pictures of Mr. Kennedy, who is to become president of the United States in January. We eat ice cream and snooze in the dark cinema. The program repeats and we leave to take a wander around T. J. Hughes's department store.

"Do you want to see Father Christmas, Willie?"

"No, I don't. That's just for wee kids, Mam—I'm nearly eleven!"

"Oh, my, we are grown up. That Kennedy's a handsome bloke, isn't he? I could go for him m'self!"

"D'you know the priest came to our school and told us that right until the last minute it was neck and neck between Kennedy and the shifty-looking fella with the long face, and it was only our prayers that made the difference and that's how he won!"

"Maybe Father was right?"

"Well, I told Dad and he said the priest was full of shit!"

"Jesus! Willie, there's no need for language like that. Never mind what that pagan of a father says to you."

"What, the holy father?"

"No, the unholy one!"

We walk back downhill toward the docks, the wind hard against us. An icy squall slashes sleet in our eyes and we take shelter in a warehouse doorway while it blows through. Mam reads the event poster pasted to the door:

The Cavern Club Presents
THE SILVER BEATLES

"Jasus, fancy calling a pop group an ugly thing like that. Silver-beetles—makes them sound like a bunch of cockroaches! Jeeezus, creepy crawly things! They should change their name to something a wee bit nicer."

Somewhere out in the Toxteth area of Liverpool, John, Paul, George, and Ringo heed similar advice and a legend is born.

We sail out of the Mersey estuary into a fierce gale. Mam is taken bad and I get her some Lucozade to sip. It is very rough and the ship pitches and rolls. I doze off and am awakened by the ship's hooter. Alarm bells are ringing and crew members are hurrying on deck from all quarters.

"What's happening? Are we sinking?"

"You lie there and I'll find out, Mam."

I run on deck. Searchlights clip the waves in wide arcs about us. A lifeboat is being lowered, and I am scared for Mam, who's feeling so ill.

"Are we going down?"

"No, son, but some other poor bugger is!"

Officers are shouting from the bridge. "Clear the boats! Clear the boats!"

The door of the radio room is open. I peep in.

"Mayday relay! Mayday relay! Mayday relay! Steam ship *Irish Prince* sinking eight nautical miles west south west of the Skerries Light! All vessels please assist!"

The wireless man is talking into a microphone.

"Mayday relay! Mayday relay! This is the MV *Leinster*. We are at the scene and holding station. Boats are away for survivors. MV *Leinster* listening out."

The great ship is turning off the wind to keep the stricken vessel in her lee. I see red, green, and white lights flickering out in the heaving black swell. Ships of all shapes and sizes form a huge circle scanning the waves with their lee lights.

There are men in the water. Our boats are pulling them onboard. A full lifeboat returns to the ship, and figures, more dead than alive, are helped onto the deck, where they lie like drowned rats. Passengers and crew members get blankets around the shoulders of the survivors and help them in out of the wind. I bring cups of warm cocoa from the galley and give it to the steward who tends to the bedraggled men. I get hot coffee for the crew and another glucose drink for my ailing mother. When I get back to Mam's seat, she is being comforted by a dapper-looking chap with a transatlantic accent. I take him for a priest and go back on deck.

A gray dawn reveals the scene of the disaster. The sea is empty now except for a long slick of oil and some bobbing clumps of flotsam. The *Irish Prince* has gone down.

One by one the rescue ships break station, leaving the cold sea to digest its prey.

Mam and I spend the next day in Dublin. She says that she can't face the long train journey just yet, so we get a chance to explore. O'Connell Street is very wide and teeming with bicycles, green buses, horse-drawn carts of every size and cargo, and a few private motorcars. In the middle of the street, a policeman stands in a black-and-white pagoda, directing the milling traffic by means of a whistle, a nightstick, and a string of verbal abuse that would shame the demons of hell. The sidewalks, broad as they are, cannot contain the press of people surging through the capital city. At each street corner and intersection, human waves of fleet-footed pedestrians break over the vehicular traffic, bringing all motorized movement to a horn-honking halt. Henry Street and Moore Street are awash with shoppers threading their way through wheelbarrow stalls of open-air markets that haven't changed much since the days when Molly Malone sold her "cockles and mussels, alive alive-o." Here the din of car horns gives way to the clatter of horse hooves and the strident cries of street traders roaring from their market carts.

"Luvelly payers, tuppence a pownd! Appuls, payers, banawnas, pick yer own fer a shillin' a bag!" The costermonger's cry gives way to the greengrocer's chant from the next stall along . . .

"Padayshaws, tomayshaws, ingons an' leeks, get yer veggies here now, missus! Grand green cabbawges, finer never grew, cawleyflowers, carrots, an' kale, get yer King Edwards, luvelly spuds, great fer chippin', sixpence a pownd!"

Tinker kids and other street urchins dive under the cart wheels to retrieve fallen vegetables and discarded bruised fruit. These they share with the tired-looking donkeys and cart horses tethered down the side streets awaiting the long pull home.

Two hundred and twelve feet above the hubbub, Admiral Lord Nelson's one good eye surveys the chaotic scene from his lofty stone column. His statue, identical to the one in London, marks the last remnant of the British occupation of Ireland.

Mam buys a punnet of fresh strawberries and we make our way back up to the main street to the bullet-scarred general post office building in the city center.

"This is where Patrick Pearse read the Proclamation of Independence in 1916."

"They shot him, didn't they?"

"They did—BloodyEnglish!"

Mam describes the Rising of 1916, when fifteen hundred poorly armed men and women rose in revolt against the might of the British Empire.

"The GPO was the first building the rebels seized. They made it their headquarters. The rest of the Irish Volunteers and Citizen Army were scattered in little units all around Dublin. They fought all week until the British shelled every building in the city and the GPO was burning around their ears. Then Pearse and James Connolly surrendered to save further loss of life."

"What happened then?"

"The British took them to Kilmainham jail and shot them for treason." She recites:

> The beauty of this world hath made me sad
> This beauty that will pass
> Sometimes my heart hath shaken with great joy
> To see a leaping squirrel in a tree
> Or a red ladybird upon a stalk

Or little rabbits in a field at evening
Lit by a slanting sun.

"That's a beautiful poem, Mam. Whose is it?"

"They are the last lines of Patrick Pearse, written on the eve of his execution."

"Oh, what a shame."

Mam sees my sad face and makes to cheer me up. At the Rainbow Café she buys me some pop called 7-Up. I've never heard of it before and when it comes, there is a large scoop of vanilla ice cream floating in it, which is very strange, but nice. Over the foaming glass I quiz my mother.

"Why did the rebels take over the post office? Surely the castle would be a better headquarters?"

"Well, the rebels tried to capture the castle, but were beaten back by the British. The GPO was a very important target, with its telephones and telegraph. It was the crossroads of communication for the whole country. In the olden days, people out in the country would stand at the crossroads for hours, waiting for travelers to come along with word of what was happening elsewhere. Since the roads went north, east, west, and south, the information they picked up was called 'news.' I bet you didn't know that, did you, Willie?" I have to admit that I didn't, but my father's oft-used call of "Encyclopedia Bullshitus Hibernicus" echoes in the back of my mind.

Leaving the café, we head west from O'Connell Bridge into a setting sun. Under an orange sky, streaked with mackerel clouds, we stroll down Bachelor's Walk and along the length of Ormond Quay. Brewery tugs pull barges stacked high with wooden barrels of Guinness under the gray wrought iron arch of the ha'penny bridge and down to the docks beyond. Bathed in the honey-hued gloaming of an Irish sunset, the great green dome of the shrapnel-pocked Four Courts shimmers up from the surface of the turgid, dark waters of the rolling river Liffey. Our walk up to Kingsbridge rail terminus is pleasant and unhurried. The train doesn't leave until six-thirty and the Angelus bell has still not called the faithful to six o'clock prayer.

At the newspaper kiosk in the railway station, an *Irish Independent* banner headline proclaims: "President Kennedy to Visit Ireland." Mam nudges me.

"Lookit! The first Christian president of the United States of America and he's coming home to the Ould Sod. Isn't that grand?"

"How is he the first Christian? I thought the others were Christians, too."

"Hmm! They were all Protestants! Nothing but pagans, so they were, except Abraham Lincoln. I think he might have been a Jew, with the beard and the big hat an' all."

"Could my dad be president of the USA? He's a pagan and you call him an old sod?"

"That's different. Yer dad can't be president because he's not an American, and anyway, he's going bald and the Yanks like their leaders to have a fine head of hair!"

"Eisenhower doesn't have much hair."

"That's his military haircut. Anyway, he was a soldier and wore a peaked cap."

"My dad has a peaked cap."

"HolyJasusWillie! Would ye ever stop yer nonsense? Ye'll have me worn out. Come on, there's our train." We board and lo and behold—

"Hello, Monica! How are you feeling? Good. This must be Liam. We never got a chance to say hi, with you helping out with the rescue an' all."

It's the American bloke from the boat and he's no priest! He hangs on my mother like an old coat. This makes me jealous and I keep mentioning my dad. Eventually the interloper feels obliged to say something.

"You're very proud of your dad, ain't you, young fella?"

"Yes, I am, and if he wasn't a bald, godless pagan, he could be your next president!"

The Limerick Express speeds into the evening shadows spreading stealthily across the Curragh of Kildare. My mother is flattered by the attentions of the American gentleman and as it's his first trip to Ireland, she fills him in on odd bits of history, mostly from her own "Irish Encyclopedia." He asks us if we want a drink, as the buffet car is now open. Mam says she would like a gin and tonic, and I ask for a Canada Dry with ice. Whether the man misheard me, or the order is placed wrong, I don't know. He brings me back a double Canadian rye whiskey on the rocks. I duly drink it down, and by the time we get to Limerick Junction, I'm half langers.

Mam's friend changes trains here and says good-bye. I give a half-hearted wave out of the window.

"Oh, Willie! Stop being a prat. I wasn't flirting with him. We were just passing the time of day. Mind you, he was a handsome bloke and he must have plenty of money. He said he was in oil!"

"What was he, a bloody sardine?"

"Willie!"

I sleep for a long while at Nana's house. When I rise on the second day, my family are all there just as before. Nana, Seán, and Frances look as I remember, but the room has somehow shrunk. The kitchen light switch is at eye level and my green spindle-backed chair looks too tiny to have ever flown me through the First World War. In the garden shed, my *Captain Biggles* comic lies on the bench, tattered and yellowed by time. I feel a lump in my throat.

Across the road, the Shannon still courses its boiling flood, and the seagulls spin above me watching my every hand movement to see if I have scraps for them. I do have a lump in my throat and it's sore, too. Inside the house I stare at the little gray gas meter, whilst Mam flattens my tongue with a lollipop stick and pronounces, "Your throat is swollen up. We'd better get the doctor."

I have the mumps.

"Live horse and you'll get grass!" Mam sits on the end of my bed while I try to eat a bowl of strawberries and ice cream. The coldness feels great on my throat and helps ease the throbbing pain. The smell of the Christmas dinner that is to be denied me wafts up the stairs. I nod off to sleep.

"Oh my sainted aunt! Will ye ever look at poor Willie?" Mam is holding up the bedclothes and with me lying there bollick naked, every-one is getting a look at my willie!

"Jasus! He's covered from head to foot with red blotches!" All my family have their own diagnosis.

"It's the scarlet fever!"

"'Tis the measles, so it is!"

"I've had the measles."

"It's the German measles!"

"I've had the German measles, too."

"It's the Irish measles, then!"

"Go'way with your measles! It's obvious—he's allergic to strawberries."

This is the first indication I'd had that strawberries are bad for me. Uncle Seán is right. When my mumps have gone away, I try some strawberries again and come up in spots within the hour.

Christmas passes without me. New Year comes and goes, but with Grandda gone there are no music sessions in the tiny kitchen. I find the end piece of his wooden flute in amongst the slabs of turf in the peat store.

"Where's the rest of it?"

"I dunno, probably burned."

Sadly I remember how lovingly Grandda looked after his blackthorn flute. How he would talk to it, and put it to bed wrapped in a red cloth, and pour Guinness into the barrel of it to sweeten the tone, and the fluttering flurries of soft notes falling gentle on the ear—jig, reel, slip-jig, and slide. Majestic march, noble air, mournful lament—all gone, gone forever.

I am ill for a long time and miss a fair bit of schooling, but eventually Mam pronounces me "as fit as a butcher's dog" and says it's time to go back to Wootton and see how Happy Harry is getting on without us. We have a last family outing to the Thomond Cinema to see *The Mask of Zorro,* and it's a great laugh as usual. People sit chewing on boiled pig's feet wrapped in newspaper and shout warnings and encouragement to the hero on the silver screen.

"Don't come in—he's behind the door!"

"Kick his head in!"

"Look out, Zorro—he's got a knife!"

"Shoot the buggers!"

And when the fighting is done and the masked marauder sweeps the girl into his arms, "Get awayoutadat, ya durty ould sod. Sure she's not old enough to leave her mother!"

Or alternatively, "Give her a tongue in the lung for me, Zorro!"

✦ Chapter 15 ✦

THE YEAR OF OUR LORD 1961 IS A GOLDEN YEAR BECAUSE, like 1001, 1111, 1691, and 1881, it reads the same upside down. It is a special year for me, too, as I have to take the eleven-plus examination. This compulsory exam decides your future at the absurdly early age of eleven, just when you're catching every bug and disease in the devil's armory. I've lost so much school that I have as much chance of doing well as a fart on a windy day.

Should I pass, I could go on to grammar school, college, and maybe even university, but if I fail, I'll have to go to secondary school until I'm fifteen and eligible for a dead-end job in some factory, or, if I'm lucky, an apprenticeship to a tradesman. Mam does a novena to St. Jude, he of lost causes, but he's still at enmity with me over finding the threepenny bits that time and cocks a deaf ear to Mother's pleas. Ah, but junior school can be boring anyway, and there are mighty things happening in the world.

Two important walls are built in this historic year: the first in Berlin, where President Kennedy, who only got elected because we prayed for him, will cry out in Cold War defiance, "Ich bin ein Berliner!" which to the crowds of puzzled Germans listening means, "I am a doughnut!" The second and more notable wall is built by my father and his pal, "Dustbin Tom," around the newly opened Sabrina Gardens annex of the trailer park.

This masterpiece of medieval engineering is two dustbins high and two hundred dustbins long. It contains twenty-five dustbins full of cement and countless dustbins full of rough field stone.

Like Laurel and Hardy before them, Dad and Dustbin Tom work on the tried and tested principle of "When I nod my head, you hit it!" It's a rare delight for us kids to watch the antics of these pair of eejits, clowning around in their Herculean labors for our amusement.

Dustbin Tom's only form of measurement is the dustbin. Even the scaffolding takes the form of two wooden planks laid across two galvanized metal dustbins. Unlike its more famous German predecessor, this wall is welcomed by all and stands as a great memorial to good old-fashioned shoddy workmanship and sacred measurement.

On a silvery moonlit night, not long after the completion of the mighty wall, I dress as Zorro in a mask and cape and for sheer devilment climb up to lie in hiding along the top of the dustbin wall.

My plan is to leap down and "Zorro" the first person to walk past by making a Z shape in the air with my car antenna rapier.

The problem is, nobody comes. I am just about to give up, when I hear hesitant footsteps coming down the path from the direction of the Country Club bar.

Perfect! An old drunk!

As the footfalls come right under my hiding place, I leap down, shrieking, "The mark of Zorro!" My rapier makes a Z in the air.

My unfortunate victim is not the reeling drunkard I was expecting, but the refinedly inebriated and elderly ex-actress, Mrs. Ayers. In her fright, she lets out a high warbling sound and, in a fit of the vapors, faints clean away! I take to my heels and don't stop until I get safely away and out of my Zorro garb.

The poor woman, on regaining her wits, is helped back to the bar, where she is plied with several double gin and tonics as she tells the incredulous customers that she has been attacked by "The Laughing Cavalier."

For the next few weeks I lie low as groups of vigilantes comb the night for prowlers, thieves, and footpads. My voluntary incarceration yields unsuspected benefits. Instead of roaming the caravan site looking for mischief, I spend the evenings working on household projects with my dad.

"This," says Dad, holding up a glass tube with three wires coming out of it, "is an EY51 EHT rectifier valve and it's buggered!" I am on all fours, staring into the back of an ancient television set.

"How do you know that's what's wrong with this thing, Dad?"

"Well, if this was all right, we would have a very high voltage on the tube anode—and we haven't, have we?"

We'd never had a TV of our own, but relied on Dad fixing one for a neighbor and us holding on to it for a few days to soak test it!

Later that day, Dad comes back from Stratford with a new tube, which we solder in, and the old TV set that I've dragged back from the rubbish tip bursts into life.

"A TV for three and six. That's a good price and no mistake!" Mam is pleased.

I find an old radio set at the rubbish dump and marvel at the pretty little multicolored bands on the resistors and the funny wee wax things called capacitors.

Dad comes in from the pub while I'm playing with it.

"Willie, what is a microfarad?"

"I don't know, Dad."

"Find out and tell me tomorrow."

I do and I'm able to tell him it is a unit of electrical capacitance. He is very pleased.

Dad, true to his word, builds a small one-tube practice oscillator from spare parts given up from the old radio and teaches me to send and receive Morse code.

I take on a fierce bent for anything scientific. Mam presents me with a belated Christmas present, a small microscope. I have great fun studying leaves, crystals, fleas, and the like.

Dad's Christmas bonus helps buy a power × 45 refracting telescope. With the aid of this beautiful instrument, I am at last able to transport myself way past this solar system and into the galaxies beyond. Nebulae, star clusters, planets, and lunar craters all become familiar as I spend night after night out in the frosty darkness seeking the rings of Saturn or Jupiter's moons.

My parents now have me looking into two cosmos at once, the macro and the micro, each as fascinating as the other and strangely similar in design.

In the daytime I turn the kitchen of our little caravan into a makeshift laboratory, where I conduct experiments with my chemistry set. My father says it is like living with Doctor Frankenstein, but I think they enjoy having a son who seems interested in the whys and wherefores of the physical world.

He laughs and quotes Kipling:

> *I keep six honest serving men,*
> *They taught me all I knew.*
> *There names are What? and Why?*
> *And When? and Where? and How? And Who?*

If necessity is the mother of invention, then I'm its bastard child! What started out as a small toddler taking his tin toys to bits with a spoon has become a series of full-scale operations. The motorbike engines, TV chassis, gramophones, telephones, and car gearboxes all give up their secrets, as the mounting piles of junk outside our caravan will attest. I drive my poor mother to the edge of distraction.

"For God's sake, Willie, you've used up all the margarine getting that grease off your hands and you've wiped the mess on a clean towel."

"Sorry, Mam. I'll give you a hand!"

I try to help tidy up and accidentally spill potassium permanganate all over the kitchen table, turning the starched white tablecloth a brilliant purple. Meanwhile my experiment bubbling on the stove produces hydrogen sulfide, the bad egg gas, stinking the entire place out. In an attempt to clear the atmosphere, I plug in an electrical fan that I'd found in the rubbish dump. This blows the fuses and plunges the caravan into darkness.

"OUT! Out, ya demon! Out before you kill us all with yer nonsense!"

Nothing, however, is impossible to the mind of the alchemist as I transmute my intellect from its base form into sublimation. I once make an egg custard pudding disappear from the oven, but I'm not sure how I did that! Ah, the quintessence of it all 'twould get the rise out of a dead man. It is grand to be young!

With spring comes the urge to venture back out into world of wickedness that I had shunned throughout the long winter nights. The game was afoot.

Neil Allen would be just in his early teens when his dad gives him an old wrecked car to play about in. It is an Austin 7 and, though it can only boast of two gears, one of which is reverse, it is a lot of fun and we all get our first shot at driving.

Most of our weekend games are precipitated by what we see at the cinema or increasingly on the television. This week we have been exposed for the first time to the American gangster series *The Roaring Twenties*.

We had all seen Edward G. Robinson in *Little Caesar* and George Raft and Humphery Bogart doing their tough-guy stuff. My favorite is James Cagney. I love all his films! "I'm on top of the world, Ma!"

Parents' closets are raided for trilby hats or fedoras and anything resembling a zoot suit. Our little mob, who last weekend had been ridding the local trees of Japanese snipers after seeing John Wayne in *The Sands of Iwo Jima,* having been demobilized into civilian life have immediately taken to a career of crime.

We cut a bizarre picture dressed in our oversized suits with wide-brimmed hats that obscure our faces. We chew imaginary gum.

"Hiya, Mack, how ya doin'!"

"Aw, it's been tough. I'm getting rubbed up the wrong way by the Feds."

We adopted new names. There is Scarface, Bugsy, Lefty, Dutch, and Dillinger. I am Dillinger. Sasha Dutton doesn't want to play as the only hoodlum names left are Pretty-Boy Floyd and Baby-Face Nelson, both of which he thought soppy.

"I can't be a gangster with a poof's name!"

"Let me fix him, Boss! I'll mess him up good! He won't need a name!!"

"Nah, nah, Lefty! We'll get some udder shmuck ta do da doity woik. Maybe we'll tell the mob on the east side that he's a stool pigeon for the cops!"

"Ah, come on, guys, I only want a proper gangster name!"

"OK, you can be . . . Hitler!"

"Hitler wasn't a bloody gangster!"

"Well, he was a bad guy anyway! So do you want to play or not?"

"OK, Hitler it is. Anything's better than Baby-Face!"

History turns on its head as Adolf Hitler becomes the latest member of the Chicago mobsters underworld.

We next check our stock of shooters. I have my trusty .22 rifle loaded with blanks, Neil has brought a .410 single and a 12-gauge double-barreled shotgun with six dressed cartridges each, "Dutch" Dutton has his Webley air pistol, and "Lefty" is carrying a wartime souvenir German Luger that mercifully has no ammunition for it.

After the incident in the woods, some time ago, we had stopped using live rounds when playing about with guns. Shotgun shells are rendered almost harmless by "dressing" open the ends and removing the lead shot, but you can still get a sting from the wadding.

We don't want to hurt anyone, though. Our sole object is to look mean and make a lot of noise, and this, like the little hoodlums we are, we achieve!

The ancient prewar automobile is a total heap and has no exhaust pipe. Its one remaining headlamp is permanently on and the under-inflation of its bald tires gives it the appearance that it waddles along rather than glides. We are supposed to drive it only in the fields or on the back roads of the trailer park, but it runs better on the paved roads and temptation is readily succumbed to by our fearless mob of outlaws.

After tearing around at fifteen miles an hour with the engine screaming for release, the radiator boils over and we are obliged to stop for a while to let it cool down.

It is then that we hear the church bells.

"Hey, O'Donnell! What's going on over at the chapel?"

"Oh, that's a wedding! They asked me to be an altar boy. I told them to stick it."

"Yeah, they asked me, too! But we're too tough to be altar boys, eh, lads?"

"Yeaah!" We spit on the ground and suck on pieces of fennel stalk like they're cigarettes.

There are times in one's life when some inner demon takes complete control of the good sensibilities of the human condition. This is to be one such occasion.

The radiator has stopped hissing, and at last we speed off on our lurching way, down Spook's Path to the old church.

The wedding party is just out of the service and is lining up between the front of the church and a large tripod camera. Here they are going to record their day to remember.

Birds sing in the yew trees, and the sun pours down on the happy couple.

"Watch the birdie!" says the photographer, as he vanishes in under his black-cloaked box camera.

The rows of teeth frozen in cheesy smiles melt into looks of astonishment as a battered car full of 1920s gangsters flies round the corner and screeches to a halt, blocking the church drive and sending a black cloud of rooks squawking from the yew trees above.

"YOU BIN ASKING FOR DIS, YOU DURTY RATS!!!"

A sustained volley of deafening gunshots rings out over the quiet serenity of the Warwickshire countryside.

To our absolute joy the entire wedding party is routed at the first broadside.

In their haste to gain the sanctuary of the moss green gravestones, members of the wedding leave top hats, high-heeled shoes, flowers, wedding gifts, and invitations scattered like confetti all over the green church lawn.

"That guy there's a G-man—let him have it, boys!"

All guns turn on the verger. We blast a parting salvo in the direction of the cowardly Timmins, who throws up his arms as if he's been hit. He drops behind an old ivy-covered tomb, whilst his pebble-like glasses curve a glinting arc in the dappled light.

"Call the police!! Someone call the police!"

"Let's get the hell out of here!"

We jerk the car around in a wide circle, decimating Timmins's bicycle in the process, and blaze off in the same direction from which we have come.

This is to be my last hurrah! We have been a nuisance far too long and what little sympathy we have amongst the site dwellers after the Grumpy episode has long since dissipated. It is decided, by the powers that be, that the time has come to bell the cat!

The village policeman, Copper Smith, rounds us up. We are disarmed and told if ever we are caught with weapons again, we will all be sent to the local Borstal prison institution for young offenders. To the great satisfaction of the wedding guests, we are lined up in the hall car park and publicly flogged. It is a barbaric but bloody effective punishment, and we vow to keep our noses clean, for a wee while anyway!

Neil, being the oldest and the ringleader, gets the worst of it and we don't see him for the rest of the summer. Poor "Hitler," even though he took no part in the actual shooting, got a licking just for being along for the ride.

"If this had gone to court, it would have been very bad for you idiots. Having a serious incident on your record at your age is no good thing, especially when it concerns firearms!" The cops get into their car and leave. Maybe Dad has picked up on his long-outstanding favor from the police, I don't know.

I inch my way painfully out of the car park, the red weals of the cane cut like the furrows of a horse-plowed field across the horizon of my arse. Paul catches up with me, mournfully holding his backside.

"God's teeth, that was a rough old paggering!"

"Too damn right, but what was worse was seeing that wee shite Timmins gloating! He blooming well fainted with fright back at the church!"

"Yeah, I saw him smirking all over his kisser. Mind you, he's probably not seen his bicycle yet!" I almost laugh.

There is an age-old saying, "If things don't alter, they'll remain as they are." The first news comes in the post. I have failed my eleven-plus with flying colors, mostly because of my inability to grasp the mathematics of the vegetable kingdom. The second and more surprising announcement comes from Mrs. MacArthur.

"Our school will close this summer and will not reopen. You will all be transferred to a nice modern Catholic school in Henley-in-Arden that is being newly built—all except you eleven-year-olds, who will be going on to a high school or a grammar school, depending on your exam results. It has been a pleasure teaching you all. Good luck, everyone, and God bless you!"

That is it. Later in the summer, just before the holidays, Mr. Bury presides over the destruction of the school's property. It is every child's dream to burn his or her school's contents. Now we were doing it under the supervision of the staff. Out-of-date books, out-of-fashion teaching papers, and out-of-the-Ark blackboard easels feed the conflagration as the enormous bonfire in the playground consumes all that has been so familiar to us. There is kind of a carnival atmosphere and everyone is very elated. I feel odd, seemingly heavy in the heart. At one point, I catch the eye of the headmistress, Mrs. Mack. She looks over to me and smiles. Somehow I know at that moment, we both have the same feeling of loss. There is a tear running down her cheek. Maybe she wasn't so tough after all.

So it comes to pass that our four-hundred-year-old school ceases to be a quaint anachronism in the brave new world. The little academy, which has seen Henry the Eighth ax the monastery and convert the flour store into a schoolhouse, is lost and gone forever.

Concrete-and-steel brutalism is to be the future of secondary schools.

As I say good-bye to Miss Hathaway, I notice for the first time how frail she is and wonder if she was always like that.

I go to shake hands with Mrs. MacArthur, but she gives me a hug.

"It's three o'clock. School's over, you can go home now."

"Will you teach at the new school, miss?"

"No, we ladies are both retiring. It won't be the same without hearing the cry, 'Willie Watkins did it!' Will it, Miss Hathaway?"

"Indeed not, Head."

I turn to the now unemployed, hapless, and harmless Mr. Bury. I feel melancholy and slightly guilty that we have taunted this poor chap, whose only sin was to try and ease some erudition into our thick heads. Guilt? Melancholy? Quare types of feelings for a young lad to entertain surely, but the history of this place hangs as heavy in the air as the smoke from the bonfire. We shake hands. I feel this is an opportunity to apologize for some of my past misdemeanors, but decide instead to pull his leg one last time.

"What will you do, sir?"

"I don't know yet. Maybe I'll apply for a job at the new school in Henley or maybe go and teach abroad for a while."

"Oh, like in Greece, maybe? I hear a lot of young teachers go over there." He shoots a nervous look at the headmistress. She doesn't take any notice. I give him a friendly thumbs-up and venture inside for a last look.

I stand for a while in the empty halls that were once filled with the hoots and stampedes of Scottish country dancing. Gone now, the swish of the bamboo cane. Silent, the cries of anguish from punished children. Hushed, the hysterical laughter at Mr. Bury's madcap antics, and stilled forever, the buzz of learning.

Certainly, I won't miss the waffling of the old parish priest droning on like a frustrated bumblebee about impure thoughts and about our parents not giving enough to the Sunday collection plate. I've finished with that load of bollocks.

Standing on a rickety old stool, I unpin my motley paper soul from the wall and inspect the blots of my past misdemeanors.

"Hm, not too bad. There's still a wee bit of white showing up there in the top righthand corner! I can't be such a bad chap after all! Sure didn't I steal *The Secret of the Old Mill* and keep the book for three weeks to see if God would strike me down—and then put it back when nothing happened! Maybe I didn't keep it long enough? Or more likely, God knew I was going to give it back anyway, so couldn't be arsed punishing me."

I wander into the infants' room and marvel at the tiny desks and the wee chairs where once we struggled with adding carrots and dividing apples.

Crossing the threshold into the daylight, dreamily aware of the other threshold I'm crossing, I stand for the last time in the tree-lined playground. Either way, I am certain of one thing: that old school bell would never ring again.

Walking past my school chums, I put my soul on the embers of the bonfire and watch it smolder, spin skyward and flutter, sparking over the beech trees and into the river. Then without further ado, shouting a general farewell to all, I leave the little medieval school and the Catholic education system forever.

Chapter 16

"COME ON, INSIDE WILLIE! YOUR FATHER AND I WANT A SERIOUS talk with you."

"Oh, Jasus! They're putting me up for adoption!"

"Am I in trouble?"

"No more than usual," says Dad smiling. He continues: "The Warwickshire County Council are offering to rehouse us in a proper house. They're trying to relocate people off of these caravan sites and into new homes with modern amenities. There would be hot water, a bathroom with a toilet, your own bedroom, and a real kitchen with a cooker, a washing boiler, and everything."

I try to tell them that I'm happy where I am, but their minds are made up and they have convinced themselves it's all for my own good.

"When will we be going?" I tremble at the reply, thinking of my friends and the wonderful life of nonsense and childish pranks that I would be leaving behind.

"Oh, not for ages yet."

"Good!" I says, and skipping out of the door I promptly forget all about it.

I spy Mike and Paul, two of my erstwhile confederates, lurking about by the service entrance to the big Georgian hall.

"What are youse lot up to?"

"Shoosh!" They are listening at the window of the site office.

"What's going on?"

Paul takes me conspiratorially aside. "I was in the office with my mum this morning, to pay the site rent. Anyway there's these three geezers in there talking to old Mr. Rice about *ghosts!* So I starts to *ear-*

wig and it turns out they're from the Sigh-kick Phenomenal Society and they're coming here to investigate the ghost of Lady Fitzherbert, better known as the Gray Lady."

"Oooh, there's great possibilities of a good wheeze looming large here! When are they coming?"

"Friday night, and they're staying for the weekend."

I give Mike, still listening at the window, the thumbs-up and add, "We must think of a good ruse to fool the Hun."

"We will, by crikey! We haven't had a good wheeze since we got the flogging."

Now, I know the Georgian hall inside and out. I have many times sat daydreaming on the elegant great oak stairway, waiting for my pal Mark to come out of his parents' apartment to play. I've always felt curiously at home in this Mecca of silk tapestries, marble fireplaces, Greek urns, and gilt-framed masters. Alone in the richness of the mahogany-paneled rooms, I have watched the sunlight dappling through the huge stained-glass staircase windows in a million prismatic fingers, savored the smell of the old beeswax-polished edifices, and I drink deep from the chalice of antiquity.

I have never seen the Gray Lady and no credible person to my knowledge has. "But she's there!" we are told by the old ones in hushed tones.

"Dad, do you believe in ghosts and the like?"

"You worry about the buggers who walk around this earth on two feet and don't be bothering yer head about any old spooks or such nonsense!"

Well, that is good enough for me. The plot thins. If my dad thinks there is nothing to be scared about, then we can enter into our dastardly plan unfettered by fear of the hereafter. "From ghosties and ghoulies and long-leggedy beasties and things that go bump in the night, may the Good Lord deliver us!" sayeth the ould Scottish prayer.

Once more the game is afoot!

Lady Maria Anne Fitzherbert had a secret—and so does the ancient, ivy-wreathed hall. Although she and the Protestant Prince of Wales, later to be Gearge IV, were secretly married, the union was illegal under the Royal Marriage Act of 1772, and Maria Anne was shunted to the sidelines when George made a legal marriage in 1795.

Wootton Hall, like so many stately homes of the eighteenth century, has a priest hole! This contrivance manifests itself in a secret underground passage from the hall to the old church. By means of this, the priest can give the banned sacraments to the Catholics in the household, under the very noses of the king's militia. Also, if caught in attendance on the papist sympathizers, he can make his ecumenical escape through the tunnel, just like a rat up a drainpipe.

This priest hole, we think would be the epicenter of the psychics' endeavors, and so we prepare to lay a trap.

I know the layout in the labyrinthine maze of underground passageways that make up the service basement of the old mansion. Oftentimes I have accompanied my dad as he stokes the main boiler when the caretaker is on holiday. Forearmed with this intelligence, we will wait until the ghost hunters are set up and then creep in and give them a fright to remember!

I have an old McMichael valve wireless that suffers from incurable I.F. instability. The frequency-changer tube has an internal short that, as it warms up, causes the entire radio set to oscillate in a most ghoulishly entertaining fashion. The resultant unearthly screeches, wails, and screams would put the heart crossways in the pope himself.

Our simple ruse is to preposition this old radio in the priest hole tunnel with a long length of twin flex running back to a mains outlet. Here, at the crucial time, when they call out "Is there anybody there?" we can switch on the caterwauling apparatus and run away giggling.

It is time to do a reccy. We need firsthand intelligence of where and what our prospective dupes will be doing. Unnoticed, our little team of Paul, Mike, and myself slips quietly into the service door of the great hall and presses forward to the inner basement door. Down into the dark abyss of the cellars we slowly ingress, like three souls descending into Anwyn, the Celtic underworld.

There is a long, dank passageway to the right that leads to the priest's hole. We turn the corner, and miraculously a light comes on. I look around, but none of us has touched a switch. There is none to be seen anywhere. We walk on through the ancient asbestos-lagged perplexity of heating pipes and archaic overhead electrical wiring. Reaching the old well, still full to the brim and incalculably deep, we hesitate. For a second we think we can hear the sound of whispers, and not too far off either! Inching forward along the wall, hardly breathing through a bristling silence so profound that the relieved sigh of a defecating rat would be clearly audible, we make our snail-like progression toward the door of the priest's hole.

"This is it!" I whisper, swallowing hard. My saliva seems to taste like frothy lemonade, and my ears are hissing with the crackling excitement of it all. Paul's huge brown eyes look like dinner plates, and Mike has a face as white as a ghost's arse! Lighting our bicycle lamps, we swing open the iron door, which replies with a spine-shuddering creak.

We step over the threshold into the rank smell of decayed soil and the lifeless humors of a long-dead tunnel. Much to my surprise, there's already a wire running along the dirt-strewn floor! As we creep nearer, I see a thing that I recognized to be a microphone sitting on a tripod. I reach out to touch it—

"Aaaaagh! Aaaaaagh! Aaaagggh!" Mike is screaming, his face completely enveloped in a giant spider's web whose disgruntled owner is still at home and biting.

Paul is already running for the exit, emitting a high warbling whimper. This all put the dread of the Devil into me, and fearing the loss of my immortal soul, I lapse into the old Latin and blurt out, "Pater noster, qui es in coelis: santificétur nomen tuum . . ." My teeth-chattering chant fades as I flee the accursed tunnel with my terrified companions. With a rush like a hot spring's geyser, we erupt into the daylight and stand in a trembling triangle staring at each other. For several minutes we drink in enormous drafts of cold clean air, then without a word, shamefacedly, make our way home. This almost became the ruse that never was, but fate had a trick up her sleeve.

"Well, there's a thing!" Dad is reading the local paper. "Do you remember those loonies from the big city who were looking for spooks here a while back? Well, they reckon they may have found proof of a murder of a young woman by a Catholic priest!"

"Go'way! Lemme see!" says Mam, peering over his shoulder with interest.

"It says that the microphone they left secretly in the priest's hole recorded footsteps and weird muffled whispers, then the old rusty door opening, and a woman's horrible screams mixed with whimpering like a lost soul—and to cap it all, the definite voice of a Catholic priest or old monk chanting away to himself in Latin! Maybe there's something in it after all?"

"Do you believe in ghosts now, Dad?"

"There are more things in heaven and earth, Horatio, than were ever dreamed of in your philosophy!" Dad replies mysteriously, and, as usual, I have little idea what he is talking about. He throws the *Stratford Herald* onto the table.

Mam picks up the paper; on page three there's a picture of the pope.

"Oh, that's a shame. It says here that the Vatican is to do away with the Latin mass. The service will be in the language of the country. That's a scandal so it is, a downright shame!"

"And why would that be, woman?"

"Because it will be in bloodyEnglish and God won't understand a word of it, that's why. Sure, he only speaks Latin—and Gaelic of course!"

"Of course!" Dad raises his eyes to the home of the bilingual God.

"I learn Latin at school, Dad."

"And a fat lot of good it will do you this day an' age. You're hardly likely to bump into a passing Roman centurion, are you? But if you do, be sure to say 'Quo Vadis!'"

"That means where are you going, doesn't it, Dad?"

"It do! So if he doesn't know where he's going, tell him. Nil desperandum et nil carborundum illegitimi."

"I've never heard that phrase. What's it mean, Dad?"

"It means, 'Despair not and don't let the bastards grind you down.'"

"Reg! Stop poisoning the child's mind with your pagan nonsense and your filthy language. All I said was, that it will be a shame when the Tridentine mass is no longer celebrated, that's all."

"Why is it called the Tridentine mass, Mam?"

"Ask your clever bollix of a father!"

"Well, Will, it's because most of the silly old sods in the congregation only have three teeth between the lot of them."

"Jasus, Reg! I'll have no more of this—get out of here before I scatter you, by Christ, you spawn of Beelzebub. Out, out, you bloody heathen!"

Mam beats my father around the table and out the door with the rolled-up newspaper. Dad runs shrieking into the night with several inky images of the Holy Father indelibly stamped on his bald head.

It's Sunday morning and Dad is sitting on the front step rubbing brown stinky dubbing into his winter boots to make them waterproof before polishing them. I sit in beside him and have at my own wee boots.

"Be careful with that stuff, you don't want to get any on your clothes. It smells like the devil's armpit and sticks like shit to a blanket."

"I'll be careful. Where's Mam? She never got me up for mass."

"No, she went away up the church, ages ago. A posse of the local witches came around for her. They're having some black mass about the Third World War or something!"

"Oh, yes! It's the women's novena for world peace today."

"Well, it must be working. I'm having a very relaxing day without your mother nagging my earholes off. Your mam praying for world peace, that's a good one! She could cause a fight in an empty house. Do you know, Will, that your mother can assemble a machine gun faster than a British army weapons instructor?"

"You're kidding me!"

"No, it's true. When I was still in the army, before we were married, mind? Your mam came down to visit me at my camp. Well, she was a little early and myself and the sergeant instructor were still putting the raw recruits through the dismantling, cleaning, and reassembly of the Bren light machine gun. This sergeant was a big-headed sod and prided himself on how fast he could put the gun together from stripped. He liked to impress the rookies with this display of old bullshit, and within a few minutes the gun was assembled, much to the awe of the young lads who had been struggling with it all morning.

"That's what you call 'putting the gun together in double-quick time!' he says. The audience lets out a gasp and the sergeant stands, preening himself with a smile on his kisser like the cat that got the cream.

"'Double-quick time, my aunt Fanny!' says yer mother. 'Sure even a mere woman like myself could do it in half the time!'

"'Well, miss, perhaps you'd like a go?' he laughs, stripping the weapon back to parts. Well, yer mam walked down to the table, picked up two wrong pieces, and with a puzzled look, tried to fit them together. The sergeant was grinning like a Cheshire cat, when suddenly, with the time nearly up, yer mam snapped that Bren together like greased lightning and pointed the barrel at him. She pulled the trigger—*click!*

"'Bang! You're dead!' says your mother, with a wicked grin, and all the squadies are cheering your mam and catcalling at the sergeant instructor.

"'How the hell did you learn to do that?' asks the sergeant, mystified, like!

"'Ah now, wouldn't you like to know, Tommy?' says yer mam in a conspiratorial Irish accent!"

"Gee! But where did she learn, Dad?"

"She worked at the BSA during the war, of course. She made thousands of Bren guns on the assembly line."

"But I thought the BSA made motorcycles?"

"They do, but it still means Birmingham Small Arms! Hmm! Remarkable woman, your mother." says Dad, staring at his reflection in a spit-and-polished toe-cap.

World peace doesn't come, but fall does and we soon need the rain-proofed boots, especially when I go for a long walk in the wilderness with my father. It is cold and the curled brown leaves of autumn lay thick and crunchy with frost. A thin, pale, wintry-looking sun floats above the lines of silver birch trees like a runny fried egg. Great deciduous giants of oak and chestnut, having shed their summer finery, slumber, swaying gently, their creaking arms communing their spirits skyward to heaven. From where the river cuts a swatch through the forest, a filmy white mist is swirling upward in the eddies of an easterly breeze.

I know Dad has wanted to talk with me for some time, and I am terrified it is going to be about "the birds and the bees." I don't know too much on the subject of S.E.X. and that suits me just fine—for the moment anyway!

Instead, my Dad tells me how he'd fallen out with two of his brothers years before the argument about Granddad's Masonic trunk, over, of all things, a wee bag of sweets! They wouldn't share with him and he told them to stick the sweets up their arses. This happened when they were little kids and they are still at enmity about it. I think this is very sad, but many bitter things have been said over the years and the hatred of brothers is said to be the most galling.

He speaks to me about greed and loss, not as father to son, but as man to man. It makes me feel very important.

"Of all the vices, greed is the worst—I reckon anyway. It makes people do crazy things. It causes wars, and murders and the like. Show me a money-grabbing man who's at peace with himself. You can't! The greed that makes people do anything to acquire riches is a hunger that can never be satisfied, a thirst that a pint of the best bitter beer cannot slake. I shudder at the unholy thought!"

We walk on, with Dad still edifying the beJasus out of me.

"We collect firewood from the forest, right? Now we only take what we need, OK? No man in his right mind would possibly take away more wood than he can use, of course not. But someone who suffers that curse of greed will chop down all the trees, whether he can use them or not, and be too mean to let you take a few bits home. He's the fella old Jesus is talking about when he says, 'What does it profit a man if he gain the whole world and suffer the loss of his own soul?' Well, avoid those buggers in your life. They are a sorry lot and bring misery to all around them, like that mangy old Blackshirt Grumpy, as you call him. If he was a ghost, he would be too mean to give you a fright. Do you see what I'm getting at?"

"I think so," I says, wondering where this is all going.

Dad takes up the charge again.

"In order to gain something, the soul must lose something first, since it must always weigh the same. The loss of your loved ones is hard, but the soul gains an understanding that in life there is death and in death there is renewal. That can be comforting in times of sorrow." I try to nod my head in the right places. He continues his theme.

"You see, it's like this. Me and your mam have tried to give you a decent upbringing, but stuck out here in the country we don't have the opportunities we would have in the big city. So . . . so . . . we're leaving for our new house next weekend!"

So *that's* what this was all about. I knew already! Mam had told me yesterday, but I don't let on because it is nice having a ramble and talking with Dad.

We stroll back to the cosiness of our little blue-and-white caravan, from which a long silver-gray plume of wood smoke issues, suffused with the yeasty aroma of fresh-baked bread.

Yet again in my short life, I am about to leave everything I have ever known and go on to new adventures and new pals.

The Irish have a saying: "A child that is not brought up in the country has only had half a childhood." I have had a fine feast of a rearing in our little Celtic enclave in the wilds of Warwickshire.

Is buaine port ná glór na n-éan
Is buaine focal ná toice an tsaoil.

A tune is more precious than the song of birds
And a tale more precious than the wealth of the world.

→ Chapter 17 ←

PULLING OUT IS A COMPLICATED BUSINESS AS WE ONLY HAVE the old Austin motorcar to move our belongings. With the car stuffed with boxes and a mattress tied to the roof, we drive like hillbillies along the twenty-eight miles of country road to the new house. Dad navigates by the only landmarks he knows: pubs and gas stations.

We arrive in Lower Beeches Road, Northfield, Birmingham. I am on the lookout for a quaint little detached house. I'm disappointed to discover that the address fits one of a number of new monolithic brick-built tower blocks. It looks more like a drab suburb of East Berlin than the outskirts of an English city.

The high-rise apartments are jerry-built monstrosities—shoddy mushrooms sprouting all over Britain, ill-designed by architects who eventually go to jail for negligence. These tower blocks are made of the cheapest materials and the flat roofs usually leak, in contrast to the ground floors, which suck up the dreaded damp like a bath sponge. The middle floors have little in the way of sound deadening and neighbors are constantly fighting over noise problems. The tower at Ronan Point in London collapses, killing many of the residents. Blocks in Yorkshire are stripped of their roofing by North Sea gales. And an old gypsy relocated in the block opposite us is ejected for keeping goats in his front room. The authorities have his goats put down and the poor sod goes insane.

Stress becomes a part of daily life in many of these hen coops. Depression and suicide are common. The one elevator in our block seldom works, and the staircase invariably smells of piss. To a flat on the sixth floor of this earthly paradise, we move our few items of old furniture and settle in as best we can. I hate the damn place.

"I have an important announcement to make!" My folks look at each other and then back at me. "Henceforth, I wish to be called Bill, like my uncle Bill. No one knows me here and I don't want a anymore of that 'Willie Watkins did it!' business. It's been the bane of my life."

"OK, Willie . . . er . . . Billy . . . er . . . Bill. Sure you can be who you want here. Make a new start. That's what I did when I came over from Ireland, so I did."

"What, changed your name, Mam?"

"Certainly not! Just the color of my hair." She flicks her blond curls.

"What color was it before you came over?"

"'Twas auburn, so it was."

"What color is that?"

"A sort of russet red."

"Did you not like it that color?"

"Well, you know what they say about redheaded women?"

"No."

"Ask yer father. Go on, Reg, tell him."

"Well, Will, it's best explained like this. A fella goes to the doctor and finds out he's only six months to live. He asks the doctor what he should do.

"The doc says, 'Go and marry a redhaired Irish woman.'

"Yer man says, 'Will I live longer?'

"He says, 'No, it will just seem longer!' D'ya get it?"

"No."

"You will one day!"

We do one more trip to Wootton Wawen. Making a last walk around the caravan site, armed with an ancient Kodak 620 box camera, I snap a handful of photographs of the people and places that have been so dear to me.

Sitting later in my lofty prison, I gaze at the circle of smiling faces that once were my childhood pals, captured forever in that last sad hour of leaving, each elfin visage brimming with mischief and merriment, now pressed like wildflowers between the pages of time, a treasury of the age of innocence. I never see any of my friends from that day forward. By the time I'm old enough to make the long trek back to the caravan site on my own, they have all left or moved off on the road, gone like leaves in the wind.

The only good thing about this bloody apartment is the view. From the living room window we can see westward clear into Wales, across open fields and woodlands. One night we hear a distant explosion, and Dad stabs the air with a clenched fist.

"The boys are at it again—Cymru am Byth! Wales forever! Up the FWA!"

"Who's the FWA?"

"They're the Free Wales Army, and they're blowing up the water pipeline that steals Welsh water from the Elan Valley to feed Birmingham's reservoirs."

This at least brings some diversion to our new isolation, and we fill the bath with drinking water as we know the taps will be dry for a few days.

My folks take jobs in the city, nine miles away. It makes for a long bus trip each day. Dad works in a factory, making car batteries, and Mam becomes a barmaid at a pub in the city center. I have to go to school, but the nearest is called Tinker's Farm and the education department deems it inappropriate that a child from a caravan site should attend a school named after gypsies. I'm sent to Colmer's Farm school, a good three miles away across country. It never occurred to me that you need to lock a bicycle. It's soon stolen and I have to walk to school. I make no friends locally, and being shy about a protruding incisor that has grown over a stubborn milk tooth, I stop smiling.

Dad is in a similar plight: the old car dies and leaves him thinking that moving here was probably a big mistake, as the local pub is both a noisy dump and a long walk away. Like myself, he misses his pals and spends his nights painting in oils, reading, and helping me build working wireless sets out of army surplus junk. We try to make the best of it.

Only Mam seems content with our new existence. Being brought up during the lean years of depression, she loves the hurly-burly of a brightly lit city enjoying the first wave of economic boom heralded by the prime minister's announcement: "You've never had it so good!"

Like W. B. Yeats exiled in the tower of Thoor Ballylee, I become a disenchanted recluse with just an old cat for company and a hand full of memories. I brood over my fate and think of the happy times, now so distant. A homemade ham radio is my only window on the world. Night after night, I put on the headphones and drift away beyond the brick walls of this citadel of solitude. Aloft on the magic ether of the wireless waves, I tune about, visiting "HCJB, the Voice of the Andes"; "FK8AZ, calling from New Caledonia in the Pacific"; "G5SS Birmingham, calling on the 160-meter band"; "Ici Radio Canada." I am on the point of dozing off to sleep when through the static-filled ionosphere crackles a sound I've heard before: "Mayday! Mayday! Mayday! This is Dutch coaster PXCC . . . PXCC, Schevening Radio! Do you read? Over!" There is no reply except the hypnotic noise of an atmospheric storm, hissing and spitting like bacon frying in a pan. I jerk awake! I remember the *Irish Prince* and know that somewhere out in the dark of the cold North Sea other men are nearing their death.

"Mayday! Mayday! All stations, all stations! Do you read PXCC . . . PXCC! Mayday! Over." I detune my transmitter from 1,900 to 2,182 kilocycles per second. Distress frequency. I know this is breaking the law, but it's obvious that the electrical storm is blacking out radio links and no one else can hear them!

"PXCC . . . PXCC! This is amateur radio station G10924 calling you! Over?"

"G10924 . . . G10924! We are sinking three miles off the Tershcelling Bank! We require immediate assistance. Please Mayday relay! Over."

"Roger PXCC. Mayday relay! Mayday relay! Dutch coaster PXCC sinking off Terschelling Bank. All stations report." There is no reply. I try several more times until in desperation I run down the fifteen flights of stairs and across the road to the telephone box on the corner.

"999 Emergency, which service please? Police, fire, or ambulance?"

"Hello! Can you get me the North Sea Coast Guard, please?"

"I'm sorry, caller. It is an offense to make nuisance 999 calls. Please hang up."

"Listen, lady, I'm a ham radio operator and I've picked up a distress signal from a sinking ship. This is not a joke. Please get me the nearest Coast Guard! Please?"

"Just one moment." *Click!* "Hello, North Foreland Coast Guard here, what can I do for you?"

"Dutch ship, call sign PXCC, aground and sinking three miles off the Tershcelling Bank. They've been calling Mayday for ages and I'm the only one they've been able to contact. I'm just a ham operator."

"What's your call sign, sir?"

"G10924. Now hurry please!"

Back at my wireless, I hear the North Foreland radio station, GNF, make contact with the coaster at the third attempt and I breathe a sigh of relief. Dad comes home and listens to the drama play out as the crew is evacuated by Dutch and British rescue vessels. As the signal for Mayday stand down is given, a voice out in the ether says, "Thanks, G10924, good job. All PXCC crew are safe." Dad hears the message too and smiles as he pats me on the shoulder.

"I'm proud of you, son!"

My interest in shortwave radio causes me to read Thor Heyerdahl's, *Kon-Tiki Expedition*. He had two radio hams on his crew, and LI2B was the call sign of the balsa wood raft he sailed across the Pacific on. This book engages me in the story of ethnic Polynesian migration, and I read more of his books. The local library becomes my second home, but on my first visit there, I ask for Heyerdahl's enormous tome, *American Indians in the Pacific*. The librarian refuses my request point blank, saying, "You kids always want the biggest books in the place, and I'm fed up with it!"

I have to explain that I am seriously interested in Polynesian ethnology, not weight lifting, and grudgingly I'm given the huge volume to take home with me.

Dad takes an interest in the subject, too, and draws parallels between the dispersion of the seafaring South Sea islanders and the Celtic sea peoples.

"The sea was always a highway to the ancients. There were no natural barriers like impassable mountain chains or deep rushing rivers, dangerous forests, or swamps to impede the progress of migration. They could sail where they wanted as long as the prevailing wind and currents were kind. On land, they might meet hostile tribes barring their way, but at sea, there were only the elements to overcome. In this way, the prehistoric travelers populated the farthest corners of the earth."

Dad sees similarities in the method of erecting the giant statues of Easter Island and the huge trilithons that make up the circles of Stonehenge.

"Levers, rollers, and ropes, that's how they moved those bloody big stones—that and a good eye to science."

"So why were the Easter Island statues erected, Dad?"

"No one knows. We know more about Stonehenge, although we don't know who built it."

"Wasn't Stonehenge just a place for the Druids to make human sacrifices?"

"No, no, it was there long before the Druids, who never indulged in human sacrifice either. That's just a load of shite dreamed up by Julius Caesar to give the Celts a bad name. Stonehenge was a clock for predicting winter and summer solstice, a calendar by which ancient farmers could read the seasons and know when to plant their crops."

A noise in the front hall brings an end to the lesson. The post has arrived and Mam comes in with a manila envelope bearing the legend: On Her Majesty's Service.

"Ooh, Billy, this is for you. It's from the government. I bet it's a commendation like your dad got from the police that time long ago."

I tear open the official looking envelope and read:

Dear Mr. Watkins,

Operating an Amateur radio transmitter without a full licence is an offence under the Wireless Telegraphy Act of 1949.

Operating an unauthorised transmitter on a Maritime Distress frequency is an offence under the above Act and also the International Maritime Treaty Piracy Laws.

Due to the nature of this offence and your age, we have decided to limit our proceedings to an official *caution*. Any reoccurrence or future offences on your part will be prosecuted to the very letter of the law.

The punishment for such misdemeanors is a fine of one thousand pounds, six months imprisonment or both. Plus the confiscation of all transmitting equipment.

The Home Office.

I let the letter drop from my hand. Mam picks it up. "BloodyEnglish."

I make a few friends at the new school and in due course some enemies.

The school bullyboy finally notices my presence. He is an ugly-looking bollix with a shock of carrot-colored hair and a face like a freshly smacked arse. He's about fifteen and has an IQ of roughly the same. I think his name is Spencer.

"Come here, you!" He grunts at me in a guttural Brummy accent. "I'm the cock of the school—the best fighter!"

"You look more like the prick to me!" One or two of my attendant classmates laugh nervously, but most draw in an audible breath and move away. It takes several seconds for this unexpected rejoinder to sink into his cartilage-filled skull, and a dilatory look of puzzlement comes over his face. Then slowly, like the sunrise over the mountains, he has it. He'd been insulted by a mere twelve-year-old student!

I'm still laughing when he hits me full in the mouth. The force of the punch dislodges my rogue incisor, which firmly imbeds itself in his hamlike knuckle joint.

Although I'm in some pain, I am delighted. That goddamn ugly tooth is gone! "Good man! Good man! Thanks a bunch!" I shake his injured hand furiously. In agony and bewilderment, he's led away to the school nurse, who sends him to hospital. He requires surgery to remove the tooth. By the time he had been operated on and gets back the use of his hand, he has left school, so I never see him again. Now I have a straight row of teeth, and I smile at everybody!

The fact that I hospitalized the school bully and laughed after he punched my tooth out spreads around the school like a measles epidemic. It offers me great kudos and I am never molested again.

The red brick and plate glass school is home to an odd complement of teaching staff. Mr. Hobbs, our wonderfully gay art teacher, is great fun to work with and his art room is a no-go area for stuffy authority. If you don't feel like drawing or painting you can make coffee and talk about art, politics, pop music, or who won the 4:15 race at Doncaster. To him all expression is art!

The aquatic-looking "Froggy" Palmer is the mathematics master. Here I stumble and fall as before. More bloody allegory!

"A farmer plants 800 potato plants, 6 out of 10 die. What has he got, Watkins?"

"Colorado beetle, sir!"

Mr. Palmer has a particularly nasty punishment for wayward students. He sends me to the washroom to soak his blackboard-cleaning rag. When I sit back at my desk he hurls it into my face with unerring accuracy. If you duck, the punishment is repeated.

At first sight, the science master, Mr. Druce, cuts a strange figure. Dressed in moss-green tweeds, he affects a wide-brimmed cowboy hat of the same color and white gloves. Sprigs of snowy hair jut out from under his sombrero and he wears thick tortoiseshell spectacles. I discover he is an albino and allergic to sunlight.

His junior in the science block is young Mr. Shaw, who seemingly is from the same school as Mr. Bury. He gives a lesson in biology and attempts a jocular aside.

"All cells must have a nucleus, just like we—all must have a belly button!"

"I have no belly button, sir!" says moon-faced Edward Hall.

"Don't be stupid, Hall. Everyone has a navel, even a worm like you!"

"I have no belly button!"

"Rubbish, of course you do!"

"I have *no* belly button, I tell you!"

"Right, smart arse, get out here!"

Edward strolls out to the front of the class and up onto the podium. Mr. Shaw spins him around toward us and whisks up his shirt.

"This is your belly butt . . ." Mr. Shaw's words trail off as he realizes he is pointing at a smooth round belly totally devoid of any trace of a navel! Edward is triumphant and afterward tells me his secret. When he was born his navel developed an infection and was operated on. When the stitches were later removed, the scar healed up, belly button and all. Mr. Shaw, however, is kept in the dark!

I like "Mad Gary" Hedges the English teacher, not just because of his projecting "Eraser Head" haircut and eyes that flicker to and fro a hundred times a minute, but also because of his unconventional taste in literature. Blaggards like us fall eerily silent when he reads aloud horror stories like, "The Forest of Fear," by Lurhendorf, a terrifying tale of being lost in the Amazon jungle. Or the sinister, futuristic politico-nightmare embodied in George Orwell's *1984*. He struts at the front of the classroom, red hair flaming skyward like a struck match, reading from banned books, uncensored books, and everything that isn't on the approved reading list. We love him for it!

An American poetry teacher arrives for a year's exchange and, with great enthusiasm, introduces me to the sacred arts of imagery, metaphor, and onomatopoeia. I spend a lot of after-school time talking to him about poetry. He is fascinated that I can remember epic Irish poems, recitations, and other gleanings of Celtic oral tradition. He writes these down with the old songs and sayings that I know. He makes copious notes.

"You could make a living singing these ancient songs and reciting this beautiful poetry."

"No one is interested in it, sir. It's all too old fashioned."

"They will be one day, Bill, you wait and see!"

"Why did you come all the way over from the U.S.A. to work here?"

"Oh, that was almost too easy! I was teaching at this university in New England, and I fancied a change of career. For a bit of divine guidance I opened a compendium of verse and read, 'Oh to be in England now that April's there.' I thought, Hello, this is a good omen, and so moved over on a teacher's swap program!"

"My grandda used to say that there is great guidance in poetry, a sacred thing to the Celts!"

The day he leaves, he gives me my first-ever book of selected poems by William Butler Yeats. I open it and there on page three is the same poem that I had heard on the wireless during my days as an infant fighter pilot.

"An Irish Airman Foresees His Death." As I read the text, the intervening years telescope and there I am in my mind's eye, still flying my spindle-backed chair through the wild blue yonder of Ireland. It makes me miss the old country terribly and I yearn to go back home.

I have no fellow countrymen worth a toss here in the big city. The kids with Irish names are more English than the English themselves. I am lonely for the ways of the Celt.

The biggest bugbear at school is the quaint preoccupation with sport, in all its torturous forms. I find this to be a right royal pain in the arse.

Soccer is compulsory, as are rugby, cricket, basketball, and field and track events. All this with the promise of nice cold showers afterward and the big eejits laughing at your willie! To avoid any future compliance in these arcane endeavors, I effect a grand *ruse de guerre* by way of which, although appearing to be exerting myself to the maximum, my total incompetence causes groans of exasperation from my teammates and appeals to the sports master to send me off. This he invariably does, and the punishment for being a duffer is to be sent to the school library.

They must think it a great agony for me to sit reading in a warm library on a freezing winter's morning, witnessing the other lads turn blue with cold whilst getting slaps in the face with icy leather footballs. 'Tis a quare castigation to be reading *National Geographic* with your feet up a throbbing radiator.

My ruse held, and eventually, after constantly own-goaling at football, running the wrong way in cricket, and throwing a javelin through the changing-hut window, I am excused from team games altogether.

"God almighty, boy! Didn't you play football where you come from, Watkins?"

"No, sir!" This was true. I'd always found more entertaining ways to expend my excess energy than running around a muddy field chasing a pig's bladder.

"Well, what games have you played in the bogs of Ireland then?"

"Only hurley, sir! It's the only one I know!" I'm on safe ground here.

"Good God, lad! That's a game for bloody barbarians! People get maimed, killed even, playing that!"

"Yes, sir, it's an ancient Celtic game from the Bronze Age, a game for warriors. It won't suit you civilized folk at all!"

"Sarcasm is the lowest form of wit, Watkins!"

" 'Tis when you're dealing with the lowest form of life!" I mutter under my breath.

"Don't get smart with me, Watkins, or I'll whip the skin off your backside. Now go on, get out!"

That was easy! Now how do I get out of cross-country running? Fate lends a helping hand.

They show me the five-mile course. This leaves the back of the school and follows the same route that I take home every day. I pace myself until, neither with the keen bunch of athletes in the lead nor the wheezing desperadoes in the rear, I find myself alone. As I jog past the back of my apartment block, I swerve into the rear door and up to my flat. This gives me a twenty-five-minute break. From the living room window, with a cup of tea and sandwich in hand, I watch the true sons of Britannia run to the top of the distant Frankley-Beeches hill and turn about. Fifteen minutes later they pass my back door and I join the gap once more, usually arriving back at the finish in seventeenth place out of thirty-six.

"William is not a natural athlete—but tries hard!" my report card reads. I have always liked the idea of being seventeenth and find the concept of any person wishing to be number one rather vulgar. The seventeenth best gunslinger in town, for instance, would be ideally suited as the sixteen above him would scarcely stoop so low as to challenge him, and the ones below him, would be so inept as to pose little threat. I begin to look upon seventeen as my lucky number, and I'm very pleased when I discover that it is the sacred number of the Druids.

From the tower of my brick Bastille I gaze on the world beyond. Through my telescope I spy a pretty young girl at the end of the street. Sadly I discover that she's one of the Kirby clan, who are the number one terrors in the neighborhood, and as lovely as she is, old man Kirby is a villain and puts me in mind of the song "Riley's Daughter." I keep well away from her.

Riley has a murderous way,
Riley has a mind to murder and slaughter,
Riley has one big red eye,
And he keeps his eye on his lovely daughter.

I'm still rather shy of girls, especially the city ones, who, with the exception of Elspeth O'Neill, seem a lot more forward than I'm used to. The sap is rising and I endeavor to overcome my coyness with the lassies. I am granted luck from an unsuspected quarter. My school is Church of England, and since I am a Catholic I'm not obliged to join in the morning assembly for prayers and hymn practice. Instead, along with the Muslims, Jews, Sikhs, and divers denominations, I am given other school duties.

The one I enjoy is late monitor. I sit inside the main entrance and take down the names of any tardy stragglers in the late book. Three consecutive bookings lead to a punishment, so I change the names of constant recidivists to give them a break.

One such offender is a pretty young lass called Sue Lloyd, and, despite living directly across the road from the school gates, she is always late.

Each day I have ample time to talk with her as the assembly meetings are forty-five minutes long and longer, if Welshman and chorister Mr. Davies gets the *Hwyl* or the Welsh religious fervor and carries the hymn singing to dizzier heights than normal.

Soon teachers and pupils alike think she's just another non-Protestant late monitor, doing her secular duty, and that is fine by us. One day I ask can I walk her home.

She laughs and says, "What, across the road? Are you nuts?" Nuts or not, I eventually do, however, and the walk usually takes at least an hour.

She is my first girlfriend.

At home, I get a marvelous picture on the old black-and-white television I'd retrieved from the dump that time. Now, plugged into the big antenna high on the roof of the building, we are able to tune in all sorts of queer transmissions, including, under certain atmospheric conditions, *The Beverly Hillbillies* in Spanish!

That year the big news in television is the forthcoming world heavy-weight title fight between Sonny Liston and Floyd Patterson, but what I want to see again are those four Liverpool guys who had been on the BBC's *Tonight Programme,* singing a song called "Love Me Do." They have a fresh new sound and mops of long hair. The stage set was a building site scene, and on the corrugated iron fence next to the band are spray-painted the words "The Beatles."

For several days I have been monitoring the shortwave broadcasts from Voice of America, Radio Moscow, and Radio Havana. The United States is convinced that the Russians have developed ICBM missiles and is not having any of them stationed in Cuba.

The great Kennedy versus Khruschev showdown is *High Noon* for real, and for three days we teeter on the brink of nuclear war. To make matters worse, coincidentally, the number one record in the top 10 is "Don't They Know It's the End of the World?"

The door of my classroom opens and a runner hands the teacher a note.

"Class, I have a notice here from the headmaster. It states that the war has indeed started. The factories are closing, and your parents will be bussed here to pick you up!"

God knows where this rumor had sprung from, but it was current all over the Midlands of England. There is no panic, just a slow sad resignation; like the Jews who knew their fate, stoically lining up for the gas chambers.

Our teachers tell us to line up in the playground class by class. All of the factories shut down and people are told to go home and prepare to die. Suddenly there are my folks amongst the worried throng of parents streaming off the buses. On a beautiful afternoon, I walk westward home down the country lane, hand in hand with my mum and dad. I have no fear of dying, I just feel cheated. Here's me on the brink of growing up and these loonies are going to end it all. We don't say much, but as I walk into the sunset with my folks, I wonder if this will be the last time I'd see the sun go down.

No one in Britain has fallout shelters except the rich, the government, and the royal family. The Civil Defense tells us that we are protected by a four-minute early warning system; radar detects the incoming missiles and we have time to hide under the kitchen table from the fifty-megaton blasts. We are urged to take off all of the doors in the house and stack them around the table for protection. My dad says he couldn't even find a screwdriver in that short time, but on the plus side, there are some athletes in the country who can run a mile in four minutes! Grim times bring on grim humor.

So this is it, the big one, and I am going to die as I was born—a damn virgin!

At home we listen on the shortwave radio to the to-ing and fro-ing of the standoff. For once, good sense prevails and the threat of annihilation is diverted. It has not been the disaster it might have been, even though Dad has drank all of his stock of home brew.

In the days that follow, a curious anger spreads amongst the populace. Most people are disgusted with the superpowers who've almost killed us, with our own government who afford us no protection, and with themselves, who have so calmly accepted the thought that we are all going home to be fried in our beds.

This wave of revulsion sweeps the country in the aftermath of the Cuban missile crisis and I commit my first political act. I join the Campaign for Nuclear Disarmament, the CND.

At the invitation of the school metalwork teacher, who is also in CND, I do my first gig as a musician. It's a benefit for a new branch of the burgeoning organization, a concert of song and poetry, located in the parochial hall. I am very pleased and honored to do it.

To say that I am nervous would be like describing the Marquis de Sade as a little eccentric. Minutes before going on stage, I am a leading contender in the brown-trouser Olympics! Total amnesia sets in, and I am convinced that my guitar's out of tune.

"Got a wee bit of stage fright?" asks my teacher.

"No!" I lie, my voice two octaves above normal. Suddenly, I think it wise to visit the lavatory. I open the toilet door and a wild-eyed bearded figure, dressed completely in black, thrusts a handful of papers into my face.

"The eagle of death sits on my head and shits down the back of my neck!"

"Oh . . . er, that's nice for you. Are you performing?"

"I do not perform, I transfigure! I am the great Kropotkin! The finest poet in the world—nay, the universe!" He thrills in a mock Russian accent, holding his sheaf of papers aloft, like the torch of a demented Statue of Liberty.

"Who in the name of Jasus is that?" I say to my teacher, as the demonic poet flits past us, black cape akimbo.

"Oh, that's Dave Patton, the awful poet. He's as mad as a hatter!"

"Well, he has me feeling much relieved! Whatever happens I won't be the worst of the night's offerings."

"Och, you'll be fine!"

Two brothers are on in front of me, and they are very good, singing in tight harmony, a bit like the Everly Brothers.

Finally I hear my name announced and I walk on stage. After a shaky start I get into the swing and I'm away. I start with an Irish song called "The Spinning Wheel," which I'd learned from Nana. Then, Ewan MacColl's, "Dirty Old Town," and I finish with a song I'd heard a lot on the American shortwave stations called "Blowing in the Wind." I announce it as "written by a chap called Tom Dillon." No one corrected me. Bob Dylan was not yet a household name!

I leave the stage and the dazzling lights to a pleasing ripple of applause. It is all over. I have done it and survived!

I feel elated. The pretty girl I'd seen earlier passing out leaflets smiles at me and says, "That was lovely! Is this your first gig? You are very good, don't you think?"

I'm suddenly a bag of nerves again. I try to nod my head no to her last question and say, "Yes" to her second question at the same time. This gives me the appearance of a badly operated string puppet with a red face. As I blush, stammer, and splutter I feel her squeeze something into my hand. My heart flutters like the leaves of the Holy Jasus Bible in a gale. *It must be her phone number or the like!* But when I look down I find I am only holding a leaflet stating "Ten Good Reasons Why We All Should Say—BAN THE BOMB."

"Bugger the bomb!"

Back home Dad is carving a wooden Tiki figure like the ones on Easter Island.

"How was your gig, Will?"

"'Twas grand! I sang a few old songs that went down well, but I was a might nervous!"

"Good lad!"

"Dad, with the Second World War over and fascism defeated, why do we need so many armies and weapons?"

"Oh, Billy boy, if it was only that simple."

"What d'you mean?"

"Well, we only got rid of Hitler and Mussolini. Half of the world is still under dictatorship. Franco rules Spain, Salazar in Portugal, apartheid in South Africa, the white racist regime in Rhodesia, not to mention Stalinism behind the iron curtain, segregation in the U.S.A. and in Northern Ireland, the war in Indo-China, the Belgian Congo, and Israel! Every bloody eejit in East and West seems to be glaring at each other! The same tired old politicians are telling everyone to 'Tighten your belt and take less money for more work!' If all jobs were based on productivity, where would these buggers be in the league tables, I wonder."

"Reg, for Jasus' sake, look at the poor child! He came home all happy and now you've depressed the hell out of him with your fascists and fatshits and God knows what else! Jasus, what do you think yer on!"

"I fought with Monty, woman!"

"I thought it was supposed to be the Germans you were fighting? Mind you, Willie, your father could cause a fight in an empty house!"

"That's what he says about you, Mam!"

"Go to bed, Willie!"

President Kennedy is shot. We cry. He was our man. We'd prayed for him, so he was ours! Now the TV brings his death right into the heart of our home. The world has gone mad, and now, even more so, I fear a nuclear war.

The electrifying events of these months of turmoil produce a couple of odd side effects: the folk music revival and the protest movement.

There begins a series of antinuclear folk concerts at Birmingham Town Hall with some great singers and musicians turning up for them. The anchor band are the Ian Campbell Folk Group, with the incomparable Dave Swarbrick on fiddle. Their guests include Ian and Sylvia Tyson from Canada, Guy Carawan, Pete and Mike Seeger, Buffy St.-Marie, Judy Collins, and Joan Baez, from the United States. British singers are represented by Martin Carthy, Ray and Archie Fisher, Nadia Catouse, Alex Campbell, Ewan MacColl, and the Scottish group the Corries. My dad knows Ian Campbell, and Ian introduces me to some of the performers. It's a great school for a lad like myself. I am very lucky to play and sing with some of these artists. From Joan Baez I learn to play the syncopated style of clawhammer picking that she excels at, and hearing Judy Collins singing Gordon Lightfoot's fine song, "In The Early Morning Rain," moves me to tears. One Saturday I sit and swap songs all afternoon with Phil Ochs.

Ian Campbell and my father are buddies from the Spanish Civil War. They both hate fascism, the destruction of which will seemingly be attained by consuming vast amounts of gargle and singing durty songs about General Franco.

Back home in Castle Doom, Dad, enlivened by several more bottles of Nut Brown Ale, continues to wax revolutionary.

"Fascism is like a nettle, laddie. You must grasp it firmly by the throat!"

"What about nationalism? Doesn't that lead to fascism, like National Socialism?"

"Not necessarily. A little of each can work together. To be an internationalist you need a nation, and the struggle of small nations to be free is the very cornerstone of the Celtic evangel." He begins to sing:

> *It is England that bade our "Wild Geese" go*
> *That small nations might be free.*
> *And their lonely graves are by Suvla's waves*
> *Or the fringe of the great North Sea.*

"Do you know, Willie, that throughout history, Irishmen, Welshmen, and Scots have joined in the liberation of subjugated nations all over the globe? The United States of America's Declaration of Independence was referred to by King George III as 'that damned Welsh document!' More people in General George Washington's army spoke Gaelic than English! Chile, freed from Spanish rule by Juan MacKenna.

The storming of the Bastille, led by Seamus Blackwell, a cobbler from Leitrim! Celts have always been to the fore! Bernado O'Higgins, chief of staff in Simon Bolívar's liberation army, hero of Latin America. Ernesto 'Che' Guevara de la Serna-Lynch, an Argentinean-Irishman, helped Fidel Castro overthrow the Cuban dictator, Batista, in 1959!"

"Reg, stop filling the child's mind with your old commie nonsense. Ye'll have him as daft as yerself!"

"Bollocks, madame!" He uses the interlude to open another beer.

"Now where was I, before I was *rudely* interrupted? Ah, yes! The Celts have long been known to be a querulous and pugnacious race, and this is seen by some to be just pure love of conflict. Standing up for your rights and beliefs can't possibly be misconstrued as bellicose, can it, young man? Hell no, indeed! The BloodyEnglish have invaded almost every country on the face of the earth, yet they still pretend to deal in fair play. A likely bloody story! Look what they did in China—got the Chinese hooked on opium and then invaded and stole every bloody thing that wasn't nailed down. Disgraceful! The British Empire was built on drug money and slavery and murder. That's why the Union Jack is known as the Butcher's Apron!"

"Well, why do they think that it's all right to have empires, Dad?"

"I touched earlier on the difference in the Celtic and Anglo-Saxon psyche and that reminds me of the time when we kept chickens. The hens wandered around the yard, pecking here and there, wherever they wished, they were no problem. Then a mate of mine gave us some ducks. Now these wee buggers have a structured order of behavior and a well-developed hierarchy. Every morning the ducks would come out of the coop and line up in a row. The leader would then take position at the front of the file and nod its head up and down. This is the cue for the line of ducks to obediently do likewise, and when they have all nodded enough, they would waddle in single file down to the pond. The problem was, if you let the free-spirited hens out first, the ducks would get hysterical trying to make the hens line up, pay homage, and toe the line. It is a comical sight, but it seems to me to be a powerful cultural analogy with overtones of Aesop's fables. It's a great pity the so-called political experts, waxing lyrical on the Anglo-Irish problem, don't keep poultry. They'd get a better idea of what they're talking about! Pour me another beer, Will. My throat's as dry as a pharaoh's sock."

Well, I'm one chicken who isn't about to be walking in a straight line anyway! My school chums leave for jobs in one of the many Austin Motor Company factories that take up most of the available land around the school. If you are smart and stay on to do fifth- and sixth-year studies you can expect a job in the drawing office or the administration block. However, if you leave at fifteen, you're a grunt, "doomed to the broom," as they say. A life of sweeping up and waiting for a grease-monkey job to open on the vehicle assembly line. Bollocks to all that!

The largest part of the school is the metalworking shops. The many full-size machines bear the legend "Kindly donated by the Austin Motor Co." Here you are taught drilling, tempering, center-grinding, capstan-lathe operating, tool and pattern making, and all the other skills you need for a life of car making. I would rather poke a pencil in my eye than go to that sausage machine existence.

My school careers officer asks me what I want to be. I answer cheekily that I'd like to be a merchant navy wireless operator or a folk singer. He says, "Why not do both?"

My schoolwork is going to shit. It never recovers from the Cuban missile scare. Algebra, logarithms, Thomas Hardy, and the bloody Magna Carta all seem so puerile in the shadow of the valley of death. What I learn, I learn at home. Dad teaches me many crafts. He shows me how to paint in oils and work in metal, wood, and stone. I study hard at my radio manuals and pass the Postmaster General's certificate of wireless proficiency.

In the long winter's evenings, Dad teaches me to play chess, drink Woodpecker cider, and hold an intelligent conversation all at the same time! This is my dad's way to get me to use my faculties—even when I might be just a wee bit tiddly!

✦ Chapter 18 ✦

"HOW OLD ARE YOU NOW, WILL?"

"I'm fourteen, Dad."

"Hmm." He stares at me as if he's measuring me up for a suit. The air about his bald pate seems electrostatically charged, and I sense one of his philosophical eruptions about to happen. I had become quite adept at recognizing the seismology of my father's periodic volcanic outflows, but it was still an unnerving spectacle.

He paces the floor, leaving plumes of blue cigarette smoke marking the quadrants of his traverse. For a while his theme eludes him; his muse is timorous. Then, suddenly illuminated, he's off, invoking the spirit within the poetry of Taliesin, the Welsh bard:

> *I was a drop in the shower,*
> *I was a torrent on the slope,*
> *I was a salmon in the pool,*
> *I was a sword in the hand-grip,*
> *I was a cry in battle,*
> *I was a bubble in the beer,*
> *For a year and a half I was the pin in a pair of tongs!*
> *I was a buck,*
> *I was a wizard,*
> *I am Taliesin. Come, ye learned Druids, and prophesy unto*
> *Arthur!*

"Don't you see, Willie? This is what it's all about! Metamorphosis, shape changing, the essence of the Celtic soul. We are born in one form and throughout our existence transmute into other levels of being, each of which is like a new skin or shape. Some changes are dynamic, like when you become seven years old and enter the age of reason. That was a sad year for you with all the death in the family. Twice seven years brings you up to the age of logical thinking and you're a fourteen-year-old coming to terms with the postnuclear world after Cuba. Thrice seven years is the supposed age of majority, the key of the door! Twenty-one. What folks forget is that the key is for unlocking the door behind which knowledge and wisdom lie. Other changes are daunting, you can find yourself between the hammer and the anvil—very unpleasant! But from the dull, raw iron is formed the pure bright steel! This is the spiritual rebirth that you hear about in almost all of the major religions of the world. We are made of atoms. The *dust* of the Bible stories. We are a carbon-based life form, and just as carbon can materialize in the appearance of coal, soft graphite, or the hardest of known rocks, the diamond, we can appear in the myriads of shapes, colors, sizes, and demeanors that are all around us. Are you following me intelligently?"

"Don't you mean that all the races are the same, Dad?"

"Yes, all mankind is basically the same. We can look different, one from another, but that's how we have evolved to suit our individual climates, locations, and diverse environments."

"So there's no point at all in racism, is there?"

"No, none at all. It doesn't bother dogs what shape or size or color they are, they treat each other as what nature intended them to be—dogs!"

"Then how is it that we think the Celts are better than other people?"

"We aren't better or worse than anyone! We are all flowers in the same garden and all have the same right to be here. It's the buggers who think they are the chosen people or the master race that cause all the problems. Never walk that path! No, no, the difference with us is purely spiritual. That, if anything, makes us a little odd. Do you know what atavism is?"

"No, Dad, I don't. What might it be?"

"It's having thoughts and remembrances that you cannot possibly have experienced in this life, flashbacks to another time, a previous existence!"

"Oh, like déjà vu, that sort of thing?"

"More like the second sight of the Gael or the *Hwyl hudoliaeth* of the Welsh. All of us only have a very thin veneer of so-called civilization, and in some folk, just below the surface, there is still the genetic memory of the ancient hunter-gatherer waiting to manifest itself. For us Celts, it comes out in our art, music, and poetry. These traits are amongst the few things we can be truly proud of, and some aspects of these wise arts are unique to our people. A practitioner of the wise arts is called, as a result, a wiz-art or Wizard! This same sense of otherworldliness is found in the ancient Druid religion, the central point of which is the transmigration of the soul. Natural phenomena become objects of worship. The wind, springs, the trees, rocks—all take on deities, and through this world the soul must travel to find its path to rebirth in a higher spiritual form."

"It sounds a bit like Buddha or the Tao."

"It isn't all that different, but our culture has suffered severely at the hands of our Anglo-Saxon neighbors, and its light has been almost extinguished. It is up to your generation to take up the challenge and rebuild the glory of the Gael. You are the rebirth of King Arthur!"

"Me? I'm the reincarnation of King Arthur?"

"Not you personally, but your generation, growing up in the first period of relative peace in God knows how long. It is up to you to build the Camelot of the mind and be the *Rex quondam, Rex-que futurus*—the once and future King. This is the start of a new golden age for the Gael, you mark my words. Strive for that which is honorable and noble, and you shall be the once and future Celts! Now give me over that bottle of beer and two glasses and I'll show you something!"

My father pours out the beer and stares into the side of the glass.

"Look at the bubbles. Where do they come from? What's their point of origin? We don't know. They start from nothing in the tiniest form imaginable and grow larger on their way to the surface, where they disappear—*pop!* This is analogous to the human existence and why Taliesin says, 'I am a bubble in the beer!' Now drink up your lesson and here's to Taliesin, the chief of the bards!"

I down my glass of Flower's Best Bitter with relish. Bubbles, lesson, and all flow sweetly down my throat.

"Who was Taliesin? I know he was a Druid and a poet in King

Arthur's court, but what else can you tell me about him? How did he come to be so powerful?"

"Well, now . . . There was a witch called Ceridwen, who had a son so ugly that he was called Morfran Y Fagddu, Great Crow in Utter Darkness. She sets a cauldron of magic herbs to boil for a year and a day from whence it will produce three drops of divine fluid. These she will give to her gruesome son and he will receive great beauty and the gift of wizardry. She makes an orphan boy called Gwion Bach stir the pot, but at the moment of sublimation, she has fallen asleep and the divine droplets leap from the cauldron and land on Gwion Bach instead. The cauldron cracks with a scream and spills poison all over the land. Ceridwen wakes and, seeing her son unchanged, realizes that Gwion Bach has taken the powers. She flies at him to tear him asunder, but now he is wise to her and turns himself into a hare and escapes. The witch takes on the shape of a greyhound and gives chase. He jumps into the river and becomes a fish. She becomes an otter. The boy speeds out of the water in the form of a bird. Ceridwen follows as a hawk, but Gwion Bach flies into a barn and becomes one of a pile of wheat grains on the floor. The witch turns herself into a chicken and eats up all the grain before becoming a woman again. And guess what?"

"What, what?"

"Now she's pregnant and in due course gives birth to a child of such beauty that she cannot bring herself to destroy him, so she casts him afloat in a coracle upon the Irish Sea. The small boat eventually is washed ashore at Cored Wyddno, the weir of Gwyddno near Conway, and is found by a poor but kindly nobleman called Elphin. He looks at the child wrapped up in the coracle and proclaims, 'Behold the radiant forehead'—*Tal iesin* in Welsh. Gwion Bach replies, 'Tal-iesin it shall be,' and the nobleman is amazed at the beautiful baby, who can speak words and prophecies, and raises him up as his own. Taliesin becomes the foremost Celtic bard in Britain.

> *I was revealed in the land of the trinity*
> *I was moved through the entire universe*
> *I shall remain till doomsday upon the face of the earth*
> *No one knows what my flesh be, meat or fish?*

I was nearly nine months in the womb of Ceridwen
I was formerly Gwion Bach,
But now I am Taliesin.'"

"Drink up your ale, Will—Iechyd da!"

"Good health to you, too, Dad!"

It is pleasant to have a wee drink with my dad, but I also mind what my mam says: "A hangover is a poor friend and makes for a rotten master."

The biggest disaster that befalls me through using too much alcohol happens in the kitchen. Dad is teaching me the rudiments of cookery, and I am the sorcerer's apprentice.

"The secret art is in knowing how much salt to put in and to always use an onion!" His fabled advice is great for stews and soups, but is total disaster when it comes to making custard, puddings, or cakes.

"We will make a Polish casserole with this." Dad holds up a small flat-sided bottle with a red label. Polish Spirit 212 proof. He has been given this fierce distillation by a Polski mate at work, along with the recipe for a vodka-based beef stroganoff–type dish. The chunks of beef are sautéed in garlic and cayenne pepper, to which Dad adds a good measure of the spirits. While this is suppurating, we both try a glass of the firewater.

"In the name of the wee man! That'll put hairs on a whale's back. Holy moly, I think me teeth have dissolved!" Goggle-eyed and wheezing, Dad regards the bottle as if it contained nitroglycerin.

I am unable to speak at all. The searing liquor has set my throat aflame and cauterized my vocal cords. I've only taken a wee sip and I will take no more! When Dad isn't looking I pour the remainder into the Pyrex casserole dish.

The gas oven is heating up to working temperature. Meanwhile, Dad stirs the vodka-infused meat and garlic, and sniffs the resultant concoction with trepidation.

"I'll give it another shot of this rocket fuel. God knows how the Poles can drink this stuff. It's little wonder they're always dancing and flinging glasses into the fireplace—pheew!" The bottle is emptied into the dish and carrots, celery, and tomatoes added to the pungent potion.

"There now, give that a couple of hours of slow cooking and it will be fit for a feast. Open a couple of bottles of beer, Will. I need to see if my taste buds still work—oh, Jasus! Put the telly on quick! The wrestling just started!"

This is our Saturday routine while Mam is away at work. We would cook the dinner and settle down to the afternoon of televised grappling matches with commentator Kent Walton. A fearsome grudge match is in progress between Jackie "Mr. TV" Pallo and the sinister Mick MacManus in his black leotard. The crowd jeers and boos as bad boy Mick picks pretty boy Jackie up above his head for a body slam. As the wrestler's back hits the canvas, a deafening explosion resounds from the kitchen behind us! Dad and me stare at each other for a split second, then dive next door. The kitchen is in ruins. flying food has spattered the walls and windows, and the oven door lies smoking in the corner. Dad scrapes a piece of beef from the doorjamb and tastes it.

"Hmm, very good! Try some, but look out for bits of broken glass."

It takes a lot of cursing and elbow grease to get the shrapnel from Dad's Polish vodka bomb from the kitchen walls and even longer to rehang the oven door. We are tidied up when Mam comes home at midnight.

"So what's for dinner?" she says, not noticing anything out of the ordinary. Dad looks sheepish. In our haste to square up the place, we have forgotten about eating altogether, and Mam's dinner had self-destructed in the oven.

"Oh, I get it! Muggins here is out at work all day while you pair of idle prats sit on your fat arses watching the bloody goggle-box and drinking Polish piss water!" She throws the empty vodka bottle into the rubbish bin and storms off to bed.

The next day is spent in a frenzy of painting to cover up the remains of the evidence of our culinary catastrophe.

"At least we didn't get found out!" says Dad, running a paint roller across the kitchen ceiling, while I paint the door panels.

"Yeah, we are lucky! If Mam had seen the mess, she would've put the house out through the window and murdered the pair of us!"

Dad smiles a satisfied smile at the newly painted kitchen.

"There now, that will please yer mam!" And it does—until three weeks later, when Dad comes home drunk, puts two pork chops under the grill, and dozes off in the armchair. He is still snoring when Mam and I come home. The chops are burnt to a cinder, the grill top has melted, and the freshly decorated walls are black with greasy soot.

Mam swears at him for over half an hour and never repeats herself once.

Whenever Dad is short of a latch lifter, which he called the price of a pint of beer, we take my guitar up to the local pub and do a bit of busking. I sing some sad old Irish songs for the many laborers from the Emerald Isle, who are temporally exiled on some building site in the Midlands. The boys like the Irish rebel songs, too, and many's the good night's craic starts off with next to no money. These lads sing along, stamping their feet in time and thanks be to God, passing the hat around afterward! There is no Irish music to be heard on juke boxes this time of day, and the workers really show their appreciation for a wee touch of home.

Most of these chaps work on short contracts in England to keep their families fed back home in Ireland. They call themselves long-distance men.

They are a hard breed of men, working out in all weathers and living out of the pubs and the fish and chip shops. Often they stay in the cheapest lodgings, or spikes, as they refer to these doss-houses. They have their own folklore about the good and bad construction companies to work for. These become the subject of the ragged-arsed toastmasters:

> *Come all you brave young navvies*
> *And you long-distance men,*
> *And don't you work for Bovis,*
> *MacAlpine or Maclean.*

"A toast: You work for Laing, but not for long!"

The glasses clink and a tidal wave of Guinness washes away the dust of a day's hard labor.

"A toast to WIMPEY: *'We Import Millions of Paddies Every Year!'*"

With a sweep of well-trained elbows, the flagons are drained and replenished.

"A toast:

> *Oh Mother dear, I'm over here,*
> *And never coming back.*
> *What keeps me here's,*
> *The rake of beer,*
> *The women and the craic!"*

"A toast:

> *'Twas the Irish built the roads of Britain,*
> *and before them, the bloody Romans!"*

They are good men, these gentlemen of the pick, shovel, hod, and trowel. They are amongst the finest lads to be met anywhere; hardworking, honest, and diligent. Politicians could learn much from them!

My activities at school continue to incur the wrath of the headmaster. I have been warned that I'm on the expulsion list. It's dinnertime and I am called to his office. On my way, I prepare my speech for the defense:

"I cannot settle to this tame, indolent existence amid the stench of fuming factories and the wantonness of pissy backstairs that lead to the concrete concussion of urban urbanity. It is easy for me to see how rats caught in a maze go mad and kill each other in frenzied savagery. This will not be my fate. I who have flown with the war heroes, survived the fury of the accursed damp, run with the sleek brown hunted otter, and roamed wild with the children of the Gael amongst the shafts of Celtic willows springing straight and lethal from the osier beds."

In the cluttered calm of the Head's study I deliver my oration, standing erect like Robert Emmet in the dock.

"Yes, very good, Watkins. Go home, your grandmother has died."

Mary-Anne the dancer had passed away, aged seventy-three.

I ask Mr. Druce, the science teacher, if I can start a science club during recess and a couple of hours after classes each night. He is delighted at my interest and readily agrees to our needs, subject to the headmaster's approval. I often helped the staff set up experiments and equipment, so he has no problem giving me a key to the main laboratory on the top floor of the science block.

One day we casually ask permission to form an amateur radio society. This, like our previous request, is granted by the headmaster, who is delighted that he has whipped one of his dissidents back into line.

We rig a huge dipole antenna and set up an ex-army W.S. No. 19 transmitter-receiver and attendant accessories: microphones, record player, tape recorder, and so on. Thus is Radio 190 born!

Our pirate radio service runs for an hour at lunchtime and two hours in the evening on a frequency of 190 meters—easily tunable on any transistor radio.

My staff of four are very professional in their delivery, and the programs soon have a wide listenership. We can be heard up to a mile away in daytime and two miles at night. For nearly three months we stay on the air.

One lunchtime, two green vans appear in the staff car park with ominous-looking direction-finding loop antennas on the roofs. We had just started transmitting when in bursts the headmaster, a policeman, and four members of the General Post Office Radio Interference Division, "The Pirate Busters." We are nicked!

I take the rap for the whole shebang and tell the doubting officials that the other kids didn't know we were radiating.

"I'm leaving soon to become a radio officer in the merchant marine."

"Best bloody place for you!" says one of the GPO men.

In view of this admission, I am not charged with offenses under the Wireless Telegraph Act of 1949 (illegal transmitting apparatus), but I'm given a hell of a row and the equipment is confiscated.

The headmaster invites me to resign from the school and thus save me the embarrassment of being expelled. This I duly do and that is the end of my formal education. I am sixteen.

My only regret is in betraying the trust of Mr. Druce. I seek him out and begin to apologize.

"You're a silly bugger, Watkins."

"Yes, sir, sorry, sir."

"Have I taught you nothing, boy?"

"Sorry, sir."

"Sticking to the same wavelength. You should move frequency, and then they'll never catch you!"

"Eh?"

"It's a shame. I like some of that folk music you played. You don't hear too much of that on the ordinary radio stations!"

So he knew all along, the cunning old fox.

"Good-bye, Watkins," he says, shaking my hand.

He is the last staff person I speak to that day, and I'm glad that we part respecting each other.

I knew I was wasting my time at school. The staff, too, knew that I was not going to pass my exams and meekly go into industry.

Dave Knaggs, the new poetry teacher, urged me to go into the theater.

"Become an actor, dear boy! God knows you have it in you!" was his advice.

Mr. Davies, our Welsh music master and part-time sadist, who had once caught me playing the blues on a harmonica, informed me that I had no musical ability whatsoever, and "a bloody cowboy like you, Watkins, should join the bloody army. It would make a bloody man of you. Look see—there's lovely, isn't it?"

I go home and that evening and tell my parents that I am no longer at school. They are surprisingly more amenable than I thought. Maybe they saw it coming.

"So what are you going to do now?" asks Dad.

"Well, I think I'll take out my wee bit of money from the Post Office Savings Bank and go back home to Ireland!"

"Hhmm! Come on!" he says, and we go for a walk into the cornfield at the back of the flats.

"Listen, Will, when I was young I wanted to be an artist. My father discouraged this and wanted me to join the Great Western Railway where he was a rising star. He had great plans for me. I would become a Freemason like him and this would help shoot me to the top. But he never thought of what I wanted. I didn't want to go against him. So I gave up my dreams for a while, thinking that after a couple of years on the railways, I could go to art school on my own money."

"So why didn't you?"

"Because Franco, Mussolini, Hitler, and the rest of the fascist bastards had a different idea about my future. By the time I'd finished fighting those sods, my chance was gone and my youth with it!"

"Oh! I never thought about it like that before." We crunch on through the stubble of dried-up cornstalks.

"Do what you feel you should do and do it well. Live your own dreams and no one else's. Never give up and don't believe the buggers who tell you it's impossible, all right?"

"Sure, Dad, I'll do that!"

"Just don't come back here later on and say I put you wrong, OK?"

"Yes, Dad, I will do no-such-a-cowardly-act, as Mam would say!"

"Remember, Willie, a man of honor may oft times have to walk alone!"

We trudge on in silence until we reach the stile. After crossing over, Dad puts his strong hand on my shoulder and heaves a shuddering great sigh. Then squaring me around face to face, he looks me straight in the eye and adds, "Remember above all things, you are a Celt, laddie!"

✦ Chapter 19 ✦

JOHNNY (J.C.) CARR, EX-SCHOOL CHUM AND HARMONICA player extraordinaire, sits next to me on the braided, horsehair-stuffed seats of the Irish boat train. He is engrossed in tuning an autoharp, the effort of which has his bottom lip sticking out like a washbasin. This time it is my mam who waves farewell and watches the train draw away into the long New Street Tunnel.

Peering out of the misted-up windows, I see Mam disappearing in a vortex of white steam as we move away. A thousand swirling images of our past travels and partings cascade through my mind. I had gone places before without my folks, but this time I know it is different, and so does my mam. She knows fine that she is saying good-bye to her little lad forever and that the person who returns from this adventure will be changed, grown up, someone new. It is all rather sad.

"You ain't gonna cry, are ya, ya big wench?" needles Johnny in his Brummy accent.

"Of course not. I've just got a bit of soot in my eye from sticking my head out of the window!"

"You are, you're gonna blub. Blimey, and to think I took you for a bit of a bleeding hard knock!"

"I'll give you a hard knock if you don't shut yer gob!" My reaction gives Johnny the rise he was looking for and he sits, contentedly chuckling to himself as the train bursts out of the tunnel into the grimy "satanic mills" of the industrial North Midlands.

I doze for a while with my eyes closed, thinking of when I was a wee kid and fond of putting my head out of the carriage window into the fragrant clouds of steam that billowed by.

"Don't do that, you'll get smuts!" said my mam, not explaining that smuts are airborne soot particles.

"OK, Mam!" I'd say and sit down puzzled.

The only smuts I'd heard of was General Jan Smuts, a hero of the South Africans, who fought the British in the Boer War, and I couldn't see how he fit into the picture.

I jolt awake with an involuntary laugh.

"Well, Wocko, it's good to see you've cheered up!"

"Aye, aye, J.C.," I mumble and begin checking my gear to make sure I have everything. It doesn't take long. I have a guitar, a sleeping bag, a woolen blanket, one change of clothes, and a bag of cheese and onion sandwiches.

"Do you want a sandwich, Johnny?"

"Fuggin' right I do!"

Johnny has even less gear than I do. Whereas I have left home with the blessing of my folks, J.C. has run away after a barney with his mother, and he thinks the police might be looking for him. His only possessions are a bag of harmonicas, an autoharp, a blanket-wrapped sleeping bag, and the clothes he stands up in. About his neck is a heavy crescent-shaped pendant fashioned by himself from a pound of pure copper; this he wears for good luck. On his head is a black derby, and the huge pocket watch hanging on a toilet chain from his waistband completes the ensemble. It's like traveling with the Mad Hatter.

Johnny and I had spent a short time on the road before. Last summer we had hitchhiked to Stourport and slept rough in the old sandstone caves with other weekend ravers. It was fun but cold in those caverns; even with the aid of a crackling log fire, the earth was damp and the air chilly. The real troglodytes, who had lived there until the 1930s, must have been a very tough breed of folk. Eventually, the way of life of these cave dwellers was made illegal by the various Health and Safety Acts of the wartime government and they were rehoused.

Sometime later J.C. immortalizes the events in song:

> Billy and Johnny, fresh from school
> Slung with guitars and playing it cool
> Out on the road, down Stourport way
> To live in the caves for a holiday-hay-hay.

The truth was, our first expedition into the wild world was a desperately ill-equipped affair: one blanket each, no tent, no matches, no cooking gear, loads of tins of beans and not a bloody can opener between us. After this initial bollock-freezing folly, we made sure that, if nothing else, our bedrolls would be adequate. "'Still, everyone makes mistakes,' as the hedgehog said, climbing off of the hairbrush." So what the hell? We're on the road!

This journey to Ireland was to be the making of us both; we planned on being away an entire year. No more would we be considered weekend ravers, traveling on optimism instead of experience. Whenever we do return to Birmingham, we'll be real heroes—long-distance men!

I'm looking forward to returning home to Ireland, and when I realize that it's nearly six years since I was last over home, my enthusiasm bubbles up.

"You won't believe Ireland, Johnny. It's beautiful. Everything is green, forty shades of it, they say. Not just the fields and the hills, even the railway engines, airplanes, buses—all emerald green."

"Yeah, yeah, and the shamrocks are green and the leprechauns are green and me arse is green—"

"Well, your face might be green by morning, matey. The sea yonder looks a wee bit on the rough side. Do you get seasick?"

"I dunno. I've not been on a ship before."

"That's right, you've never been out of England, have you? God knows what you're expecting to find in Ireland—lions, elephants maybe, camels, or whatnot!"

"Little green women, an' little green men, an' little greenhorns like you, so don't be taking the piss out of me, Wockins, ya cheeky wee bastard. I'm older than you, remember, so have a bit of respect!"

"Oh, aye, that eighteen days makes all the difference. Who do you think you are, bloody Methuselah?"

"Who the hell's Mafoosela?"

"You know, the bloke in the Old Testament who lived nine hundred and sixty-nine years—blimey, Johnny, haven't you read the Bible?"

"No!"

"Why?"

"Because it's full of bollocks, like blokes living nine hundred and sixty-nine years!"

Holyhead, the gray granite springboard of so many of my past adventures, comes into view. The boat train pulls into the seaport and the west wind whips hard at the wave tops, sending white breakers crashing over the harbor mole. Rising from the quayside like a floating city is a shiny new passenger ship, owned by British Railways, but called the M.V. *Hibernia*. The old steamship *Princess Maud,* which had survived countless hurricanes, two world wars, and the curses of my mother, had finally met her fate in the scrap yard.

The new vessel is clean and spacious. We promenade the deck like Edwardian gentlemen, nodding to fellow passengers and crew members alike. Below decks, we find the seclusion of an empty linen closet and roll our sleeping bags out on the wide wooden shelves. It's perfect.

There's a singsong in the lounge bar, and grabbing our instruments, we join in. The Irish are famous for impromptu get-togethers like this and we have a good session, marred only by Johnny being refused service by the English bloke at the bar.

"Can I get two pints of Guinness, please?"

"Are you of age, mate?" says the barman in a London Cockney accent.

"What d'you say?"

"How bleedin' old are you, sonny?"

"I'm sixteen."

"Then come back in two years, sunshine. Now bugger orf or you'll get my boot up yer arse!"

We dock in Ireland next morning. Although the sea remained rough, the crossing had been smooth as the ship was fitted with stabilizers. Johnny was not seasick and, indeed, proved to have a "cast-iron" stomach after surreptitiously drinking all the dregs he could find in the bar. A comfortable night's sleep was had in our makeshift cabin, and before long we were making our way down the gangplank onto Irish sod.

"Welcome to my country, Mr. Carr." I make a sweeping arm gesture.

"Merci beaucoupus fullbus maccabeeus, Mr. Wockins." Johnny bows in mock reply.

"What's that mean?"

"I've no idea."

The tang of sea air, fresh and salty, is great for the appetite, and along the dockside a greasy-spoon café offers an Irish breakfast we'd be fools to ignore. After supping on a belt-bursting meal of sausage, bacon, eggs, fried black pudding, tomatoes, soda bread, and hot black tea, we waddle like penguins over the cobblestone forecourt to the Dublin train.

The port rail terminal is not quite as I remember. Dun Laoghaire has changed a lot in six years. Long rows of horse-drawn jaunting cars once queued here waiting for fares; now it is rows of motor taxis that ply the trade.

Sadly, the hissing green CIE steam trains of yesteryear have been replaced with oil-dripping diesel locomotives in grimy orange livery. Nearing the engine, the sweet ocean ozone, wafting in from the bay, is quickly soured by the belch of acrid exhaust fumes from the revving loco. Johnny pulls an equally acidic face and belches himself.

"Hey, Wocko, you bullshiter! You told me they had green steam trains here, not these stinky things." I have no answer for him, so I just shrug my shoulders.

From the vantage point of the long curve of raised railway line, J.C. stares down on the shops and houses comprising the outskirts of Dublin. The quick ride into the city has convinced my friend that Ireland was England with more shit in the streets. The brisk walk from Westland Row station to the city center confirms his belief.

"These buses look exactly the same as the buses in Birmingham!"

He was right. The buses, once green with gold trim, were now a drab cream and black, but something else looked different, too, something about the view down O'Connell Street. What the hell was it?

"These building are just like the ones in Brum, same stone, same shape, same—"

"Of course they are. They were built by the same British architects when Ireland was a colony! But something has changed since I was last here," I mumble, still puzzled by the "new look" Dublin.

"What's changed about it?"

"I'm not sure. People seem better off than I remember, better dressed. There's more motorcars than there used to be and hardly a horse and cart to be seen. These shopfronts all had quaint old Dickensian windows. I wonder why they got replaced with plate glass?"

"Maybe it's just modernization, you know? Getting with it, as they say."

"I guess you're right, J.C. You can't expect a place to stay frozen in time, like the Olde Worlde pictures on a toffee tin, but it's a shame that things have to change."

"That's the trouble with nostalgia, Wocko, it ain't what it used to be."

"Yeah, maybe that's it. Wait a minute! Oh, my God, he's gone! Totally gone!"

"Who's gone?"

"Admiral Nelson! Horatio *bloody* Nelson. He's gone, completely gone!"

"I think you're bleedin' gone, Wockins, gone in the head! Nelson's been dead for donkey's years!"

"Johnny, you don't understand. He was standing right there, outside the GPO, on a bloody great two-hundred-foot column, like the one in Trafalgar Square, and it's gone!"

"What d'you think happened to him?"

"I dunno, wait and I'll ask someone. Hey, mister, what happened to old Nelson?"

"Aw Jasus, son, sure wasn't he blown up last March by the brave boyos!"

"What boyos?"

"The Eye Or Ay, so it was, in the middle of the night. Blew the ould Brit from his perch—an' good riddance to the one-eyed ould tosser. Ould Nelson is up there now, orbiting the fookin' earth with John Glenn an' Yuri *fookin'* Gagarin!"

"What did he say, Wock? I didn't get a word of that."

"He says the IRA blew up the statue in the middle of the night."

"That's right, son. The lads blew the beJasus out of the column, without even cracking a pane of glass in the GPO. When the fookin' Irish Army were called in to blow up what fookin' remained of the fookin' thing, they broke every fookin' window in Dublin! Boom!" says the stranger, throwing his arms in an arc about his head.

The spot where Nelson's plinth had once stood is now a flowerbed burgeoning with daffodils. We take our ease for a while, sitting on the concrete wall surrounding the nodding yellow blooms. On the parapet, some Dublin wag has scribbled "Nelson's Grave."

"The GPO, over there, is where the rising of 1916 started fifty years ago."

"Oh, that's nice," he says, surveying the scene.

"Nice? There was bugger-all nice about it. The British shelled the city flat and killed hundreds."

Johnny isn't listening; his mind is elsewhere and, in a feat normally the sole province of the owl, he nigh-on turns his head full circle when checking out a bevy of passing office girls.

"Wow! They've got some nice looking bints here and no mistake. D'ya think we'll get the ride?"

"No bloody chance. You know what they say in Holy Catholic Ireland, 'No Fling Without a Ring!'" J.C. pouts and cranes his gaze in the opposite direction; there is a sharp crack like the snapping of a stick of chalk.

"Oh, shit! I think I've got fighter pilot's neck!" He rubs the bones at the base of his skull as pain dampens his ardor and more mundane thoughts reappear.

"So where's this other station we have to go to. Is it far?"

"Aye, it is. Kingsbridge station is a good long walk from here, a couple of miles away up the back of Guinness's brewery."

"That's a drag. Why didn't they build the station in the city center?"

"Well, they thought of that, but decided it was better to put it where the railway tracks were."

"Oh, very funny, Wocko. You're so bloody sharp, be careful you don't cut yerself."

"Forward march!" I signal. Johnny follows and we swing briskly up the banks of the Liffey to the railway station. Although encumbered by our bedrolls and instruments, we exude a jaunty air and enjoy the inquisitive looks from passersby and the curious gaze of the many young lassies we meet on the way. Imbued with all the confidence of victorious soldiers on a looting spree, we know there is nothing in Ireland the likes of us!

The Limerick Express thunders across the great open expanse of the Curragh Plain. All around, fine thoroughbred horses are being exercised for the flat-racing season. Like the white chalk figures our ancestors carved into the hills, these creatures look so well adapted and content in the lush, green landscape. It is easy to see how these Irish horses excel in soft-going racing conditions when they have been running on moist malleable moss all their lives. Sure I like the soft-going myself.

"Glac bog an saoghal agus glachgig an saoghal bog tú!"

"Yeah, Watkins, and the bleeding same to you with knobs on! What sort of bloody bog Latin is that? Roman?"

"No, it's Irish! That was the favorite saying of a venerable old Irish tailor. It means, 'Treat the world softly and the world will treat you softly!'"

"So you bog-wogs have yer own lingo, do you? I thought you were just ignorant paddies that can't speak English proper—like what I do!"

"And a lovely job you make of it, too, Johnny! No, Irish is a very ancient language, far older than Greek or Latin, a remnant of the old Celtic tongue once spoken all over Europe and the British Isles, until the Romans pushed the native people into the most out-lying fringes of the continent, where they live to this day."

Johnny chants a kiddies' street rhyme much used by girls jumping rope or skipping, as we would say:

> *The Germans speak Krautish*
> *The Frenchies speak Frog*
> *The Romans speak I-tie*
> *The Noggies speak Nog*
> *But the English speak English*
> *The language of God!*

"Hmm, very nice, but 'dogs' would be a better rhyme and a lot more accurate."

"Bollocks!"

"That's an Irish word, Johnny!"

"Well, how about *bugger off?*"

"Now you're talking. That's good old Anglo-Saxon, or as you would say, the language of God. By the way, do you fancy a beer?" He looks up suspiciously.

"How are you going to manage that? We're both obviously under-age."

"You're not in England now, sonny!" I say, mimicking the Cockney accent of the barman on the ship. "This is Ireland!" I make my way to the buffet car, where I buy two bottles of Time beer. The barman hardly looks at me.

Beer in hand, J.C. is very impressed.

"How did you pull that one off?"

"You see, my friend, no one thinks it odd that a sixteen-year-old would be up at the bar getting drinks. The parents often send the kids up to get the rounds in."

"Cool! Is it the same in the towns—kids allowed in pubs and the like?"

"Yeah. All the big pubs employ young lads as potboys to fetch and carry pints for the grown-ups, and if someone is sick, a child might be sent to the local pub for a bottle of medicinal whiskey. No one's bothered if a teenager has a beer or two, as long as he don't get stupid and start showing off. You can have a good piss-up as long as you don't advertise it to the whole bloody world! You'll not get away with that in Birmingham, will you, eh?"

J.C. nods his head and sucks at his beer bottle, cross-eyed, like a calf getting its early morning feed. He makes me laugh, and humor is a good leaven and succor in times of travail. I reckon, deep down he's carrying a heavy load and hides his problems under a facade of japing and jesting that gives him a reputation for being a bit of a bumsteer. At school his taste for practical jokes was legendary, and he drove the teachers to distraction.

Johnny could emit a high-pitched scream, ventriloquist-like, and then become part of the crowd of puzzled passersby, looking around and speculating on the origin. When some poor innocent bugger runs past him at speed, "Stop thief!" Johnny shouts. The unfortunate victim of this prank was often grabbed or banjaxed by some civic-minded member of the public, who instead of receiving praise for their actions, are at pains to explain the nature of their random act of violence to the injured party. He transforms the mundane world around us into a maelstrom of mischief and mayhem, whilst seemingly aloof to the consequences. Johnny was born on April Fool's Day the same year as myself; a date that, considering his taste for the bizarre, has to be more than coincidence.

I first met him when he was made to sit next to me at school. He was loud and brash with a puckish sense of humor and liked to get up the teachers' noses. However, he wasn't much of a student and left school early to become an apprentice cable joiner for a firm of street-lighting electricians. He says that working in the roadside trenches gives you great opportunity to look up girls' skirts, and heating up pennies with a blow lamp, for some mean old sod to pick up, is a good source of fun on an otherwise boring day.

Johnny sits staring at the label on his beer bottle, his eyebrows alternately meeting and blenching; like two shy caterpillars waiting to be introduced.

"Why call a beer Time? Seems like an odd name. Time goes by, maybe? Ah, ha! That's the joke—Time for another!" Finger aloft in realization, he makes for the bar and returns somewhile later with: "Look, Wock, more Time on me hands!"

He lies full length across the carriage seats, gawping at the green fields flitting by. His well-rounded face has a girlish "peaches and cream" complexion, which, combined with his shoulder-length blond curls, makes him look rather effeminate. This most certainly is not his nature. He's a tough little bugger and can be a downright nasty little bollix when it suits him. It's as well that he makes me laugh or sometimes I'd have to strangle him.

I had helped him to play music and he was quick to learn the guitar and mouth organ. Now J.C. has an autoharp to add a little zest to our folk duo, and we look forward to singing for our supper in the green womb of Holy Ireland, where so much music and poetry have been conceived, nurtured, and often banned by the BloodyEnglish.

We arrive in the same old Limerick station and go to my nana's house, where there is tea, soda bread and jam, and a bed made up for us in the spare room.

After swapping family news, I sit scanning the entertainment column in the *Limerick Leader* newspaper, for word of a folk club or traditional music event where we might make our debut.

To my chagrin, I can't see anything that looks even remotely promising. It seems that country and western music has taken over and there is no shortage of these gigs. The big venues are being packed out by the many showbands, like "Big Tom and the Mainliners" and "Dickie Rock and the Miami." This is a blow. What has happened to the come-all-ye folk clubs? Is our trip to end in disappointment?

"So what's the big event in this one-horse town?" Johnny enjoys taking the piss out of my mounting frustration.

"Well, Latchford's Cinema in Newcastle West is opening with *Mary Poppins* on the twenty-first of August. Admission prices: threepence, two and six, and one and six. Do you want to go?"

"I'd rather eat my own shite, thank you very much!"

"You wait there, Johnny, and I'll get you a spoon!"

Dad is right. The Lamp of the Gael is burning at an all-time low. Poetry is becoming the province of academics, and traditional music is disappearing from areas of the countryside, like frost on a fire grate. Something has got to be done, but what?

"What has happened, Uncle Seán? What's happened to Celtic culture?"

"Jasus, Willie, you will be hard put to finding a piece of Celtic culture outside of a museum. Sure the Gaelic tunes, songs, and stories are being torn asunder by immigration and death and apathy and sure Hollywood movies have a lot to answer for. Radio Eireann hardly ever plays Irish music anymore. Now it's all Frank Sinatra and Elvis Presley and all them Bobby whatsits—Vee or Vinton or Darrin. Jasus, there's no end to them! Sure I have the feeling that Irish music is on the run and has little chance of surviving for long, unless a miracle happens!"

He's right, judging by the fact that it is almost impossible to get traditional Irish music on modern LP records. Most of the stuff we have is on old cracked wax seventy-eights. I worry it might all be going down the tubes, doomed to oblivion in my own lifetime.

"Auntie Maura, would you ever sing me 'Bridgín Bhan Mo Stór?'"

"Ah, go'way now, Willie, sure no one sings them old come-all-ye songs anymore, sure they went out with the Ark! How about 'When Irish Eyes Are Smiling' or maybe 'Tu-ra Lu-ra Lu-ra'?" They're grand little ditties altogether! You need to get with it, Willie!"

"Maura, if Tin Pan Alley is with it, I'd rather be without it!"

It seems that the old ways are dying out and a new era of modernism is sweeping the last vestige of the Gael into the wild Atlantic, with folks looking on who think that Bing Crosby is an Irish priest who sings nice songs and does a bit of acting on the side!

It isn't all bad news though. Seán tells me that Irish music and folklore are still alive and safe in small pockets scattered throughout the country and even more so overseas in Britain and America.

"You need to get out into the country and seek ye the festivals called 'Fleádh Cheoils.' Organizations like Comhaltas Ceoltóiri Éireann are working both sides of the Irish Sea trying to promote traditional music and dance. Seán O'Rioda, Paddy Tunney, and Séamus Ennis are doing grand work, and so are the Dubliners and Paddy Maloney's group Ceoltóri Chuilinn. I'll ask around the boys at the post office and we'll see if we can't find you a Fleádh Cheoil to get your teeth into!"

"Thanks, Uncle Seán. I promised my dad that I would do something to help save our culture and that will give me a start."

"Strike a blow for the Gael, Liam! Ceol an Gael Abú!"

Seán brings news of a Fleádh in Kilrush, County Clare, where I had once seen the tinkers and the drunken horse. With spirits high, we hitchhike down to Kilkee and sleep the night in one of the beach changing huts. In the wee small hours, the door bursts open, giving me the fear of Christ.

"Oh, sorry lads! It's the police here—I'm just checking!" The civic guard looms large on the other end of his flashlight, his torch picking out our musical instruments in the gloom.

"Are you down here for the Fleádh, boys?"

"We are, sir, yes. We've come down from Limerick!"

"Good lads. I'll maybe see you in the morning, so! Goodnight now."

After sunup we arise to leave. I find that some kind person has left a pint of milk and a bunch of bananas outside the hut for our breakfast.

"It must have been the policeman. What a nice chap, eh, Johnny?"

"A.C.A.B."

"What's that supposed to mean?"

"All Coppers Are Bastards, Wockins, you mark my words." Shaking my head, I leave him sitting on the sand dunes, the policeman's milk running down his peach-fuzzed chin.

Alone I walk up to the cliff tops and stand eating my banana, watching the ever crashing, luminous green Atlantic rollers basting the bay with rhythmic repetition.

The sky is alive, iridescent with bands of mingling color: red, gold, green, and blue. Great white gulls and kittiwakes wheel and squawk overhead, spiraling upward, then descending dartlike into the foam-topped waves. Although I am alone, I have no feeling of loneliness. I feel a part of all this. Like the prodigal I am, I have returned home to where my heart lies. Way out, far past the edge of the silvery bay, I see a ship hull down to the horizon.

"Must be going to America. More immigrants, I suppose. Just why do people pull up their roots and leave such a beautiful place?" I am still full of the inward glow of the returned wayward son, wandering and wondering, being young, naive, and most of all oblivious to the economic realities of recession-cursed Ireland.

"Wockins! Wocko! Where are ya?" J.C. is calling me from below, his foghorn voice cutting through the hiss of waves on the shape-shifting shingle.

I make my way back down and pack up my gear. It is a testament to the times that sleeping bags, guitars, or what have you can be left unattended almost anywhere without fear of theft or damage. Johnny is waiting.

"What yow bin doing, Wock?"

"I was communing with nature." I am still dreaming the small dreams of the protopoet.

"Yer, me too. I had my shite over there!" replies my nefarious nemesis, pointing to a little pyramid of turds and newspaper, steaming amongst the golden sand dunes.

> *As I roved out one midsummer's morning,*
> *For to view the fields and to take the air,*
> *Down by the banks of the sweet primroses,*
> *'Tis there I spied a sweet maiden fair.*

Singing at the top of my voice, I march my way along the green-dyked undulating road, from the seaside town of Kilkee, to the inland market town of Kilrush.

Strolling along a few feet behind me, Johnny is striking great swelling chords of accompaniment on the autoharp. We are a pair of medieval minstrels on our way to the fair to find fame and fortune. Bardic vagabonds, celebrating a tradition as old as humankind itself. Songsters, rhymesters, clowns, and jongleurs. The Gentlemen of the Toby, as all true Gypsies call the road. We are the dedicated artisans of the muse, resolved to play our souls to the very heavens and, if at all possible, please God, get ourselves fixed up with a couple of young lassies.

The soft wind pulls the summer trees over to hear our song. The sun tumbles blithely across the blue sky, the meadowlark soars from the furze in sublime vivacity, and we, just as carefree, ramble through County Clare.

Cars full of reprobates, rakes, and revelers occasionally pass us by, the folks all waving and beeping their horns in merriment.

Although we do not stick the old hitchhiker's thumb out, to our great surprise, a venerable old Morris Minor car stops next to us and its equally ancient driver asks, "Arroo going to the Fleádh, boys? If you am, get yerselves in. I'm away down to sell da sheep and ye'll be most welcome to come along fer da ride!"

We are quick to take up the farmer's kind offer, but when I open the door, I realize that the driver has the only seat left in the vehicle. Where the passenger seat and the rear seats once were, there is just a bed of straw and a disconsolate-looking blackface sheep that stares back at us as baleful as Bacchus during the holy hour.

Anyway, we make the most of it and our journey down is full of songs and jokes. On the outskirts of town, we run into the crowds, and it takes almost thirty minutes to navigate through the festive throng to the central square.

So like Christ's triumphant entry into Jerusalem on the back of a lowly donkey, we young hopefuls arrive at the epicenter of the "1966 All-Ireland Fleádh Cheoil," not as the rising stars of the folk music revival, as we had hoped, but covered in straw and sheep shit and smelling like the bottom of an owl's nest.

The Fleádh is a unique experience. Since I have little interest in sporting events and seldom do the Stations of the Cross, I'm not used to large crowds at all and it is at first a bit intimidating. Before long, however, the good nature of the participants and the other musicians quickly wins me over and I feel as at home as a pig in a midden. Johnny is in his element, doing his long-range ventriloquist act and puzzling the beJasus out of the folk in the market square. I am plucked by the arm by a big fellow with a shock of wiry red hair and a square ginger beard.

"Come on, youngfella, there's a grand session inside of the green barn here. Come and sit in, and we'll hear some of your stuff."

I recognize this man from an LP record of my mam's. It is Luke Kelly from the Dubliners! Johnny follows us inside, grinning with devilment.

In the dim light of the old corrugated iron barn, several tiers of wooden benches have been erected, and on some of the lower ones sits a clutch of musicians battering out the reel "Rakish Paddy."

The thing I find most peculiar with this scene is that the audience sits behind the players and can only see their backs. When I ask Luke why this is, he says, "This is a session, not a concert, so you don't need folks staring ya in the face!"

I am very glad of this fact, when after being invited to sing, my nervous state of excitement causes complete amnesia in the middle of "The Wreck of Engine 143." My red face is saved by my fellow musicians filling in an extra-long instrumental break until I can recover my wits and sing the ending to the old American railroad song.

Johnny and myself, gaining in confidence by the minute, play almost everything we know and soon are the *corps célèbre* of the assembly of fine musicians, made up mostly from the Pipers' Club in

Thomas Street, Dublin. These wonderful people take us under their collective wing, and we become sort of mascots for our much older and wiser companions.

Brendan Byrne, or Brendan Bodhrán, as he is known, being a virtuoso on the ancient one-sided Irish skin drum, is taken up with J.C. and, like him, has an autoharp. He spends a good while teaching Johnny new techniques and how to get the best out of his old yoke, as most folk refer to any unknown or seldom seen instrument.

I have a good deal of time chatting with Luke Kelly, who is very interested in some of the old songs that I can remember and is pleased when I help him fill in some missing words or verses from a song he is trying to master.

Luke is a truly great singer and a lovely man and, like myself, sports a "Ban the Bomb" badge on his jacket lapel. He is as politically aware as he is talented, and it is reckoned that his voice is loud enough to blow the froth off of a pint of Guinness at forty paces!

I'm glad to say that he is very patient with me when I put up my half-arsed arguments against his communist beliefs. Also, he is delighted when I sing Spanish Civil War songs like "Viva La Quince Brigada" or "Los Cuatro Generales" in which he and Brendan would join in with gusto, their clenched fists waving the air!

For the four days of the Fleádh, our mentors do us proud, imparting that which you cannot learn at school or from your family and treating us as young adults, not as older children.

We are successful in everything, except chatting up the girls. I am far too shy and Johnny is far too blunt. Between the pair of us, we either bore them to death or scare them off. A couple of blond girls with Swedish flags sewn on their rucksacks seem poised to speak with us. J.C. jumps in quick, snatching defeat from the jaws of victory.

"It gets on yer wick, don't it?" he says, indicating the enormous press of the crowd around us. I stand beside him nodding assent and grinning like a torn slipper. The darling daughters of Odin regard us in mystified silence, whilst trying to decipher our meaning. Then, assuming they are in the company of a pair of village idiots, they leave us in their wake.

"Fuggin' Viking virgins!" Johnny curses. It's as well he has a "cast-iron neck"; rejection never seems to bother him.

In every house, pub, and street the festival is a seething sea of wild goings-on that would have inspired a dozen paintings by Brueghel, or in some back lanes, the lewd triptychs of Hieronymus Bosch. There is a huge wooden stage made of farm carts in the town square, on which beautifully uniformed Irish dancers clack out their knotwork of intricate steps. On smaller stages all around, competitions are being held for poetry, dancing, singing, piping, flute playing, and fiddling. Harps send their silvern notes drifting heavenward suffused with the smell of roast ox, chicken, and pork. Reminiscent of the medieval pageants, velveteen-tabarded dancers, in vividly embroidered smocks, mingle in the throng, calling to mind the colors of a patchwork quilt. Like camels at the oasis, the imbibers know no limit, and the many hundreds of pubs are serving strings of people well outside their premises and down into the streets.

To one such tavern we push our way through the merrymaking, and it is pleasing to note that folk give way to the musicians, so as to let them into the heart of the sessions. There are so many people crammed inside this old pub that half of the assembled players are having to stand up on the sill of a great stained-glass window to get room to swing the elbow. The music is mighty, and the jigs and reels that we're playing reach a climax of speed, involvement, and dexterity.

Suddenly without any warning, there comes an earsplitting crack and a dozen or so musicians and the multicolored window disappear out onto the cobbledstoned street below. I am one of them, but luckily for me, I land on top of the pile and am thus saved from injury. The ones who fell first seem to fare no lasting harm and even instruments are spared any bad damage. I guess many are too drunk to notice otherwise, as overindulgence leads to great immunity! We climb back through the gaping casement and into the newly air-conditioned pub, where we continue playing until a visiting civic guard calls us to order.

"Quiet! Quieten down now, all of youse!" he shouts, waving his arms in a sit-down movement. "This is no good, no good atall atall!" he continues. "Youse will all need to make some reparations to the good folk of this establishment!"

And with that, he takes off his policeman's hat and passes it around to take up a collection for the damages. By the time it is handed over to the grinning landlord, it is overflowing with pound notes and fivers. He and his staff give us a round of applause in thanks and we bend back to the task of raising the roof—musically, that is!.

It was very strange to see a cop indulging in such a noble gesture and although neither of us could contribute to the fund, I'm glad to have witnessed it. At the insistence of one of the farmers present, we later adjourn to a private house that is having a chélidh. We eagerly dig into the huge buffet of food that is provided for us.

"God, Johnny, this is good scran."

"Yeah, no kidding. I'm as hungry as a pig with worms!"

Our group of six or so plays for the dancers, who thunder across the bare floorboards of the front room. Sitting on the floor, the vibrations of the assembled jarring the bones of my arse, I'm wondering how the deck can take such punishment when a teacup hits me on the head! Looking up I see the Welsh dresser, from which the cup had tumbled, swinging some six inches out from the top of the wall with each syncopated stomp of the dancers. I decide to move to a safer spot as the dresser continues to jive around, shedding its china contents and no one paying any heed to it. Amazingly, the two-hundred-year-old floor stands firm and is probably used to such extreme testing.

But all good things must come to an end, even Fleádhs. On the following Tuesday it is time to say good-bye to our new friends and hit the road once more.

I have learned a lot in these four days. Not just about playing music, but how to conduct myself with a wee bit of decorum. As Luke says, "Always remember that a musician is the guest of his audience and not the other way around!" I am grateful for this wisdom and thank him as we say "Slán leat" to each other. He is a great man with his loud voice, wild red hair, and graceful demeanor.

About five or six miles out of town, there is a Bronze Age "fairy fort." This takes the form of a circular enclosure with a central stone-slabbed chamber that you can access by a shallow tunnel. The locals are very superstitious about these and seldom go near them. This is a useful taboo, as it prevents vandalism and helps to preserve the monuments for future generations. It also means that we can camp out there with little chance of interference from the police or the intrusion of blaggards.

A southwest wind, soft on the cheek, blows warm and moist from the Gulf of Mexico. It has all the makings of a fine night. Content with our lot, we lie in our sleeping bags on the dewy grass, wishing, like most sixteen-year-olds, that we had the company of a couple of lassies. However, I have the moon for companionship; a silver, pockmarked surfer riding the curls of the scudding clouds above. Johnny is soon snoring, but I've a bet on with myself and won't go to sleep until I can remember all of a poem about the moon.

> *Whenever the moon and stars are set*
> *Whenever the wind is high* . . . *dum te dum*—oh, bugger!

Try another one:

> *The moon was a ghostly galleon*
> *Tossed upon cloudy seas* . . . *de-dah-de-dah-de-dah*—no better!

There must be one I know all the way through:

> *The man in the moon came down too soon*
> *And burnt his tongue on his porridge*—there, done it!

Good night!

I doze off in the throes of trying to remember any other moonish verse. An hour later, I'm rudely awakened by rain splattering in my face. The moon and stars *have* set, and the wind *is* high. In the cloudy seas above, the ghostly galleon has foundered after the man in the moon abandons ship.

In the sudden squall, my sleeping bag is fast sinking in the mud and Johnny, cursing like a whore on holiday, is trying to wriggle out of his waterlogged bedroll. The storm gathers pace, and we crawl into the open mouth of the underground burial chamber.

Our shadows gyrate on the walls of the mortarless stone vault, as the breeze from outside snatches at the flickering flame of a candle stub. By our feet, a rivulet of peaty rainwater vanishes, gurgling, between the cracks of the flagstone floor. Sitting hunched up in the confined space, we speculate on the existence of yet another crypt below us. This conjecture is short-lived when a successful grab of wind snuffs out the candle. Attempts to relight it fail, and embalmed in our bedrolls, we sit like motionless mummies in the thick blackness, two entombed mortals sporadically illuminated by the blue sheen of lightning flashes from without.

Thunder pounds the grassy roof of the dank Bronze Age sepulcher. Between thunderclaps, the dribbling water splatters onto the stones of the mysterious chamber beneath. Sitting on the numb bones of my arse, knees under chin, I eventually slip into a fitful sleep.

A white-robed Druid invades the dank sanctuary of my tormented dreams. Grasping my wrist, he pulls me down into the dripping catacombs below. A fire flares at the end of a long tunnel, upon which sits the great boiling bronze cauldron of Dagda. The priest causes me to gaze therein. Under its bubbling surface, I see a hideously demonic visage twisted and contorted in a ghastly grimace. Against my will, my own face is drawn inexorably nearer to the wraithlike specter, grinning maniacally up at me. The horrid head opens its raw mouth and, instead of speaking, belches a stench of the foulest imaginings, searing into my stinging nostrils.

"Ahggh!" I shake myself awake into an equally malodorous environment. The fetid air of the musty tumulus has taken on the clinging miasma of a putrefying corpse.

"Silent but deadly, eh, Wockins?" says Johnny, sitting smugly in the clammy midst of his early morning fart.

⇥ Chapter 20 ⇤

A BRISK ATLANTIC BREEZE SWIRLS DUST DEVILS ALONG THE
cracked concrete streets of Milltown Malbay, chasing the last of the
summer heat haze from the late afternoon. The town seems deserted as
we two vagabonds drift through empty lanes with nothing to do and all
day to do it. Autumn is coming and the fresh westerly trade wind threat-
ens to dislodge a goat, feasting on the fruits of windblown cabbage
seeds growing green and luscious in the diseased roof thatch of a white-
washed cottage shop. Having failed to intimidate the animal, the wind
snatches up a faded newspaper, rending the pages asunder in rage. In a
fit of spite, the gust deposits most of the fragments over the half door
of the tumbledown emporium below. A girl's voice from within strains
over the tinny dirge of pop music from a transistor radio.

"Would ye ever close the top door out, Connie? The bloody wind
has all the shite in the universe blowing in and me trying to clean up."

"We've an hour to go yet, Patty-Jo. If I close the door, how will anyone know we're open at all?" comes a second voice.

"Put the sign up in the window, Concepta, fer Jasus' sake and don't
be coddin' me!" The yellow-stained sunshade jerks aside and a slender
hand places a card in front of the cobweb-embroidered corner of a con-
spicuously empty window.

'Yes, We Are Open!' the Day Glo orange message proclaims to a heap
of dead wasps and bluebottles gathered behind the grimy glass.

Johnny makes his way over the road to investigate the derelict shop
and its young female proprietors. As he ventures to peer into the dark
interior, the top half door, squealing in torment on its rusty hinges,
bangs out in his face, revealing the name of the establishment neatly
picked out in fine Art Nouveau lettering: A Touch of Class Boutique.

⇥ 267 ⇤

J.C. gets a fit of the giggles at the shop's optimistic claim and his derision is met by a bleating rebuff from the roof above. The goat leaves off chomping cabbages and from his vantage point regards Johnny with defiant contempt. Lord of all he beholds, the capricious creature reaps his revenge. With a triumphant bleat, the puck lifts its tail, releasing a shower of sticky black grapeshot, skittering down the rotting thatch roof and all over the pair of us. Pursued by the bouncing nodules, Johnny and I scurry for the safety of an old pub up the road that is advertising a music session.

Sitting in the back bar of a west Clare public house picking goat shit out of my collar was not how I'd imagined the life of a wandering balladeer, but as luck would have it, we had stumbled into one of the finest traditional music sessions in Ireland. Amongst the customers in the tavern, the mood is quiet and expectant. Conversation is muted, and Johnny, somewhat awed by the ambience, sits like he's in church .

"That old geezer over there is going to play the fiddle," he whispers over his pint of stout.

With a conceding creak, a coffin-shaped violin case opens. There is a soft rustle of velvet, then the sonorous squeak of a ball of rosin rubbed gently upon the ghost-white horsehairs of a centuries-old bow. In the center of the room, the old man stands tuning the antique walnut instrument resting beneath the stubbled jowls of his chin. Silent, except for the wind in the chimney, the audiences wait impassively for the release of the fiddle's secret soul. The fiddler pays no heed; he takes his time plucking the strings and adjusting the pegs until, content with the tuning, he stiffens his frame and presents bow to string. With his eyes seemly fixed upon a far-distant point in time, a torrent of triplets spill out heralding the arrival of "The Lark in the Morning." Feet tapping in six/eight time, we return to our pints. The maestro takes us on a gay-spirited ramble down "The Road to Lisdoonvarna," and by way of a merry hornpipe, introduces us to "Madame Bonaparte." Finally comes the heart-wrenching lament for lost youth, "An Buachaill Caol Dubh."

I had never before experienced such a mystical force emanating from one human being. It was obvious to me that the fiddle played itself, but the man played the very souls of his listeners. For the first time, I realized the power of music and why it struck fear into those whose hearts were cold to it. If the pen is mightier than the sword, then the fiddle bow is a veritable cutlass in the hands of a noble warrior such as this. This fact didn't escape the BloodyEnglish. Under the Penal Laws of the seventeenth century, possession of a musical instrument was punishable by death! Mind you, come to think of it, under the Penal Laws anything an Irish person did was punishable by death.

A prolonged applause abates, and acknowledging the audience for the first time, the old musician hands the violin to a fresh-faced girl of about eleven. She plays a fine slip-jig, without scratch nor screech, then amid hoots and cheers, hands back the fiddle with a curtsey. A young lad, who might have been her brother, pulls a tin whistle out of his sleeve and begins to play "The King of the Fairies." Every musician in the house joins in and a whale of a session primes the autumn night. I am reborn!

Milltown Malbay, Lahinch, Lisdoonvarna, and Ennistymon become the radials of our circuit as we pass from session to session through the pubs and taverns of wild West Clare. We find a little-known village called Doolin at the back of the Cliffs of Moher. Here we play in a tiny bar in the rear of O'Connor's grocery store.

Although we are seldom paid any money for our entertainment, we are bought lots of pints and provided with plenty of food by our various benefactors. It is a grand apprenticeship to serve, playing the music I love and living rough. However, as winter draws on, we decide to go back to Limerick and the warmth of Nana's house.

There is a poetry and ballad session in the Turret Room of King John's castle and we offer our services. The resident musicians include accordionist Joe Collopy with his pal Jimmy Martin on the bodhrán, and a lovely young girl called Martina, who plays guitar and sings the Irish ballad "Buachaill on Eirne." She is an invocation of pure beauty and I'm immediately smitten with her.

I play one of my own compositions, "The Beatnik's Lament," which despite its lack of subtlety, is well received, rough edges and all. Afterward a reporter from the *Limerick Leader* asks for an interview, which duly appears in the local paper under the headline "Castle Recitals Appealed to Birmingham Pals."

It is a start. From this we get a couple of gigs at Limerick's White

House Tavern, a long-famous place of poetry, music, and sundry bo-hemian carryings-on. Robert Graves, the poet and author of *The White Goddess,* is a frequent visitor and we also are befriended by the local artist and poet Peter Jackson. We are at last getting recognized; this just might be a twin-edged sword.

We had made friends in town, but unbeknownst to us, we had also fostered some enemies. After a night in O'Brien's Bar, we are making our way down the back lanes behind Denmark Street, when two big men call across to us from the doorway of a derelict shop.

"Hey, lads! Come over here and see this," says one of them, and like fools we oblige.

"See what?"

"This!" says the other one, punching me in the head and dragging me into the shop doorway. Recovering quickly from the shock, but find-ing myself in a headlock, I get a side-angled view of Johnny grappling with the taller of the two, in the orange silhouette of the streetlight.

"Gerroff, ya bastard!" I roar, but my cries are lost in the rank stench of my assailant's tweedy armpit. Wriggling away from the acrid reek of sweat and urine tearing at my senses, I try to grab his balls, but he ma-neuvers sideways, turning us like a two-man Rugby scrum. Luckily, I get in range of the other guy and let fly a well-aimed kick into his bol-locks. Still spinning, I lose sight of him briefly, but on the next turn, I see Johnny has the upper hand and the blaggard is scrambling away on all fours. As I'm dragged around again, there is a whooshing crack above my head and the grip on my neck relaxes as my attacker, blood gushing from his ear, stumbles cursing into the darkness. Johnny stands gasping in the shadows of the doorway, the great half-moon copper pendant swinging like a blood-spattered medieval mace from his trem-bling fist.

We never discover the identities of our attackers, let alone their motive. An overcast day becomes the first of many and finds us loiter-ing in the local railway station. Now, boredom is an awful thing, and the devil soon finds work for idle hands. Temptation comes in the form of an old penny vending machine standing in the corner of the main hall. The ancient contrivance is a green-painted, cast-iron apparatus, with a large brass dial lettered A–Z and numbered 0–9. By swinging the pointer to select letters, a person can emboss words on small strips of aluminum. I waste a penny printing a tag with my name on it, and Johnny wastes another making one that reads, "THE POPE IS A JUNKIE." That night at the dinner table I show off my neat little name tag, which I intend to put on my guitar case someday. Johnny has lost the tag he made, which is no big deal until Nana finds it in the bathroom and goes doolally. We think it prudent to cut out until she calms down. After a spell of staying with friends, J.C. and I find an old deserted farm cottage and move in.

On a rainy evening, Garda officer Patrick Carmodhy clanks down the road on an antediluvian bicycle and, seeing us, shudders to a testicle-jarring halt across our path.

"I want a word with ye lads," he says, pulling the bicycle clips off the cuffs of his blue policeman's trousers.

"It has been braawt to my notice that you have been blaggarding in the street and shouting rude things about His Holiness the Pope." We stare at each other making noncommittal wiggly faces.

"Don't be shtandin' there like butter wouldn't melt in yer mouths, an' don't be denying it eithur. Shure I have it on the besht arthority: ye were seen by the priest! Two longy-haired amadawns, he said, and there's no one else in this town with hair down to their shoulders like a gerral. It's disgustin' so it is?"

"It was good enough for Jesus. He had long hair—and a beard!" tries Johnny.

"Don't ye be taking the Lord's name in vain, by Christ, or I'll be marching ye off to the slammer right now!" He turns a maddened eye on me.

"And ye, I seen ye sitting laffin' like a fooly one, across on the steps of Tait's clock. Is it the drugs ye'd be after taking?"

"No, no, I've never taken drugs in my life. It's just . . . that old clock makes the funniest clangs and boings when it strikes. It's a source of amusement." The old civic guard shakes his head in resignation.

"Jasus, if shoutin' yer bollocks off in the street and laffin' at old clocks is the best diversion ye can find, then God help the yooth of today!" He replaces his bike clips and pedals off.

"I have my eye on ye—be warned!" he roars over his shoulder, nearly spilling himself from the saddle in the process.

"Silly old sod. Who rattled his cage?"

"I sure as hell don't know, Johnny."

We trudge through the splattering rain to the derelict cottage, which we had commandeered as our own. Last week it was cozy and dry, but the change in the weather has revealed it as a bit of a bum gaff. With the roof a mass of holes, the decayed stone building has become a miserable old kip for sleeping in. I try to light a fire, but the thin cold rain, pissing down the chimney, puts it out. I sit by the dead hearth wrapped in my blanket.

"This place is a hellhole, Johnny. We should go back to my nana's."

"No, not likely! Look on the bright side—we can come and go when we like and if we do pull a couple of tarts, we can bring them back here and ride them. We can't do that at yer granny's!"

"If . . . that's a big bloody *if.* You wouldn't get a decent lassie to come back to a dump like this if your arse was dripping with diamonds!"

"I'm not looking for a deeecent lassie, I want a tart who ain't a fuggin' virgin!"

Silence falls and I take to watching the rain-soaked clouds scud the gray heavens through the gaping hole in the roof. Just to cheer me up, God sends a lightning storm that keeps me awake all night. I've been through this movie before and it's shite!

A dreary drizzle mists the windows of the main railway station as we begin the chore of drying ourselves out. We hang our socks and underwear on the heaters in the waiting room, and the smell rising up soon ensures that we have the place to ourselves.

The sun comes out and we trail our way down to Authur's Quay, a looming complex of rat-infested warehouses that had once been converted into small cupboard-sized dwellings by some unscrupulous bastard of a landlord. Sitting on the stone quayside, we drop rocks into the fetid, still water of the dock and watch the oil released from the sediments bursting on the surface of the dark brackish water like a psychedelic light show. Nearby in the flaccid back reaches of a tidal eddy, a dead dog floats, bollocks to the sky, in a slowly rotating dance of decay.

When the tide is out, the smell of putrefaction oozes from beneath each stepping-stone as we mudlark in the mucky shingle hoping to find treasures. Sometimes we find old bullets and cartridge cases from the civil war, but more often, we end up just getting covered in shite.

When not engaged in wasting time on the waterfront, we sit in the Muileann d' Ór Café, or the city library, wasting more time.

After being told by Robert Graves that the beatnik movement lacked ethics, I'm not sure what he means, so I steal a book on the subject from the public library, but after reading it, I realize I'm duty bound to put it back. We have our own code of conduct anyhow and don't need Immanuel Kant to tell us right from wrong. In the impecunious state we have found ourselves in, it would be all too easy to sell drugs, rob people's houses, or mug unsuspecting folk in dark alleys—like what had happened to us—but that is not our way. We were poor, others were rich, but were they any more moral?

The poor man toasts the rich man thus:

> *Here's to us, as good as you are, and as bad as I am*
> *But as good as you are, and as bad as I am*
> *I'm as good as you are, as bad as I am!*

If we were guilty of any sins at all, I suppose lust, unrequited as it was, would be top of the list, followed by sloth and on rare occasions gluttony. Our lives have become akin to that of the snake: always on the lookout for food and when gorged, sleeping night and day until hunger spurs the quest forward again. Pride, avarice, envy, and covetousness, all seemed the damnation of the wealthy and so hardly our affair. What was our concern was the state of the moldy old cottage now crumbling around our ears. Attempts to fix the holes in the roof have been repeatedly sabotaged in our absence, probably by the landowner to discourage unwanted tenants. No matter, Johnny comes back all excited after discovering a new doss-house.

"I've found a great place, Wock, just up opposite the castle in the old graveyard. It's a little stone shed with wooden benches and it's bone-dry inside."

"Maybe it's a workman's hut for the sexton or the grave diggers?"

"I dunno, it was too dark to see. Come on before the rain starts again and the doss bags get soaked."

We bundle our kit up and run through the dark lanes to the graveyard wall. With much humping and pushing, we scale the stone parapet and drop into the Protestant cemetery.

"Over here! This is it!"

He swings open the iron gate of a rectangular limestone sepulcher. It's as black as all hell inside.

"I'm not sleeping in there, that's a crypt!"

"Is it? Like in, 'The cat crept into the crypt, crapped, and crept out again'?"

"Yes, and it's full of—"

"It ain't full of fugg all, it's empty—feel?" Johnny waves his hands around in the air. I try to strike a match, but they're too damp to light.

"Just roll your sleeping bag out on one of these benches and we'll be fine." In the inky blackness, we doss down for the night. The first fingers of a deathly dawn poke impious probes into the vapid vault. My one eye peering from my blanketed cocoon reveals that fear to which, last night, I could give no voice. The wooden benches of J.C.'s dream home were the rotting lids of ancient coffins.

"Johnny, fer Jasus' sake!"

"What is it!"

He sits bolt upright in fright as, with a noise like a pistol shot, the ancient wood beneath his arse gives way. Johnny is interred in a cloud of dust as he drops in to visit the previous incumbent. Lying cheek by jowl with an eighteenth-century woman is the nearest he's got so far to fulfilling his ambition of sleeping with a tart who wasn't a fuggin' virgin!

The Muileann d' Ór Café boasts even more unsavory characters than us, most of whom are tinkers and petty criminals. One particular little herbert, who was as shifty as a shithouse rat, informs J.C. of an empty house up in Farron Seon that is still fully furnished and had been mysteriously abandoned long ago. It remains undisturbed by the thieving classes only because it is supposedly cursed and haunted. No doubt, the informant wishes to test the veracity of the haunting rumor before burgling the place over.

Johnny neglects to tell me this bit of the plot as we creep into the back kitchen of the long-empty house. Like the famous ghost ship, *Marie Celleste,* everything from daily life is left as it had been thirty years before: dishes on the table, pots and pans on the stove, coats hanging on their pegs, and beds still neatly made upstairs and in the attic. All is covered in a thick layer of dust and cobwebs. The detritus and decaying fur of three decades of neglect, unexplainable, uncanny, and sure to make the hair rise on your neck!

We select a room at the end of the long upstairs hall. For reasons of security, I put a piece of straw into the lugs of the backdoor lock, which, if found broken, will show us that someone has entered. I also place some of the glass-framed pictures face up, along the corridor, so's no one can launch a surprise attack without a foot breaking the glass and giving the alarm.

The house does indeed feel creepy, but it is weather tight and the next morning, in daylight, it seems not so scary. In getting ready to leave, we feel confident enough to leave our gear behind and even some small change sitting on the bedside table.

It is easy for us to wriggle through the tight gap we have created by pulling the heavy, marble-topped table over and jamming it in behind the bedroom door. Anyone bigger than ourselves will never be able to slip through this narrow passage.

For the first week all is well and we've grown used to our new abode. I have a part-time job doing a bit of modeling at the art college, which consists of sitting on a dais, playing guitar, whilst the students paint the scene. Some of these portraits even look like me, which is flattering. One lassie paints enormous purple pussycats, and I wonder at how much paint she uses. It must be great to be a student.

J.C. hangs out with his mates at a small café in the town center and does odd jobs for them. On a misty, cold night, I go into the house alone and venture upstairs. We both know where the glass frames are lying and can easily step between them. We reason that a would-be intruder will not be so nimble and so give the game away.

I have left Johnny talking to his mates under the streetlamp outside. As I wriggle into my sleeping bag, I hear what I take to be Johnny's footsteps coming along the hall. The door handle turns and, not in any way perturbed, I start a conversation with him. To my puzzlement the door opens, but there is no one there. I get up and peer into the hall—not a soul. I look out of the window and, as before, there is Johnny still chatting with his pals below. When he finally comes up, I tell him the news of the odd occurrence and that I think it is supernatural! J.C. says that I'm full of shite and being a wimpy prat.

Later that night, the footsteps return twice, and this time Johnny hears them as well. Leaping up, he challenges the interlopers.

"Who's there? Who's there, ya bastards!" Just as before, the hallway is devoid of human form! We have a restless night with our fleet-footed phantoms.

The next morning, I try to put it all down to being overtired. As I walk down the stairs a silver tabby cat shoots past me and runs into the upstairs passageway. I turn and follow it back up. It sits at the end of the hallway regarding me with jaundice eye and as I approach it, quick as a cobra, it darts into a hall cupboard. I ease the door a little more ajar and gaze in. The closet is totally empty except for the skeleton of a small cat!

When I tell Johnny this, he thinks I'm pulling his leg.

"You'm off yer rocker, Wockins. Bloody spooks, my arse! Who's ever heard of a ghost cat, fer God's sake?"

"Well, I'm only telling you what I saw! You heard the footsteps last night, didn't you?"

"I heard something, but it might have been the wind!"

"The wind from your arse maybe. Anyway, I'm not dossing there tonight. I'd rather sleep in the park!"

"Look! Let's give it till the end of the week and if it's still getting weird, we'll move out, OK?" Johnny is beginning to have his doubts, too.

When we get back at night the glass is still intact, as is the piece of straw across the backdoor lock, but our room is totally ransacked. The heavy marble-and-oak table has been pushed with such force that the iron bedstead is buckled in the middle. Whoever is responsible for this act possesses superhuman strength. Nothing is missing—not the musical instruments, nor the wee bit of money sitting on the bedside table. The only thing that can't be accounted for is my red neckerchief that traditional traveling people like to wear, "for to keep away the evil spirits!"

Snatching up my scant belongings, I run so fast out of that damned room that I break every plate of glass in the hall! With my heart pounding like a steam hammer, I can only hope and pray that whoever is running behind me, breathing acrid hot air down my neck, is Johnny Carr and not the spawn of Beelzebub!

That night we do indeed sleep out in the concrete changing rooms at the football park. It is unbearably cold, but with the aid of some candles nicked from the local church, I manage to hard-boil two eggs in a water-filled milk carton. It's hardly a warming supper and doesn't stop the dank cold seeping right through me.

We wake to a light snow falling and dejectedly trudge down to the Coliseum Cinema where we often sneak into the gents' toilets for a wash. The warm water feels good on my frozen face and fingers. After some minutes, there's a knock on the lavatory window from the outside. When we pop it open, unseen hands push in buns, cakes, and other fancy confectionery from the bakery next door. This is akin to the miracle of the loaves and fishes to me, and, although some pieces fall in the soapy water, like half-starved dogs, we eat everything greedily.

It is plain that our daily routine is becoming well known to the general populace, and before long we are banned from the cinema washrooms. We begin to look more like tramps than travelers, grimy ghosts haunting any warm place until ejected by store owners or pub landlords who get pissed off when we don't buy anything.

St. Mary's Cathedral is one of our few places of sanctuary, because no one bothers us here. It is damp and in a bad state of repair, but it's wind- and watertight, and we spend hours sitting on the pews talking or dozing in fitful catnaps. There is an odd plaque on the west wall of the church that reads: "Here lies the body of Dan Hayes who died in 1767. An honest man and a lover of his country, who was the author of 'The Tragedy of Hamlet,' originally written by him and inserted into the works of William Shakespeare."

I am dreaming of walking with old Willie Wagglestaff through the summer-filled country lanes that surround Stratford-upon-Avon.

"Did you write *Hamlet,* Willie?"

"Hamlet? Hamlet! Quotha! I fain I knowest not aught of this Hamlet. Perchance it be an omelette containing ham, foresooth?"

I am laughing at Shakespeare's jibe as the sun slips behind a dull, gray cloud and an icicle chill seizes me.

"Wocko! Wocko, wake up! You're rambling in your sleep. We'd better go and warm up. Let's get out of here. It's fuggin' freezing." We stumble through the winter streets to a new location. I dream and I stagger through my dreams. Cold, cold and damp seeping into my body, the pavement slides underfoot and I fall. Numbness, no pain from the fall, nothing to drive out the chilly humors. Cold, damp, death, dancing in my footsteps. I can feel its icy breath on the back of my neck. I hold on to J.C.'s arm and stumble on, eyes closed.

I wake up in the boiler room of a school. This is the warmest I've felt in weeks, but we are discovered by the janitor and the next nightmare is spent in an abandoned Austin A40 hatchback car, out in the wintry wilds. Somehow, in the middle of the night, the police appear.

I wake first and wind down the window. Three civic guards surround the derelict vehicle.

"Is that a girl you have in there?" says a hopeful cop, shining his flashlight into Johnny's effeminate face.

"No, it fuggin' well isn't, ya dozy prat!" says Johnny and then wonders why the cop opens the door and thumps him!

I'm feeling too weak to do more than answer few a questions in a hoarse whisper. They leave us alone that night, but when we return the following evening all of the windows of the car have been smashed.

"You see, I told ya. ACAB—All Coppers Are Bastards!" Johnny smiles with the grim satisfaction of belated vindication. I cannot walk back to town, and so we try to sleep where we are sitting, in the midst of the frozen crystals of shattered glass.

The winter days wear on, and I drift in and out of reality. We have taken refuge in the basement of a vacant shop near the city center, but although it is warmed by the boiler rooms in the buildings adjacent to it, I am cold and ill.

It's all I can do of a morning to get up and make my way down to the library, where I can sit and pretend to read. That night we sit in the small dockside café, and the waitresses try to sneak us the odd cup of tea and a bite to eat when the boss isn't looking. Day turns to night turns to day. I see the faces of two art students, John Connolly and his girl-friend, Adrianne, who know me from the college. They are speaking to me, but I can't make out what they're saying. They realize that I'm sick and take me to their flat and call a doctor. I'm suffering from pneumonia and am seriously ill. Christmas comes and goes, and in my illness I'm oblivious to it. These good people nurse me back to health and pay my expenses out of their own pockets.

"How are you feeling, Bill?"

"I feel better, Adrianne, very much better. Was I out of it for long?"

"Oooooh, yes! And you kept saying that the damp had eaten your cowboy suit!"

"Dear God! So the dreaded damp had nearly done for me, after all was said and done!" I mutter.

"What was that?"

"Oh, nothing! Just thanks, thanks for everything!"

Whilst I've been poorly, J.C. has been working with some dodgy-looking traveling folk dealing in scrap metal. I imagine the job isn't all quite aboveboard, as it is only referred to in hushed tones and deals are furtive affairs in back streets and on pub corners.

Amongst the other Flash Harrys that Johnny has befriended are a bunch of young spivs who hang around the street corners in their shiny Italian suits, spitting on the pavement and smoking king-sized cigarettes. They remind me of Derrick Davies's Bulldog Gang, who hung around the post office corner when I was young.

J.C. is chin-wagging with this gang of young turks one evening, as I'm walking down past Cannocks's clock. I stop to chat with him for a while when I spy the young lassie I'd once seen at the castle, walking down the road with two other lassies. She is dressed in a dark green Aran sweater and a gray skirt, her long ash-blond hair flicking over her shoulders. As she sweeps past me into the ice cream shop, my head turns with her like the periscope of a U-boat scanning for a ship.

"You fancy her, don't ya? That's young Martina, ya know?" says a lanky chain-smoking eejit who goes by the name of Wayney.

"Er . . . no! . . . I mean, er . . . yes . . . sort of!"

"Do youse want me to put in the good word for ye? I used to go out with her big sister, so I know her well enough!"

"Would you do that for me, Wayney? I'd be ever so grateful to you!"

With a giggle, the three girls come out of the shop licking their ice creams and turn to go back up the hill.

"Hey, Martina! I've something to tell you!" The matchmaker is doing his work. This is great! I can hardly believe it!

"What is it now, Wayney?" she asks coyly, looking a vision of loveliness.

"BILLY WATKINS WANTS TO BREAK YOUR FEATHER FOR YOU!" he roars across the street, nearly choking on his own laughter.

She glances at me for a split second and I hoped she could see my hurt and bewilderment. I am devastated by this foul-mouthed traitor, but too taken aback to do anything but stare like a fool. Wordlessly, with a toss of her lovely head, she is gone and, with her, my hopes of romance. The night is sickly sweet with the derisive laughter of know-nothing knaves.

Head bowed, I shuffle off to the café. Each black crack in the pavement becomes a yawning crevasse, wide and deep enough to swallow my shame and sorrow. It's my own fault, putting my trust in the likes of corner boys. You'd think, with all the time I'd spent studying Taliesin, I'd have learned by now!

> They despoil Mary's chaste maidens
> Their lives and times they waste in vain
> They scorn the frail and the guileless
> They drink by night, sleep by day
> Idle, lazily, making their way
> They despise the Church
> Lurch towards the taverns;
> In harmony with thieves and lechers.

Johnny strolls in and sits opposite me in the steamy café, all smiles.

"Cheer up, Wocko! Things could be a lot worse!'

"What the hell could be worse than this? What could be worse?"

"He was only having a little bit of fun, Wock!"

"Don't try to placate me, Johnny. These folk are morons, especially that Wayney fella! I don't think it was funny, embarrassing the poor girl like that! There was no need for that at all."

"It was you that got embarrassed, Wocko! You looked as red as a baboon's arse and just as sore!"

J.C. sniggers away to himself as he stuffs yet more pieces of bread and butter into his already overfull gob!

"Grow up, for crying out loud!" I mumble to my teacup.

Suddenly Johnny starts and stares goggle-eyed at me. His cheeks begin to puff out like a hamster and his eyes begin to bulge. He is bursting like an overripe boil!

I lean back from this swelling apparition, wondering whatever can be amiss? As I open my mouth to inquire, J.C. explodes into my face, the loudest, wettest cross between a sneeze and a cough imaginable. I am suffused with half-masticated bread and butter particles, snot, and phlegm. On the verge of throwing up, I jump up from the table. Johnny is howling with laughter and pointing to the mirror behind me, on the surface of which, outlined in his expectorated slime, is the fine silhouette of my head and shoulders.

Thank God, winter is now a distant memory and the weather is getting warm and wet. The moist Caribbean southwesterly winds blow up along the Gulf Stream, draping films of fluffy white clouds across the Shannon estuary and over the mountains, where they hang swirling and twitching like lace curtains at a gossip's window.

"It's soft over Clare—there'll be rain today!" says a familiar voice behind me. I spin around. It is my uncle Seán, out taking his bicycle for a walk.

"When did you get back in town? Why didn't you pop over to see us?"

"I'm just back now!" I lie, anxious not to hurt his feelings by letting on that I have been there all the time.

"Well, come over for Sunday dinner so. I'm sure Nana will want to hear all of your news. How's yer mam and dad?"

"Er . . . grand enough when I last saw them, a wee while ago!"

He held out his hand to shake mine, and as he does so, I feel him slip something into my palm. It is a five-pound note, riches above the dreams of avarice!

"Get yerself some sweets, Willie—or is it beers now?" he says with a twinkle.

"Go raibh mile math agut, Seán." (A thousand thank-yous, Seán.)

"Fáilte romhat, Liam." (You're welcome, Willie.)

Johnny is off on one of his forays into the country with his traveler pals. I am making my way over Baal's bridge in the cacophony of a barrage of bell peals. It seems like every church in Limerick is trying to outdo the other; Methodist, Proddy, and Pape all going like the clappers of hell . . . bell, book and candle . . . and buckets of blood. What is it they're saying?

> *Catholic, Catholic, going to mass,*
> *Riding on the devil's ass!*
>
> *Prody, Prody, ring the bell,*
> *All the vicars, down to hell!*
>
> *A rope, a rope to hang the Pope,*
> *and a lump of cheese to choke him!*
>
> *Jacky the minister, four foot high,*
> *A baldy head and a winky eye!*

Cannonade and broadside bounce off each corbeled stone edifice with little damage to anything except the ego and the eardrum. You'd be hard put to, thinking that these rivals are all praising the same God! But I suppose it makes for a more interesting life. Sure aren't we all flowers in the same garden—with the occasional weed thrown in?

On the way to Nana's house, I walk behind two venerable old women, both wearing waist-length, black knitted shawls draped over their heads and large hobnailed boots. These are the last real "shawlies" in Limerick. The one is as large as the other is small, and in their anti-quated garb they look like the peasant women from the Ukraine and wouldn't look out of place doing washing on the banks of the Dnieper. It would have been a wonderful thing to sit down to a slice of soda bread and a heat of the tea with these women and listen to their chat. I bet they have stories galore. When they are gone, we won't see their likes in Ireland again, and we'll be impoverished by their passing and that's a fact.

I cross the Shannon at the Thomondgate bridge and put my fingers in the indented scratch marks made by the fingernails of the Bishop's Lady when Drunken Thady tried to throw her into the river. As a child, I always wondered about this folktale and its incongruities. How did a woman, struggling for her life, manage to scratch deep into a solid rock parapet with her nails? What was the bishop doing with a lady anyway? Why did Drunken Thady want to drown her? And how come, judging by the twelve gouges in the granite bridge, did she have six fingers on each hand? Ah, Limerick, thou city of mysteries!

Sunday dinner at Nana's is just as I remember and as luck would have it, it is bacon and cabbage, the Irish national dish and a great favorite! After dinner, Nana, Aunt Frances, Uncle Seán, and myself sit around the peat fire chatting, and I play some classical pieces on the guitar.

When questioned, I'm more than a bit evasive about what I have been doing recently and make certain sure that I don't mention sleeping rough.

Nana has no such reservations, however.

"Guard Carmodhy says he saw you downtown dressed like a tramp and laughing at a clock. So what, in the name of the Good Savior, is that all about?"

"Sure I don't know, Nana. Maybe he's been having a wee drink of the poteen."

To avoid further questioning I take the boiled potato skins outside for the seagulls. There they are, lined up on the Shannon wall, waiting to be fed, just like when I was a tiny child. This visitation only takes place at Nana's house, and somehow the kittiwakes and blackheaded gulls always know when our dinnertime is. This inherent skill must have been handed down through the generations, and I would guess it is these gulls' great-great-grandparents that I'd fed all those years ago, when I was wee!

I'm invited to stay the night and I take up the offer of a hot bath.

Lying in the warm suds, I decide it is time to give up the traveling life for a while and see if I can find regular work. The next day, leaving my gear at Nana's, I go down to Jacky Glynn's music shop to see if I can get a job as a musical instrument salesman. He is very sympathetic, but says there is just not enough work to justify taking someone on. He says to call back in the summer.

Meantime, rumors are spreading in the town that Johnny and I had pissed in the holy water tank outside the Augustinian church. I knew I hadn't, but had J.C.? So one night, sitting in the dockside café, I ask him outright.

"Did you take a leak in the holy water tank?"

"No, I couldn't get the top off . . . it's padlocked."

"Why did you try? You're not even a Protestant!"

"'Cause I don't like any of the religious bastards, Caflick or Proddystans!"

"Why not? You never had to suffer all the kneeling on cold floors, praying for the conversion of Russia, or that Jack Kennedy would be elected president, like we did!"

"No, I never went to church. I didn't have to do the relige bit!"

"Why not?"

"'Cause they're wankers and if you go to church you're a wanker as well, you're all a bunch of wankers!"

"You're f——ing nuts!"

"I'll show you fuggin' nuts, Wockins!" he says, picking up the teapot and holding it above his head with a deafening shout of, "The pope's a wanker!"

He does a little jig in the middle of the café floor. Then emitting a high-pitched cackle, rather like the Australian kookaburra, he leaps through the café door and vanishes into the misty night.

"Where's my bloody teapot?" demands the café owner.

I can only shrug my shoulders.

"Come on, where does that hairy eejit live?"

"In truth, I have no idea. I didn't ask him. I don't know where he is dossing at all. He moved from where I stay some time ago."

"Well, if he doesn't bring me pot back soon, I'm calling the civic guards!"

"It's bugger-all to do with me, and so I'm leaving!"

The owner puts a big hand on my head and presses me back down into the seat.

"Oh, no, you're not! You're staying right there!"

"Would you like another cup of tea, Bill?" asks one of the pretty waitresses.

"NO, HE BLOODY WELL WOULDN'T!" my captor shrieks.

I watch the grease-covered café clock, as the seconds turn to minutes and the minutes to an hour.

"Right! That's it! I'm calling the police! Your mate has had enough time to return my goods and he hasn't!" The man is indignant as he picks up the telephone.

To his consternation, no sooner has he replaced the receiver than the door flies open and in rush three policemen! The bewildered owner stands blinking, looking perplexedly from the telephone to the latest arrivals. Then seizing the moment, points at me, crying out, "Him! There! That longhaired sputnik fella! He's one of them! He's the accomplice to the thief, so he is!"

The spluttering owner rubs his hands and does a little jig of delight.

"Would you come with us, sir?" says the sergeant, and I get up resigned, to my fate.

As I'm marched past the grinning patron, I hiss, "The word is *beatnik,* you ignoramus!"

"By Jasus, I'll not have that sort of language in my establishment!" he is roaring. "Come ye back here and I'll give ye a good hiding!" he says, going purple in the face.

"I fight with men, not their underpants!" I needle, as I'm whisked out the door.

He hops up and down, fists raised, shadowboxing the air!

"You cheeky young bollix . . . I'll . . . I'll . . . !"

"Shit his pants if he doesn't calm down!" says the sergeant, and even I laugh.

I am taken to William Street Garda Barracks and into the interview room. A detective comes in and offers me a cigarette.

"I don't smoke, thanks."

"Do you know why you're here, son?"

"No, not really . . . I don't . . . no."

"Well, we have a report that someone has committed a very serious crime, something we haven't had in this town since the Black and Tans were here, a crime I have never had to deal with in all my years on the force, a crime, not just against man, but against GOD! Jasus, lad, they used to hang people for it!"

"Hang people for what?"

"Sacrilege! Do you know what sacrilege means?"

I nod yes with my head. I know fine what it means. It means that holy water tank.

"We have a report that one of ye beatnik fellas ran into the Augustinian church, just after benediction tonight, and put a red teapot on top of the tabernacle and that a cry of 'F——the Pope!' was heard by the sexton. So was it yourself?"

"How could it be me? I was in the café all the time."

"Can you prove that? Do ye have witnesses?"

"Of course I have. Wasn't I being held a prisoner by the manager?"

"Oh, yes, sure I never thought of that! Well, if it wasn't ye, it must be the other fella." He opens the office door and shouts down the hall, "Is there any sign of the other eejit, Michael?"

"There was, sir, yes. Officer Carmodhy saw him in the street a bit ago and chased him. If he hadn't stopped to put his bicycle clips on, he would have caught him, too."

"OK, keep me posted, so." He turns back. "So this is nothing to do with you!"

"No, sir, nothing."

"Well, I believe you, thousands wouldn't," he says, indicating the door.

"Can I go now?" I ask the detective.

"Well, that's up to the duty sergeant. I have no more use for you!"

I'm told to stay put and from where I sit, strange shadowy shapes pass the frosted glass of the charge room windows. I imagine it's Johnny being led to the interview room in handcuffs.

"OK, youngfella, what's your address?" asks the burly desk sergeant, filling in a form.

"What am I being charged with?"

"Just give me your fuckin' particulars, laddie, and less out of ye, and don't you worry your little head, I'll soon find something to hang ye on."

I give him my folks' address in England so as not to embarrass Nana with a visit from the police.

"So where are you staying in Ireland, son?"

"I'm just traveling about, all over."

"How much money do you have on you?"

"I think I have about one and six left, that's all."

"Well, you need at least seven and six so's not to be a vagrant! It is my belief that you are living without visible means of support and that is an offense against the Vagrancy Act."

"Oh, dear, I didn't know! What will happen to me? This is all very worrying."

"Let me see now. We can send you up to court, or get rid of you quietly and no questions asked!" he says, cleaning his earhole with his pencil.

"What! What d'ya mean, 'Get rid of me quietly'? Good God, man, it's only vagrancy!"

"No, don't worry. We give you a rail pass and a second-class ticket back to Britain, from out of the public purse, and then you're someone else's problem! You will stay here in the cells tonight. And tomorrow, I have a man going up to the Bridewell in Dublin and he will escort you to the boat. Get it?"

"Yes, OK, so I'm being chucked out of the country through no bloody fault of my own!"

"Yer breaking my heart! Now empty your pockets into the tray and give me your belt. You'll get them back in the morning. Now sign this and good night!"

"What do you want my belt for?"

"So you don't hang yourself, of course!"

"Jasus! Do ye think I'd hang myself for vagrancy?"

"You haven't seen the state of the cell yet. Now come along quietly or it will be the worse for you!"

He slaps the palm of his hand with a heavy black truncheon as he leads me to a black, iron-studded door that has a peep hole in the center. The policeman swings it open with a sinister screech like a cat caught in a mill wheel. To my horror, the cell already has an occupant. As the door clangs shut, the acrid stench of piss and neglect overwhelms me. A shadowy figure resembling a hastily assembled bag of rags rustles in the corner of the only bunk in the room.

"Get away! Get ye gone! Yer not having my blanket—yer not!"

"I don't want yer poxy old blanket! Now shut up, fer God's sake, before the guard comes back and takes the night stick to ye!"

The poor old tramp mutters a string of demented oaths as he pulls his maggoty army horse blanket around himself. Even in the half-light, I can see it is crawling with body lice. Sitting on my haunches on the other side of the chilly cell, I pass a tortuously wearisome night. My dreams are the only escape from the living nightmare of waking up. These, too, would suddenly lurch from the pastoral bliss of a day fishing by a gentle stream to the mockingly, maniacal spectacle of a giggling Johnny Carr dressed in priest's vestments, celebrating Holy Communion with chocolate wafers handed out from a red enamel teapot.

Of the events the next morning, I recall little as I seem transfixed in a dreamlike state. Having survived that hellish night, I am given a cup of tea that tasted like creosote and has most likely been stewing on the gas all night. This at least gives some heat to the couple of bits of cold toast the guardians of the law have provided for breakfast. On the trip up to Dublin, I sleep most the way to Nenagh. The policeman is a cheery Dubliner and is transferring back up to the big city. He jokes that although I am a bloody Englishman, I'm the best prisoner he's ever had.

"No need for the bracelets to be put on a sleeping man!"

"Thanks!"

"So what are you being deported for? Tell me, I can't be bothered to read your paperwork."

"Well, apart from being broke, which I didn't know was a crime, I haven't done anything wrong at all! It's all just lies and rumors."

"They still haven't caught your pal. Is he some sort of a Protestant Orangeman or the like?"

"No, not at all, he wouldn't know an Orangeman if one leapt up and bit his arse! He just jokes around. He likes to shock people, that's all. He's no threat to anyone."

"Now I'm supposed to take you all the way to the boat. If I just see you just up to Kingsbridge and onto the boat train, you won't be running off anywhere now, will you? It's just I don't want to be traipsing all the way down to Dun Laoghaire and back, baby-sitting a fine big fella like yerself!"

"No, no, I'm just as anxious to get home as you are. You can trust me not to scarper. God knows I've no intention of going back to Limerick for a good while."

The cop accepts my assurance of good behavior and kindly buys me a cup of coffee and a hot bacon roll. It is the ambrosia of the gods.

He is more than pleased to be out of the Confraternity City, as Limerick is known for its straitlaced Catholic airs. He's going back to the bright lights of dear debauched Dublin. Stationed up at the Bridewell nick, he explains, is nice and handy for getting a pint or two in John Mulligan's pub in Poolbeg Street or a quick gargle in the Palace bar, on Fleet Street.

After arrival at Westland Row we take the bus to Kingsbridge railway station. Here he gives me my second-class boat ticket and we shake hands. He is a decent sort of a chap with a merry twinkle in his eye. He straightens up and touches his cap.

"Slán leat. That's Irish for good-bye!"

Well, if all coppers are bastards, at least this guy was a decent bastard.

"Bu'ochas a' chara, agus slán abhaile anois!" (Thanks, my friend, and safe home now!) I shout from the door of the departing Dun Laoghaire train. I am pleased to see him crack up laughing at being had on! He's a good egg.

Alone in my compartment, high on the railway viaduct above the slate roofs of backstreet Dublin, I gaze down as the game of daily life plays out on the cobbled streets below.

Raincoated men with greyhounds and whippets scurry in and out of pubs and betting shops. Others, in suits or overalls, hurry off to work or off to avoid work, either joining or avoiding the commuter queues, standing at bus stops, waiting in vain for the black and cream, *just like Birmingham,* buses to come along.

Garrulous groups of women, in floral pinafores and paisley pattern headscarves, chitchat on street corners, pausing only to plug fallen baby bottles into infant mouths, light cigarettes, or scold scruffy-arsed kids hanging on rope swings from lampposts.

Descending into a railway cutting, the train slows, giving the passengers a chance to read the spiderous graffiti scrawled across the blackened brick walls. It caters for all tastes: "Up the IRA"; "Mickey is a wanker"; "Whitworth F.C. We are the Champions"; and my favorite, an insult complete with the element of choice, "Helen is a pig or cow."

After idling in the cutting for some minutes, the train jerks forward again. I am fighting the fatigue now closing in upon me. For all I know, this might be my last view of Ireland for a long time. Maybe I won't be allowed to return at all! Spurred by this fear, I greedily grasp every last image of my Irish motherland.

Through half-closed eyes, I spy a Rugby game scrumming down on a college pitch. The young buckos, in their green striped jerseys, have the advantage over the lads in red and white and push them over. Oblivious to all but their own world, two lovers dawdling along the banks of the Grand Canal steal a long, lingering kiss. Behind the canal wall, a tinker lad, standing upright on the back of a speeding horse-drawn cart, darts down the lane toward Pembroke Road. By Beggar's Bush Barracks, a black-faced coalman dumps bags of "Tadcastle's Best Anthracite" into a coal cellar, watched by a tail-flicking cat proudly enthroned upon the dented roof of a rusty, wheelless Volkswagen.

Behind the long rows of terraced houses, one woman hangs out damp washing on her backyard clothesline, whilst a few doors down another gathers dry washing in.

An old man, in shirtsleeves and cloth cap, shakes the creases out of his daily newspaper before entering the privacy of an outside lavatory. In the adjacent alleyway, a small brown dog strains in tail-quivering ecstasy on the threshold of his own evening evacuation. Life, when viewed from a passing train, has a wonderful symmetry about it.

Yellowed by the honey-faced sun peeping demurely from behind the shadowy crests of the far-off Wicklow Mountains, all of Dublin seems to be busy doing something; as busy as bees around a hive. I close my eyes, but the honeycomb of my brain remains abuzz with a swarm of bittersweet images; montaged mementos, frozen in the moment, always there to be recalled, something that no one can take from me, my personal experience, my own ramshackle vignettes of my island, my Ireland.

⇥ Chapter 21 ⇤

SAILING, AS MANY'S THE TIME BEFORE, FROM THE OLD QUAY-side that I know so well, again, I leave Ireland. But on this occasion, instead of leaving a piece of my heart behind, I'm leaving my child-hood innocence. I have experienced a good slice of adult life with its mixture of great beauty and callous ugliness; losing old friends and finding new ones. I've discovered that both the kind and the crass na-ture of people is as universal as it is unpredictable. I feel likened unto a snake that has outgrown its skin; a serpent leaving Ireland, not at the behest of St. Patrick, but because of the need to expand my horizons way past the confines of miscreant youth.

Leaning on the ferry's stern rail, the green, white, and orange tricolor above my head snaps in a fresh, westerly breeze. The great golden orb of the sun sinks below the ribbon of pastel-colored houses that form the skyline of the township of Dun Laoghaire.

I gaze down.

Keen, phosphor bronze screws slice through the emerald green water, turning effervescent eddies of boiling white foam into a hissing dissipating wake.

The last lone finger of the setting sun stretches out from between the darkening hills and anoints the ship with a rich amber light. I too feel anointed, as if heaven has seen fit to forgive my misdeeds in her ver-dant green colony upon this small earth.

Great gulls and kittiwakes follow our progression, the souls of dead sailors shining in their round black eyes. Above, a cloudless sky is turn-ing a deep indigo and small strings of streetlights twinkle out from the headland, like dancing decades of a fluorescent rosary.

Wild, tempestuous Irish Sea, you have broken the backs of ships, the spirits of men, and the hearts of wives and sweethearts, but tonight, without my mother to torment, you lie fetid and flaccid, as content as a fishmonger's cat. You beguile the foolish with a placid calm that belies your true nature. Who can trust you, you fickle witch of wicked water?

In the secret realms of your deep, the sea-god Mananan Mac Lir rides his wave-cutting currach *Ocean-sweeper* out from the Isle of Man. Aloft he waves the Answerer, the magical sword that no armor can resist. Through storm and tempest, he guides sailors to and from Ireland. Not only does he protect that sacred isle, but also the Islands of the Dead that lie beneath the rolling waves.

To you, Tír na nÓg, the souls of the dead seafarers descend. To you, Land of Eternal Youth, is given the name Davy Jones's Locker or Fiddler's Green. Yours is the enchanted land that lies beneath the white-crested breakers. Yours is the roar of defiance when chilly arctic drift currents and the warm Gulf Stream clash in the midst of your ebullient maelstrom. Yours is the magic that seduces the hearts of men. Yours is the—

"Excuse me, lad. I don't want to disturb you, but I need to take the flag down," a Scouse deckhand wakes me from my reverie.

"We take down the colors at sunset."

"Oh, sorry, mate! I was away with the fairies there for a moment. I didn't see you." I smile as he gathers in the ensign.

"Are you going on holiday or coming back from one, like?"

"Yeah, I was on holiday, the holiday of a lifetime!"

"Now what? Are you working or trying a job over in England?"

"No, I suppose I'll have to find something to make a living."

"Ever thought of going to sea? Being a sailor, like?"

"Yeah, when I was a kid it's all I wanted to do. I used to dream about it."

"Then why not do it? What would youse like to be? A skipper, I'll bet?"

"Naw, maybe a wireless operator."

"What, a sparks? Blimey, you know a cushy job when you see one. Nothing to do but sit around listening to the radio. Fair play to ya, son!" He wanders off.

I take one last look into the west and, with a sigh, make my way to the ship's aft-deck saloon. Unlike the trip to Ireland, there is no party atmosphere celebrating the exiles' return home and no session in the bar. These passengers sit in muted groups, reading or quietly playing cards. Some stare out of the lounge windows and others into space, no doubt contemplating the return to the daily grind of work in the pubs, factories, and construction sites of England:

> 'Twas the Irish built the roads of Britain
> And before them, the bloody Romans!

I go below and locate the comfortable linen cupboard, but find it fitted with a Yale lock and a sign reading, "Crew Only."

Above deck I have better luck and find a warm place to curl up in the lee of the vessel's smokestack, just behind the wireless cabin. Lulled by each soporific swell, I soon drift off to sleep.

My subconscious dreams rise and fall on the peaks and troughs of the undulating waves. Across the dark rolling sea, the voices of the fabled sirens of old beckon to the mariner within me, not in the ancient language of Greek myth, but in the modern staccato notes of the International Morse Code. Dah di Dah dit . . . Dah dah di dah . . . the temptress nymphs call: CQ . . . CQ . . . Seek you! Seek you! they solicit.

On the morning of March 14, 1967, I walk warily down the gangplank of the M.V. *Hibernia* and, for the first time in nearly a year, set foot back in Holyhead, Wales.

There is no police reception committee, no passport control, just a ticket inspector who punches a hole in my chit and wishes me a good morning.

Seagulls wheel overhead, squawking their enticements as a new flame kindles the ashes of my childhood yearnings. I look at the ships riding at their moorings, each craft a mystery. Where has it been? Where is it bound? I need to know. The sirens of the previous night have done a good job, and one day I will surrender to their entreaties. But for now, I must turn my back to the sea and its calling and strike out across the long causeway connecting Holy Isle to the beautiful Isle of Anglesey.

Ynys Môn, as it is in Welsh, is the age-old sacred island where the Druids had their holy groves and chief seats of learning until its destruction at the hands of the Roman general Suetonius Paulinus, in A.D. 61.

> *Romans, long departed,*
> *Your name liveth on in Welsh*
> Rhufeinig, *you are in that tongue.*
> Roughnecks *and* Ruffians
> *The English will call you, in their turn.*

Wales! Wales! Here I am in the land of my fathers and like my father before me, deported from Ireland through no fault of my own. A Celt, son of a Celt, deported by Celts, from one Celtic country to another. It's a ridiculous scenario. I mind well the words of my father, the great exponent of internationalism and erstwhile professor of fermented beverages: "Never be seduced into playing the English imperialist game. It's a game of divide and rule, and the dice are loaded in favor of the conqueror. Scots, Irish, Manx, Cornish, and Welsh, we are hewn from the same stock. We may be different tribes, but we are the same people—Celts! It has always been in the interest of the English empire builders to split us up and use one tribe to subjugate the other. It's something they learned from the bloody Romans!"

Sure enough, Welsh is just the Saxon word for foreigner; Scot means an Irishman; Cornish comes from the Celtic tribe, the Cornovii; and Manx from Mananan Mac Lir, the Irish god of the sea. The Angles, the folk that most English people claim descent from, were never a people; the name is derived from Gaelic: *An Gaul,* which just means the foreigners. Likewise *regal* comes from *Ri Gall,* or stranger king.

Strange parlance, English. In the medieval period it was so akin to that of the Frisian areas of modern-day Germany and the Netherlands that there is an old folk rhyme recording this similarity:

> *Bread, butter and green cheese*
> *Is good English and good Frise.*

Language be buggered! A cheese sandwich sounds great. I'm starving and neither have I a penny to my name, nor a pot to piss in.

A steady stream of vehicles trickles through the Holyhead ferry terminal. I pause for a while at the dock gates, hitchhiking the little knots of traffic leaving the customs post. I'm wasting my time. No one returning from their holidays can be bothered picking up a scruffy-looking bugger like me, and I can't say I blame them. Ah, well! As Dad was wont to say, "nil carborundum illegitimi"—or should that be ille-gitemus? No matter, no bastard is going to grind me down, either way!

Head up! Stiffen the sinews! Summon up the blood! It will be a long hard slog to the mainland, but if the Roman legions could march twenty-four miles a day, then surely a Celt like me can make the twenty-one miles to the Telford Bridge before evening. The long march begins into the interior of the Isle of Anglesey.

As the crow flies, it must be seventy miles to the English border, but since I have little chance of wings in this life and even less in the next, shank's pony is my only means of transport. Borders, what a pain in the nawney! I'll be glad when no one gives a bollocks about divisions anymore. Aren't we all born naked on the same planet?.

I'm put in mind of my American poetry teacher. He liked to quote the words of the Russian poet Yevgeny Yevtushenko. What was that he said about international borders? "Frontiers are imaginary lines in the minds of men," or something along those lines and fair play to him, he's right enough. Sure aren't all of us just Jock Tamson's bairns or the sons of Adam or whatever you like to call it. It seems very odd that individuals can be racist, let alone the governments of the world classifying people by what side of a dotted line you were born on.

"If a cat has kittens in a bakery, does it make them currant buns?" No, Mother, it does not and all hail to the day when the word *xenophobia* can only be found in a crossword puzzle. Aye, aye, we're all flowers in the same garden, so we are, but I wish one of these fine specimens, whizzing by in their fancy cars, would stop and give this wilting violet a ride!

The spring sun beats down relentlessly and there is little shade on the flat central plain of the island to comfort the traveler. The sacred oak groves of the Druids, once burned down by the BloodyRomans, never grew back. God's curse on the ruffians!

Ah, but despite it all, the sense of freedom you have on the road is intoxicating:

I have traveled over the earth
Before I became a learned person
I have traveled, I have made a circuit
I have slept in a hundred castles
I have dwelt in a hundred cities.

Taliesin's words set me off thinking about my seventeen-year quest through life. Did my father plant the seeds, full knowing the effect the poetry of this ancient adept would have on me? Did he envisage how closely my own life would parallel that of Taliesin, the wandering bard? The poet began life as little Gwion; he became Taliesin. Who am I?

I try my hand at a shape-shifting poem:

I was William, I was Willie
To my father, I was Will
In Wales I was Gwylym
In Ireland, Liam
To J.C. I was Wocko
I was Billy, I am at last Bill.

Shakespeare asked, "What's in a name?" I wonder if he managed to collect as many nicknames as I've had over the years?

"To be or not to be? That is the question."

Who am I? Who was he? Some of the world's scholars reckon he never wrote a play in his life and others maintain that he was never born at all and was an invention of medieval Stratford's Tourist Board!

Great Britain's Poet Laureate lies
In fear of church and crown
It must be hard to satirize
The state when kneeling down
And so his art becomes the crap
Of sycophant and craven
Unless you count the bearded chap
From Stratford upon Avon
But Shakespeare's wit was in his plays
His verse was quite limp-wristed

Its drama's muse deserves his praise
—If ever he existed!

Well, poor Willie Wagglestaff might not have been born, but he definitely died! I've seen his grave, and judging by the size of the massive stone on top of him, he'll have a fierce job getting out of bed when Gabriel blows his horn to wake the dead on the last day. So when he doesn't turn up, ye'll have all those intellectual clever bollixes saying, "See, I told you so. Those plays were written by Francis Bacon over there!' And old Bacon would just smile and wave and wouldn't be fool enough to tell the buggers any different, after them giving him the cold shoulder first time around. Dan Hayes, from Limerick, would be scandalized and jumping up and down screaming that Bacon was an impostor, too, and that he'd written *Hamlet* himself! Then Shakespeare, being a very merry wit, would arrive late at the gig and wisely decide to say nothing to nobody and instead make a grand play out of the whole carry-on—which, since Shakespeare didn't appear to exist, would end up being attributed once again to Bacon!

Bacon? Oooh, Jasus, I could just go a big bacon butty, dripping with grease. What was it Dad used to say in times of hardship?

"If we had some bacon, we could have bacon and eggs—if we had some eggs."

It's amazing the stuff that tumbles through your mind when you are hungry. Maybe that's why religious folk like to fast as a way to clean out the attic of the soul. It's little wonder they have visions. Daydreams are handy vehicles drowning out the cries of an empty stomach and two sore feet.

I am so involved in my dilly-dallying that I fail to notice an open-topped Land Rover that has stopped for me.

"Do you want a lift or don't you?" the farmer quizzes me.

"Yes, sorry, I was dreaming away to myself."

He has a crate of live chickens in the front seat, so I sit in the back in the company of a trussed-up, blackfaced ram and three black-and-white border collies. The ram glares at me, but the dogs seem to like my company and give me their own version of my mother's face-cleaning technique.

We cross the Menai Bridge into North Wales. The farmer is delivering the livestock locally and can only take me a further six miles, but I'm more than grateful. As I wave good-bye to the departing jeep, the three sheepdogs sit in line abreast, barking their farewells in triple harmony. Ah, yes, the Welsh love choirs!

Dad was right. "A man of honor must oft times walk alone," but he didn't mention getting corns on the toes. I walk on until my boots feel like they are full of hot sand.

At a wayside stream, I stop to drink and bathe my feet. The cool mountain water is sweet and refreshing, and I fancy that the bubbles arising from my toes are caused by me boiling the water with my feet. Completely knackered, I rest up for a while in a lush spring meadow near Penmaenmawr, which is the Welsh for "The Head of the Big Rock."

I catnap and in turn, dream of Palug's Cat, a spotted kitten given to the people of Arvon by the evil goddess Hen Wen. The feline grows into a savage monster, killing all in its path and becoming one of the three plagues of Anglesey. This mighty leopard is eventually killed by the warrior Cei, who was destined to become the Sir Kay of the Arthurian legends:

> *Cei went to Ynys Môn*
> *To kill lions*
> *Polished was his shield*
> *Against Palug's Cat*
> *Nine score warriors*
> *Would fall as food for her.*

Awakening, I feel renewed enough to walk onward toward the distant fortress town of Conway. My eyes follow the curve of the coastline to the Weir of Gwyddno, where Elphin found Taliesin cast ashore in his baby coracle on All Soul's Eve, all those centuries ago. The railway line that had been my umbilical to Ireland runs along the same route. How many times had I traversed that track? Dozens, maybe scores!

Still I amble on. The wind at my back, the merciless sun above, and the hard metal of the A55 North Wales trunk road driving into my feet. I am dehydrating quickly and, like a parched pilgrim, beginning to feel the mystical effects of drought and hunger.

My thirst is quenched at the drinking fountain in the village of Gwalchmai. As clarity returns to my addled brain, I ponder upon the origin of the place-name. It must be called after King Arthur's nephew, who the medievalists renamed Sir Gawain. The lines of an ancient stanza fleet in my mind:

> *Gwalchmai they call me, enemy of the Saxons*
> *For Anglesey's king I have lunged out in battle*
> *And to please a girl, bright as snow on the trees*
> *When Chester was fought for, I have shed blood.*

I trudge on toward Chester, feeling like my boots are shedding blood and wishing I had a girl to please, "bright as snow on the trees."

I had slaked my thirst with a drink at a fast-flowing stream outside of Llangefni, again at a tap in the gents' toilet in Colwyn Bay, and now in desperation, with a bottle of yellow-green pop that I find lying in a ditch near Llysfaen. I smell and taste it with the greatest of trepidation, being more than wary of yellow liquid in bottles, but it is good!

The punctual orb of the sun is beginning to slip silently below the horizon, drawing its covers of purple night behind it. This is a welcome relief. There is still a stiff breeze to assuage my sunburned forehead and cool a brain that is boiling like the cauldron of Ceridwen.

I have fasted for almost twelve hours, and I am now seriously feeling the pinch. "An army marches on its stomach," said Napoleon. I feel like an army has marched over mine! "An empty stomach has a loud voice," another old saying goes. Well, if that's true, mine is singing the old Welsh marching song "Men of Harlech."

Descending into the seaside town of Rhyl, I root amongst the discarded trash of the early holiday makers and glean some half-eaten fish and chips. Although they are cold, I am more than glad of what I have found. As luck would have it, I pick up a silver sixpence from the gutter and use it to buy a packet of Cadbury's chocolate wafers. This is good high-energy food and I ration them out to myself. The long jaunt continues back up onto the main road and into the crooked arm of North Wales. No one notices my passing except a few inquisitive brown bullocks, with whom I share a respite and some handfuls of juicy green grass.

Night falls thick and treacle black as I tramp my way from Rhyl to Prestatyn. There is hardly any traffic, and what there is speeds by. The length of highway I am now navigating is undergoing repairs. New curbstones are being laid, and every other one is lying out in the road. I take some small diversion by walking up and down on each of these, just to break the monotony of walking and cursing my pathetic plight. Up-down-up-down, I swing—like Long John Silver on his wooden leg.

The stars sizzle bright overhead in a moonless sky, and several times I see the streak of meteors blazing across the inky heavens, leaving luminous, powdery trails arching behind them. Mars glitters like a discarded cigarette end in the crystal cosmos above.

I know the names of the stars in their places.

I think of the night that Dad showed me the constellations and Mam sang "O'Ryan the Hunter." I was so young then and now I feel so old and weary. Seventeen—the lucky number of the Druids. I went to Ireland a child. Now I am cast ashore on the coast of Wales, a changeling; neither child nor adult, neither fish nor flesh, reborn, but still growing, hardening my form, shaping my spirit.

On the road behind me, I perceive a single light making its erratic course up the way toward me. It is either a one-lamped motor car or a motorbike.

Motorcycles and their riders often give lifts and, judging from its speed, the bike would take about another six ups and downs of the curbstones to put me within hitching distance of it.

Having walked the calculated interval, I turn with my thumb out, expecting the motorcycle to be about ten yards away.

"Whoa!" It's right on top of me! I get such a fright that I lose my footing and spiral into the ditch.

"You crazy bastard! You nearly knocked me over!" I scrabble for a stone to fire after my assailant, when something odd occurs to me. I rise up to get a better view.

The motorbike's taillight is a pale pink. The rider, in old-style goggles and helmet, wears a long army-type trenchcoat with a gas mask bag over his shoulder. The bike has a fishtail silencer, ancient flat-sided rear mudguards, and rigid suspension. I stand in the road, and the pebble drops from my grasp as I realize that the machine and its rider make no sound whatsoever. Shock overwhelms me; the entire vision vanishes in full view on the open road, fifty feet away. It was a ghost—a ghost on a motorcycle!

For a long while afterward, I walk alone down the center line of the road, now dark and lined with trees on both sides. "God is good, God is good, and the Devil isn't such a bad fella when ye get to know him!" Every noise of the night, every creak and hoot seem sinister portents of doom. I try to apply cold logic over sweat-forming fear. Whereas the events at the haunted house in Ireland may have had some rational explanation, this time, seeing is believing and the evidence of my own senses had to be reckoned with. Surely it can't be possible that I might be dreaming with all that amount of adrenaline coursing through every vein in my body!

I am still in a state of shock when another strange thing happens. Without me even noticing, a posh white sports car stops and the driver offers me a lift. I climb in with trepidation, expecting to see Old Nick or one of his demons behind the wheel, but the car is driven by a well-dressed young business type. Zombie-like, I sit quietly stunned whilst the poor young fella tries to elicit some sort of conversation out of me. Then suddenly, I'm off, bursting forth like a torrent from a fractured dam! I can't stop babbling about what's just happened. The unfortunate driver has every reason to think that he has either picked up a demonically possessed drug addict or an escapee from the local lunatic asylum. When he drops me on the Chester bypass, the poor man is as white as a sheet and tears off with the passenger door still open!

In the ensuing silence, I have time to recap and make some sense of my experience. "Right, Billy boy! There's nothing to be frightened of. Form a theory, try to think like a Druid. OK, here's what occurred. What happened was, the two worlds of the parallel universe brushed briefly together; one materialized in the other and by chance, I had been there in the middle, like the pin in a pair of tongs! Yes, that must be it." Comforting myself in this way I cease to be frightened as I walk on.

To my great relief, as soon as I lie down on a thick wooden bench in a country bus shelter, I go fast asleep with no thought of ghost, ghoul, or goblin. Even without the aid of blanket or pillow, I sleep the sleep of the just, or if you like, *the dead!*

I awake at first light to the tinkle of rain and the awareness that people are shuffling about somewhere near me. When I look around I realize that the early morning commuters have stood out in the shower rather than wake me up. I nod my head in appreciation of their kind gesture and vacate the bus shelter. I've nothing to eat except food for thought.

Resuming my walk toward the M6 motorway, my mind goes back to Ireland and J.C. I didn't like the thought of leaving him on his own, but who knows what fates lie in store. Johnny will have to pursue his own dreams in his own way. Everything happens for a reason, says my mother, and this is probably just the kick in the pants I am needing to set me on a new vision quest. I hope Johnny does all right. He too had played his part in reviving the fortunes of the Gael, and together we had made sweet music and opened many a deaf ear to it. In our small way, we rallied the songs and tunes of our heritage and brought them back to the people who had almost forgotten them. Was it worth it? Time will tell.

"Retrospection is the handmaiden of history," which I think means about the same as, "Even the fool is wise after the event."

Who knows if the Celtic culture will survive into a new millennium? It's the smallest stone that starts the avalanche. Maybe we did nothing to help and were just playing at it. Time will tell, time will tell.

> *Fish swim, bees gather honey*
> *Vermin crawl; everything bustles*
> *To earn its keep . . .*
> *except minstrels and thieves.*

Aye, Taliesin! As you say, *"except minstrels and thieves"*!

A spot of rain is the hitchhiker's friend. Drivers are much more likely to give you a lift during a downpour, and I cover several miles in small local rides.

Later that day, somewhere near Warrington, I get a lift from a bored Yorkshire long-distance lorry driver in need of a chat to keep him awake. He's heading south to Walsall and he can take me near enough to where I need to be. At his insistence, I tell him some of the bizarre events and whimsical stories of the past few years: the school Christmas pageant, the exploding pike, the haunted house, and the ghost of the North Wales bypass. He laughs like a drain as his eighteen-wheeler rumbles on.

At the Keele service station on the M6 motorway, the truck driver buys me the first hot meal I've had since leaving Ireland: steak-and-kidney pie, mashed potatoes, brussels sprouts, and gravy. It is the ambrosia of the gods, and despite the hunger, I eat it slowly for fear of throwing up!

He finishes his pie and mash, but leaves his sprouts.

"Don't you want them, the sprouts?"

"Er, no, I don't much care for them. They came with the meal."

"Is it the taste or the shape?" I scrape them onto my plate.

"What do you mean, the shape?"

I tell the trucker about Uncle Seán and his spherephobia. He laughs.

"Come to think of it, I've read about folk like that in the paper. It only effects certain types of people. He must be very odd?"

"No, not at all, there's nothing odd about him! He's a postal worker!"

For some reason this sets him off laughing and he goes up to the counter, coming back with two big steaming mugs of hot tea.

"By heck, lad! You've got some tales to tell and no mistake! How old did you say you were?"

"I'm seventeen."

"I'll tell thee this, lad! You be nowt but an old head on young shoulders. Them be some adventuring thee's has, and you hardly out of the egg."

Back on the highway the eighteen-wheeler eats up the miles on the downhill run to the Midlands of England. When he drops me off at the Brownhills interchange, the kindly trucker flips me a half crown. I try to refuse, but he won't take no for an answer.

"Thanks a million, pal, and drive safely!"

"You're welcome, mate, and thanks for the stories. Good luck!"

The truck pulls away, leaving me standing on the outskirts of Birmingham's new industrial sprawl. I marvel that the city has grown so huge since I'd first visited just a few years after World War II. Skipping across the road, I catch a black and cream bus—just like the ones in Dublin, Johnny!—to the city center. I sit upstairs at the front.

Brick upon brick, the crusty old metropolis rises from the Mercian plain. Two hundred years ago it was a hamlet of thirty people, belonging to the Norman-French family of Berminghame, who also owned lands around Limerick.

The Industrial Revolution saw the tiny village mushroom into the second largest city in Britain, a mighty powerhouse of industry and invention that became a magnet for rich entrepreneurs and itinerant laborers alike. Curiously, it is the only town in England to have a bullring.

Between angular lines of corbled stone banks, long reaches of sluggish green water crisscross the landscape, marking the course of the once-bustling inland waterways called navigation cuts. Tradition has it that the water filling these puddled-clay channels came from the living sweat of the Irish navvies who dug them.

For reasons lost on locals and Italians alike, the city fathers like to boast that Birmingham has "more miles of canal than Venice." That may well be true, but imagine two lovers enjoying a gondola cruise along the stagnant backwaters of the second city, serenaded by a Brummy gondolier's rendition of "O solo mio!"

Maybe I should write a tourist brochure?

"The romantic fantasy is further enhanced by perusing the canal's accumulation of abandoned cars throughout the ages. Lean back and enjoy, as we punt gently through the floating lilypads of household garbage to terminate our idyllic voyage in Birmingham's delicately named Gas Street Basin."

Gas Street, Oxygen Street, Broad Street, New Street, Corporation Street—when the city bigwigs named this lot, what were they thinking?

The bus stops near the bullring, now a shopping center. "Brummy-jum," as the natives call it, has the same run-down, grimy warmth as usual, and the air is filled with the incessant chatter of millions of little starlings clinging to every parapet and ledge of the soot-blackened Victorian buildings. The trees in the park are so densely infested with the wee birds that they look like sticks of black cotton candy.

"Sharpen Your Elbows and Show Your Teeth" should be the slogan of the spring sales. Purchase-hungry shoppers mass the doorways of C&A and Marks & Spencers. Swift as sharks, they close in on the scent and furious feeding frenzies erupt as they haggle over marked-down bargains. It's a tough call to make my way down through the greedy hordes of latter-day hunter-gatherers toward the entrance of New Street Station.

Reaching the station clock, I have returned to the very spot where my journey with J.C. had begun almost a year ago. I have come full circle, and in keeping with the old traditional ways of the traveler, I spit on the ground for good luck.

"Dirty hippie bastard, get off out of it!" shouts the old geezer selling hot potatoes and roasted chestnuts from a cart-wheeled, black iron oven.

"No, you don't understand. I was just—" I smile back at him, but he's in no mood to parley.

"You were just gobbing on the floor, ya dirty bastard. Go on, get out of it, and get a bloody bath while yer at it, you bloody hippie!"

"I'm telling you, mister, I'm not a hippie."

"Piss off, before I call the police, hippie bastard!" A small crowd of toffee-nosed suburban commuters gathers around him, tutting and clucking in agreement.

There's no arguing with this bloke, and I retreat from his peculiar world as mystified as a visiting Martian.

What did he mean, hippie? What, in the name of God and his holy angels, is a hippie? I'm not a bloody hippie, I'm a long-distance man!

I quote a verse by the nineteenth-century Irish poet Arthur O'Shaughnessy, partially in memory of Johnny and our bizarre journey, but more to raise the spirits than anything else:

We are the music makers
We are the dreamers of dreams
World losers and world-forsakers
On whom the pale moon beams
Yet we are the movers and shakers
Of the world forever, it seems.

→ Chapter 22 ←

"HAAANDY CARRIER! HAAANDY CARRIER!" AN OLD SOLDIER sells brown paper shopping bags at the corner of Corporation Street, his rows of medals from two world wars glinting in the spring sunshine. I pass on.

"*Daaaily Worker,* Vanguard of the Revolution! *Daaaily Worker!*" The clarion call issues from beneath the cloth-cap of an old commie agitator hawking his red-star tabloid to an oblivious tide of people, who as ever, always seem to be going in the opposite direction to myself.

"Le papier! Le papier!" cries the oldest of all street vendors. I remember him since I was a little kid, standing in the same spot, peddling his pile of *Birmingham Evening Mail* newspapers. Sick Dick the Beatnik once spoke to him in French, only to discover that *Le papier* was the sole extent of the old boy's repertoire.

Fumes from the vehicles idling in traffic jams tear at my throat, whilst the human current streams against me, rude and unapologetic. I feel like a salmon trying to get up the rapids, swimming in an aggressive river of clamoring clods. Diving out of the melee into the relative quiet of a doorway, I get my breath. A tufty-haired waif, selling flowers from a street stall, shouts over to me.

"Hey, mister! Hey, you, hippie! Flower power, man!" He throws over a daffodil and I stick it in my buttonhole.

A pretty young girl in a cotton cheesecloth sari stops. She flashes a seductive smile at me and says, "Peace and love, man. Are you a real hippie?"

"Ah, yeees! Yes, of course I am. Yes, indeed!" She kisses me on both cheeks and gives me the two-fingered peace sign. Before I can overcome my surprise, she is gone, swallowed up by the mad rush, to God knows where.

Well, that was a turnup for the books! Whatever this hippie thing is, I better keep my options open.

With renewed vigor, I press up Corporation Street, leading a thirst that would choke a camel, to the oasis bearing the legend:

Yeats's Wine Lodge
(Licensed for the Purveyance of Alcoholic Beverages)

My soul, once soaring aloft, thirsty for Mr. Yeats's poems, now prepares to land with parched palate squarely in the brothers Yeatses pub. In from the bright street I fly, touching down in the cool entrance hall of the saloon.

The Wine Lodge is a distillation of the city itself, thronged as it is with a multiethnic ensemble of late afternoon tipplers, poets, scallywags, besuited businessmen, thieves, and fur-coated old hookers. All human life is here.

This is a truly great house. The design is every bit as varied and eclectic as the clientele: a jumbled mishmash of classical, baroque, and rococo motifs thrusting out their tobacco-stained glory at the drinking fraternity below. Few customers are English, and most are Irish, but the languages of Sikhs, Hong Kong Chinese, and jaunty Caribbean Rastamen can all be discerned in the hubbub.

The ornate vaulted ceiling resembles a medieval cathedral nave, as does the great stained-glass windows portraying nymphs, satyrs, centaurs, and other zoomorphic imaginings of the ancient Greeks. These fabled beasts blaze from their intricately carved casements above the walnut bar. It is how Nero's mausoleum would have been, if indeed he had one.

One hundred feet of bartop, the longest in Britain, supports gargantuan oak casks upon a gantry, their brass stop-taps supplying the world's finest wines, ports, and sherries. Each sweet elixir emits an aroma, which, suffused with beeswax polish, fresh ground coffee, and cigar smoke, produces an olfactory cocktail heady enough to put you spinning!

Service is obtained by entering a long wooden-railed chicane. Here you wait to be served by one of the white-aproned counter staff. They give you a ticket with your order, which you pay for at the checkout at the end of the rail, rather like in a supermarket. It is all rather quaint and reminiscent of the old luxury ocean liners: *Lusitania, Mauritania,* or, if you've had too much to drink, the *Titanic.*

Standing atop of the white Connemara marble steps, it takes a few minutes for the eyes to adjust to the interior ambience.

To my left is the great bar and to my right the smaller speciality bar, whose blond-curled keeper is smiling and craicing away with her admiring customers.

Sideways is the only method to slip through the press of folk, and with some jostling, I gain a foothold on the edge of the walnut bar.

"Hey, watch out, mate! You nearly spilled my drink."

"Sorry, pal, it caught my sleeve, I just want a word with the bar lady there."

"It's OK, no harm done, son. Hey, miss! There's a hippie-looking bloke here wanting a word with you!"

The server strolls down the long counter as if she owns the place.

"Good day, sir, and whaat can I do for yew?" She says, nonchalantly, polishing a cocktail glass and half-looking in my direction. Somehow this barmaid has recently acquired a rather refined English accent. She turns to put the glass up on the shelf.

"How's about you and me going for sausages an' stuffing at the Oxford Restaurant!"

She spins around like a cartoon cat, her eyes round and large!

"Jasus, Willie! I'll kill you, you bleeder, giving me a bloody fright like that, you bugger. Ye put the heart crossways in me, so you did!" Gone is the affected BloodyEnglish accent and thanks be to Christ and his Holy Family, she lapses back into her native Irish brogue.

"Holy mother of God! Will you look at him—he's all grown up! You were never that tall when you left home. And look at all that hair. You look like a Beatle!" She clasps her hands momentarily over her mouth. "Jasus, I don't know what your dad's going to say? No matter, bollocks to him! Are you well so? Will you have a drink, a pint or something? Do you want a pork pie? Are you hungry? Oh, Jasus! I can't get over it! Would you Adam and Eve it? The cat came back."

Hopping about like a flea on a griddle, she takes out a small white handkerchief, and for a moment I'm feared that I'm about to get the dreaded spit-and-rub treatment, but mercifully, she dabs at her eyes instead. The crowd at the bar are all smiles and nudge up to let me in.

"Easy now, Mam, I'm fine! Grand all together, tickety-boo, just."

"By all the saints, Willie, you look so different. Just take a gander at yourself. You're like no one's child!" She moves sideways, revealing the glint of the scalloped-edged mirror enshrined in the dark wood cove of the bar. I stare at a stranger!

"You are no one's child," mocks my reflection in the glass. "Not any more. This weather-beaten bloke with the wee red whiskers is you—and you have become a man!"

Every bit as mystified as Alice, I'm mesmerized by the apparition reflected in the looking glass. For an all too brief moment, on the threshold of metamorphosis, my existence hangs in the space between the mirror and myself.

"I was many shapes before I was born . . ."

The distance between my mother and me widens, but not in an uncomfortable way; it's more the sense of sweet loss felt when sailing from the familiar pierhead of a beloved country. The seventeen-year voyage into manhood has all but ended, leaving in its wake a mere decaying reflection in the smoky glass mirror. I have come full circle again, back to the mother that bore me, back to the harbor of her heart.

My wee Celtic childhood is over, gone like snow on the water in a cascade of infinitely repeated images reflecting the world betwixt the child and the long-distance man. And that was that! Having shed the soft skin of infancy, I emerge from the chrysalis transformed; reworked in the image my father had envisioned, that time long ago, when we walked and talked in the woods.

The umbilical cord to the past is finally severed. Destiny ties the end in a trefoil knot: a trinity of three faiths. I hope my father will approve of my efforts. I trust I have become "a man to ride the river with." I pray that I am on my way to becoming "the once and future Celt."

Above our heads, the great oak gantry clock strikes two and, as is the custom, Mam closes the bar down for the afternoon holy hour. We step into the street.

Arm in arm, we trip through the backstreets, avoiding the crowds. Before us lies the legendary Oxford Restaurant. It's just like old times, except I'm the tall one now. I'm the long-distance man.

Mam squeezes my arm. She is proud of me, I can tell.

"Is an leanbh athair an fhear!" she says. "The child is the father of the man!" I squeeze her arm in reply.

"Mam?"

"What is it?"

"Sing 'Bobby Shaftoe' for me."

Some of My Family's Traditional Songs as Alluded to in the Text

Bad Luck to This Marching
Air: "Paddy O' Carroll"

Bad luck to this marching
Pipe claying and starching
How neat we must be to be killed by the French
I'm sick of parading
Through mud and snow wading
And standing all night to be shot in a trench.

Now I love Garryowen
When I hear it at home
'Tis a marvelous tune, with an elegant lilt
But the strength of the beat
Doesn't sound half as sweet
When you're facing the French and about to be kilt.

Though we're up bright and early
Our pay comes so rarely
The devil a farthing we've ever to spare
Some say a disaster
Befell the paymaster
But I fervently think that the money's not there.

Like a sailor that's nigh land
I long for ould Ireland
Where even the kisses we steal as we please

With no Sarge to abuse us
We fight to amuse us
And we've nothing to do but to stand at our ease.

Now I'd dance like a fairy
To see ould Dunleary
My discharging papers cannot come too soon
To the tune of a fife
They'll dispose of your life
So think on, my lads, 'er you join the dragoons.

Brighidín Bhán Mo Stór (Bright Bridget My Treasure)

I am a wandering minstrel man and love's my only theme
I've strayed beside the pleasant Bann and the Shannon's winding
    stream
I've piped and played to wife and maid, by Barrow, Siur and Nore
But never met a maiden yet, like Brighidín bhán mo stór.

She wears her ringlets rich and rare, as nature's fingers wove
Loch Cara's swans are not so fair or gentle as my love
As she walks out in her Sunday sheen, all by my cabin door
I'd forsake a high-born Saxon queen for Brighidín bhán mo stór.

It's not alone her smile so sweet, or soft her voice in song
That causes me to oft times repeat her name the whole night long
But that does rest all in her breast, a heart of purest core
Whose pulse is known to me alone, my Brighidín bhán mo stór.

Oh, I'll take ship to Amerikay, good fortune for to find
And every day lament the heart I had to leave behind
But soon in riches I'll return, unto my native shore
With pomp and pride, I'll make a bride of Brighidín bhán mo stór.

An Maidrín Rua

Ar ghabháil ó thuaidh dom trí Shliabh Luachra
'Gus mise 'cur tuairisc mo ghéanna
Ar bhfilleadh aduaidh sea fuaireas a dtuairisc
Go raibh Donncha Rua á n-aoireacht.

Curta.

Maidrín rua, rua, rua, rua,
An maidrín rua atá dána
An maidrín rua 'na luí sa luachair
Agus bárra a dhá chluais in áirde.

Nil cnoc ná coill ná cnuasach poill
Ná lub ná leadhb in Eireann
Ná go rabhas is mo mhuintir de ló 'gus d'oíche
I ndialadh an mhasa rua ar saothar.

Curta.

O' greadacdh croi craite chugat 'mhaidrin ghranna
A sciob uaim m'ál breá géanna
Mo chearca beaga bána mo choilligh is mo bhárdal
Is mo lachain bheaga b'fhearr a bh' in Eirinn.

Curta.

Dinny Burns the Piper

In the year '98 when our trouble was great,
It was treason to be a Milesian and the blackwhiskers said we would
    never forget,
And our history tells us there were Hessians
In these troublesome times; everything was a crime and murder it
    never was riper
In the town of Glensheed, not an acre from Meath, lived one Dinny
    Burns the piper.

Neither wedding nor wake would be worth a shake if Dinny was first
    not invited

For at squeezing the bags, or emptying the kegs, he astonished as well as delighted.
But in these time poor Dinny, he could not earn a penny
Martial law had him stung like a viper, and it kept him within,
Till the bones of his skin, were grinning through the rags of the piper.

Now day it did dawn as Dinny marched home back from the fair at Lafangen
And what should he see, from the branch of a tree, but the corpse of a Hessian there hanging.
Says Dinny, "These rogues, they've got boots—I've no brogues" and the boots he laid hold with a gryper
And he pulled with such might and the boots were so tight; legs boots and all came away with the piper.

Well, Dinny did run, for fear of being hung, till he came to Tim Haley's cabin
Ah, says Tim from within, sure I can't let you in, and you'll be shot if your caught out there rapping.
So he went to the shed, where the cow was in bed; with a wisp he began for to wipe her
And they laid down together, in seven foot of heather, and the cow took to hugging the piper.

As day it did dawn Dinny did yawn, and he pealed off the boots of the Hessian
And the legs, by the law, sure he left in the straw, and he gave them leg-bail for his mission.
Now breakfast being done, Tim sent out his young son, to get Dinny up like a lamplighter
When the legs there he saw, he rose up like a jackdaw, "Jasus, Daddy—the cow's ate the piper!"

"Well, bad luck to the baste, she has musical taste to eat such a jolly old chanter
Arrah Phadrig a vic, get a lump of a stick, drive her off on the road and we'll cant her."

The neighbors were called, Mrs. Kennedy bawled, they began for to
humbug and jyper
And in sorrow they met, and their whistles they wet, and like divils
lamented the piper.

Now the cow it was drove 'bout a mile or two off till they came to the
fair at Killaley
Where there she was sold, for four guineas in gold, to the clerk of the
parish, Jim Daly.
They went to the tent, where the pennies were spent, the clerk being a
jolly old swiper
And who should be there, playing "The Rakes of Kildare," but yer
bould Dinny Burns the piper.

Tim gave a jolt, like a half-drunken colt, and he stared at the piper like
a gamuck.
Says he, "By the powers, I thought for the last eight hours, you were
playing in the ould cow's stomach!"
And Dinny observed that the Hessians, when served, began for to
humbug and jyper
And in grandeur they met and their whistles they wet—and like divils
they danced round the piper.

Seán Ui Dhuir a Ghleanna (John O'Dwyer of the Glen)

After Augrhim's great disaster
When our foe in sooth was master
It was you who first plunged in and swam
The Shannon's boiling flood
And through Slieve Bloom's dark passes
You led your gallowglasses
Although the hungry Saxon wolves
Were howling for your blood.
And as you crossed Tipperary
You rived the clan O'Leary
And drove a creacht before us

As our horsemen southwards came
Through flood and field we bore them
To the very heart we gored them
Ah Seán O'Dwyer a ghleanna
You were worsted in the game

Long, long we kept that hillside
Our path hard by the rillside
The sturdy knotted oaken boughs
Our curtain overhead
The summer sun we laughed at
The winter hail we chaffed at
Depending on our strong steel swords
To win our daily bread
But the Dutchman's troops came round us
And with fire and steel he bound us
And he blazed the woods and valleys
Till the very sky was flame
But our sharpened swords cut through them
To the very heart we hewed them
Ah Seán O'Dwyer a ghleanna
You were worsted in the game

Here's a health to yours and my king
A sovereign of our liking
And to Sarsfield underneath whose flag
We cast once more a chance
For the morning dawn will wing us
Across the sea and bring us
To take a stand and wield our brand
Amongst the sons of France
And although we part in sorrow
Still, Seán O'Dwyer, a chara
May our prayer be God save Ireland
And pour blessings on her name
May her sons be true when needed

May they never fail as we did
Ah Seán O'Dwyer a ghleanna
You were worsted in the game.

The Jackets Green

When I was a maiden fair and young on the pleasant banks of Lee
No bird that in the greenwood sang was half as blithe and free
No love have I for to call my own, nor he call me his queen
Till down the glen rode Sarsfield's men, and they wore their jackets
    green

Young Donal sat on his high gray mare like a king on a royal seat
And my heart went out on its regal wave for to worship at his feet
Oh love you have come in those colors dressed and woo with a sol-
    dier's mien
I will lay my head on your throbbing breast for the sake of your jacket
    green

No costly attire did my true love wear but the good sword that he
    bore
But I loved him for himself alone and the colors that he wore
Ah love had you come in England's red for to make me England's
    queen
I would roam the high green hills instead for the sake of the Irish
    green

When William stormed with shot and shell at the walls of Garryowen
In the breach of death my Donal fell and he sleeps near the Treaty
    Stone.
That breach the foemen never crossed while he swung his
    broadsword keen
But I do not weep for my darling lost for he fell 'neath the flag of
    green

And when Sarsfield sailed away I wept as I hear the wild Ochone
And I felt as dead as those who slept 'neath the walls of Garryowen

Whilst Ireland held my Donal blest no wild seas rolled between
I still would fold him to my breast all robed in his jacket green.

I saw the Shannon's purple tide flow by the Irishtown
as I stood in the breach by Donal's side when England's flag went
    down
But now it glowers as it reaches the sky like a blood-red curse be-
    tween
And I cry, "It is not women's tears will raise the Irish Green."

Watkins Ale (This version c.1590)
A Ditty delightfull of mother Watkins ale
A warning well wayed, though counted a tale.

I

There was a maid this other day
And she would needs go forth and play
And as she walked she sithed and says
I am afraid to die a mayd,
With that behard a lad
What talke this maiden has
Whereof he is full glad
    And do not spare
To say, faire mayd, I pray
Whether goe you to play
For I will, without faile,
Mayden, give you Watkins ale:
Watkins ale, good sir, quoth she
What is that I pray you tell me?

II

'Tis sweeter farre then sugar fine
And pleasanter than muskadine
And if you please, faire mayd, to stay
A little while, with me to play

I will give you the same
Watkins ale cald by name
Or els, are I to blame
In truth, faire mayd
Good sir, quoth she againe
Yf you will take the paine
I will it not refraine
Nor be dismayd
He toke this mayden then aside
And led her where she is not spyde
And told her many a prety tale
And gives her well of Watkins ale

III

When he has done to her his will
They talkt, but what it shall not skill
At last, quoth she, saving your tale
Give me some more of Watkins ale
Or else I will not stay
For I must needs away
My mother bade me play
The time is past
Therefore, good sir, quoth she
If you have done with me
Nay soft, faire maid, quoth he
Againe at last
Let us talke a little while
Good sir, she then do say
With that the mayd begin to smile
What do you care?
And sayse, good sir, full well know
Your ale, I see runs very low

IV

This young man then, being so blamd
Did blush as one being ashamde

He takes her by the middle small
And gives her more of Watkins ale
      And sayse, faire maid, I pray
   When you goe forth to play
      Remember what I say
         Walke not alone
      Good sir, quoth she againe
      I thanke you for your paine
      For feare of further staine
         I will be gone
Farewell, mayden, then qouth he
Thus they parted at last
Till thrice three months are gone past

This mayden then fell very sicke
Her maydenhead begin to kicke
Her colour waxed wan and pale
From taking much of Watkins ale.